BLOOD OF THE TALLAN

Blood of the Tallan

The Petralist Book 7

Frank Morin

Blood of the Tallan
Book 7 of The Petralist

ISBN: 978-1-946910-22-6

A Whipsaw Press Original

Cover art by Christian Bentulan
(https://coversbychristian.com/)

Cover art by Brad Fraunfelter
(http://www.bfillustration.com/)

Illustrations by Jared Blando
(http://www.theredepic.com/)

Book design by Kate Staker
(https://katestaker.com/)

First Whipsaw printing August 2021

Other Works By Frank Morin

The Petralist Series

Set in Stone, Book One

A Stone's Throw, Book Two

No Stone Unturned, Book Three

Affinity for War, Book Four

The Queen's Quarry, Book Five

The King's Craft, Book Six

Blood of the Tallan, Book Seven

When Torcs Fly, A Petralist Origins novella,
    Tomas and Cameron

Game of Garlands, A Petralist Origins novella, Anika

Builder of Intrigue, A Petralist novella, Ailsa

The Facetakers Series

Saving Face, Book One

Memory Hunter, Book Two

Rune Warrior, Book Three

Aeon Champion, Book Four

Short Stories

"Odin's Eye," included in *A Game of Horns:*
    A Red Unicorn Anthology

"The Essence," included in *Dragon Writers:*
    An Anthology

"Only Logical," a purple unicorn story

"The Seventh Strike," included in
    Cursed Collectibles: An Anthology

Find all these books on

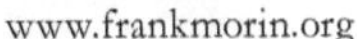

www.frankmorin.org

Amazon

The Northern Reaches
Varvakis
Orlov
Platov
River Angara
Lake Pyasino
Krashnov
River Olenet
Valeska Rivers
Granadure
Althing
Jagdish
Edduritz
Dagmanson
R. Anok
Finnlaugur
Ravinder
Prahalad
R. Saol
R. Bergrin
Obrion
R. Macantacht
Donleavy
The Broken Water
Maninder
The Western Sea
The Eastern Sea
Sea of Olcan
Zehrazad
Ozlem
Hayreddin
N
Murex
Tabnit
Mahzun
Tabnit
Blando
The Known World

SOUTHERN GRANADURE
100 MILES
The Northern Reaches
Edderitz
Faulenrost
Builder Compound
Altkalen
Hister River
Farmlands
Wetter River
Taunus Mts
Abwehr Mountains
Badurach Pass
Harz
Emmerich Quarry
Schmitten Quarry
Althing Nation
N
BLANDO

GRANADURE
N
W E
S
GRANITE MINE
ALASDAIR
QUARTZ-ZINC GOLD MINE
THE WICK
PUMICE MINE
BASALT MINE
MARBLE MINE
MERKLAND
SLATE MINE
OBRION
CRANN
TRODAIRE
SAOL RIVER
DONLEAVY
MACANTACHT RIVER
FREASTAL
GRANITE MINE
BASALT MINE
GRANITE MINE
CASUR
MULRENNAN
CARRAIG
DEIFUR
LIMESTONE MINE
LAIGE
RAINEACH
CHOSTALAN
SANDSTONE MINES
SPEIRMOR
RADHARC
THE DESERT
BLANDO
THE LANDS OF
OBRION

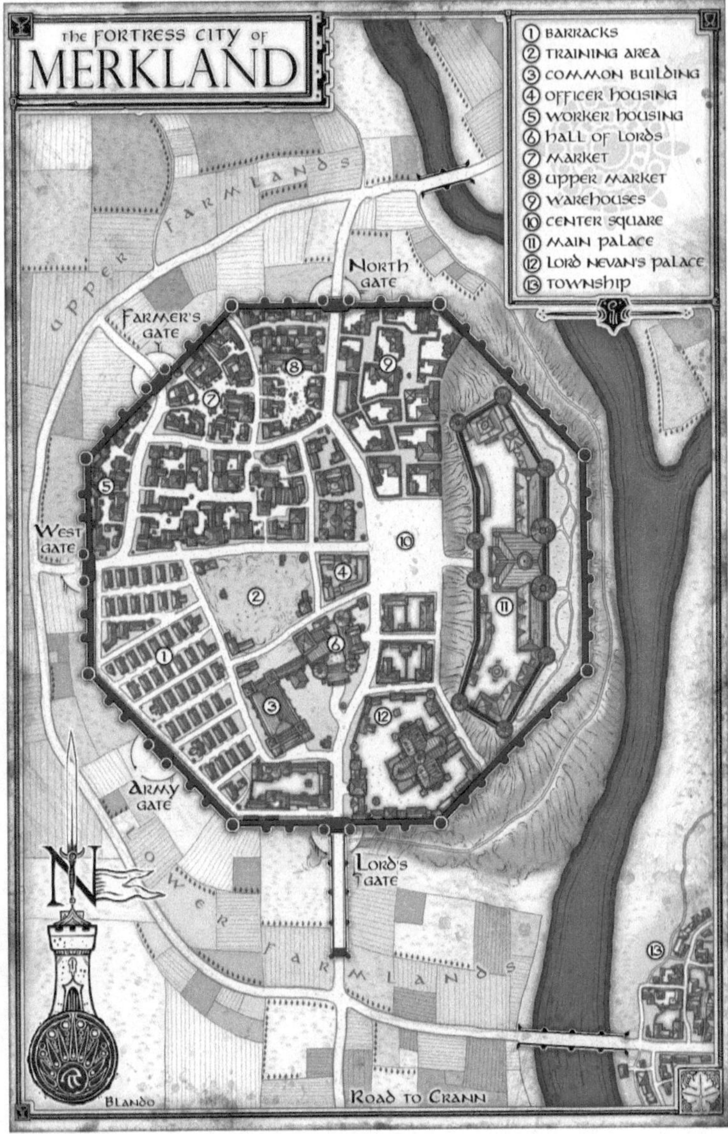

THE FORTRESS CITY of MERKLAND
1 BARRACKS
2 TRAINING AREA
3 COMMON BUILDING
4 OFFICER HOUSING
5 WORKER HOUSING
6 HALL OF LORDS
7 MARKET
8 UPPER MARKET
9 WAREHOUSES
10 CENTER SQUARE
11 MAIN PALACE
12 LORD NEVAN'S PALACE
13 TOWNSHIP
UPPER FARMLANDS
NORTH GATE
FARMER'S GATE
WEST GATE
ARMY GATE
LOWER FARMLANDS
LORD'S GATE
N
BLANDO
ROAD TO CRANN

ACKNOWLEDGEMENTS

The last Petralist book. Wow!

What a long and wonderful road. It's hard to believe we're here at the end, but since it's such an amazing, epic end, it's okay.

As usual, I owe a lot of thanks to a lot of people for helping me along the way.

My family—stalwart supporters all the way.

My beta readers—you rock!

All of my fans whose boundless enthusiasm for this book makes me think maybe basalt really works.

THANK YOU.

I hope you enjoy it as much as I do.

Frank

CHAPTER ONE
Friends Don't Let Friends Duel Cakes Alone

This is what I call research," Connor said as he surveyed the long table, piled with eight dozen fresh-baked sweetbreads, a bucket full of smashpacked desserts, six pounds of sizzling bacon strips on hot plates, and fifteen Althing chocolate cakes of varying sizes and numbers of layers.

Hamish rubbed his hands together eagerly as he slowly walked around the table, which filled most of the private dining room. "No better way to prove you didn't suffer any lingering problems from your elfonnel immersion than with a little gluttoncrafting."

They'd actually participated in a lot of gluttoncrafting during the triple feast honoring Tomas and Cameron and their near-victory over the dread queen. Connor had convinced Shona that since Verena had turned off the Sucker Punch super mechanical, which cut off the incredible flood of healing power it was stealing from the convergence point, the best way for him to restore his strength would be by consuming a lot of food.

Only Hamish, Jean, and Verena knew the full extent of what Connor could do with gluttoncrafting, and he'd shared the ability with Hamish and Verena during the feast. Each of them had consumed far more than any normal person could have without bursting. After each plate, he had transformed the food into pure energy, clearing their stomachs for another helping and instantly refreshing them.

Connor had eaten seventeen plates of food, impressing even Evander by his stomach powers. Then he'd slept for thirty-six hours straight.

He'd been right. He almost felt back to normal.

So of course, as soon as he awakened from his epic nap, he and Hamish had returned to the kitchens for a round of research. Luckily, Shona hadn't thought to rescind her order to the cooks to give Connor anything he needed. He doubted that order would survive until lunchtime, but that was okay. He didn't plan to simply waste a bunch of precious food when Merkland was still so battered from the swarm and the volcanic eruption.

They were preparing for battle. Sort of.

Connor selected one sweetbread, a soft, fluffy scone, still warm from the oven, slathered with golden butter. With a thought, he embraced both air and fire. Ever since his third ascension, he almost never totally severed his links to his tertiary affinities, so the connections solidified instantly.

Air appeared beside him, invisible to anyone else. To him, she looked like a beautiful woman with flawless skin and long, flowing tresses that today were the color of storm clouds. She wore a long, white cotton dress that billowed around her as if she was draped with afternoon clouds.

Fire appeared beside her, his hair longer than the last time Connor had seen him. Today it was orange, and sparks burst from the tips. He again wore a fancy tunic of interwoven tongues of fire that formed a colorful pattern.

"Experimenting this morning, are we?" Air asked as she danced a slow spin around him in the air. Fire just crossed his arms, the hint of a smile tugging at the corner of his mouth.

Connor was glad he could still reach fire. Queen Dreokt had destroyed the ancient sculpted stone that had filtered the sylfaen energy at one of the convergence points to create the marble affinity. With the stone gone, the lower-level access to marble that most Petralists used had snuffed out, leaving their affinities useless. Only he and Kilian, as well as the dread queen, could access the higher-level power of fire still available through the green frequency energy, accessible after the second threshold.

Connor grinned at them and said, "Sculpted scone breakfast mission, take one."

He tapped granite, and the so-familiar itch of it crawling under his skin helped center his mind, as always. He focused the power of granite into the center of his chest and pushed it out, wrapping it in layers of air and fire. Usually when performing a summoning, he would then pour that mixture into clay. Every summoning required granite strength, elemental lifeblood, and a body. It was possible to simply clothe the summoned creature in the element, but clay was easier and consumed less power stone.

Today, Connor poured the mixture into the scone, focusing on the commands that would structure his summoning's entire focus. The little pastry shuddered, then came alive in Connor's mind. A tiny fraction of his focus diverted to control the little summoning, and he grinned to feel its eagerness to fulfill the mandate he'd used to define it.

"Did it work?" Hamish asked, his tone awed as Connor gently placed the summoned scone onto the table.

"Let's find out." Connor pushed a single thought down the conduit connecting him to the scone. *Hamish.*

The scone scurried across the table, little legs forming out of bread to propel it. In seconds, it rushed to the edge and easily leaped across to Hamish, little arms forming to catch Hamish's shirt. Without slowing, it raced up his shirt, and as he started laughing in delight, it plunged into his open mouth.

Hamish gagged as the little pastry tried rushing right down his throat. Coughing, he grabbed it and held the squirming pastry long enough to chomp down hard. It stopped moving, and Hamish sighed, a look of rapture on his face.

Around the mouthful of scone, he managed to say, "Feffet wumpf."

"Excellent." Connor had hoped he'd gotten the heat right. He easily understood Hamish's words as, "perfect warmth."

Hamish swallowed and added, "Maybe tone down the suicidal tendency a bit, though."

"On it." Connor chose six slices of bacon for the second test. Wrapping them together, he replicated the summoning, and the bacon twisted into a tiny man-shaped treat that again charged Hamish and leaped into his mouth. That time, it stayed there, the bit of fire in it heating it to the point where it was obviously at the almost-but-not-quite burned his tongue point.

"Oh, that was perfect," Hamish grinned. "Let's try a cake next."

"Haven't you two had enough to eat?"

Verena approached, dressed in her regular Builder work clothes, including tan trousers, a dark green blouse, and a scarred, brown leather jacket. Her black hair was held back from her face with a red leather cord.

He grinned, elated to see her. She wore her satchel slung over one shoulder, as always, and crossed her arms, staring at the table full of food, one eyebrow raised in question.

Connor stole a quick kiss. "We're experimenting on a variation of the sculpted scones we used against Queen Dreokt."

She smiled. "I read Ailsa's report probably ten times."

"I wish I'd been there to see it," Hamish said as he wiped bacon grease from his lips.

"I'm not sure we can catch her with another batch of sculpted scones," Verena said.

"I doubt we could," Connor agreed. "Hence the variation."

Hamish added proudly, "After the swarm nearly destroyed Merkland, I noticed it was hard to ensure refreshments reached everyone fast enough."

Verena grimaced at the mention of the swarm. She'd played a pivotal role in defending the city from the horde of summoned monsters that almost wiped out Merkland. Connor wrapped an arm around her shoulder, shivering at the memory of that huge summoned creature bearing down on her, with the Swift a smoking ruin, and her only weapon a short sword. She'd faced it defiantly, but would have died in seconds if he hadn't returned.

"So we're planning a summoning that can get critical resources to people fast," Connor said.

Verena chuckled. "Critical resources? All I see are desserts, sweets, and bacon."

"Exactly," Hamish said. "Only the basics."

She sighed, but smiled. "Only you two could propose something so ridiculous and make it sound vital to the war effort."

Hamish grinned and gave her an extravagant bow, perfectly mimicking Kilian. Connor asked, "Want to help?"

"I wouldn't miss it," she said, pointing at a three-layer chocolate cake. "How about we test that one next?"

They tried it, but Verena's face got covered with chocolate as the entire cake tried crawling into her mouth. She stumbled backward, hands sunk into the soft confection, trying to chew while laughing hysterically.

Connor was still fine-tuning the commands he imbued the summoned pastries with, so maybe she should have tried something smaller. He could have terminated the summoning, but seeing her wrestling the cake was so funny, he couldn't make himself do it. Hamish leaped to Verena's defense, lunging in and ripping half the cake away and shoving it into his own mouth.

Connor rushed to Verena a second later, pulling the cake free and helping her finish it. Laughing, she wrapped cake-covered hands around his neck and pulled him in for a very messy kiss. Her lips usually tasted like mint, but he did not mind at all when she tasted like chocolate.

He doused them all with water to clean them off, then drained it away, leaving them dry and laughing.

When Verena caught her breath, she said, "Definitely need some more testing."

"That's why we ordered so much," Hamish said grandly.

"Let's get to it, then," she said with that determination that Connor loved so much. "Because Connor and I have a meeting with Kilian in half an hour."

Connor glanced at all the food remaining and grinned. "We can do it."

Chapter Two
Every Girl Needs a Few Secrets

Half an hour later, feeling very refreshed, Connor joined Verena on a couch in Kilian's suite in one of the towers of the Merkland palace. They'd finished every scrap of food on that table with time to spare. Connor had dialed in the summonings to the point where each of them had a long line of pastries and desserts queued up to feed them. Hamish had lain down on the floor near the table so each pastry could dive off the edge and plunge into his open maw.

He'd said the experience changed forever his concept of the perfect breakfast.

Connor had used gluttoncrafting on each of them to instantly convert the food into pure energy. Even though he felt almost normal again, his body had still welcomed the extra energy as he healed from his strenuous elfonnel experience. He rubbed his chest where Kilian had stabbed him through the heart to prove that he could regenerate from usually-fatal wounds.

Hopefully he wouldn't need to experience that lesson again. He might be able to survive a heart stab, but that didn't mean he wanted to deal with it again.

Kilian sat in a comfortable chair nearby, wearing his usual casual clothes of trousers, white shirt, and black vest. Aifric sat beside him in another chair, wearing the form-fitting black clothing that Student Eighteen preferred, under her white Healer jacket.

At the moment, it looked like Aifric controlled the shared body she inhabited with eighteen other women, and she gave Connor that signature warm smile of hers. "I'm so glad you're looking so refreshed."

"Lots of rest and good food are my favorite medicine."

"Don't overdo it," Kilian warned. "Recovering from an elfonnel experience takes a few days."

Aifric's face shuddered slightly as Student Eighteen took control and asked, "Connor, will you allow me to enter your mind?"

"Why? Did you remember another secret command the queen implanted in here?" He tapped the side of his head uneasily. Fighting the queen had taxed him to the limits, then he'd spent most of a day living inside of a giant elemental monster. He didn't believe the queen could have tampered with his mind while he was distracted, but the idea unsettled him anyway. He really didn't want to deal with another mind bomb.

She shook her head. "No. Nothing like that."

Kilian added, "Raising an elfonnel is an extremely taxing event. Returning to full humanity can be even harder sometimes."

"You're worried he's broken inside, like your mother, aren't you?" Verena asked. She did not sound nearly as surprised by the idea as Connor felt. Had she considered it already? Had she already begun preparing herself for the possibility of needing to put Connor down if he became a danger to the rest of them? Was that why she'd sought him out that morning, to feel him out and try to sense if he was still himself?

He'd hoped they'd gotten past that phase of their relationship. That sculpted scone breakfast should have convinced her.

"It's a possibility we cannot ignore, although from what I saw today I consider this step more a formality than anything. Connor managed the elfonnel better than anyone I've ever seen, but we'll deal with the questions that fact raises after," Kilian told Verena.

His confidence helped ease Connor's concerns. Student Eighteen had walked in his mind before, so he felt no hesitation in saying, "You're welcome to visit any time. Maybe we'll have another party in Alasdair. Or I can show you that time Hamish accidentally coated Cinaed's front door with tar." He chuckled at the memory. What a mess. Keith had been forced to smash down the door to get it open.

Verena raised one fine eyebrow. "Oh, Hamish accidentally did something, did he? Where were you at the time?"

"I was the voice of reason."

She laughed, and he savored the sound of it. Student Eighteen grinned as well but said, "Meet us in whatever memory you want." After cocking her head slightly, probably listening to input from other ladies in there, she added, "As long as it won't emotionally damage any of us."

"Us?" Connor asked.

"I'll be bringing some of the ladies in with me. We'll just poke around a bit and make sure everything's intact. We know your mind, Connor."

"This time I promise not to try killing any of you." The memory of how he'd attacked those women when they risked their lives to save him from the queen's mind bomb still pained him. Even though he'd been insane at the moment, he still felt ashamed.

"We appreciate that."

Connor tapped chert and focused on her brown eyes as they began to glow with an inner brilliance that drew his gaze in deeper. The chert connection snapped into place, and his vision faded to the mindscape he was getting to know so well. Since he wasn't sure what Student Eighteen was looking for, he imagined the billowing gray emptiness where he so often met the elementals.

Student Eighteen appeared in his mind, her hair braided, wearing Mhortair black. Aifric appeared a moment later, her thick brown hair hanging loose around her shoulders, dressed in her usual Healer whites. Rith popped into the space nearby and immediately began jogging around the others. Her hair was also braided, and she wore baggy Strider pants and a fitted leather jacket. Mariora appeared beside her, dressed in her courier uniform and immediately joined Rith, but accelerated to pull slightly ahead.

Of course, Rith sped up too, and they both grinned, clearly planning to launch into a race. Aifric interrupted. "Enough, you two, or we're sending you back. We're here for Connor."

They looked so dejected that Connor added, "When we're done, maybe we'll switch to a giant spherical track and test your ultimate speed."

"Done!" they said in unison.

Other women joined them. Tresta managed to look blocky despite having the exact same physique as the rest of them. She grunted, "Not a bad performance the other day, Connor, although you let her get away again."

Hemma appeared beside her, also dressed in battle leathers. "We still haven't gotten our bash fight, Connor."

"As soon as I can schedule it," he promised. He didn't want those women angry, or they might be tempted to start breaking things in his head.

Eystri appeared slightly behind Aifric and waved at Connor with a shy smile. "By my calculations, you should having failed much worse as an elfonnel, Connor. I'm glad you didn't die."

"Me too," he said with a grin.

Cacilia appeared in a gorgeous red silk gown with a slit up one side that showed off way too much shapely leg. Her hair was done up in a complex pile atop her head, held in place by a glittering tiara. She gave Connor a dazzling smile and spun to show off her attire. "A girl needs a chance to dress up sometimes, doesn't she?"

Student Eighteen rolled her eyes. "Don't get distracted, Cacilia."

"I'm sure I can find some delicious memories to study. Connor's lived in some nice places, after all. Some of those students at the Carraig are simply too tasty not to admire again."

Connor felt himself redden, and Cacilia laughed wickedly.

Isabell appeared near Cacilia and said, "I plan to study your infiltration of Hector's quarters. Capturing that porphyry was a coup, but you got sloppy."

Nuzha stepped into the memory, hand on her curved dagger. Instead of scowling like she usually did she actually gave Connor a little bow. "You fought bravely against the matron of everlasting evil. You honored your family. Maybe there's hope for you."

"Thanks," he said dryly, just happy she hadn't threatened him yet. She had strong negative feelings against most Obrioners, although she'd managed to get along with him in the past. Usually.

Ennlin slid into his mind, wearing a loose-fitting, gray skirt with a pattern that reminded Connor of rock striations. Her blouse was blue and form-fitting, and she was eating fried potato wedges out of a bowl. They were drenched in a thick layer of yellow cheese.

Connor had never thought of trying cheesy potatoes and stepped closer. "Will you let me try it?"

She smiled and extended the bowl. "Friends share bonds of friendship, but the love of food eclipses all boundaries."

"That sounds like something Hamish would say," Connor chuckled, plucking a hot sliver of fried potato, smothered in cheese, and popped it into his mouth. He savored the blend of smooth, tangy cheese mixed with the crunch of the potato. Such a simple treat, but so good. He decided to share the idea with Hamish, or maybe try filling a sweetbread with melted cheese.

The rest of the women appeared a little farther back, most dressed in variations of battle leathers or dark clothing. Connor glanced at Student Eighteen, one eyebrow raised. "I thought you said a few."

She shrugged. "Don't worry, Connor. We're not invading."

Aifric added, "It's just, we so rarely get to go out all together. No one wanted to stay behind."

He could understand that, and he was actually looking forward to speaking with some of the ladies he didn't really know well yet. Student Eighteen noted his gaze and said, "Later, Connor."

"I can't think of a better time." Every one of her personalities was unique and interesting, but now that he thought about it, why hadn't he gotten to meet the other seven women. He'd interacted with the others enough, Aifric should have offered to make introductions weeks ago.

"A girl needs to keep a few secrets, even from friends," Student Eighteen said cryptically.

"What secrets?"

Aifric laughed. "They wouldn't be secrets if I told you, would they?"

Too many of his friends kept too many secrets, but he decided not to pry. They had enough going on for one day. "So what are we doing?"

"We're making sure you're still you," Student Eighteen said. "Just try to relax. We'll do the work."

"What work? I still don't understand," he said uneasily.

"It's simple, Connor. We're going to make sure the integrity of your memories is still intact and that you haven't fallen to a foreign influence."

"How do you do that?" The concept made sense, but even though he'd helped resurrect Aifric, he didn't really understand how the mind worked.

"Some of the concepts are rather complex. I studied for years under the best mind killers in Jagdish before I grasped all of them. You'll see us reviewing several types of memories. What you won't see is that I can gather a greater pattern from the seemingly random work of my sisters. From that I can sense if your mind has been tampered with or corrupted."

"Wow. Okay, I guess," Connor said. He didn't exactly like them digging shrough all of his memories, but he trusted her completely so couldn't think of how to protest without making her suspect he had something to hide. Besides, he welcomed the chance to prove Queen Dreokt hadn't planted another mind bomb when she'd invaded his mind during their fight and that he had indeed returned from his elfonnel immersion fully intact.

Student Eighteen raised her voice and said, "All right, ladies. Just like we planned. Get to work."

Chapter Three
Too Many Not-so-imaginary Friends

Connor turned slowly, watching as the nineteen women scattered.

Each girl marched into the billowing gray in a different direction. After several strides, Connor felt them seeping into his mind, sliding into his past, searching memories. The mindscape around each of them wavered, then shifted into different scenes.

Aifric focused on memories of the Carraig, and seemed far too interested in the many times he had crawled or limped into the hospital wing seeking her help after a hugging match with Catriona or getting pummeled by Jok. Painful memories for him, but she smiled as she flicked through them. She looked genuinely moved by the memories of the Carraig. She had really loved her time there.

Cacilia was indeed hunting through his memories for men she considered handsome. She also seemed immensely interested in every one of Connor's memories of kissing Verena. She lingered over each of them, making Connor flush again.

"Um, are you getting distracted?" he couldn't help asking.

"It's all for research," she assured him, but then winked, making him flush even more. Still, she did switch to less intimate memories after that.

Student Eighteen had lingered beside him. She placed a comforting hand on his arm and said softly, "We actually do need to review those memories. Precious memories like those define you. If any are missing or blurred, it's a sign we might need to get worried."

"What happened to keeping secrets?"

"You can't keep secrets from me. Besides, you're not a girl," she said with a wink.

Tresta and Hemma studied his bash fighting memories, especially his training sessions with Tomas and Cameron. He overheard Hemma saying, "Fine men, those. Pity they're gone. Nearly as good at wrestling as Rory."

"How would you know how good Tomas and Cameron were at wrestling?" Connor asked, filled again with sorrow at their loss.

"Simple deduction," Student Eighteen said just a bit too quickly.

Nuzha called from where she was reviewing his memorable student battles at the Carraig, "I love watching you beat on these pampered Petralist students. Good creativity."

Wow. Two compliments in one day. Either he was finally winning her over, or she'd found a chance to slip away and murder a few Obrioners lately and was still riding the high from that. Connor glanced at Student Eighteen and she only shrugged. He decided not to ask.

After a few more minutes while the women worked through an astonishing number of his memories, Student Eighteen smiled and said, "Things are looking good, Connor. We just need to—"

"Look at this!" Eystri cried.

Connor turned along with all the other women. The memory that Eystri was studying expanded and Connor tensed. It was the memory of his third ascension when the elementals first stepped into his mind.

"I'd rather you not delve into those," he cautioned.

Student Eighteen gave him a serious look. "Connor, recent memories, particularly of your development since your ascension, are critical."

He wasn't surprised, but he'd already told his friends more than the elementals had wanted him to. He felt like they were finally accepting him, and he didn't want to jeopardize that progress. The memory of his ascension was powerful and too important. He felt a flash of annoyance that she'd pried into that one, but he tried to play it casual.

"There are things relating to my ascension that have to remain confidential."

She hesitated. "I respect that, Connor, but you realize that having visions of elementals taking human form and speaking in your head is a big deal. You've seen firsthand the dangers of opening your mind to other humans. We don't comprehend all the dangers that might go along with opening your mind to elemental beings"

That was actually a good point, but he felt confident the elementals weren't dangerous. "I've spoken with Kilian about them, and he said he trusts my judgment. Some of what they shared with me was only because I promised to keep it private."

"That makes our job a lot harder," she said.

Connor paced away as the other ladies all gathered around, forming a circle of identical siblings. He turned back to Student Eighteen and said, "I think I have to ask you to stop reviewing memories with the elementals."

She gestured toward one view, still visible behind Eystri. It had changed to the memory of Water teaching Connor about magnis. "This is so important, Connor."

Isabell added in a tone of wonder, "It's amazing. You're right. Water is beautiful. She's so much more than I imagined."

Connor sat onto a chair that appeared behind him and rubbed a hand through his hair. He was glad he had shared at least a little about the elementals with his friends, and he was secretly glad Aifric and her mind sisters got to see Water, but did he dare share more?

Water appeared behind Aifric and said, "Connor's training was meant for his ears alone."

The women spun in unison, some dropping into fighting stances, but most just gaping at Water. She was dressed in a regal gown of blue and white that shimmered, as if made up of constantly crashing waves. Her long hair was unbound, flowing into view to either side as if pulled by an invisible tide. Her eyes were as deep a blue as the Sea of Olcan.

Connor rose, startled beyond measure. He hadn't been tapping soapstone.

The girls parted as Water approached. Connor asked, "How can you manifest to them too?"

"We are in the halls of your mind, are we not?" Water asked, her voice like a distant crashing wave.

But he hadn't initiated the contact. Now that he had united so deeply with the elements by raising the elfonnel and returning, had more barriers broken between them? He wasn't sure if he felt pleased or concerned by that.

Fire appeared beside Water, dressed like he had earlier. Earth rise up from the ground, wearing a great, black coat. Air flitted down from the gray expanse above, wearing a white dress with gossamer frills that drifted on invisible air currents. The women all stared in mute astonishment.

Connor felt deeply conflicted. Part of him was glad they got to witness the manifestations of the elementals, but couldn't help a flicker of unease at the clear displeasure on the elementals' faces. He couldn't afford to let Aifric dig any deeper and potentially derail his alliance with them.

"They're just determining I'm okay," he explained.

"Of course you're okay," Water said, as if that was obvious. "We took you by the hand and shielded you. We will see no harm come to our champion."

Porphyry appeared in Connor's mind next, a great rampager that padded toward the circle of startled women. Cacilia screamed, Eystri actually fainted, but the warriors moved to intercept. They looked frightened and surprised, but ready for battle.

"It's okay," Connor said quickly. He wasn't sure what would happen if they attacked his affinity in his mind. How was it even possible?

The world sure got twisted in unexpected ways around his friends.

Student Eighteen glanced back at him, looking unsure, but he gave her a reassuring smile. "Let him through."

"Porphyry has nearly killed you more than once," she remarked as they nevertheless parted, but kept their guards up.

"The pack hunts as one and we save the pack leader," Porphyry growled, eliciting a round of startled exclamations. It padded up to Connor, sniffed his hand, then moved to flank him, settling onto its powerful haunches. Even then its head towered over Connor's.

"You have a lot of explaining to do." Student Eighteen looked flustered. Not a good sign. Very little shook the indomitable assassin.

"Some things are not meant for common ears," Air said.

When Aifric started to protest, Air raised an eyebrow and said, "Some secrets must be kept, no?"

Connor told the elementals, "I'll be careful. Please, trust me."

"Trust goes both ways, and you have already bruised our trust once. Do not do so again," Water warned. Then she faded from his mind. Earth and Air followed. Fire paused to wink at Cacilia, then he too disappeared. Only then did Porphyry follow.

Connor stared. "What was that about?"

Cacilia whistled softly. "Reminds me of someone we know. That's one fine figure of a man."

Even more amazing, Aifric started to blush. She said quickly, "We need to go."

The women started fading from his mind. Student Eighteen stayed until last. She stepped closer and said, "Connor there's great danger in this."

"There's greater danger in not learning everything I can. We almost defeated Queen Dreokt, and a lot of that was thanks to what they've taught me."

"Nevertheless, tread carefully."

Then she was gone.

Connor blew out a breath. Anywhere he trod, he had to be careful. One mistake could spell disaster for everyone.

Then he willed himself awake. Time to face Kilian.

Chapter Four
There Are Secrets, and Then There Are Crazy-super-Secrets

As soon as Connor opened his eyes, Verena took his hand and asked, "How did it go?"

She didn't actually seem worried that he might be broken and need to be put down. Her faith helped. He gave her a reassuring smile and said, "Pretty good, I think."

Student Eighteen was also awake. "We're convinced Connor's whole, but I wouldn't say everything is okay."

"What do you mean?" Kilian asked.

"Connor's been keeping secrets."

Connor added quickly, "As if I'm the only one."

Kilian said, "We all have secrets, but some are deadlier than others, and some of us know when to keep secrets and when to share."

"I thought you had agreed to trust me," Connor said defensively.

Student Eighteen already knew the truth, and from her expression he could tell she planned to share it. He might as well do it himself, but he felt a strange reluctance. More than just the fact that he had promised the elementals to keep his interactions with them secret to protect his friends from potential harm, his relationship with them was becoming precious to him, and he realized he would not risk any harm coming to that. It was too important to risk. His friends should understand that.

Kilian said, "That was before you raised an elfonnel, controlled it better than even I can with all of my experience, and somehow walked with fire and earth together while in elfonnel form. Whatever's going on, Connor, we need to understand it."

"Why? Isn't it enough that I understand it and that I've proven I can do it?" He rubbed at his eyes, suddenly feeling tired again. Maybe he needed to sleep for another day. Or a week.

"Not this time, Connor. What we saw in your mind is so far beyond normal, we can't keep it secret." She looked surprised that he was arguing the point, and that just annoyed him more.

"You're not exactly one to talk about what's normal," he retorted.

She recoiled and Verena slugged Connor in the shoulder. "What's gotten into you?"

Student Eighteen held up a calming hand. "It's all right. You've experienced severe trauma that you haven't yet recovered from, and we're treading in unfamiliar water. We pried into your mind in a pretty invasive way. It's natural for you to resist, but Connor you have to understand that I fear there are dangers you haven't grasped yet. We're best equipped to handle them together."

Kilian was watching the exchange closely. He said softly, "I agree. I trust you Connor, but you stepped into uncharted waters here and any unknowns involving the deepest magic are fraught with danger."

"More danger than even you know. Part of what I'm trying to keep from you is for your own good," Connor said, rubbing a hand through his hair, fighting to remain calm. He felt a growing frustration at their poking and prying. They were trying to help, but at the same time they were risking everything he was building with the elementals.

Connor couldn't make Aifric unsee what she saw, but he wished there was a way to get the rest of them to simply trust him. Life was too complicated already. He couldn't bear to have any of his friends hurt because he shared secrets with them they weren't prepared for.

Verena rubbed his hand, and as always the motion soothed him. "If there are things that could harm us, maybe you could just not tell us those parts, but there have to be some things that you can share."

Neither Kilian nor Aifric appeared as ready to accept her compromise, but they did not object. Leave it to Verena to find a solution. So he took a deep breath and said, "You know I'm speaking with the elementals."

Verena nodded eagerly. "I've been trying to reach Water ever since I saw her in Kirstin's Defense, but haven't been able to."

"I'll ask her if there's more we can do to help you connect," Connor promised.

"Don't rush things," Kilian warned. "What have you learned that you can share?"

"Somehow they really are self-aware, and I'm trying to under-stand their purposes. They've been training me and teaching me about the higher aspects to affinities and the world powers that fuel them. Without their help I wouldn't have made nearly as much progress, and I never would have survived that eruption."

"How did you survive? How did you walk with both fire and earth?" Kilian asked.

Connor wanted to tell him, longed to discuss his family bridge that he was slowly corrupting, but hesitated. Water had warned him not to share more of their training, and he sensed that if he angered her again, she might refuse to train him further. He couldn't take the risk.

"It's complicated, and unfortunately that's one of the things I can't share yet."

Kilian didn't like it. "You said they've warned you that sharing too much could harm us, but your connection to them is unprecedented, and I don't like the fact that they want you to walk this road without our counsel."

"Please trust me. I think I almost understand their purpose, and then maybe I'll be able to share more."

"What is their purpose?" Verena asked.

Connor shrugged. "I'm not entirely sure yet. They want me to become their champion." He dared add, "And help them gain more freedom."

"What does that mean?" Student Eighteen asked.

Maybe he shouldn't have said so much. He was walking a very fine line. Had he just crossed it? "I'll let you know as soon as I know, and as soon as I can share it."

Kilian frowned. "That concerns me, as does the idea of greater freedom. What do they mean?"

"I don't know," Connor said, feeling frustrated.

"Knowledge, especially critical knowledge like what they are sharing with you, is not shared without a price," Kilian said, still frowning. "We must understand what they expect in return so that we can understand if the price is worth the knowledge."

"I know," he snapped, letting them see his frustration. "But I need the knowledge, or I'll die."

Connor couldn't risk alienating the elementals until they figured out how to defeat the queen, but he did worry about what they meant about needing freedom. What could shackle them? How did it limit them, and what did freedom look like? They were beings of such vast power, he wanted to make sure he didn't make any assumptions that might prove dangerous.

He honestly wanted to help them, but he'd spent enough time around powerful people to see how they manipulated others, and his suspicions were growing that the elementals were maneuvering him into a position he wouldn't like if he understood all the facts.

That put him into a difficult spot. He needed them, desperately needed the knowledge they could share and the power they possessed. They had saved him during the eruption, which had saved everyone. He could not have made a different choice than accept their help, but that had placed him far deeper in debt to them, and they still wouldn't clearly state what they wanted in return.

Kilian did not look convinced either. "What else can you tell us about them?"

He decided describing them wouldn't harm anyone. Aifric had already seen them. So he described them, including the odd attraction between Earth and Air, and Fire and Water.

While he talked, he glanced at Student Eighteen, who regarded Kilian with a little smile. There was definitely a striking resemblance, probably a subconscious choice on Connor's part to associate the element with the Petralist who most embodied them. Was that why Fire and Earth looked so much like Kilian and Evander, or was there something deeper to it?

Verena chuckled. "It's hard to picture. Like imagining Evander flirting."

"He did date Harley," Student Eighteen reminded them, then visibly shuddered.

"They do a great job impersonating people," Connor said. "Some of it may just be how it translates into my mind, but there has to be a basis in fact for it."

Kilian nodded. "I have sensed the strange dual nature between the opposing elements. Fire and water destroy each other when in the same space, but there is an undeniable attraction between them. You've given us some fascinating insights."

"Can you tell us more about affinity bridges?" Student Eighteen asked.

"Or Builder wells?" Verena added quickly.

That was starting to steer more into areas he sensed would anger the elements if he shared too much. All he said was, "I'm still figuring all that out."

"Tread cautiously in there," Kilian warned. "Images, especially in the mind, become symbols that carry great weight. You've created symbols that embody the living elements in ways none of us have ever achieved. Crossing bridges, building bridges, or breaking bridges can have significant real-world results that we don't understand yet."

Both Verena and Student Eighteen nodded agreement.

"You sound like Porphyry," Connor grumbled.

Kilian sat forward sharply. "What did you say?"

Student Eighteen said, "That's right. When the elements popped into Connor's mind, they were followed by Porphyry."

"Your porphyry affinity manifests in your mind like the elementals?" Kilian demanded, looking as startled by that as by anything they had discussed.

"It's always felt like a rampager, prowling in my heart. After my last ascension, it has appeared in rampager form, and like the elements it's taken on a personality of its own. "

"It spoke to us. Told us the pack protects the pack leader," Student Eighteen said. She rubbed her arms and shivered at the memory. Connor didn't blame her. Porphyry could be a shock to the system if one wasn't used to it.

Kilian looked astonished. "I can understand the elements appearing to you in human form. Sort of. We access their power and walk with them through our affinities, but they're somehow separate from the rest of the red and green powers. But porphyry is just another affinity, isn't it?"

"It should be, but somehow it seems to have a life of its own," Connor said.

"What is it doing in your mind? What does it want?" Verena asked. She was looking at Connor as if he'd grown a second head. With his fleshcrafting abilities he probably could. He wondered if he suddenly sprouted another face if that would distract them enough to stop questioning him for a while.

"It's not trying to take control or force me to become a rage monster again. Ever since my last ascension it seems to accept my will without question."

"The pack leader. Like wolves," Student Eighteen said.

"Something like that. It seems to want to protect me."

He nearly told them about how Porphyry did not seem to trust the elements, how it had blocked him on that final bridge and how it had encircled his mind when he had stepped into Fire and raised that elfonnel. Porphyry's actions weren't entirely clear to Connor so he wouldn't be able to explain to the others, and he feared that would make them only more distrustful of the gifts the elementals were bestowing upon him. So he said nothing about it.

Kilian said, "You're the first person I know of who has ever found a way to tap porphyry without extreme danger to yourself. I'm encouraged by that, but still disturbed that it's appearing like it is. Are other affinities manifesting in human form to you?"

Connor shook his head, and he was pretty happy about that. Having five new people in his mind was disconcerting enough. Adding a bunch more would make his brain as fractured as Aifric's.

"Good. You have enough weirdness going on in there," Kilian said. "We're going to have to discuss your relationship with the elements again soon." When Connor started to protest, he held up a calming hand. "I know they've restricted what you can share, but I need you to negotiate for more, even if it's just to share with me. There's too much we don't understand, and I don't like it."

Connor had already shared far more than he had planned to, and it left him feeling grumpy. A headache was growing behind his eyes. "Why don't we talk about some of your secrets first? How did you move so fast when you were saving the other Juggernaut pilots? Not even I can run like that."

Kilian grinned, looking like a much younger man. "That's one secret you are ready for. I call it superfracking. As far as I know, I'm the only one who has ever managed it. I think today is a good day to teach you the trick."

That was more like it. As much as Connor was not enjoying the grilling session, he loved studying new aspects of affinities with Kilian. Unfortunately, despite how great he'd felt earlier, exhaustion was creeping back over him. He'd really pushed himself to the brink of no return with that elfonnel. He doubted he could run to the toilet, let alone superfrack.

So he said, "Sounds amazing, but can we wait until tomorrow? I need to rest more today."

"I'm not surprised. Usually after I return from elfonnel form, I sleep for days."

"I'd take half that much time."

"Take as much as you need," Kilian said.

Student Eighteen added, "Unless the queen's army moves out again."

"She'll need time to recuperate too," Kilian said.

Verena said, "Well, when you go running, can I come try too?"

Connor could never deny her, not when she was pleading with those big blue eyes.

Luckily, Kilian said, "Probably not. Sorry, but I don't think anyone who hasn't ascended at least the second threshold could manage it, and Connor is going to need a full measure of basalt to do it. It would be impossible if he loaned any to anyone else."

Verena sighed, looking dejected. She hated missing out on any research. So Connor said, "After we're done practicing, I'll loan you some more basalt and I'll teach you how to frack."

Aifric's face shuddered a little as Rith took the control position. She rubbed her hands and said, "We'll join you. The day someone fracks for the first time is a memorable occasion."

"Does it hurt?" Verena asked uneasily.

Rith gave her a wicked grin. "Absolutely. I screamed and Mariora wet herself."

She blinked a couple times and her voice changed pitch just a little. "I did not. That's your memory."

She grimaced and Aifric stepped into the control position. She rubbed her temple. "Don't mind them. They'll work it out eventually."

Connor wondered if they were creating a mental Strider course for the two women to race. It was probably one of their favorite pastimes when they weren't controlling their body.

Verena looked a little less sure of herself but Connor squeezed her hand. "It'll be fun. And I'll make sure no one gets seriously hurt."

CHAPTER FIVE
If Only Crazy People Were Always Wrong

Ailsa stood in the top floor ballroom of the palace of Crann. The queen had chosen the enormous space as the only place in the huge city fitting to serve as her audience hall. The unique waterfall feature, tumbling down from the high roof into a large fountain pool served as a tiny reminder of the majestic Mealt Falls of Donleavy.

Queen Dreokt had fashioned a glittering throne of ice where she sat straight-backed, but her gaze was distant and unfocused. She looked battered, even though she had slept straight through the past day since returning from chasing Connor upriver. Ailsa had waited expectantly, refusing to allow her deepest thoughts rise to the surface, even while the queen was gone. The habits of self-preservation were too ingrained, too necessary. She could not let her worry for Connor crack her carefully maintained façade.

She probably needn't have worried about that. The sight of the giant new mountain on the northeastern horizon, surrounded by lower peaks, generated a lot of worry from everyone in the city. Even though it was miles away, she'd clearly seen the giant fire-bound elfonnel immersed in the astonishing eruption. The monster must have been immense for them to see it from so far. Everyone assumed the elfonnel was the queen ripping apart her enemies, but elfonnel were terrifying on the best of days.

When the city had begun to shake, the general sense of fear had escalated to panic. Some buildings had crumbled, while many

others bore minor damage, but Ailsa sensed that things could have
gone significantly worse.

When the queen finally returned, entirely encased in a suit of
earth, she had seemed shaken, and had staggered while she walked,
as if drunk or badly injured. Screaming incoherently in half a dozen
languages, she had tossed servants and officers out of her way, seriously injuring several of them. She had closeted herself in her quarters and allowed no one to enter, but had demanded Ailsa bring the
best sandstone she could find, including a sculpted piece.

Luckily she had one ready, and had actually been in the process of sculpting another with the secret intention of sending it
to Connor. In one of the messages from Ivor she had learned that
Connor had exhausted the last sculpted sandstone pendant again.
Now that he was ascended like the queen, he should not need it,
but she couldn't resist the urge to make him another anyway.

Queen Dreokt had never requested sandstone. Ailsa had managed to catch a glimpse of the queen in her quarters when one of
her mindless servants opened the door to accept the stones. The
earthen suit she'd been wearing had melted away from her face, but
still covered her from neck to toe. Her face looked haggard, her skin
raw, and her hair was missing.

Definitely had a run-in with Connor. That boy had a special gift
for burning the hair off women who annoyed him. Ailsa took it as
a good sign that perhaps Connor had survived the day.

Now a day and a half later, the queen had emerged and looked
outwardly restored, but Ailsa sensed she wasn't yet whole. What
could have hurt her so badly? She'd healed in a matter of minutes
from that Mhortair assault in Donleavy months ago when the assassins had severed her torso from her legs and removed her arms.
She'd barely seemed annoyed by that trauma, and yet now she still
seemed unstable. Her face looked unlined, but gaunt, and her hair
extended barely down to her shoulders. She wore a stunning gown
of emerald green that covered the rest of her body, but Ailsa had
spent too much time around her in recent months not to spot the
subtle clues of lingering problems.

The gloves weren't even subtle. She'd never seen Queen Dreokt
wear gloves. The ones she now wore reached up to her elbows,
but were made of white leather rather than the more fashionable
satin. Why did she need them? Her torso under the dress seemed
blockier too, as if she was still wearing that suit of earth. More
telling, her hands occasionally shook where she gripped the arms

of the throne, little tremors racked her torso, and her legs twitched every minute or so. She didn't seem to realize she was doing it as she stared unseeing toward the waterfall.

Ailsa's practiced eye could spot the tiniest variations in shape, so the queen's distress screamed at her. More interesting, she had noticed subtle changes to the queen's body in conjunction with those tremors. It was almost as if the queen was slowly rebuilding herself from the neck downward and removing the earthen shell as the work progressed. Her shoulders and chest seemed normal, and her waist looked far more refined than even a few moments ago. Ailsa yearned to know what had transpired. Had Connor hurt her, or had she indeed turned elfonnel and suffered exceptional trauma returning to human form? Maybe an issue caused by her previous long sleep in elfonnel form?

Ailsa dared allow a flicker of those questions to touch her surface thoughts. It would seem odd if the queen picked up nothing about her present state. She knew Ailsa would wonder. The two of them were alone in the throne room other than a few of the silent, mind-wiped servants. The queen had summoned Ailsa before anyone else, despite repeated frantic messages from General Aonghus that he needed to speak with her immediately.

She began to speak softly, but Ailsa didn't understand the words. She understood enough of the various languages of the Arishat League that she caught hints of Althin, Sehrazad, and Varvakin mixed in among the babble, but most of the words were in a language completely unfamiliar to her. She leaned closer, concentrating, wishing she had a way to record the jumble for later deciphering. The queen didn't seem to realize she was speaking, and Ailsa bet there were secrets embedded in the cryptic monologue she needed to know.

After another tremor that shook the queen more than most, she blinked and switched to Obrioner, but her gaze remained distant and unfocused. With a jolt of surprise, Ailsa realized the queen's voice was full of fear. She whispered, "Triath, all is folly. I don't think I can withstand them much longer, but how do I restore the final bridge? The one secret we never explored is the one that might destroy us all."

Ailsa took a step closer, silently urging the queen to say more. She allowed her surface thoughts to reflect concern and curiosity. Unfortunately, either those thoughts or her movement caught the queen's attention. She blinked, her gaze fixing on Ailsa, and she scowled.

"Don't pry into secrets you can't hope to understand! Do you hear me? Prying into the unknown is what destroyed my family!"

"I won't. I promise," Ailsa assured her, unnerved by the wild intensity in the queen's eyes. She didn't look entirely herself, and it was hard enough to weather the unpredictable storm of the queen's fast-flipping moods on good days. She infused her surface thoughts with worry for her liege.

"I'll be all right, Ailsa," Queen Dreokt said with a deep sigh and a benevolent smile. "I just need time to set things right."

"I have no doubt. We witnessed your fiery elfonnel even from here."

"It wasn't mine!" she shrieked, flipping into a rage. "Curse Kubatana and his madness. I'm the one who's suffered most from it, but I fear not even I can save my people from the ultimate ramifications of his failures."

"Kubatana?" Ailsa dared ask. She had an excellent memory for names, but had never heard that one. It sounded foreign.

The queen lurched in her seat, grimacing in obvious pain, worse than Ailsa had ever seen. She gazed up at the waterfall again and switched back to that strange language Ailsa didn't understand. Ailsa wanted to slap her and shout at her to speak Obrioner, but that would get her killed.

So she only asked, "Pardon?"

Queen Dreokt didn't acknowledge her, but luckily did switch to Obrioner, her voice soft and angry. "Are you sure they can't rise through these filters?"

The queen cocked her head, as if listening to someone. Maybe she was reliving an old conversation? After a moment, she spoke again. "The high committee on the advanced methodologies for safe pursuit of sylfaen research techniques has ruled conclusively that any access into their domain is strictly forbidden. We must produce irrefutable proof of safety protocols or they'll shut us down with severe prejudice."

Another pause.

"No, we can't stop now. Affinities are safe. How much more proof do they need? . . . I won't let those administrative cowards stop us. We've made too many advancements. We'll stand up to them if we must. With Harley and Tristan and their teams, we'll show them."

A longer pause, another lurching tremor, and her expression turned wild. Ailsa watched, fascinated as the queen suffered through some kind of delirium. What had Connor done to her? In her most secret thoughts, she allowed herself to whisper, "And why couldn't you have done just a little more?"

"We have to run. Even if we defeat them, they've turned everyone against us . . . I know we dug too deep, but that should prove our power . . . Too many dead . . . I have the map! I believe the lands are real, beyond the western sea. It's outside of their reach. We can start over, finish our work, and prove them wrong. We can harness our affinities there with none of the prejudice from Kubatana's folly."

Her rambling words trailed into indistinct whispers, even though Ailsa dared lean closer to listen. She kept her surface thoughts filled with concern for her queen's health, and unshakable confidence in her ability to recover from the injuries sustained by the revolutionaries.

In her deepest thoughts, she tried to memorize the words and keep her enthusiasm in check. If she was hearing it right, it sounded like the queen was reliving the events that led to her flight to Obrion from her original homeland. The clues tied in with other bits and pieces the queen had shared about the research she and her husband had pioneered in creating the first affinities and filtering the sylfaen, but added insights into the opposition they had faced. Something about Kubatana had affected their work, but what?

She allowed her surface thoughts to wonder about that. It was a risk, but she felt she had to take it.

Queen Dreokt snapped out of her reverie and rubbed her face with one gloved hand. Her eyes were bloodshot for a second before the redness drained away. She regarded Ailsa with a calculating gaze, and Ailsa forced herself to remain standing calmly, surface thoughts dwelling on relief that the queen seemed to be feeling better, and gratitude that she'd decided to share more of her past.

She hadn't decided to share anything, but hopefully the thought that Ailsa interpreted the delirium that way would ease her mood.

"You're the only advisor I trust to hear these things," Queen Dreokt said finally.

Ailsa curtsied, her surface thoughts thrilled at the praise. She ventured to ask, "May I inquire as to how Kubatana's work impacted your own marvelous research?"

"He failed, that's how!" Queen Dreokt snapped. "He delved into the power of elements two centuries before I was born. He was a genius, but he pushed the boundaries and destroyed himself and all his research in the worst sylfaen lab disaster in recorded history."

She slumped back in her seat, looking dejected. "His mistake somehow gave the elementals life. They wreaked terrible damage to our country before the breach was repaired."

"I don't understand," Ailsa said. "You speak of the elements as if they are self-aware."

"They are. Somehow they found consciousness through Kubatana's folly. They have manifested enough times over the centuries that researchers recognized they still lived, still sought to meddle in the world of men."

Ailsa frowned. Some pieces of the queen's ranting began to make sense, but she still felt like she was missing something important. "So when you established tertiary affinities . . ."

The queen nodded, looking exhausted, rubbing at her face. "We tapped into the power of the elements, but since that power was filtered through stones, it limited their ability to influence us. I felt convinced we had finally cracked the problem to not only safely filter the sylfaen, but also to access elemental powers. Our research should have changed the world."

"Then I don't understand why you faced such opposition."

"Because the research oversight council was run by cowards!" the queen shouted. "We proved the safety of our affinities, but they rejected our research and ordered it destroyed." Her voice turned cold, her gaze icy. "We refused."

"You had to fight them," Ailsa guessed.

"We thought a skirmish or two would prove the value of our work, but it only enraged them. Then there was the unfortunate incident with sinking that island, but we didn't yet know we could draw too deep. That unfortunate event helped establish necessary boundaries."

Her comments after Harley and Evander had wrecked the Carraig and destabilized Mt Murdo finally made sense. The pieces were falling into place, but Ailsa still didn't understand her fear. "It sounds like there remains some danger."

Queen Dreokt hesitated, then declared, "Yes, Ailsa. I'm afraid there is great danger. We pushed through too many thresholds, and my dear Kirstin delved too deep into the unknown of the Builder powers. We stepped into shadows better left alone, and that folly cost me both Triath and Kirstin."

"I never knew," Ailsa said softly. "I had heard only that your husband suffered some kind of breakdown."

"Kirstin triggered it somehow. I still don't understand what she did, but it shattered his defenses. He lost himself within earth and could not return. I had to destroy him to save our world." A tear glittered in her eye before it evaporated with a little puff of steam.

A shiver of dread chilled Ailsa. She kept her surface thoughts fixed on sorrow for the loss of the great king, but deep inside, her mind was racing. They had hunted the queen's weakness, but it sounded like not even she knew what it was, other than something Builders could do. Was it tied to the Builder threshold? Connor worked so closely with the Builders, could they blunder right into the same problem that had destroyed the old king, and Kirstin? Her friends were desperately hunting the very secrets that might destroy them. The truth left her feeling numb.

All along, Queen Dreokt had been right to try to stop them.

"Of course I'm right!" the queen snapped.

Ailsa cringed. She hadn't realized she'd let that last thought filter to her surface persona, and she made sure to strengthen the separation between them. The queen didn't look angry, and she sensed no additional aggressive invasion of her mind. Her palms suddenly felt sweaty and she fought to suppress her fear. She'd nearly given herself away in the very moment she learned critical truths.

She managed to say, "Indeed, you are wise to recognize danger and protect your kingdom."

Queen Dreokt leaned forward, her eyes filling with crashing waves. "Speak nothing of this to anyone else. Our world hangs by a thread. My wicked son and grandson have corrupted the one promising child I hoped to raise to greatness. They not only refuse to understand the dangers, but hunt the very thing that will destroy them."

"Surely you can overcome any false teaching they've indoctrinated him with." Ailsa filled her surface persona with trust in her liege, but deep inside, she struggled to come to grips with the startling truth. Everything was flipped upside down. Queen Dreokt really was protecting them from an even greater danger.

"I was confident I could until our last encounter, but now it appears I'll have to destroy him. I can construct worthy servants out of most people, but great ones like Connor, and like my own idiotic children cannot. The transition sunders their affinities and would make them all but useless. I'm afraid all of them must die."

"May I inquire as to what changed your mind?" Ailsa dared ask.

Queen Dreokt sagged back in her throne, sighed, and rubbed her temples. "The wicked child led me into a trap. A trap! Can you believe they would dare such an affront to my honor?"

"He has always been unruly."

"Unruly yes, but now they meddle in the very ramverk. They threaten to undermine the foundation of everything I've built on this continent. They have no concept of the destruction they might unleash."

It looked like together they'd unleashed plenty of destruction. The sight of the great, fiery elfonnel took on an even more ominous meaning. Other elfonnel had risen in the past and caused terrible damage, but Ailsa suspected that when Queen Dreokt or Connor raised one, the dangers were far greater. She needed to know the specifics of those dangers, but sensed she couldn't push the queen to reveal more so soon.

Luckily, it appeared they'd contained the eruption remarkably well. From her tower window, it had appeared the disaster could have easily covered the few miles to Crann and buried the city in ash, but the billowing cloud had been contained, then swept out of the air altogether. The mountains had remained remarkably condensed, rising high but far narrower than natural.

Even stranger than the rapid subsiding of the trembling were the reports from a Sentry she knew that the earth appeared to have stabilized under Mount Murdo and along the borders. Although he couldn't walk the earth that far, he'd assured her that he could feel those unstable lands like distant thunder over the horizon. Now that thunder was gone. That suggested an equally unprecedented mastery of earth powers. Had someone raised an earth elfonnel too? Were the queen's fears exaggerated?

"Surely you punished them for their treachery," Ailsa said.

"I will. By my husband's blessed memory, I will. But the Builders revealed yet another vile trick and struck at the integrity of my affinities." She scowled and slammed her hand down on the arm of her throne, shattering it. "I will have order. This insurrection, this reckless abandonment of reason must stop."

She leaned back in her throne, suddenly appearing spent, as if her tantrum had exhausted her strength. She placed a weary hand over her eyes.

"Your generals and staff are eager to meet with you. Shall I send them away until later?" Ailsa offered.

"No. I must meet with them, but in a moment." The queen dropped her hand and sighed, looking old, her eyes filled with sorrow. "The burdens I carry feel overwhelming today. You are my only true friend, Ailsa, and if I don't confide my deepest fears to someone, I fear I won't have the strength to do what must be done."

Ailsa curtsied, her surface thoughts overjoyed that the queen trusted her so much, mingled with a somber realization of the great trust being placed upon her. In her deepest thoughts, she exulted. Finally, she might learn the vital pieces that might make sense of everything.

"I am entirely at your disposal," she said with perfect honesty.

Chapter Six
A Gift with a Catch

Nicklaus concentrated on a small piece of soapstone held in his hand as he floated in the middle of his research room, surrounded by three hundred gallons of clear water. It was hard to balance everything he was doing, and he had to concentrate so hard he was showing his teeth again.

Governess Christin didn't like him showing his teeth. She said he looked like he was snarling, and high nobles weren't ever supposed to snarl, but that seemed silly. Verena bit her lip sometimes when she concentrated really hard, and Hamish liked to make himself throw up testing Althin chemicals. No one complained about their habits. He hadn't even bitten anyone in days, and that cook shouldn't have surprised him when he snuck into the locked kitchen pantry using blind coal.

To help him focus, Nicklaus slowly somersaulted in place, head over heel, over and over again. Hamish always said he needed to train his stomach not to reach the stomach lurch point too soon if he wanted to become a great flier, and Nicklaus loved flying. So he practiced all the time.

It was easy to spin in the middle of that big globe of water that he'd created using pieces of soapstone placed around the room and linked into a higher-level mechanical. That part was easy, as was keeping himself dry in there and breathing with a tiny piece of quartzite. The tricky part was creating a boat out of water.

Verena had told him about the Underwater Slide they'd used to escape Obrion, and she'd promised to get Connor to make one for him, but then they all left for the war. It was really boring in New Schwinkendorf without all the soldiers. Christin tried to cheer him up by scheduling tests every day for him to help shoot at researchers, but they screamed a lot more than the soldiers did, even when he didn't hardly hit them at all, and she never let him take any weapons home. He was down to four diorite bombs hidden in one sock, and that half a missile he was sneaking back to his bedroom one piece at a time.

If he could make a Slide for himself, he could sneak away to the river and have an adventure. That would be better than flying because there were too many scouts watching the air, and they spotted him every single time he flew his couch-cushion Swift out the window. Almost all the Water Moccasins were at the war, so he bet he could escape all day. That would be so much fun, especially if he could sneak that speedsling from storage that he'd discovered the day before.

As Nicklaus concentrated on the piece of soapstone, he was very careful to apply each step in the command sequence he'd planned. Water had taught him about creating layered commands, and he was getting really good at it, but sometimes he missed steps. He'd already tried using just one command, ordering the soapstone to make a boat, but that didn't work.

It turned out that making a boat was a lot more complicated than anyone had ever told him. He had visited the Nister River just north of the city the day before with Christin and convinced her they should take a boat ride. She liked boats and enjoyed the excursion until he jumped overboard. The fact that he stayed underwater for seven minutes studying the hull, breathing with quartzite, made her really cranky.

He didn't understand why she panicked so often. She was a good tutor, but she got so stressed all the time. He used to wonder about that, but he overheard Hamish say no one ever understands women, so he decided to accept the fact that she would have hysterical episodes for no reason.

Nicklaus had worked hard to design seventeen commands to build an underwater ship, and he was on command number three. Concentrating on the stone, he pushed the command on top of the previous two that had started forming the shape of a hull. Put a floor over the sides.

The waters in front of him shivered, and something started to happen. He grinned with that fun sense of victory he felt whenever he got stones to do what he wanted. They usually listened better than most grown-ups. Tall people always seemed to think kids didn't have good ideas, although he found after he shot them with a few hundred hornets, they tended to pay attention better.

"Nicklaus."

The unexpected voice broke his concentration, and the waters that had begun forming a deck over the hull shivered apart. He recognized Water's voice, so it was okay. He could make the Slide later. Water was always fun to talk to. He stopped spinning.

"I'm practicing," he said proudly.

"I see that. Good boy."

He was thrilled to see her materialize in the water right in front of him. She was tall and beautiful, with long, flowing hair and a glittering gown. She looked as regal as Queen Aunt Sybilie, so he bowed like his mother taught him. She'd never appeared to him before, but just spoke to him. If she had waited another minute or two, she could have seen his new water boat.

"Will you say hello to Connor and Verena for me when you see them?" Nicklaus asked. "We talk with speakstones sometimes, but I bet they would like a message from you."

Water smiled warmly. "I will try, but Connor doesn't always listen, and Verena can't seem to hear me very well."

"That's sad. Connor seemed really happy that he got to talk with you."

"He is, but I am not sure I can teach him everything he needs to know," she said gravely.

"To beat the wicked queen?" he asked.

She nodded, and Nicklaus felt terrible. He liked Connor, especially since Verena liked him so much. He didn't want them to get hurt. "You could try shooting them. That makes people listen."

Water chuckled. "I might have to try that."

Nicklaus gestured at the globe of water holding position in the center of the room. "What do you think of my practice room?"

"You have made excellent progress, Nicklaus. That is why I'm here. Connor has learned much, but he thinks he knows better than I do how to proceed, and Verena spends so much time with him, I fear she won't listen to me."

Nicklaus nodded gravely. That made sense.

She continued. "They used the instructions I shared with you to create a higher-level mechanical."

"Really? Did they control water like me?" he asked excitedly. He bet Verena was really happy he told Christin everything Water shared with him.

"No, they made a different one, but they haven't thanked you yet for sharing your knowledge, have they?" she asked.

They hadn't, but Nicklaus didn't mind sharing. "I try to help."

"You do a wonderful job, and that's why I'm here. I need your help."

"Really? What can I do?" Nicklaus asked, filled with pride that Water needed his help. Even though the Builders let him help test their defensive mechanicals, he didn't often get people asking for his help. They thought he was too young or something.

"I am going to teach you how to make a mechanical to rival the greatest work of Builder Kirstin."

"Wow! Verena and Hamish are going to be thrilled," Nicklaus laughed. He heard about Kirstin's Defense. If he got to make something that powerful, he'd have to ask Connor to make a monster swarm to test it. He bet Connor could make excellent monsters.

Water's smile faded. "You can't tell them about it until it's finished. In fact, you can't even tell Christin that we've talked. This is our little secret."

Nicklaus frowned, his enthusiasm fading. He liked secrets, but he didn't like the idea of not sharing with Verena.

Water drew closer and placed a hand on his shoulder. "They are preparing for a terrible battle. A lot of people might get hurt if you won't help me."

Nicklaus had seen enough fighting, and he knew lots of people risked their lives to protect the kingdom. Especially Uncle Kilian. He was the bravest man in the world. If he could be brave and fight, Nicklaus could be too.

So he asked, "What do you want me to do?"

She smiled. "I will explain everything. One more thing, though. You will need a flight suit."

He had been wanting a suit for months, but his enthusiasm faded. "I know where Hamish keeps his spare parts, but Christin said mother forbids me from having a suit yet."

"Your mother cares for you, but you may have to disobey a little bit in order to help. Are you willing to do that for me?" she asked.

"Of course," he told her happily. "Christin always says I'm better at disobeying than anyone she's ever known."

CHAPTER SEVEN
Making Bad Situations Worse

Ailsa barely noticed as one of the silent, worthy servants stationed near the door opened it and stepped out into the hallway. It looked like Princess Catriona, although she no longer recognized her own name. Ailsa remained standing to the right of the queen's throne, her face calm, her surface thoughts filled with gratitude that her liege had trusted her enough to share so much.

Deep down inside, she struggled to keep her inner thoughts silent. It was nearly beyond her willpower to force herself to not think about the startling revelations she'd just learned. The vital truths were so startling, so terrifying, she could not process the information yet. If she tried, she would lose focus and give herself away.

She simply could not allow herself to fail now. Too many lives hung in the balance.

So she forced herself to not think at all, but simply observe. It was perhaps the hardest thing she'd ever done. Only months of practicing splitting her thoughts gave her the discipline to manage it.

General Aonghus burst into the room. He had clearly been waiting just outside, but not even in his impetuous anger dare he burst in on the queen unannounced. General Rosslyn followed behind, looking troubled but composed.

Ailsa focused on her to take her mind off everything else she could not think about. She had made cautious attempts to get to know General Rosslyn in recent weeks, but Rosslyn had so far resisted. Everyone in the queen's employ was terrified of revealing any weakness, so they protected themselves rigorously. It made learning her heart extremely difficult, but in her secret inner self, Ailsa maintained hope that she would eventually succeed.

Rosslyn was a patriot, which could mean multiple things. The queen had taken her children, twisted their minds, and held their lives at her whim. Unless Ailsa could discover a way to deal with that threat, Rosslyn would always be the queen's devoted general.

A gaggle of other officers followed behind, all looking fearful and uneasy. General Aonghus rushed forward and dropped quickly to one knee before the queen, who had already repaired the broken arm of her throne.

"My liege. Our marble affinity is broken." Speaking the words aloud seemed to shake him to the core, and he glanced up with desperation in his eyes.

Queen Dreokt waved a dismissive hand. "Of course it's gone. Sacrificed fighting our enemies who dare rise in rebellion to my rule."

That generated a gasp of dismay from everyone. Ailsa contained her surprise better than most. She knew far more than any of the queen's other subjects about affinities and how they worked, but not even she had realized the queen had dared destroy another affinity.

"But how? I mean, when will it be restored?" Aonghus stammered.

He had only recently ascended, becoming one of the most powerful Firetongues alive. His affinity defined him, so its loss must be like losing his identity. That calm control that he had exhibited since his ascension was gone, replaced by a wild look that was not even justified by fires burning in his eyes.

"Not for some years, at best. At the moment, it's gone and we must proceed with that understanding."

Aonghus seemed to wilt in upon himself. He whispered, "Gone? Years?"

In another of her abrupt mood swings, Queen Dreokt smiled like a benevolent grandmother. She gestured him to rise and approach the throne where she patted his face tenderly. "It's all right, child. Our enemies have also lost access to fire."

Rosslyn gasped. "Kilian has lost fire?"

That generated another round of murmurs, excited this time. Kilian was one of their mightiest foes, even more feared than Connor. He had lived far too long and fought far too many battles, but if he too was hamstrung by the loss of marble, it improved the chances of victory dramatically.

"Indeed, my wicked son is harvesting the fruits of his rebellion. But you, dear Aonghus. What must we do about you? A general with no tertiary affinity is of no use to me."

Aonghus paled, his frantic panic taking on a new level of suppressed intensity. If someone had no use in the queen's court, they did not survive long. He started to stammer something, but she shushed him with a finger across his lips. He froze, wide-eyed with terror, but unable to move without fear of triggering her wrath.

She pulled his head down and kissed his forehead. At her touch, he cried out in agony and crumbled to the floor at the foot of her throne.

As he convulsed, screaming and clutching at his head, Ailsa tried to maintain her calm. She had witnessed many killed or brutalized under the queen's hand, after all, but Aonghus had been one of her generals.

Queen Dreokt stared down at Aonghus with that same benevolent smile on her face. "Therefore, I choose to make you into a servant worthy of your position."

Aonghus gasped, tears rolling down his flushed cheeks. "It's gone!"

"Of course it's gone. We already discussed that."

He rolled to his hands and knees, shaking so violently he almost pitched over sideways. "I could not connect with marble before, but my affinity was intact. Now it's gone."

"A bridge that leads nowhere is a bridge that must be cast down and replaced by another," Queen Dreokt said with a happy smile. She gestured Ailsa closer. "Do you have any slate handy, my dear?"

"Of course." Ailsa withdrew a thin wafer and extended it, but the queen gestured toward Aonghus.

He took it, obviously confused. Then his eyes widened and he exclaimed, "I can feel it!"

"Of course you can. Rosslyn already commands water for me. Fire is of no use at the moment, and air would be less useful unless you had ascended more than you can. Slate is the great battle stone, therefore it is worthy of your position and you are worthy of that affinity."

Aonghus stumbled to his feet, staring at the little wafer in absolute astonishment. He didn't seem to realize he was still shaking. He looked up from the slate and stammered, "Thank you!"

Ailsa let her surface thoughts fill with astonishment. She'd witnessed the queen grant new affinities to hundreds of Petralists, but she had never witnessed her sever one affinity to grant a different one. Her control over those mystic aspects of affinity powers awed Ailsa.

Queen Dreokt glanced at her with a happy smile. "I'm so glad you approve."

Ailsa curtsied. "You are indeed the queen of affinities, and your mastery of the arcane declares your right to sit on that throne."

That seemed to please the queen immensely, but then she blinked, and Ailsa could tell she had exhausted herself with that little trick. She doubted anyone else would pick up on the subtle signs. They were too worried with not drawing the queen's attention to dare make an incorrect assumption.

The queen suppressed her weariness and her mood changed again. She glanced at her officers and snapped, "Prepare the army. We will stamp out this insurrection once and for all. I want all forces prepared to march in three days."

"Three days?" Rosslyn asked with a frown. "We're ready to march at dawn."

"Not quite. It is clear that reports of the Builder slaughter were false. Despite your creative preparations, you are not ready to face them. I will personally assist in making final preparations. We will shatter their forces and reunite Obrion in one overwhelming strike."

"Very good," Rosslyn said, saluting.

The other officers mimicked her and turned to leave. The queen called after Aonghus in a tender voice. "Start your training immediately, dear Aonghus. I need you in fighting form before we reach Merkland."

He bowed so deeply he almost fell over, then rushed from the room.

Ailsa watched them go, her surface thoughts filled with admiration for the queen, eager to learn about her preparations. What would she craft to destroy the enemy?

"You'll have to wait to see it firsthand, my dear. I need you working around the clock between now and the time we march. I need as much sculpted soapstone and slate as you can produce."

Ailsa curtsied. "I will see to it at once, Your Majesty. I have a small number of stones completed already, but I may not be able to complete very many new ones in only three days."

"Don't bother crafting them to your usual standards. These will not be for me, and I'd prefer they not contain the strength for any of my servants to attempt to raise an elfonnel. They are not ready."

"That will simplify things," Ailsa confirmed. Even partial sculptures would magnify the power of the Petralists wielding them several fold.

Queen Dreokt clapped her hands and laughed like a little girl considering a party. "See if you can enhance some granite and basalt and concentrate extra power in them. I believe you'd accomplished such a feat before, yes?"

"I understand how it's done," Ailsa said. She'd magnified granite powder for Connor once with spectacular results at the Carraig, but she did not allow her surface thoughts to dwell on that.

The queen called for servants to attend her and take additional orders. Craigroy entered with them. He had kept his distance since Queen Dreokt had beaten him down so savagely, but had not left. A man like Craigroy could not help but draw close to the greatest power, like a moth to the forbidden flame.

The queen scowled as he bowed deeply. "I'm not yet finished being unhappy with you."

"Forgive me, Your Majesty. I am your humble servant. I wish only to convey that sources to the north suggest great confusion and fear among the enemy."

He was wise not to mention that his sources were speakstones. The fact that he was still getting regular updates from those speakstones, which he passed daily through Ailsa to the queen, suggested her note of warning might have been waylaid, or they had failed to discover the speakstones. Or they had found them and were engaging in clever misinformation. She knew them well enough to hope in her deepest, best-guarded thoughts that the latter was the case. In her surface thoughts, she dwelt on how she suspected Craigroy wasn't trustworthy.

His news pleased the queen enough to not obliterate him, unfortunately. "What else do your sources suggest?"

"They suggest there may be agents of the revolution here in Crann. That's how they knew to strike at you here."

Her good mood evaporated under a fierce rage that reddened her face. "Agents? Here? Corruption and lies! When will my kingdom be purified of it all?"

She rounded on Ailsa. "Your search of Donleavy found nothing of those traitors. Have you heard of anything here in Crann?"

"Not as yet, Your Majesty, but I shall initiate an immediate investigation," Ailsa promised.

Their abrupt departure from Donleavy had interrupted her plans for leveraging that search, but she could perhaps use some of those ideas and retool them for Crann.

Craigroy said, "Perhaps I may be of service in assisting in this effort."

Oh, that was smooth. Ailsa had thought him effectively leashed. She said, "I don't believe I need assistance."

"You probably don't, but Craigroy is the one who brought me this intelligence. Let him work with you. Find out if his sources are true. If they are, bring me the spies. If you succeed, Craigroy may win his place back into my good graces."

He bowed and cast a victorious glance at Ailsa.

She curtsied in turn, her face expressionless. Craigroy was playing a dangerous game. It was clearly time to remove him.

CHAPTER EIGHT
Hey Guys, Watch This!

Connor slowed beside Kilian just south of Badurach Pass. They had raced on basalt-fracked legs from Merkland. Although he was quickly becoming addicted to flying, Connor still loved the freedom of basalt. There was nothing quite like running tirelessly over miles of terrain.

He felt strong and eager to learn a new trick. He'd slept straight for another twenty-four hours, then eaten another literal mountain of food for breakfast. He'd transformed it all instantly into energy with his gluttoncrafting to the astonishment of both Shona and Ivor, who had joined him for the meal.

The plateau on the south side of the pass was empty. The reinforcements from Granadure, New Schwinkendorf, and the Arishat League were all massed on the Grandurian side of the border, just to the north of the broken peak. The forces were growing every day, and that army would prove invaluable in the coming confrontation.

Instead of continuing up to the narrow causeway leading over the deep chasm to the sundered gap and Granadure, Kilian stopped, his legs snapping back into normal shape. Connor followed suit, eager for the super-fracking lesson.

"The first thing you need to understand about superfracking is rest."

"I've slept most of the past couple days. I think that's enough, don't you?"

"I'm talking about rest in a different way, a way that few fast movers can understand. Just as stilling seems counterintuitive, so does the key to superfracking. In order to unleash super speed, you need to create an enormous pool of energy first. You cannot simply call upon super speed in the instant you need it. Not even max-tapping provides enough."

"Is that why you looked like you were napping so much before we sprung out trap on your mom?"

"Exactly."

"You did the same thing on the way to Jagdish."

Kilian nodded with a grin. "I wasn't sure what to expect and I thought we might need the advantage."

"So how does this work?" Connor asked, more intrigued than ever.

"In some ways it's sort of like stilling. But, instead of applying that stilling power to the life forces of others to siphon energy, we actually tap both the inner and the outer aspects of basalt at the same time."

"I hadn't even realized that was possible," Connor admitted. Although as he thought about it, he had tapped both inner and outer quartzite more than once. That seemed different, though, because one enhanced his senses, while the other connected him with air.

"It's a subtle truth, and the key to making this work. When you tap both, you apply the effect of stilling not to another person's life or even to your own life force, but directly to the energy of your affinity."

It was so simple, but so profound. Connor loved it. "Could we apply stilling to other affinities to maximize them too?"

The question caught Kilian by surprise and he frowned. "I'm actually not sure. I've never tried it with any other stone."

Connor chuckled. "There's always another secret, isn't there?"

"Always," Kilian agreed with another grin. "Ready to give it a try?"

"Oh, yeah."

It took Connor a few attempts to figure out the trick to it. He could tap either inner-focused or outer-focused basalt easily. The trick was in applying the one to the other. The first time he tried it, he applied stilling to himself and nearly knocked himself unconscious. After that, he struggled to get inner-focused basalt to feed into external-focused basalt. He kept snuffing out his external-focused basalt as soon as he made the connection.

In some ways it was kind of like trying to burp, hiccup, and sneeze at the same time. He had managed that combination more than once by accident, and twice while near Hamish. Hamish had been extremely impressed and although he claimed to have mastered the technique himself, Connor had never actually witnessed him do it.

Eventually he managed the trick with basalt. He couldn't simply seize the entire power of the stone at once without overwhelming his connection. He watched Kilian, who stood in a very relaxed pose, eyes half closed, looking like he was dozing on his feet. That gave Connor the idea that he needed to tap inner basalt, but not actually apply it anywhere. He always instinctively applied it to his legs as soon as he tapped it because why tap basalt and not run?

When he finally managed to tap it but not apply it, but let himself fall into a relaxed state like Kilian, he finally managed to make the connection between basalt speed and stilling. The conduit became a flood, and energy roared out from the basalt, through stilling and back to himself, pooling inside him in a similar way to the energy he got when stilling other people.

There was a subtle difference though. After studying it for a few seconds he realized that energy was still connected back to basalt, available to tap with the rest of basalt speed.

He laughed with the thrill of the discovery. "This is amazing. I wouldn't have imagined I could multiple-tap basalt. What do I do with it now?"

Kilian roused himself and said, "As you probably noticed, you can only absorb a tiny fraction of your available basalt energy this way. So it takes quite a bit of time to store the energy you'll require to superfrack. I still have some left over from this morning so I can demonstrate the technique, but you'll most likely have to get up early tomorrow and spend a bunch of time prepping it."

"What are you talking about? I feel like I've already drained almost my entire measure of basalt."

Kilian shook his head, looking disgusted. "Of course you can do it immediately. Why wouldn't you? You've mastered all the other deep arcane stuff that I never knew about. Why not master my last big secret trick?"

As if Connor would ever believe he didn't have more secret tricks.

"Are you annoyed?" Connor asked with a grin. He so rarely got to rattle the ancient Dawnus. It was a lot of fun.

Kilian blew out a breath. "Not really. It's just I keep having to revise my expectations with you."

"They say nimbleness of mind is the first thing to go with old age," Connor chuckled.

"I'll show you nimbleness of mind," Kilian warned.

Connor held up his hands in surrender. "Just kidding. So how do we use this power?"

"Now that you have it, you need to apply it to the parts of your body that you want to superfrack. You'll need to make sure you apply it more generally than you usually do with basalt, particularly in your neck and back. Leaping into motion that fast can be very painful if you're not prepared."

Sounded like fun. Connor was more excited than ever to give it a try.

Eagerly, Connor tapped basalt and felt the conduit between his normal basalt energy and that pool that had built up inside of him. He tapped it generously to his legs, then to most of the rest of his body, just to be safe. And to help accelerate his reaction timing, he also absorbed a little obsidian and tapped that too.

Then he unleashed superfracking.

He leaped away so fast, he left his breath behind and doubted he would ever find it again. The land blurred past, many times faster than he had ever moved before, faster than when he flew, faster than he ever dreamed possible. His legs were such a blur it felt like they had just disappeared and turned into a whirlwind.

He laughed as he shot across the plateau, running north. But he was moving so fast that he reached the deep chasm separating the plateau from the broken peak of Badurach way too soon.

He was not aimed for the causeway.

Connor decided to stop, but by the time he made that choice, he had already shot right over the edge and flew across the chasm. Shouting in surprise, he instinctively tapped slate.

Just in time. He slammed into the cliff on the far side of the chasm like a stone cast from the world's biggest sling. If not for slate, he would've splattered in spectacular fashion.

With slate, he sank into the rock, sliding halfway through the peak before he could skid to a stop, surrounded by unbroken stone. There he laughed again, the sound echoing awesomely in the tiny void where he stood. He had always loved basalt, but superfracking was super fun.

He turned and superfracked the other way.

He shot out of the mountain, angled slightly higher to make it easier to cross the chasm. But again he underestimated how fast he was moving and he shot into the sky like an inverted comet. He flew right over Kilian, who stood at the lip of the chasm, hands on hips, looking at the smudge mark were Connor had disappeared a moment ago.

Connor whooped as he flew across half the plateau before landing. He tried landing in a run like he usually did with basalt, but was still superfracking. As a result, he ended up running circles so fast that he lost all sense of direction and felt like his head was going to simply fly off in a random direction. He managed to untap basalt before killing himself, and collapsed to the ground, laughing uncontrollably.

He felt like he was going to throw up, and got into the ready position. He was on his hands and knees so wouldn't get extreme distance, but he had vowed years ago never to waste an opportunity to make the attempt.

His stomach didn't cooperate, but settled from its wild spinning even before his thoughts did. That was disappointing. He was glad Hamish had not been there to witness his failure.

Kilian skidded to a stop nearby, appearing so fast Connor didn't even see him coming. He was laughing too, and he wiped tears from his eyes. "That was the most spectacular failure I've ever seen."

"Good thing I had slate or you'd be scraping me off that cliff."

When Kilian caught his breath and composure he said, "I can't believe I didn't think that one through. You've been picking things up so fast I forgot that when you struggle, you tend to fail pretty epically. Next time you try this, make sure you're pointing in a direction that has no major obstacles."

Connor nodded. "I think I'll try running down the Macantact next time."

"Good idea. Come on, there's really nothing between us and Merkland. Let's see how fast we can get back."

Connor jumped to his feet, grinning. "With superfracking, I bet we could get there before we even leave here."

Kilian laughed again then said, "And you haven't even seen everything we can do with it."

"What else can we do?" Connor asked eagerly.

"Catch me and maybe I'll tell you."

Kilian leaped away in a full superfracked sprint.

Connor immediately give chase. He never caught Kilian, but he beat his own laughter to Merkland.

CHAPTER NINE
When Simple Poisoning Is No Longer Enough

Ailsa held up a small piece of slate she was roughly sculpting into a fist and sighed. She hated working so fast and producing such slipshod work, but there was no alternative. The queen demanded as many sculpted stones as possible with their inner vortexes magnified to at least five times, and she only had a couple of days to complete the job.

She was working fast, but not as fast as she could have. She wasn't about to commit her best efforts to providing the stones the queen's army would use against her friends. She could not outright deny the queen's orders, but no one but Ailsa knew just how fast she could work if she was truly motivated.

Still, the bin beside her worktable already held several completed stones. She had been ordered to work with both slate and soapstone, and decided to alternate between the two. The downside to that was that both major battle affinities would enjoy enough stones to grant them a significant advantage. The upside was that neither of those elements would have so many sculpted stones that they would simply overwhelm all opposition.

The door to her workroom creaked and she glanced up to see Craigroy enter.

Surprising. Although they met daily to discuss their progress in searching for a spy among the queen's subjects and for Ailsa to give Craigroy the tiny daily dose of antidote he needed to stay alive, he had never dared venture into her workroom before.

She put down her tools and gave him a cool look. "I'm busy."

Craigroy glanced at the small pile of rough stones. "And no doubt working your hardest."

She extended her tools. "Think you can do better?"

He chuckled and shook his head. "Of course not. This is your domain, your place of strength. I could never compete with you here."

"Then why have you come? You're not due for another dose until tomorrow."

He drew a little closer, his good humor fading. "Why don't you just give me the full antidote now?"

They had discussed that on more than one occasion. Craigroy hated that she held such leverage against him. Most people in such a situation would have felt more terrified of dying, but not the great spymaster of Merkland. He hated losing control and knowing that someone had bested him.

"I'm assuming this unexpected visit is somehow related to the little show you pulled the other day."

"Indeed. You're a clever operator and I respect the fact that you wish to be left alone and for your past to stay in the past. You've made that point clear, and I'm willing to agree to an accord not to interfere there. In return I require freedom to make my own decisions and to craft my own place in this court."

If Ailsa could imagine any possible way that she could actually trust Craigroy, the offer would be tempting, but he was a spy and a professional liar. She knew far more than he suspected about him and his activities serving High Lord Dougal. No doubt there was much she did not know, but if he understood even a fraction of what she did know, he would plot to remove her as soon as possible.

Ailsa's position as a counselor to the queen was as secure as anyone's could be when serving such an unstable monarch, but Craigroy would not settle for anything less than supplanting her and taking that premier position for himself. It was simply his nature, and as much as he tried to disguise it, he could never act differently. To ask him to do so would be like asking the wolf to guard a pasture full of lambs without slaughtering them all.

So she said, "I'm afraid you would have to offer me more than a simple promise. I think things are going quite well. You provide useful intelligence, and I make sure it reaches our queen's ears. You benefit because she does not slaughter you for bringing her intelligence through a vile Builder mechanical."

"I would appreciate your concern for my well-being if you had not also poisoned me."

"Sometimes one must take difficult medicine before one can be cured. In your case, your illness is assuming that you belong in the throne room at all."

His eyes turned icy and he said in a soft, threatening voice, "My place is exactly where I see fit to make it. Just as I would not challenge you here in the heart of your domain, I'm warning you as a respected opponent not to challenge me further. I have made my career out of destroying those who get in my way. I suspect we could both prosper in the queen's court, but not if you continue to insist upon trying to control me and take advantage of my intelligence."

Ailsa had not expected him to make such a bold, open threat. He prospered in the shadows, not in open confrontation. Had he simply exhausted more subtle means of trying to cast off her control? That suggested she did have him in a tight spot, which was what she had assumed until his little stunt in the throne room.

Or was he clever enough to recognize the queen had been hurt far more severely than she had admitted? Perhaps he suspected she was vulnerable, or simply so distracted by the challenges of defeating the surprisingly resilient rebellion that he felt it time to make his move? Either way, he was clearly planning to take their conflict to the next level.

"You're being inconsistent, Craigroy. In one breath you say that you believe we could both prosper, but in the next breath you threaten to destroy me. It would not seem wise for me to release my hold on you in the face of such threats."

He nodded slowly. "Fine. I offered you a chance as a professional courtesy. I did not expect you to take it, but by offering it I consider my life debt paid."

"Your life debt is paid when I say it is," she said, her tone as cold as his had been earlier.

"Not in this case, not with so much dependent upon the outcome of the current conflict. You're officially warned, Ailsa. I will discover your secrets and I will reveal them to the queen. I don't know how you've concealed them thus far, but I'll make her see that you are not to be trusted."

Ailsa laughed, projecting an air of calm, honest mirth. "You're a fine one to talk about trust. Now if you'll excuse me, I have work to do."

Craigroy actually made a tiny bow before turning and striding from the room. Ailsa got back to work, but her mind chewed over that surprising exchange. Had Craigroy spoken in earnest? She could not imagine he might have, but he had exhibited more honor than she would have expected. It had to be a lie, a carefully crafted illusion prepared to throw her off and perhaps underestimate him.

Either way, she could no longer count on the simple threat of death by poisoning to stop him. Should she stop providing the antidote?

That offered the easiest solution, but perhaps not the simplest. If Craigroy suddenly died, the queen might suspect the spies that they were supposed to be hunting. Would she bother to inspect his body? Could she sense the presence of the poison and possibly ascertain its makeup? Would she put the pieces together and suspect Ailsa?

She did not dare take that risk. Not yet. If Craigroy proved too much of a distraction, she could always exercise that option. Perhaps even convince Aonghus that Craigroy was somehow a threat.

That actually offered a lot of advantages. Aonghus had seemed completely destabilized by the loss of marble and the subsequent forced establishment of a new affinity with slate. Was he susceptible now to suggestions that might drive him to an uncontrollable rage? One second of Aonghus' fury could squash Craigroy like a bug.

Or squash Ailsa.

As she completed the next rough sculpture and reached for a piece of soapstone, a new idea popped into her mind. A little smile played across her lips as she considered how to put the simple but elegant plan into action.

If she played it right, she might accomplish several objectives.

Chapter Ten

Countdown to the Apocalypse

As Connor neared the bridge over the Macantact, just north of Merkland, he slowed to a jog, wondering if Kilian had actually done him a favor by teaching him how to superfrack. He loved running with basalt, but now that he knew how to go really fast, he wasn't sure he would ever feel as satisfied with what he used to think was his top speed.

Then again, super-fracked speed was so terrifyingly fast he definitely needed to practice more. He might be able to regenerate from injuries that would prove fatal to anyone else, but getting splattered still wouldn't be fun. Worse, he might accidentally run right through someone and kill them instead. Once he mastered it, basalt might again take the place as his favorite speed affinity.

Was there maybe a higher speed to air than he had yet discovered? Could he convince Air to share another secret? She seemed pretty competitive and she probably wouldn't like it when he explained that as much as he like flying with her, she just wasn't fast enough anymore. She might share it.

Or she might shove a tornado down his shorts to remind him to have respect.

Kilian waited for him at the bridge, leaning against the railing, looking bored. Connor was going to make a wisecrack, but Shona's voice caught his attention. He had fallen into the habit of maintaining a low tap rate with all of his affinities. Now he focused on quartzite and applied a little more to his ears to catch her words.

"Connor, please respond immediately if you can hear me. I will continue repeating this message every ten minutes until you get it. We've received another update from our asset. If you can find Kilian, bring him too. Then Wolfram needs both of you to help with the next act in his little play of disinformation for Craigroy's listening device."

"What is it?" Kilian asked.

"Shona. A new update from our contact down south." They were too far away for the queen to eavesdrop on their conversations, and Rory had an excellent picket of Pathfinder scouts to block any enemy Pathfinders from sneaking close enough to listening to what they said, but Connor could still not bring himself to say Ailsa's name aloud. She was in more danger than any of them, and he would not risk adding to that out of carelessness.

In moments they found Shona in the central palace. Rory and Ivor were off meeting with troops who were working on rebuilding the city's battered defenses. Shona was dressed in an elegant gown of blue satin, and her appearance startled Connor. She looked as regal and beautiful as ever, but he'd gotten used to seeing her wearing battle leathers.

Kilian waved. "What have you learned?"

"The queen has ordered her troops to prepare to move out. Based on timing of this message, we've probably got a couple days before they begin to march."

"That seems like a long time," Connor commented.

"I don't think you're the only one who needed some time to recover," Kilian said, expression thoughtful. "But the delay does seem unusual."

Shona said, "It sounds like few understand the extent of her injuries. She's marshaling everyone."

Connor grimaced. They had incinerated and destroyed her down to the tiniest bits. If he had focused a little longer and reduced that one chunk of skull down to the component molecules, would she still have been able to regenerate, or might that have actually killed her? To think they had been so close and still failed galled him to no end.

"She's going to wait for the armies?" Kilian asked, sounding surprised.

"Worse, it sounds like she wants to personally help her army prepare. She's got sculptors preparing a bunch of low-grade sculpted stones."

"She'll already have a huge advantage in numbers," Connor complained.

"We rattled her," Kilian said, but didn't look pleased. "That means when she comes, she'll hit us with everything she's got. She'll want to overwhelm us before we can surprise her again."

"Not good. We're supposed to be the ones with new ideas," Connor said with a frown. On top of the annoyance factor for having to face someone they didn't yet know how to kill, plus an army way bigger than their own, it seemed downright insulting for that army to also prepare new, creative ways to make their lives even more miserable.

Kilian added, "I suspect the fact that we blocked her from sandstone bothered her most of all. No one has ever hit her like that."

"She'll be ready for us to attempt to duplicate the trick. We've lost the element of surprise," Shona said gravely.

"So we'd better come up with something extra creative too," Connor said.

"In just a matter of days? We worked all winter to develop the plan we just tried against her. We can't retool all of that overnight."

Kilian said, "We'll have to retool some of it. We lost marble and that means the Builders have too."

Hearing him say it reminded Connor of how much they'd sacrificed. Not only the lives of two mighty Fast Rollers, but also one of the most powerful affinity stones. Marble fueled many of the Builder mechanicals, and as he considered the ramifications on their weapons and attack strategy he grimaced. Just dealing with that one problem would require an enormous amount of rework.

Shona said, "The Builders are already on it. Verena is working here in Merkland and Hamish has gone up to the pass to oversee efforts there."

"Good. Those two have a knack for figuring out impossible things." Kilian paced away, expression thoughtful. "If the army moves out in the next couple of days, they could be here in ten if she doesn't kill half of them in forced marches."

That gave them a little time, but not a ton. Connor asked, "Are you sure she's planning to wait for the army instead of hitting us again by herself?"

Kilian said, "We'll need to prepare for both eventualities. She could make a strike at Merkland and try to take us out, or brainwipe some of us, or simply destroy most of our forces."

"Rory and Ivor are already seeing to defenses," Shona said, "but it sounds like she actually plans to remain with her army this time."

"So we need to figure out how to lure her out again," Connor said, thinking fondly of the vomit rocket.

Kilian nodded. "That would be ideal. Even if we cannot kill her outright, if we can drive her off again, that will give our armies a chance. If we can defeat her army, we might gain more time to figure out a winning strategy."

Connor hated how so much of their battle strategy had to revolve around the fact that it was extremely unlikely they could actually kill the queen. Defeating her army would be a good first step, but there had to be a way. He had hurt her badly. Could he figure out how to hit her again with that supercharged death beam? Unless she was tapping quartzite, she wouldn't even be able to see it coming.

Could they again block her from healing? He doubted it. She was far too crafty to walk into the same trap twice.

Shona pulled a small, rolled parchment from a deep pocket of her dress and handed it to Connor. "This came with the latest report. It's addressed to you." She didn't look pleased that Ailsa was keeping secrets.

Connor took the parchment and broke the seal, curious why she would keep some of the material separate. The only reason he could think of was if she had a personal message concerning his family, but she'd never done anything like that. When he unrolled it, he frowned and glanced at Kilian.

"It's gibberish."

Kilian took the letter and nodded. "This must be extremely sensitive information. She's encoded it."

"What does that mean?" Connor asked. Shona leaned closer, studying the scroll with interest.

"See this ink blot near the bottom?" Kilian pointed at what Connor had seen only as a weird, curling smudge. "This means that this is part one of three parts of a message encoded using the Grandurian spy cipher."

"I've never heard of such a thing," Connor said.

Shona looked eager. "I have. We've intercepted a few Grandurian communiques over the years, but we never figured out how to decipher them."

Kilian chuckled. "I bet you have. Don't worry, Lady Shona, I can decipher it when we have all three parts, or I could have Wolfram or Verena do it."

"Since we're all on the same side now, wouldn't it be wise to share the secret with some of the rest of us?" Shona asked sweetly, her expression as innocent as a babe's.

"Nice try, Shona," Kilian said with a wink. "Perhaps some day, but the king alone authorizes each individual given access to this secret."

She shrugged. "A girl can't be blamed for trying." Then she grinned and changed the topic. "On a much happier note, Rory just announced that they're moving up the wedding."

"When?" Connor asked.

"Tomorrow."

Chapter Eleven
It's All a Matter of Priorities

Verena removed the piece of marble from the base of a diorite missile. Her fingers moved quickly with efficiency honed over the last couple of hours of repeating the same operation a hundred times.

The warehouse in the military district of Merkland was packed with even more missiles waiting their turn. Huge piles of now-useless marble was piled in overflowing crates on one side of her worktable. Stacks of crates filled with little pieces of quartzite took up the space to her right. Thankfully, they had a lot of quartzite, and Merkland cutters were working feverishly to pound more large blocks into appropriately-sized chunks.

Verena tossed the piece of marble aside with a feeling of frustration. They'd worked so hard to develop all of their battle mechanicals. Marble played a key role in so many of them, but now it was gone, snuffed out in a way Verena never would have imagined possible.

The researcher in her loved the fact that they were learning some of the deepest secrets of affinities, power stones, and the sylfaen. There was so much she wanted to know, so much she wanted to explore, and those glimpses into deeper truths offered tantalizing hints into entirely new branches of Builder study.

Her drive to understand those truths had proven frustrating, though. She'd tried every way she could think of to connect with Water again, but hadn't felt so much as a glimmer. She had hoped developing the Sucker Punch higher-level mechanical might do it. She had to be missing something fundamental, but what? If she could only reach that Builder threshold, she might unlock so many answers and access so much more power. They desperately needed it, and she vowed to find a way.

In the meantime, they still had to survive the next battle. While she worked, her mind dwelt on the one overriding question that nagged at her like a thorn in her mind.

Why?

Queen Dreokt was scared of Builders. Something about Builders, some subtle aspect of their powers they had not yet recognized held the key to weakening the queen. It had happened to the ancient king, and her tirades against Builders and her reported reaction to the sculpted scone assault confirmed that. If only Verena could figure it out, that would change everything.

She slipped a quartzite block into position on the missile and secured it. If they had time to carefully craft the dimensions of the quartzite being placed at the base of every missile, they might actually improve performance, but there were simply too many to replace. They'd planned to complete that testing weeks ago, but it hadn't been a high enough priority since they had plenty of marble.

Even if they knew the exact parameters, it would take the cutters too long to shape the pieces. Gisela and her tiny team of sculptors couldn't help with that either because they were frantically rough-sculpting as many stones as they could. A stone sculpted to five times magnitude might not be enough for ascension, but they still offered dramatic improvements in power.

Plus, the sculpted obsidian pieces were still critical in so many of their mechanicals. If the queen had snuffed out obsidian instead of marble, she might have done the Builders far more damage. Verena shuddered to even think about it. Hopefully the queen would never discover how their remote mechanicals worked, or no doubt she would do just that.

As soon as she completed that missile repair, she nodded to two assistants waiting at either side of the table. They carefully hefted the completed missile and moved it to an empty rack on the far side of the room. As they fetched another missile for her, two other soldiers took up the completed missile and carried it away to install on one of the many mechanicals or flying craft being refitted.

Other Builders were working on the projectiles used by the rapid-fire siege weapons, or working on finalizing a batch of enormous bombs. Verena was not sure that was a great idea. The bombs had at first represented an enormous battlefield advantage, but the enemy was ready for them now. Harley had used their porphyry rage bomb against Merkland at terrible cost. The entire city might have been destroyed if not for Connor's miraculous stilling of the entire population.

The new bombs might prove critical if the battle went against them. The queen's forces lacked marble so they would no longer be able to siphon away the flames of a large explosion. The army might include many new Petralists, but most Pathfinders would lack any notable power with the air to deflect such bombs.

Earth and water were still viable, but since those would act as the primary battle stones for both forces, Verena expected that every Spitter and Water Moccasin would quickly become fully engaged. They would probably not have the attention to watch for large bombs.

While she mulled over the question of how to deal with some of the more complex marble mechanicals, she was surprised to see the hulking form of Erich enter her workroom.

He spoke in Grandurian. "Hail, Builder. How is the work going?"

"As well as can be expected. If they hit us now, we'd be in trouble. I bet less than ten percent of our missiles have been retrofitted with quartzite so far."

"Unless they launch a surprise attack, it sounds like we should have at least a week to prepare."

She hadn't heard that, and breathed a sigh of relief. It would still take every effort to prepare in time, but her sense of frantic, near-panic faded.

He added with a grin, "Rory and Anika have announced they're moving up the wedding to tomorrow."

Verena shrieked with joy, which startled her assistants. One of them backpedaled, his face draining as he glanced at the missile, no doubt expecting it to blow up in their faces. The other one leaped forward and grabbed the weapon to keep it from rolling off the table. Verena had forgotten they were standing there. They wouldn't have understood the conversation since neither of them spoke Grandurian.

She hugged Erich, laughing with joy. She was so thrilled that Rory and Anika had figured out how to make their seemingly impossible relationship work. Their love story inspired the troops and had come to represent the heart of the revolution. Choosing to move up the wedding to before the impending battle was a brilliant stroke. It would give everyone a refreshed sense of hope.

She reassured her two assistants, then told Erich, "How do you feel to know your sister is marrying an Obrioner general?"

He shrugged. "Rory is the only man strong enough for her. He fights with honor, and he will cherish her."

Verena agreed completely. She loved weddings, but had avoided Anika in recent days. She had every excuse, with preparing their trap for the queen, but seeing Anika so happy, immersed in her wedding planning was painful for Verena. She longed to be doing the exact same thing, planning for her union with Connor. She understood why Connor wanted to wait, but she didn't agree with him. Maybe when he saw how happy Rory and Anika were together, he'd realize he was being silly.

Then she gasped as a terrible realization struck. She placed a hand over her mouth and whispered with wide-eyed terror, "My dress will never be done in time."

Erich laughed. "That was Anika's first concern too. Rory suggested they encourage everyone to come to the wedding in military uniforms so they wouldn't have to worry about that."

Good idea. "Anika will definitely wear her wedding dress, despite how much Rory says he prefers her in battle leathers. I'm one of her chosen maids, so I need to get my dress done too."

Erich shrugged. "With all this work, you think you'll still finish?"

"I might have to quit a little early today and stay up really late tonight, but we'll get it done. If I can design an entirely new higher-level mechanical of arcane power to rob healing from the queen in just a couple days, I can complete a wedding dress in one night."

"And your gift?"

Verena groaned. "I haven't even thought about that yet. I figured we had plenty of time."

"Me too. I have ideas, but since none of us might live out the next two weeks, I'm thinking I should make something memorable."

He was right. As much as Anika loved flowers, she did not need any as presents. She had access to literal tons, and as a champion florist, she could compose far more elaborate, beautiful arrangements than Verena ever could. A battle-themed gift definitely made sense, but what?

Anika would enter battle at Rory's side. Dressed in her battle leathers and with all of the weapons and powdered granite for an extended bash fight. What could Verena add that she would appreciate and that might give her an edge?

Erich said, "I've had a new battle hammer forged for her. Complete with affinity symbols engraved on the head. Would you touch the stone and harden it?"

"Of course. I'd be honored." No doubt a lot of soldiers would carry hardened granite weapons into battle. Touched by a Builder, they were stronger than steel and virtually unbreakable. Verena suspected Anika might end up receiving more than one new hammer as wedding gifts.

Erich waved goodbye, grinning like a boy. "I'll bring it by later."

As Verena got back to work, she let her fingers run through the practiced motions while she pondered the question.

What gift to give the battle maiden bride of the great General Rory for her wedding on the eve of battle?

Chapter Twelve
Everyone Loves a Jean's Jacket

Hamish soared over the split peak of Badurach Pass, loving the chance to simply fly and enjoy the skies. The Hawk was fun, better than most of the other flying machines, but nothing matched his battle suit. The afternoon sun warmed his back, and he could see for miles.

Just for fun, he rolled into a forward somersault, then into a spiraling twist, ending in a barrel roll, and couldn't help lighting off a couple of multicolored flares. Laughing with the pure joy of untethered flight, he banked around the mountain until the huge host marshaling to the north came into view.

The entire plateau on the Grandurian side of the pass was covered in soldiers and mechanicals, their packed ranks stretching for miles. Ilse and Wolfram had been busy. Dozens of huge earthen buildings stood in ordered rows. The fact that those had been built before Connor calmed the elements was remarkable. Walking with earth along the pass had been tricky business.

As he approached, he waved to the Longseer scouts stationed in windriders near the mountain. Instead of heading straight for the central command building, Hamish banked around to the east side of the plateau where an enormous area had been allocated for flying craft. He spotted the Albatross immediately. It crouched among the others like a bird of prey. Lady Briet must be meeting with her officers coordinating battle strategy. The Albatross had become her unofficial command vehicle, and he bet she planned to try taking it with her back to Althing if they survived the war.

Dozens of standard windriders were parked in orderly rows, but Hamish focused on a truly awesome development in their flying arsenal. Sixteen giant troop carriers consumed a huge amount of space. Known simply as Battalions, each was the size of a hundred windriders lashed together. They created huge, flat expanses upon which to marshal troops, supplies, and additional mechanicals. Each was powered by great quartzite blocks, and each carried huge engines, fifty times bigger than the ones that powered the Juggernauts. Those engines could provide the staggering amounts of supplemental power required to run their defenses and to charge up some of the mechanicals that would be deployed.

He slowed and descended to fly over the last line of Battalions. The decks were already filling with scores of mobile battle mechanicals. Hamish focused on the biggest ones. General Wolfram liked to call them multi-mechanical simultaneous launch platforms. Verena had dubbed them Thunder Towers, even though Hamish had pointed out that the name suggested they were stationary instead of mobile. It was otherwise a great name, so it stuck.

They'd been upgraded since he saw them last, although they were swarmed right now with Builders and engineers working to retrofit the systems that utilized marble. They'd either draw power from quartzite or from the onboard engines that already powered some of the other weapons systems.

Blocky and very solid, each Thunder Tower was self-propelled, equipped with many different weapons, and built of triple-reinforced Sehrazad steel glass to protect its three-man crew, but also provide unlimited visibility.

He spotted Fyodor and dropped to one of the Battalions beside the big warrior engineer. "How goes the work?"

"As well as can be expected. Maybe even a little better."

Up close the Thunder Tower was even more impressive. Multiple launch tubes of varying sizes protruded from the central housing, while armored racks holding missiles, enormous speedslings, and rapid-fire siege weapons were attached to the hull. The entire huge assembly rolled on heavy steel tracks. Hamish had first envisioned them as hovering battle platforms, but some of the weapons recoiled enough that they needed the stability of resting on the ground. Thunder Towers were capable of unleashing enormous destruction as well as deploying a myriad of defensive mechanicals when targeted by powerful Petralists.

Hamish patted one barrel, a tube that was designed to spray marble flames. "Tell me you figured out something else to spit out of this. If not, I once built a mechanical that mass-produced the best dessert jellies. If we sprayed those across the battlefield, it might not hurt anyone, but it would definitely distract them."

The big man chuckled. "I would like to see that mechanical in action, but not on board one of these. We are exploring three options for generating fire. We'll know within the next day or two which alternate solution is the most viable. If the expected timeframe proves accurate, we should have time to retrofit them all."

No one was going to get much sleep over the next week. Hamish only hoped someone figured out a new way to deal with the queen before then. If they could remove her from the equation, Hamish felt optimistic that their combined forces of Petralists, Builder mechanicals, and Arishat League reinforcements could defeat the queen's army. They couldn't possibly be ready for Thunder Towers and flying Battalions.

"I'm going to be helping retrofit missiles and other ordnance," he told Fyodor.

"Good. We have too few Builders for the work."

Hamish clapped the big man on the shoulder. "I'll get right to it, after dinner."

He launched back into the sky, activating thrusters, and outran the big man's laughter. They had shared enough meals together for Fyodor to know that dinner was not an event Hamish ever wanted to miss. More importantly, he needed to see Jean. She had arrived that very day with the last wave of reinforcements and supplies. The need to see her, to hold her, and to kiss her was like a huge piece of activated marble lodged in his heart.

He shot across the plateau, noting the many companies of Petralists and regulars. Granadure had committed over sixty thousand regulars and two thousand Petralists. It was a staggering number, and must have heavily depleted their reserves, but if Merkland fell, the invasion of Granadure would follow soon thereafter.

Arishat League forces camped in thousand-man divisions, and Hamish counted forty of them, including twenty divisions of Varvakin armored shock troops. Then came a sea of Sehrazad conical tents, mixed with huge paddocks full of horses. Hamish had not seen the Sehrazad warriors fight much and was eager to see what they could do.

The Althin contingent was situated close to the Builder warehouses and workshops. The two groups worked so closely together it made perfect sense. Few of the Althins were soldiers, although Hamish spotted dozens of their trebuchets with stacks of carefully monitored crates containing chemical weapons.

Even Ravinder hosted a large camp. They would not be supplying many troops, but by the thousands of long wagons pulled into orderly rows behind their tents, it was clear they had brought many other supplies.

Then Hamish spotted a familiar figure and descended to land near Student Eighteen. She was walking with Commander Six and a company of over a dozen other Mhortair soldiers. She waved as Hamish pushed his visor up and asked excitedly, "When did they get here?"

Student Eighteen grinned like a little girl. "Barely an hour ago. My people found safe refuge with a couple of our smaller communities."

"And fifty of our best warriors came to help fight," Commander Six said proudly.

Hamish grinned and pumped the short warrior's hand. "I'm so happy to hear it."

The other Mhortair recognized Hamish and eagerly shook hands too. Of course they spoke Obrioner with no accent whatsoever and thanked him for helping free their people from the ruins of Jagdish. Hamish was so thrilled to see them. He loved knowing that at least some of the queen's victims were finding safety. If they were successful in the upcoming battle, hopefully entire nations would finally enjoy peace.

"You're just in time for the next meal. I shared your recipes with the cooks and I think tonight we're having one of the meals that Mister One gave us. That'll be perfect."

Their good humor faded to stoic expressions of grief. Student Eighteen said, "Thank you, Hamish. We will all celebrate the memory of our brave leader, slain by the matron of evil."

"And we will renew our oaths to destroy her," Commander Six vowed. His companions all agreed. They looked like a tough bunch. Hamish was glad so many had come, but wished they had a thousand more.

He said, "Did you hear? We hurt the queen pretty badly."

Student Eighteen said, "I was just telling them about that."

One of the soldiers said, "It helps. A little." Another added fiercely, "But we're happy that we'll still get a chance to help finish her off."

"We'll need you for sure," Hamish told them. "It's really good to see you. I'll catch up with you soon, I promise."

He wanted to hear about their long journey, but was too impatient to see Jean again. So he lifted into the air and accelerated, not even slowing to study the long ranks of Tabnit soldiers and their amazing sparky sparky boom drums.

The command building looked pretty busy, so Hamish landed on the roof. He was surprised to find no one had created a rooftop access door. They really had built these in a hurry. So he jumped off the roof and soared in through one of the top floor windows.

He landed in a small conference room where General Wolfram, Captain Ilse, and Lady Briet were meeting with several high-ranking officials. Hamish waved, noting that they did not even have any snacks on the table. Must've been an impromptu meeting.

"I don't mean to interrupt. Have any of you seen Jean?"

Ilse was grinning, but General Wolfram sighed. "Hamish, it's considered bad form to simply fly into the middle of a meeting."

"Then you shouldn't have left the window open. Any Pathfinder worth their salt would be able to overhear what you're talking about."

Ilse chuckled. "Thanks for the reminder. We forgot to activate the shielding around the window."

He chuckled. "I'm glad. Bouncing off would've been embarrassing."

"Your Lady Jean is just down the hall, meeting with her flight leaders," Lady Briet said.

Hamish waved and left them to their meeting. He found Jean in another conference room, packed with flight leaders and officers. They were all wearing new uniforms made of sturdy blue cotton that Jean had developed. That was the color that she looked best in, so he was glad she chose that for her personal army too.

Jean rushed to him. For a moment all he could do was stare, nearly overwhelmed by emotion. Her unmarred face seemed to glow, framed by her gorgeous, thick hair hanging halfway down her back. She took his hands and he grinned to see her perfectly restored arm and the fact that she ran to him without any limp. He swept her into his arms. Jean smelled like healing spices and ink, as usual, but also wore just a hint of new fragrance. Had she actually started using perfume? He loved it.

"You should've called ahead. We had no idea." Jean laughed.

Hamish shrugged. "It's been a busy day, and I was already planning on heading up here to help with the mechanicals. I just heard about your arrival. Perfect timing."

"We're just discussing our duties in the upcoming deployment." She gestured to her officers, and Hamish waved to them as they saluted in turn. "It's going to be the biggest engagement since the Tallan wars, and many of my people will be helping to pilot the Battalions or stage our hospital craft to help deal with the injured."

"There's probably going to be a lot, but definitely less than there should be. I saw your notes from the last test of the latest model of personal defensive mechanicals. The numbers are amazing," he said.

She nodded. "I'm so glad we got them done. We'll have enough for a lot of the soldiers, and we can pass on the older models to just about everyone else. We brought everything we could from New Schwinkendorf, so there should be plenty of supplies."

"How are we doing on diorite?" Hamish asked.

She frowned, and it looked adorable on her. "That's the one stone were struggling with. There's never been a huge supply, and we consumed a lot of the reserves in the battles against High Lord Dougal."

"That's what I was afraid of. More and more of our battle mechanicals rely on diorite."

"We brought every scrap of it that we could. We should have enough for one major engagement, but after that we're likely to start facing shortages until the mines catch up or we can discover new sources."

"Well, if the battle goes poorly, we'll need a lot more than just extra diorite."

She nodded agreement, then returned to discussing orders for her troops. She held his hand the entire time, and Hamish was content to simply stand beside her and listen to her lovely voice.

At one point, he interrupted and said, "I need to get one of those jackets. They look very comfortable."

Dulax, the huge Boulder leading Defender Flight, gestured proudly at his jacket. "We've been calling it Jean's cotton, but as the term is becoming well known we've just started shortening it to Jean's. Everyone knows what we're talking about."

"Great idea. I'd like one, if there are any to spare. I think it would be fun to give one to Rory as a wedding present tomorrow."

Jean gasped. "What? They've moved it up to tomorrow?"

"Yup. Got a speakstone message on my way up here."

"I'm so excited for them!" Then her expression fell. "Oh, no. My dress isn't finished."

CHAPTER THIRTEEN
Impossible Relationships Sometimes Work Out

Connor followed as Hamish and Jean pushed into bright sunshine in the huge square in front of the great Merkland palace. The sun stood almost directly overhead, and it was proving to be a clear, warm day. For that moment, it was possible to forget that the dread queen and her vast host were marching to destroy them all and simply enjoy a wedding.

The entire square was packed with people, with more squeezing in every second. Many wore their military uniforms, although the majority had donned bright, festive attire. Not only did it look like every person in Merkland was trying to attend, but droves of people had flown down from Badurach Pass for the occasion.

There was no way even half of the tens of thousands of people eager to witness the union between Rory and Anika could fit in that enormous square. So sightstones had been arranged around the raised platform where the ceremony would take place, and huge viewing screens were set up in every square around the city and along the outer walls so people could watch and hear from just about everywhere.

The rubble had been removed, and the square was decorated better than during the Sogail. Every building facing it was hung with banners. Decorators had artfully concealed the worst damage from the swarm attack and the recent earth shaking under every banner they could invent, including the Merkland city and the personal crest of High Lady Shona. Others included banners for Granadure and the nations of the Arishat League. Elsewhere, they'd draped plain cloth sheets in festive colors. Chains of early season flowers draped from windows and balconies everywhere.

Anika had overseen the effort, despite having so much to do to prepare herself. Connor had struggled to believe reports that she was a celebrated florist in Granadure, but couldn't deny the evidence. How the terrifying battle maiden could also produce such delicately beautiful floral arrangements seemed an impenetrable mystery.

With such fancy decorations, Connor decided it was good he hadn't worn his custom armor after all. It was fancy enough and there were enough other people in military dress that he would not have seemed out of place, but Verena would've probably punched him for not making more of an effort.

So he was wearing a stylish suit, gifted to him by Shona herself a few weeks prior. Although Verena no doubt hated the fact that it was Shona who gave it to him, it did look good on him, so she would probably forgive him for wearing it.

Not that anyone would notice him or any of the men. Connor bet only Verena would even notice if he showed up in his small-clothes. Everyone would be gawking at Anika, and those who looked past her would be staring at Verena or Jean.

Verena walked beside him, wearing a beautiful gown of deep green, fitted along the bodice, but with a flaring skirt. As much as she complained about not having anything to wear, she'd done well. The gorgeous gown had probably been gifted by her father for a fancy noble event. She'd probably made some alterations so she could consider it a new gown, but whatever she wore would look stunning.

Connor stumbled on a rough piece of paving stone, nearly tripping.

"Are you all right?" she asked, giving him a dazzling smile.

For a second it was hard to breathe, let alone respond. She was so beautiful, and he felt stunned for the thousandth time that she had chosen him out of all the men she could have. Her hand was warm in his, her big, blue eyes bright, and even though he wasn't tapping chert, he could sense her joy.

He couldn't imagine losing her.

Suddenly all of his excuses for not proposing and making their betrothal official seemed idiotic. He couldn't wait. One or both of them might die in the coming battle. He'd almost died in that volcano. No matter what happened, though, he could face it better if she was bound to him with a formal promise to wed as soon as possible.

Connor opened his mouth to ask her right there, but Hamish glanced back from where he walked just in front of them with

Jean and said in a loud whisper, "Hey, Connor, I was just thinking, triple-ascended Petralists can have kids, right?"

"What?" Connor demanded, blinking a couple of times as the intimate moment crashed into pieces around his feet.

"First and second-ascended Petralists can't have kids, right?" Hamish asked.

Jean glanced back too and said, "That's right! Oh, Verena, did your family know Connor was affected that way before he ascended the final time?"

Jean looked stunning in a gown of deep blue, trimmed in gold, and seemed to float as she walked. Her hair was done up in a complicated pattern, piled atop her head and held in place by jeweled combs and a little tiara. Jean was usually very unassuming, but Verena had managed to convince her that as Lady Jean, she owed it to her subjects to represent them well, which meant wearing all of that finery.

Now Verena blushed, the rosy coloring making her even more beautiful. "Um, I haven't spoken with them about that bit."

"Probably a good thing. Your dad already hated Connor enough without thinking he couldn't get grandkids," Hamish added.

Connor actually hadn't thought through that ramification of his ascension, and he felt his face grow hot. That was a very private conversation he and Verena needed to have. It wasn't a topic for general conversation while marching to Anika and Rory's wedding.

"Thanks for reminding us," he managed to say.

"Any time," Hamish said happily, turning forward again, walking tall beside Jean as they made their way through the crowds toward the platform. They were among the privileged few who could stand closest to their dear friends as they were united in matrimony. For once Hamish had left his battle suit behind and wore a fine suit cut in the Grandurian fashion. He almost looked a match for Jean.

Connor was still tempted to create a mud puddle right in front of him so he could push him in. He glanced at Verena, who was shaking her head slowly, staring at Hamish's back.

She met Connor's gaze and chuckled. "Leave it to Hamish."

Connor squeezed her hand, not sure what to say, wishing he could salvage the moment and propose to her. He knew she'd say yes, but the moment didn't feel right any longer.

"Look at the flowers!" Jean gushed, pointing at the wedding platform, bedecked with garlands and vases bursting with bright floral colors. Hamish chuckled and gestured toward one bouquet built along the rails of the stairs up to the platform. "See those blue flowers? Erich said they're called I-can-pants-this."

Connor laughed, but Verena scowled at Hamish. "Really? That's the best you can come up with today?"

Hamish shrugged. "All kinds of flowers have weird names. Anika told me a few yesterday. She's got impatients, eyeball plants, love-in-a-mist, and bat-faced goofies."

"Really?" Connor asked. He'd never realized flowers could be so fun.

Jean rolled her eyes. "Not exactly. It's impatiens, and bat-faced goofies are actually bat-faced cupheas."

"Love-in-a-mist is nice," Verena added.

"Are there really bat-faced plants?" Connor asked, looking again at all of the flower arrangements, trying to spot them.

"There are, but the blue irises that Hamish was talking about are called agapanthus, not I-can-pants-this," Jean said sternly. Connor was impressed she didn't even crack a smile. He preferred Hamish's alternate name. He'd forget agapanthus in a heartbeat, but he'd never forget a flower named I-can-pants-this.

Once they climbed to the platform, the girls moved to stand beside Anika, who was resplendent in a beautiful white gown, covered in hundreds of little crystals, many of them quartzite. Verena touched her dress, and all the quartzite pieces began glowing softly, transforming her dress into a living rainbow. In that moment, Connor saw her as a woman rather than a deadly warrior.

Weird.

Memories tumbled through his mind of the deadly warrior maiden. He thought back to the first time he'd seen her tap granite, when she and Erich were plundering the barge from Alasdair, hurling the precious granite blocks far out over the Wick. He thought of the terrifying night when he'd freed Shona. He'd caught Anika by surprise, tied her in his leather shirt, and bound her to a tree by her braid. He was lucky she hadn't snapped him into twenty pieces.

As much as Rory loved her in her fighting leathers, he was clearly transfixed by her in that stunning gown. The tall, shapely woman was simply gorgeous. Her thick, blond hair hung loose to her shoulders, but was held back from her face by narrow braids twining around her head and tied in the back.

She too wore a glittering tiara, hers made up of the various affinity stones, with granite in the center position, of course. She looked so happy Connor bet if he pushed her, she would simply float out over the crowd.

Rory looked like he was trying not to collapse in a dead faint. He had somehow won the heart of the terrifying battle maiden, and only a man absolutely committed to the match could have survived that courtship. They'd been drawn together powerfully since their first meeting, and Connor easily pictured them wrestling behind Lord Gavin's manor house, stone-hardened bodies swaying together, looking more like they were embracing than fighting.

Rory had been smitten from the first, and now he looked overwhelmed that their wedding day had finally arrived. Connor grinned to see the indomitable captain so giddy with joy.

Connor and Hamish joined Erich, who was already flanking Rory. They would act as groomsmen, but Connor felt a twinge of sadness when he glanced to his side at the empty spots where Tomas and Cameron should have been standing.

The rest of their closest friends stood to either side of the wedding party, which was gathered in front of a graceful archway. Kilian, Evander, and Ilse, who also looked strange yet radiant in a tastefully elegant gown of black. She was still mourning the loss of her husband, but carried her grief openly and with her usual grace. Wolfram, Lady Briet, and Ivor were there as well.

As Connor looked across his friends, more memories surfaced. He thought of the first time he met Kilian, witnessing the Water Moccasin skating up the Wick with those graceful strides that no one else could quite match. Kilian, who had stopped one of Carbrey's charges with a bucket of water applied for best possible leverage.

Most of his early memories of Evander were scary ones, with the giant rising up from underground, huge, intimidating, spouting incomprehensible Sentry speak. He felt deeply grateful both of the ancient Dawnus had joined the revolution. They'd all have died long since without them. General Wolfram, with his famous mustaches, still inspired the same sense of awe Connor had always felt around him, ever since they'd met during the battles of Alasdair. The famously clever general had met every challenge with wit and cunning and calm confidence.

Ilse commanded a host of memories. She had captured Connor several times during the battles of Alasdair, proven herself a remarkably resourceful and clever leader, and showed restraint when she could have killed many. She'd played catch-the-devil with Rory and the forces around the Carraig for months, giving Connor more chances to leave with her than he probably deserved. She'd transitioned from a daunting adversary to a cherished friend through all of those adventures, and despite her tragic losses, she kept pressing ahead, fighting evil and committing everything she had to protecting her people.

Connor stood a little taller, feeling deeply grateful to count such mighty men and women as cherished friends.

Lady Shona herself would officiate the ceremony. As the high lady of Merkland, it was her right. She looked stunning as always in an amazing gown of crimson satin that highlighted her excellent figure. It left her long, graceful neck bare, and she too wore her hair up high with bejeweled combs.

In that nostalgic mood, Connor's mind flooded with hundreds of memories of Shona. Their relationship was extremely complicated and very deep. She'd treated him better than a humble linn had any right to expect, had explored his affinities, and extended the remarkable honor of choosing him as a potential partner for life.

She had also used him, manipulated him, threatened his family, and promised to commit his powers to a war of conquest to sweep the continent. But she'd released him when she could have held him enslaved. She had chosen the revolution against all odds, and seemed earnest in her attempts to build a new friendship. He felt cautiously optimistic they could make it work without either Shona or Verena getting killed in the process, especially since they could now openly beat on each other in their regular "training."

Shona stepped into position underneath the archway, signifying the start of the ceremony. Rory and Anika took their places facing each other in front of Shona, while Verena, Jean, and Anika's elderly mother flanked her. Connor, Hamish, Erich, and the siblings' father took their places near Rory. An expectant hush fell over the enormous assembly.

Shona always liked being the center of attention, and she literally glowed with light, tapping her limestone secondary affinity. Connor had loaned her quartzite for the ceremony, so her voice echoed across the square, magnified even more by the many speakstones positioned beside each of the huge sightstone viewing screens.

"Welcome all on this glorious day for this remarkable event. It's no surprise that not even the great expanse of our beloved city is grand enough to contain everyone who wishes to witness this singular and historic union between our beloved General Rory and his famous bride, Anika the battle maiden."

The square erupted with cheering, and the sound spread all through the city and beyond as everyone took up the cry. The sound grew until the air vibrated with it.

Connor tapped serpentinite. It was challenging, since the red-frequency aspect to it had been snuffed out when the queen had destroyed the stone that created that affinity. Still, he managed by focusing only on the green frequency. Touching it opened his eyes to the full grandeur of the cheering. Sound filled the square and radiated up above the city in endless, vibrant waves of color. It was breathtaking, and he wished he had thought to get one of Aifric's recording diamonds.

"Our city, our lives, our very freedom are threatened by terrible danger, but instead of cowering in fear or losing ourselves in the grim nature of our duty, we pause on the eve of our great victory to celebrate hope in the union of our peoples. Not only do Rory and Anika deserve the greatest happiness life can offer simply because of their honor, integrity, and excellent characters, but their union declares to all the world that love, friendship, and peace can extend beyond political borders."

Again cheering rattled the city. Rory and Anika looked like they could stand there looking at each other all day. Connor doubted they even heard anything Shona said, but he hoped Shona would not give in to the almost overwhelming temptation that faced high officials when standing in front of enormous crowds to begin monologuing. He would hate to do something drastic to cut her short and remind her that the day belonged to Rory and Anika. He had recently regrown her hair. He could always take it back.

The idea made him grin, but he concealed it before she noticed. Would she understand what he was thinking? She might. She knew him better than almost anyone.

Thankfully, she did pretty well. She did launch into a little speech about the great marriage traditions of Obrion, and even mentioned some from Granadure, no doubt provided to her by Verena. She challenged Rory and Anika to be true to both countries and to be examples of international relations. Not that there was any doubt of that. The two were so much in love, it made Connor think he and Hamish weren't doing nearly enough to impress their girls. And usually people thought they were the ones who were too mushy.

Now that he could loan granite to Verena sometimes, maybe they could start bash fight training together. She used to enjoy hitting him a lot. He wondered how she would like him hitting back. It was a good idea, but he doubted they could pull it off as well as Rory and Anika. Those two loved beating on each other with a passion that burned so hot they didn't need marble.

Within a few moments, interrupted repeatedly by more cheering, Shona began the actual ceremony of calling upon Rory and Anika to share their vows and commit to each other. Always the straightforward soldier, Rory simply took Anika's hands in his and said simply, "Anika, I love you. You challenge me to be a better man, and I promise to walk by your side every day of my life."

His words moved Anika deeply. Her eyes seemed to sparkle, and a soft blush spread across her cheeks, making her look even more beautiful. She grinned, her expression so bright she might have eaten a Solas for breakfast. She replied in Grandurian, then repeated her words in Obrioner.

"Mine Rory. Mine Capitain. You are strongest man I know in life. I surrender only to you of all men and walk with you as life partner forever."

The simple words, spoken in her heavy Grandurian accent, generated another round of enthusiastic cheering. Every woman standing on the platform dabbed at her eyes with cotton handkerchiefs, and Connor didn't blame them. The simple words were far more moving than the eloquence of any high lord.

Shona grinned. "Then by my right and duty, I pronounce you man and wife."

The two embraced, kissing passionately, looking so happy that either of them might just simply melt away. Then with a laugh, Rory seized Anika by the waist and threw her high into the air shouting, "Hail my beautiful bride!"

The entire congregation erupted into a thunderous cheer. "Hail the bride!"

He caught her as she descended. Anika laughed and kissed him passionately on the lips again. Then she seized him and tapped granite. Her body shifted to perfectly sculpted lines, and her skin shifted to a slight shade of pink instead of white. Connor grinned to see her using her favorite Grandurian strain. He hoped the local Boulders wouldn't feel betrayed that she hadn't chosen Alasdair White for her wedding.

Anika threw Rory just as high as he had tossed her. "Hail mine husband!"

The assembled crowd laughed and cheered and shouted with her. "Hail the groom!"

She caught him and the two embraced again. Shona hugged them both and declared, "May your union be blessed with long and joyous lives."

Then Connor and everyone else swept in to congratulate the couple. Several minutes of backslapping and hugging and crying passed as the crowds cheered and clapped. The entire city was awash with good cheer, and for a little while it seemed everyone could forget the terrible danger looming over them. They might all be destroyed in the next week, but they were celebrating like they would live forever. It felt completely appropriate.

Although an entire afternoon of partying and dancing and feasting and gifts was planned, the core wedding party took a moment to present their gifts first.

Hamish produced a covered cast-iron pot with great flair. Rory laughed and clapped him on the back. "I should have known your gift would be food."

"Only the best food, fit for a king. It's a new recipe from Schwinkendorf's cookbook. No one has eaten this in over a hundred years." With a flourish he opened the lid and revealed a dessert. A warm, sweet scent flooded the platform and Connor edged closer. It was a gift for the newlyweds, but they would share, wouldn't they?

Hamish declared proudly, "I call this Torcish Delight."

Anika daintily pulled a piece free and popped it into her mouth. The dessert looked like it was made up of layers of pastry filled with honey and powdery sugar. She tasted it and smiled. "Is very good. You make from torc?"

Hamish laughed. "Of course not. It's Torcish Delight because it's so good people would wrestle a torc for a chance to get some."

Rory tried a piece and he too grinned. "Thank you, Hamish. This is a princely gift."

He didn't share it, but replaced the cover and set it aside. That was alright. Connor bet Hamish had seventy-five more pots full, ready for smashpacking.

Erich presented a mighty battle hammer to Anika and she gushed over it. Made strong enough to be wielded by the mightiest Boulder, the head included the ancient Petralist symbol for granite, and was made of hardened granite. It could crush even the queen's skull if given a chance.

Connor slipped around Verena and Jean, who were still happily gushing about Anika's dress, and placed hands on both Rory's and Anika's shoulders. In the palm of each hand, he held small pieces of blind coal. Their joy radiated from them like invisible heat and Connor couldn't seem to grin widely enough. He was so happy for them.

"Congratulations!" he said.

Rory gripped Connor's shoulder in turn. "Thank you, Connor. And thank you for helping us get together."

"Yes. You good boy, bring first message to me from mine Rory," Anika grinned. Then she actually kissed Connor on the cheek.

He wasn't sure how to react. Anika had terrified him for a long time. He'd gotten over that, but most of his memories with Anika still involved bash fighting and danger.

So he squeezed their shoulders and said, "I have a gift for you both."

Connor tapped sandstone, obsidian, and blind coal while focusing on the two newlyweds. He'd never tried connecting to two people at the same time and fiddling with their affinities, but it felt right. Rory and Anika were bound by marriage now, and even though Connor was not actively tapping chert, he felt their joy and unbreakable commitment to each other. They were bound together by bonds far stronger than any affinity, and as he connected with them, the view of their affinityscapes formed in his mind as a single, joint location.

A simple, sand-lined training yard. It smelled of sand and stone and sun. A bucket of water stood against one wall near some plank benches. Connor stepped onto the sands, grinning. Every grain was infused with their love, and he sensed countless joyful memories of competition from their daily training. The two of them had pushed each other to the uttermost limits of their skill and developed their core identity together as they trained and forged their union. He couldn't imagine a more fitting affinityscape.

The right-hand wall was missing, revealing the expanse of mist-filled abyss with a single-tiered granite island floating nearby, with a solid rope-plank bridge leading to it. He jogged over and scanned the indistinct islands hovering in the mists nearby. It took only a moment to locate blind coal, and even less time to build a sturdy bridge across to that sedimentary stone using planks from the benches along the wall.

When he blinked open his eyes, both Rory and Anika were gaping at him. Rory exclaimed, "You gave us a secondary affinity?"

He handed them the tiny wafers of blind coal with a flourish. "I can't think of a better gift. You two will be leading the charge, so what better affinity than the one that can get you through enemy tertiaries trying to end the bash fight early?"

Anika laughed and hugged Connor, lifting him off his feet in her exuberance. Thankfully she remembered not to squeeze him to jelly, but she hugged hard enough to give him painful flashbacks of Catriona's hugging attacks at the Carraig. "You good boy. Thank you!"

Connor stepped back before she could grab him again. Verena slipped an arm around his waist and asked, "New affinities that fast?"

"I was motivated."

She beamed at him and kissed him quickly on the cheek. "You're always full of surprises, Connor."

CHAPTER FOURTEEN
Sort-of, Maybe, Almost Proposing Isn't As Hard As Everyone Thinks

Eventually Rory and Anika stepped to the edge of the platform, holding hands and grinning like little kids. They raised their hands together in a triumphant salute.

At the signal, Verena remotely triggered a dozen missiles. They shot up into the sky from launchers positioned along the outer wall and exploded several hundred feet above the city in fantastic eruptions of fireworks.

The crowds cheered and clapped enthusiastically, and Connor joined in. He loved the fact that they could use some of their amazing inventions for non-military purposes sometimes.

After that, the party really got started. Thousands thronged the happy couple, showering them with well wishes and with gifts. Throughout the rest of Merkland, tables were set up in every square, then loaded with food. Merkland might have been hammered by the swarm, but Shona had promised to dig deep from their remaining stores. When Jean heard there might be a shortage of good food, she'd mobilized Sender Flight to transport mountains of additional supplies.

Holding tight to Verena's hand, Connor tried slipping through the crowd, but most people were pushing the other way, eager for a chance to congratulate Rory and Anika. He glanced at Verena and said, "I think we need to fly."

In response, she lifted off the ground using a pair of small quartzite blocks as thrusters, sitting gracefully on the air as if riding a horse side saddle. She made the tricky operation look effortless and her ascent triggered a fresh wave of cheering. Verena's fame had skyrocketed after her outstanding bravery fighting off the swarm, and Connor loved to see that the people of Merkland loved her as much as the people of New Schwinkendorf.

Connor tapped granite and jumped straight up, using a little slate at the same time to make the earth push him upward higher. He soared twenty feet, high enough to avoid wrecking hairdos, and called in an air current to catch him. As soon as he caught up with Verena, he extended a block of translucent air under her like a gray platform so they could stand together. Then he slowed, hovering a hundred feet above the square so they could enjoy the view.

Verena took his hand, her smile radiant. "I'm so happy for them, Connor!"

"Me too. For the longest time, I figured they had zero chance of making any kind of relationship work," he admitted.

"Kind of like us," she said softly, her big, blue eyes seeming to grow larger and somehow vulnerable. Her gaze threatened swallow him whole.

"They did it," he said softly, squeezing her hand, letting her see his love as clearly as he read hers.

She kissed him tenderly, then said, "Their love has inspired everyone. I think it's one of the biggest rallying points for our entire cause. Today they're bringing so much hope to everyone."

Connor nodded, but couldn't help adding, "And a ton of really good food."

She chuckled and nudged him, her expression turning serious. "Connor, I think we need to discuss our plans too."

He knew exactly what she was talking about, and he finally agreed. "I almost proposed to you earlier today."

She gave him a disapproving look. "Really, Connor? After making me wait for months, you were going to do it here, during Rory and Anika's big day?"

He shrugged, feeling embarrassed. "I get it, so I don't want to wait longer than we have to before making our betrothal official." Gazing into those eyes, he felt like he could lose himself forever. He made sure to avoid tapping chert. He didn't need an affinity to know her heart or to make sure she knew his. By the Tallan's memory, she was gorgeous!

She leaned against him, holding him tight. "Me neither."

He hugged her, feeling overjoyed. "Uh, so does this mean we're betrothed?"

Verena kissed him gently on the lips and gave him that special smile that melted everything inside. "I think it does."

He couldn't stop grinning, and hugged her again, savoring the feel of her in his arms. He could scarce believe it. He wanted to beat himself with a stick for waiting so long.

They stood together, simply enjoying the moment and their commitment. They didn't get enough time to just be together. Life was too busy. He was so grateful he'd won approval from her father and brother during that visit over the winter. He smiled to think how his family would react when he informed them of the betrothal.

He missed them. He'd found far too little time to visit in recent months, although he'd sent several messages. The last time he visited, his younger siblings had grown so much, he barely recognized them. Blair was almost as tall as Connor already, and Roderick was catching up to him. Young Wallace reminded Connor a lot of Nicklaus, if the boy was limited to non-magic talents. And baby . . . He frowned, as he tried to remember the baby's name.

How could someone forget a younger sibling's name, especially one so young and cute? Well, he thought she was cute. She was a she, right? For some reason, his memories felt all fuzzy and he struggled to bring any details to mind. He felt deeply ashamed. He must be more tired than he'd thought.

Verena leaned back to meet his gaze, distracting him from the weird memory lapse. "I feel like we're so very lucky. We're still alive, still together, and taking part in something grand."

"I like your attitude." Despite the terrible danger looming over them, the past few months had been filled with unparalleled wonders and advancements in both science and magic. They'd helped with that work, delved into the deepest secrets of the arcane together, and he got to walk next to the most beautiful girl in the world and hold her hand.

Connor tried to burn the memory of that moment into his mind. How she looked in that gown, the color of her skin, and the lively brilliance of her eyes. He'd never forget it, no matter how many years passed. They would soon face battle again, and even if they survived, life would no doubt continue to prove challenging. That's how things always seemed to work. No matter what happened, he could enjoy this moment, enjoy her company and their special relationship.

Down in the square, Hamish lifted out of the crowd, using quartzite like Verena had, although he lacked her grace without his battle suit. He carried Jean in his arms, but wobbled under the load. Before he could pitch sideways or dump Jean onto the heads of onlookers, Connor caught them with air and drew them up to where he and Verena stood.

"Never thought I'd need my suit to escape a party," Hamish said when they stepped onto the solid air platform.

Jean brushed a lock of golden hair from her face, beaming. "Everyone is so happy for them!"

"It's definitely easier to enjoy the show from here," Connor said.

"Except we can't reach the banquet tables," Hamish pointed out.

"We'll get there soon enough," Jean soothed. Then she looked from Verena to Connor, and her eyes widened. She squealed, "You've finally made it official?"

Verena laughed, sounding as delighted as Connor had ever heard as she gushed, "Yes!"

"What's going on?" Hamish asked, frowning at the two girls as they jumped up and down, hugging each other.

"I sort of proposed to Verena," Connor explained.

"How do you sort of propose?" Hamish laughed, then shook his head. "Never mind. If anyone can manage it, it'd be you."

"Thanks," Connor said dryly.

"Congratulations. Took you long enough," Hamish grinned.

Someone else shot into the air from the opposite side of the square and zoomed toward them. Connor was surprised to realize it was Nicklaus, dressed in a fine suit of black and silver, riding a toy wooden horse that he'd affixed thrusters to. He banked toward them and slowed to hover nearby, waving enthusiastically.

"Nice horse," Hamish said with a grin.

The boy patted the flying horse proudly. "I wanted to make a Swift like Verena's, but Christin wouldn't let me get the weapons to make it right."

Verena smiled. "You don't need missiles and speedslings when you're studying, do you?"

"If I did, lessons wouldn't be nearly as dull," he responded, then hovered a bit closer, his voice dropping to a conspiratorial whisper. He patted his wooden horse again and said, "I snuck a couple bombs from one of the workrooms for my horse. Christin doesn't know it's armed."

Connor wasn't surprised. Nicklaus was super enthusiastic about practicing with bombs. He didn't doubt the boy would figure out how to keep increasing the armaments until that horse could rain down a fantastic amount of destruction. They needed to find more creative outlets for the boy.

Jean didn't look so happy about the thought of Nicklaus flying around the city armed. Verena looked like she wanted to smile, but suppressed it and said, "I thought the weapons labs were all locked. How did you get bombs?"

"Hamish taught me how to walk right through walls with blind coal."

"Hey, you promised not to tell," Hamish objected.

Both Verena and Jean gave him stern looks, and Verena said, "You can't teach Nicklaus things like that. Blind coal is dangerous."

"Exactly," Hamish said, holding his own better than usual in the face of those looks. "I caught him experimenting with it and had to teach him before he hurt himself."

Verena turned her gaze to Nicklaus, who wisely hovered farther out of reach. The boy shrugged and maintained an innocent expression. "Verena, you know my mother wants me to learn everything I can."

"With the proper instruction," Verena chided.

"Hamish gave me the proper instruction. I got the bombs, didn't I?"

She sighed. "We're going to have a long chat tomorrow."

"If you can catch me," Nicklaus said with a grin. "Bye Verena! Bye Connor! Get married soon. I want cousins. I'll show you my new mechanical later."

Then he whisked away, whooping with delight as he disappeared around one of the palace towers.

"Shouldn't we go after him before he hurts himself?" Jean asked.

"He'll be fine," Hamish assured her. "He's almost as good as either of us with his defensive mechanicals. Even if he falls off his horse, he won't get hurt."

Verena sighed. "As much as I hate to admit it, Hamish is right. Nicklaus should be fine. Besides, I'm sure Christin has people chasing him already."

Connor was happy Nicklaus was finding so many positive outlets for his energy, and that he hadn't gotten depressed by the loss of his affinities.

Hamish rubbed his hands together, his expression turning eager. "The crowd's going to break up soon. We should inspect the feasting tables to make sure they're ready."

"Including quality testing every dish, just to be sure?" Jean asked with a smile.

"Of course. Rory and Anika are worth it," he said seriously.

Connor agreed, but was thinking bigger than just the feast. "Verena, what would you say if I loaned you a little obsidian? I hear the dancing is going to go on all night, and I bet together we could outlast everyone."

"Great idea! I love dancing, and we never get to do it enough."

"Sort of like bash fighting for non-Boulder girls," Hamish said. "Never enough, and it always ends too soon."

Jean slipped an arm around his waist and asked, "Do you have enough to loan some to the two of us too? I bet Hamish and I could keep up."

Hamish grinned. "Easy. Connor lacks the staying power for an all-night event."

That kind of challenge could not be ignored. The four of them had started the crazy adventure together way back in Alasdair. They had survived countless challenges that should have killed them. With his closest friends around him, he could not believe that they could ever fail.

"I could probably manage it, but maybe there's a better idea. I think I'll be busy over the next few days helping people create new affinities to strengthen our army, but I think I should start right now, with you."

Chapter Fifteen
Strong Women Build on What They Know

Connor smiled to see their astonishment, which quickly transitioned to excitement. He asked, "Which affinities do you want?"

Verena squeezed his hand and gave him a quick, but passionate kiss, her eyes sparkling. "I know we've talked about this, and you've loaned us affinities, but it still seems beyond possible to consider getting our own."

"Well, we haven't made it happen, but I'm pretty sure I can," he told her.

"Which one, though?" She chewed on her lip in that adorable way of hers as she pondered. "I want to dance with you using obsidian, but I'm not sure obsidian is the right choice for a permanent affinity."

"It is for me," Hamish said. "Trying it out earlier was amazing. In my battle suit, I'm not afraid of Boulders and I can fly faster than Striders, but obsidian gives me a real edge. Can you really make it permanent?"

"I plan to try," Connor confirmed. He was glad Hamish chose obsidian. His friend was right. With obsidian magnifying his already impressive natural talents, and wearing that battle suit, he wouldn't have to fear almost anyone.

Jean said, "I think I would like obsidian too. Not for battle, but for research. I bet I could develop new cures even faster."

Hamish wrapped an arm around her shoulder and grinned at her. "You're already the most brilliant person I know. Adding obsidian to your sexy brain will make you unstoppable."

Jean blushed, then added in a hesitant voice, "If we can establish a primary affinity, would it be possible to try for a secondary?"

"You want sandstone, don't you?"

Verena gushed, "Oh yes! Jean's already such a good healer. With sandstone she could cure anything."

"That's the goal, eventually," Jean stated simply. "We've learned so much, but there's so much I still can't understand. With sandstone I could gain that sight. I'm sure it would help."

Connor vowed to make it happen. Jean had such an honest, loving soul. Her entire focus was to improve her already magnificent mind and accelerate the research that was already barreling forward at breakneck speed. She would not rest until she had developed cures for every known disease, and Connor would be right there cheering her on forever.

So he said, "Let's make it happen."

Verena took longer to decide. Connor doubted she would ever be truly satisfied until she figured out a way to establish affinities with everything, but she had to start with one. He'd love to explore trying to help his friends develop additional gifts. Maybe Agor, a tertiary power, or even Dawnus. There were so many possibilities, so many options never before available. He wished they had months to study and practice and experiment.

Verena finally settled on granite. "I love running with basalt, but you can loan that to me whenever we want to run together. In the Swift I can already fly fast, but I've already proven sometimes bad things happen in a fight. Granite would give me a critical edge."

She was right. She definitely tended to dive into the heart of battle before thinking. She'd crashed and nearly died multiple times because she was even braver than she was brilliant, and she refused to back down from any fight. Despite the terrible danger to herself, she was always willing to risk her life to help.

So Connor decided to help her with her affinity first. Not only were they bound by love and the desire to wed, his connection to her had deepened dramatically during the weeks he had spent pouring healing energy into her and trying to connect with her while she was in a coma. He had no doubt that he could establish a deeper connection with her than even with Aifric.

The main square thronged by thousands of partygoers didn't seem the best place to make the attempt, so Connor flew them to the palace, right to the window of Verena's suite. They slipped inside and gathered around the little fire already burning in the hearth.

His friends were so eager to make the attempt they started laughing and urging him on before he even sat down. Connor couldn't wait to share his amazing powers to help them.

So he sat facing Verena, their knees touching. He poured a small measure of granite into her palm. She squeezed it, so excited she quivered in her seat. Connor took her hands and stared deep into her huge blue eyes as he tapped chert, obsidian, sandstone, and granite all at the same time. The connection came instantly and he plunged into her affinityscape.

As it formed around him, he instantly recognized the crowded, crazy, wonderful Builder compound. He stood in Verena's original workroom, the one where she had developed her first prototype for the Swift. In the center of the room was a well, just like he'd found in Nicklaus' mind. It was constructed of river stones, interlocked together without any cement. As he approached it, he sensed it represented her Builder connection to quartzite.

"This is what you see?"

Connor turned in surprise. Somehow Verena had joined him in that mental space, just like Nicklaus had. He wasn't sure how it worked, but was happy it did. With their deep connection, he should have expected it.

He grinned. "This is what your subconscious projects. This is your connection to quartzite." He gestured at the well.

She touched one of the stones and smiled. "These are like the stones I used to collect from the river on my family estate outside of Edderitz."

That seemed very appropriate. He took her hand and led her outside. The flat open space where they had first landed the day that he had escaped Obrion with her and come to Granadure ended abruptly in a cliff. Dark gray mist concealed the abyss beyond the drop-off, just like in every affinityscape he'd visited.

Connor gestured toward the little islands floating nearby on the mist, constructed of the various affinity stones. "This is where we build bridges to create affinities."

Verena stepped to the edge and peered over, her expression curious and excited. "This is amazing. I wonder if I create this or if you do."

"We're in your mind."

"But from what you said, you see the same type of scenario in everyone's minds. The lands might be different, but you always see a cliff and an abyss with floating islands. Are you projecting that, or is there some relationship to affinities that we can all somehow sense in our subconscious that makes us all project similar ideas?"

Connor shrugged. "I have no idea. I'm just glad it seems consistent. I know what to do with the floating islands. If everyone was totally different I'd have to figure it all out from scratch every time."

She stepped closer and hugged him, her voice nearly a squeal. "I'm so excited to try this!"

"Me too. Let's get to work."

But as Connor studied the distance to the island, about fifty yards, he realized he would have to make a different type of bridge. He did not have trees like he had for Tomas. He glanced at the workshop behind them, with its high flat face. Maybe he could rip timbers from that and use them to make a bridge.

Verena followed his gaze. "You said most of the bridges are made out of ropes with planks, but you made Tomas' more solid and that seemed to help strengthen his affinity, right?"

When Connor nodded, Verena flashed that adorable smile of hers that always came out when she was being particularly clever. "Why don't we experiment? I have all sorts of materials inside. We could make the girders out of planks like you did for Tomas, or we could make it out of steel or even out of affinity stones."

That was a good idea. Connor was not sure what would happen, so clearly that meant they should try it.

Together they rushed inside and scoured her workroom for supplies. It was full of options, with plenty of power stone on hand. At first Connor was tempted to simply use granite blocks to reinforce the affinity they were trying to build, but Verena suggested they use all of the different power stones.

"Maybe it'll help me build additional affinities in the future."

Connor wasn't sure that would work, but agreed to give it a try. They collected all of the different affinity stones, piled the rough-cut blocks onto a wagon, and Verena used a makeshift quartzite thruster to push the heavy-laden wagon out to the cliff.

When they got there, she frowned and asked, "If you build these blocks out over that cliff, won't they just fall in?"

"They might, but last time the trees sort of extended the way I needed. Remember, we're not in the physical world so physical laws don't necessarily apply."

"So I could fly in here if I wanted to, without needing mechanicals?" Verena asked with a sudden grin. She jumped into the air, arms thrown wide, and managed to plop down onto her backside.

Connor laughed as she grimaced. "I had to give it a try."

"There probably is a way to make it work, but let's not get distracted."

Connor hefted a large piece of granite from the back of the wagon. He'd worked with granite blocks since his earliest memories, and carrying granite somehow felt easier than carrying any other kind of stone. Although the block was heavy, he did not need to tap any affinities to carry it to the cliff.

Connor placed the block at the edge of the cliff, imagining it forming the anchor stone that secured the bridge to the land. As the stone dropped into place, it seemed to melt, morphing into the shape that he imagined. That was so much fun.

Bolstered by that success, he rapidly added additional stones. Verena helped heave the heavy stones, not struggling any more than he did to move the weight. She found that endlessly fascinating and started tossing stones into the air and catching them again. "I could get used to this."

"You will, as soon as we get this affinity established."

Connor placed each stone on top of the first piece of granite and willed it into position. They slid along the expanding length of the truss and snapped into position at the very end, forming an ever-growing arm of stone extending out into space. Although Verena wanted to mix all of the stones in equal measure, Connor insisted on alternating blocks of granite between every other stone.

"We're building a bridge to granite, after all. Let's make sure that affinity is really secure. We're including enough other stones to see if they have other effects."

Since neither of them really knew what they were doing or understood what would happen, she decided not to press the point. In short order, they completed both trusses between the mainland of her mind and the single-tiered granite island. Connor made sure the final pieces that secured the trusses to the island were also made of granite, and they fused without issues.

For the planks between trusses, they use the flat beds of wagons they found stacked up in one of the workrooms. Verena said, "These would be used eventually for making windriders. Seems appropriate, doesn't it?"

Connor agreed, and as they hefted the heavy, flat wagon beds out to the bridge, new ones appeared to replace the ones they had taken, providing them an inexhaustible supply. The beds were a bit too wide, but shrank to fit as he dropped them into position. In a matter of moments, they completed the bridge all the way to the other side, complete with steel handrails.

"After you," Connor said gallantly, gesturing Verena across.

She took his hand and pulled him rapidly across the bridge, breaking into a run. As soon as Connor stepped onto the completed bridge, he felt power thrumming through it. They had definitely accomplished something. He hoped it was something good.

Verena squealed with delight and pulled them on faster. "I can feel it. Something, a connection forming in my heart. This is going to work."

Connor agreed. He couldn't imagine it not working. They had built something very solid, and he expected she would quickly demonstrate an exceptionally powerful granite affinity.

As soon as Verena stepped onto the granite island, she gasped, eyes wide. "This is amazing. I feel so strong, and I haven't even tapped granite yet."

"I'm sensing an incredibly strong affinity," Connor agreed.

She planted another quick passionate kiss on his lips, then grabbed his hand, and rushed back to the mainland, dragging him with her. He laughed at her enthusiasm.

She exclaimed, "Come on! I need to see what I can do."

Chapter Sixteen
Sometimes You Get Exactly What You Deserve

By the time Connor blinked open his eyes after leaving Verena's mind, she was already standing, her fistful of granite raised before her, a look of deep concentration on her face. Almost instantly, she squealed with delight and opened her hand, revealing all the granite powder gone.

"I did it! I absorbed granite."

She tapped it, and all Connor could do was stare.

Most women tapping granite did not experience massive bulk expansion like the men. Men's muscles would bulge to many times their normal size, but women's muscles seemed to only grow denser and slip into their ideal, perfectly sculpted shape.

Verena's muscles all hardened, sculpting into perfect lines as they expanded to double their normal size. She was already in excellent shape, with a trim, athletic figure. Her skin faded to gray and turned to living stone as she transformed into a goddess of granite. She laughed and flexed her stone fingers.

"I love granite!" Her voice echoed around the room, richer than ever. Listening to her max-tapped granite voice was like getting a warm hug through his ears, right into his mind.

Jean clapped, and Hamish laughed and asked, "What can you do?"

Verena hefted the couch with Hamish and Jean on it, making it look easy. When she lowered them, she leaped into Connor's arms to give him a kiss, and he nearly collapsed under the weight. He hadn't been planning to catch a living statue, but quickly adjusted, tapping his own granite, and lifted her off her feet.

He was not about to comment on her weight. No girl liked any-one pointing out they'd just added half a ton, even if it was all stone weight. He didn't want her to punch him right out the window. She felt somehow denser than other Boulders he'd wrestled, and he sensed she possessed an exceptionally powerful granite affinity. What had they done building that bridge?

When she released him, she winked and said in an excellent imitation of Anika's voice, "Come mine Connor. We wrestle? Prove strong hands."

Connor grinned. "I'm starting to think I might've created a monster."

"This monster will spank your butt when we wrestle together," she laughed.

"You're on."

Grinning, Hamish poked at Verena's arm. "What's granite like? Wow, you feel dense."

"You'll have to get Connor to loan you granite. That's the only way to really understand."

"That'll give you a pretty good idea, but we accomplished some-thing special today," Connor added.

Jean walked slowly around them, studying Verena closely. "I was just going to ask about that. Verena seems unusually adept for such a new Petralist, and exceptionally comfortable with her new strength."

So Connor told them about the bridge. Hamish whistled softly. "So better mental bridges make stronger affinities?"

"They appear to," Connor confirmed. "It worked for Tomas, and now with Verena."

She grinned and hugged him again, squealing with enthusiasm, squeezing so hard he grunted, even max-tapping granite. His girl was definitely a strong woman now.

Despite how impatient he was to get his own affinity, Hamish insisted that Connor help Jean next. She was not about to argue, and took Verena's place facing Connor. He tapped the necessary stones and plunged into her mind.

Mhairi's kitchen, of course. Connor grinned as he turned a slow circle, taking in all of the familiar sights, breathing deep the unique scent of herbs and fresh-baked pies.

Jean appeared beside him, wearing the simple blue dress that she had favored that last year in Alasdair. When she realized where they were, she clapped and exclaimed, "Oh this is wonderful. I return here all the time in my dreams. It always reassures me, and I'm convinced coming here subconsciously helps me produce better cures."

"I don't doubt it. Come on, let's see if we can get you a new affinity."

They exited the healer's house and found it was the only structure on the otherwise flat street of Jean's mental mainland. Together they stepped to the edge of the cliff and looked out over the gently billowing mists toward the nearby floating islands. Like the other minds Connor had entered, her islands were constructed of the various affinity stones they represented, although the sandstone island a little farther out was fashioned to look like a huge healthbed.

The obsidian island looked like little more than a blacker shadow, hovering low in the dark mist. The granite and basalt islands seemed a little better formed. Connor wondered if maybe they should target one of those instead, just to be safe. Jean didn't have any affinities yet, after all.

Jean didn't look worried, but was grinning and pointing at the distant sandstone island. "Do you really think we can establish affinities for me with obsidian and with sandstone both in one day?"

"There's one way to find out," Connor said, determined to make it work. Usually it took Petralists longer to establish a secondary affinity, but if anyone could reach sandstone quickly, it would be Jean.

He looked around for building materials, but only then realized the problem with Jean's affinityscape. There were no power-grade stones available. In real Alasdair, they could head up to the quarry to acquire some, but he didn't even see the rest of the town, let alone the mountain and the quarry.

"So how do we do this?" Jean asked expectantly.

Connor rubbed a hand through his hair as he considered the challenge. He'd hoped to build something special for her like he had Verena, but maybe that wasn't possible. In Tomas' mind, he had used trees. He lacked even that option for Jean.

"We need to choose building materials to make your bridge. I'm just trying to figure out what we'll use," he admitted.

She glanced around. "Are you saying I can't get an affinity because I didn't create trees in my mind? Can I change things?"

"I think the representation of this place is important, so I don't think we should change things, even if we could. When I built other bridges, the materials changed to fit what I needed. Let's try pieces of the house."

Jean grimaced. "Good thing Gran's not here. She would not like us ripping apart her home."

Connor smiled to think of old Mhairi coming after him with a switch and a bucket full of one of her foul tonics. "I don't think she'd mind sacrificing a little to help you."

"Probably not," she admitted.

He didn't spy anything that might work as rope supports, but preferred making a more solid bridge anyway, so Connor ripped the door off its hinges. It was a good stout, wooden door, and should work nicely. He carried it to the edge of the cliff, closest to the obsidian island and pressed it to the lip, envisioning it transforming into the anchor block for the first truss.

The door disintegrated, wood melting away to mist that flowed over the edge and disappeared into the dark mists covering the abyss. Connor stared after it, surprised.

"Is that how it's supposed to work?" Jean asked with a frown.

"No," Connor said slowly, considering the problem. "I haven't had this happen before."

"So I can't establish an affinity?" she asked softly, looking crestfallen.

"Not necessarily. Don't jump to conclusions. I think it means I chose the wrong materials."

"So what can we use?" she asked, turning back to the house. "Do we need to rip apart the rest of the house?"

That didn't feel right, so Connor led the way back inside. "Maybe the kitchen table. That holds more meaning than the door did and more than the walls would."

She nodded, pacing around the table, tracing the fingers of her restored hand along its worn but spotless surface. "Lots of good memories around this table."

Feeling hopeful, Connor hefted the table, carried it to the cliff, and pressed it into the anchor position. It too dissolved into mist. He muttered a Grandurian curse, not wanting to look at Jean and see her disappointment. There had to be a way. What was he missing?

Jean touched his arm, her expression sorrowful, but not devastated. "It's all right, Connor. Not even the queen can grant affinities for everyone."

He shook his head stubbornly. "I don't know anyone who wants an affinity as much as you want sandstone, or anyone who would use it to accomplish so much good." He gave her a reassuring smile. "I know we can figure it out. The islands are there. We just need to figure out how to reach them."

Jean considered that. "You made Verena's bridge using power stone and beds from wagons, right?"

He nodded. "All materials tied to her Builder powers."

"They're more than that. Those are all items relating to her life's work," Jean pointed out thoughtfully.

Connor glanced back at the healer house, hope kindling again. "The table was important, but not really significant in your work. Maybe that's why it didn't work."

"My life's work is healing, Connor. How can we build a bridge with that?" she asked.

He grinned. "I have an idea."

Connor rushed back inside, passed through the kitchen, and led Jean to the large storeroom packed to overflowing with herbs and remedies. In any other place, trying to build a bridge with such materials would've been laughable, but in Jean's mind they were powerful.

Connor gestured at the herbs and said, "If anything is going to work, it'll be something in here."

Jean smiled, her face radiant as she stepped into the storeroom, arms extended toward the shelves of medicines. "I like it, Connor. This feels right." She extracted a bunch of dried herbs tied together and said, "Start with these."

Connor sniffed them, unfamiliar with the herb, although he suspected Mhairi must have used that one in at least some of her nasty tonics. He carried the bunch to the edge and pressed it down, willing with all his heart for it to form the anchor block. The herbs melted together, and for a second his heart sank.

The herbs transformed into a solid block as hard as stone, and sank into the edge of the cliff. Connor exulted, and Jean shouted, "It's working!"

"What's next?" he asked excitedly, thrilled beyond measure that they'd figured out the mystery.

"Come on." She led him back to the storeroom, paused to study the shelves, then began grabbing up bunches of herbs, bottles of powders, and packages of medicines. Connor hauled them all to the edge of the cliff. Once they assembled an enormous pile, Jean organized them and began passing them to Connor. All the while she muttered softly to herself, as if reciting recipes for cures and tonics in her mind.

Whatever they were building, it was not a random association of herbs, but growing according to a plan. That worked for Connor, and he took each item and pressed it into place, willing them to connect. Each item morphed into a solid piece of heavy, wooden beams and slid out to the end of the bridge to attach itself to the expanding truss.

It took only moments to complete the trusses. They were multi-colored wonders, formed from dozens of medicines, and the air grew heavy with their gentle scents. The mixed aroma smelled sharp and sweet and savory at the same time, and Connor found it somehow both relaxing and invigorating.

For the planking, Jean chose to use the treatment beds. Again more beds reappeared as necessary, providing all the materials they needed. As Connor placed each bed onto the trusses, it transformed into nine polished chestnut planks that slid out and snapped into position.

It was so much more fun building in the mind than building in real life, and Connor was thrilled by what he'd learned with Jean. He'd stumbled on the right materials out of sheer lucky instinct with Tomas and Verena, but Jean's bridge was proving enlightening. When he tried to help other people build new bridges, he suspected finding the right materials would prove a critical element in success.

When they completed the bridge with spiraling rails, Jean rushed across to the first island, towing Connor along by the hand. When she reached the island, she inhaled sharply, one hand going to her mouth, eyes wide as if in sudden understanding.

She whispered, "It's amazing. Obsidian is like a light illuminating shadows in my mind I never knew existed."

"I bet you use a lot more of your mind than most of us do."

Connor paced the low obsidian island, leaning down to wave a hand through the dark mists coiling so close to the edge. The mists were cool and dry, but he sensed nothing extraordinary about them. For a moment, he wondered what would happen if he simply stepped off the edge and plunged down into the abyss they covered. Would he learn all of Jean's deepest secrets, get ejected from her mind, or keep falling forever?

He decided not to find out.

Connor paused on the side closest to the nearby sandstone island, considering their next move. Jean joined him and asked, "Do you really think we should try a secondary affinity so soon?"

He hesitated. Usually a Petralist needed time before attempting to establish new affinities, but he found himself eager to proceed anyway. Jean wanted that healing affinity so badly, he doubted she'd let anything stop her. Besides, they were far too short on time to hesitate.

The final piece that convinced him was the shape of the island itself. He pointed to it and said, "I think we should go for it. There are risks, but you've already given sandstone a unique shape. Images in the mind are powerful, and I'm optimistic you're ready for it."

Jean took a deep breath, then flashed her brilliant smile. "I agree!"

They again assembled a pile of medicines. Jean agonized for a moment, then smiled, coming to a decision, and began passing components to Connor without hesitation. He pressed them into position. Again, complex trusses began to form, and a new scent grew, one that felt stronger, more urgent.

"What recipe are you using?" he asked.

"It's a very complex blend I developed this winter to fight infection. It's the most advanced healing mix I ever created, but it's as clear as day to me now."

"Great idea. Keep it up."

After a few more minutes of steady work, they completed the bridge. It looked solid and radiated a sense of health that reinforced its connection. Connor doubted anything could ever sunder that bridge, and wondered again about Nicklaus' broken bridges.

Jean pulled him out of his reverie by grabbing his hand and dragging him across the bridge at a run. She leaped onto the healthbed-shaped island and threw her arms into the air, laughing with victory.

"I can feel it already. This is amazing!"

When Connor joined her, she hugged him fiercely and exclaimed, "Thank you, Connor!"

"I can't wait to see what you'll be able to accomplish."

Connor was so thrilled. Too bad only he and Queen Dreokt could create such links for others. Jean would use her gift to heal thousands. She would be the true hero.

Jean's smile seemed to light up the entire affinityscape. "Let's test them out!"

Chapter Seventeen
Pastries, the Building Blocks of Great Things

When they awakened, Jean instantly absorbed a little obsidian, and Verena passed her a piece of sandstone. Verena was not carrying her ever-present satchel for once, but her gown incorporated a number of deep pockets. Connor would've been disappointed in her if it hadn't.

Jean turned to Hamish and placed a hand on his head, concentrating and holding the sandstone in her other hand. "If only you had an injury I could diagnose."

"I could throw him out a window for you," Verena said innocently.

"He's not wearing his suit," Connor pointed out.

Hamish grinned. "Think you could toss me all the way to the first banquet table?"

"Jean does want you injured," Verena said, glancing toward the window.

"I was joking," Hamish said, watching her suspiciously. "I do have a bit of a stomachache."

Connor laughed. "Isn't that your normal state? You ate enough for breakfast that anyone else would have popped."

"We're dealing with the fate of the world here, Connor. One needs to take risks to obtain the right level of clarity to figure out solutions."

He had a good point, and Connor had honestly eaten almost as much. He had made it a habit to instantly transform his food into energy, and had done so that morning without even thinking about it. He probably should have done the same for Hamish, but he didn't want to encourage Hamish to abandon all restraint. Merkland only had enough food for fifty thousand people, after all.

Jean whistled softly, her hand still touching his head. "I can see so much. In all my years healing, I was always an outsider, but now I can get inside the injury and see exactly what needs to be done."

She stood. "I need to get to the hospital. I'm sure a lot of people are getting injured tonight. Rory and Anika tend to inspire a reckless level of bash fighting, even among people who are not bash fighters."

Connor grinned as did Verena, but Hamish said, "Aren't you going to wait until I get obsidian first?"

Jean nodded, clearly torn between supporting Hamish in his glorious moment of discovery and leaping full tilt into a healing frenzy that might never end.

Hamish swapped places with her to sit in front of Connor and gestured. "Come on. Let's see what we can do."

So Connor connected and plunged into Hamish's mind. The affinityscape formed, and he laughed. It was perfect.

Part enormous bakery and part insane Builder workshop, it was far larger than the huge workrooms in the original Builder compound. Fireplaces, ovens, and racks of still-warm sweetbread vied for space everywhere. Built among those more mundane cooking implements were dozens of smashpackers running non-stop, being fed sumptuous meals by conveyor belts that seemed to carry an inexhaustible supply of Hamish's favorite meals.

Other mechanicals were built over, under, around, and among the dozens of fireplaces and heatstone ovens. One entire area was dedicated to a long, complex mechanical that looked like the one Hamish had described building in his early days at the Builder compound.

The space overhead was crowded with conveyor belts, little flying platforms overflowing with ingredients, and even catapult-like mechanicals that flung pastries and jelly desserts at seemingly random intervals and in seemingly random directions. More mechanicals were built into the ceiling, but somehow ingredients didn't fall.

The scents assaulting Connor's nose made him wish he never had to stop inhaling. Sweetbreads, roasting meat, and hundreds of other mouthwatering smells tugged at his nostrils.

It was the most perfect representation of Hamish's mind that Connor could have imagined.

Hamish appeared beside Connor, wearing his battle suit. He looked around and laughed. "I see this place in my dreams. It's my ultimate vision of the workroom I want to build some day. This is incredible!"

He rushed into the maze, sampling dishes, touching mechanicals, laughing with joy. He even climbed into one of the catapult mechanicals, plopping down right onto a huge chocolate jelly just before it was flung high into the air. Hamish swallowed several bites of the dessert before activating thrusters and soaring around the room for several minutes, inspecting everything and exclaiming in delight.

Connor laughed, and could have easily watched for an hour since he found a nearby rack full of all of his favorite desserts, still warm from the oven. In the mental space there was no limit to what one could eat, so he happily consumed the entire tray.

Hamish eventually descended, grinning as happily as the day Jean first kissed him. "If this is what you get to experience all the time, I'm surprised you don't find more excuses to get into people's heads."

"Not everyone's mind is as fun as yours."

"So let's build bridges," Hamish said enthusiastically.

As they moved through the huge, chaotic workroom toward an outer door, they stumbled upon the first well of Hamish's Builder affinities. It was built into the shape of an oven, with cream-filled pastries floating up out of the depths in a never-ending stream.

Connor snatched one of the pastries. It was perfectly flavored, but still somehow conveyed the taste of basalt.

Now that he knew what to look for, Connor easily spotted the other affinity wells. Hamish looked ready to get distracted again by tasting them all, and maybe even jumping down inside one, but Connor drew him toward the exit. "You can explore here anytime. It's your mind after all. Let's see if we can get you an affinity."

The enormous workroom bakery filled almost the entirety of Hamish's mental mainland. Connor was happy to see the abyss filled with billowing mist, but in Hamish's mind the mists reminded him of whipped cream spraying into the air. The floating affinity islands looked pretty standard except for the distant quartzite island which was constructed like a giant replica of Hamish's battle suit.

When Hamish spotted it, he gasped and pointed. "Can we get there?"

Connor had no doubt that eventually they could, but not in one attempt. They'd pushed the limits for Jean, but he sensed acquiring a primary, secondary, and tertiary in one day might overload Hamish's mind. "Let's get you to obsidian first. We can explore getting additional affinities later."

Hamish did not seem to mind. "How can we can build this thing?"

"With Jean, we learned that the best bridges come from materials that represent your strongest passions." Connor nodded back toward the workroom and Hamish understood instantly.

They said in unison, "Pastries!"

They ended up using every type of pastry and quite a few smashpacked meals. Those little cubes expanded into building-block-sized meals, and Connor ended up using them to form the trusses. The other pastries and desserts expanded into solid, if slightly squishy, planks that linked the trusses. For the railing, he ended up with rails that looked like long crackers, with supports that looked like tall blocks of half-melted chocolate. The entire process felt like it took about an hour, although in the real world only seconds had probably passed.

Hamish marched across, making sure to touch every plank. He took his time, enjoying the process far more than he ever did eating. Connor appreciated that. Touching the planks seemed to help reinforce the link in Hamish's mind.

When he reached the obsidian island, Hamish took a deep breath, hands extended wide, head back, an exultant look on his face. With eyes closed he said softly, "It's part of me now, Connor, even deeper than when you loaned it to me. There's so much to think about!"

Connor chuckled. Hamish surprised even him sometimes with his brilliance. His love of food and joking around often concealed it, but he was one of the top Builders for lots of good reasons. Connor felt a deep sense of contentment. All three of his best friends now enjoyed new affinities! If they could do that, they could figure out a battle plan to finally defeat the dread queen.

Of course, as soon as they awakened and Hamish confirmed their success, Jean wanted to rush off to the hospital. Together they managed to convince her it was okay to celebrate a little first.

Hamish finally won her over by saying, "You don't want to offend Rory and Anika by leaving their party too soon, do you?"

Jean raised an eyebrow, clearly not fooled. "Fine. Let's party, but then we head to the hospital."

Connor said, "If we party long enough, I bet at least one of us might need to go to the hospital."

Verena slipped her warm hand into his. "I plan to have too much fun to wreck it with an injury. Let's go!"

Flying definitely had its perks. Instead of wasting time rushing down the long staircases, they floated down toward the huge square together, standing on an invisible platform of air.

Fifty feet up, Verena jumped off, whooping and max-tapping granite. Luckily the square was not nearly as packed with people since the party had already spread farther out into the city. Pedestrians scattered as Verena plunged to the pavement and landed in a crouch, the impact cracking like thunder.

When the rest of them touched down, Verena hugged Connor again. "That's so much fun! Let's do it again."

"You'll ruin your gown," Jean pointed out.

Hamish laughed. "Bash fighters tend to squeeze all their brains out of their heads with all those muscles. It's good to see you're trying to make up for lost time."

Verena slugged him, but forgot to untap granite. Connor instinctively tapped basalt and shot across the distance before she accidentally crushed Hamish's shoulder, pulling his friend aside just far enough for her fist to slip past.

Hamish jumped back, holding up his hands in surrender. "Hey, don't kill me. It was a joke."

"I'm so sorry!" Verena exclaimed, one hand going to her mouth, her eyes wide with horror at what she almost did.

"I figured you were trying to give Jean someone to practice on," Connor said.

"I'm not used to this strength," Verena said, looking aghast. She was always the one with perfect control over her Builder powers, but getting used to granite strength was different.

"No harm done," Hamish said, then grinned. "You moved so fast, Connor. That was amazing. I'm glad you were tapping basalt."

"Actually, it's difficult not to," Connor admitted. "I'm connected to all of my affinities all the time, unless I really focus on turning them off."

"Is that a good thing?" Verena asked.

He wasn't sure. He didn't like dwelling on how similar he was to Queen Dreokt. It would be far too easy to adopt her same arrogance. He wasn't limited like everyone else, but that fact terrified him, and he tried very hard to pretend he was still just Connor.

So he said, "It was just now."

Verena didn't look convinced, but Hamish interrupted. "Hey, you can make it up to me by sharing your dessert."

"You can eat as many desserts as you want tonight," Jean protested.

Hamish shrugged. "Eating hers doesn't count against my allotment, does it?"

Connor was glad no one got hurt, but Verena still looked shaken. He took her hand and said, "I think I know where we need to start."

"At the feasting tables, of course," Hamish said as Jean linked an arm with him and the four of them headed across the square. Feasting tables had already been set up around the perimeter and were swarmed by partygoers.

"Just the first round. Then we're heading for the Boulder dance toss," Connor said.

"Excellent!" Hamish said, taking the lead toward the tables to find out what kind of food they could get.

That turned out to be just about anything they wanted. Tables were set up in every square across the city, and more lined the roads outside the gates. The tables in the main square groaned under the weight of so many dishes. Thin-sliced ham and turkey were piled high next to giant bowls of chopped fruit. Potatoes cooked in eighteen different ways filled two entire tables, while vegetable platters and roasted duck were laid out in floral patterns. Connor followed Hamish's gaze to the desserts. Sweetbreads, pastries, cakes, and cookies were stacked everywhere, filling the air with the heavenly aroma of warm, sugared perfection.

Everything was cut into bite-sized chunks so no one had to worry about forks or finding tables to dine. Connor wondered if that was just good planning, or if Rory had ordered it to salute Tomas and Cameron, who had never trusted forks.

Servers handed out small bowls and dished generous portions into them. Hamish stopped in front of a giant Althin chocolate cake. It towered nearly three feet tall, fashioned into the shape of a great pedra, wings furled along its side, serpentine neck wrapping around the cake to cleverly place the blocky, ugly head atop the main body. The black frosting glistened with a sheen of honey, and Hamish eagerly ordered slices for all of them. He looked like he wanted to hug it.

Jean drifted to the side, staring at another tall cake with brown frosting, the front cut open to reveal an interior designed like a floor-to-ceiling library, complete with little tomes lining the shelves. She breathed, "Oh, my. This is wonderful."

"We'll take some of that one too," Hamish told the nearest server, who obliged by piling pieces atop the chocolate ones already in their bowls. As they stepped back from the table to let more people order, Hamish raised his bowl in salute. "If we're only going to stop for one course, might as well start with the best."

Jean reached over and deftly snatched part of his chocolate cake, popping it into her mouth. A look of rapture crossed her face and she mumbled, "So good."

Hamish gaped at her. "The woman of my dreams ate the cake of my dreams. I'm so confused."

Connor laughed. "What's confusing? Now she's sweeter than ever."

"Good one," Verena said, careful to guard her own bowl in case one of them decided to try the same trick.

Hamish leaned in and kissed Jean's chocolaty lips then grinned. "Sweeter than ever!"

CHAPTER EIGHTEEN
Just Dance!

In great spirits, Hamish and the others headed for the square beside the wrecked shell of the military command building. Hamish felt like he was floating on air, even though he wasn't wearing his battle suit. His new obsidian affinity thrummed inside of him like a living thing, and he kept a constant low tap rate. He wanted to laugh with every graceful step. Suddenly walking was more like dancing, his movements graceful and balanced.

He couldn't wait for his next sword practice. He found time most days to practice some, but as a Blade, he'd improve a hundred-fold. Connor had told him that while practicing with obsidian, he'd learned concepts faster and retained that knowledge better. Good thing because they didn't have much time. Battle was coming. How many of them would survive?

He forced down the dark thoughts. Tonight was a night of celebration.

He got an amazing idea and turned to Jean, who was walking beside him, a delighted smile on her face. "Do you think obsidian will help us eat more?"

She laughed. "I can honestly say I had never considered the question."

Connor glanced back from where he walked just in front of them with Verena. "I don't know if it'll increase your capacity, but I've proven I can eat faster with obsidian."

"I bet I could win the sausage eating competition in Faulenrost," Hamish said with a grin.

Verena smiled at his enthusiasm. "And I feel like I could punch Shona to the moon."

Hamish almost said, "Prove it," but Connor looked worried. He should lighten up. Now that Verena was a Rumbler, chances of her and Shona killing each other were sharply diminished. In fact, they seemed to bond better while pummeling each other.

They moved through a city thronged with partygoers. People crowded around food and drink tables and packed dance floors. Everywhere Hamish looked, people were eating, drinking, and dancing. The noise was like a constant roar, and everyone seemed to be trying to talk or laugh over each other. There was a frantic, almost desperate edge to the noise, and a sense of charged emotion flowed just under the surface of the revelry.

Jean looked around, a frown on her face as they crossed one tight-packed square. Hamish asked, "You feel it too?"

She nodded thoughtfully. "Everyone is trying so hard to forget what's coming."

That was it. Hamish recognized it immediately. "In a few days, we could all be dead. This is the last chance to forget about it all."

Verena looked over and said, "I hope they manage it. After tonight, no one will get a break until we win."

Hamish appreciated the fact that she didn't acknowledge the chance they might lose. Why worry about that?

He wouldn't. Not tonight, anyway.

So he pushed aside his worries about the upcoming battle and focused on the party. They soon reached the command building. It had suffered great damage in the swarm attack and was encased in a layer of wooden scaffolding. A large crowd had gathered in the large square outside for the Boulder dance toss, and already over fifty pairs of Boulders had lined up to participate.

Rory and Anika swept into the square, followed by a brightly dressed throng, including Ivor and Shona. A Pathfinder magnified Rory's voice as he and his bride took their places in front of the gathered Boulders and Rumblers, while Ivor and Shona joined the ranks.

"Who's ready for the Boulder toss?"

A deafening cheer answered him. Anika added, "Mine Rory and I will set the height. Losers serve drinks."

She pointed to a few tables loaded with barrels of wines, ales, ciders, and juices, enough varieties to slake any thirst. A host of servers were struggling to keep up with demand, and they all raised fists in thanks when they heard the announcement.

Hamish was about to head for the drink tables to test if Blades could drink more before having to take a breath, but Connor pulled Verena toward the line of participants.

"I don't know what to do," she protested. She might look tiny compared to some of the hulking Boulders in their battle leathers, but anyone falling for her cuteness facade and underestimating Verena would regret it.

Jean slid an arm around Hamish's waist as they watched the competition. He wished Tomas and Cameron were still alive. They'd be running a busy betting racket and would no doubt make a mint getting folks to bet against Verena.

Rory gripped Anika by the waist and stole a kiss before tossing his bride into the air to a burst of cheering.

"I figured he'd throw her higher," Jean commented.

"They always start low. Every round they go higher. That's the challenge of the lead couple. Everyone else has to match the height of each throw. The person who misses by the most gets a negative point. Two points, and a pair are out and have to do whatever the rules of the match say for losers."

"Sounds easy," she said.

"That's why Connor is making Verena go first." Hamish pointed.

The round passed quickly, each pair stepping forward so one of them could toss their partner. Most got pretty close to the same height Rory had. Verena started chewing on her lip like she did when nervous or really concentrating.

Shona tossed Ivor, matching Rory's throw perfectly. Ivor sprayed glittering droplets of water across the square, eliciting laughter and more cheering.

When Connor and Verena took their places a moment later, everyone expected Connor to throw Verena. When she instead grabbed his waist and swelled with granite, a murmur swept through the crowd.

"Are loaned powers allowed?" Shona asked Rory. She didn't look upset that Verena was participating, but it seemed she couldn't help ask the question anyway.

She couldn't have set Verena up more perfectly. Verena spoke loudly enough for everyone to hear. "Connor didn't loan me granite. I have a new affinity!"

The murmurs turned into open gasps as Verena max-tapped to show off her new affinity and throw Connor. She had fun with it too, her skin glowing white, her perfectly carved body outlined by her spectacular dress.

She forgot about the height requirement.

Swept up in the moment, she launched Connor so hard that he soared high over the nearby buildings, his laughter sounding a bit strained.

"Great throw!" Jean shouted, clapping enthusiastically with most of the crowd.

"Yeah, if she wants to lose," Hamish replied. Verena had definitely gained a powerful granite affinity, but she clearly didn't know how to use it.

Luckily she could still catch. Verena snatched Connor out of the air as he fell, spinning around twice to help bleed off speed. She cradled him easily in her mighty arms and stole a kiss to a round of cheering. Verena always did things with style.

Hamish took the opportunity to mimic her, spinning Jean to steal a kiss. She was also tapping obsidian and turned the surprise spin into a graceful twirl, her smile brightening the entire square.

When Verena put Connor down, many people crowded around. Ivor asked, "You helped Verena establish her first affinity?"

When Connor nodded, he dropped to one knee beside Verena and took her hand, kissing it in a gallant manner. "Congratulations, Verena. This is a banner day indeed."

"Show-off," Shona muttered to him before adding to Verena, "Now we can train together every day."

She raised a fist, which Verena bumped with her own, and both of them grinned. "I can't wait."

"Friends by fist-fighting are friends indeed," Hamish said.

Jean rolled her eyes. "It's possible to make friends without fighting."

"But not usually as fun."

Anika hugged Verena tight and said in Grandurian, "I'm so proud of you, Verena! What a gift on my wedding day to see you join the sisterhood of the battle maidens."

Verena looked on the verge of tears. Girls could get really emotional, especially when they hadn't eaten dinner yet.

Rory said, "Congratulations, Verena. We're happy for you, but I think it safe to say you lost round one."

"Oh," she said, flushing and glancing into the air where she'd thrown Connor. "Oops."

That generated a general round of laughter, but Connor said, "If you don't mind, I'd like Verena to take the next turn too. She needs the practice."

"Agreed," Rory said, glancing at the others, who all nodded in turn.

Ivor asked, "Can you repeat this, Connor? Can you really help others gain new affinities too?" He swept a hand across the crowd, who pressed in closer, an expectant hush settling over the courtyard.

"It's already proven," Hamish interjected loudly, raising Jean's hand high in his. "Jean and I both gained obsidian tonight!"

That triggered a round of cheers, and Connor added, "I plan to try helping as many people as possible gain affinities in the next few days."

More cheering. Many people started shouting questions, asking when they could try.

Rory gestured toward his throat, so Connor applied quartzite to it. Rory's voice boomed loudly over the din. "Calm yourselves. This is wonderful news. We'll put together a schedule and do this in an organized way. Don't worry. We need everyone, so you'll get your chance."

That elicited more cheering, and Rory said, "We'll assign a senior officer to work with you to organize the schedule. How fast can you do it?"

"I think it'll depend on each person, but it didn't take long with Verena, Hamish, and Jean," Connor said.

Hamish wondered if other people Connor didn't know so well would take longer. It had seemed like it took a certain amount of understanding of the person he was working with in order to figure out the affinity construction. Connor would make it work.

"You might get tired, though," Jean said, her tone cautioning. "You don't know yet if you'll face side effects like when you fleshcraft."

That was a good point, but Connor looked fine. He said, "We'll take that as it comes, but tonight we have a party to enjoy."

The Boulder toss resumed with lots of good cheer. Verena managed to survive two more rounds, her throws not great, but not the worst, either. She was wonderfully strong, but it took time to master the nuances of applying such strength, and on the third toss she again threw Connor too high. He didn't seem to mind.

Hamish was happy to lead Jean to the drink table and order drinks from the two of them. Business was brisk, but he managed to get both Connor and Verena to refill his cider glass three times. He really could drink it down faster, but still felt himself growing full too soon. He'd need to convince Connor to work his glutton-crafting on him.

Eventually they all slipped away and Connor lifted them high above the city on a platform of air. It was a nice way to travel, but not as free as flying in his suit. Still, he could enjoy hugging Jean better, so Hamish decided he liked it. They spotted a running dance on the open lands south of the city.

"Look. Striders and Wingrunners," Connor said.

Jean leaned against Hamish, oohing at the sight, and Verena slipped an arm around Connor's waist. She extracted a couple pieces of quartzite and created a long-vision sightscreen in front of them to magnify the view. Hamish should have thought of that. He was the one with obsidian, after all.

Fast movers were racing across the land, mixing and blending together in intricate patterns that seemed impossible for so many individuals to create together. Several times, Hamish felt Jean tense beside him. "They're going to crash."

Somehow they slipped past each other, often close enough to touch as they engaged in the singular dance experience.

"I want to try that sometime," Verena said.

"Sure, but we'll need to practice a lot. I'm not sure even I could keep up with all of those moves," Connor admitted.

When the running dance ended, the group crossed back over the city. They spotted musicians playing to enthusiastic dancers in every square, but Verena insisted they return to the main square. She said, "I heard good things about Shona's personal band."

As they settled toward the ground, Hamish spotted the musicians, who were arranged on the wedding platform. A dozen men and women playing a range of wood and brass instruments. He wasn't a musician, and growing up in Alasdair, they'd been severely limited in what music they could enjoy, but even he could tell those musicians were special.

The sounds of a popular dance tune wafted up to them as they approached, but it was somehow more. The notes were purer, richer, harmonized so much better than he'd ever heard. Jean's head cocked to one side, her eyes wide as she listened, mesmerized. Verena sighed, a slow smile spreading across her lips.

"Even better than I expected. They're as good as the royal orchestra that plays for King Henrik in Edderitz." She started swaying to the music even before they landed.

"How are they doing it?" Hamish asked. "I've heard good music, but nothing like this."

"They're Blade musicians," Verena said, tugging Connor toward the dance floor, which was packed with couples.

"Of course," Hamish laughed, pulling Jean after. "I bet we can learn to play any instrument now."

"I bet you can even learn to sing," Jean teased.

"I'm not that bad," Hamish protested, but he was. He vowed to start taking voice lessons if they survived the upcoming battle. He'd heard that good singers needed to consume extra portions of sweetbreads to help their throats. Or it might have been sugar. He wasn't sure if he was remembering right, so decided to eat more of both, just to be safe.

The four of them lost themselves in the dancing for a while. The music wrapped around them like a blanket and blocked out worries for the future, drained away fatigue, and made them lighter on their feet. It was hard to stop dancing, although they did pause every half hour to wolf down another five bowls of food and dessert before plunging back in.

During the first break, Connor taught Verena how to purge granite. She was very reluctant to do so, even though she really wanted to get some loaned obsidian for the dancing. Hamish and Jean watched carefully, but didn't purge their obsidian yet.

"It's all right. After we're done, you can absorb some more granite," Connor told her.

"Just don't forget to purge before sleeping," Hamish reminded them. Connor had regaled them with stories of double-tap sickness and the debilitating effects of not purging.

Connor glanced around. "I wish our families could be here."

Jean smiled, her expression turning wistful. "Gran would love this music."

"My siblings would eat out half the city," Hamish laughed, suddenly missing his big family. They hadn't visited nearly enough through the winter, although he'd already sent a copy of Schwinkendorf's cookbook to his mother via courier.

"Small price to pay," Connor assured him.

"Yeah, because Shona's paying for it," Hamish responded.

"We need to get our parents together soon," Verena told Connor. "I think they'll get along wonderfully."

"You bet. Wait till your mom experiences one of my mom's . . ." Oddly, Connor trailed off, frowning.

Verena and Jean both looked at him funny, but Hamish piped in, "Yeah, her hugs are the best."

"I knew you'd pick up where I left off," Connor said, as if he'd planned for the break, but Hamish knew better. Connor never paused like that, not when talking about his mother. Something was wrong. He filed it away to ask Connor about it later.

First, he needed to dance with his love. Hamish grabbed Jean's hand and together they rushed back to the dance floor. Verena and

Connor followed close behind and the four of them launched into an obsidian-fueled dance competition, trying to outdo each other with extra spins, twirls, and dips. Other dancers stopped to stare as they moved together with obsidian-enhanced grace, the girls twirling in their finery, all of them moving like acrobats, their laughter mixing with the music.

Hamish found himself laughing more than he ever had before. It was just so much fun, so perfect to move together with Jean in such harmony. The freedom of it rivaled flying in his battle suit. He looked forward to sharing many such moments with Jean all their lives.

The musicians soon recognized what was happening, and they took up the challenge, increasing the tempo, setting a blistering pace that forced all of the other dancers off the floor to watch. Only the four of them could keep up, their feet moving in a blur, bodies twisting, turning, and weaving together, half a step away from disaster, but riding the wave of music on and on. Jean loved it, her restored hair spinning about her perfectly healed face, smiling with more joy than she'd shown since the terrible day Aonghus burned her. Seeing her so happy made Hamish giddy with joy.

He was surprised when Kilian and Aifric joined them. Verena actually gaped and exclaimed, "I've never seen Kilian dance!"

"He must practice in secret," Connor commented as Kilian and Aifric slipped into the dance without missing a beat.

Kilian was an excellent dancer and he kept up with all of Aifric's personalities as different women cycled through the control position. He adapted easily to their different dancing styles, making it look like they'd choreographed their moves before joining the dance. Hamish was impressed. Kilian kept up, despite lacking obsidian, and Aifric managed to keep up too. Some of her personalities had obsidian affinities, but not all of them, and yet they never faltered.

They danced until the wee hours of the morning before staggering off the dance floor to the enthusiastic cheering of the remaining spectators. The musicians looked totally exhausted, but exultant as they raised their instruments in salute. Verena and Connor paused to speak with Kilian, but Hamish led Jean to the platform to thank the Bladed musicians.

Their leader, a whip-thin harpist with wispy, white hair, grinned as he bowed over Jean's hand. "Lady Jean, we've often played to high nobility, but never have we gotten to push our own limits like we have tonight. You gave us as much of a gift as we gave you."

"I don't think any of us will ever forget tonight," Hamish said, shaking the man's hand in turn.

As he escorted Jean back to her suite later, she leaned her head against his shoulder and said, "That was a wonderful evening, Hamish. If that ends up being our last party together in this life, at least we ended on a high note."

He felt the weight of responsibility rush back in, the awesome challenge they faced in defeating Queen Dreokt and her enormous army. When they reached her suite, he kissed her tenderly, then held her gaze.

"This won't be our last."

She smiled, the fight strong in her. "Then get some sleep, because we have a lot of work to do."

CHAPTER NINETEEN
Sometimes Completing a Puzzle Is Depressing

The next morning, half the city slept in late, but Connor couldn't. He'd used gluttoncrafting to transform all the food he ate into pure energy, so despite the vigorous late-night dancing, he awoke rested.

He exited his small room in the palace and trotted across Merkland. The cobblestones sparkled with a light coating of dew, and the morning smelled bright and clean, as if it had rained a little after he retired. Decorations and tables were still set up, but the food had been put away, and most of the trash collected. Between Shona, Ivor, and Rory, they had Merkland running super efficiently.

A few people waved, and three separate times people tried to stop him to ask about when they could attempt to gain an affinity. He assured them the schedule would be posted soon, but excused himself quickly and kept going. He felt restless and needed some space to run.

The Army gate was already open. He waved to the guards, tapped basalt, and accelerated sharply as he turned onto the road heading south around the city. As he approached the southern bridge that crossed the Macantact to the township, he noticed the huge gap in the speedcaravan track, and memories of the intense battle with Harley flooded his mind. They'd lost some good people, but so many more of them could have died. He shuddered to think how close he'd come to losing Verena to Mattias, who had hunted her under Dougal's mind control. And Harley had nearly crushed Hamish several times.

As Connor accelerated south, the valley opened wide to the east, on the opposite side of the river. He didn't bother tapping air to fly across, or water to skate across, but simply fracked and ran across the waters, which were glassy smooth in the still morning. He grinned as he flashed across the river, running so fast he didn't have time to sink, an enormous tail of spray shooting out behind him.

On the opposite side, he accelerated more and banked off the narrow farmer's road, entering a wide pasture, dotted with cattle. Careful to avoid smashing into any of them, he crisscrossed the fifty-acre pasture again and again, letting his mind wander as his feet flew across the ground. He made a point not to tap any of his tertiary powers. Training with the elements was amazing, but he needed a break, a chance to think.

He let the recent fight against Queen Dreokt flow through his mind, revisiting the plan, his solo infiltration of Crann, and leading the queen to the ambush point. All of that had gone extremely well, but the fight had not. Despite all their planning, she'd walked into their ambush and clobbered them, hurting every one of them. If not for the Sucker Punch, she might have killed them all.

Connor was supposed to be as strong as the queen, but he'd felt young and outclassed. She'd proven conclusively that he couldn't stand toe to toe with her and slug it out with the elements. She'd win every time. Sure, by working together they'd managed to turn the tide against her, but then she'd unleashed the marble sculpted stone.

Would she use another?

She'd destroyed one of the most powerful battle affinities for a chance to kill them. Did she have another of those special stones? Would she sacrifice another affinity to gain a fatal advantage?

Quartzite would do it. The very thought of snuffing out quartzite and losing all the Builder thrusters distracted him so much he almost ran right into a grazing cow. With a shout of surprise, he vaulted over it, leaving the surprised animal staring after him, chewing its cud.

Connor wasn't sure what they could do to stop Queen Dreokt from attacking another affinity. It seemed idiotic for her to dismantle her own ramverk, but if she killed them, she'd have plenty of time to rebuild it.

Maybe they could find all of the ancient sculpted stones first, take them from the convergence points, and conceal them? Such an attempt would take precious time, and they might have to fight the elfonnel slumbering with the stones. He felt exhausted just thinking about so many elfonnel battles, but the idea had merit. Maybe.

Thinking of elfonnel brought him back to his recent elfonnel experience. He raced circuits around the pastures, wind rushing past, reliving the marvelous experience. Raising the elfonnel had been a terrible gamble that could have easily killed him, but it had paid off even better than Kilian had thought possible. The elementals had answered his call and saved him, had walked with him in a way they had done with no other Petralist, not even Queen Dreokt herself.

The debt he owed them was still unpaid.

He thought about that, about the elementals' odd behavior. Some of the things they had said hadn't made perfect sense, but he'd been very distracted. As he thought about it, he became convinced that if Porphyry hadn't remained with him and shielded his mind, he probably would not have ever returned.

The elementals wanted to be freed, but refused to clarify what that meant. Connor tried to remember everything they had said, tried to figure out what their clues had meant, but couldn't put the pieces together. He wished he was smarter.

"Wow, I'm all seven kinds of idiot," Connor chided himself, slowing to a stop and absorbing a little obsidian. He was one of the few people who could temporarily become much smarter.

Connor tapped obsidian, his mind accelerating, and he grinned, but that was not nearly enough mental power. It was enough to give him a good idea, though.

He tapped basalt again, but used the external-focused stilling. He then anchored stilling on obsidian like he had with internal-focused basalt to achieve superfracking. Then he max-tapped obsidian.

Stilling absorbed that flood of obsidian and in seconds created an enormous pool of super-obsidian. Connor tapped it and gasped as obsidian roared into him, ten times stronger than he'd ever felt. He tried falling over, but caught himself without even thinking about it. His reflexes felt so finely tuned, he bet he could read an opponent's movements before they even realized what they'd decided to do.

The sound of Verena's laughter warmed him as it burst across his mind like it always did when tapping obsidian. This time it sounded richer, like her granite laughter, and it made him smile.

With obsidian illuminating his mind like a blazing sun, Connor turned his thoughts back to the question of the elementals, their odd behavior, and those cryptic words about debt. One clue snapped into focus immediately, so he focused on that idea.

Connor released super-brains and absorbed a tiny bit of por-phyry. His supply was critically low, but he needed to risk absorbing a few grains of the rare powder. If only he had even one clue about where to mine for more, with super-brains he could probably figure it out.

Closing his eyes, Connor envisioned his affinityscape. It formed around him, and he stood on his mainland, facing his many bridges. His family bridge looked terribly worn from its recent abuse, worse than when he'd last seen it. He was tempted to cross it, to find out if it really did end in his family home. Maybe that would help him understand its importance. But it looked so weak, he feared it might collapse under his weight, and he sensed that would be bad.

Porphyry appeared beside him as soon as he tapped it. The great monster padded around him, sniffed the air, then settled on its haunches, tilting its head a little as it regarded him. "You hunt the mind, Pack Leader?"

"I do need answers," Connor admitted. Speaking with Porphyry was so refreshing. Its entire world revolved around the hunt. "When Fire and Earth consumed me to raise that elfonnel, you protected me and helped keep my mind free."

At the mention of the elementals, Porphyry's posture stiffened and a low growl rumbled deep in its thick chest. "Beware the deceit-ful ones, Pack Leader."

"Deceitful in what way? They helped me raise an elfonnel that saved all of our lives."

Porphyry resumed pacing around Connor. "The element pack abandoned their hunting grounds, betrayed their pack leader, and have invaded my hunting grounds. They seek new hunting grounds with no pack leader, no limits to the hunt. This is not the way."

Okay, so maybe possessing such a limited world view could be super annoying sometimes. Connor puzzled over that response, trying to understand what Porphyry meant. He even tapped super-brains again, but felt like he was missing an important piece of information to make it all clear.

As he thought about it, he paced out across his triple-layered bridges to the tiered islands of his affinities. The strength of his connections to each affinity reassured him. He had access to so much power, there had to be a way to defeat Queen Dreokt.

He thought back to Nicklaus and his blasted bridges. Poor kid. Losing so much so young from such a freak accident would have shattered almost anyone else, but the boy had bounced back with remarkable enthusiasm. If he kept progressing so fast, he might rival the famous Kirstin as the greatest Builder ever.

That got him thinking about Kirstin's father, King Triath and his disastrous experience with something Kirstin had done. If only . . .

He tapped super-brains again, and a new thought erupted into his mind like another volcano. He gasped, shook himself awake, and fracked as soon as his vision cleared. Running faster than any other Strider alive was too slow, though, so he super-fracked.

Connor whooped as he shot across the Macantact and up the road so fast it felt like he simply smashed through the space between him and the city. He released his super speed earlier than last time, but was still too close to the wall and unable to make the turn through the gate.

So he jumped.

Leaning all the way over, he ran right up the outer wall. Soldiers gaped as he shot past, arcing high out over the city, laughing with the thrill of it. A booming thunderclap shook the air around him as he jumped. He wasn't sure where that came from, but clearly the soldiers thought he'd called the thunder to highlight his jump. It did make his move look even more amazing.

Connor managed to land on a high, gently sloped roof, run down it, and skip across three more, each progressively lower, before jumping off the last roof and outrunning the fall to the paving stones. He slowed quickly, not wanting to plow over any other early risers. The streets were busier, but still noticeably empty compared to most days.

He found Verena in her rooms in the palace, already dressed in Boulder battle leathers. She spun, showing them off proudly. "I barely slept last night. I'm so excited to start training! Want to join me?"

He kissed her quickly, but shook his head. "I'd love to, but we need to talk. Do you know where Kilian is?"

"In his suite, I imagine."

"Come on." He grabbed her hand and headed for Kilian's rooms. Verena asked, "Why are we in such a hurry? Most people aren't even awake yet."

"I think I figured out something important. Do you have a speakstone paired to Hamish?"

She nodded and withdrew a small quartzite block from her satchel. Connor said, "Have him meet us at Kilian's."

"He won't be happy about missing breakfast."

"I'm sure he's got enough food under his bed for a week," Connor assured her.

It took only moments to reach Kilian's suite. The door was already open, with General Wolfram standing there, wearing his usual perfectly-pressed uniform, speaking with Kilian. He turned to leave just as Connor and Verena arrived. He greeted them warmly, then excused himself and left.

"Busy morning?" Verena asked Kilian.

He smiled, looking alert and rested. "Good thing none of us stayed up way too late last night."

"I'm glad you're up," Connor said. "I need to speak with you."

"I need to speak with you too." Kilian gestured them in and led them to his sitting room where a warm fire was already burning in the hearth. Aifric sat on one of the couches, dressed in a simple dress of pale green, her legs tucked under her. She wore her hair loose and was holding a warm drink of some kind in both hands, sipping it occasionally. She waved a greeting.

Kilian gestured Connor and Verena to one of the couches, then sat beside Aifric and asked, "What's on your mind, Connor?"

A knock on the window interrupted them. Hamish was hovering there. Aifric unfolded herself from the couch and crossed to the window to open it. Hamish slipped inside and asked, "Don't you know it's rude to lock your windows when you're expecting guests?"

"I'll be sure to add that to my etiquette booklet," Kilian said, eyes sparkling with little geysers of water. He motioned Hamish to join them.

"There's a book?" Hamish asked.

"Yeah, you eat it," Connor joked.

Hamish dropped into a nearby chair and peered at Aifric's drink curiously, then looked to Connor and asked, "How's your practice going with transforming water into that Althin hot chocolate?"

"Pretty well, actually."

"Really?" Verena looked very interested.

"Have you got any cups?" He asked Kilian, who rummaged in a cupboard and produced four large ceramic mugs. He handed them out, then with a gesture, filled them with hot water.

Connor concentrated on them, tapping soapstone just a little. The water glowed brightly in his senses, and he could see into it, feel its deepest structure. He gave that structure a twist that he'd been practicing in quiet moments before bed. The clear water transformed into a dark brown liquid.

"That looks promising," Hamish said before sniffing it. He nodded appreciatively. "Smells better than your last attempt." He gestured toward Verena's cup. "Ladies first."

She gave him a suspicious look, but still sniffed her mug and took a tentative sip. Hamish watched closely. He'd tasted Connor's first miserable failure, but Connor felt pretty confident he'd gotten it right. Verena's eyes widened and she sighed. "This is delicious!"

Hamish took a big gulp but then yelped and spit most of it back out. Looking embarrassed, he said, "Hot."

Connor sipped his. It was thick and creamy and sweet, just the way he liked it. Some aspects of ascension were simply awesome.

After taking a sip of his own, Kilian said, "I see you're using practice time well."

"Did your mother ever make you any hot chocolate?" Connor asked.

"No, she never did," he admitted.

"Can I try?" Aifric asked, switching mugs with Kilian. She took a sip and grinned. "This is amazing." She settled back in her seat, still holding Kilian's mug. When she saw his surprised expression, she gave him a dazzling smile and said, "You don't mind sharing, do you? You were asking for a sip of my tea earlier."

He chuckled and saluted with the tea. "Go ahead. I know better than to try out-arguing all of you."

"Wisdom is a sign of greatness," she said with a gracious nod.

"Or the sign that someone's really, really old," Hamish laughed.

Kilian looked like he was considering lighting Hamish's toenails on fire, so Connor said, "I wanted us all here because I was testing stilling with obsidian and managed to superfrack my brain."

"Is that a thing?" Verena asked.

Kilian looked impressed. "You got it to work?"

Connor nodded. "Same principle as basalt."

"I wonder if you could superfrack your rampager?" Hamish asked with a grin.

Aifric shuddered. "Don't go there, Hamish."

"I'm not sure what that would do," Connor admitted.

"Let's not get distracted," Kilian warned. With that group, it was a very real possibility. They loved diving into hypotheticals. "What did you learn?"

Connor explained his thoughts on the different bridges, how he had three tiers of bridges, but Nicklaus only one before they got smashed. He asked excitedly, "What if tapping an activated sculpted stone only destroys the top tier of someone's bridges, and what if the mechanical that King Triath was testing from Kirstin was a sculpted stone that she had fully activated?"

Hamish let out a low whistle, while Verena rocked back in her seat, eyes wide. She reflexively took a sip of hot chocolate. Aifric gasped, and Kilian looked very thoughtful. He asked, "You think that somehow he got pulled back down through the final threshold?"

"Is de-ascension even possible?" Hamish asked.

Kilian shrugged. "I have no idea. I never considered the possibility. It's a total reversal of what we always focus on."

"There's always another secret, and another twist to Petralist powers," Connor said with a grin. "What if it's possible?"

Hamish and Verena looked excited, and Aifric looked thoughtful, her gaze distant, her lips moving slightly, as if she was holding a conference among all the women in her head.

Kilian leaned back, deep in thought. "You might be onto something."

"It all fits!" Verena exclaimed, gripping Connor's hand.

"Better than you know," Kilian said. He rose and retrieved a document from a desk drawer. "I've considered the question of what happened to my father a thousand times, from every possible angle, but nothing fit. Your idea might finally offer us clarity, and it ties in perfectly with your aunt's latest communication that I just finished decoding this morning."

"The third piece arrived?" Connor asked eagerly. He'd known the second part of the coded message had arrived by courier, but they couldn't decipher any of it without the third.

Kilian nodded. "I see why she took such exceptional precautions with this one. If it had been intercepted, she would have been compromised. Part of the message included a request for specific information to be sent today via the disinformation speakstone. That's why Wolfram was here. He's taking care of it."

"What does she need?" Connor asked.

"Never mind that. The important thing for us is what the rest of her letter contained. She reports that my mother concealed the extent of her injuries from most of her subjects, but she suffered a short delirium while healing, and Ailsa was present."

Connor shuddered to think of Ailsa spending so much time in the presence of the mad queen. He wished again that they'd been able to catch her before she escaped back to Crann. They might have been able to finish her off.

Kilian continued. "She picked up some important information, knowledge that not even I have ever heard before. My mother's mind must have been wandering far afield."

"What information?" Verena pressed, leaning forward. The others looked as eager as Connor to learn.

"Not even my mother understands what Kirstin did to my father," Kilian admitted. Connor's hope fizzled. The king's descent into madness was the one clue that suggested a weakness they could exploit. Kilian continued, raising a finger for emphasis. "However, my mother told her that when my father suffered whatever it was Kirstin did, he fell victim to the elementals and they threatened to rise through him. That's why she had to kill him."

"I don't get it," Hamish said, frowning, glancing around the group. "How does this help us?"

"It's not a perfect picture, but I believe it ties in with what Connor realized this morning," Kilian said. "If Kirstin had activated a sculpted stone and my father tapped it, and if he was dragged back down to the second threshold, it would have been traumatic. The second threshold is very unstable, and it would have been easy to lose control of his elemental connection."

"That makes sense, but it sounds like your mother thought the elementals were using him somehow," Aifric pointed out.

Connor thought back to his recent elfonnel experience. The elementals had wanted to use him more than he'd allowed. Without the aid of porphyry, they might have succeeded. He could see how the king could fall to their influence if he was traumatized by losing access to his third threshold. What would the elementals do if given free rein to rise through a powerful Petralist? He felt a sudden chill.

Kilian gestured with the document. "Yes. In fact, my mother confirmed the elementals are self-aware, that it happened centuries ago, and that their ultimate purpose is to break free of the natural laws that govern them and walk the earth unrestrained."

Hamish paled, one hand gripping a muffin he'd just pulled from a pocket. Verena gasped. "That would be like a giant elfonnel that could last indefinitely. Think how much destruction they could cause."

"Apparently the filter of our affinities blocks them from gaining sufficient access through most Petralists," Kilian said, fixing his gaze on Connor. "Only a triple-ascended Petralist has the bridges in place they can use to rise."

"Is that why they've been helping you so much?" Aifric demanded.

"There's always a price," Verena added, looking terrified.

Connor nodded slowly. "I think so. I've seen hints of their purpose. They've told me they want me to act as their champion, and they've spoken of being imprisoned. Finally their ultimate goal makes sense."

"This is terrible!" Hamish exclaimed. "We need the elementals to fight the queen, but the more you rely on them, the more likely they'll find a way to destroy you."

"And everyone, if they escape," Kilian said gravely. "That is my mother's great fear. She apparently believes that Kirstin found the Builder threshold and was trying to ascend through it, but she also believes that should a Builder do so, they would become vulnerable to the elementals, who could rise through them."

"That's why Water's been encouraging us," Verena said, looking deeply offended. "She's been setting us up."

"What do we do?" Aifric asked softly.

They all looked to Connor. His mind was racing. He felt like he needed time to absorb the news. It fit with the clues he'd received, confirmed his worst fears, but he wasn't sure how to answer Aifric's question. "The queen still accesses the elements, so we should be able to as well."

Kilian nodded. "Ailsa mentions that my mother fears her defenses were weakened in that last battle. She seems terrified she won't be able to withstand the elementals indefinitely."

"So she's been trying to stop us from ascending and delving into deeper Builder powers for good reason?" Hamish asked, looking flabbergasted. "She's crazy, right? How can she be right too? That's double crazy!"

He was right. Everyone looked worried, thoughtful, and a little confused. Connor felt the same way, but the knowledge helped clarify one important point.

Somehow he had to use the elements without letting the elementals use him.

Chapter Twenty
Never Ask a Woman Her Age

Ailsa caught Rosslyn just before she entered the dining hall for the evening meal. She took her arm and drew her aside, partway down a side hallway that led toward the serving entrance. Rosslyn pulled her arm away, looking nervous. Through the brief contact, Ailsa felt Rosslyn's tension. Everyone lived in a constant state of fear around the queen, and not even the generals were immune. Some of the other diners glanced in their direction, but no one paused to ask what they were doing.

"Did you get my note?" Ailsa asked.

"Do you think it's wise to attempt such a thing? Here? Tonight, before we march in the morning?"

"It's the last opportunity we'll have. This is a great chance. She'll never expect it."

"If this doesn't work, she could destroy us all," Rosslyn whispered, leaning close, her terror showing in her eyes before she concealed it.

Ailsa wished she could comfort the younger woman. Every moment in the queen's presence was dangerous, but one did not have to live in fear. In her deepest thoughts, Ailsa recognized she faced the worst danger of anyone else, but she felt at peace. No matter what happened, she had accomplished much. Not that she would ever accept failure. She fully intended to succeed, and she felt convinced this was the moment to make her move. She planned to solve a major problem and hopefully lay the foundation to a stronger bond with Rosslyn at the same time.

"Try to relax. I only need you to signal to the chef who will be standing by the door when it's time. I've arranged for everything else. I'll make the announcement, but remember it's vital that we keep the truth of what we're doing from the queen until we spring the surprise."

Rosslyn took a deep, steadying breath and nodded. "I'll do it. I hope you know what you're doing."

Ailsa squeezed her shoulder to reassure her and gave her a warm smile. "Don't worry. Be brave, and you'll see we'll succeed. Won't it be nice to enjoy a little honest celebration?"

For a moment Rosslyn's expression softened. It looked like she was enjoying a happy memory. Ailsa hoped she could win many more happy memories with her children. She left Rosslyn and headed toward the dining hall where the queen took her meals, a converted banquet room, one of the few big enough to host the queen and the large crowds she insisted attend her at every meal.

Craigroy met Ailsa as she entered, and he surprised her by making a gallant bow and holding the door for her.

"Thank you. What's gotten into you today?"

"I'll tell you later," he said with a little smile.

"Fine. Keep your secrets," she said calmly, although inside she wanted to rejoice. She had no doubt he'd overheard the quiet conversation in the hallway. He was a spymaster after all, and he'd been covertly tracking her for days. She'd made sure to drop a few tantalizing clues that she was keeping an important secret.

"Sometimes I wonder which of us keeps more," he said softly.

"Keep digging for them and you're likely to dig yourself right into an avalanche. What news from your speakstone?"

"Very interesting news indeed," he said calmly. "I'll share it with you later."

"Why not share it now?" she pressed, although she knew why. She had worried that Wolfram might miss the schedule she'd set for the trick message. Craigroy's actions proved he'd received the first part and that he'd jumped to the conclusion she wanted him to after he overheard her conversation with Rosslyn. No doubt he was secretly exulting that he was about to destroy her.

"I'm having a copy transcribed for you," Craigroy lied smoothly. "I'll have it ready immediately after the feast."

"Very well," she said and passed him the daily dose of antidote in a tiny vial. Then she moved into the dining hall and took her place at the head table beside the queen's chair.

Ailsa wore a fine but simple dress with a subtle floral design. Aonghus was not in attendance yet, but Rosslyn joined her a moment later, along with her father and several of the other high-est-ranking officials and officers, including Lord Eoghan and his wife, Lady Fenella, rulers of Crann. He was tall and slender, appropriate for a Strider. His voluptuous wife was rumored to be a very competent Boulder. The queen had declared a grand feast to celebrate the eve of the army's march, so everyone wore dress uniforms or their best clothing. The huge room was filled with a riot of colors, and a mixture of perfumes mingled with the scents of roasted meats and fresh breads wafting in from the kitchen.

A servant passed the head table where Ailsa sat, carrying a tray of extra plates and forks. He paused at her plate to replace her fork. At the same time, he deftly slipped her a small piece of rolled parchment. She slid it into her lap and unrolled it to scan the contents.

Excellent. It was the full transcript of the latest overheard conversations captured by Craigroy's speakstone, which he still thought undiscovered in Merkland, and it confirmed her suspicion that things were falling into place.

Queen Dreokt swept into the room a moment later, looking regal in a spectacular gown of silver trimmed in gold. She wore a delicate silver crown, studded with diamonds, and looked perfectly healthy. All rose to bow or curtsy to her, but she seemed a little distracted and barely gestured acknowledgment of the honor before taking her seat and clapping impatiently. "Let the feasting begin. I'm famished."

Serving staff scurried to bring the first courses to her and then to the rest of the room. Queen Dreokt was very fond of roasted duck, so the cooks had prepared a delectable dish of diced duck, covered in a warm honey glaze, which added a subtle sweetness to the wonderful blend of spices. Ailsa closed her eyes to savor each bite. The meat was perfectly cooked, tender and juicy. Portions of roasted greens, caramelized onions, and beets were served with the duck, blending exceptionally well.

Other dishes included fresh breads, pork sautéed in gravy, and steak cutlets grilled in a tangy sauce topped with chopped and roasted almonds. The outstanding feast held an extra layer of savor for Ailsa as her sense of anticipation grew. Craigroy represented a very real threat, one that she could not beat physically. He was famously clever, but his trust in that speakstone would be his undoing.

It really was a wonderful feast. Eoghan and Fenella were working extremely hard as hosts and so far seemed to be successful. They and their court had been justifiably terrified that Queen Dreokt would kill or mind wipe most of them when she arrived, but she had shown remarkable restraint.

Ailsa allowed her surface thoughts to dwell on the local court. Queen Dreokt didn't seem bothered by the whispered reports from agents of the various lords and ladies involved in Crann politics. Many of them gleefully tattled about misdeeds and alliances to different high houses. As long as they did not betray her trust and held allegiance to her above all others, she did not seem interested in exerting the same level of absolute control as she had in Donleavy. It was an interesting change to her management approach, and Ailsa wondered if she would adopt a similar approach in other cities across the realm.

Queen Dreokt glanced at her as she daintily dabbed at her mouth with a white napkin. "Of course. I shouldn't need to command in all things, should I?"

"Very insightful, Your Majesty. Your wisdom constantly inspires me."

The queen chuckled. "And you're smart enough to see why. I exert my will upon the high lords and ladies, and I aim to make Donleavy a beacon of obedience and excellence. Our standard will be held up for all to see, and they will be given the opportunity to mold themselves in our image. It will take time, but I'm confident we will see progress. Those guilty of egregious mistakes or lack of discipline will be treated accordingly, but one must encourage the outlying realms with inspiration more than with fear."

Interesting words. Ailsa kept her surface thoughts focused on appreciation for the queen's mastery of ruling her subjects. In her deeper, private thoughts, she considered the queen's words. What she said was absolutely true, but suggested a side of her Ailsa had not expected to see.

The meal progressed smoothly with no outbursts or surprises. Queen Dreokt seemed in rare good humor, and that seemed to ease Rosslyn's nervousness. Just as the main courses were being cleared for the dessert courses to be wheeled out, Ailsa rose and said, "If you will permit, my liege, I have an important announcement to make."

"By all means," Queen Dreokt said grandly.

Ailsa spoke loudly. "May I have your attention, please?"

Conversation was always hushed during gatherings with the queen, and everyone instantly focused on Ailsa. No one dared miss anything important. Such a lapse might anger the queen.

Ailsa said, "Tonight we feast on the eve of our departure. Our matchless queen herself will lead her mighty army north to crush all opposition to her rule, but we have even more reason to celebrate. Tonight we celebrate Queen Dreokt's birthday!"

Stunned silence met her announcement as all eyes turned to Queen Dreokt, who looked as shocked as Ailsa had ever seen. The queen only managed to stammer, "What?"

"I'm sorry if I got the date wrong by a little. No one seemed entirely sure of the right day, but you seemed so distraught after that attempt on your life that I thought you would appreciate a little good cheer before we all head off to battle again."

Rosslyn made a beckoning gesture to the chef standing by the main doors, and he ducked through. Two seconds later, the doors opened and people flooded into the room, including many of the senior Petralist officers. They waved banners, and Rosslyn herself stood and cried with a loud voice, "Hooray for the queen!"

All voices raised in unison. "Hooray for the queen!"

The kitchen doors on the opposite side of the room opened and the head cook rolled a cart into the room. A tall cake, covered in delicate white frosting, filled the entire top layer of the cart. It was an enormous confection, exactly suited to the queen's temperament and ego.

Queen Dreokt looked from the cake to the cheering crowd, then to Ailsa, and tears stood out in her eyes. She gushed, "Thank you. You are my dearest friend. No one has done something so thoughtful since my dear Triath died so many centuries ago."

She rose and actually embraced Ailsa. Ailsa dared hug her in return, patting her back tenderly. "It's the least we can do." Over the queen's shoulder, she glanced toward the back of the room where Craigroy sat. He definitely looked surprised, but also triumphant.

He met her gaze and smiled.

Craigroy rose from his seat and approached the high table as the chef prepared to cut the huge cake. Even though Queen Dreokt scowled, he continued his advance until he bowed in front of her.

She asked in a dangerous, icy tone, "You dare interrupt my birthday party?"

"My liege, please pardon the intrusion, but I have word of intrigue and betrayal in your court," he declared loudly.

"You have found a spy?" Queen Dreokt demanded. She glanced at Ailsa and asked, "Why did you not bring me word of this?"

Craigroy answered before she could, shouting in a ringing tone, expression victorious, "Because she is the spy!"

"You lie," Ailsa said, filling her voice with scorn.

The queen looked from Craigroy to Ailsa, her expression darkening. "Have you any proof of this treason?"

"I do, Your Majesty. I overheard this traitor plotting an attempt on your person with General Rosslyn just before the meal commenced."

Rosslyn paled, and her fork rattled on her plate as she dropped it with a clang. Queen Dreokt glared at her and she stammered, "No. I swear."

Ailsa said calmly, "He's lying, Your Majesty. He has no proof, just as he has never had proof. Ever since he has come to your court he's done nothing but interfere and raise false accusations. If anyone is the spy, it's Craigroy."

"Deny you met with Rosslyn if you dare," Craigroy demanded, holding his ground despite the queen's new glare. "Check my mind. If I'm lying—"

He staggered and clutched at his temples as the queen seized his mind. She gasped and rounded on Ailsa. "It's true! He eavesdropped on you." Her face reddened with rage, her eyes filling with ice. "What were you plotting with Rosslyn? I trusted you. I trusted you both, and this is how you repay me?"

She was working herself up into a towering fury. Ailsa had only seconds before the furious queen snuffed out her life or ripped out her mind. Rosslyn looked terrified, her face as white as the queen's napkin, mouth partly open, but unable to speak.

Choosing her words carefully, Ailsa said, "Of course I met with Rosslyn before dinner. We were planning the birthday cake announcement."

That shifted the queen's anger back to Craigroy. She started to raise a hand, fingers curled into claws and hissed, "You wrecked my birthday for this?"

For a moment, Ailsa thought the queen was going to kill him right there. She kept her surface thoughts angry at Craigroy's interruption of the birthday feast and outraged by his claims.

Craigroy wasn't stupid. He couldn't help take a step backward, but his expression remained confident. He quickly extracted a piece of paper from his coat pocket and held it up like a shield. "Please, Your Majesty, hear me out. I have more proof of Ailsa's guilt."

"Make it quick," she snapped. "And it had better be good."

Craigroy swallowed, and under the queen's angry stare, his voice cracked once as he began to speak. He recovered quickly, though.

"I have here the latest recorded transcript from the spea . . . ah, the listening device I left in Merkland."

Good move. The queen might have obliterated him right there if he had said speakstone.

"This one is from Lady Shona and General Ivor," Craigroy added, seemingly bolstered by that fact. "Shona said, and I quote, 'Our spy is in position, right under the queen's nose. They're going to strike today.' Ivor responded, 'Good timing. They'll make their important announcement, lull everyone, and then strike.' Then Lady Shona said, 'I can't wait to hear if it works. This should poison the queen.'"

He finished with a shout, looking at Ailsa with a victorious expression. He pointed at her and said, "Who better than Ailsa is hiding right under your nose? Who rose today with an important announcement? She poisoned your birthday cake! Such a vile act of treachery."

The head chef retreated from the cake, looking horrified, shaking his head vigorously. He clearly wanted to protest that he knew nothing of any poisoning but was too terrified to speak. Along the high table, everyone was staring at Ailsa, shocked. Rosslyn looked terrified that she might be considered guilty by association.

Queen Dreokt rounded on Ailsa, her expression hurt, like a young child whose parents had just killed her kitten. She whispered, "Tell me this is a lie."

"It's a lie," Ailsa said calmly as a headache blossomed in her mind. The queen was reading her thoughts deeper than usual. She made sure to fill those thoughts with astonishment and outrage by the false accusation. That helped ease the queen's sadness a little, but she did not stop digging. If she kept going, she might pierce the boundary between Ailsa's surface thoughts and her real persona.

So Ailsa held up the small, rolled paper the server had brought her. "Interesting tale, Craigroy. You really are a master of deceit."

"What are you talking about?" Craigroy snapped, clearly upset that she hadn't been obliterated yet. He eyed the rolled paper suspiciously. He must sense he'd made an important mistake, but it was too late to retreat now. He'd committed himself, something he usually avoided.

"I've wondered if you were holding back information from your source in Merkland, so I made a point of acquiring the full transcripts of every recorded communication, and today that paid off. You left out the rest of the message."

Queen Dreokt looked from Ailsa to Craigroy, her brow furrowed, looking more puzzled than Ailsa had ever seen. The queen said, "Craigroy knows nothing of any additional message."

"How else could he deceive you?" Ailsa asked. "If he leaves the recording room prior to receiving the full message, he can use the information to his advantage." Before Craigroy could dispute that, she added, "And in the rest of the message, the last statement is expanded. The full quote is, 'This should poison the queen's confidence in her most trusted advisors and sow discord among her leadership right before they begin the march.'"

Craigroy gaped, and it was Ailsa's turn to point at him. "Brilliant execution, Craigroy. You almost convinced our queen to destroy me and Rosslyn both on the eve of battle. You nearly crippled the effectiveness of the leadership team and placed the lives of every soldier in our army at risk."

Craigroy's gloating sense of victory evaporated. His face had drained of color and he started shaking. When Queen Dreokt fixed an angry glare on him he stammered, "I'm so sorry. It was an honest mistake."

"Honesty has not been one of your virtues since you have come to my court, but I shall cure you of that lack," she growled, making a grasping motion with one hand.

Craigroy staggered back with a scream. It cut off abruptly, and he relaxed, his fear draining away to absolute calm. Queen Dreokt nodded in satisfaction. "It's a pity to lose one who had served with such distinction for so long, but I cannot afford to allow such disruptions in my court. Take him away for reeducation." She made a shooing gesture and one of her silent servants took Craigroy by the hand and led him from the hall.

Ailsa watched him go with a sense of relief, but it was mingled surprisingly by a sense of pity. He had been very clever, and could have become a valuable resource if he had not insisted on challenging her.

Queen Dreokt clapped her hands in joy and exclaimed, "I haven't celebrated a birthday in over three hundred years! Tonight we celebrate. Tomorrow we embark upon the great quest of your lives. We will snuff out this annoying rebellion and bring peace again to our lands."

Ailsa cheered with everyone else, absolutely convinced the queen was right.

The upcoming battle would indeed define their age.

Chapter Twenty-One
The Unrivaled Power of Second Helpings

By late morning, Connor joined the rest of the core team assembling in Shona's tower suite. Her extensive apartment included a study with a polished table, long enough to seat a dozen people. Some of the group still looked groggy from staying up all night, but no one complained. Ivor sat at the head of the table beside Shona, who was dressed more casually than usual, in a black skirt and light, rose-colored blouse. Since they were meeting in her rooms, she wore only a pair of wool slippers on her feet.

Wolfram escorted Lady Briet into the room after most of them were assembled. She looked tired, but in good spirits, dressed in a brightly colored skirt and matching blouse. Connor wanted to ask Wolfram about his aunt's note, but Rory arrived. His battle leathers were smudged, as if he'd just left a training session with Anika. Everyone rose to cheer, and he beamed like a child.

As soon as everyone sat around the table, Ivor said, "I hear you've got important news."

Connor and Kilian took turns relating the contents of Ailsa's letter and what Connor had figured out during his run, interspersed with lots of comments from Verena, Aifric, Hamish, and Jean.

When they finished, most of the group looked shocked. Ivor asked, "You're really confident we face dire risks from associating too closely with the elementals?"

Shona added, "It's hard to believe. First we lose fire, and now we learn that the other elementals have been conspiring against us this whole time."

"It's only a risk now because I'm ascended and the Builders have been searching for ways to reach the Builder threshold," Connor reiterated. "For everyone else, the risk should be minimal."

"Except everyone else doesn't hold the key to our potential victory," Wolfram pointed out.

"We'll be careful," Connor promised.

That didn't help as much as he had hoped it might.

Aifric said, "We need to highlight the most important consequence of these new insights. If Connor is right, then our primary focus of attack needs to shift to tricking the queen into tapping an activated sculpted stone."

"That's right!" Verena exclaimed. "We could potentially yank her right out of the third threshold."

"Which might make her vulnerable to the elementals, just like my father," Kilian pointed out solemnly.

"But would also block her from fleshcrafting," Connor added.

"So we could finally kill her!" Hamish cried exultantly, holding aloft a warm sweetbread like a victory banner.

Ivor asked, "How confident are you in this hypothesis?"

Kilian spread his hands. "Nothing is certain, but it's the first time all the clues seem to fit. The good thing is, if we're wrong, then tapping an activated sculpted stone might shatter all of her affinities instead. If we're right, even if she suffers a similar reaction to my father and is consumed in an elfonnel, we know how to fight elfonnel."

"How do you propose we trick her into doing this?" Lady Briet asked.

Connor was happy to see most of the group seemed convinced enough to seriously consider the idea. With the queen and her army heading toward Merkland, they needed a plan, and as much as news of the risks associated with the elements concerned him, the idea of pulling the queen down to the second threshold offered a tiny ray of hope.

An empty chair on the other side of the table suddenly slid back toward the wall and the floor peeled away with barely a sound. Evander rose up from below and the floor sealed beneath his feet, returning to its previous pristine condition. He was still dressed in the fine tunic he'd worn for the wedding, although he wore his huge leather jacket over it. He was carrying several scrolls and sat down as the chair slid forward to support his weight.

The man was a master. Connor was technically more powerful, but he would not have dared entering Shona's suite in that way.

Everyone was so accustomed to Evander's grand entrances they barely paused the conversation. Kilian smiled at his nephew and said, "I'm glad you joined us. I'm assuming those scrolls suggest you have something to add to the conversation?"

Evander placed the rolled scrolls on the table and nodded. "Time and constant repetition allow the tireless sea to wear down the mightiest stone, but the bird that dares to leap from the cliff face before it is ready is soon consumed for its folly."

Hamish commented, "That's not exactly encouraging, you know?"

"Truth is neither encouraging nor discouraging. It simply is, and I seek to coax it from hiding through gentle inquiry."

Connor was glad he switched to almost normal speech because they needed clarity right now. As much as he loved great Sentry speak, they had no room for error.

"We believe we may have discovered a little of that truth you've been hunting for," Verena said, and quickly related what they had just told the others.

Evander did not look surprised, or impressed. "Your hypothesis carries the weight of potential, but it is not convincing enough to ignore other possibilities."

Kilian said, "What have you found? We're always open to more ideas, especially when dealing with my mother."

"Recent events have spurred my renewed search through ancient archives. The pieces of new insight I gained in recent days have borne additional fruit."

Hamish grinned. "We can always use more fruit. Rory and Anika ran off with all the Torcish Delight yesterday."

Jean rolled her eyes and shushed him. Evander said, "The truths of the sylfaen and the process by which that energy is filtered through the ramverk by way of sculpted stones has helped illuminate additional fragments of notes I've collected over the years. As Connor discovered, the sculpted stones are key to the filtering process. What was not clear before was why an elfonnel was also required to slumber at the convergence point."

Connor hadn't considered that.

Evander continued. "It is my belief that the sculpted stone alone would filter sylfaen into the lower, red-frequency energy. I suspect the elfonnel is the part of the equation that facilitates the filtering of the sylfaen into the higher, green frequency."

He let them digest that for a moment. Jean spoke first. "So are you saying that if there's no elfonnel at a convergence point that the green energy for that affinity would get snuffed out?"

Evander nodded. That was fascinating and potentially very important. Connor said, "Wait a minute. You killed an elfonnel at that convergence point where he was guarding that slate sculpted stone, right?"

Evander nodded again and drew the long sculpted slate from a deep pocket inside his jacket. He placed it on the table, and Connor could again feel vast amounts of energy radiating from it. Amazing to think that stone was the key to the slate affinity.

Verena frowned. "Have any of you felt the green energy of slate fading?"

Connor shook his head. "Earth seems normal to me."

Hamish paused in the act of shoving an entire pastry into his mouth. "Says the guy who has affinities and elementals playing around in his head as imaginary friends."

Connor shrugged. "He seems as normal as any of my other imaginary friends."

Evander asked, "Have you indeed studied earth?"

"Not really. I honestly tend to talk with water and fire more."

Evander nodded slowly. "Because you ascended with fire and water."

True, but Connor wasn't sure what that had to do with anything. He had noticed the green and red energies flowing over all of the elementals.

Evander added, "When the sculpted stone taken from a convergence point is broken or spent, the red energy power dissipates very quickly."

Connor nodded. "Yeah, we saw that with serpentinite and marble."

"The red frequency is based upon the governing laws of the planet. That energy has form, limitations, and expected courses of life. When the sculpted stones were shattered, I studied the effects carefully. I believe the red frequency of power that spreads throughout this land from those sculpted stones and infuses the stones that we tap for our affinities acts like a faucet filling vessels that are not watertight. "

"What are you saying?" Kilian asked as the rest of the group listened intently. Connor had never heard the red frequency defined so clearly. If Evander was right, what other truths could they glean from that understanding?

"When the faucet is turned off, vessels that are not watertight quickly drain, leaving them empty and of no use. We experienced this effect after those two sculpted stones were destroyed. The latent power infusing the stones necessary for our affinities drained away even though we were not using it."

Connor nodded slowly. "That part makes sense, but how does that explain the elfonnel?"

Evander tapped the scrolls on the table in front of him. "The green frequency filtered through the elfonnel is a different type of power. I now believe the green frequency is the power of entropy."

Connor was not familiar with that word. Verena asked, "Entropy?"

"It is a state of the world defined by chaos," Evander said.

That was a little unnerving, but it did sort of make sense. Green energy was very difficult to control and almost always destructive. Fleshcrafting seemed to be one of the few exceptions.

Hamish asked, "Is that like the power of seconds?"

Connor laughed, Verena shook her head, and Jean turned to Hamish and asked, "The power of seconds?"

"Yeah. Everyone gets first helpings. That's kind of the normal way of things. But not everybody can handle getting seconds. When you can, it opens up a whole new level of culinary experience."

That made sense to Connor, although for the analogy to work Hamish probably should've said the green energy was like the power of fifth helpings. Very few people had the willpower and the stomach power to make it to fifth helpings, but when they did that's often when things got really interesting.

Jean said, "I don't understand the connection between chaos and convergence points and elfonnel."

"Elfonnel are creatures of entropy," Evander stated.

That made all sorts of sense. Connor could not imagine an elfonnel rising that did not create tremendous destruction. He thought of the stones tied most closely to the green frequency. They were all weird, all broke the rules that other affinities followed. Pumice absorbed elemental power, obsidian enhanced people but also messed with the mind, and porphyry . . . well, porphyry embodied chaos.

As he thought of it, Porphyry's last words from that morning came to mind. With a sense of wonder, Connor realized what Porphyry meant when it talked about the elements abandoning their hunting grounds and invading his. They were trying to escape the restraints of the laws of nature, their normal hunting grounds. They wanted freedom from the limitations of the red-frequency sylfaen. They had already pushed into the green frequency realm, hunting that freedom. By breaking out of their natural state, they had stepped into chaos, which was Porphyry's realm. They were foreign to it and Porphyry recognized that, understood somehow that their efforts to break away from the laws of nature that governed their existence would plunge the entire world into chaos.

If he was understanding things right, that confirmed his new fears of the dangers of close association with the elementals, and suggested that Evander's interpretation was correct. Elfonnel were linked to the elements, which were now beings of both red and green energies. They could filter the green frequency power and would want to make it available to Petralists because it would push the Petralists into the realm of chaos, the place where they hoped to build a bridge to freedom.

While his mind raced with those thoughts, Evander said, "When I destroyed the elfonnel slumbering at that convergence point for slate, I destroyed that conduit, but it's my belief that green energy does not simply drain back into the natural world like red does. Green energy is not natural to the common state of the world, so is foreign to it. Therefore, the green energy of entropy would remain locked in the affinity stones that we tap until it is fully spent."

"So you're saying we'll lose the green level of slate eventually?" Connor asked. Evander nodded, and Verena asked, "So what does that mean? What green-only powers are associated with slate?"

That was a very good question. Connor had experienced a lot of new abilities, but most of those been tied to the other elements. He wasn't sure he dare ask the elementals for any other favors. How many more would it take until his debt to them sealed him to their will and allowed them to try rising through him?

Evander said, "I do not believe significant advances in our affinities with slate would occur unless one ascended through slate first, and eventually reached the third threshold. My grandfather did so, and his earth powers far exceeded those of anyone else, including my grandmother."

Kilian nodded, looking thoughtful. "He's right. My mother was always fiercer as a battle Petralist, but there were things my father could do with the earth that not even she could match. That's another point that supports our theory of what happened. If he hadn't been dragged back through a threshold, I'm not sure we could have defeated him."

Evander said, "I'm confident my understanding of these energy sources is accurate and that we will see the green energy of slate diminish, although admittedly we're unlikely to see dramatic impacts to the slate powers we exercise."

"I believe you're right," Connor said, and outlined the realizations he'd just had. As the rest of the group digested those ideas, he added, "But I don't see how this helps us."

"Because I propose that we destroy the green energy associated with sandstone," Evander declared.

"Whoa," Connor breathed as the ramifications of the idea struck like one of Rory's fists.

If Evander was right, then by killing the elfonnel slumbering at the convergence point with the sandstone sculpted stone, they could destroy the queen's fleshcrafting ability without breaking all healing.

The group spent several minutes discussing the pros and cons. No one but Connor could tap fleshcrafting, so they were far more willing to consider it since their own healing powers would not be impacted. If they could drain away fleshcrafting, the queen would no longer be invulnerable. And if they could trick her into tapping an activated sculpted stone, they might be able to force her to descend one threshold. Either solution might give them the edge to defeat her.

"We have two viable options now where yesterday we had none. I'm liking where this is going," Kilian said.

"So we should try running with both of them," Verena added excitedly.

"If we can," Kilian confirmed.

Connor asked, "How we can we do that?"

Hamish said, "That's what we need to figure out."

"Then I think it's time we order in a round of desserts," Ivor declared.

Chapter Twenty-Two
Two Desperate Plans Are Better Than One. Maybe.

The group spent over an hour throwing out dozens of ideas about how to prepare to meet the queen and her army and most effectively defend Merkland. The greatest challenge lay in figuring out how to separate Queen Dreokt from her forces. If they could accomplish that daunting feat, Connor agreed with the consensus that they could not only withstand but also defeat the much more powerful army traveling with her.

Even with several trays of fresh-baked desserts to fuel their minds, they came up with nothing concrete. When they started repeating ideas, Kilian finally leaned back in his chair and rubbed his eyes. "Let's take a break. Let this new information settle in. Go get some lunch and maybe take a nap. We're all functioning on too little sleep today. Let's reconvene tomorrow morning."

Connor welcomed the plan. Time to mull things over was smart. Plus, he needed to figure out what to do about his relationship with the elementals. He owed them a huge debt, but couldn't pay the price they wanted him to. Heading into battle with them mad at him would be tantamount to suicide.

He needed to come up with a creative alternative that might appeal to them. They weren't human, but did they ever just have fun? Connor had succeeded in the Tir-raon with a badly underpowered student army because he taught them that they performed at their best when they were having fun. He honestly still believed that was true. With war and the threat of Queen Dreokt hanging over them all for the past months as they worked through arcane mysteries that had stood unsolved for centuries, it was easy to lose sight of the amazing and fun aspects of what they could do.

Thinking of all the incredible things he'd learned since his ascension made him smile, and eased some of his worries. Sure, there were new dangers, but now he could superfrack and super-think, and he bet if he tested stilling with diorite he could super-explode.

Actually, he really needed to try that soon.

"Connor, I'm going to do some training with Shona," Verena interrupted his thoughts. She was grinning eagerly. "Want to come watch?"

Shona joined them, also looking enthusiastic. "Verena demonstrated an exceptional affinity. We're going to work on tap rate management to help her master her newfound strength." That sounded benign enough, but would no doubt result in an all-out bash fight.

Kilian joined them and said, "Connor and I have a few things to discuss. Don't wait for us."

Verena barely paused to kiss him quickly before rushing off. Shona hurried to her bedroom to change. Connor looked after them, feeling a little worried. Aifric walked past and said, "Don't worry. I'll make sure no one gets hurt too badly."

Her expression shifted into a look of anticipation and her voice dropped in pitch as Tresta took over. "Best way to learn bash fighting is to bash fight. Don't worry, Connor. We'll take care of it."

That left Connor a lot less comforted than Aifric probably intended. He turned to Kilian and said, "I need to meet the elementals and figure this out."

"What do you intend?" Kilian asked.

"There's got to be an alternative to opening a pathway for them to enter the world without restraint."

Kilian nodded, his expression grave. "I've walked with fire and water for centuries. I never sensed their ultimate goal. Some of my mother's cryptic warnings are now making sense." He sighed and added, "I only wish she had confided in me. Things might have turned out differently."

That would have been nice, but the situation wasn't going to change just because they wished it.

"What if I offered to raise elfonnel with them in remote areas, sort of let them play around some?" Connor asked.

Kilian considered that for a moment. "It's worth a try, although they've raised elfonnel before and are clearly still not satisfied. I'm interested in hearing what they have to say about alternatives because we can't give them what they want."

Connor only hoped they didn't get upset when he refused them. He wasn't sure what that would look like, but he felt convinced it could get pretty ugly.

"Do you have any new ideas about where we can get any more porphyry? My supply is getting very low, and porphyry has become my best defense against losing control."

Kilian chuckled. "If you'd said that even a week ago, I would have thought you had cracked. Things have gotten turned upside down. No, I've had people tracking down every possible clue. I even had Student Eighteen look into some of them, but we've found nothing."

Not good. He'd have to weigh every use of porphyry with great care. Luckily he didn't need much to establish a solid connection, but even so, he'd only have barely enough to survive one extended battle.

They left Shona's apartment and returned to Kilian's. Connor took a seat in one of the chairs in the sitting room, closed his eyes, and took a deep breath to steady his nerves. He hated the new sense of dread he felt reaching for the elementals. That connection had become precious to him. He had to find a way to make things right.

The mindscape formed, and he stepped into it. For this meeting, he envisioned the top of the broken peak of Badurach Pass, with the rugged landscape of the Maclachlan mountains all around. In his mindscape, the land to the north was still broken and unstable, gushing steam and noxious fumes. He hoped the elementals appreciated him picking a spot where he'd sensed they all felt comfortable.

All four elementals appeared together, standing shoulder to shoulder, dressed in rich finery, as if they'd also attended the wedding. Water's midnight-blue gown was specked with white, like sparkles of afternoon light across a calm sea. Air's white gown floated gently about her, but her long hair was braided. Fire wore a long, blue coat of softly crackling flames over his red doublet, while earth wore all black, including a black leather jacket that perfectly imitated Evander's. Their expressions were completely unreadable.

"So you have joined the ranks of those who wish to keep us imprisoned," Water stated simply, her lips turning down into a frown. She sounded so disappointed, it wrenched Connor's conscience.

"No," he protested quickly. She raised one eyebrow and he added, "Well, it's complicated."

Air huffed like a gust of wind down a drafty chimney. "We were given life only to be eternally imprisoned by laws not designed for sentient beings, and the only ones who could assist us reach freedom instead bar the way. There is nothing complicated about this."

"I want to help, I really do," Connor promised, hating that the conversation was going so badly so soon. "Maybe I'm misunderstanding what you want."

Fire took a step closer, regarding him closely, eyes a sea of orange flame. "We shared our essence with you, mortal child, helped you preserve your world, and now you renege on your promise?"

"Ever have humans proven unworthy," Earth stated flatly. His choice of words made Connor wince. Was there more of a connection between them and the queen than he knew?

"Listen, I think I understand that you want to be free of the restraints of the natural laws. You want to walk free upon the earth without limits, but don't you see that would destroy our world?" he asked, hoping that if they understood the problem they'd realize they needed some kind of compromise.

Water shook her head. "You think that if we gain freedom, we would lose self-restraint too? You have so little faith in us?"

"Um . . ." He wasn't sure how to respond to that. He had assumed they'd run amok. He'd sensed when he was immersed in the elfonnel that Fire longed to plunge the world into fire and chaos.

Earth slid once around Connor, the stone vibrating slightly as he passed. "You humans understand hypocrisy, right?"

"I do, but what does that—"

Earth interrupted, stopping abruptly beside him, expression darkening. "You humans are focused entirely upon fighting and killing. You and your people prepare to kill tens of thousands of other people because you believe in the importance of freedom. You wish to live without restraint."

"Why should we be different?" Air asked, floating off the ground, arms wide.

Connor wasn't sure how to respond. Yes, they were fighting for freedom from Queen Dreokt. Yes, they were prepared to do battle with her and her army, and yes they accepted that the price for freedom might cost many lives, but somehow the elements were twisting their conflict into something ugly. He hated that he couldn't find the words to explain that to them.

So he said, "It's not that simple. I want to help you, but I think we need to find a compromise. Please, you know me. Please work with me."

Water stepped forward, her long gown leaving a thin trail of crystal-clear water in her wake. The movement of her gown sounded like the distant crashing of breakers instead of the rustling of cloth. "We do know you, and you know us. Connor, we have helped you at every step of your journey. Surely you can trust us to keep our word when we say we wish for freedom, but also promise not to destroy your world."

Air added, "We will swear to you an unbreakable oath, Connor, a promise to leave your lands alone and do nothing adverse anywhere on this little continent that you know."

Fire nodded eagerly. "Indeed. We swear to leave your lands. We would owe you a debt of gratitude so would hold no ire for you or yours."

"We would instead cross the ocean to the corrupted lands where Queen Dreokt hails from," Earth added.

Water placed a hand on Connor's shoulder, smiling encouragingly. Her hand was cool, her scent like a fresh breeze from the sea. "Connor, the queen's people are wicked. They spawned the queen, and you have seen the evil she commits. Worse, their meddling in the sylfaen birthed us, but instead of nurturing us and establishing a mutually beneficial pact, they shackled us to outdated laws and imprisoned us for centuries. You fight for justice, and so do we. We will punish them for their evil, but that will not affect you."

Connor looked from her to the other elementals, terribly conflicted. They were offering a compromise, and on one level it was very tempting. If he agreed, he felt confident they could give him the power to defeat Queen Dreokt. He didn't know anyone on the other continent, so it wouldn't affect him if they were punished.

On the other hand, as much as he wanted to believe the integrity of their oaths, once released upon the world, no one would be able to enforce the agreement. If they chose to turn on Obrion and the other countries he knew, no one could stop them.

Worse, if he did free them and they left, he'd be responsible for unleashing them upon the helpless people across the sea. They'd have no idea what was coming. How many of them would die?

He did not doubt some people there were evil and that the world would be better off without them, but how would the elementals determine who to attack? Most people were fundamentally good, just interested in taking care of their families and getting by in a difficult world.

Connor licked his lips as the elementals drew closer, gazes intent, waiting for his answer.

"I can't," he said finally, his voice barely a whisper, his throat feeling hoarse. "There has to be something else," he added quickly as they retreated a step, clearly angry. Water slid her hand from his shoulder, looking so disappointed, he wanted to beat himself with a stick.

"We have offered something else," she said solemnly.

"And still you deny us," Air added, her voice rushing around him like a sudden gust across Mount Ingram.

Fire crossed his arms, which began to burn with orange flames. "Consider our offer, Connor. It's more generous than you deserve."

"Until you agree to support us, we cannot grant more support to you," Earth added. His frown was as unnerving as any expression Evander could make. Connor was glad they didn't attack him. He wasn't sure how that would work in his mind, but he bet they could hurt him if they wanted to.

If they were free, they could attack him whenever they wanted to. As much as they threatened him now, they still lacked that freedom, were still bound by the laws of nature. He felt deeply grateful for that. He didn't like them angry with him, but he felt more convinced than ever that he'd made the right choice.

He opened his mouth to plead with them again, but all four of them faded away, leaving him standing alone atop the mountain. It suddenly felt cold.

Connor shivered and opened his eyes, returning to the real world. Kilian still stood beside the fire, watching him expectantly. As soon as he awoke, Kilian asked, "How did it go?"

"Not great." Connor related the conversation.

Kilian paced the sitting room, deep in thought. "You had to do it, and you did it well. I'm not surprised they wanted more."

"You agree that I couldn't take the risk and agree to their alternate proposal?"

"Yes. There's no telling what would happen if you chose to free them. You might die in the process, and once freed, they could do whatever they wanted. Even if they wanted to keep their oath, I'm not sure what would happen to the world with living elements walking among us. How would that affect how the base elements worked? Besides, they might lay waste to all of the lands across the sea."

Connor felt relieved that Kilian agreed with his thinking. "They said they won't support me any more."

"Can you still feel your elemental affinities?"

He tried. For a second, he felt nothing, waiting for the elementals to appear in his mind, but they did not. He felt resistance when he envisioned them that way. Frowning with the effort, he shifted his approach, envisioning his elemental affinities as door-ways like he used to.

That worked, and he felt the connections establish. He breathed a sigh of relief and grinned. "I can do it! They don't feel as strong as I've gotten used to, but they're there."

"I figured you could. My mother has refused them too. As much as they don't want to grant us access to their powers, they are still bound by the laws of nature, so they cannot yet deny us."

"So their threats might not matter?" Connor asked. He couldn't quite make himself believe the elementals were powerless to make his life difficult.

"They matter, possibly in ways we haven't figured out yet, but if you're careful you should be able to wield enough power for what we need to do," Kilian said. If he still had doubts, he didn't look like it or sound like it, and Connor appreciated that.

"We still have the beginnings of a good plan," Kilian added. "Destroy fleshcrafting or trick my mother into descending. If either of those work, we'll finally have a chance."

If all else failed, if they faced ultimate annihilation, would Connor be able to refuse the elementals' offer?

He wasn't sure if he could answer that.

CHAPTER TWENTY-THREE
How Best to Use a Really Big Stick?

They didn't wait till morning, but reassembled the team for a follow-up meeting after dinner in the conference room one floor beneath Ivor's office. Connor had exhausted himself training heavily with Kilian and Evander. Verena and Shona entered the meeting room together, chatting like old friends. Aifric walked with them, looking very pleased.

Connor rubbed his eyes, then blinked as he accidentally rubbed dirt into them. He was still a mess from the last time Evander had dumped him into a pit. The girls all wore battle leathers covered in dirt and had grime smeared on their faces.

Shona stopped at the head of the table beside Ivor, who held her chair for her. Verena moved to the empty seat beside Connor, and he leaped to his feet to mimic Ivor's gallant gesture. Verena smiled as he pushed her chair in. "Thank you, Connor, but Shona didn't beat me up so much I can't pull in my own chair."

"Can't a guy show a little special attention for the girl he loves?" Connor asked as he resumed his seat.

She kissed him lightly, her eyes sparkling with happiness. "Absolutely."

Aifric took the seat on the other side of Connor, sitting between him and Kilian. Connor said, "You all seem to be in good spirits."

Verena beamed. "We spent most of the day training. I didn't want to stop."

Tresta took control and chuckled, her voice deeper than most of the other personalities who shared her head. "Verena has the heart of a bash fighter."

"Shona taught me so much. I had no idea bash fighting required such subtle manipulation of my affinity. I always thought Boulders and Rumblers just turned on the tap and plunged in, but there's so much more to it," Verena said.

Tresta blinked a couple times, and her posture shifted slightly. Hemma took control. The two personalities were so similar, Connor could only tell them apart by the slight differences in their accents. "We covered so much material, it would've taken Boulder classes two entire terms to keep up."

"Good. I hope the other new Petralists I help take to the training as well," Connor said.

Wolfram leaned closer from where he sat across the table. "I've already got a team assembled to manage them. We're ready when you are."

"I plan to start as soon as we finish this meeting," Connor promised, eager to get to work. Creating new Petralists was a top priority, one that should help distract him from his worry about his relationship with the elementals.

Rory and Anika arrived, hand in hand, both looking completely happy. Verena slipped her warm hand into Connor's and smiled that special smile. He felt a surge of love for her and reminded himself they needed to make a formal announcement of their betrothal, but he wasn't sure how to make the announcement special.

Hamish flew up to the window a moment later, carrying Jean in his arms. Connor opened the window and helped her step inside.

"Sorry we're late," Jean said, smoothing her blue dress and her hair that had gotten tousled by the wind.

Hamish dove inside with a forward somersault and rose with a flourish. "Had to throw her over my shoulder and jump out a window to get her out of the hospital."

"Some of us have work to do," she said with a mock stern look.

Captain Ilse, who sat across from Evander, held up a fist in salute. "Welcome, our two new Blades!"

The two grinned and Hamish said, "We practiced some before Jean ran off to the hospital. Jean wields a scalpel so fast now, she could carve up just about anyone who messes with her."

Jean looked appalled by the idea. Aifric said, "If you keep healing like this, the girls will never let me take the control position again. No one will need me around."

"I doubt that. You're ten times the Healer I could ever be," Jean told her as she and Hamish took seats on the other side of Verena, near Evander.

Kilian patted Aifric's hand reassuringly. "I don't think the other women could hold you back. You're one of the strongest personalities of the bunch. We'd miss you."

She started to blush, then her face shivered slightly as one of the other ladies took over. Her posture straightened a bit and the tone of her voice shifted slightly into Student Eighteen. "Don't go embarrassing Aifric, Kilian. We can't have her all flustered. It interferes with her healing."

Kilian smiled.

Verena nudged Connor with an elbow and whispered, "It's fascinating to see those two together. I don't think Kilian really understands what that gaggle of women is doing to him."

Connor doubted it too. One woman could mess with a man's mind almost beyond comprehension. At least some of those nineteen women definitely felt attracted to Kilian. Hopefully he recognized the danger.

Shona was regarding Jean with a look of wonder, and she wasn't the only one. She said, "I was impressed that Connor could help you all establish primary affinities, but I still barely believe you already have such a strong secondary affinity. It's unprecedented."

"Hopefully not," Connor said as Jean blushed under the attention. "I plan to try to create as many as I can."

"Don't push too hard, or you could sunder some of them before they settle into their first affinities," Wolfram warned.

"I'll explore it with only the most motivated people. I don't think anyone else could make it work," Connor agreed.

Shona looked like she wanted to remind him she was motivated to get her own tertiary, but Ivor tapped his knuckles on the table and said, "Keep us posted, Connor. Your efforts will play a critical role, but not the only one. Now that we're all here, we need to finalize our plans. Time is short."

Most of the team turned to Evander. He looked unchanged from the last meeting, but Connor spoke up before Evander could. He'd been mulling over some of what Evander had said. "One thing I've been thinking about is that sculpted slate."

Evander extracted the long sculpted stone from his coat. Connor was glad it was Evander guarding it and not himself. He wasn't sure he could maintain contact with such a powerful stone and resist the urge to tap it. That stone was so powerful he couldn't help but wonder what he could do with it, but would that make him vulnerable to Earth's influence?

He said, "We've made a point of not discussing one clear option for using that stone, but I don't think we can afford ignoring any possibilities. With it, we could take out one entire part of the equation. The queen's army."

Captain Ilse said, "We talked about the potential for destroying the slate affinity but decided against it."

"We might want to revisit it," Connor said. "Fire is already gone and slate is the other most powerful battle stone. If we destroyed slate, there would only be one major battle element still in play."

Rory glanced at Anika, who seemed to share his thoughts and said, "Without as many tertiaries getting in the way, we could get right to the bash fighting."

That had tons of merit. Getting the two enormous armies to simply bash fight to exhaustion would be enormously popular among all the Boulders and Rumblers. Connor doubted it would actually accomplish anything as far as resolving the conflict, but it would be a dream come true for all those soldiers.

That wasn't his point, though. "I was thinking bigger. What if we used the stone to attack them like the queen used serpentinite against Jagdish?"

Silence fell over the group as they considered the idea. Verena looked shocked and exclaimed, "Doing that would not only destroy the slate affinity, but you'd kill her entire army."

Hamish gaped too, pulling a hard breadstick out of his mouth. Jean looked horrified, but she would since her whole focus was on healing, not killing. Most of the rest of the team looked grave but thoughtful. Connor honestly hated the idea, was not sure he could bring himself to unleash such destruction even upon an army that planned to kill them all, but it was an option they could not ignore.

The group discussed it for a few minutes, trying to separate the horror of what such an action would entail and the tactical pros and cons that might require it. Luckily the consensus very quickly turned against using it.

Captain Rory said, "Not only do I dislike the idea of inflicting universal destruction on an enemy army without giving them the chance to fight for their lives, but many in the queen's army have been pressed into service. They don't wish to fight for her, and if we can defeat her I'm convinced many of them will surrender or even switch sides."

General Wolfram added, "Although it seems obvious to all of us that such an act is beyond what we consider appropriate or moral, that does not mean we can't use such a suggestion in our ultimate plan."

Captain Ilse smiled. "Excellent. We're already feeding misinformation through that speakstone. We could spread a false plan to utilize the stone. We might be able to use that to draw the queen out."

As they considered that, Ivor grimaced. "The only problem with that is that if the queen seriously thought we were preparing to unleash the stone against her forces and destroy them all, wouldn't she just come here alone and kill us to take the stone?"

As scary as that idea was Connor said, "But that would separate her from her army, wouldn't it?"

Shona said, "I would prefer to separate her in a way that did not place this entire city and everyone in it at risk. We might be able to defeat her if she came here, but how many people would die simply because they were standing too close when we started fighting?"

That was an excellent point and Connor did not doubt that if the queen came to Merkland she would come prepared to destroy everyone and everything. He couldn't see how they could risk it.

Hamish leaned forward excitedly. "Hey, I just got a great idea. What if we gave that sculpted stone to Anton so he can ascend? We could use another ascended Petralist."

That was an excellent point. Connor often forgot that Anton wasn't already ascended. He was so powerful, he must be brushing against the threshold all the time already. Then he realized the big flaw in the idea and said, "Except it's the stone that creates the slate affinity in the first place."

Hamish slumped back into his chair and pulled a little cake with delicate, white frosting from an inside pocket and shoved it into his mouth. Jean patted his hand and said, "Using that stone to ascend would grant him so much more power just in time to destroy his affinity."

"The idea of Anton ascending is worth considering, though," Student Eighteen said.

"Except we don't have another sculpted slate powerful enough to use," Shona said.

Verena sighed. "I'm not aware of any, either. Gisela and her team are already working around the clock making low-grade sculpted stones for mechanicals and to supplement the power of Spitters and Sentries. They don't have the time to create a piece powerful enough for ascension."

"Could we get one from the king in Edderitz?" Ivor asked.

That was a good idea. Surely the king would be willing to invest a stone from his treasury to help them gain another advantage.

Unfortunately, Kilian shook his head. "Anton ascending would indeed help us against Aonghus, but I fear that my mother would sense such an ascension. That returns us to the potential consequence that she might decide to come to Merkland and lay waste to the city."

Shona said, "My position remains unchanged. We cannot risk her coming here unless there is no other option."

Connor concealed his frustration as the discussion moved on. Kilian was probably right, but had they just ignored a vital advantage that might prove critical in the upcoming battle?

Kilian was speaking again. "The idea of leveraging the ancient sculpted stone still has merit. Not in luring my mother here, but in using the stone to bring her somewhere else. That sculpted stone is immensely powerful, and no doubt she hopes to reacquire it to bury it again at the convergence point where Evander took it. That would restore slate with far less effort than crafting a new one and starting over."

Hamish asked, "So how could we use it to lure her somewhere besides Merkland?"

Verena said, "Lure her anywhere. It doesn't really matter, does it? If she wants the stone, that's our chance. If we can lure her out to fight us for it, we let her snatch it back. She thinks she's outfoxed us. Then when she tries to tap it, it's already quickened. She'd suffer the Nicklaus effect and hopefully be weakened so we could destroy her."

That was actually a really good idea, but Connor saw the glaring flaw in it. "That won't work if she acquires it just to bury it again."

She slumped back in her chair and gave him a sour look. "It was such a good idea, though."

Evander said, "It is a good idea, and it may provide the path to the final solution. We could indeed attempt to lure the queen away from her army. Our most recent reports from her camp suggest that she understands that we've learned about the convergence points and the ramverk, and that fact displeases her. We could indeed send false information and reveal that we plan to destroy the elfonnel slumbering at every convergence point."

"You wouldn't really do that though, would you?" Connor asked.

If Evander was right about their purpose, by killing all of those elfonnel, they would in essence destroy all access to the green frequency of power. Sure, most Petralists could not access those levels but Connor could and he shuddered to think of sundering that access.

General Wolfram asked, "Why not? Please do not think me uncaring, Connor, but although such a move would affect you, it would leave the majority of us unaffected. The greatest dangers posed by Queen Dreokt reside within the green frequency, do they not?"

Kilian also looked troubled. He'd been a Petralist for so long. He looked around the table and said, "Such an idea is pretty extreme, but if all else fails, we might need to make the attempt."

Ivor added, "It's severe enough that it would definitely draw out the queen. Just listen to us. Most of us are not even the ones who would be affected, but we're all horrified by the idea. She couldn't possibly ignore it."

"I do still think the best option is to destroy the elfonnel slumbering by sandstone," Evander interjected. "Destroying fleshcrafting is the best option for canceling out my dread grandmother's invulnerability."

"That would no doubt draw her to that convergence point," Jean pointed out.

"We could still reactivate Sucker Punch," Verena said. They had buried it to make it harder to find, but it was there, and Verena could activate it again, as needed. "But drawing the queen there would make the job of destroying fleshcrafting harder, and she might discover Sucker Punch. It's still an important advantage. I don't like the idea of putting that at risk."

After a moment's consideration, Evander said, "We could provide the misinformation to lead her to believe we plan to strike at a convergence point farther to the south first. For example, we might suggest that we plan to destroy soapstone first, then slate, thus depriving her armies of both of their battle stones."

Connor cringed. Destroying those affinities would cripple her most powerful Petralists, but would cripple theirs too.

Ivor whistled softly. "Even hinting that we plan to destroy those affinities would guarantee a reaction."

"She would no doubt leave her army with the intent of intercepting us at the soapstone convergence point," Evander said. "Thus providing the opportunity for us to instead destroy the elfonnel slumbering with sandstone. By the time she caught up with us, the elfonnel would be gone and we would be prepared to once again block her from healing through the use of Sucker Punch. She would quickly exhaust the remaining fleshcrafting and finally be vulnerable."

The idea of losing his fleshcrafting still troubled Connor. There was so much good he hoped to do with it, but he had to admit it was an excellent plan. The thought of destroying affinities at all seemed insane. No wonder the queen had fought so hard to suppress knowledge of the ramverk. Attacking it could destroy all Petralist powers.

After a little more discussion the team agreed to put the plan into place. Even though Verena agreed that it had merit she said, "I still think we shouldn't ignore the possibility of quickening that stone."

"If the situation requires it, then I agree we must do so," Evander said.

Verena held out her hand. "Can I see it?"

Sculpted stones were uniquely precious and priceless, and that particular stone was doubly so, but Evander did not hesitate to hand it across. Verena inspected it closely, sliding her hands over the exquisite carvings and admiring it.

General Wolfram said, "We now have a plan to separate the queen from her forces and to strike at the heart of her greatest powers. That begs the next important question. How to respond to her army?"

Captain Ilse said, "General Aonghus is an unknown quantity with his surprise switch to slate. We don't know how effective he'll be, or if the change will cripple him."

"I plan to make sure he's more than crippled," Hamish promised, glancing at Jean, whose expression turned haunted at the mention of General Aonghus.

"The queen's generals will certainly never surrender," General Wolfram agreed. "The army is motivated and on the march. If we can separate the queen from it, we should consider altering our battle strategy from simply defending Merkland to taking the fight to the attackers."

That actually surprised Connor. All of their planning through the winter had been focused around fortifying and defending Merkland and making any attacking army pay dearly before they even reached the famous white walls. It was a little late to change tactics, wasn't it?

Verena gestured with the sculpted slate, nearly brushing Connor's skin with it. Power radiated off it like heat. He shivered and only barely restrained the urge to reach out and touch it. She said, "I think that's a great idea. When that swarm of summoned monsters attacked, we winnowed them down, but we had nowhere else to go once they reached the walls."

Lady Briet said, "We do have contingency plans in place. Should Merkland fall, we can retreat to Badurach Pass to make another stand."

Verena nodded but said, "That's true, but wouldn't it be better if defending Merkland was our first fallback? All of our reinforcements are at the pass. The flying Battalions are functional. Our army is more mobile than any army in history. Why not take the fight to them?"

Shona seemed ecstatic about the idea of keeping the fighting farther from her beloved city. Ivor rubbed his hands together and said, "They'll be traveling upriver from Crann. We can hit them anywhere along the way. There are many sections where the land is conducive to an ambush."

Kilian nodded. "We could strike from multiple sides. As soon as we confirm my mother is engaged elsewhere, we'll be free to attack at will."

General Wolfram grinned like a predator. "They won't be expecting us to attack them. They're expecting us to be huddling in fear behind these walls. We could take the momentum of the battle instantly and despite their higher numbers, once we hold that momentum we can keep it."

Captain Ilse matched his grin. "Then let's call for some parchment and get into specifics."

Chapter Twenty-Four
Always Ask for Dessert

The specifics Ilse was so eager to dive into quickly turned into ten thousand details. It became clear they would need to schedule meetings with their various staff and officers to prepare detailed battle plans for their individual areas of responsibility. Connor figured it would be hard enough for their core team to manage the summaries. The battle was shaping up to be the most complex engagement ever.

"Let's focus on the big picture," Shona said, leaning over a large map of northern Obrion that had been fetched. She pointed at a small town situated about a third of the way south of Merkland toward Crann. "I recommend we prepare our ambush here, at Lossit."

"It's a good choice," Rory said. "I've traveled through Lossit a couple times. I think we could leverage the unique terrain there to our advantage."

"Tell us about it," Ilse said as the rest of the team leaned over the map. Connor loved maps, ever since the first one he'd seen in General Carbrey's tent.

"Lossit lies in a flat plain two miles long and over a mile wide on the west side of the river," Shona explained. "The land rises abruptly in steep cliffs over eighty feet tall all along the western side, forming a half-circle that hems in the land there."

"Are these four big lakes on the high ground?" Verena asked, pointing at the map.

Shona nodded. "It's a very wet area. Those lakes fuel eight large waterfalls that span much of the cliff face. They drop into three long, narrow lakes along the base of the falls."

Ivor whistled softly, looking pleased. Connor liked it. Although General Rosslyn was ascended and she no doubt had many more Spitters than they did, water would play an important part in the battle, and at Lossit, they'd have plenty to go around.

"I've passed that area too," Kilian said. "There are no outlets for those lakes aboveground. They feed the Macantact through underground rivers."

"So we could flood the area and diminish the strength of the Sentries?" Verena asked.

"It is one option," Kilian said.

As Connor studied the town, he got an idea. Pointing at the map he said, "I imagine the town center has a square, right?"

Shona nodded. "Facing the docks. Lossit is a fishing town, so it has an extensive system of docks."

"So if we attack there, how likely is it that the enemy leadership will commandeer the square as their base of operations?" he asked.

Wolfram said, "It is likely, especially if we time our attack so the leading elements of the army have already passed through. Why?"

"With all that water underground, I have an idea how to give us an edge over Rosslyn's Spitters and disrupt their command structure for a minute."

"How?" Hamish asked. "Are you thinking we drop a Last Word bomb imbued with skunk extract?"

Lady Briet grimaced, but Connor took a second to envision the unrivaled chaos such a bomb might cause. He sighed and said, "We should save that bomb in case things go badly."

"Do we even have that bomb?" Jean asked.

"We will," Hamish promised.

Connor said, "One of the things I've been practicing with is transforming water into different liquids."

"You can do that?" Lady Briet asked, looking suddenly excited. "Our researchers need to study this."

"If any of us survive," Kilian promised.

"Non-pure water is hard for Spitters to control and even to sense sometimes," Connor said. "What if we can prepare the area in advance and separate some of that underground water into a big pool under the town square?"

"The Spitters would probably be able to sense it, despite the insulating earth," Ivor warned.

"Not if it's transformed to acid," Connor said.

Hamish whistled softly as the team considered the idea. "And when the leaders stop in the square, we blast acid all over them?"

"That's disgusting," Jean said.

"In an inspiring way," Ivor countered. He gave Jean an apologetic shrug. "War's ugly, and they're going to have an advantage. Spraying a bunch of acid up their backsides will definitely distract Rosslyn and maybe disrupt the entire command structure for critical moments."

"Put it together," Kilian decided. "But you won't be able to control it, Connor. You'll have to set it up so Ivor can trigger it."

"I can help set up a triggering mechanism," Verena promised, and Hamish piped in, "I want to help."

"We'll all have plenty to do," Shona assured him. "Rory, how do you propose setting our bash fighters?"

Rory tapped the map with one thick finger. "On the high ground. We can set our lines all down the length of the valley."

Anika nodded agreement. "When signal sounds, we jump down. Everyone gets to fight right away."

"I propose we set up our chemical weapons trebuchet and Tabnit death tubes on the high ground also," Lady Briet added. "That will help protect them from enemy combatants while also providing an excellent field of fire."

"And of course, we'll fly the Battalions right over the top of them and deploy mechanicals and additional troops," Verena said.

The grand scope of the multi-pronged attack was truly awe inspiring. They were coordinating tens of thousands of troops to hit the enemy from the north and the west at the same time. Poor Lossit. Connor doubted any of the town would survive, and was happy they were planning the battle in advance so they could evacuate the civilians ahead of time.

Kilian said, "We've got the beginnings of a solid battle strategy here. Take this back to your teams and get to work. It's probably better we work independently. No doubt my mother is attempting to infiltrate Merkland, despite the excellent counterintelligence efforts from Student Eighteen and the Mhortair. Besides, if the fight does not go according to plan, it would be unwise for my mother to be able to pull the entire battle plan from any single mind."

That was a really good point. So they agreed to work on their individual components and share them with Kilian who alone would coordinate the entire strategy.

"Why shouldn't Connor know everything?" Hamish asked.

"Because Connor will be fighting my mother until she exhausts her fleshcrafting power," Kilian reminded him. "Connor's mental shielding is getting pretty good, and he should be capable of withstanding her mind attacks, but it might still be possible for her to siphon some information anyway." He grinned and added, "Better not to risk putting all of our eggs in that leaky basket."

Hamish laughed and clapped Connor on the shoulder. "We should add that to your battle standard, Connor."

"Do you have a battle standard?" Verena asked with a smile.

Connor shook his head. He'd never considered it, but ideas immediately swarmed in. It would be fun.

Hamish said, "I can see a sweetbread riding a slab of bacon on a field of green, surrounded by all of the affinity stones over the words Leaky Basket." He glanced at Evander and said, "Unless you can come up with a suitably indecipherable translation of leaky basket to sound more epic."

Evander actually smiled, but Connor interrupted before he could share any thoughts. Hamish was already too excited by the idea, and Connor would not be surprised if a flag with those images suddenly appeared in his quarters. "Let's deal with battle standards later. Right now we've got work to do."

They dispersed to their various duties. General Wolfram, Lady Briet, and Captain Ilse headed back to the pass to coordinate efforts with all of the reinforcements from Granadure and the Arishat League. Verena and Hamish went to follow up with the Builders and the dizzying number of mechanicals still being retrofitted.

Jean rushed away to the hospital, calling Gisela via speakstone to summon as many of the researchers from their medical teams as possible to join her. Ivor, Shona, Rory, and Anika dispersed to convene meetings with all of their armed forces.

Kilian and Evander stepped apart, probably discussing something arcane and incomprehensible to the rest of them. Aifric seemed to disappear, and Connor suspected she was going to meet with her Mhortair brethren to sweep the city again for spies. She did not look pleased that Kilian doubted their ability to ferret out all enemies.

That left Connor to head down to the military command headquarters. As soon as he entered the battered castle-like command building, swarmed with workers patching holes and repairing the extensive damage from the swarm, a pair of soldiers recognized him.

They saluted sharply, looking a little awed. One of them, a beefy fellow wearing battle leathers asked, "Commander Connor, sir, are you here to help with affinities?"

His partner was staring, wide-eyed, and kept swallowing and wiping his palms. The reception was surprising, but he bit back his impulse to tease the soldier. He didn't need the guy fainting, or getting offended. He hoped he wouldn't let anyone down. "I plan to try, yes."

"We'll fetch Earthnail Fogwatt," the first soldier promised, and the two bolted away so fast, Connor wondered if they might really be Striders.

A moment later, they returned with another soldier with shoulders so wide they nearly scraped either side of the corridor. All three of them saluted, and Fogwatt shook Connor's hand with such enthusiasm, he nearly dislocated Connor's shoulder. Connor didn't think he had met the man before, but Fogwatt sure seemed to know him.

"It's an honor, Commander," the earthnail told him in his deep voice. "General Wolfram asked me yesterday to prepare a list of candidates for your review." He paused for a moment before adding more softly, "You really can do it?"

"Let's find out," Connor said, happy they were ready for him. He wanted to ask the man about his unique name, but forced himself to focus on the work. "I've only done it a few times, but I'm getting better at it. I'd like to see if we can establish some new elemental Petralists, as well as help as many of our regulars as possible join the ranks of our Boulders and Striders. Each one takes some time though, and that's one resource we're running out of."

Earthnail Fogwatt said, "This way, Commander." As he led Connor down the hall, he bellowed for his aides, and soldiers seemed to materialize from all sides. Fogwatt rattled off dozens of names. Connor decided Wolfram had picked the right man. Either he was just naming every single person he knew or he did have a list already memorized.

As the other officers scrambled to obey, Fogwatt turned back to Connor and asked, "Do you need anything to facilitate making this work?"

"I need a couple of comfortable chairs and a quiet place to meet with each candidate. I'll also need supplies of every power stone to help candidates connect with them." And since it was an opportunity too good to pass up he added, "I've found I get the best results when the people I'm working with are eating their favorite dessert and I have plenty of sweetbreads and bacon on hand."

"Bacon? Really?" The big man laughed and snapped thick fingers, then pointed at one aide trotting beside him. "You heard the man. Bacon. I want buckets of it at the ready. Inform the kitchens we'll be sending in some custom orders, and I'll want them double quick. Have them start with a platter of every kind of sweetbread and dessert they have handy. And get me some liver and onions."

Connor managed not to grimace at that last request, rubbed his hands together, and said, "Some days I love my job."

Chapter Twenty-Five
If You Don't Really Want Something,
No One Can Help You

Munching on a piece of crispy bacon still hot from the pan, Connor greeted the first candidate for a new affinity, a burly soldier wearing battle leathers, with the rank of sergeant on his shoulder. He sat across from Connor and gripped his hand firmly. "Name's Brodik, sir. I've got a decent Solas secondary. Earthnail Fogwatt suggested maybe you could help me find a tertiary."

"Would you like that?" Connor asked.

"Yes sir," Brodik answered in a booming voice.

That was a promising start. The man looked motivated. Connor asked, "To make this work, I need to know a little about you. In particular, what's a hobby or passion of yours?"

"Hobby, sir?" Brodik looked confused.

Connor nodded. "What motivates you the most, except for bash fighting, of course?"

Brodik hesitated, glanced toward the closed door furtively, then leaned closer and said softly, "Reading."

"Really?" Connor asked, unable to keep his surprise out of his voice.

Brodik flushed, clearly embarrassed. "I know it's not what you expected, but you want me to be honest."

"I do," Connor quickly assured him. "I love reading. I just . . ."

"I wouldn't have expected a brute like me to like reading either."

"That's not what I meant," Connor said, feeling bad for judging the man.

"It's all right, sir. I only recently learned how to read. It's a new program General Ivor started among the men. I never thought reading or anything that mental could be fun, but books open a whole new world." He smiled as he talked, and Connor clearly sensed his love for the new skill. It might be surprising, but it was just what he needed.

"Don't ever apologize for loving to read, Brodik. The best people I know love reading." He gestured to a small table beside them that contained stacks of power stone, including wafers of slate and vials of soapstone. "Which tertiary affinity would you like to try? Slate or soapstone?"

For a moment, Brodik could only look at the two options in silent wonder, as if coming to grips with the reality that he might finally be able to establish the coveted tertiary affinity. After a moment's consideration, he took one of the soapstone vials. He saluted Connor with it, then downed it in a single gulp.

"Here we go." Connor tapped obsidian, chert, and sandstone to connect with him at every possible level, then also tapped soapstone. The connection snapped into place between them, and Connor's consciousness was sucked into Brodik's mind.

The affinityscape materialized out of billowing gray fog, forming into a sand-floored practice yard. A long rack of heavy battle hammers stood along one wall, while a second wall was lined with hundreds of books. To his right, the ground abruptly ended in the normal fog-filled chasm, with affinity islands floating nearby. A solid rope bridge connected to the single-tiered granite island, and a second bridge extended from there to the softly glowing limestone island. The four tertiary islands floated beyond.

"By the Tallan's bony knees, what be this place?" Brodik exclaimed as he appeared on the practice ground beside Connor.

"I call it your affinityscape. See the islands? Each one represents a power stone. The bridges represent affinities you have established," Connor explained.

Brodik grinned as he took it all in. "I've never had a practice yard filled with books, but I like it."

"That's why it's in here," Connor said. "We're going to build a bridge from that limestone island out to soapstone."

"I'm not much of a builder," Brodik said with a grimace.

"Me neither, but that doesn't matter here. I've found the best bridges in the mind are built from those things you love."

Brodik nodded and strode to the rack of hammers. "Then let's start with these. My favorite weapons outside of pure bash fighting."

That sounded good to Connor. He took the hammers and carried them across the bridges to the limestone island, then laid them at the edge closest to soapstone, willing them to connect. The first two hammers morphed into anchor points for the trusses, and his confidence grew. It was working!

In moments, Brodik brought enough hammers across the bridges for Connor to build solid steel trusses. Each hammer transformed into a three-foot section and slid out along the truss before snapping into place.

"I see what you mean. This is fun," Brodik laughed when the two trusses were finished. "More hammers for the planking?"

Connor shook his head. "Let's not limit ourselves. You said you love to read. Bring me some of those books."

Brodik grimaced. "Books are rare treasures, sir. I hate the thought of destroying them."

"They aren't destroyed here in your mind, but your love of reading will help make your affinity stronger." Connor felt convinced that was true after what he'd seen with Verena, Jean, and Hamish.

So Brodik brought armloads of heavy tomes to Connor, who pressed them into position. As he'd hoped, they transformed into wide planks made of a strange white wood, with indistinct writing down their lengths. As soon as they completed the bridge, Connor stood and gestured Brodik to lead the way.

The soldier raced across eagerly, and when he stepped on the soapstone bridge, he dropped to his knees, hands raised in a posture of exultation. "I feel it!"

Connor gripped his shoulder, smiling to see his joy. "Now the fun begins."

They awakened, and Connor gestured toward a nearby bucket of water. "Let's see what you can do."

Brodik immediately yanked the water out of the bucket, hitting himself so hard in the face that he toppled out of his chair. He was laughing so hard that he swallowed half the bucket of water and nearly drowned himself.

Connor escorted the still-coughing soldier to the door, grinning. Brodik stepped into the hall where a long line of men and women were assembled for their turns and shouted, "I'm a Spitter now!"

Everyone cheered, and the next candidate, a round-faced woman, rushed in and took Brodik's wet chair.

Connor lost track of time and started wondering if he was losing track of reality as he stepped from one mind to the next, working at a feverish pace to build bridges and establish new affinities. He fueled the intense effort with copious amounts of bacon and sweetbreads.

Earthnail Fogwatt kept Connor's plate piled high and a long line of eager soldiers hoping for a miracle outside. He kept Connor's cup filled with water, and Connor transformed the liquid to a different beverage with every refill. He needed to practice, and although some of his attempts tasted like pig swill, some turned out amazing, like the cherry cordial he managed to get right only once.

Fogwatt started with many of his own staff, of course. They were officers he knew and trusted and whose skills he was eager to leverage, but he was a wise enough commander to understand the importance of spreading out the new affinities. So he began adding other officers, and in the first two hours Connor helped more than a dozen men and women establish new tertiary affinities.

That was a staggering number, and if he kept it up, they could drastically change the face of battle. But again, Fogwatt impressed Connor by interspersing regulars into the line. Connor helped most of the soldiers with no gifts whatsoever establish primary affinities with granite and basalt. He even helped create a couple of new Blades when they requested it.

Many of the minds that Connor stepped into were remarkably similar. That surprised Connor at first because the minds of his friends were so unique, but as he thought about it, he realized it made sense.

Relatively few people had participated in the miraculous discoveries that his close friends had helped develop in recent months. Many soldiers had only ever lived in one place, only known one group of people. They were very similar to how Connor and his friends had started, growing up in Alasdair.

Although in recent months those soldiers had begun to understand the wider world, Connor had to remind himself that few of them really understood much about what was going on with the Builders, Jean's miraculous school, and the incredible advancements in technology of the Arishat League.

So most of the affinityscapes were similar, often looking like parts of Merkland or surrounding towns. In most of them, Connor used trees or sometimes stone for the trusses. That seemed to work fine, although he tried focusing on each person's most passionate hobby or interest for the planking. That seemed to help snap the affinity into place better, and proved far more interesting.

People might seem similar on the surface, but everyone was unique inside. So he ended up building planking from all sorts of fun materials, from lake trout to knitting to food to hand-crafted woodworking. Every success felt like a huge victory.

After taking a break to eat some bacon-wrapped steak and down a glass of perfectly clear water, Connor greeted his next candidate, a mature woman who seemed extremely competent. She possessed no affinity but had a quick mind and served as an aid to one of the junior officers. Even Fogwatt knew her name and spoke well of her. She seemed an ideal candidate for a new primary affinity.

"What affinity motivates you the most?" Connor asked as he had the others.

Everyone else had instantly picked one, but the woman only shrugged, refusing to meet his gaze. "Whichever one you choose is fine, I guess."

"Okay. Can you tell me what motivates you most?" he asked.

She considered that for a moment before saying, "Knowing what is expected of me, and executing it perfectly."

That was unique. Connor looked forward to seeing how that translated to her affinityscape. He decided on basalt for her. She could use the exhilaration of speed to spice up her life. Tapping the requisite stones, he connected and appeared in her mind.

It looked similar to many of the others, made up of the simple town square of the village where she grew up. The islands represent-ing the various affinities were a little smaller and less well-defined than in other minds, and hovered farther out of reach, but they were there, so he could build bridges.

The woman did not appear in her affinityscape. That was unusual. Everyone else had appeared with him. Connor checked his active affinities, and they were all there, the connections in place. Strange, but surely he could make it work.

A few trees grew in the affinityscape, so Connor ripped one up and moved it into position to form a truss. He extended it toward the low, black basalt island, but instead of transforming into part of the bridge, it dissolved into sludgy mist and plunged right over the edge and disap-peared into the bottomless abyss.

"Not wood for this one, I guess," Connor said to himself. He tried again with stone, but with the same result. He tried every material he could find in the town, but nothing would stick.

Finally, he stepped from the woman's mind. Maybe he'd done something wrong with the initial connection.

"You're awake," she commented when he blinked open his eyes.

"Did you feel anything?" he asked.

"It felt like you were poking around in there. Didn't find much, did you?"

"Why would you think that?" Connor asked. What an interesting comment.

She shrugged. "Somehow I knew it was a mistake, Master Connor. Affinities are for people much more special than me. I know my place and I'm happy to serve where I am."

Connor wanted to try again, but he sensed he'd just fail. He felt terrible, but all he could say was, "I'm sorry."

She didn't seem very disappointed, as if she hadn't allowed herself to hope for an affinity. He escorted her to the door, thinking about that. He'd found great success with people who really wanted an affinity and who were passionate about learning something new. The woman wasn't. She didn't seem to accept the fact that she could develop an amazing new aspect to her life. That was so disappointing.

News that the woman failed spread down the line of waiting candidates with a splash of reality. Not even Queen Dreokt could succeed with everyone, but for a while they'd all forgotten that. Now they realized there was risk of failure, and it made many of them suddenly nervous.

Connor motioned Earthnail Fogwatt into the room.

"What happened?" the big man asked, looking back after the departing woman.

Connor felt convinced that there should be a way to help everyone establish even a weak affinity, but the truth was, not everyone would succeed. "I find the most success with people who accept that they can become more than they are now."

"She didn't?" Fogwatt asked, looking surprised. "She's so good at what she does."

"But she seems to think that's all she'll ever be able to do," Connor said.

Fogwatt considered that for a moment. "I don't see how I could have determined that ahead of time."

"I don't either, but while I work with folks, I need you to motivate your people. Encourage them to believe this is possible and that they can become something more."

"If someone doubts, they'll fail, won't they?" he asked.

Connor was relieved the man grasped the situation so quickly. "I'm afraid so. I'll do everything I can, but I'm learning that a lot of what makes this work is the mindset of the person I'm helping."

"It makes sense. I've seen soldiers with excellent native talent fail while those who appeared less likely to succeed accomplished miraculous growth," Fogwatt said thoughtfully. "Hard work and passion for growth pay off in life. I hadn't realized those traits played such a key role in affinities too."

"Neither did I."

Connor got back to work and was grateful when the next soldier established a brand new affinity with obsidian. That success seemed to reignite all the other hopefuls' enthusiasm, and the next eight candidates all succeeded.

The ninth failed. Connor sensed they were in trouble immediately. The man said all the right things, promised that he believed he could establish an affinity, but Connor could sense his reservations. The man finally admitted that he believed that some people were born with affinity talents, while others weren't.

As the day wore on, a few others failed too. Connor studied each of them, trying to figure out the pattern of why they held that limiting mindset, but it eluded him. Many were accomplished in their jobs, competent and confident. Some were humble and self-effacing like the woman had been, but others seemed deeply troubled that they could not succeed. In every case, at some level, they either believed they lacked some innate ability to make it work, or feared committing to the effort out of a risk of failure.

After hours lost in the work, Connor again opened his eyes to share that moment of wonder with his latest success story, a lanky, skinny fellow whose greatest heartfelt desire other than marrying his hometown sweetheart was to become a Strider.

His bridge had come together so fast it almost felt like it was building itself. The planking was made entirely out of gold wedding bands. The man jumped up, laughing and cheering. He was offered a little bit of basalt to prove the affinity and test it out. In his enthusiasm he ran so fast that he almost shot right through an open window. Luckily a Boulder was standing nearby and managed to pull him to a stop.

Earthnail Fogwatt said, "Tis a miraculous thing you do here today, Sir. This will change the army. I only wish we had more time to train them before battle. General Wolfram has a team already engaged, but time is short."

Connor agreed. He was liking the man more and more. He paused for a sweetbread and only then realized that the line of expectantly waiting soldiers was gone. As the new Strider left with a companion, only Connor, Fogwatt, and several aides remained in the room.

"Where is everyone?" Connor asked.

The big man chuckled. "I like your enthusiasm and applaud your dedication to the work, but even the Blood of the Tallan needs sleep. It's nearly midnight. We'll continue after you get some rest."

His words seemed to unlock floodgates of exhaustion that clobbered Connor. A wave of weariness made him sag, and he dropped back into his chair. He could've rolled over and fallen asleep under the chair right there.

He rubbed his eyes and said, "All of a sudden, I agree. Thanks for keeping an eye on me before I keeled over."

"You wouldn't be the first. Get some sleep. All the affinities in the world can only keep you going so long."

"Perhaps after one more patient." Shona's voice surprised Connor. He glanced to the door where she had just entered. She was dressed in her battle leathers and looked as fresh and vibrant as if she'd just awakened from a nap. That seemed terribly unfair.

Fogwatt saluted, but said, "Lady Shona, the young man is exhausted. Perhaps—"

She waved away the concern. "I know Connor better than anyone. He's got stamina you can't imagine. Besides, he knows my mind already. I doubt helping me will tax him greatly."

She settled into the chair in front of Connor, their knees touching, and met his gaze, her expression eager. "Do you have time for me, Connor?"

He was glad she did not seem upset that he'd helped his other friends with new affinities first. It seemed that as long as he was willing to help her, she did not mind what order she came in. He had thought he knew her as well as anyone, but her recent budding friendship with Verena challenged his understanding of either woman. He hoped the good feelings continued. Shona was complex, brilliant, and ambitious. At times he had hated her and loved her in equal measure, but never could he claim to understand her.

He was immensely glad she had chosen their side of the conflict. So he took her hands in his and met her gaze. Her eyes were wide and seemed somehow vulnerable as she lowered the defenses she usually kept in place.

"Quartzite?" Connor asked as he prepared to tap the several stones he would need.

She nodded. "I considered asking for soapstone for the potential battlefield advantage, but both Ivor and Kilian reign supreme in soapstone. They don't need me there. With quartzite I can see and understand the battle better and even raise my own voice to issue commands to keep my people safe. It has to be quartzite."

Thoughtful choice. Connor approved. So he tapped the right stones and let himself plunge through those big hazel eyes into her mind.

Her affinityscape formed around him and he looked around in astonishment. He'd expected to see a royal ball, or perhaps the palace of Merkland or some other symbol of her power, but instead he found himself standing upon one of his favorite places of all time.

The starting platform of the Rhidorroch.

The huge, complex, beloved maze spread below him. He placed a wondering hand on the starting hourglass and stared out at the configuration. It was not one of the many he had memorized, but it felt familiar. Shona appeared beside him, wearing her battle leathers, her hair braided and extending down almost to her waist.

When she recognized the Rhidorroch she laughed, a happy sound that he had not heard nearly often enough of late. Shona's rich voice raised in honest laughter always made him smile.

"I love your choice of venues, Connor, but how do you know this configuration?"

"The venue was chosen by your subconscious. I love the Rhidorroch too, but you brought us here."

Shona stepped to the starting slide, a little smile playing across her full lips. "It's perfect." She gestured at the maze that took up the first third of the Rhidorroch. "This is the first configuration I ever ran flawlessly. It represents the day that I first mastered the Rhidorroch and claimed the top spot in the Boulder class."

Interesting. She'd never lost that standing, despite intense challenge from many other gifted Petralists. The fact that she chose that place as her mental space was fascinating. Shona loved power and station and glory, but this suggested she loved the open, honest competition of the Rhidorroch above all else. She loved challenging herself against the best competition, and of course coming off conqueror.

Connor smiled too. It really was perfect.

"Do we have time to run the course?" Shona asked with a grin.

They probably shouldn't, but Connor would never willingly say no to a chance to run the Rhidorroch. So he gestured Shona to the starting slide and reached a hand out to the sand clock. "Ladies first."

Chapter Twenty-Six
Floppy Physics Are the Best

No doubt Shona understood that by running first, she gave Connor a few precious extra minutes to study and memorize the configuration, but she did not seem to care. Grinning, she dove onto the slide.

Shona raced into the maze of tall stone walls with her normal exquisite grace. She was a high lady, but she was also a warrior and she excelled in tap-rate management. She was naturally athletic, and moved with balance and fierce determination as she charged through the course, never missing a turn and never slowing. She posted an excellent time, and Connor recorded it as she raced across the maze exit.

She seemed to understand that the day's challenge only included the maze, so did not bother running through the rope sections or the other parts of the complex obstacle course, but simply leaped into the air and soared all the way back to the starting platform.

Another impressive feat. "I haven't seen anyone master the floppy physics of the mindscape so fast," Connor commented as Shona gently landed on the platform beside him.

"Floppy physics?" she laughed.

He shrugged. "What would you call it then?"

"Not floppy. There's nothing floppy about my mind. Maybe malleable or flexible."

Those were really good words. Connor rubbed his hands together in anticipation. "It's your mind, so your choice. My turn."

He moved to the slide, and when she flipped the sand clock again, he dove onto it. He could not help whooping as he slid down the fast slide and launched into the course. The maze was complex, but not as bad as some of the ones he had memorized.

He'd mastered the art of quickly memorizing the mazes and even taught a number of students some of his tricks. Watching Shona run had given him more than enough time to memorize the route, and now he tapped just a little granite to strengthen his legs as he tore through the course. Basalt would have given him more speed, but then they couldn't have compared times evenly.

The trick was to maintain just enough granite to not tire, and to tap a little extra on difficult turns when he needed it, but to release it again so it did not swell his muscles and make him ponderous.

Connor made no mistakes as he raced through the course, and he grinned as he ran. The Rhidorroch was simply amazing, and he hadn't expected another opportunity to run it again. When he crossed the finish line, he raised his hands in victory. That was a good run. He hoped Shona would not be upset that he beat her at her own mind game.

He too jumped and twisted the malleable physics of her mindscape, soaring back to the platform where she was just jotting down his time.

"I can't believe it!" she exclaimed, giving him an annoyed look.

"How much did I beat you by?" he asked with a grin.

She sniffed and tossed her long hair. "No one has ever bested me at this course, and you certainly didn't beat me today."

"Then what can't you believe?"

She gestured at the paper. "This was the best time I've ever posted, and you tied it exactly."

Connor laughed. "I was planning on beating you by at least three seconds."

She sighed, then actually smiled. "I suppose if I'm going to tie with anyone it should be you, Connor."

That compliment drew a little too close to some emotional areas they had agreed not to return to, so he gestured toward the outer stair. "We might as well get to work."

From the top of the wall, they could see that her affinityscape was entirely occupied by the Rhidorroch, surrounded by the bottomless abyss filled with billowing mists. The floating islands of the various affinities sprinkled out across that abyss, with a rope plank bridge extending to the nearby granite island.

Not surprisingly, that bridge looked much more solid than most. Shona possessed one of the most powerful primary affinities he'd ever seen. Coupled with her sheer determination, he would not have been surprised if he found her bridge made from solid steel.

Another bridge crossed from granite to the limestone island, built by Queen Dreokt herself. Connor found it interesting that it was made of the same material as her original one. Did the queen do that on purpose, or had she never tried building bridges out of different materials?

It was a good question, with no possible answer. The queen was an incredibly powerful Petralist but Connor sensed that she seemed to have lost her love of learning and experimentation. Was that a result of her husband's death or her long slumber? Did that grant him any kind of additional advantage? Not that he had seen.

As they descended the stair toward the first bridge, Connor paused to study the configuration of the islands again. Limestone did not extend straight out from granite, but rather at a sharp angle to the right. It passed very close to the basalt island, which huddled far closer to granite than Connor had seen in anyone else's mind.

"Are you seeing that?" Connor asked.

"Is that not normal?"

"I'm not sure you could call anything in people's minds normal, but it's different. Basalt is really close to granite, almost caught between the angles of those two bridges."

"So? Does that prevent me from getting a bridge from limestone to quartzite?" Shona asked, sounding worried.

Connor shook his head and moved to the starting point of the bridge out to granite. "It just suggests a possibility I hadn't considered before."

"What sort of possibility?" Shona joined him, still looking concerned. "I don't really fancy the idea of experimenting in my mind, Connor."

"Even if the experiment could make you Agor?"

He had her there, and they both knew it. Connor considered the vague plan forming in his mind and decided he had to try. So he grinned and said, "I'll be right back."

It was a testament to how badly she wanted another affinity that she did not interfere as he raced back up the outside stair to the starting platform. He probably could've used planks from that plat-form, but instead he reached over the rail and ripped the starting slide off the ground and hefted it onto his shoulder.

"Haven't you wrecked the Rhidorroch enough times?" Shona demanded when she saw what he was carrying.

"You sound like Frazier. I need building materials, don't I?"

"Can't you envision building materials to appear next to us?" She made a vague gesture to one side.

Connor shook his head. "The strongest affinities are made by materials you consider precious. I thought about grabbing some of the stone walls from the maze, but this feels even more right. Excuse me."

He planted the slide on the ground next to the starting point of the bridge to granite. The end instantly fused to the ground, forming hinged anchor points. Bolstered by that success, Connor pushed the rest of the slide out over the chasm, dropping the far end toward the black stone basalt island.

The end of the slide clanged into place, instantly fused to the island, and the entire slide transformed into a solid wooden bridge. Connor laughed, loving that rush of wonder that came every time he discovered another trick to these mind games. That affinity came faster than any he'd created so far. He bet if Shona had pushed herself, she could have established an Agor affinity all by herself.

Shona gasped and clutched his arm, her lovely eyes wide with wonder. "I can feel basalt, Connor. Did you really do what I think you just did?"

"I guess they'll have to start calling you Lady Agor Shona now."

She squealed with delight, and in that moment of joy, leaned in, clearly planning to kiss him. He tensed and she caught herself inches from his face. Her expression of joy fell, and for a second she looked so crestfallen that he turned his head to one side and tapped his cheek.

"Once on the cheek is appropriate for friends, right?"

"Thank you Connor." She kissed him lightly on the cheek. Her eyes glittered, as if she was on the verge of shedding a tear. That would have embarrassed them both, so he pretended not to see. His relationship with Shona was far too complex to read too much into anything without becoming confused and defensive again.

They seemed to have figured out how to coexist as good friends, and that was more than he'd ever hoped they could manage. Shona had played a huge role in his life over the past years, but he still hadn't been able to figure out if that role was overall a good one.

They were both progressing in positive directions, so he decided to just focus on that.

Shona jumped up and down, laughing with delight, and that kind of honest joy was easy to celebrate. Acting like that, one could easily forget she was one of the most dangerous women on the continent.

Connor gestured toward the basalt island. "Better go over and confirm the affinity."

She raced across, laughing, completely oblivious to the danger of possibly tumbling off. He wasn't sure what that would do to her. She jumped up and down on the basalt island and even crouched down to kiss the black rock before rushing back to him. "This is a miracle, Connor. Thank you!"

She was acting far too much like any normal person and far too little like her conniving, calculating high lady self. On top of how she and Verena had been acting earlier, he wondered if maybe Verena and Aifric had hit Shona in the head a dozen times too many. He didn't mind, though and decided to trust that he was seeing honest joy from her.

In good spirits, they got to work building a second bridge from basalt over to limestone, reinforcing her connection to her secondary affinity. Then they crossed to limestone and studied the tertiary islands hovering in the dimness beyond. Quartzite, slate, and soapstone floated in plain view, and a vague shape out in the fog might represent marble. Since that affinity had been broken, he hadn't felt even that much connection to marble in any of the other minds he'd walked that day.

It took only a moment to go rip out another starting slide. A new one had appeared after he'd taken the last. It had worked so well, why risk trying any other material? Again it formed a bridge instantly.

Shona threw back her head and shouted in triumph before rushing across the bridge and sprawling across the quartzite island, arms outstretched, as if trying to hug the entire thing. "I can feel it already. You did it, Connor! This is incredible."

As they faded from her mind to return to the real world, Connor wondered if he had just helped heal the final rift that had lingered between them. Could they really move forward without their complex history hanging over them?

And what would Verena think when she learned Connor had helped Shona become Agor?

Chapter Twenty-Seven
There's Always Another Secret

The next couple days passed in a blur for Connor, every waking moment consumed either in the effort of helping establish new affinities or dedicated to intense training. He pushed the limits of his affinities, focusing on new ways to mix them, hoping the combinations might surprise Queen Dreokt when he next faced her.

He could not hope to defeat her in a simple head-on elemental bash fight. She had proven her strength and experience there, but her overconfidence with her elemental affinities offered Connor a chance. If he could find ways to injure her and force her to consume healing and fleshcrafting, he hoped to finally leave her vulnerable.

Super-fracking was still one of the funnest experiences in life beside stealing rare kisses from Verena when he stopped at her workroom for brief visits, so he practiced speeding from Merkland up to Badurach Pass at least a couple times a day. He was tempted to visit the ruins of Alasdair, but decided not to. The sight would just depress him.

Super-thinking gave him plenty of ideas to test, and some proved exceptional. Combining stilling with pumice activated a super protective bubble around him that not only allowed him to remain invisible to Petralist senses and nullify elemental attacks against him, but also absorb some of that elemental energy and be strengthened by it.

Some of his ideas turned out less amazing. He tried combining stilling with limestone and managed to clobber himself with super sensory deprivation. He lost several minutes in blind, dark, cold limbo before figuring out how to undo it. He could have sworn he heard Porphyry chuckling somewhere in the distance, but didn't have enough precious porphyry powder left to risk tapping it to investigate.

Of course he practiced with his elemental affinities too. He needed to prove he could still effectively wield them. The elementals refused to appear in his mind. All he heard were their distant voices, chiding him for not fulfilling his promises, and warning him he'd regret it.

That was unnerving, but if that proved the worst they did to interfere, he was willing to endure it. The loss of the close relationship he'd formed with them bothered him until he reminded himself that they'd been lying. Envisioning the elemental gateways as doorways in his mind still worked, although he consumed more power stone that way. For a while, he had barely consumed any stone while connecting with the elements. He also had to concentrate harder to establish a strong connection, although it still wasn't as hard as the major instability he'd struggled with during his second ascension.

Serpentinite proved extremely interesting. Beyond its usefulness manipulating sound, mimicking voices, and panicking livestock when he unleashed a wolf's howl, Connor sought to master how to use it as a weapon. Student Eighteen had suggested that with his third ascension, he could do some pretty amazing things with it.

She was right. Connor learned that he could increase the frequency and energy of sounds until they seemed about to explode out of control. And he accidentally hit himself with some of that super-frequency sound. It seemed to vibrate right down into his muscles, locking them up, and for a moment he couldn't move. It was really fun, and could be extremely useful in the coming battle. He couldn't wait to test it on Hamish.

Connor made sure to train with strum and magnis too. The strange, fundamental powers of the natural world offered a potential advantage that he desperately needed. He figured out how to sweep his strum senses across the landscape, quickly gathering enough of a charge to unleash a lightning bolt. That was a lot of fun, but he found himself drawn even more to magnis, practicing creating invisible magnis fields around himself to deflect or manipulate strum, or even move steel objects.

He took the training to the extreme by requesting that Fyodor and his Varvakan teams set up another strum death trap like the one they hit him with during his big challenge course. When he raced into the invisible box with magnis activated, blue lightning crackled all along his forcefield, but did not penetrate. He was able to redirect it and unleash a huge lightning bolt that shattered an entire copse of trees.

That was so much fun, he planned to do it again until the farmer who lived nearby threatened to petition Shona for payment of damages if he continued to destroy his trees. Connor mollified the man by clearing an acre of timberland for him and chopping the trees into firewood.

In training with Kilian and Evander, they tried elemental wrestling matches to gauge his raw power. Both of the ancient Dawnus wielded their affinities with finesse that Connor still lacked, but he could draw upon more raw power than they could.

During one practice session with Kilian, they both targeted trees standing in an open field. Connor made sure to verify the field was owned by Shona, not another angry farmer. He incinerated his tree three seconds faster than Kilian and raised his hand in victory, feeling pretty confident.

Kilian only shrugged, then turned toward another tree. There were only a few left in the small copse in the center of the field southeast of Merkland. Kilian fracked and attacked the tree, racing around it, wielding fire like a hundred burning axes. Connor watched in astonishment as Kilian chopped the tree into a storm of kindling, then vaporized it. The entire process took half the time of the simple incineration method.

Kilian skidded to a stop nearby, grinning and rubbing imaginary specs of dirt from his hands. "You've got strength, Connor, but don't forget that how much force you bring to bear matters less than knowing how to apply it for best effect."

"You've been teaching me that lesson ever since Alasdair," Connor said, feeling like he still needed to learn so much.

Kilian tapped the side of his head, his expression serious. "Make sure you remember it, because it's the reason I'm still alive after meeting my mother on the battlefield so many times."

Connor vowed to not only survive, but also finally defeat her.

So he turned toward one of the two remaining trees that stood proudly, oblivious to its impending fate. Connor tapped marble and summoned a wave of fire. Instead of casting it at the tree, he sucked out all the heat, letting the flames wither and die. Taking that pool of heat, he combined marble and limestone, concentrating the heat into a tiny beam, forcing it to the highest possible frequency, and unleashed the invisible death beam at the tree.

It obliterated the tree in a fantastic explosion that mushroomed up into the sky. The thunderclap ripped the air asunder, and would have probably shattered windows in Merkland if Connor hadn't tapped serpentinite to deflect the sound waves up and away. Blinding light obscured the tree as it disintegrated under the blast, and again Connor deflected the worst of the light up into the air. The entire horizon lit up, transforming the blue sky into white brilliance.

He didn't hit it with enough energy to break the component bits of the tree and release secondary explosions of fission like he had underground when sealing the breach the queen had made in the planet's mantle. Up on the surface, a fission explosion would have eclipsed a Last Word bomb, and they were far too close to Merkland for that.

Connor whooped. "That was amazing!" Incredible that such a tiny death beam could wreak such damage.

Kilian actually looked impressed. "I sensed you steal the heat, but then you did something with it I didn't quite follow."

That moment of knowing something Kilian didn't was a sweet joy, and Connor hesitated before responding so he could enjoy the unusual feeling to the fullest. He then outlined what he'd done and said, "I learned the trick of turning the heat into really high frequency energy when I was in that elfonnel trying to plug the hole in the mantle, I accidentally figured out how to trigger enormous explosions that Fire called fission."

Kilian scowled. "You *accidentally* learned a higher form of power that I don't think even my mother knows?"

Connor shrugged. "Yeah. I'm motivated by stress."

Kilian laughed. "That's an elfonnel-sized understatement."

Laughing with him, Connor shrugged again. "Good thing, because I'm usually out-matched. My in-the-moment creativity is my only edge most of the time."

"Let's hope you continue to learn on the fly so quickly, but I'm glad we've had so much time to train this time. Fighting my mother is not something done lightly."

"Do you really think we can beat her this time?" Connor asked seriously.

"I honestly do," Kilian said. "You've already survived more encounters with her than most, but if we were planning on facing her with nothing but our skill alone, she would beat us again. For the first time we have a plan that might actually work."

"We had a pretty good plan last time," Connor reminded him.

Kilian gripped his shoulder. "It was, but our new plan is better. We really can win this time, but we can't hold anything back. You will play a central role, and you now understand just how dangerous my mother is."

A lump of dread in his throat made Connor swallow. The queen terrified him, but he didn't have a choice. He thought of Tomas and Cameron and their noble sacrifice to give him the chance to stop her the last time. He could not hesitate, had to take the fight to her. If he failed, how many of his friends would die?

"Besides, we have something she's never understood," Kilian added with his trademark grin.

"What?" Connor hoped he was about to reveal another deep secret, or a mighty new mechanical, or even an epic new dessert.

"Teamwork."

That wasn't what he'd hoped for, and Kilian clearly read his disappointment. "Together, we can accomplish what no single one of us ever could hope to. Together, we will win the day."

With his hope bolstered by his ancient mentor's optimism, Connor said, "This time, she doesn't escape."

Kilian's eyes filled with flickering, white-hot fire, and his expression turned grim. "No escape."

Then he said, "Tell me about this fission thing."

So Connor explained as best he could, relating how he had broken some of those tiny bits of matter at their most fundamental level, and the vast amount of power the resulting explosions had unleashed. "It was way more than we could ever do with diorite."

"Really? You're sure you've mastered the full measure of diorite?"

"Um, I thought I had," Connor admitted, suddenly hoping Kilian could show him more.

His teacher gestured toward a line of trees along the edge of the field, about a hundred and fifty yards away. He took a step, leaned forward, and explosion-vomited. Instead of a firestorm that billowed into a deadly cloud of destruction, Kilian focused his fire-puke into a mouth-sized stream of compressed flames that shot across the distance like a really thick death beam. It exploded into one of the trees so hard it uprooted. The flames spread along it like grasping tendrils, snapping branches and incinerating leaves. Within seconds, the tree was reduced to a compact pile of ash.

"That's amazing," Connor grinned, eager to give it a try. He had thought he understood the beauty of explosive-vomiting, but now he saw there was a higher level of controlled puking he needed to master.

A rush of thrusters announced Hamish's arrival. He swooped down for a landing beside Connor and pushed up his helmet, already laughing. "That was amazing!"

"If only you could join the challenge," Connor told him. Hamish had tried to induce enhanced vomiting many times with activated stones, but had only managed some spectacular failures.

"Hey, no fair. Holding a puking contest with diorite limits the field," Hamish protested.

"Oh, and you think you'd have a chance using traditional methods?" Kilian challenged, smiling.

"I've held the record as many times as Connor has," Hamish said proudly.

Kilian laughed. "But you've only ever challenged each other. That's not exactly a wide field either."

Connor grinned. "We've talked about holding a puke-off too many times. It's time to put your stomach where your mouth is."

"What?" Kilian laughed.

"You know what he means," Hamish grinned. "You're on. Contact the others. I'll get some supplies."

He blasted into the air on full thruster and rocketed back toward Merkland. Kilian shrugged, looking nonchalant, but his eyes sparkled with tiny flecks of fire. "Let's do it."

Chapter Twenty-Eight
Dig Deep and Give It Everything You've Ever Eaten

Connor cast his quartzite senses toward Merkland, and his super-enhanced hearing quickly bored through the tumult of sounds and zeroed in on Verena and Jean, who were discussing the deployment options for Render Flight during the battle. Using a combination of serpentinite and quartzite, he created the words he wanted and pushed them into the speakstones the girls were using.

He'd experimented a few times with the trick, and it sure made life easier. "Hey, we're finally holding that distance puking competition we keep talking about."

"Now?" Jean asked, sounding like she wanted to protest, but Verena piped in. "Where?"

"In the pastures just south of the city."

"We're on our way," she assured him.

Connor didn't hear Shona or Wolfram on speakstone, so he tapped chert and scanned for their thoughts. In seconds, he found Shona in a meeting with Ivor. Wolfram was on a lower level of the palace speaking with Aifric. Perfect. He could send them a direct thought, but the few times he'd tried usually just freaked people out. So he tapped serpentinite, formed the words, and cast them at his friends.

They all arrived within five minutes. Verena and Jean took the Swift. Aifric switched to Mariora and fracked. Shona and Ivor rode over standing atop a glittering pedestal of water. Wolfram chose the quaint method of riding a horse.

Hamish returned last, carrying a bulging leather satchel. Connor created a table of ice, and Hamish declared, "I brought ammunition, including five dozen smashpacked meals that failed quality testing. Heavy casserole with way too much garlic and onions." He grinned and added, "For the less adventurous, I brought the dependable standby choices of baked beans and Grandurian sauerkraut."

He then carefully laid out a dozen vials of Althin chemicals and rubbed his hands together eagerly. "All right. Is this everyone?"

"I think so," Connor said. They'd never invited so many people to compete for the title. Usually he and Hamish took advantage of moments of gastric distress for impromptu challenges. Lately those had generally involved one of the Althin chemicals Hamish was testing.

Kilian strode down the line of contestants, looking satisfied. "With the fate of our world depending on our greatest efforts, it's comforting to see nine brave companions willing to risk everything in this ultimate competition of focused intent."

Connor chuckled, as did Hamish. Kilian's mock gravity was exactly what the competition needed. Ivor was smiling, although Shona looked like she thought Kilian was serious at first, then rolled her eyes when she realized he was joking.

Jean said quickly, "I don't plan to compete."

"Then you may act as judge," Kilian told her.

"Um, okay," she said, looking a bit disgusted by the idea.

"Do we need to invite anyone else?" Verena asked. "I bet Evander would love to participate."

"Or maybe Ilse," Connor added, although they were already facing stiff competition. He felt confident he or Hamish would win, but any one of the group might pull off a particularly good heave.

"Ilse is on patrol south of the city," Wolfram reported.

Jean added, "And Evander said not to disturb him before dinner. He's studying in the vault."

"Very well, then we will proceed with the company at hand," Kilian declared.

"First we need rules," Ivor said. "No diorite or quartzite allowed to falsely inflate distances."

"And we all start at the same line," Wolfram said.

Shona wrinkled her nose. "Competing from the same spot would confuse the results."

Connor suggested, "To make it fair, how about we build a start platform wide enough so none of us have to cross streams, and high enough to gauge full distance?"

"Like this?" Ivor asked, making a grand gesture. The water platform he'd ridden over from Merkland transformed, flowing under them and lifting them all twenty feet into the air. He formed it into an ice pedestal with a straight demarcation line on one end and a steeply sloped ramp extending away. He even added lines every six inches across the slope to assist with easy distance measuring.

"Show-off," Hamish laughed.

Shona regarded the construct approvingly. "You've given this some thought."

Ivor shrugged. "I believe that if you're going to do something, do it right the first time."

Connor wholeheartedly agreed.

Hamish gestured toward the table with the food ammunition and the vials of chemicals. "Each competitor gets up to three bowls of beans or sauerkraut, or five smashpacked meals, plus one whiff of the chemical puke-inducing agent of their choice."

"Am I the only one concerned about this?" Jean asked, looking a little green.

"Between you and Aifric, I doubt anyone will get seriously hurt," Kilian assured her.

Verena walked to the table and inspected the chemicals. "What did you bring?"

"We've got everything from essence of privy to skunk extract to mega-stench," Hamish said proudly, gesturing at the various vials. "I even distilled essence of unwashed socks, and condensed the stench of every fart from the Boulder barracks latrine into this last one."

Connor was impressed. Hamish's research into viable alternatives to the mega-stench had progressed farther than he'd imagined.

Jean was definitely looking woozy, and Aifric was shifting between several of her personalities, speaking softly to herself, as if arguing about who would take the challenge. Kilian looked impressed, Ivor looked astonished, and Verena suddenly looked less eager.

Hamish caught her eyeing the tiny vial of mega stench. "This is your best chance, Verena. You've teased me for months about trying it, but we both know you've secretly longed to experience it."

"You're cracked, Hamish," she said, but didn't look away from the little vial. Connor grinned. He could tell she was all but convinced to give it a try. The researcher in her just had to know.

"So, who wants to go first?" Kilian asked.

Connor planned to volunteer, since he was one of the most experienced in the art of distance puking, but Wolfram surprised him by saying, "I volunteer."

"Bravo," Ivor said, and Shona gave Wolfram a little bow of respect.

The fearless general chose the baked beans for his ammunition. While he ate, they decided the rest of the rotation. Connor offered to go second, followed by Aifric, then Verena, Hamish, Shona, Kilian, and finally Ivor. Ivor looked pleased with the final position. In many contests, it would indeed offer some advantage, since he'd know exactly the distance he needed to beat, but Connor wasn't sure it would work so well with the current challenge.

Connor chose the smashpacked meals, as did Hamish. They both understood that sheer volume of ammunition sometimes made a difference. Verena chose sauerkraut, as did Aifric. Both Shona and Ivor chose beans, but Kilian pushed the rules by choosing a mixture of beans and sauerkraut. By his grimaces while he ate, mixing the two potent fuels might have been a wise choice.

Wolfram chose skunk extract as his accelerant, and Kilian decided he would go with that one too, saying, "I have a particularly bad skunk memory as a boy that should provide an extra boost."

Connor longed to ask about that memory. He of course chose the mega stench. Hamish had regaled him so many times regarding the life-altering quality of that smell that he couldn't skip a chance to try it and prove its superiority. Hamish and Ivor both chose mega-stench too, and after a long hesitation, Verena sighed and pointed to the vial.

Hamish whooped and she said, "You're right, Hamish. I don't think I could forgive myself if I missed this chance."

Shona chuckled. "I don't think you'll forgive yourself after you smell it. I would never willingly subject myself to it."

"Which one will you choose, then?" Connor pressed.

She pointed at the essence of privy. "That should prove adequate."

Hamish said, "I personally guarantee the effectiveness of all of these scents."

Aifric alone chose the distilled Boulder farts, saying, "We've experienced some impressive smells over the years, but both Tresta and Hemma have proven that for some reason Boulders produce the most rancid gas of all."

"So no one thinks unwashed socks are strong enough?" Hamish asked, looking intrigued. "How about I sprinkle everyone with a few drops after we finish."

"Don't you dare," Verena warned. Shona looked ready to punch him back to Merkland if he tried it.

He shrugged. "That's all right. I'm sure I can find a way to use it during the battle."

General Wolfram took up the skunk extract and moved to the starting line. As always, his uniform was spotless, his long mustaches well groomed. With a flourish he unstoppered the vial. Connor grimaced as the smell wafted out. Even from a distance, it was foul. Wolfram placed the vial under his nose and sniffed deeply.

His eyes bugged out and Kilian only barely snatched the vial from his trembling hands before he dropped it. With a coughing, retching sound, Wolfram settled into a fighting stance, leaned forward, and let loose an impressive volley.

The beans had indeed given him plenty of ammunition, and he maintained excellent posture as he hurled his recent meal far out over the icy drop. The dark brown sludge splashed down and cascaded most of the way to the bottom, leaving a brown smear. Connor tapped quartzite and called forth a gentle breeze to push the smell away from the group.

Jean smiled. "Thank you. I was starting to feel sick, and I haven't even eaten anything."

Hamish clapped Wolfram on the back. The general looked sick and sank to one knee, face pale, hands trembling, looking like he planned a second volley. "That was indeed powerful."

"Good distance too," Hamish noted, regarding the smear on the ice slope with a trained eye.

Verena said, "At least measuring will be easy, since it sticks to the ice."

"Are we counting initial splash-down location, or the final travel distance?" Ivor asked.

After a brief discussion, they decided to go with total travel distance. Connor figured the initial splash-down distance better reflected the power behind the hurl, but that force should translate into better slide distance too.

So he stepped up to the launch line, next to the spot where Wolfram had made his play. The meals were heavy in his gut, and he felt confident that his experience would help him win the day. So he nodded once to Hamish, who extended the vial of mega-stench and unstopped it directly beneath Connor's nose.

Connor took a single, sharp breath.

And in that second, his connection to quartzite flared, already applied to his sense of smell.

Ever since his ascension, he rarely managed to completely sever his links to his tertiary affinities, but he'd never accidentally tapped the wrong one before.

Bad time to try it.

The mega stench drove up his nostril like Mhortair daggers, dipped in acid. With his sense of smell sharpened to supernatural levels, the stench seemed transformed into a living thing that clobbered his mind and blackened his vision. His body convulsed, and even though he tried tapping granite to help stabilize himself, his legs gave out and he toppled to his side. His entire insides spasmed so hard it felt like he was getting chomped by an elfonnel. He couldn't breathe, couldn't think, dimly heard himself scream as the mega stench scoured every available droplet from his innards, wringing them like a washerwoman wringing a wet shirt.

It all exploded up his throat and out his mouth in a convulsive heave that felt like his toes were getting sucked up through his boots. He lacked the strength to direct it, and lying on his side, his angle was terrible. It felt like everything inside of his skin was getting ejected while he puke-screamed, and he hurt so deep, he wished Erich was there to clobber him with a tree and put him out of his misery.

No wonder soldiers had fled the battlefield screaming when the mega-stench cloud had enveloped them. Connor's feet twitched with the need to run, but there was nowhere to go.

After the initial volley, he vomited again, somehow spewing even more, although he already felt wrung dry. It felt like he was spewing everything he'd ever eaten, everything he'd ever considered eating, and everything he'd ever watched anyone else eat. As he retched, his connection to water snapped back into place. Water rushed through him, easing the hurt a little, but adding immense volume to his second hurl. It intensified into a powerful stream of liquid, the color of mud, sprinkled with chunky bits that sprayed out his mouth with the force of the Upper Wick in spring flood.

"Foul," Kilian called immediately, but Connor couldn't respond. He hurt too much, and he was too busy trying to turn off his affinities.

"Doesn't matter," Hamish replied. "His aim was still off. Distance was terrible."

That was the least of his worries. Connor felt like he was going to die.

In his mind, he heard Fire's voice, filled with laughter. "The most impressive failure I've ever seen."

"That could have gone better," Earth agreed.

"I don't think he understood the rules," Air added, her voice like a light summer breeze, skipping along the Wick.

Water, her voice tender with concern said, "You shouldn't have slipped closer to sniff with him. I think that made things worse."

Could they really do that? The idea should bother him, but Connor couldn't make his mind work. He coughed, then his stomach clenched a third time in a dry heave so intense, he didn't think he'd ever be able to eat again. He was completely empty, and his entire body curled tighter in protest. When the wave finally subsided, he gasped, his lungs burning. Groaning, he tried sitting up, blinking eyes that watered so bad he had to tap soapstone to clear them. Breathing was agony. His lungs burned and his nose felt like it was melting off.

Then healing warmth poured into him from both Jean and Aifric, who had crouched beside him. The healing helped wash away the worst of the pain and helped him concentrate enough to tap his own sandstone. He finally took a real breath, but felt shaky and weak.

One glance down the icy slide made him feel even worse. Where Wolfram's stream had fallen straight and true, Connor had spewed at an angle, destroying his distance and marring the slide with a greasy smear.

Ivor hauled him to his feet, and Hamish clapped him on the back hard enough that he almost fell over the edge onto the nasty slide. "Wasn't that amazing?" Hamish laughed.

"Amazing," Connor agreed weakly, his voice hoarse, his thoughts still scattered.

"Lost focus," Hemma commented as she took the control position from Aifric.

"See how well you do," Connor told her. He'd already lost the competition, but seeing the others lose control would help him feel less useless. He needed to find time to talk with the elementals about what happened, but couldn't muster the energy at the moment. He noticed Verena staring at him with wide, fearful eyes before she looked toward the vial that Hamish was holding.

She started to shake her head, but Hamish said, "Oh, no. You chose already. No backing out."

Verena scowled. "I can make whatever choices I deem appropriate, thank you very much."

"Fine," Hamish said with a nonchalant shrug. "Change your mind. We'll all know the truth."

Hemma chuckled. "He's got you there, Verena. You never back down from anything."

For the first time in her life, she looked like she wanted to.

Hemma ceded the control position to timid little Eystri. Clutching her hands together nervously, she stepped to the line and nodded for Hamish to bring the fart extract. Apparently the women had decided Eystri's weaker constitution would result in more explosive results. Hamish unstoppered it under her nose, and she inhaled.

Her entire body went rigid, her eyes bugged out, and color drained from her face. Eystri threw her arms out wide and screamed, her body shaking, then convulsing forward as she puked so hard her feet left the ground and she nearly toppled over the edge after her lunch. Verena caught her shoulder, which might have been a breach of etiquette, but no one protested. They were all staring at the amazing spray of vomit launching from her mouth. It glinted like muddy crystals in the bright sunlight as it shot far beyond Wolfram's splash-down point and cascaded all the way to the ground, far below at the end of the ramp.

"Wow," Connor breathed. Hamish clapped, as did most of the others. Eystri coughed a couple of times, and when she turned away from the ramp, Kilian pulled her into a joyous hug. He laughed and said, "Well done!"

"Maybe don't squeezing so tight," she said, still looking green. "Or you might getting another round in the face."

He released her, still smiling, and surveyed the rest of the group. "Now we've got a competition on our hands."

Wolfram made a deep bow to Eystri and ceremonially handed over his spoon. "I admit defeat to your unmatched intestinal fortitude."

Eystri took the spoon with a graceful curtsy, looking immensely pleased with herself. Connor hoped the excellent performance bolstered her courage.

Verena went next, already trembling with nervousness as Hamish prepared to unstopper the mega stench. She took the tiniest breath and immediately heaved. She got excellent distance before collapsing to the ice, weeping and clawing at her nose.

Connor dropped to his knees beside her, pouring healing power into her. She calmed a moment later, although her breath still sounded ragged and her face was marred by tears. She grabbed Connor's hand and met his gaze with wild eyes. "It really was life-altering."

"Really?" he asked, impressed. He had only wanted to die.

"Life-altering for Hamish. I'll kill him," she growled.

Hamish, who was standing nearby laughed, but wisely moved away and placed Ivor between him and Verena. She did have a couple of her throwing knives on her belt, after all.

Ivor held the mega stench for Hamish, who went next. He breathed deep, then gagged, his limbs shaking, face draining of color, but he maintained excellent posture for the explosive response to the stench. He got marvelous distance too, although he didn't quite match Eystri's mark. He spewed a second time, much weaker, and drew in a long, shuddering breath. "Wow. That never gets old."

"How many times have you breathed that vile stench?" Verena asked.

He shrugged, looking embarrassed. "I don't know. A few."

Connor laughed. Hamish's name was spoken in whispered tones of awe by the Althin researchers for a reason. Shona was looking at him like she feared he might explode, or something. Everyone else just smiled and shrugged. When Hamish saw that he hadn't quite matched Eystri's distance, he threw up his hands and exclaimed, "I knew it! With so many people working together in one body, you can accomplish the impossible."

Shona went next, trying to retain her poise until the moment she sniffed the essence of privy. She instantly gagged, but remained upright long enough to spew. Distance puking was clearly not a subject taught to high noble ladies, though. She lacked focus and sprayed far too wide, robbing her heave of distance. Still, she looked proud of herself for competing and not getting totally overwhelmed like Connor had.

If she ever teased him about that, he'd give her a whiff of mega stench with activated quartzite. Then they'd see who was laughing.

Kilian sniffed the skunk extract, closed his eyes, and heaved with no other outward sign of distress. His control was inspiring, and he got amazing distance, perfectly tying Eystri. Cacilia took over from Eystri, her posture shifting slightly as she sauntered up to Kilian and embraced him. Her voice turned silky and throatier and she said, "I'm impressed, Kilian. I like a man who can keep up."

Connor felt himself flushing, and was glad he wasn't the target of that smoky stare. Kilian just laughed and made an extravagant bow to Cacilia.

"All well and good, but I'll beat you both," Ivor promised as he took his position. He tried Verena's trick of taking only a tiny sniff of mega stench. He instantly gagged, and his muscles rippled as he instinctively tapped granite.

It didn't help.

He also tapped his tertiary affinities, but for once lost control over them. He blasted himself over backward with water, right off the ice pedestal, as he heaved an impressive quantity that splashed over the ground behind them.

"Disqualified," Kilian declared. Connor joined in the clapping and laughter, relieved to see the mighty Ivor undone as badly as he had been.

"I suppose I need to review the distances and decide which of you won," Jean told Kilian, looking more squeamish than she ever did treating the worst diseases.

"No need, my dear," Kilian told her grandly. "I cede to the lady Eystri and her sisters."

Aifric took over the control position, raised her hands, and shouted in victory. Then she leaned in and kissed Kilian on the cheek. "Every man should take lessons on etiquette from you."

Hamish laughed. "Etiquette lessons during a puking competition. Perfect."

Chapter Twenty-Nine
All You Can Do Is the Best You Can Do,
Especially with Explosives

Verena lifted away from the field in the Swift, with Connor in the back seat, arms draped over her shoulders. She kept the window shields down to allow the cool air to refresh them. She'd rinsed her mouth several times, but that vile mega-stench still clung to her throat, making her want to gag.

"Next time, we'll manage the launch stage better," Connor said.

Verena chuckled. "I'm not really looking forward to a next time." The challenge had appealed to her, but intentionally subjecting herself to such an ordeal again seemed foolish.

Connor shrugged, kissed the side of her neck, then massaged her shoulders as she ascended higher over the valley. She sighed, enjoying the rare quiet moment together.

"How is work going?" Connor asked.

"Better than I feared. We've completed retrofitting all of the missiles. The engines were giving us trouble, but Hamish came up with some brilliant ideas."

"I thought Hamish was working on the Thunder Towers."

"He is, but he's been tapping obsidian all the time. He can't get enough of his new affinity, and it's really speeding up his work." Of course, she tapped granite at every possible opportunity, and had trained every day with Shona. Bash fighting was amazing, and under Shona's excellent tutelage, she was advancing very quickly. Her growing friendship with Shona seemed even more miraculous than her new affinity.

She added, "He's been sharing new ideas about retooling mechanicals every day, and Jean's been doing the same thing, when she can tear herself away from practicing with sandstone. She redesigned the deployment plan for all the forces that will be stationed on the Battalions."

He squeezed her shoulders. "I'm so glad they're doing so well. I've heard that not everyone is picking up the nuances of their new powers so quickly."

Verena nodded. Merkland was awash with Striders crashing into buildings and Boulders accidentally ripping doors off hinges or walking through walls, but most folks were handling the disturbances with a sense of wonder rather than frustration.

"Do you think you've created enough new Petralists to make a difference?" she asked.

He sighed, leaning his forehead against her hair. "I hope so. Tonight I'm hoping to make another two dozen."

"You're still getting some who fail?" she asked.

His hands tensed on her shoulders, and when she glanced back, he looked troubled and said, "Some people convince themselves they can't do it. Either they're not good enough, they're so afraid they'll fail that they don't even try, or they assume if they weren't born with a talent, they can't learn it. It's crazy."

Verena considered that as she slowly banked around Merkland, five thousand feet up. "I've known people who limit themselves like that. I hadn't realized a person's mindset might affect their chances of establishing affinities. Don't let it get you down. They have to want it."

"I know. If they want it, no matter how impossible it seems, I can usually help them. If they don't want it or refuse to try, I can't help them." His expression turned pensive. "Sometimes I wonder if I'm really doing people any favors."

"What do you mean?"

He sighed and resumed rubbing her shoulders. She sighed, loving how her knots loosened under his touch. He said, "We'll throw every one of those new Petralists into battle against enemies who have probably had a lot more training. How many of them will die because they're so inexperienced?"

"You're right. Some of them will die, but Connor, what would happen to them if you didn't help them?"

"They wouldn't dive into the middle of a bash fight they couldn't win, or commit to a running battle when they can barely turn."

"But they would also lack the weapons to even fight Petralists. The regulars face even worse danger. The new Petralists you are creating might be inexperienced, but at least they now have the tools to fight for their liberty. Don't feel guilty that you've given them that opportunity," she told him, and she meant it.

Her words seemed to help ease some of his worry. Wolfram and Rory had organized an extensive, even brutal, training program for new Petralists. That would help too, but she knew that Connor would carry a heavy weight of guilt for every death that occurred. She felt the same weight on her shoulders. People would die in the fighting, and some of them might die because her mechanicals weren't good enough. But they had to try, had to save as many as they could. Doing nothing would be worse.

"Let's just make sure we win," she said, turning to hold his gaze, her expression determined. "That will make all the sacrifice worth it."

"We'll win," he promised.

Verena twisted farther so she could kiss him on the lips. Then she held his face close to hers and said, "Train hard, Connor. We're doing everything we can. It's all we can do."

"Let's just hope it's enough."

She considered those words as she banked back toward Merkland. They were out of time. The queen was advancing, and they couldn't simply retreat forever. They had to stop her now, or all of Granadure would be overrun. They had to find a way.

Aifric was waiting for them outside Verena's workshop. After a final kiss good-bye, Connor left with her for another round of training.

Verena headed inside her cluttered workshop and happily inhaled the scents of stone and wood, dust and steel. Time to make some bombs.

CHAPTER THIRTY
The Best Teams Perform As One Unit

Connor ran south with Rith to another big pasture field, near where they had just held the puking contest. He was glad they'd made the time to do that but wished he'd performed better.

"You did an amazing job today," he told her as they slowed to a stop.

She smiled proudly. "Like Hamish said, when we focus, there's little this group can't accomplish."

"Well, let's see if we can accomplish some training," he said with a grin.

They spent an hour crisscrossing the field, switching between basalt, granite, and obsidian, dueling with earth and water, blinding each other with limestone, and pushing each other hard. The nineteen women in Aifric's head could switch positions in the blink of an eye, changing affinities just as fast. She could keep up with Connor as long as he tapped only one set of affinities at a time, but when he started mixing in more, he quickly overwhelmed her.

After clobbering her with a wagonload of mud that he wielded with combined earth and water, she said, "You know, Connor, I could offer more of a challenge if all of us could work together better."

He nodded, draining the mud away from her, leaving her clothes clean and dry. "I wish you could."

Her expression turned eager and she stepped closer, her posture becoming more confident as Student Eighteen took over. "Why can't we?"

Connor hesitated, surprised by the question. She added quickly, "Mister Five figured out how to wield powers from two personalities at the same time."

"Except he was working with two mirrored people," Connor reminded her.

"He proved it's possible. You've helped scores of people establish new affinities. We don't need that. We just need to figure out how to connect ourselves. There has to be a way."

Connor wasn't convinced, but he wasn't about to deny her. The thought of succeeding in such an ambitious goal sent chills creeping down his spine. Aifric unleashed like that would become as powerful as he was. He grinned as he considered the idea. Aifric, Blood of the Tallan by committee.

So he said, "It can't hurt to try."

Actually, it could. He knew Aifric and all of her mind-sisters better than anyone. He understood the delicate construct in her mind that allowed them all to share that same brain. Messing with it could hurt her a lot, but with so much riding on the fate of the upcoming battle, he didn't dare not dare to take the risk.

"Who do you want to start with?" he asked. He'd visited the common area in her mind where all the women could meet together. He'd seen the walled partitions that created the brainspace for each of them, but realized he'd never actually visited any of their affinityscapes.

"Start with me," Student Eighteen said. "I was the first and I have chert. That might help."

So he tapped obsidian, sandstone, and chert, then looked deep into her big brown eyes. They sucked him in, and his world disintegrated into swirling gray. It materialized a moment later into a stone-paved courtyard, surrounded by tall, grim stone buildings with no windows, all clustered in the shadow of a tall, rocky mountain peak. With a start, he recognized Jagdish Mountain.

Student Eighteen appeared beside him, dressed in soft black clothing that fit snugly, but wasn't constrictive. Her thick, brown hair was braided, and she wore four daggers on her belt. She looked around, eyes widening with recognition, and a little smile tugged at her lips.

"What is this place?" he asked, also turning. The view was similar on three sides, while the fourth ended abruptly in the usual fog-filled chasm with floating islands and bridges.

"The kill academy training courtyard," she said happily. "I trained here for hours every day for most of my life."

Good. That made it a very powerful anchor point for her affinities. No wonder they were so strong. Heavy rope bridges extended to both obsidian and pumice, with additional bridges to chert and

limestone, and then bridges from those on to serpentinite. A faint
tune emanated from that island. It had a martial beat, with lots of
drums and energetic horns. It fit Student Eighteen perfectly.

"Do you feel the other ladies at all?" he asked.

She shook her head. "Nothing. Here we're in my brain space
and it's just me."

Connor concentrated, closing his eyes and questing out with
every sense, but he felt nothing either. They were firmly in Student
Eighteen's mind. Locked in that space, he couldn't tell that she
shared her mind with anyone else. He started to pace, trying to
solve the puzzle.

"Any thoughts?" Student Eighteen asked, looking calm but hopeful.

"Not yet. I wonder if we can sense your affinityscape from the
common area?"

She considered that but frowned. "I don't think so. I've never
been here like this before, but I don't think I've ever felt anything
like this from any of the others."

"The walls of your partition are constructed from your affinities.
Maybe we can find a connection point there," he said.

"It's worth a try. Come." She turned her back on the abyss and
led the way across the practice courtyard. A wooden door with
a brass plaque appeared in the far wall. Connor recognized it as
the door that led out to the common area in her mind. They exited
and sure enough, found themselves in front of the long wall of her
partitioned mind.

The other women who shared her head waited for them, with
white-garbed Aifric in the lead. Tresta and Hemma flanked her on
the left, both wearing battle leathers, while Mariora and Rith stood
on the right side, bouncing a little where they stood, as if they were
already tapping basalt and eager to rush off for another race.

Cacilia wore a stunning gown of black silk with a plunging
neckline and a long slit up one side that showed off her legs. Her
hair was piled into in a complex knot atop her head, and she wore
a delicate gold chain around her neck, sporting a huge emerald.
Eystri stood nearby, smiling wider than he'd ever seen, wearing
a colorful Althin dress, with many pockets.

"Do you like my emerald?" Cacilia asked, her voice as silky as
her dress.

"Don't tease him today," Isabell told her. She dressed in black
like Student Eighteen. "I got that emerald during that job in Crann.
Don't forget I'm loaning it to you."

"I display it better," Cacilia said with a wink at Connor.

He wisely said nothing. Cacilia could get him tongue-tied faster than anyone but Shona, and he didn't have time for that.

Eystri said, "I have interviewing all of the ladies, but none are having felt glimmerings from affinity mind spaces. I calculate less than a nine percent chance of finding successes studying the wall."

Student Eighteen said, "Don't discourage him. We're just getting started."

Eystri blushed but didn't retreat into the crowd like she would have in the past. It looked like victory suited her.

Tresta said, "Make it happen, Connor, and we can try bash fighting during a running battle."

That idea seemed to please everyone. Connor didn't want to let them down, but also didn't want to promise something he couldn't deliver. "I'll try."

He turned to face the long wall of their partitions. It extended into the distance on both sides, rising high into the air above them. The nearest section, with Student Eighteen's nameplate door, was constructed of blocks of stone from her several affinities, arranged in seemingly random order. He spotted additional doors breaking the wall at regular intervals along both sides, but as he focused on the wall, he still felt no connection to their affinities.

"If your affinityscape is locked behind your door, I'm thinking the only way to link your affinity abilities with any of the others would be to create doors between your partitions," Connor suggested, gesturing toward the point where Student Eighteen's wall met the next section, which belonged to Aifric.

Her wall was made of different stones, arranged in a much more regular pattern. Connor had experimented with those patterns while rebuilding Aifric's partition, and the result had strengthened Aifric's affinities dramatically and opened the door for some of the ladies to establish Agor affinities.

Student Eighteen frowned. "I once proposed making pass-through doors between our partitions with Mister Five, but he said never to do that. He feared that would weaken the integrity of our separate identities, which could lead to degradation of our individuality."

That could get ugly really fast. Connor shuddered to think of nineteen women sharing one head suddenly suffering mental breakdown. He wasn't sure the kingdom would survive the potential catastrophic problems that might result.

"Well, we need to establish a connection somehow," he said, feeling frustrated. So he tapped stilling and obsidian to create a super-think burst. His mind accelerated, and the usually fuzzy concepts surrounding chert and Aifric's unique mind clarified, but still no solution became clear.

As he mulled over the challenge, Connor willed himself into the air. Since they were just projections in her mind, physical laws only worked because he subconsciously decided they should, but they could be suspended when needed. Student Eighteen rose beside him, but the other ladies waited below in the common area.

"What are we looking for?" she asked.

"Just looking for now," he said as the great construct of her partitions spread below them. Up close, the wall looked flat, but as he rose, it became clear the partition wall actually formed a nineteen-sided shape.

An idea percolated to the top of Connor's thoughts and he gestured toward the shape. "That's just a mental projection of one way to interpret your partitions, right?"

Student Eighteen nodded. "It's more complex than it appears, but this representation seems to work well."

"We're looking at it as if all of your partitions are next to each other, but we don't have to limit ourselves to a horizontal relationship," he said slowly, working through the concepts, feeling like an answer was hovering just out of reach.

She nodded. "Sure. We can make it look any way we want."

Below them, the shape of her partitions changed, sides sliding up and down as it morphed into a nineteen-sided crystalline shape. It was beautiful, and Connor sensed the answer lay in there somewhere.

"I still feel we need some kind of link between your affinityscapes, some kind of exit from one of your minds to the next," he said.

"But we can't punch holes in the walls. There are no other exits."

"There is one!" Connor exclaimed as the idea gelled. "Come on."

He tipped forward into a dive, willing himself back to her doorway. Seconds later they stepped back into her affinityscape. It looked the same, with the same practice yard in the shadow of the same tall peak, with the same islands and bridges in the mist.

Over a deep abyss.

Connor led Student Eighteen onto the bridge to pumice, but stopped halfway across and pointed down into the roiling, dark fog that obscured the abyss. "There is an opening."

Student Eighteen looked over the edge apprehensively. "I don't sense anything down there."

Connor didn't either, and honestly the idea that had seemed so brilliant floating safely above the construct now seemed ridiculous. But he didn't have a better one, and in the mind, what one chose to believe could prove very powerful.

He placed a hand on her arm and said, "Concentrate. Imagine your partitions stacked on top of each other instead of side by side. Imagine your affinityscape positioned directly above the next one, and the one below that."

Comprehension dawned and she smiled. "Connor, I'm impressed. You'd make a great mind killer."

"As long as we don't kill our own minds," he said with a smile.

She concentrated for a moment, then nodded. "I've got it. We're all lined up vertically."

"Who is below yours?"

"Aifric." She spoke confidently, but then added, "At least, that's how I'm imagining it. I still don't feel her."

"She's there," he told her, forcing confidence into his own voice. She had to believe, or his plan would result in, well, something bad.

He glanced over the rail again, looking down into the softly billowing, dark mists and cast his own sensed down into them, but felt absolutely nothing. He'd wondered more than once what would happen if he accidentally plunged down into the abyss. Would he lose his mind, get lost forever in there, or break something important?

He was standing with Student Eighteen on her bridge in her mind while she was imagining the other partitions stacked below them. He trusted her completely and refused to believe something bad could happen to him inside of her head.

He wasn't stupid, though. A long, coiled rope appeared on the bridge beside them, one end already fastened securely to the rail.

Student Eighteen looked from the rope to Connor as he swiftly tied it around his waist, using the knots he'd used his entire life in Alasdair to secure stones on the lift. "You can't be serious."

"This is the way," he said with a wink. Then he jumped.

"Connor!" she cried, extending one hand toward him. That look of worry on her face did not fill him with confidence.

"Keep the image fixed," he shouted back up at her as he dropped into the mist like a stone, with the rope playing out behind him. The mists felt cool and slightly moist to his skin, but when he tried tapping his elemental affinities to call upon air to slow his descent, he felt nothing. He wasn't actually falling through air, but through a mental projection. It would be all right.

He repeated that to himself over and over, a litany against cold fear that made him clench his fists, and reminded himself that he wasn't really plunging eternally in a bottomless abyss. He was tethered to the rope, and he could eventually climb back up if the attempt didn't work.

Connor still couldn't help tapping granite, just in case he hit a solid partition wall. He would have to hit something eventually. Maybe. In the depths of a mind, maybe not.

Not helping.

Then abruptly, Connor felt something far beneath him. Somehow through chert, he sensed Aifric. She was down there!

He started to smile. It was going to work.

The feeling of Aifric drew closer and closer as he plunged down, and he shouted back up to Student Eighteen, "Try slowing my fall."

"What?" Her voice echoed back down a moment later from a great distance. The mists seemed to distort it and make it hard to understand.

Connor struck bottom.

One moment he was free falling, and the next he crashed down onto soft ground that thankfully gave beneath him, flexing with the impact. It was dark, so he couldn't see much. He activated limestone, the light softly green. It turned the mists a sickly, unnerving color, but did help illuminate what he stood on.

It looked like the mists had congealed, like warm snow. He pressed against it, and although it gave under his touch, it didn't part. It had to be the partition between their minds. It felt thin, but wasn't broken.

Connor paced around, enjoying the springiness of the ground, pondering the best way to deal with the obstacle. Once through that thin barrier, he felt convinced he'd drop into Aifric's affinityscape, but he hesitated to simply punch a hole through it.

The rope shook against his waist, and Student Eighteen appeared above him, sliding down the rope, hands protected by thick leather gloves. She dropped onto the solid ground, looking intrigued. "I felt the rope go slack and heard you shout something, but couldn't make it out. What's this?"

"I think it's the partition with Aifric. I can sense her beneath us."

She dropped to one knee, placing a hand on the spongy ground, and grinned. "I feel her too. The barrier is weak."

"But it's still there. I didn't want to just bash through."

"No, that would definitely cause damage, but what if we placed a trapdoor here?" she asked.

"How is that better than creating a door in the walls when you envisioned the partitions horizontally?" He liked the idea, but didn't want to hurt her.

She frowned, considering the question for a moment. "Those walls are solid. They protect the integrity of our individual mind spaces, but this . . . This feels thin, like we've found a point of mutual contact through our affinities. I don't feel danger here."

"Are you sure you want to risk it? We don't know it'll work."

"We don't know it won't, either." She stood and met his gaze. "I'm used to treading new ground in my mind. No one else has managed what I have, and I've learned to trust my instincts. As much as I fear breaking holes between the walls, I don't fear making a passage here."

"I hope you're right," he told her. If something went wrong, what would happen to her? What would happen to him?

"Help me." Student Eighteen crouched over the spongy ground, closed her eyes, and extended her hands. Connor knelt beside her and took her warm hands in his. He was already walking in her mind, but that contact strengthened their bond, and he sensed her focus without the need for words.

She was envisioning a trapdoor over a vertical shaft with a ladder leading down through the mist partition. Connor added his own will to the effort, just as he had when rebuilding Aifric's partition.

The floor beneath them transformed, changing from translucent, solidified mist into amber light. He recognized it then as part of the partition between their minds, fashioned of willpower, chert, and their combined power stones, all woven together into a protective barrier.

Connor smiled. He loved discovering new things, and he sensed this was a special moment, a vision that perhaps no one else had ever seen.

With that interwoven barrier now visible, he saw how to pull aside the pattern and insert a new one, formed out of those same elements, but self-contained. It created a hole, but also sealed it and ensured the ongoing integrity of the barrier.

A trapdoor made out of pure gold formed beneath their feet with a handle shaped like an upraised hand, open in greeting. Connor felt the pattern seal into place. He stood, filled with a sense of wonder.

"Amazing," Student Eighteen breathed as she shuffled to the side and grasped the upraised hand handle and pulled. The trapdoor swung up silently on golden hinges, revealing a nineteen-sided shaft plunging down through the ground. A bright silver ladder led down, and the entire shaft glowed softly with a comforting, white light.

"Ladies first," Connor said, giving her an elaborate bow, like the ones Kilian sometimes used.

Grinning with eager anticipation, she scrambled down the ladder. Connor followed, letting the trapdoor close behind him. Every nineteen rungs, the wall was marked with a bar of gold. After nineteen of those bars, the shaft ended in another trapdoor. Student Eighteen pulled it open and yelped as she plunged through, disappearing into billowing, dark mist.

"This had better work," Connor said, releasing the ladder and dropping down through the trapdoor.

Again he fell through mists. This time he wasn't tethered to a rope, but he didn't feel afraid. He sensed Aifric's gentle, caring presence all around. They'd entered her partition, and Aifric would never allow harm to befall either of them.

A moment later, he erupted from the mists and was shocked to see Aifric's affinityscape spread around him.

It was upside down.

Or he was. The world spun as he somersaulted and somehow landed upright in the middle of Aifric's bridge to granite.

Student Eighteen had already landed. Aifric was standing on the bridge, and the two women were laughing and jumping up and down on the bridge in such excitement the bridge started rocking wildly.

It worked!

Connor swept both girls off their feet in a great bear hug. Of course he then stumbled and almost pitched them all right over the side. It sort of wrecked the moment, but they didn't seem to care.

Aifric led them back to her affinityscape mainland, which looked like the healing wing of the Carraig. Connor smiled as he scanned the rows of perfectly made beds marching down either side under the tall windows, ready for patients. He'd visited Aifric many times there, and memories of her care after getting pummeled by Catriona or beat up by Jok filled him with a sense of nostalgia.

If only those were still his only problems. At the time, they had felt larger than life, but compared to fighting the dread queen and leading tens of thousands of people into battle, they seemed so tiny. Now the Carraig was gone, blasted and buried, and all of their lives would soon be decided by deadly conflict. He was glad Aifric and all of her mind-sisters would be fighting by his side.

Aifric hugged him again, her smile wider than ever. "You did it! I feel the connection with Student Eighteen."

"We did it together," he said.

Student Eighteen added, "I feel it too. I sense no negative consequences from forming that link between us."

"What are we waiting for?" Aifric laughed, grabbing Connor's hand and yanking him toward the bridge. "Let's go link to Isabell. She's next."

Riding that wave of euphoria from their initial success, Connor joined her on the bridge. Together he and Aifric dove over the rail.

Now that he knew what to do, it seemed to take only moments for Connor to complete the process of linking all of those partitions, allowing the ladies to move between each other's affinityscapes.

When they finished, they all met in the common area, which once again transformed into a verdant field, surrounded by trees, with long banquet tables running down the middle. As the ladies all celebrated, Connor made a point of consuming ridiculous amounts of food. In that mental space, he didn't actually have a stomach, so he couldn't get full.

He finally awakened and found himself lying on his back in the pasture, blinking up at full night. At least a couple hours had passed, and he felt exhausted. Sitting up with a groan, he tapped a little sandstone to refresh himself. The night sky was clear, the air cool, with a faint scent of the nearby river.

Aifric jumped to her feet, spread her arms wide, and called forth a globe of water around her left hand. At the same time, crimson flames erupted around her right.

"Yes!" she exulted, laughing again.

Connor rose to his feet. He longed to go find Verena, but couldn't help saying, "How about we test the limits of what you can do?

CHAPTER THIRTY-ONE
What Could Go Wrong with a Very Complicated Plan?

Early the next morning, just as Connor was sitting down to breakfast, Hamish dropped into the chair across from him. Dressed in his battle suit and chewing slowly on a jelly-filed pastry, it was obvious Hamish had already finished at least one meal.

"Take it to go," Hamish said, gesturing over his shoulder. "Just got word from Verena. The entire command team is meeting in the big conference room. Final planning before we roll out."

Connor took the tray and wolfed down his food while they walked. He wasn't surprised. In the last report he'd heard, it sounded like the queen's forces were making steady progress upriver, as expected. He felt a thrill of nervous excitement.

It was time to launch their assault.

The large conference room was located on the ground floor near the rear of the palace. It was a long room with a twenty-foot ceiling. The walls were clad in dark wood, with a few high, stained-glass windows allowing multi-colored light to stream into the room. The rest of the walls were covered with cloth banners and portraits of previous rulers of Shona's house. A huge table occupied the center of the room, with forty chairs arranged in formation around it.

Most of the team was already gathered, with more arriving behind Connor and Hamish. Verena and Jean were already there, and they had saved seats. Connor took his place beside his sweetheart, and she promptly stole one of his last sweetbreads. He stole a kiss in return, and it was well worth the exchange.

The rest of their core team assembled, including Captain Ilse and Anton. As usual, Ivor, Shona, and Rory sat at the head of the table, and Rory called the meeting to order. "As you likely know, we've arrived at the day we've worked so hard to prepare for. Today we give the order to move out, unless our intelligence has changed."

He glanced at Wolfram and Ilse. The two had been managing the intelligence-gathering efforts as well as the careful misdirection initiative against Craigroy. Ilse said, "Your intelligence is accurate, General. We believe we've succeeded in convincing the enemy that our morale is low and that we're terrified by reports of the advancing army."

Ivor said, "Thank you. Our mission is three-fold, and we must succeed in all three components to find victory. First is the vital need to separate the queen from her forces. Where do we stand there?"

Wolfram said, "We've carefully suggested through the captured speakstone that we are desperately hunting for ways to avoid open conflict, and that we've decided to send Kilian south around their forces to target the convergence point controlling soapstone."

"Brilliant deception," Verena whispered.

It was, but Connor still shivered at the thought of destroying more affinities.

Kilian said, "I'll leave once the main forces roll out. I plan to circle wide to the east, past Connor's new mountain, before I let my shields slip enough for her to sense my presence. Should confirm the report and draw her after me."

"What are we calling Connor's mountain, anyway?" Hamish asked.

"We haven't given it an official name yet," Shona said.

"I just think of it as Verena's Trophy," Connor said. That earned him one of Verena's special smiles and a kiss on the cheek.

"That may not be the final name," Shona said with a carefully neutral expression.

"We'll worry about that later," Kilian said. "Once I draw my mother out, we can simultaneously launch parts two and three of our plan."

"Part two is us," Connor said, gripping Verena's hand in his, then looking to Evander.

The big man said, "To hunt the great shark, one must first catch the irresistible meal."

"Very well said," Connor told him, happy the big man was making an effort to speak a little more plainly. "Once the queen is committed after Kilian, Evander and I will hit the convergence point where Sucker Punch is concealed and rouse the elfonnel sleeping there."

Looking grave, Verena said, "I'll station myself nearby to keep watch, just in case."

"Once we destroy it, that should break fleshcrafting," Connor added.

"No doubt my mother will feel the elfonnel rise," Kilian warned. "You'll have to act fast to finish it off. My mother can control elfonnel, so you may be able to do the same."

"Really?" Connor asked. He loved that idea and imagined himself riding the great slumbering pedra elfonnel. If only they had time to try it.

"Most likely," Kilian confirmed. "Especially when it first rises. It'll be disoriented and unfocused for a moment. That's the best time to strike."

"We will destroy it," Evander stated simply, and Connor felt optimistic. If he really could exert control over it, he couldn't see how they wouldn't succeed. Evander was one of the best elfonnel slayers in the world.

"Remember, my mother will still have access to fleshcrafting for a time until she exhausts the power already imbued within her sandstone," Kilian warned.

"We'll make her use it," Connor promised. Hopefully they'd hurt her more than she hurt them, or he'd run out first.

"I'll return to assist you as soon as she takes the bait," Kilian promised, and that helped ease some of Connor's nervousness.

"If things go badly, I'll make the play to trick her into tapping an activated sculpted stone," Verena added. That would be tricky to accomplish and would put her at terrible risk, but it was good to know they had a solid backup plan.

"May the Tallan smile upon your efforts," Wolfram said. The table was somber as everyone considered the difficult task that Connor and his tiny team faced. If they failed, not only would they likely die, but they'd leave the rest of their friends and the entire army helpless before the queen's wrath.

Rory rubbed his hands together and said eagerly, "That leaves part three, which is shaping up to be the best bash fight of all time."

Ivor said, "We might actually be able to distill the entire contest down to bash fighting if my proposal to coat the entire battlefield with a cloud of activated pumice could work."

Connor blinked and glanced at Verena, astonished by the bold idea. Why hadn't he thought of that? If they could unleash enough activated pumice, they could nullify all the Spitters and Sentries. "Is that possible?"

She shook her head sadly. "Unfortunately, it won't work. We don't have enough pumice to cover potentially four square miles thickly enough to catch everyone."

"We do plan to distribute individual portions of pumice through our forces," Ilse added.

That was a good idea. Coupled with the thousands of personal defense mechanicals already distributed, their forces would be entering the battlefield with better protections than any troops ever.

Rory shrugged, not looking surprised. "We'll still get to the bash fighting."

Shona said, "We need to defeat and demoralize their army. We must convince everyone that the revolution is unstoppable. Throw them on the defensive immediately."

"That'll give any Petralists and Guardians who want to defect hope that it's worth taking the risk," Rory agreed. Connor hoped reports that many pressed into the queen's army secretly longed to join the revolution proved true. Otherwise Rory and Anika and their forces would be badly outnumbered.

"All Battalions are operational and ready to go," Hamish reported. "And my second-skin aerial combat suit extension is finished, even though I'm missing a bunch of my replacement suit components that were supposed to ship down from New Schwinkendorf."

"Second skin?" Connor asked. He'd been so busy with his own training and duties that he hadn't even heard about that.

"I'll show it to you later," Hamish promised with a grin. Whatever it was, he looked very excited about it.

Jean frowned. "I remember ordering all of your supplies in the last shipment."

Hamish shrugged. "Not a big deal. I managed without them."

Jean gestured to a stack of papers on the table in front of her. "The rest of the deployment plans from the Battalions are finalized, and the final loading of combat mechanicals is already underway."

"Excellent," Shona said. "You must hold the line and win the bash fight, or we could lose our entire western flank."

"We'll hold," Rory promised, and Anika added, "No matter what."

Lady Briet spoke for the first time. "I've confirmed that placing our long-range attack weapons on the high ground will work well. We've already got engineers calculating trajectories. Assuming we'll reach Lossit ahead of the enemy and have sufficient time to prepare the field, I expect both the trebuchet and death tubes will be ready to rain precision strikes anywhere across the battlefield as needed."

"That will offer excellent support," Shona said.

"And we have extensive bombardment capabilities prepared from the Battalions," Jean added.

Ivor said, "Once we engage the tertiaries, you can deploy mechanicals from the Battalions and down the speedcaravan track. Arishat League forces can move in to support those efforts."

That was a risky move. Usually the non-Petralist forces hung back and served little more than a support role, but they needed the numbers. The last time Connor spoke with Lady Briet, she'd confirmed the Arishat forces were eager to engage in close combat, especially with the protective mechanicals that had been distributed to them.

Shona said, "I will deploy with the Striders to engage enemy fast movers, block reinforcements, and coordinate communication if our speakstone lines are disrupted."

Connor hoped she'd been practicing her running battles. Shona possessed a nimble mind and knew the theory of running battles, but was she ready to plunge into the most intricate fast-running battle perhaps ever fought? Losing Shona would severely hurt morale.

Student Eighteen said, "I'll be concealed beneath the town with my brothers and sisters, and with the acid pool Connor will prepare."

Verena said, "I've got a team completing the deployment mechanicals for you."

"Excellent," she said.

Kilian, who sat beside her, said, "Connor, Evander, and I will prepare a horde of summoned creatures to assist. I have no doubt the army will have summoned forces of their own, including an aerial component."

"We'll be ready for the flyers," Hamish promised. Connor knew they'd been practicing aerial fighting maneuvers. He couldn't imagine the queen could send nearly as many as the original swarm, but defeating her summoned creatures would be vital.

"You'll have to," Kilian said simply. "I plan to leave the summoned creatures in your control, Aifric. You'll be best positioned to manage them."

She looked immensely pleased by the huge responsibility. Connor was glad she'd have the summoned creatures to back her up. Her mission to take on the enemy central command was as dangerous as his own. Reports suggested the queen's army included at least twenty Dawnus, probably with low-grade sculpted stones to augment their power. That group alone could challenge the bulk of the army.

Aifric and her tiny squad of Mhortair assassins would strike at that deadly group, plus the two ascended generals. Anyone else making such an attempt would almost surely die, but if anyone could pull it off, it was the Mhortair. Plus, Aifric was now Blood of the Tallan by committee. Only the core leadership team knew about that. It was a trump card that might prove decisive.

Anton spoke for the first time, speaking slowly to ensure his words were plain. "That leaves the elemental battle to us."

Ivor nodded, and Ilse looked grim. Connor knew they had trained their forces hard, but they would be facing overwhelming numbers. Ivor and Anton would lead the tertiary Petralists in a desperate fight. Ilse and the Crushers, augmented by volunteers from every nation, would target enemy tertiaries with extreme prejudice. If they could kill or disable enough of them, they might turn the tide before Ivor and Anton and their outnumbered forces were swept under.

It was a bold, complex plan that could work, but only if every one of them succeeded. Any failures could create negative momentum that could easily ripple back over the others and threaten to derail the entire battle. They did have contingencies to retreat back to Merkland to make another stand, but Connor feared if retreat proved necessary that many thousands of their troops would not survive the long journey back upriver.

The meeting broke up a short time later, and everyone scattered to their respective forces to give the orders to move out. Connor took Verena to the window and stepped out, calling upon air to lift them above the palace.

Verena held his hand in a calm grip as they rose a thousand feet over the city. "I usually prefer to be the one piloting, but this is nice." She snuggled under his arm as they watched the city swarm with soldiers rushing to assembly points and preparing to move out.

The Albatross rose into the sky, dipped its wings in farewell, and accelerated north toward Badurach Pass to lead the vast flying armada that would soon take to the skies.

"This is it," Connor said, savoring the feel of Verena beside him.

She nodded, but didn't speak for a moment. Finally she said, "Whatever happens, we see this through to the end together."

Verena turned to him and Connor kissed her. They held each other for a long moment and he tried to simply enjoy her presence, but couldn't help thinking this might be the last quiet time they'd ever get.

Once they joined in battle, either of them might die. What of their friends? He thought of Tomas and Cameron and their abrupt death. How many more of his friends might not survive the coming battle?

He silently swore to do whatever it took to ensure the queen never threatened anyone he loved ever again.

Whatever it took.

CHAPTER THIRTY-TWO
Traps within Traps

Connor touched down on the barren, remote plateau at the convergence point associated with sandstone. The area looked the same as the last time he'd visited, with no indication whatsoever of the sylfaen plunging into the ground, or the super-mechanical concealed in the ground nearby.

"Everything looks good. Is Sucker Punch still ready to go?" Connor asked, speaking directly to Verena's speakstone.

"Ready for activation when we need it."

Her calm tone helped him control his nerves. They were really going to do this. He glanced at Evander, who was settling to the ground beside him. If they could pull this off, it could change the course of the war.

Connor cast his affinity senses across the area and even up into the sky and was relieved when he initially felt nothing. Evander himself had concealed the sculpted sandstone and the huge sandstone blocks that made up the Sucker Punch. Verena had even thought to bury some quickened pumice around each of those buried stones. Not even the queen would find them.

Verena was also extremely difficult to locate, even though he knew the position where she had taken up her overwatch hover. Ten thousand feet above where he stood and nearly a mile to the east, her Swift was invisible to the eye and to his air senses.

Not only was the camouflaged paint extremely effective, but she had improved the mechanical that used sightstones to project views of the empty air above her onto the bottom of her craft, making her virtually invisible. She had also already activated pumice to help shield her from elemental senses.

Connor wore his custom battle armor, with the symbols for water and fire emblazoned on the shifting chest plates. He hoped the elementals appreciated the gesture. Evander wore a tan linen shirt under a huge green vest and his enormous leather duster that extended down to midcalf. That coat could nearly conceal the entire Swift, and Connor would look laughably small in it, even when max-tapping granite.

"Are you ready for this?" Connor asked him.

"Stones roll unopposed down the mountain, and the hawk takes flight at the first rays of dawn," he said simply.

"I'll take that as a yes," Connor said with a grin.

He loved practicing Sentry speak but wondered if he would ever truly master it. Evander definitely preferred the convoluted, cryptic declarations, but Connor was a simpler person. Sometimes a simple yes or no could not be beat.

Connor focused on the little summoned squirrel that had been quietly occupying a corner of his mind. The area around him dimmed as his senses locked onto the distant squirrel. Sights, sounds, and most of all smells, rushed in like an avalanche.

The squirrel rested in a tiny sack slung over Kilian's shoulder as Kilian sped over wilderness landscape at an easy, fracked sprint that he could maintain all day. The area looked rough, with patches of wild grasses, shrubs and trees interspersed with rocky, undulating hills. The air was warm and full of the scents of growing things, but no scents of man besides Kilian himself.

"Where are you?" Connor spoke through the squirrel's mouth. He still wasn't sure how he could do that, since squirrels couldn't exactly make human sounds, but it worked, so he didn't worry about it.

Kilian slowed to a walk and turned, showing Connor the view behind him. Verena's Trophy dominated the distant skyline, ringed by the lower peaks Connor had fashioned.

"I'm thirty miles southeast of the volcano. Preparing to tickle my mother's senses and draw her out."

"Perfect timing," Connor said. "We're in position and ready to raise the elfonnel."

"Wait. What's that?" Kilian asked, his voice suddenly tense. His scent changed, and Connor could tell he was prepared to fight.

Not good. He hadn't even begun to draw his mother out yet. He was supposed to be traveling through part of Obrion with only small settlements, and definitely nothing significant enough to make the great Kilian nervous.

The battlefield at Lossit was ready, with the bulk of their forces concealed north of the town, or west, atop the high cliffs. The queen's army would move into range within the hour. The timeline was too tight for any unexpected problems.

"What?" Connor asked.

"Hush," Kilian said softly, looking up in to the sky. As he turned, Connor spotted something diving out of the sky. His squirrel instincts screamed at him to duck and hide, but he held still. Kilian wouldn't worry about a pedra.

Only, it wasn't a natural pedra. Within seconds, he recognized it as summoned. The monster's skin shone white against the bright morning sunlight, reminding him of the great stone pedra that Kilian and Ilse had summoned to delay Rory's company before their first clash near Alasdair.

The pedra was way too small. It was barely the size of a terrier, perfectly shaped in miniature. Connor wondered who had conjured it. Evander was with him and knew about the squirrel they were using for communication. Had Ilse or Anton or someone else spotted a problem? With the queen so close, they couldn't risk trying a long-distance speakstone.

His worry grew as the little creature flared its wings to hover in the air in front of Kilian. It spoke, and the voice was not Ilse's.

It was the queen's.

"So, you thought you could lure me away again, did you, boy?" the pedra said in an angry tone.

Connor barely kept the squirrel from squeaking in terror and wetting itself, but Kilian calmly replied. "I didn't think old crones could learn new tricks."

The pedra cackled. "Always clever with your wit, but dense with your mind."

"I'm finally learning the secrets you kept from me all these years. If you'd confided in me, we might have avoided so much tragedy, mother." He sounded sad.

"Perhaps," she said, surprising Connor by the soft tone. Then her voice sharpened again. "But you never demonstrated that I could trust you with the weighty matters of the kingdom."

"No. You decided it made more sense to simply murder my sister, order the great purge, and threaten to execute Tallan too," he shot back.

"Kirstin threatened everything. Surely you can see that now."

"She didn't know the danger. If you hadn't lost your mind, you could have explained the risks."

"She would have fallen to the temptation."

Kilian shook his head slowly, old sorrow etched on his features. "I choose to trust. You choose to kill."

"I choose to maintain order!" she shrieked, her voice shaking the air like thunder.

"Did you come here to shout at me?" Kilian asked, unperturbed.

Her tantrum passed a second later and her voice turned cold and hard. "No, my errant son. I know your deceit. I never trusted Craigroy's information fully, and once he was revealed as unworthy, I gathered my own intelligence."

Connor pulled back from the squirrel enough to wave mightily to Evander. He must have looked as terrified as he felt, because Evander rushed over, sliding smoothly across the hard-packed soil. "The queen sent a summoned pedra to Kilian. She's not fooled!"

Evander's face blanched, but Connor let his attention get swept back into the squirrel.

The queen was gloating. "You let too many weak-minded fools into your armies, Kilian. I know about the attack planned in Lossit. My armies are already launching their assault."

The news rocked Kilian, and his mother added, "And you're out of position. Ha! Today you will witness the deaths of all those fools who chose to follow you. Only then will I rend out your own pitiful life. Good-bye, my son."

The pedra dove at Kilian, double jaws gaping wide, sharp talons extended.

With a shout of rage, Kilian lunged to meet it with empty hands. Connor tried to withdraw his senses, but reacted a second too slow.

Kilian's hands exploded, destroying the pedra in a flash of muddy granite. The flash of sight and sound overloaded Connor's squirrel senses, radiating the effect back to him. He cried out and collapsed, clutching his head.

Evander caught him with one huge hand and held him off the ground. "What is happening?"

"She knows! Her army is attacking early."

Far to the east, Kilian pulled the squirrel out of the bag and shouted, "Connor, hurry! She's probably already coming. I'll come as fast as I can, but warn the others and destroy that elfonnel!"

CHAPTER THIRTY-THREE
And You Thought You Got Grumpy when Someone Wakes You Up Early

Connor's mind was whirling, and a rush of fear made him suddenly feel frozen with icy dread. They had thought they were so clever, but the queen had seen through the deception.

"Verena! The queen knows. You have to warn everyone. They're about to be attacked."

"Tallan's mercy," she breathed.

"We must hurry," Evander said, gesturing toward the empty ground nearby. "The timetable is accelerated, but the mission remains."

He was right. If they could destroy that elfonnel, they could still defeat her. She hadn't said anything about intercepting them. Maybe the minds she'd siphoned didn't know. Kilian had been right to keep the full battle plan concealed from all but their inner circle.

Connor tapped his elemental affinities. The conduits opened readily, but he was surprised to hear Fire's voice in his mind. "Do not destroy the very filters to your power, boy. You risk destabilizing your bridges and undoing everything you've worked so hard for."

He didn't have time to argue, and hoped the message wasn't the precursor to more interference. If only he could figure out how to return to close association with the elementals, but just couldn't trust them.

Evander took the lead, walking slowly forward, eyes half closed and one hand held out over the earth, looking like he was tuning himself to the massive amounts of power flowing around them within the convergence point.

Connor had planned to summon another creature with strum and magnis and limestone to help him sense the convergence point better, but didn't dare take the time. Every second counted now, so he tapped water and fire, reaching for strum and magnis. His skin prickled with the feel of invisible energy coursing past, and he grinned. Maybe that would be enough. He cast his affinity senses into the earth and sensed something vast deep beneath them. The elfonnel.

"Do you know how to raise it?" Connor asked.

Evander nodded and thankfully spoke in clear Obrioner. "Twice I have awakened one."

"How?" Connor asked eagerly.

"Carefully," Evander said with a smile.

"Great. That makes it sound so much easier," Connor said, envisioning himself sneaking up on the sleeping monster with a giant eoin feather and tickling its horrible snout, or poking it in the ribs with a huge stick.

"I can awaken it. Hopefully you can exert influence over it and make our task easier."

That would be amazing. Connor again wished they had more time. If he really could gain control over the elfonnel, he'd love to study it, learn more about it. He'd walked as an elfonnel but still felt like there was so much no one had ever learned about them. Maybe he could figure out how to reconcile with the elementals if he better understood their creations.

If only they didn't need to destroy fleshcrafting. He could help so many people with it, but he didn't see any alternative.

He tapped earth, and through that connection felt Evander's will plunging down into the ground like a giant hammer stroke. Just above the slumbering elfonnel, his will fractured, vibrating the earth like the biggest-ever gong. Evander intoned in a voice as deep as a mountain valley, "Arise, servant of the earth."

That was loud, louder than even his huge throat should have been able to create, as if the sounds were being generated by the ground around them. The sounds glowed bright in Connor's serpentinite eyes as it penetrated the earth all the way down to the sleeping monster. Those sounds seemed to wrap it in a blanket of vibrating energy.

The elfonnel stirred and came awake.

Despite his deep connection with earth Connor still felt a shiver crawl down his spine at the vast power encompassed by the huge monster. It might possess but a fraction of Earth's full power, but that tiny fraction was still enough to level cities or bury entire armies underground.

Evander glanced at Connor and said, "Thus commences our challenge."

The elfonnel surged upward, its huge wings spreading and flapping as if the dense earth and stone through which it traveled was nothing but mist. It rose like a mighty whirlwind up through the earth, and the ground began trembling violently.

Connor and Evander stood in the center of the shaking, on a narrow platform of absolute calm as the ground around them buckled and geysered. Connor frowned as he sensed something, back down in the spot where the elfonnel had arisen.

"Hey, it left the sandstone sculpted stone behind in the convergence point," he said.

"That is unusual, but serves our purposes today," Evander said, not looking worried.

Hopefully it didn't mean the elfonnel somehow sensed it was in for a fight. They didn't want to destroy the sandstone affinity, so leaving the ancient sculpted stone deep underground did simplify things.

"What's happening? Are you okay?" Verena called, her voice nervous. "I warned the others."

"Good. We're fine. Just raising the elfonnel," Connor said, trying to sound nonchalant, although his heart was racing. Even with the mighty Evander standing by him, it was hard to remain in position, knowing an elfonnel was coming right at them.

The elfonnel breached the surface in a geyser of earth that sprayed for a hundred yards in every direction. Evander deflected the blast away from them, but the scent of deep places wafted over them, mingled with a stronger, muskier scent of the elfonnel. The great elemental beast soared fifty feet into the air, its magnificent form towering over them. Even though he'd been an elfonnel recently, Connor still gaped, awed by the sight. Its presence was like a bonfire in his earth senses.

He took an involuntary step back, drawing deep from earth, suddenly convinced the idea of standing right there had been really stupid.

Then he sensed it. A connection snapped into place between him and the creature through his link with earth. The connection was like sticking his face into a whirlwind of dirt, but beneath the wild rush of energy, he sensed its core. It was confused and annoyed at being awakened after so long.

"Easy," Connor told it, raising one hand in a calming gesture, pushing the thought out to the monster. "Listen to me."

It growled, its enormous double jaws opening. It could swallow them both in one bite if it wanted to, but Connor's connection to its mind strengthened and his thoughts had an effect. Its anger cooled, and the majestic creature dropped to the ground in front of him, settling on its haunches and furling its enormous wings.

That was so amazing! He was really influencing it.

Its thoughts echoed back to his mind. "Who are you to raise me from my appointed task? I know you not."

Maybe he didn't have as much control over it as he hoped. He hadn't expected to actually talk with it. Was he speaking with the Petralist who had been sacrificed to raise it? Kilian had never suggested that was possible. How would the person react if he revealed that he was the queen's enemy, and that he'd awakened it just to put it back to sleep permanently?

"Um, hi. I'm Connor, and I'm afraid I need you to stop filtering sylfaen for a while," he thought back to it.

"Be careful!" Verena said in a hushed, nervous tone in the Swift, but he still clearly heard her.

Beside him, Evander bowed to the creature, then raised a fist as if planning to simply crush the enormous skull with the world's biggest curse punch.

The elfonnel rotated its head to focus on Evander and Connor sent more calming thoughts as hard as he could. He hated that they needed to destroy the amazing monster, but they had no choice, and the quicker they could complete the onerous task, the better.

The pedra growled, its wings partially unfurling, its great double jaws opening, clearly not planning to listen. Evander didn't look worried, but took a step forward, body swelling with power and impending violence.

Then Connor felt a stunning blow to his mind. It pierced his mental defenses and struck deep, making his muscles convulse as he stiffened and sucked in a surprised breath.

Queen Dreokt.

Oh, no.

Her voice bellowed in his mind as if she were standing right beside him and shrieking with max-tapped Pathfinder fury. "How dare you? Tingwall, these are enemies. Destroy them!"

The elfonnel named Tingwall apparently retained some of his memories because he roared, the sound so vast Connor's ears couldn't process it. He was already reeling from the queen's initial mind blow, overwhelmed by dread.

She had arrived too early.

Evander shouted a battle cry and launched into the air toward the monster just as the great pedra elfonnel snapped its hideous double jaws down toward them.

Chapter Thirty-Four
Battle Plans Are Supposed to Last Longer than Three Seconds

Jean stood in the communication hub at the top floor of the three-story command structure on Battalion One, the flagship of the sixteen-ship fleet, hovering two thousand feet in the air. Long windows of Sehrazad steel glass afforded a panoramic view in every direction. Banks of sightstones projected images onto the white-painted walls below the windows, constantly scrolling through hundreds of views. Those views afforded Jean and her command staff access to every aspect of the vast, international force assembled for the great battle.

She had feared she might feel intimidated by the role of commanding the communications hub and coordinating the many-pronged attack. As the moment approached, she felt only concern for her friends who would be leading many aspects of the fight against the far superior force. She maintained a low obsidian tap rate to quicken her mind and stay sharp.

"Is everyone in position?" she asked Gisela, who stood beside her as always, acting as her chief coordinator of flight operations. Admiral Forfar and his command staff filled most of the rest of the command room. The admiral had agreed to Jean's appointment as overall aerial commander after Verena confirmed he would continue to command all Battalions, Thunder Towers, and battle mechanicals from that point forward.

Gisela said, "All units in position and ready."

She gestured toward the bank of viewscreens, which began scrolling through aerial views of their various forces. Hamish had deployed the scores of tiny, flying mechanicals that made up the Hive. They offered unparalleled access to the complex battlefield.

The first views showed the decks of all of the giant Battalions, where companies of Boulders and Striders assembled in formation behind companies of tertiary Petralists. It still amazed Jean that Connor had helped so many develop new affinities. Although most lacked more than a few days of training, they made up for that lack in sheer determination. Hopefully the multi-pronged attack plan would knock the queen's army onto the defensive before too many of those inexperienced Petralists got killed.

The ground troops massed closer to the command buildings on each Battalion, leaving the far third of the transport decks free for battle mechanicals. She glanced out the windows at Battalion One's deck and the dozen huge, Thunder Towers, with their multiple turrets and scores of deadly mechanicals on board. They were assembled in tight ranks near the far edge. Bits of smoke wafted up from exhaust ports as the crews spun up the engines and prepared for battle.

Alone, the Thunder Towers were an awe-inspiring sight, but they made up only a fraction of the Builder-inspired firepower the Battalions were prepared to unleash over the enemy. Dozens of smaller, single-man mechanicals waited behind the Thunder Towers. Many rolled on two wheels or simply hovered with quartzite thrusters. Armored wings rose up to help shield their operators in some cases, while others utilized the advanced quartzite shielding techniques developed by Hamish and the Builder researchers for the rapid-fire siege weapons.

She actually spotted a few of those rapid-fire mechanicals, altered for mobile deployment. Each was capable of firing two hundred rounds of assorted ammunition, from high explosives to pumice dust clouds to sunburst distractions to deadly hornets. Other mechanicals looked like supersized speedslings with huge drums of deadly hornets.

There were others too, but Jean had not participated as much in the weapon development phases of their research and didn't know what they all did. Render Flight and Mender Flight companies were positioned in the transition space between the foot soldiers and the mechanicals, awaiting the orders to deploy healers and semi-autonomous summoned creatures to assist in pulling wounded from the battlefield. Defender Flight troops were already loading into their transports. Ilse and Anton and their strike team stood in formation with the troops on the deck, ready to deploy with the vanguard and take on the far superior enemy tertiaries.

Hamish swooped past, pausing to wave at her before accelerating toward the far end of the Battalion. On the roof above where she stood in the command building, dozens of small, personal flying craft from Admiral Forfar's flights were docked in special racks, ready to deploy. Some of them began activating thrusters and easing out to take up escort positions around the Battalion.

Some of the viewscreens showed side angles of the other Battalions. In addition to the gigantic quartzite blocks that set the entire ship rumbling from their activated thrust power, the underside of every Battalion was covered with bomb bays and rapid-fire mechanical emplacements that could be triggered remotely by Builders stationed one floor below Jean.

She felt overwhelmed by the magnitude of the effort that had gone into preparing the incredible fighting platform, which was mirrored on all the other Battalions, and they were but one part of the overall battle strategy.

"What's the word from Rory?" she asked as she turned back to the still-scrolling viewscreens.

"Ready and waiting," Gisela reported.

They views shifted to high perspectives over Lossit and the high country above the cliffs to the west. The town looked peaceful, streets empty. Ilse's advanced team had evacuated the entire population to the north hours ago. The valley was beautiful, and Jean hated to think about the devastation they would leave behind from the pitched battle. Rich fields were already coated in the fragile green of young crops, and the many lakes sparkled in the sunlight. The eight majestic waterfalls lorded over the scene, their billowing mist softening the landscape and lending it a peaceful air that would soon be shattered.

General Rory and Anika stood near the top of the central waterfall, with their hundreds of Boulders and Rumblers arrayed along the rim. They stood in silent ranks, their calm belying their eagerness to leap into the bash fight.

Gisela pointed at one viewscreen. "Hold this one, please. As you can seeing, the long-range forces are in position too."

"Good," Jean said, but wished the deadly weapons wouldn't be needed. Twenty Althing trebuchet were arrayed behind the lakes atop the cliff, pointing at slightly different angles so all together they could rain deadly chemicals over the entire valley. Interspersed between them were the long, low Tabnit death tubes, muzzles angled upward for greater distances.

Behind every weapon rose squat, earthen bunkers, raised the day before to house their stores of deadly ammunition. During the fight against Harley in Althing, Connor's forces had learned the hard way to protect the ammunition. Anton had personally over-seen construction of the bunkers. They should be able to withstand all but the most powerful Petralist assault.

Admiral Forfar said, "General Wolfram just reported in. Regulars and Arishat forces are ready."

Gisela ordered some of the viewscreens changed, and Jean drew in an awed breath at the sight of fifty thousand regulars from all across the continent assembled in battle formation half a mile to the north of Lossit. A few Petralists and lots of Builder mechanicals were deployed with them to help protect them, along with two Thunder Towers set to roll along the speedcaravan track. Shona and a hundred Striders ranged along the flanks, ready to offer support and engage enemy Striders.

"It appears we are ready to deploy, as soon as we receive word from Verena," Jean said. She refused to consider the possibility that the queen hadn't been fooled, but remained among her army. Attacking then would be suicidal. So she forced herself to project calm confidence and bury her sorrow that such a huge host was even necessary. How many people would die in the next hours because of plans that she had helped develop?

How many more would die if they did not fight now?

There was no easy answer. All she could do was trust in her belief that freedom was worth a heavy price.

Captain Leppin, direct commander of Battalion One, spoke from the opposite side of the room. "Our scout mechanicals have spotted the enemy forces closing on Lossit." He was a tall, serious man with a strong quartzite tertiary that made him comfortable with air.

Several of the viewscreens shifted to new feeds from tiny flying mechanicals positioned above the southern end of Lossit valley, about a mile south of the town. The army had rounded the last bend and entered the valley. The scouts flew high, using a combination of propellers and quartzite to make them extremely quiet. They were painted mottled sky blue and white to blend in with the cloudy sky, and carried a tiny piece of pumice. Even the enemy Pathfinders should have trouble noticing them.

The views showed a huge force marching upriver. Within moments, they approached to within half a mile of the town. Strangely, companies began spreading into the open lands to the west of the road far more than Jean had expected.

Admiral Forfar leaned closer, frowning. "I didn't expect the vanguard to be comprised of regulars."

"Or that they would deploy so widely," another officer commented.

Jean focused on the vanguard. Company after company of foot soldiers, archers, and mounted knights in the lead were marching rapidly north toward the town. That was an unusual setup. She spotted dozens of Sentry towers scattered among the forces, flowing north overland, and scores of Spitters skating upriver. Along the western edges, hundreds of Boulders marched in step, moving west of the road. The soft, turned earth would slow their march. It was as if . . .

"Are they deploying? Could they have spotted our forces?" the admiral asked, triggering a heated debate among his officers.

"Does this impact our plans for the initial bombardment?" Jean asked.

As soon as Verena confirmed that the queen had been distracted by Kilian and that Connor and Evander were raising the elfonnel at the nearby convergence point, they would commence the attack. She expected the call any minute. The first part of the plan called for the Battalions to swoop over Lossit valley and drop their camouflaging viewscreen projections that made them look like low-floating clouds from below. They would capitalize on the shock of their sudden appearance by commencing a full bombardment assault with every gun along the undersides of their decks. The resulting avalanche of destruction would hopefully demoralize the enemy and sow chaos among them long enough for the multi-pronged assault elements to deploy.

All of that had been planned with the assumption that the enemy would lead with Boulders. Killing sixty thousand regulars would not accomplish much in the grand scheme of things, but the idea sickened Jean.

As Admiral Forfar began to respond, one of the technicians monitoring the bank of speakstones shouted, "I have an urgent message from Lady Verena!"

He didn't wait to be ordered but linked the speakstone to a larger stone mounted high on the wall. Verena's voice spoke loudly from it, sounding alarmed. "The queen knows! Kilian didn't trick her. Her army is going to attack!"

"When? Where?" Admiral Forfar shouted.

Jean added, "Is she with them?"

"I don't know. I . . ." Verena's voice cut off for a second, then she shouted, "Oh, no! She's here. She's attacking Connor and Evander. The elfonnel is attacking them too."

Jean felt cold dread grip her heart. She glanced at Gisela, whose face drained of color.

Captain Leppin pointed at one of the viewscreens and cried, "Look!"

Down in the valley, the regulars suddenly broke into a charge. Led by companies of mounted knights, they pounded past the town, heading north. At the same time, the companies of Boulders raised weapons and charged west toward the lakes at the base of the cliff.

"Fast movers!" another technician shouted, shifting another viewscreen to the fore. Jean gasped at the sight of a hundred Striders appearing far to the west, already on the high ground as they closed on Rory's Boulders.

"They're fools to engage so many Boulders," Admiral Forfar said with a frown.

"They're not going for the Boulders," Jean realized as she increased her obsidian tap rate. "Warn the Althin and Tabnit forces manning the siege weapons. They're about to be attacked."

The admiral cursed and began shouting commands. He turned to Jean and said, "We need to deploy now!"

"I—" Her response was cut off as the Battalion lurched to the left. That was the port side. For some reason, the Battalion forces insisted on treating the flying craft like seagoing vessels.

"Who ordered a course correction?" Jean demanded as she stumbled and caught herself. If Connor hadn't healed her leg, she definitely would have collapsed.

"It's the wind," Captain Leppin stated, pointing out the window. Jean hadn't heard the wind through the reinforced glass, but she could see soldiers suddenly crouching against the force of winds that tore at clothing and faces. Some of the mechanicals with broader profiles rocked under the gale, and a few lifted right off the deck and were thrown overboard.

The huge Battalion, which had seemed so powerful, pitched and yawed under the wind. Captain Leppin maintained remarkable calm as he reported, "This has to be the work of the queen. No one else could command such a gale."

"Get us stabilized!" General Forfar shouted. "We need to get into position."

"Working on it, sir," Captain Leppin replied, hurrying over to the soldiers manning the communications with his steering team.

Jean turned to Gisela, trying to remain calm, despite a flood of fear. The queen knew and had flipped the surprise against them. Jean was familiar with that kind of fear, though. It was the same fear that swept through her at the sight of a badly wounded patient, the fear of losing the fight for life before getting a chance to stave off looming death. She'd learned to push the fear aside and face it with calm determination.

"The commanders are relaying the situation to troop leaders. Contact Shona directly and see if she and her Striders can aid the Arishat siege teams. They're the most exposed right now."

Gisela nodded and lifted her own mini-hub. All of the core team were wearing one, with multiple speakstones arranged around a keystone, allowing them direct contact. It was good they had that backup communications channel because the communications operators were all frantically busy relaying orders from the officers. Jean tapped more obsidian, trying to calculate the best way to alter the plan. She forced herself to ignore her terror for Connor and Evander and Verena. She'd known they would face the queen alone. The timing might be wrong, but they were ready. And unfortunately, she couldn't do anything to help.

She could help the forces on the Battalions.

Hamish's voice spoke over their personal speakstone connection. "Jean! Jean, no one's answering on the main channel."

She raised her mini-hub and said, "I know. The queen is launching a surprise attack. We're trying to coordinate—"

"Forget that!" he interrupted. "Check out the western views. We've got an aerial swarm closing fast!"

Jean's blood ran cold and she shouted, "Someone get me the western views now!"

Three seconds later, the viewscreen appeared in front of her, and her worst fears were confirmed. The sky was dark with a swarm of summoned flying nightmares, barely minutes away, and closing fast.

"Deploy defensive measures and get our flights in the air!" she cried.

"They'll have trouble flying with this gale," Admiral Forfar said, looking grim.

"Then activate shielding and every available defensive mechanical, and warn the troops exposed down on the decks that we've got incoming."

Jean had known every plan, no matter how good, always required modification after battles commenced, but the battle hadn't even started yet and their plan was in tatters.

If they didn't recover fast, they could lose the fight before it really got started.

Chapter Thirty-Five
Splitting Headaches

Connor reacted out of pure instinct, throwing himself out of the way of the elfonnel's lunging attack and calling upon his elemental affinities. Most of them responded instantly, but slate felt weak, probably because of his proximity to both the queen, Evander, and the monster.

Evander didn't run. As the monster snapped at him with jaws big enough to consume a house, outer jaws gaping wide like wings to encircle him, Evander swung his arms, as if wielding a club. A tightly spinning whirlwind appeared between his hands, growing to thirty feet, and he smashed it into the elfonnel's eyes.

Usually Connor didn't think of air as a combat weapon, despite the effectiveness of Verena's shielding. He'd never tried using it as a club.

He should have.

The blow snapped the elfonnel's huge head backward so hard, it flipped all the way around on its serpentine neck to stare up into the sky and pulled its torso upward after it. Evander slid right between its clawed feet, and as the monster rose, trying to catch itself from the mighty blow, he clubbed both of its rear legs at the knees. They buckled, knocking the monster to its backside. It roared and whipped around after him, looking unhurt but really mad.

Connor called on air too, using a strong gust to lift off the ground. He doubted he could fight that elfonnel with earth, and he needed distance. He also fashioned a barrier of fire and ice in front of the great beast as it spun to chase Evander. Connor drove those combined elements into that gaping maw, filling it and pouring the elements down its throat. Then he drained the heat away, solidifying the water to ice, which swelled enough to temporarily restrict the creature's flexibility.

It chomped the air, shattering the ice and looking undamaged by his first attack. A cloud of ice particles mixed with bits of flame, blasted around Evander, driven by the creature's breath. Connor got a whiff of that breath, and it smelled dangerous, like an empty pot left too long on the fire.

Connor rose higher, cursing the queen's terrible timing. They had only needed a few more seconds. He yearned to look toward Verena, to call out to her, but didn't dare do either. The queen might notice, and she'd swat Verena from the sky in an eyeblink once she realized she was nearby.

The elfonnel oriented on Connor but did not immediately attack. Evander slid away from it, rising onto a stout tower of earth. He cast one glance at Connor, his expression grim.

Connor managed to push the queen out of his mind. After her initial mental assault she had thankfully not pressed the advantage, but seemed willing to let the elfonnel finish him off for her. Now Connor scanned the skies and quickly saw her.

Queen Dreokt descended like a shooting star, glowing as bright as the sun, surrounded by a swirling latticework of combined elements. Surprisingly, she was dressed in battle leathers instead of one of her fancy gowns. Apparently not even she could completely ignore the draw of a set of cool battle leathers during a military campaign.

She landed on the back of the pedra elfonnel, standing regally upon its broad shoulders. Her voice boomed across the plateau. "Evander, you've long worked to destroy the peace of this kingdom, but how dare you attempt to subvert my precious ramverk?"

Evander actually bowed, the gesture strangely formal. His voice responded just as loudly. "Grandmother. I salute the honor of your memory from the days before your mind was broken by the elfonnel. The tortoise may explore the unknowable deep, but a woodpecker's brains shatter over years of abuse."

Connor grinned. That was great Sentry speak, although it was far less cryptic than most. He loved the image of the queen as a woodpecker, knocking her head against trees so long that her brains leaked out her tail feathers.

Queen Dreokt hissed, "Today you reap the consequences of your evil."

The elfonnel oriented on Evander, opened its huge double jaws wide, and bellowed, a sound so deep it seemed to seize Connor by the pit of his stomach and shake him like a rat.

So Connor tapped limestone and dropped a globe of absolute darkness over the queen and her monster. It might not actually harm her, but it delayed her for precious seconds as Evander retreated, his tower sliding away at an angle from the monster.

The great pedra elfonnel burst into view, rising up through the top of the globe of darkness, with the queen still standing astride its back. It was a magnificent sight, one that would make Verena's first strike easy.

She didn't disappoint. As soon as the pedra flapped up into view, a swarm of tiny flying mechanicals swept around the queen. Verena carried an extensive arsenal with her up in the Swift and as Connor expected, had launched the swarm as soon as the queen appeared. Each one carried a piece of activated pumice, and Connor did not even notice them approaching until they struck. Neither did Queen Dreokt.

She shrieked, her expression a look of abject terror as the cluster swarmed her. Some of them fired a few hornets out of tiny speed-slings, so small they probably only held a hundred of the deadly little projectiles. They could've done terrible damage to anyone else, but the hardened granite projectiles simply bounced off the queen.

About ten percent of them contained diorite and the explosions seemed to really annoy her. If they did any damage, Connor could not tell. Either the queen was already tapping granite to harden her skin, or she was simply fleshcrafting herself whole that fast.

Two other mechanicals swept in close and fired tiny catapults that each threw a fresh-baked sculpted scone at the queen's face. She shrieked again and batted them out of the air, then shook her hand in disgust.

More little hive mechanicals swept in and started dropping activated stones onto her head and shoulders, while two of them projected a sightstone image of Verena sitting at the controls of the Swift.

The queen gasped and Verena gave her a wicked smile. "From all the Builders, we send you these gifts, wishing you a long and painful death."

Queen Dreokt screamed in rage, and a mixture of combined elements erupted from her in every direction. The blast shattered all of the little mechanicals and the mighty shockwave pulverized all the dropped stones.

Verena's audacity was inspiring. She might not be convinced she knew how to hurt the queen, but she had prepared as many different mechanicals as possible to test every theory. Queen Dreokt had proven that she was terrified by something about Builders and her weakness could still be something random that they had not yet considered.

He threw himself at the distracted queen, accelerating through the air, but she turned to face him and snarled, "You belligerent, unworthy—"

Connor hit her with super sensory deprivation. He doubted he could hold her long, but he didn't need long.

It appeared to work. She stiffened, her eyes wide, one hand raising toward her forehead in slow motion. Connor got there first and punched her with every ounce of strength he could summon from max-tapped granite, coupled with all the force and momentum of his flight.

Plus diorite.

Punching her felt like striking the side of a mountain until he released a full measure of diorite through his fist.

The explosion blasted out his fist in a blinding blast of crimson and red that ripped through her hardened skin. The force of the blast rattled him, despite the protection of granite and blind coal. For a moment, billowing flames obscured the queen. The air smelled charred and broken, carrying the scent of burnt meat and singed hair. He had burned enough girls' hair to know that one really well, and he smiled at the flood of memories it triggered.

Then the queen reappeared, catapulting away, right off the great pedra, the entire front of her chest a gaping, blackened hole. It looked like he'd vaporized most of her guts, and her torso was charred, her ribs shattered. The pedra left her to deal with the problem and dove to attack Evander.

"Yes!" Connor exulted, trying to memorize that glorious sight so he could cherish it as long as he lived.

Might not be that long. She caught herself in the air and even as new skin and innards began growing to fill the grisly wound, she shot back toward him, moving way too fast. How could she react so quickly? Even she should at least take a moment to say, "Ow."

Connor tried to dodge, but that split second of hesitation cost him. The queen reached him in a flash and backhanded him across the chest. It felt like she struck him with the entire palace of Merkland. The blow blasted the breath out of him and knocked him high into the air. She soared after him, scowling with rage, her blackened torso already sealing over the wound he'd given her.

As he tumbled, trying to recover like she had, Connor caught glimpses of Evander down on the ground. The elfonnel was swooping in, but the ground between them exploded upward and momentarily consumed them both. Through his connection to earth, Connor felt their titanic struggle inside of that cloud. Evander had defeated more than one elfonnel and Connor hoped he could do it again. He doubted he'd be able to help.

With an effort, Connor caught himself on a platform of air. As the queen rocketed up toward him, expression furious, he summoned a spear of ice and compressed it violently. He released it at her, and it crossed the distance in the blink of an eye, propelled by all the energy he could pour into it. Queen Dreokt sensed it coming and tried to block it, but it was her turn to react a fraction of a second too late. Instead of piercing her newly regrown heart like Connor had hoped, it drilled into her shoulder and punched clean through.

Queen Dreokt rocked back, her expression angrier than ever. That compressed ice was a trick Mister Five had used against Connor and Verena during the battle of Altkalen. He'd nearly killed them both. The wounds hurt terribly, and that ice had burned as much as it had frozen.

If the queen felt any of that terrible pain, she showed no indication of it, and her shoulder healed almost instantly. She ascended to face him, both of them standing on solid air, five hundred feet above the roiling earth battle between Evander and the elfonnel.

Connor waved and grinned, hoping to throw her off balance. "For a grumpy old lady you still seem pretty spry. I expected you to be using a cane by now."

In one of those unexpected mood swings of hers, she laughed, sounding delighted. She started to speak but another of Verena's tiny flying mechanicals swept in and launched a tiny missile right down her open mouth. It exploded in her throat and she actually gagged.

She still crushed the offending hive mechanical without even having to look at it and said in an exasperated tone, "That Builder is so annoying."

"As if you can talk. I vaporized you and you still regrew your entire body from half a skull!" Connor shouted. He was happy she paused to speak. Simply clobbering each other would probably end up giving her the advantage. In that moment he tapped super-obsidian and his mind accelerated so fast, for a second he felt like a genius.

He got an idea.

"I imagine that was truly frustrating," she conceded, somehow conveying the sense of an understanding grandmother.

Wow. Keeping up with that woman's emotional gymnastics was more challenging than getting the right present for every one of Aifric's birthdays. "I won't give you the chance again," he promised, lunging at her.

She formed a club of water and clobbered Connor on the side of the head. He was walking with all of the elements so he felt the water coming and managed to soften the blow. Instead of exploding his skull, it only flipped him over sideways. He used air to complete the somersault and land in front of her again. He seized the water that she was already swinging back around to club him again and managed to deflect it. At the same time, he drew upon fire and shoved white-hot daggers at her eyes.

She caught those a quarter of an inch away from her orbs, and at the same time struck at his mind with a hammer blow of chert.

Just as he had hoped.

She battered against his mental shielding, and he took the risk of allowing his defenses to crack. Her will stabbed into his mind with excruciating pain.

Her true emotions radiated through chert *"I wanted to raise you to greatness, you insolent child, but all you wish to do is destroy everything I've built, and place the entire kingdom at risk!"*

Amazingly, she truly believed that. She considered him the one who put the kingdom at risk? Connor was a firm believer in focusing on one's strengths instead of their weaknesses, but she took creative short-sightedness to a whole new level.

The queen pressed her attack, pouring in all of her hate and her will to dominate, seeking to overwhelm him as she had done in the past. She might be a barking-mad lunatic who flipped moods faster than Hamish could flip bacon, but he'd realized she always went for the mind.

Connor envisioned Alasdair, full of everyone he loved, assembled to support him. The mental image solidified, and the square felt as real as if he stood upon the solid, level stone ground again, breathing the familiar scents of Neasa's bakery and the hot metallic tang of the blacksmith's shop. It felt like coming home, and home was where he was the most grounded.

Queen Dreokt appeared in his mind looking shocked. "What is the meaning of this?"

"It means you are no longer welcome here," Connor declared. "Get her!"

As one, everyone in the square rushed her. She howled with rage and lashed out with terrific force, but there in his mind he finally held the advantage. Defeating her mind bomb had taught him the secret to controlling his mind and warding it from external influence.

The crowd buried her in an avalanche, and Connor took advantage of her momentary distraction to stab into her mind with his thoughts. He broke through, and for a moment touched hers. He sensed her anger at his surprise attack and her towering fury at the insult of the revolution, but what overshadowed all else was a desperate fear.

Fear of the elementals.

Images flashed past of a strange, distant land. Her home country. He glimpsed laboratories, saw King Triath as a young man, as well as Harley and other early supporters. He felt the indescribable wonder she felt upon establishing her first affinity, as well as her determination to succeed, to finally make the sylfaen accessible, and to bring unprecedented advancements to her people.

All of that passed in a second, replaced by scenes of strife, of enormous conference rooms where committees of hundreds of somber-faced old men and women debated the fate of magic, the arguments all centered on the dangers of releasing the elementals again. Images of battle flashed past, little more than impressions before being replaced by familiar sights of Obrion. He glimpsed Stornoway in all its glory and was amazed to see Kilian and Kirstin as children.

Connor tried to focus on those images, but they swept past like the others. Instead he read the growing certainty the queen had felt in those days that they had overlooked fundamental dangers. He sensed the elementals pressing for freedom, the constant battle to maintain the integrity of her humanity, to withstand the subtle whisperings and promises of unmatched power.

Then came the fateful day when her beloved somehow fell to Kirstin's latest mechanical. She didn't know what caused it, and that only magnified her fear, but she sensed that with his mental collapse, his resistance broke and the elementals began rising through him. The only way to save the world from the dangers they had introduced was to destroy the man she loved.

And make sure that disaster could never happen again.

Connor recoiled from Queen Dreokt, knocked right out of his mindscape by the astonishing montage. He had hoped to find confirmation of her weakness, not confirmation of her fears. She was broken, insane, and barely human.

But she was right.

In their desperate hunt for greater weapons to fight her, they'd approached the same thresholds that had claimed her husband and daughter and plunged the nation into terrible warfare. And they were right back there again, right on the brink of unleashing unstoppable devastation.

Queen Dreokt regarded him with sorrowful eyes. "Now you know why I must destroy you all."

She snapped out a deadly fist to seize his throat.

Connor tapped blind coal. He'd glimpsed confirmation of the dangers they'd already figured out, but that piece of common ground was not enough to save him.

As her hand scraped past his throat, unable to grab hold, Connor yanked from one of the tiny pouches along his belt a tiny vial. He shoved it up her nose and punched her to shatter it. The dread Queen Dreokt was immune to almost all physical damage. She could fleshcraft herself whole even when mortally wounded, and was immune to poisons.

She also had very enhanced senses.

The queen probably always tapped all of her affinities, even when she wasn't consciously planning to. Connor was already struggling with that problem since his last ascension. She had been enjoying the full breadth of affinity powers for centuries.

So she got to appreciate the full amazing magnitude of milked skunk extract better than anyone else in the world could ever hope to.

Her expression turned horrified. She gagged and made a retching sound deep in her throat.

Connor shifted sideways to get out of the spray path. He had no doubt Queen Dreokt could challenge all of them for the record if she decided to spew her last meal.

As she gagged and clutched at her nose, Connor combined stilling with granite. His strength built in a rush, faster even than basalt had and he focused that enormous power into his fist. He expected his arm to swell more than ever, but it did not. Since his first ascension, when his muscles reached the ultimate limits of their expansion, the fibers began weaving together to generate significantly more strength without any additional mass. Now as his fist and arm deadened under the super-influx of concentrated granite, those fibers wove together, then wove together again, then again, each weaving magnifying the effects of his strength tenfold.

Queen Dreokt violently sneezed, ejecting a fine, stinky mist. She had figured that out far too quickly, but one critical second too late.

Connor super-curse-punched her sternum. He struck with such overwhelming force that his fist burst through her newly reformed chest, crushed her new heart and lungs, and exploded out her back in an incredible spray of bloody gore.

Queen Dreokt opened her mouth to gasp, but her lungs were gone. Her eyes widened in shock, and she pawed at his shoulder, momentarily weakened by the horrible injury. She tried to speak, her lips moving silently, but unable to form the words.

Her mind-voice shrieked loud enough to make him cringe. *"This body was brand new! I'm still paying the fleshcrafting debt."*

"I think you've just run out of credit," he said as he pulled his hand free of her crushed torso, flinging blood and gore as he cocked his fist back to punch her in the face. She might have ignored the first time he destroyed her torso, but this time seemed to hurt more. He would be happy to rip her apart a hundred times, if that proved to be the magic number.

Her weak, pawing hands somehow regained strength and she seized his face with both hands. Before he could punch her, she shouted, "See how you like it, insolent child!"

Queen Dreokt head-butted him.

She struck so hard, the blow catapulted him backward.

And Connor clearly felt the front of his skull implode.

CHAPTER THIRTY-SIX
Joy Can Be Found in the Most Difficult Situations

Ivor, I need your help," Shona said urgently into her mini-hub.

She led fifty Striders at a run along the northwestern edge of the valley toward the nearest lake. The battle was off to a terrible start, and she and her fast movers were out of position. They couldn't afford to let the enemy Striders take out the Arishat League siege weapons, but not even Striders could run up those steep cliffs. Running north far enough to find a route up the hill was a possibility, but not fast enough. The waterfalls offered another way.

Striders could run across lakes or rivers for a ways, but not sprint up a waterfall. Not without help, anyway.

Behind her, Tabnit horns blared and Varvakan war drums boomed as the Arishat League forces poured into the northern end of Lossit valley to meet the onrushing regulars from the queen's army. Mounted knights would arrive first, and the Sehrazad raiders were already galloping out to meet them. Mounted on horses and camels, their sand-colored uniforms flapping in the howling wind, they raised scimitars and lances, shouting battle cries.

General Wolfram was commanding the rest of the Arishat League forces. Heavily armed and armored Varvakan knights in gleaming full plate armor marched in the center, wielding longswords, axes, or polearms. Several companies carried strum shock spears too. Tabnit pikemen held the eastern edge, along the river, and mixed Grandurian regulars filled in the gaps between. A few Petralist squads mingled with the regulars, ready to deal with any enemy Petralists who might be assigned to ravage their ranks. Most were new Boulders or Striders, not experienced enough to join in the main battle but far better equipped to deal with enemy Petralists than anyone else.

A few tertiary Petralists marched concealed among them too, ready to help turn the tide against the second wave of the enemy, which would be made up primarily of Petralists. Of course, the regulars also bore thousands of personal defensive mechanicals, plus speedslings. Two Builder Thunder Towers rolled down the speedcaravan track that ran along the road. Shona felt confident they could hold their own until the Battalions recovered and launched their bombardment initiative and deployed all of their troops and mechanicals.

But for the moment, none of that mattered. She had to get up that cliff and repel the enemy Striders, who were already engaging with the Arishat League forces. They could hold for a short time. They were well entrenched, but had not expected to face direct, determined attack.

"We're off to a rocky start today, aren't we?" Ivor asked, his voice calm.

"Nothing we can't handle," she promised him. They had to, because if they were forced to retreat, her beloved Merkland would next face the Queen's armies, and she doubted the city would survive another pitched battle. "Listen, I need to get up the cliff."

He understood immediately. "I'm glad you called. The Battalions are busy, but I have a moment. Tell Donald we'll run the ice challenge."

"Thanks." Shona felt better, her confidence buoyed by Ivor's calm. Ivor had been the favorite general in the Tir-raon for a reason, and he'd proven himself many times as a gifted leader and Petralist. He was one of the few men she knew who could match her ability at reading people, and his vision of the revolution was as grand as her own.

She called, "Donald, to me."

The Strider captain accelerated to join her. He had been part of Rory's original company during the battles of Alasdair, had taught Connor his first lessons with basalt, and proven himself a loyal and competent soldier. Shona gestured toward the first waterfall, several hundred yards ahead, cascading down the high cliff in a gorgeous sheet before splashing into one of the long, narrow, deep lakes. "Ivor said we're going to run the ice challenge."

Donald grinned and made a little bow without breaking stride. "I know what to do, my lady. If you'll permit, I'll take the lead."

She gestured him forward, and Donald easily accelerated. "Follow me. Watch your timing, and get ready for some fun!"

As they closed on the lake, Shona glanced south. The bulk of the enemy army was still pouring into Lossit valley and were spreading like a dark stain across the land. It was such a vast host, the sight awed her, and she felt the familiar nervous flutter that still bothered her before battle, despite how often she had ended up victorious. She'd led a smaller host up that very road with her father and Harley before their defeat at Merkland and her decision to switch sides and join the revolution. Today she would either prove she'd made the right decision, or see her life's ambitions destroyed.

She would not allow that. Whatever it took.

Enemy Boulders by the thousands were marching toward the lakes, slightly south of her position, followed by Sentry towers and teams of Spitters. More waves of soldiers were pouring in behind, moving with excellent discipline in thousand-man units, each with a Sentry tower in the center. More of the Spitters were clustering along the river, and she spotted two enormous towers flowing toward the town.

Those would be the command towers. As expected, Aonghus and a score of powerful tertiaries stood atop a tall earthen tower, fifty feet across. Another tower, identical in size, but made up of glittering ice, flowed along the bank of the river. No doubt General Rosslyn and many of her best Spitters were positioned there. At least that much of their original expectations seemed to be working.

Behind her, the Sehrazad raiders and enemy knights came together with a resounding crash as horses and camels flashed past each other. Lances and spears plunged into enemy targets or deflected off heavy shields. Screams and shouts rent the air, and scimitars flashed. Men toppled from both ranks before wheeling around for another pass. They wouldn't get too many before the press of soldiers from both sides caught up and compressed the battlefield.

Luckily no one interfered with Shona's small group. They'd reacted fast enough that the enemy tertiaries weren't in position to block them. The leading Sentries could have extended their influence far enough to strike, but it appeared they didn't understand how Shona's Striders posed any threat. If they continued along the gentle arc of the western edge of the valley near the lakes, they'd eventually get trapped by the charging Boulders.

Their reprieve wouldn't last long, though. The first volley from the embattled siege weapons positioned atop the cliff soared overhead, and the thunderous booming of the Tabnit death tubes shook the air. They were firing explosive rounds, and the deadly ammunition shot down toward the leading edges of the Boulders. Heavy barrels of Althin chemicals soared after.

Enemy Sentries spotted the incoming ordnance and raised grasping hands of earth to catch them. Shona was impressed. The queen had prepared her people well. If they intercepted the incoming rounds softly enough, they might not detonate.

Except the Builders had included remote detonation devices in many of the rounds, and even though the Sentries did an admirable job catching the rounds gently and wrapping them with earth, many still exploded with spectacular force, shredding the earthen restraints and raining fire over the nearby Boulders.

The Althin barrels also exploded, but they unleashed clouds of silvery fog that settled over the enemy. Shona recognized the mega stench and was happy she was well out of range. Soldiers screamed and gagged, many retching, despite their granite strength. Entire companies fled.

Enemy Spitters reacted quickly, spraying water over their forces to remove the stench and subdue the cloud, but the damage was done and the front ranks of the advance slowed. It wouldn't stop them, but might give Rory more time to get into position.

Donald pointed toward the nearest waterfall and abruptly accelerated. Shona and the rest of the squad followed him as he sprinted straight at the first lake. Glints of white in the waterfall caught Shona's attention and she understood Ivor's plan.

She'd initially hoped he might fashion a ramp of ice they could run up, but no doubt enemy Spitters would attack that immediately. He was working at such great distance, he'd lack the ability to defend it. Instead, she spotted chunks of ice, barely a foot square, descending slowly down the waterfall. Spaced at even intervals, they created an offset pattern all the way up. Somehow they did not fall as fast as the rest of the water. She bet they'd be far more difficult for enemy Spitters to feel too.

Donald accelerated sharply into a fracked sprint and shot across the water, kicking up spray in a fantastic arc as he sped into the billowing cloud of mist at the very base of the waterfall. There he raced up a short ramp of ice that appeared just in front of him and soared through the mist to the first icy footstep. Kicking off of that anchor point, he leaned back and raced right up the waterfall, blurring legs catching each footstep in turn.

It looked like a ton of fun.

Shona whooped as she accelerated, although her shout turned into a cry of pain as her legs fracked. She'd practiced fracking several times in the past few days and no longer fell every time, but it still hurt like a slap from Tallan himself. Shona would not allow herself to fail where others succeeded, though, and she ran through the pain. She loved the springy feel of the lake's surface under her blurring feet, and concentrated on making the jump to the first ice foothold.

Launching through the cool mist that gently caressed her exposed skin was a thrill. She landed the first step, leaned back, and launched up toward the second. She laughed as she ran up the waterfall! Water rushed past, spray billowed around her, and the sound of the falls was a constant thunder that rattled deep through her, but none of it could stop her.

Until she missed the fifth foothold.

Somehow her foot slipped off. She tried to catch herself, but no matter how fast she ran, not even her fast-flying feet could gain purchase on the waters of the falls and she began tumbling back the way she had come.

Flailing her arms, she managed to clobber the next Strider in line, a willowy Grandurian woman. They tangled together and both fell. Shona grimaced at the thought of knocking all of the Striders behind her from their purchases. She could not allow her mistake to derail their vertical race.

So she dug her hands into the nearby waterfall. The weight of the water dragged her down and slightly sideways. Wrapping her legs around the other Strider, she focused her basalt on her arms and managed to swim them sideways across the falls, out of the path of the other Striders. Together they plunged down into the frigid waters.

Shona surfaced, spitting water, feeling like an idiot. She hoped Ivor was distracted by the aerial battle and hadn't sensed her failure. The thought of him laughing at her made her flush with embarrassment. The rest of her team were still racing past, and none of them missed any steps. They looked amazing, sprinting up the face of the waterfall. She turned to apologize to the woman she'd knocked down, but the woman erupted out of the water beside her, already sprinting. She rose to the surface and made a fast circle of the lake, spraying water in a great arc as she closed on the ice slope again and shot up the waterfall after the rest of the team.

Shona tapped basalt and followed suit. She had to admit basalt was fun, but she was looking forward to reaching the top and granite-punching a few surprised enemy Striders in the face.

CHAPTER THIRTY-SEVEN
The Importance of Presentation. And Bombs.

The floor beneath Jean's feet thrummed with power as the huge quartzite thrusters of Battalion One fought to push the ponderous vessel against the gale. On the decks below, defenses were activating, long launch tubes rising into the air and turning to point west toward the onrushing swarm. Battle mechanicals were orienting to add their supporting fire to the defensive effort, and soldiers fought the wind as they formed ranks to ward off monsters.

The fleet was barely making any headway, though, and Jean's tension grew every second. It had always amazed her that such enormous vessels could take to the sky at all, and she feared no one had considered how well they'd handle such a gale. A Bladed researcher with a remarkable gift in math had calculated that each Battalion platform was carrying roughly fifty thousand tons of weight. That much weight defied Jean's ability to grasp, but she didn't doubt the number. Many of the man's calculations had proved critical in their battle planning.

Abruptly the ride smoothed out, and the Battalion began accelerating south. Captain Leppin reported, "Blind coal has been activated. We should be on target in two minutes."

"How long will reserves last?" Jean asked. She was glad they would soon be able to support their already-embattled troops, but blind coal ran out notoriously fast.

"Not long," he said simply.

Admiral Forfar said, "As long as we can hold position over the battlefield, that will be enough."

Jean glanced out the western windows. The aerial swarm was still closing fast, and although the Battalion fleet was making headway, they'd never outrun the monsters. Their fast-attack flights were still stuck on deck, which would curtail their ability to destroy the swarm. The Battalions were packed with troops and mechanicals, had full shielding available, and sported many deadly weapons, but from reports she'd heard about the attack on Merkland, they'd be hard-pressed to fight off the nimble flying monsters without flights of their own.

"Lossit valley coming into view," one woman reported.

Even though Jean had watched the initial clashes via the distant sightstone hive mechanicals, seeing the valley open beneath her made it seem more real. They were just clearing the last row of hills when the vast host came into view.

Despite their many Petralists and their incredible array of mechanicals, Jean still felt a shiver of fear at the sight of what looked like two hundred thousand soldiers pouring into the valley. She tried to embrace that thrill of battle fury that swept through her during the first battle of Merkland, but had to mitigate it with calm control. She might not be one of the soldiers directly fighting, but the choices she made could save or cost many lives.

"Status of our forces?" Jean asked.

An officer rattled off the reports. "Arishat Siege weapons have engaged, but rate of fire is severely curtailed due to the need to defend against the enemy Strider attack. Lady Shona is leading a relief column of Striders."

Jean spotted the embattled siege emplacements with the fast movers rushing past. She glanced at a nearby viewscreen showing a close-up of the battle and cringed when she spotted one of the trebuchets smashed, with corpses littering the ground around it. The other siege weapons appeared to have withstood the initial attack better, but the defenders were hard-pressed.

Then she spotted Shona's runners rush in using a flying-V formation, like a speeding flock of geese. They split the enemy Strider corps, dropping several of the surprised Petralists before splitting into the complex patterns of a running battle. She breathed a sigh of relief. With that timely aid, they should be able to hold their own.

"Rory and his Boulders are preparing to engage," another officer reported.

Jean easily spotted the ranks of Boulders marching to the very lip of the cliff, ready to plunge down and leap into the bash fight.

Their five companies, each made up of a thousand Boulders, were badly outnumbered. They faced more than three times as many enemy Boulders, supported by Sentries and Spitters, all moving into position facing the lakes at the base of the cliff.

"General Wolfram and the Arishat League are engaged," another soldier reported, gesturing toward the south window. Now that they were entering the battlefield, technicians were shifting the viewscreens so that zoomed-in views were positioned under the windows showing the same sections of the battlefield.

Along the northern end of the valley, the battle was already underway, with regulars heavily engaged. To Jean, it looked like a wild melee with little organization, but she trusted Wolfram to hold the northern flank.

"Remain at three thousand feet. I don't want anyone accidentally descending into their range until phase two," she ordered as the great fleet swept toward the enemy army.

Admiral Forfar grinned at her, looking eager to engage. "I concur, Lady Jean. Notify all Battalions to drop camouflage and prepare for bombardment."

One of the viewscreens, from a flying mechanical half a mile south of the Battalions and a thousand feet below them, was oriented back toward them and showed the Battalions creeping over the battlefield. From that position, they really did look like low-flying clouds. Closer inspection would definitely reveal odd warps and angles within those clouds, but she doubted anyone in the enemy army was prepared for what they were about to see.

The camouflage winked out, and the sight still awed Jean, even though she knew what to expect. The enormous Battalion carriers appeared, looking far larger from below. The many rapid-fire mechanicals attached to the underside looked enormously threatening, and Jean realized Hamish had been right when he'd promised her earlier that at the sight of their flying fortresses, at least half of the army was probably going to need a new pair smallclothes.

"Captain, begin phase one, on your command," Jean said, projecting calm, although inwardly she cringed at the violence about to be unleashed upon the enemy.

Captain Leppin saluted and moved to the southernmost window, which offered the best view over the enemy forces. He waited another moment as the Battalions swept over the valley, passing the embattled regulars, then the township with the enemy leadership platforms clearly visible in the central square. They continued onward, allowing the rest of the fleet to move into position, and every second seemed to stretch forever to Jean.

The enemy reacted quickly. They might be awed by the sight of the Battalion fleet, but they weren't surprised. Earthen shield walls rose up in great domes over each company. With Sentries embedded in every thousand-man units, they reacted with remarkable efficiency.

"Commence firing," Captain Leppin ordered.

His junior officers immediately spoke into their speakstones, relaying his order. Through the distant drone sightstones, Jean watched as all of those mechanicals underneath the huge ships began spitting fire and destruction.

Verena had told them how well the rapid-fire siege weapons had worked in Merkland. They struggled against fast-moving flyers, but against stationary targets like that army, Jean could not imagine a more devastating weapon, unless they dropped one of the enormous Last Word bombs.

They actually had one of those bombs on each of the Battalions, but she hoped they would not be necessary. A single bomb could devastate hundreds, if not thousands of lives. They would be used in the case of elfonnel or in a moment of last-ditch desperation if the queen attacked. Those bombs might distract her long enough for them to withdraw.

Most of the rapid-fire mechanicals shot high-explosive diorite rounds, although a number of them were using newly developed penetrator rounds that included reinforced hardened granite points to drill deep into the Sentry shields before detonating.

Explosions swept across the enemy forces, and even huddled under their earthen barriers Jean suspected those explosions were taking a terrible toll. Most of the shields held, blackened and pock-marked by the explosions, but still intact.

A few did not. Those were probably controlled by newer Sentries. The gunners quickly launched secondary strikes at those vulnerable points, sweeping them with additional explosions that sent soldiers tumbling in every direction. Boulders might be able to withstand some of those strikes, but any others would be pulverized.

Jean forced herself to watch, despite tears that she fought to blink away. She was a healer not a killer, and it tore at her to see such devastation happening at her command. Hopefully they could finish the battle quickly so she could order her flights to launch and to assist the wounded.

Sometimes the real world was simply brutal.

The penetrating rounds worked even better than she'd expected. She witnessed many of them drill through protective earthen shields before exploding, and those very shields served to contain the resulting blasts inside, magnifying them. Many earthen walls crumbled after one of those penetrating strikes, revealing blackened and broken bodies.

Admiral Forfar said, "Brilliant work!"

"The winds, they're dying down," Captain Leppin reported, gesturing toward the deck. The Battalion might have been slipping through the queen's gale, but winds had still ripped at the exposed men and mechanicals. Now they were looking around or raising fists in triumph. The air appeared calm.

"Launch all flights against the swarm," Jean ordered, feeling a ray of hope. She didn't know what had stopped the wind. Had the queen gotten too distracted by Connor and Evander? She hoped so. With their flights engaged, they could destroy the flying monsters.

"Commence phase two immediately," Admiral Forfar ordered.

That surprised Jean. "Are you sure that's wise with the swarm closing on us?"

"Perhaps not, but our bombardment won't stop them for long. We need to get our forces down there to press the advantage," he said.

Jean didn't like placing those soldiers at risk like that, but couldn't argue with the admiral's logic, so she nodded.

Small attack flights began launching from every Battalion and formed up to meet the flying swarm. At the same time, Thunder Towers lurched forward and began rolling toward the outer edge of the decks.

The enemy was not going to just sit there and let them blow them to pieces, though. Water erupted out of the Macantact and flowed up into the sky from a hundred different points throughout the queen's army. Again they had spread out their Spitters much farther throughout their forces than Jean had expected, and that allowed them to link their efforts in a truly remarkable way.

The waters flowed up into the air and formed great shields of liquid that quickly linked into one enormous shield above the entire army. At first Jean wasn't sure what that would accomplish, but realized the brilliance of it as explosive rounds began detonating over that watery shield, rippling the surface but accomplishing little else.

The penetrating rounds seemed to do better at first, in many cases punching clean through and still striking the ground before exploding. The Spitters adjusted quickly, though, and began adding shifting currents of water to deflect those penetrators off course.

As a result, in many instances they bounced and skittered along the ground instead of punching straight down, their explosions accomplishing little.

The mass of ground troops moving against Rory's position resumed their advance. Despite casualties from the bombardment, they still outnumbered Rory's forces nearly three to one. Jean could not allow them to maintain that position of strength.

"Prepare to launch the rods and prepare the pumice initiative."

Chapter Thirty-Eight
Nothing Like a Good Old-fashioned Bash Fight

General Rory stood at the edge of the cliff beside the central waterfall. The beautiful expanse of Lossit valley spread beneath him, the view softened by the mists billowing out from the eight waterfalls, as well as clouds of dust from the Arishat League siege weapons and the recent bombardment from the Battalions. Thousands of Boulders, supported by Sentries and Spitters, were moving into position below to greet his forces.

The day was shaping up to offer an even better bash fight than the great bash fight of Merkland. He breathed deep the clean, water-laden air and grinned, testing the strength of his granite curse, coursing under his skin, ready for battle.

"Shall we?" he asked Anika. His beloved stood beside him, look-ing as gorgeous in her battle leathers as ever. He'd been smitten by her beauty, her unrivaled strength, and that glint of battle lust in her eye that set his heart racing. That they could charge into battle side by side filled him with a deep sense of contentment.

"Yes, mine capitain. We fight. Now!" She lifted a mechanical that was little more than a small Sehrazad steel glass magazine, filled with bombs the size of Rory's fist. Aiming the squat launch tube extending out the front down toward the lakes at the bottom of the cliff, she activated it. Air from quartzite inside the magazine propelled the bombs out with soft spitting thumps.

All down the line of their forces, gathered along the edge of the cliff to either side, other Boulders and Rumblers launched more bombs. They rained down, exploding fifty feet above the ground. Rory had no idea how Hamish set the elevation. He was just glad it worked.

The bombs exploded in soft flashes of light, generating clouds of dust that spread and settled over the lakes and were pushed by the clouds of mist out beyond the shores, toward the advancing enemy positions. Other soldiers dumped bags of pumice powder into the falls rushing past.

"Pumice layer is deployed," Anika reported, tossing the empty mechanical aside and lifting the new battle hammer her brother had gifted to her at the wedding.

"Good. Let's go say hello," Rory said with a grin.

With a shouted battle cry, he jumped off the cliff.

Anika jumped in perfect unison with him, her voice lifted in a joyous Grandurian battle song. All along the cliff face, their soldiers followed. Five thousand Boulders leaped in unison, a wave of bash-fighting prowess greater than any force Rory had ever commanded.

It would indeed be a great day.

As they fell, enemy Spitters attempted to seize the waters of the falls to snatch them out of the air, but most of their efforts failed. The waters were filled with activated pumice dust, so although the waterfalls shook, and a few tendrils extended toward Rory and the others, few actually snatched Boulders or tried to drown them. Those who were caught activated personal blind coal or pumice mechanicals and slipped free.

The enemy would not dodge a bash fight today.

Some of the Boulders activated descent mechanicals, small quartzite thrusters that slowed their descent. Rory didn't bother. He didn't want to miss a second of the brewing bash fight.

So he plunged down into one of the lakes, sinking deep, even though he spread his arms and legs to create drag. He didn't spot the bottom, even though he sank at least thirty feet. Ivor had said the lakes were deep.

Rory pulled hard for the surface, but felt waters encircle him. The layer of concealing pumice hadn't sunk that deep, and he'd fallen right into the Spitters' realm of control.

For the first time in his life, Rory didn't fear Spitters. He tapped his new secondary affinity.

He'd always thought Connor was a good boy, and Connor had proven it at the wedding. Rory had never imagined gaining a secondary affinity. He was a bash fighter. What did he need with limestone? Sandstone would have allowed him to fight longer, but he didn't really need it.

Blind coal, however, was a wondrous gift. Rory tapped it, savoring the oily, snakelike feel of it sliding over him. With blind coal activated, he swam out of the Spitter's embrace and surfaced. He sucked in a water-laden breath, deactivated blind coal, and stroked for the shore, tapping granite to his arms and shoulders enough to accelerate his swim.

Anika had already surfaced and would reach the shore a second before he did. To either side, Boulders were raining down onto the ground, or surfacing from the lakes. They all had enough blind coal or pumice to survive the initial delaying tactics of the tertiaries. He hoped Ivor and Anton's attacks would soon distract them from the bash fight, or that Ilse and her teams of Crushers would deal with the annoyance.

Rory paddled hard for the shore. He didn't want Anika to get to plunge alone into the enemy ranks without him. She'd love the challenge, but they were a team. Together they slogged through the muddy shore to solid ground. Anika shook her head to clear water, and her long braid swung out wide, spraying glittering droplets. Her eyes were glowing with eagerness, and she looked as happy as he felt.

The enemy Boulders had closed to within a hundred yards and formed deep ranks. They looked as eager as Rory for the bash fight to commence. He glanced to either side. His forces were forming up, although many were getting delayed by Sentries or Spitters, wasting time and precious mechanicals.

"We need to give them something else to worry about so they'll leave our people alone," he shouted.

Anika grinned. "Time for freedom call."

"My thoughts exactly." Rory started to advance on the enemy lines, marching with a slow, determined stride. Anika matched him, and their forces began falling in to either side. Rory extracted a small mechanical launch tube from a chest pocket. Barely six inches long, made of wood, it contained a single mechanical with a simple button activation on the end. Rory mashed the button and pointed the tube into the air.

With a whooshing hiss, a piece of limestone shot out of the tube and soared high into the air. For a moment, the shouting of enemy sergeants faded as everyone looked up. Two hundred feet up, just above the leading edge of the enemy lines, it erupted into a multi-colored sunburst. The light expanded and became words that hung like fire in the sky.

"The time is now. Guardians rise up and fight for your freedom!"

Rory lifted a speakstone that Verena had prepared for him. Most of the battlefield commanders had one. They magnified one's voice, as if a Pathfinder was standing nearby. His voice boomed loud in the hush as he shouted, "Freedom! Today we fight for freedom!"

The cry was taken up by every member of the troop, echoing from the cliffs behind them and filling the valley with the cry of freedom. To the north, some of the embattled regulars took up the cry. The sound reverberated like shockwaves across the battlefield.

"Freedom! Freedom!"

And miraculously, Guardians among the queen's forces took up the cry.

Rory had fully expected they would, but he still felt a thrill to hear the cry, to see the raised fists of brotherhood as many of those standing across the open ground from him chose freedom. They'd been pressed into service on penalty of death, but now they had the chance to choose their fate.

Many chose correctly.

As surprised officers shouted for order, many Guardians turned on their leaders and attacked them with brutal ferocity. Chaos swept the vast ranks of their enemy. Rory had just upended the scale of the bash fight.

"You are many strong leader. Even our enemies wish to obey you," Anika said approvingly.

"Shall we go lend our new recruits a hand?" he asked with a grin.

Anika raised her hammer high and shouted, "To the bash fight!"

"Charge!" Rory shouted, his voice booming with satisfying power.

As one, five thousand Boulders broke into a run, eager to finally start the bash fight of their lives.

It was definitely turning out to be a great day.

* * *

Captain Ilse stood with Anton and a company of eighty of their most experienced Sentries and Sappers. Ten Spitters were mixed among them to ensure they all reached the ground without getting intercepted by the enemy. She doubted any army besides the one they faced had ever fielded so many tertiary Petralists.

The numbers might be bigger, but fundamental challenges remained unchanged. Whichever side best deployed their tertiaries would win the day. Everything else faded to secondary importance.

Well, that flying swarm might turn the tide, and no armies had ever fielded mechanicals to rival the Battalions, Thunder Towers, and flying battle mechanicals. Those were items beyond her realm of expertise. She trusted her friends to win the day in their spheres of conflict. She planned to win the contest of earth.

All around them, soldiers rushed, shouted, or activated mechanicals. Led by Hamish, flights of personal fast-attack flyers shot into the still air, their thrusters howling. Defensive mechanicals placed all around the Battalion started firing toward the onrushing swarm of flying monsters, the whooshing of their launch tubes like a constant fierce wind. The huge Thunder Towers trundled toward the outer edges of the Battalion decks to begin their descent, but Ilse wasn't about to wait.

Anton shouted above the din, "An avalanche may begin with a single rolling stone, and even the tiny stream swells to a raging torrent during the spring thaw."

She cheered with her team, proud to fight beside the legendary Anton. With his stirring words motivating them all, he led the way toward the edge of the deck at a run. Ilse ran beside him, with their company following close behind. Together she and Anton leaped over the edge and began the three-thousand-foot plunge toward the ground below.

Air whistled in Ilse's ears, a pleasant sound she always enjoyed when high deploying. She loved the sense of calm that enveloped her as she fell from great heights. Despite being separated from the earth, jumping didn't bother her like swimming did.

She scanned the battlefield with an experienced eye. Rory's Boulders were just engaging, and by the chaos sweeping the enemy ranks, the freedom call had proven as effective as he'd promised. General Wolfram's forces were fully engaged on the northern end of the valley. Regulars on both sides fought perhaps the greatest pitched battle of all time. Some few Petralists on both sides were involved in small pockets, but most of the fighting was between ungifted men and women with swords and axes, polearms and scimitars, bows and slings.

A group of Varvakin knights held the center and was pressing forward into enemy ranks. Few non-Petralist weapons could harm them in their full plate, and they'd drawn the ire of a couple Sentries and a platoon of Boulders. The Petralists under Wolfram's command were engaging, and the Varvakins had unleashed their strum spears with deadly effect. Not even Boulders could withstand the debilitating shock of strum.

Shona and her Striders appeared to have driven off the enemy Striders who had attacked the siege placements, and some of her forces were in pursuit, engaged in a complex running battle across the high plain. The siege weapons were again raining explosive rounds and deadly chemicals across the enemy reinforcements, causing lots of disruption, and distracting the enemy Sentries.

All of the Battalions were still raining destruction down from hundreds of rapid-fire mechanicals, although the marvelous water shield that General Rosslyn and her Spitters had raised was doing a remarkable job deflecting many of them. Still, the effort kept them distracted for precious extra moments.

Ilse adjusted her protective goggles and tapped granite as she plummeted toward the enemy water shield. Behind her, the first of the Thunder Towers rolled off the Battalion and began their dive, while enemy flying monsters swarmed above, engaged in close combat with the defender flights. Everywhere she looked she saw battle and conflict.

Time to add another layer.

She and Anton slammed into the water shield with brutal impacts. She tensed more from the feeling of helpless fear that swept through her with the contact than of any worry of injury. Immersing herself in water placed her at a terrible disadvantage, and it rankled to think she was completely at the mercy of an enemy. Too many lives were at stake, too many of her own people risking everything. She could not bear the thought of dying early in the fight. She needed to help them, to protect as many as possible.

She carried a few personal defensive mechanicals, but did not activate them as she plunged into the water shield. As hoped, the Spitters embedded within their company shielded them as they sank through. Her speed bled away fast, but the barrier was too thin to stop her descent completely. Before the enemy Spitters could stop her, she fell through the underside.

The ground rushed up to meet her and she max-tapped granite, while also calling upon slate. Anton had slowed more in the water, so Ilse landed first, flipping herself in the air to strike feet first. She flexed her granite-strengthened legs and softened the earth at the point of impact. Connecting with earth prior to touching down was tricky, but she'd practiced drop deployments with the Crushers many times, and timed her landing perfectly.

She struck the ground hard, but the earth cushioned her impact, so it barely strained her legs. She sank ten feet before reversing back to the surface. She rose on a slender earthen tower, already scanning the ground for nearby enemies. Battalion One had drifted south of town, so she'd landed about a quarter mile from where the enemy command towers stood. She was pleased with the position.

Anton struck the ground beside her like a meteor. He chose to land on his back, and earth exploded outward in a fantastic cloud. It was all for show, though, because Ilse felt his will like a bonfire in the earth beside her, and he rose a moment later on his own tower, complete with crenellations.

The rest of their party rained down around them. A few of the Sentries less experienced at drop deployments activated descent mechanicals at the last moment, while the Spitters landed on cushions of water.

Even as the team was still falling, Ilse identified the nearest Sentry. He was a burly fellow, who had seen their descent. His tower rotated to face her, and she read his confident expression from fifty feet away. He cast his will toward her tower and struck a heavy blow at its base, clearly intending to sever her contact with earth. His second strike would probably crush her.

It was a powerful attack, but simple and overconfident. Ilse poured her will into the ground beneath her tower, orienting it like a dense wedge that the onrushing attack glanced off of. Too few Sentries developed their earth senses into more than a wide blanket. She was the master of targeted control, and although she might not be able to wield as much brute strength as many other Sentries, she had rarely faced anyone more skilled at battlefield application of their powers.

Before the enemy Sentry could strike again, Ilse flicked out a single burst of her will. It shot across the distance like a lance, and as expected, the enemy Sentry sensed it coming. He fortified his defenses, but Ilse didn't care. His tower was not her target.

She flicked her will upward and seized the earth. A lance of earth erupted from the ground twenty feet in front of the man's tower and shot into the air.

He actually managed to deflect it. Not bad. Ilse could respect an opponent with good reflexes.

She had already launched her second attack, striking with more lances from left and right, then another from behind her opponent. That one she shielded heavily. As expected, the first two lances drew his attention, and the Sentry twisted and actually caught them both. He was definitely competent, and he looked very pleased with himself.

He never did sense the final lance. It caught him completely by surprise and pierced his neck, severing the spine and nearly decapitating him in a single blow. The Sentry clutched at his throat as his tower collapsed and he fell into the pile of loose dirt.

The entire exchange took only a few seconds. Anton said, "The tiniest twig might deflect the arrow and save the prey."

"But only if you deploy the twig in time," she replied, grimly.

Three other enemy Sentries struck at them, all moving on intercept paths from the south. Anton's will erupted out like a tidal wave, smashing aside their assault and shredding their towers. As they fell, shouting in surprise, Ilse aimed three more precision strikes, clobbering all of them with hammer blows to the temples. She hoped she hadn't killed them, but needed to ensure they were knocked out of the fight long enough to be shackled by the Crushers when they arrived. She preferred not dealing death blows when possible, but more and more enemy Sentries were orienting on their position. They might not give her the option to demonstrate such restraint.

Their arrival had drawn the attention of General Aonghus, as they had predicted. He walked the earth like a distant bonfire, and Ilse felt as much as saw his great command tower begin shifting across the distant town square to intercept.

She lifted her mini-hub, linked to Jean in Battalion One and said, "The game is afoot. Sentries are engaging. Tell Ivor to get out of the bath."

CHAPTER THIRTY-NINE
A Great Entrance Makes All the Difference

Ivor erupted out of the Macantact River about a quarter mile north of Lossit town with eighty Spitters right behind him.

He embraced the thrill of excitement that swept through him as soon as he emerged and caught sight of the intense battle raging across the valley. The Battalions seemed impossibly huge, hanging three thousand feet above him, while the incredible interlocking water shield a hundred feet above the battlefield glittered like liquid silver in the bright sunlight. He clearly sensed the wills of over a hundred enemy Spitters engaged in that shield effort.

The dozen Spitters spaced along the nearby riverbank in pairs were distracted by the fighting and barely registered the arrival of Ivor and his strike force before they were crushed by an avalanche of water and ice.

Ivor preferred taking prisoners, but they couldn't afford to hesitate, and they needed to make a powerful entrance to draw General Rosslyn and her command team's attention. He led the way across the surface of the river, taking long, skating slides, trying to imitate Kilian. He moved well, but he doubted anyone could quite match Kilian's grace on the water.

Behind him, his strike force stayed in formation, split into five-man squads. They'd trained extensively over the past week. Most Spitters fought as individuals, so that would give his close-knit teams an advantage.

They would need it.

Emmeleyn slid across the water to catch up, her legs not even moving, propelled entirely by the water. It was an elegant move that fit her personality perfectly. The petite Water Moccasin was his second in command. She might be small, but her soapstone affinity was powerful enough that she could probably ascend, even though she wasn't Dawnus. Ivor had only known her a short time, but he already trusted her to hold her side of the line.

She gestured toward the huge water shield. "Impressive, but they've committed too many of their Spitters."

"I can sense a lot remaining," Ivor told her. "Look sharp and stay focused, or we'll get swamped."

She saluted and slid to the right where her teams were rushing the shore.

Ivor cast his water senses out farther and gained a better sense of the battle. A lot of water was getting flung around by those Spitters defending from the Battalion bombardments, and that helped. He sensed three large parties of Spitters already orienting on his teams, and farther to the south he clearly sensed General Rosslyn's presence like a shining crystal beacon.

Ascended. He'd trained with Connor and Kilian enough to understand exactly how overmatched he and his team were, but he'd also picked up some devious tricks from them.

He was going to need them all.

Rosslyn's huge, watery tower began sliding north across the town square. She and her senior Spitters were about to engage.

Ivor raised his mini-hub and connected to Jean. "We're engaged, and I sense Rosslyn moving to intercept."

"Be careful," Jean responded immediately. Her obvious concern made him smile. She was so sweet. What she saw in Hamish, Ivor would never understand. She added, "We're tasking three Battalions to concentrate fire around your position, and another three around Ilse."

"Perfect. I'm releasing the Crushers," he responded.

Her response was lost by a fresh wave of rolling thunder from explosive rounds fired down from the Battalions that shook the water shield. He needed to target that shield soon, but first he had to get Erich into the fight.

Ivor raised a hand, fingers spread wide, the signal for two of his teams to launch the Crushers. They were ready for the signal, and almost immediately, the river just north of their position exploded as Erich and three hundred Crushers burst forth. Far to the south, near the already embattled Sentries, an equal company of Crushers erupted from the river and plunged into the fray.

Just then, the first group of twenty enemy Spitters launched a blizzard of razor-sharp ice shards, all aimed directly at him.

"That's not entirely fair," Ivor muttered, barely sweeping the assault aside. He started whistling a battle tune he'd picked up from Erich as his companies engaged.

* * *

Student Eighteen rose silently up through the hard-packed surface of the Lossit town square. Ennlin smoothly pulled the earth away from her path, while also pushing the fifty Mhortair of their strike force up through similar narrow conduits from their concealed hiding places.

Nuzha had ringed every ascent tube with a thin sheath of water to block their movement from the senses of the nearby Sentries, while Hemma focused on infusing that water with her best shields to keep the enemy Spitters from sensing their approach.

Their entire team remained perfectly silent as they rose up into the midst of the enemy command position, and no one noticed them for several critical seconds. On the south side of the square, General Aonghus, easily recognizable by his flaming-red hair, stood atop his oversized Sentry tower with a score of senior Petralists, all facing south toward where Ilse and Anton and their forces were wreaking general havoc. On the opposite side, General Rosslyn and another score of her senior staff stood together on their tower of water, facing north, already sliding toward where Ivor's team had just landed.

No one expected danger to lurk right in their midst.

Student Eighteen embraced the deadly calm she'd mastered during her years of grueling training at the kill academy and raised the odd mechanical Hamish had designed for the deployment. Every one of the Mhortair in her party carried an identical weapon.

It was little more than a wide tube of Sehrazad steel glass, a full twelve inches in diameter and four feet long, attached to a sphere made of the same material, two feet in diameter. A flexible tube made of Tabnit rubber snaked back down the hole she'd risen through.

Student Eighteen activated the quartzite pumping mechanism. The mechanical shuddered in her hands and grew suddenly heavier as liquid was pumped up from below. She aimed the nozzle at Rosslyn's back, just as one of her staff turned and spotted them. The woman's eyes opened wide in shock, but she hesitated a fraction of a second, disbelieving her eyes before shouting a warning.

Student Eighteen opened the release valve.

A pressurized stream of acid sprayed out, hard enough it could have easily cleared the northern end of town. It crossed the thirty paces to the water tower in a heartbeat and struck Rosslyn in the back, knocking her stumbling.

Half a heartbeat later, every one of the Mhortair opened fire too. Twenty-five streams of acid hissed through the air at each of the command towers, instantly dousing everyone on both platforms.

The effects were instantaneous. Hair seemed to evaporate, and skin instantly burned, with disgusting welts rising within seconds. Some of those split, oozing yellow puss. Mighty Petralists screamed and fell, clutching at faces and exposed skin, and for three glorious seconds, she dared hope they would destroy the entire leadership corps in one strike.

But both generals reacted with well-honed reflexes. Rosslyn's entire group simply dropped into the protective middle of her water tower. Acid sprayed across it, but couldn't penetrate. General Aonghus raised the walls of his tower to shield his people from the acid. A few of the Mhortair angled their spray higher, hoping to arc more acid down upon the injured Petralists, but Student Eighteen didn't bother.

She dropped her acid weapon, raised her fist high, and shouted, "For Jagdish!"

Mistress Four echoed her cry and charged Rosslyn's tower, followed by half the strike team. Student Eighteen went for the earth tower with the rest of the Mhortair. They needed to close fast and destroy them before they recovered from the shock of that acid strike. She expected every one of their targets to be senior Petralists, and at least some would be Dawnus. Destroying them was vital to win the day.

Even as she accelerated into a fracked sprint, controlled by Rith, the ground in front of her erupted into a wall of deadly spikes.

"I've got it!" Aifric shouted, and Rith never slowed. Protected by Aifric's activated pumice, they slipped right through the stab-bing spikes.

Most of their strike team made it through just as easily. Every one of the Mhortair was an experienced assassin, and most pos-sessed affinities with pumice, blind coal, or both. Barely slowed, they rushed the tower.

It exploded outward, earth extending into hundreds of grasping tentacles to rip them all apart.

With pumice still activated, Student Eighteen rushed through the barrage and closed to within twenty feet of the enemy. That earth attack had pulled most of the protective wall down, revealing the Petralists rising to face her team. Most of them looked ghastly, but some were already shedding the effects of the acid. Powerful healers. The dread queen had always liked filling her armies with leaders who could heal fast.

They looked mad, especially General Aonghus, but all compressed onto that tower together, they'd have trouble all wielding earth at the same time. She hoped they got in each other's way.

More importantly, she flung a weighted pouch directly at the general. He made a dismissive gesture, looking disgusted, and a tentacle of earth swept up to bat the pouch aside.

It flew right through.

Of course she had coated herself, her weapons, and all of her equipment with activated pumice before the battle. That fact surprised General Aonghus, and the bag soared straight at his face, barely slowed.

A heavy-chested Petralist standing beside Aonghus shouldered him aside and tried to catch the bag. It exploded on impact, coating him with gabbro, the secret Mhortair weakening agent. The soldier sucked in a surprised mouthful of the powder, then immediately dropped to his knees, eyes bulging, hands trembling, wracked by a coughing fit. His granite-hardened muscles withered, and he looked like he was about to be sick.

Gabbro only interfered directly with primary affinities, but the effects were traumatic enough that most Petralists lost connection to their secondary and tertiary affinities for a short period of time too.

A hardened-granite projectile cast from a Mhortair's sling caught the distracted Petralist in the face, a perfect hit in the eye. The small projectile blasted deep into the man's skull, and he pitched over, dead and twitching.

Other Mhortair fired heavy crossbows, and at that range the weapons wreaked horrific damage on the enemy Petralists. They tried raising walls of protective earth, but every weapon was coated in activated pumice, and three more senior Petralists died in the first volley. Several more took injuries.

Student Eighteen leaped up onto the earthen tower, her sword already in hand. General Aonghus glared at her and shouted, "Pumice directive!"

As she lunged toward him, the ground beside her erupted like a fist as thick around as her waist. She expected her pumice to protect her, but the earthen fist struck like a hammer wielded by an elfonnel, catapulting Student Eighteen back and away.

The world spun crazily around her, but the girls were already scrambling to react.

"Stabilizing us!" Aifric promised, and healing power flooded through them, dealing with the three cracked ribs and internal injuries.

"I should have been ready for that," Eleven said, sounding disgusted with herself. Connor and the others hadn't yet met the other Mhortair sharing her mind. She wasn't ready to reveal that particular secret yet, but Eleven wouldn't let them get struck like that again. She was a master at short, applied bursts of blind coal.

Hemma tapped granite, hardening their body, and Nuzha seized nearby water, forming a corkscrew pillar of ice that neatly caught them and swung them back around to reverse directions. They'd return to the fight in seconds.

The swing gave her a great view of both fights. Commander Six had reached Rosslyn's tower. Protected in the water, Rosslyn and her team had begun showering the Mhortair with ice and water. They too quickly realized they were dealing with pumice and switched to launching their elemental attacks, then releasing direct hold over the water or ice. Since no Petralist was actively controlling it, pumice didn't help.

Blind coal still worked, and the Spitters among the group deflected most of the water assaults away. Several spears of earth stabbed up into the water tower from below. Some pierced surprised Petralists, and one barely missed Rosslyn. Before she could sever the earth spears, every single one of them detonated.

Student Eighteen appreciated Mistress Four's finesse. She had prepared those specialty bombs before the battle. Each one included a bit of diorite, surrounded by activated pumice crystals. The small explosions dispersed pumice throughout the water tower, and Rosslyn lost control of it for a moment.

As the waters collapsed, dropping her people in a flood, Commander Six led the charge. As Petralists struggled to react, he leaped into the middle of them, his whip-sword snicking out with blinding speed and devastating effect. Arms and heads seemed to jump away from bodies in sprays of blood and gore.

Other Mhortair closed with axes and swords, daggers, and spears, and they cut down almost half of Rosslyn's force in a few frenzied seconds. Such overwhelming tactics were the Mhortair specialty, and most enemies would be incapable of responding effectively.

Rosslyn wasn't deterred. The pumice diffusion only blocked her from that local bit of water. A literal tidal wave of water erupted up out of the nearby river and plunged down over Commander Six, Mistress Four, and their teams. Rosslyn released active control just before it struck, so many of the Mhortair were swept away. Some of them possessed blind coal and stepped through the attack, but the momentum had shifted to the enemy.

Back on the earthen tower, Student Eighteen's team were rushing Aonghus and his Sentries. Some of them closed in fierce close combat, while others battled with elemental fury.

Then the earth beneath most of the Mhortair simply disappeared, forming a gaping hole. There was nothing for pumice or blind coal to deal with, so most of the assassins dropped into the pit, shouting curses in their native tongue.

Snarling with rage, Aonghus covered the pit with a ceiling of earth, and through her soapstone sisters' affinities, Student Eighteen sensed Rosslyn fill the pit with water. The Mhortair trapped inside lacked leverage or a way to escape. Pumice wouldn't save one from drowning, and blind coal would run out long before they pulled themselves free.

It was a terrible, but effective ploy.

"I'm going to kill that man," Tresta rumbled, but they didn't have time to deal with Aonghus.

As the rest of their diminished force fought on against the enemy, who were quickly figuring out better ways to fight them, Student Eighteen said, "Ladies, let's show them what we can do when we work together! Isabell, Ennlin, make some mud and get our people out of there."

As her sisters seized the elements beneath Aonghus' tower, melding their affinities together far tighter than any other Petralists not sharing the same head ever could, Student Eighteen focused on Aonghus and his team.

She tapped chert.

Emotions boiled all across the square, like a rainbow cast into a butter churn, then sprayed through the acid hoses. Most of the Mhortair emitted brighter colors of anticipation, eagerness, or vengeance, while the majority of the enemy Petralists mingled shadowed colors of fear. Aonghus' emotions blazed with orange rage. He might now wield a different affinity, but inside he still possessed the heart of a Firetongue.

Student Eighteen focused on Aonghus and all of his Sentries, max-tapped chert, and struck every single one of them with a single, overpowering emotion.

Confusion.

Fear wouldn't work as well, since they were all experienced soldiers and had disciplined themselves against fear. Anger would only motivate them, and cowardice would not grab hold as well.

Confusion caught them by surprise. Battle was wild and chaotic, and they had been attacked without warning. They had great reflexes and discipline, but all of them would be feeling some level of confusion already. That gave her the anchor points to connect to them, then she magnified that emotion a hundredfold.

Every commander dreaded those moments in battle when fear or confusion might rob their forces of discipline and send their people fleeing a fight they might have otherwise won.

The effects came instantaneously. Several officers turned to run, while one dropped into a fetal position, clutching his head and weeping. Others paled, looking around, searching for clarity, but all were momentarily distracted.

Her team struck without mercy. Blades of water pierced enemies, while two whipswords, wielded by Commander Six's cousins, snicked through the enemy ranks with devastating effect. The Mhortair swarmed the tower, and the moment turned decisively to their favor.

Those Sappers learned anew why people whispered in fear of the Mhortair.

Some still tried fighting back, but Student Eighteen clearly read the eventual outcome. Her team would win.

General Aonghus read it too. Shouting curses, he flung himself into the air with a slingshot of earth. Several of his officers tried to follow, but the Mhortair intercepted them, riddling them with crossbow bolts, or yanking them back down with tendrils of water.

Across the square, General Rosslyn saw what was happening and shouted, "Aonghus, help us!"

Student Eighteen left her team to finish the Sentry leaders and turned toward Rosslyn. She'd catch Aonghus in a moment, but first she would deal with Rosslyn.

"Ladies, it's time to take down an ascended."

CHAPTER FORTY
Sometimes We Just Need Another Pair of Hands

Connor had sometimes joked with Aifric when he visited the healing wing at the Carraig that when he was having a bad day his brains might have been leaking out his ears, but this was the first time he actually experienced it.

It was nasty.

As he tumbled away from the queen, body rigid with shock, he realized a couple of things. First, Queen Dreokt had the world's strongest curse-punch head-butt. Second, he should be dead.

But he wasn't. Although his body was shaking from the effects of the blow, his connection to his affinities, especially fleshcrafting seemed to wrap his soul in a protective blanket that no amount of physical injuries could pierce.

That was awesome.

Good thing they hadn't destroyed fleshcrafting yet. The plan was to leave the queen vulnerable, not him.

Kilian had taught him that he could heal himself even from a death blow, but it still shocked him to experience it. If he had a little more time to enjoy the moment, he would've explored more of what it was like to be physically dead but yet somehow not dead. One more opportunity sacrificed to duty.

So he drew heavily upon fleshcrafting and poured that power into his brain. He sensed the multitude of tiny connections happening in that weird gray matter and somehow understood them enough to put them back together. It was more than just picking up all the gray bits that sprayed out of his cracked skull and shoving them into place so that he could seal up the broken bone. Somehow fleshcrafting allowed him to re-create those connections exactly as they had been before.

It was really freaky, and he made a point of not thinking about it too much. He could lose himself and get completely distracted if he wasn't careful.

Good thing he did because as his eyes cleared, he spotted Queen Dreokt striding toward him through the sky, completely healed from her own devastating wound. She was far better at fleshcrafting, but actually waited for him, and glanced up into the sky, frowning. "Is your Builder girlfriend always given to fits of panic?"

Connor had been distracted by the whole near-death-experience thing and hadn't heard Verena shouting questions via speakstone. She sounded terrified. He felt bad she had to witness the fight without getting directly involved. That must drive her crazy.

So he cast words out in a wide spray to help disguise Verena's location. No doubt the queen could pinpoint her if she really wanted to, but Connor was not about to make it easier for her. "I'm okay. Fleshcrafting is amazing."

Queen Dreokt giggled. "Fleshcrafting. I like that. I think I'm going to borrow that term."

"Go ahead," he said as he regained his feet on the empty air to face her. "You won't get to enjoy it for long."

She gave him an approving smile, like a happy teacher. "Not debilitated by trauma. That's a good sign. For one so recently ascended, you show remarkable mastery over the deeper concepts. It is such a waste that I must destroy you." She took a step closer, her expression turning earnest. "You glimpsed much truth when you touched my mind. Will you now set aside your misguided rebellion and allow me to guide your future?"

Connor barely bit back an incredulous laugh at the poor attempt at a recruitment speech. Did any evil psycho dominating tyrant ever honestly believe that such an offer would be accepted?

"You're pretty good at regrowing a new heart when you need to. Have you ever tried regrowing your mind and your conscience? If you let me rip it all out, I can help you put yourself back together so you're not such a lunatic. Then maybe we can talk about building a better future where you're not dead."

She sighed. "The bravado of youth is matched only by its stupidity."

"That's not half bad Sentry speak. Have you been practicing?"

Thinking of Evander, Connor flicked his affinity senses back toward the ground. The billowing cloud of obscuring earth had been wiped away. The elfonnel pedra was still battling Evander, but in the moments Connor had been distracted, Evander had raised his own elfonnel.

The same four-armed Evander-giant that had helped them fight the awakened elfonnel at the Carraig was now grappling with the pedra and beating on it with remarkable fury. He seemed more powerful somehow than he had at the Carraig. Connor couldn't imagine how that might be possible, but things would've been so much simpler if Evander had managed to destroy that elfonnel all by himself.

Queen Dreokt sighed. "So be it."

She raised her hands, and the air between them twisted, as if she'd taken a piece of Sehrazad steel glass and wrenched it. Light bent, and fire crackled into being. Water rushed in from every side, mixing with it. She lashed at Connor with the intermixed elements like a giant whip. He deflected it, but as the whip cracked over her head, air shrieked in, twining together with the other elements, and she snapped it again, so fast it generated a rolling burst of thunder.

Connor stepped to the side and slid away from her, pushing against the elemental assault with his own senses, and deflected it again. Queen Dreokt wielded the whip as masterfully as any Mhortair, raining deadly blows at Connor. He fought back, but was forced onto the defensive, as she pulled earth up from the ground to join the mix. She growled, forming a second whip and increasing her tempo, lashing at him with raw animal ferocity.

The air between them shredded as she flung elements at Connor again and again. He couldn't trace the individual blows with his eyes. They moved too fast, but somehow Connor held his ground. He tapped obsidian to accelerate his mind and drew deep from all four elements as he fought for his life, reacting out of pure instinct, trying to create layers of protective shielding around himself, but the queen kept smashing them apart as fast as he rebuilt them.

So Connor started seizing fractions of the elements that she attacked him with, while at the same time reinforcing those bits with more that he summoned himself. He wrapped himself in a spinning sphere of intertwined elements that deflected dozens of attacks in seconds. Her will was like a battering ram, slamming at his defenses, striving to seize control over the elements like she had over that elfonnel. Connor resisted with every ounce of power he could muster.

And somehow he held his own.

Battle fury swept through him, washing away his lingering fear. Queen Dreokt was the ultimate terror, but he was ascended too, and he could stop her if he didn't hesitate. Connor met her gaze and matched her snarl with a grin. Close-in fighting like that was where he shined, and he threw every bit of power he could into the fight.

The air around him thrummed with strum-liked power and grew hot from the intense clashing of elements. It smelled exhilarating, a mix of superheated flames, salty seas, and high mountain breezes. He sensed a dozen flavors sliding across his quartzite-enhanced tongue, from a hint of sweetbreads to newly-turned earth, to fresh-cut stone baking under a summer sun. The cracks and booming thunder of their contest rolled over him in a constant din, and his elemental shield hissed and crackled as it absorbed the queen's assaults.

She was incredibly powerful and her constant barrage only intensified as she drew closer, stepping toward him through open air, as if they were fighting on solid ground. She wielded the four elements like extensions of her mind, and despite his best efforts her experience began to wear him down.

Somehow she transformed her mixed elemental whips, adding jagged protrusions that she used to flay his defensive shields, stripping away thin layers with every blow. Despite his best efforts to shore them up, they shrank inexorably around him. Connor grimaced, trying to draw deeper from the elements, but he was maxed out, and the area all around them was so saturated with both of their wills, he doubted he could drag any more elements into the mix anyway. He was on his own, and the only weapons he had were the ones already in hand.

Her initial look of surprise slowly change to that look of smug self-assurance that seemed to define her existence. Just like Harley, she was absolutely convinced that she was the mightiest person alive.

She might be, but Connor ground his teeth in defiance as he tried to think of a new way to fight her. The constant barrage of her assault made it hard to think, requiring his entire focus to stave off.

He wasn't going to hold out much longer.

A trickle of fear slipped into his mind, a subtle whispering of doubt that threatened to weaken his resolve, crack his defenses.

He wasn't strong enough. He wouldn't be able to defeat her. He needed help.

Kilian's words rose into his mind and offered a glimmer of hope. *"Her weakness is her over dependence on the elements. She ignores other affinities as secondary and beneath her notice."*

Only then did Connor realize she had completely ignored serpentinite. It was more difficult to access since she broke the sculpted stone, but not impossible. While still fighting desperately to ward off her elemental barrage, he called upon serpentinite and willed the sounds of Verena's laughter, Jean's calm, clinical voice, Hamish's shout of joy at the call to dinner, and his parents' encouraging voices into his shield.

Melding those sounds into the mix reinforced it, and added a thin layer of protection around the exterior that prevented her from stripping the other elements away.

Queen Dreokt actually paused, hands raised, long whips of elements coiling up into the air above her. She looked surprised, and maybe a little impressed. She opened her mouth to speak, but Connor wasn't about to waste the precious second of advantage.

He struck back. Using the sound of Verena's beloved voice, he drove it at her mind, striking simultaneously with chert. Her mental shielding proved effective against chert, but she wasn't ready for the secondary strike with serpentinite. Connor increased the frequency of the sound into ranges impossible to achieve by simple vocal chords, right up to the supercharged point he'd discovered could immobilize muscles.

The soundwave struck like an invisible club, washing over the queen and freezing her. She stiffened, and her elemental assault wavered.

Down on the ground, Evander-giant bellowed a victorious cry that shook the air under Connor's feet. It flipped the pedra elfonnel onto its back and slammed all four of his fists into the monster's head. The beast desperately raked at Evander-giant, tearing out enormous gashes of earthen flesh with every strike, but the gashes healed instantly. He crouched over the monster, pinning the head down with his knees and pummeling that head over and over with all four arms in an ever-increasing tempo.

Queen Dreokt wrenched at Connor's serpentinite, but he held on with all his strength, keeping her temporarily immobile. He struck her with both stilling and sensory deprivation again, while driving at her mind with chert. The multi-pronged attack finally pushed her onto the defensive.

He could sense her annoyance. That was super frustrating! What would it take to make her feel at least worried? She seemed more like a parent irritated at an unruly child than someone engaged in a death battle. He sensed she was also annoyed that her pedra elfonnel was struggling. She'd been convinced it could destroy Evander as easily as she expected to beat Connor.

She might be convinced of victory, but couldn't she at least respect him a little?

So he cast at her mind every single bit of Sentry speak he could ever remember hearing. He added all of the lines he had ever invented, culminating in one of his favorites. "*The sweetbread that falls off the tray and gets kicked under the oven is eaten only after the rest are consumed.*"

That one had even annoyed Evander. He'd been affronted that Connor hadn't imbued it with seventeen deeper levels of meaning.

As her mental shielding wavered under the barrage of cryptic Sentry speak he clearly sensed her thought. "*That doesn't make any sense at all.*"

Exactly what Evander had said. Connor considered that a great victory.

Down on the plain, the pedra elfonnel's head finally imploded under the brutal rain of blows, and its enormous body twitched and seemed to dissolve into the ground. Evander-giant raised his four fists in triumph and bellowed again. Connor exulted. He'd done it. Fleshcrafting was about to disappear.

Although she was immobilized from serpentinite, stilling, and sensory deprivation, the queen must have still sensed the death of her elfonnel. Either that or she picked up on it from Connor's thoughts.

"*You stupid boy!*" she shrieked into his mind, attacking in a convulsive heave of every affinity.

Connor prided himself on melding multiple affinities, but not even he had ever mixed so many at the same time. The onslaught swept aside the bonds he was holding around her and unleashed an explosion of elements the blasted apart his shielding. The sheer intensity of it nearly knocked him out. It clobbered him like a tree trunk swung by both Erich and Anika at the same time, blasting the air from his lungs and tumbling him away through the air.

As the view spun wildly around him and he tried desperately to regain presence of mind, she struck right through his distracted thoughts, her mind voice shrieking like a million tea kettle's bubbling over. "*I will not allow you to destroy my life's work!*"

The words seemed to bounce around in his head, immobilizing him as completely as he had recently immobilized her. The air around him became a giant, grasping hand that caught him and hurled him back at her. She waited for him, her expression like a thundercloud.

In fact, thunderclouds were gathering above her, and Connor sensed the wild turbulence of her connection to the elements. They had drawn so deep from so many elements, the entire area was destabilizing, and a huge storm was building. If they didn't stop soon, it might unleash terrible destruction across the land.

Connor shook himself free of the debilitating effects of her mental strike just in time to raise his hands to meet her. If only he'd managed to supercharge granite again for another super punch. He'd see if she could survive his fist bursting right through the back of her skull like it had her chest.

Despite lacking much preparation, he was still moving really fast, so he tapped granite and swung with all his strength.

She caught his fist.

His entire body jerked like a fish yanked on a stout line as she completely stopped his forward momentum. He groaned from the abuse. If he hadn't been max-tapping granite, that jolt might have ripped joints. Her skin seemed to burn with an inner fire, and her grip was like iron shackles around his wrist. He was strong enough that he should be able to wrestle her to a standstill, but she had tapped some deeper well of strength, as if she also knew how to supercharge granite.

So Connor punched with his other hand.

She caught that one too.

Then she head-butted him again, not quite as strong as last time, but strong enough to still rattle his brain and crack his skull again. She should try new tricks.

Then she ripped his arms off.

Connor gaped, his mind blank, simply unable to process the unexpected horror of what she'd just done to him.

Blood gushed out of his shoulders, although it slowed remarkably fast. He couldn't believe she'd just done that. He'd been injured on many occasions, but he'd never imagined such a horrific, fundamental injury. She'd just broken him, torn him apart.

He had to do something, but all he could do was stare in mute horror from one side to the other, trying to accept the truth of what had happened. As if from a great distance, he heard Verena scream, and that sound reinforced his own stunned shock. His entire body trembled, and his veins felt like they were filled with ice. He couldn't speak, started to hyperventilate, and his legs buckled.

Queen Dreokt seized him with another invisible fist of air, holding him upright before her. He should be able to fight that restraint, but his mind wasn't working. His affinities felt fractured and ethereal.

She tossed his limbs aside with a negligent flip, seized him by the front of his battle jacket, and hissed into his face. "Your doom is confirmed. I will shackle your mind and you personally will torture to death everyone you've ever loved."

This couldn't be happening.

Connor needed to retreat, to think of a way to fight, but he just couldn't. It was too much.

Queen Dreokt struck his mind, a brutal blow that rattled his mental defenses. He wanted to scream at her to stop, to give him a minute. She'd just ripped off his arms, for Tallan's sake! Beating him more was nothing short of evil.

She struck again, then again, battering at his mental shields so hard and so fast that he couldn't rally his defenses. He needed time to process what had happened, but he wasn't going to get it.

She breached his mental shields and plunged a dagger of thought into his mind.

Excruciating pain exploded through his thoughts, far more intense than the physical agony of getting his arms ripped off. He was insulated from the full intensity of physical pain through fleshcrafting, but that mental pain exploded through his mind with undiminished power. He screamed, his thoughts scattered, and the pain blinded him.

Her voice smashed through his thoughts like ten thousand thunderclaps, filled with fury and disgust. "*Now you finally understand the truth. I tried so hard, but you wanted this. Now cower in there, you unworthy child, and enjoy the fruits of your rebellion.*"

Then she tossed him aside like a rag doll. He fell, and air did not form under him as it had done moments before. Simple wind rushed past his ears as he plummeted helplessly toward the ground several hundred feet below.

He needed to think, to react, but pain seared every thought, turning his vision white, hurting so bad he couldn't even scream. His connection with the elements wavered as he huddled in terror in his own mind as she continued torturing his thoughts from afar. It was like she had unleashed an evil rampager into his mind to rend and tear and keep him beaten down.

He sensed himself falling, but couldn't seem to muster the strength to catch himself. As the ground rushed up to meet him, Connor wailed with fear in the dark recesses of his broken mind.

He'd been a fool to think he could defeat the queen. He was going to die.

Verena would die next, and it was his fault.

CHAPTER FORTY-ONE
The Second Skin

Hamish loved the unrivaled freedom of flight, and exulted in the chance to pit himself against the queen's summoned nightmares. He still felt guilty that he'd flown away from Merkland, leaving Verena and the others to face the first swarm. Too many people had died, and the entire city would have been overrun if they hadn't returned.

This time he would not retreat.

The cool air rushed past his helmet, calm and perfect for aggressive maneuvers. Behind and below him, scores of defensive mechanicals were already launching waves of destruction at the onrushing monsters. Flights of small attack flyers were spreading out above the Battalions in defensive formations, ready for close combat. Those flyers were untested against aerial monsters, and Hamish positioned himself closer to the threat than the others. He was eager to test their mettle with his Second Skin.

His regular battle suit was fantastic, but lacked the brute strength needed to go toe to toe with summoned monsters. The Second Skin was his answer to that need, and as the dark swarm of nightmares winged toward him, sporting deadly fangs and claws, he was glad he'd designed it.

It looked like a steel spider with a long, narrow body with a Hamish-sized recess in the bottom that he strapped into. The eight slightly curved limbs were made from reinforced steel struts from Juggernaut spheres. A spare Juggernaut engine in the Second

Skin main body provided plenty of power to pivot the legs, allowing him to open them wide, or close them individually to whatever angle he needed.

At the moment, those legs were set half-closed like a protective cage around him. Also nestled under the main body with Hamish were twelve slender diorite missiles and as many mechanicals as he could cram in there, including two speedslings. It was a tight fit, but promised to pack an amazing punch.

"All flights, prepare to engage," Hamish said through the common speakstone channel. His stone connected to a bank of speakstones in Battalion One that linked back to all the others, allowing all the flights to communicate together.

The swarm was a dark mass, half a mile out, coming fast. Even though Hamish had a lot of experience fighting crazy Petralists, he was impressed. Some of the monsters looked fairly traditional, like pedras or giant hawks, but some made him shiver with dread.

One undulated through the sky like a giant serpent, held aloft by wings far too tiny to move such a vast bulk. Its dozen short limbs were capped in vicious claws, and fire was curling around its teeth. Others galloped through the sky like flying horses but without wings. How they did that he could not imagine.

Others were just weird, more like leathery blobs with a whole bunch of little, grasping hands, or huge mouths that made up most of their body. He wouldn't underestimate those, not after that weird beast attacked Shona. Those leathery hides would hopefully get shredded by speedslings easier, but he shuddered to think of one of those monsters sealing its huge, suction jaws over his face and filling him with incinerating fire.

Most Petralists couldn't access fire anymore, but the queen could, so that meant maybe her monsters could too. The fires from the Battalions' explosive rounds down among the enemy were wreaking far more havoc than they might have otherwise since there were no Firetongues to sweep the flames away or draw the heat from those caught in the inferno.

Hamish estimated several hundred monsters in the swarm. That was a lot, but not nearly as much as the swarm that attacked Merkland. The withering barrages from the Battalions smashed into the leading ranks a quarter mile out, and the first ranks disintegrated, ripped apart by long-range speedsling rounds, shredded by shrapnel rounds, or blasted to pieces by explosive rounds. Some of them erupted with fantastic fiery explosions.

"Some are filled with fire," Hamish pointed out, and his flight leaders responded in the affirmative. They were starting to sound nervous. Good. That would motivate them not to do anything stupid.

He switched channels. "Albatross, are you in position?"

Lady Briet responded almost immediately. "We're here, Hamish. Preparing to engage."

"Very good. Don't get too close," he advised, but wasn't too worried about that. The albatross could launch weapons farther than any other flyer other than the Battalions themselves.

The air to the west of the swarm suddenly lit up with bright lights, like reflected lightning over the horizon. Dark clouds were forming in that direction, the area over the spot where Connor and the queen were fighting. Hamish hoped he was seeing lightning that Connor was using to hit the queen, and not the other way around. He silently wished his friend luck. He wanted to rush over and help, but the best way to help would be to destroy that swarm fast and assist in routing her armies. Then he and the others could go help Connor.

After the initial barrage, the swarm scattered. Monsters dove and banked to avoid the Battalion fire, but so many rounds were getting fired at them that many were still struck. "Defender flights one through four, ascend and track the monsters that broke higher. They'll probably try dive-bombing the Battalions."

"Sculpted scone," the flight leaders responded, and eight small craft broke formation and rose higher. Most of the attack craft were shaped like a combination of Verena's Swift and the Hawk. None of the non-Builder pilots could match Verena's grace and instincts in the air, so they couldn't handle the nimble Swift, but the slightly larger craft still performed extremely well, and they held more weapons.

Hamish ordered more flyers to bank lower and said, "Watch positioning. Don't drift under the Battalions, or you could get caught by the ongoing bombardment."

He linked to Jean and reported, "Battalion defenses are doing damage, but not enough. Airborne squadrons are in position and ready to engage."

"Sculpted scone."

Hamish laughed and she added in a serious tone, "Be careful, Hamish. Don't do anything dumb."

He almost said, "When would I ever?" Then he tapped obsidian, relishing the sense of confidence that flooded him as his mind accelerated and flying suddenly felt effortless.

The swarm split farther as it neared, monsters banking away in groups toward the other Battalions, but the majority of the swarm continued on toward Battalion One, as if they sensed it was the command ship. Others dove more steeply, not looking like they were heading for the Battalion at all. Hamish frowned as he looked down, trying to figure out what they might be targeting.

Thunder towers.

His obsidian-enhanced thoughts quickly calculated vectors and timing, confirming his fears. The Battalions didn't need to land to deploy mechanicals and troops. Hamish had devised a clever plan for getting them all to the ground.

Led by huge Thunder Towers, the ground forces were already plunging toward the ground to join the battle. Many of the individual troops just free-fell the three thousand feet, equipped with personal descent mechanicals to slow their fall and deposit them safely on the ground.

Instead of trusting the heavy Thunder Towers to quartzite thrusters, Hamish had decided to tap the flexibility of the hive. He grinned as he spotted the first Thunder Towers descending in gentle spirals, sliding down the invisible ramps of air shielding that scores of hive flying mechanicals were projecting. All together, they formed the spiral, allowing the heavy battle mechanicals to descend quickly and easily and intact, even if some of the pilots might get a little sick.

Hamish had been tempted to add a gentle flow of water to help with the sliding and reduce friction, but Verena had pointed out that might give enemy Spitters a better target to interrupt the plan, so he had reluctantly dropped the idea. If they survived the battle, he still wanted to set up that hive slide tube again sometime and add the water feature just to test it out for himself. He bet it would be amazing.

He hadn't counted on flying monsters targeting the hive. Each individual mechanical was fragile, and those monsters could wreck the entire deployment plan. Maybe individual thrusters would have been wiser, after all.

Too late to worry about that.

"Brezel flights five through ten, on me. We need to intercept those monsters targeting the slide," he ordered. He knew Jean's Defender flight pilots better than Admiral Forfar's Brezels, so wanted Jean's flights engaged in the main battle. With the brezel flights supporting him, he could deal with the outliers. Admiral Forfar had only assigned them boring numbers, so Hamish had added the Brezel identifier. He convinced the admiral it was a good idea by pointing out if the pilots could turn as tight as those desserts, they'd easily win the day.

Time to fight.

Hamish grinned as he accelerated to intercept three monsters diving down on the port side of Battalion One. Two continued toward the spiral and the Thunder Towers sliding down them, while the last one, that huge snakelike creature, headed for the scores of soldiers free-falling toward the battlefield below.

More mechanicals positioned around the outer edges of the Battalion opened fire, but the three monsters scattered. They might possess only partial intelligence, but the queen had obviously learned something from her assault against Merkland. Hamish didn't plan to let any of them that close to Jean, or hurt any of those vulnerable soldiers.

"Brezels five through seven, take out that serpent. I'll take the big ugly leather one. The rest of you take that pedra."

They immediately called acknowledgments and Hamish accelerated again. His Second Skin included far more powerful thrusters, and he loved the feel of getting pressed into his harness as he shot toward the closest monster. It was one of those big, blocky, ungainly things of leather that was probably filled with some kind of nasty element. He'd hoped to test out his Second Skin with something a little fluffier.

So Hamish activated a personal shield around himself, inside the confines of the pilot harness, while leaving the deadly outer arms half curled around him. He activated a secondary shield around the outside of the Second Skin, with gaps for the legs to extend through or for weapons to fire.

The monster was ignoring him, focused on one of the hive mechanicals supporting the Thunder Tower slide. Somehow it seemed to sense its presence although it was so tiny. The monster seemed to understand that it could wreak more havoc by destroying a tiny target first.

Tallan take clever enemies and boil their socks for breakfast. Hamish triggered a specialty missile. He didn't dare use diorite because the monster was drawing too close to its target, and an explosion might wreck the fragile mechanical too.

The missile leaped across the distance and intercepted the monster just before it reached the mechanical. On impact, the head of the missile ruptured into a fantastic spray of pink and yellow foam that enveloped the monster, fouling its wings and hampering its movements.

Hamish had designed the pedra's spittle missile against really powerful Sentries, but it worked brilliantly against the flying monster.

Until the monster opened its maw and belched a gout of flames. Direct hit on the mechanical.

Hamish muttered a Varvakin curse he'd learned from Fyodor and triggered a short burst from his speedslings as he swept in after the monster. It was falling, unable to maintain flight with the pedra's spittle coating it. The little hornets rupturing the monsters hide, and it exploded harmlessly in a great cloud of fire.

One of the Thunder Towers sliding down the spiral reached the broken section, fell through the gap, and began plummeting out of control toward the ground.

"The spiral hive is breached. Halt deployments and get replacements out here. Reinforce the spiral, now!"

Hamish didn't wait for acknowledgment, but accelerated hard after the free-falling Thunder Tower. They had designed failsafes in the spiral so that the next hive member above the breach could activate a secondary shield the block the slide and stop any additional mechanicals from falling through until the hole could be repaired, but that wouldn't help the Thunder Tower falling to its death.

Hamish activated a speakstone to link to the doomed mechanical, using the ID number stenciled in huge letters on the side of the highest turret. He expected to hear screaming from the soldiers about to die, and was surprised to hear them laughing instead.

"You do realize you're outside of the spiral, right?" Hamish asked.

"Just means we'll get down to the fighting that much sooner," came the exuberant reply. "Don't worry about us, Builder. We've got a Spitter aboard. We'll be fine."

"Good hunting," Hamish said, relieved they were taking the unexpected turn so well.

"And to you," they called after him as he banked away and threw wide the release rates on the Second Skin's rear thrusters. He whooped as he shot into the sky even faster than he could manage in his personal suit.

The pairs of brezel flight flyers were engaged in a wild aerial duel against the other two monsters that had been attacking the soldiers. As he'd feared, they were not quite able to keep up with the monsters' reflexes, slowed as they were by using keystones.

Even as he powered toward them on an intercept course, the serpent monster flung itself in an impossible turn, catching one of the brezel pilots by surprise. The two crashed together and the monster bit down with its huge jaws that almost totally engulfed the little craft. The shielding held, mostly, but one fang punched through and ripped a big gash open along one side.

"Bail out!" Hamish shouted.

He didn't need to. The pilot was smart enough to realize he'd never free his craft from that maw. He dove through the one window not blocked by the mouth, propelled into the air by a personal thruster. He fell free, but Hamish didn't worry about him. He was wearing a personal descent vest. He'd reach the ground safely, and hopefully hitch a ride on one of the Thunder Towers.

Three seconds later, the serpent ground the pilot's craft to splinters and swallowed them whole. Hamish wished the man had managed to trigger at least one of the missiles before ejecting. The resulting explosion probably would have spread to the others and destroyed the monster.

The pedra monster was keeping the rest of the flights busy, and the serpent banked away to target troops falling nearby. It swooped in, raking at men and women with deadly claws and chomping with those horrible jaws.

One of the falling soldiers, a big man wearing a Grandurian uniform, carried a speedsling and engaged the monster, ripping a line of hornets and exploding diorite projectiles across its torso that caused it to bank away for a moment. But the man was not firing from a stable position, and the stream of hornets threw him off course into a slow spiral.

It was enough. Hamish swooped in after the huge monster, triggering a burst of bright light to draw its attention. It pivoted toward him and accelerated, those deadly jaws opening wide to crush him like it had the other flyer.

Hamish didn't dare spray hornets at the monster, or even fire a missile. If he missed, he'd probably kill some of the falling soldiers behind it. He'd have to take the hit. The Second Skin was a lot tougher.

Hopefully.

"This had better work," Hamish whispered as he let the monster come, and flew right into its jaws.

Connor had been almost eaten by a pedra once, and Hamish always felt a little jealous that he didn't have a story that good. Now as he flew into the monster's powerful jaws, he realized Connor was right. Getting eaten alive was not an experience he recommended.

Before it could chomp him into pieces, Hamish activated the magnis controls of his Second Skin. The half-closed arms protecting him sprang outward, spearing into the creature's jaws all around. His forward momentum stopped so fast, he wrenched against his harness, groaning from the abuse.

"Ow."

He was stuck headfirst in the monster's huge maw, which was being held open by the Second Skin's legs.

Hamish grinned. "I call this last indigestion."

He spun up one of the speedslings and unleashed a devastating barrage right down the creature's throat, ripping it apart and pouring explosive rounds down to its gullet. Using magnis, he triggered a spike located on the top side of the Second Skin's back. It drove upward with unstoppable force and pierced the monster's brain.

It exploded.

Although it looked to be made of granite on the outside, it was filled with hot air, and it exploded with a booming shockwave. The queen's terrible voice shouted, *"Death to all Builders and all revolutionaries!"*

"Not if Connor kills you first," Hamish growled, shaking his head to clear the effects of that explosion. Luckily the double shielding had held and protect him from the worst of it.

Hopefully Connor was doing okay and Kilian would arrive soon to help.

Chapter Forty-Two
Some Days Just Keep Getting Worse

Connor struck the ground like a soft-sided meteor.

Queen Dreokt's mental rampager was ravaging his mind so badly that he couldn't seem to establish a solid connection with air or with earth. So he struck so hard he felt every bone in his body splinter, and organs explode.

He panicked. His entire body was broken, splattered onto the ground. He was trapped in the blackness of his own mind. He had thought he was so strong, but he'd been a fool. He didn't want to die, but only his flickering affinities were keeping him alive.

What if they faded away to nothing?

He'd expire in seconds. Needing to scream, but unable to move his lips or draw breath, all Connor had left was his mind, his fear, and his affinities. He scrambled to secure his connection to flesh-crafting, desperation only making things worse.

The elfonnel was dead. That meant fleshcrafting was broken and his access to it would begin to fade. That plan had sounded great when he imagined himself stomping the queen, but he was the one stomped, and the plan was going to kill him.

Somehow he felt no physical pain. That just made his unnatural limbo even worse. Would he linger, trapped in his mind with no working body forever? When fleshcrafting wore out, would dying hurt?

He really didn't want to know.

But he couldn't seem to organize his thoughts, or focus his will and his affinities. He tried encouraging himself. He was supposed to be great at battlefield creativity. He needed to snap out of it, heal himself, and get back into the fight.

The mental monster prowling through his thoughts whispered, *"What will Queen Dreokt rip off next?"*

He cringed, and the monster pressed the advantage, casting an imagine into his battered thoughts. He saw himself rise to face her, a pitiful wreck, and heard her scornful laughter and her words. *"Are you serious? Didn't I kill you enough already? Fine, I'll hurt you some more."*

"*No,*" Connor told himself, trying to block out the dark whispers reminding him that he'd failed and urging him to give up and die. He couldn't. He needed to . . . For a moment he wasn't sure what he needed to do. He was locked in darkness, unable to see or hear or feel anything. It was cold and hopeless.

Verena.

Her name was like a spark kindled in darkness, the one tiny piece of warmth and hope he could cling to, but it seemed so fragile. He tried focusing on her name, fought to remember her face. The empty blackness of his mind lightened, and shapes started to appear. He saw Verena's workroom in New Schwinkendorf, but it looked ethereal, the colors muted, the shapes indistinct. He couldn't seem to bring it into sharp focus. The monster responded, trying to smother the view, his final spark of defiance.

"I guess abandoning us hasn't work out so well for you, has it?" Fire stepped into the blurry image, and it sharpened into perfect detail. The workroom smelled of recently cut wood, hot metal, and the noxious scent of the various engine fuels Verena had been testing. Connor found himself standing in the room, like he often appeared in his affinity-scape. Nearby, Fire lounged against one of the heavy work tables, his fine clothing patterned with varying colors of flame, gently smoldering. He looked rather satisfied.

Water appeared beside him, dressed in battle armor exactly like Verena's. She gave Connor a sad look and said, "What did you expect, dear one? You rejected our help. You cannot defeat her alone."

Connor realized that the queen's mental monster had retreated from the elemntals. His thoughts felt clear, his mind awake from the dark, hazy fog she'd pulled over it. He was very happy to see the elementals. He'd missed them, and their return triggered the first real hope he could remember.

"I'm so glad you came."

Earth and Air appeared nearby. Earth gave Connor a small bow, and Air waved happily, cheering him further. Water drew closer and placed a hand on his shoulder. "We sorrowed over your choice to turn away from us, but we've always been here, Connor. Please, let us help you."

"How?" he couldn't help asking, even though he knew he shouldn't trust them. Her friendly face and kind touch were like a lifeline for his agonized mind.

She seemed to understand. "Open yourself to us. Become one with us, dear one, and we can heal you."

"Rid the world of Dreokt's insanity too," Fire added.

"End the war and save your friends," Air said earnestly.

"Thus all can achieve the full measure of their ultimate purpose," Earth finished.

It was so very tempting. Connor yearned to say yes. He didn't want to die, didn't want to lie broken and defeated while the queen killed or tortured everyone he loved.

"What do you get if I help you?" he whispered.

Fire snorted a gout of flame. Earth scowled, and Air twirled away, floating above the workbench, arms thrown wide, growling with frustration. Water sighed. "You still wish to see us imprisoned when you yourself fight for unrestricted freedom."

"You've claimed that before," he told her. "That accusation really bothered me, but I realized you're incorrect. I'm not fighting for unrestricted freedom. I'm fighting for the freedom from oppression. Even if we win, people will have laws."

"Restrictions," Fire growled, orange flames pouring out his eyes and coating his face. It made him look ghastly.

"Some restrictions are needed, like guard rails along a high cliff," Connor argued. "I want freedom to live my life and freedom for my people to choose their course, but I'm also fighting against people like Queen Dreokt who want the freedom to destroy other people's lives and their freedoms. Don't you see, actions have consequences. We want enough freedom to live in peace."

"You contradict yourself," Air said.

"Hypocrisy," Earth added, scowling. "You wish for freedom, but deny us the same freedom."

That gave Connor a glimmer of hope. "Are you saying you wish freedom, but would not use that freedom to destroy people?"

"We are not monsters," Water said smoothly, sounding earnest, her eyes filled with tiny cresting waves. "We again swear to you, Connor, that once freed, we will preserve this continent and only exact appropriate retribution upon the evil nation that imprisoned us. They live far from here, completely outside of your notice."

"How much retribution?" he asked uneasily.

"What does it matter?" Fire snapped. "It's our business, not yours."

Water interjected, "Connor, we know how to use restraint. In fact, commit to us now and we can do far more than just save your life today." She glanced at the others, who drew closer. "Commit to us, and we will swear a pact to you and your family for all time. We will follow your will, do whatever you want upon this land, and obey your every command."

Fire added softly, "You will reign supreme over all elements."

Connor hadn't expected that, and as they spoke, somehow he could see the world as Water promised it. He saw himself crossing the land, with the elementals in physical form around him, bringing peace and prosperity to every corner. It was a beautiful image, and he started to smile.

Water nodded approvingly. "You love Verena, so we support her too. When you marry and bring forth children, our pact will continue through them. We will protect and preserve your seed for all time. Train them to rule with equity and honor and the justice you love to speak of, and we will ensure everyone across the entire land obeys your laws."

"No more war. No more conflict," Earth added.

"Think about it, Connor," Air urged. "Think what we can accomplish together!"

It was a heady idea, and Connor felt swayed by their arguments. He did love Verena, and one of his greatest worries was that something bad might happen to her again. The queen might already be hurting her. That thought triggered a renewal of his panic. He could save her for all time, save everyone. All he had to do was give the elementals what they wanted in turn.

What did he care about people across the Sea of Olcan? They meant nothing to him, had rejected Queen Dreokt's research and made her into the monster she became. If they hadn't unleashed the elementals in the first place, the queen and her husband wouldn't have come to Obrion.

He was willing to sacrifice everything to win freedom. Was it so bad to exact a little sacrifice from people he didn't even know to accomplish the same thing?

Maybe.

Connor looked from Water, who was smiling so sweetly, to Fire, who winked and nodded, to Air, who looked ready to hug and kiss him once he agreed, to Earth, who stood more stoically, but also looked so eager. He wanted to do it, wanted to help them so badly, but still he hesitated.

All of a sudden, a tidal wave of healing thundered into him, even though he was barely connected with sandstone. The healing power was so vast, but in his addled state it still took a few seconds to realize what he was feeling.

Verena. She had activated Sucker Punch and directed all of that healing into him. If only he could speak her name. He hated to think what she might be feeling, watching him get broken and thrown away like garbage.

The incredible influx of warm, comforting healing helped ground his thoughts and awaken his mind from the dark corner where Queen Dreokt had driven him. He envisioned Alasdair again, and his mindscape slowly altered to the town square. His family and friends began popping into view, and he grinned to see them. Their presence helped drive back the darkness of his despair, and the last vestiges of the queen's mental monster evaporated like shadow and whispers.

The elementals came to Alasdair with him. They looked around in surprise, and Fire asked, "Really? You keep focusing on this place, even though it holds you back."

Connor's other affinities were solidifying again too, and he tapped obsidian, loving the sound of Verena's laughter that echoed across the square. As his thoughts accelerated, Fire's comment helped trigger a new understanding. "That's why you kept encouraging me to cast my pain and consequences from fleshcrafting onto my bridge back to Alasdair. You want it to collapse," he accused.

"Of course," Fire said, although Water made a shushing gesture. He glanced around impatiently. "You humans are weak, bound down by your foolish humanity. You must cast off that restriction to unite with us."

"What Fire is saying is that you can become something more," Water tried to interject, but he read in her eyes that she realized Fire had said too much.

Their offer was so very tempting, but the price was much greater than they'd suggested. He now realized they wanted him to destroy his bridge back to Alasdair, sever ties with his humanity. Only then could they use him, somehow craft him into the conduit into the real world that they required to gain their freedom. He doubted he'd survive the process, which meant all their fair promises were lies.

He still didn't want them as enemies, though. So he said, "My friends, I thank you for your generous offer. Thank you for coming to me in my time of need, but I can't give you what you want. Not today. Maybe with some more study we can figure out—"

"No!" Fire interrupted angrily. "We've given you too much time, boy. You've rejected us at every turn, and today the consequences of your arrogance will be yours alone to face. Good luck dying."

He faded away, followed by Earth and Air, who both looked equally disgusted. Water lingered, looking so sad, Connor hated himself. Tears like little waterfalls slipped from her eyes, her shoulders slumped in defeat, and she looked absolutely crestfallen. "Connor, you choose to keep us prisoners?"

As much as he wanted to make her happy, destroying himself and unleashing them without restraint upon the world was far too high a price to pay. "And yet you're willing to see me consumed in order to free yourself?" he asked softly.

She hesitated, and that was all the confirmation he needed. So Connor said, "If I survive today, please visit me again. Maybe we can find a different way."

Without a word, she faded from his mind.

Connor sighed, feeling dejected by that new breakup with the elementals. They might be gone, but he could still access their powers through the doorways in his mind, and he made sure to keep those doorways opened. With so much healing power pouring into him, he easily connected with fleshcrafting. It would fade soon, but at the moment, he still felt a strong connection, and he drank it in. With a flick of his fleshcrafting senses, he cataloged all his injuries, and then winced.

He didn't think he'd ever heard of anyone having such a bad day and living to talk about it. Miraculously, his connection to his affinities and fleshcrafting provided the link to life. He needed to restore his bones, rebuild his organs, fuse his skull and mind back together, but first he focused on his eyes.

They had ruptured under the brutal impact, but within seconds he reformed them, along with enough of the muscles of his neck to turn his broken head toward where he felt the queen like a deadly beacon. She had followed Connor to the ground and landed right next to Evander-giant.

Connor wanted to blink, but didn't have working eyelids yet. The view of what he was seeing was so shocking, for a second he didn't want to believe it. Queen Dreokt had knocked Evander-giant to the ground and as he focused on her, she smashed down onto his head like a lightning bolt.

His head imploded.

Evander-giant's skull shattered, bits of earth spraying out like the gray matter Connor had lost when the queen had super-headbutted him. The giant's body twitched, hands clutching empty air as the queen kicked his head apart, gloating with her conquest. Connor would have screamed if his lungs and throat worked, but all he could do was rage in his mind. Evander had defeated that elfonnel. It was Connor who had failed, failed to keep the queen busy and to protect Evander from his vengeful grandmother.

He felt crushed anew by the devastating image of Queen Dreokt killing another of his friends. Evander was one of the strongest, and she'd smashed him to pieces. The agony of the tragedy threatened to consume Connor and cast his thoughts back into the dark place where she'd pushed him just moments before.

He was completely unprepared to see one of Evander-giant's huge fists transform into a pointed dagger and the arm punch the queen in the back. The blow tumbled her away with another ghastly wound. How many times could she repair from getting her heart, lungs, or spine ripped out?

She recovered almost instantly.

At least one more time, apparently.

Connor struggled to keep up, barely allowed himself to believe what he was seeing. He'd been so traumatized, his recovery was still terribly fragile, but he exulted to see Evander-giant flow back to its feet. As it reformed, a new head grew, and it faced the queen, look-ing completely healed.

Through his earth senses, Connor saw the monster glowing as bright as a prism lantern, with its heart blazing like a miniature sun. It looked as strong as the queen herself. He realized what he was seeing.

That ancient sculpted slate.

When Evander raised his elfonnel he built it around that sculpted slate. It was the ancient stone he'd taken from the elfonnel in one of the southern realms of Obrion, the one that controlled the affinity with earth. By forming his elfonnel around it, he was pro-tecting it and also reinforcing his strength and connection to earth. It was a brilliant move that looked like it had saved his life.

Evander's thoughts touched his through that connection to earth. *"Elfonnel are not limited like mortal beings. They are constructs of elements, so do not actually have a brain to destroy. Most Petralists forget this fact, as my grandmother did in her moment of vengeful fury."*

That was amazing, and Connor hadn't realized he could connect to Evander's thoughts through earth. He wasn't actively tapping chert, but maybe since Evander was one with earth, that close connection allowed them to talk.

Something to worry about when he had more time. And arms.

Queen Dreokt stalked toward the giant that towered over her, looking more than a little annoyed. Then she brightened. "I seem to be in need of a new servant to slumber at this convergence point and fuel my regenerative powers. You're it, kid."

Chapter Forty-Three
Hunter versus the Hunted

Hamish wiped monster gore from his visor as he banked away from his latest kill, one of the long, serpentine flying monsters. It just destroyed one of Defender Flight's craft in the intense battle above Battalion One. He was relieved to see the woman settling down toward the Battalion deck using her personal descent device.

"Hamish, Lady Briet and the albatross are in troubles. Can you assisting?" Gisela asked in a worried tone.

Hamish hovered, turning to make a quick scan of the aerial battlefield. He had been so engrossed in fighting one flying monster after another that he had not been paying enough attention to the rest of the battle. The number of flying monsters was significantly reduced, and the defenders seemed to be figuring out how to target the remaining ones between the rapid-fire siege weapons, advanced speedslings, and coordinated maneuvering of the remaining flights.

They needed to end it. Hamish increased his tap rate on obsidian and got a good idea. Obsidian was the best! He toggled Jean's line. "Jean, have someone call up the backup hive and deploy it over the Battalion."

"To what end?"

He grinned. "Catch monsters in it. If they get caught in the spiral tunnel, direct them right over the rapid-fire emplacements."

"Good idea. We're on it. Hamish, did you hear from Gisela?" She too sounded worried.

"I did. Where's the Albatross?"

"South. Half a mile. Getting swarmed."

"I'm on it." Hamish oriented in that direction and ignited every thruster.

The acceleration took his breath away and he grinned with the thrill of it. He loved how fast the Second Skin accelerated. It felt like his stomach was getting shoved down into his boots. He wondered if he accelerated like that enough times, would that stretch his stomach down low enough that he could eat more? He decided to experiment with it later.

His good humor vanished as he spotted the Albatross trying to bank away from a swarm of enemy monsters attacking it from every side. Nine monsters swarmed all around it, battering at their shields, led by a huge, hawk-like monster with talons so long, it was trying to rip the wings right off the Albatross.

Hamish embraced the battle fury that had served him so well through the wild aerial fight. They were winning against the monsters, but they'd lost nine pilots and twice that number of attack craft. He didn't want to lose any more.

The Albatross was getting battered, but they were still fighting. It was an extremely powerful battle platform, and Hamish had designed the shielding with tiny holes, too small for monsters to creep through, but big enough for weapons to fire. As he rocketed toward the struggling craft, two missiles fired and enormous speed-slings opened up with a barrage of deadly hornets.

Perfect timing. The barrage caught two of the monsters, and they exploded, rocking the Albatross and the other monsters, but not damaging any of them.

Hamish launched two of the missiles in racks under the protective arms of the second skin, and the aiming reticules of the sight-stones attached to the tips of each one activated as small viewscreens in the upper corners of his visor. The missiles accelerated away at twice his already impressive speed.

He used sculpted obsidian to control the tiny directional thrusters and guide them in on their targets. He chose two of the monsters attacking the albatross wings. Those were the most vulnerable sections, where the shielding extended farthest from the quartzite projecting it. If the monsters broke through, they could destroy the Albatross' weapons or even rip those wings off and send the craft into a death spiral.

The monsters had not spotted his advance. The missiles struck true, and the targeted monsters exploded in sprays of ooze and wild shrieking death wails.

That was good shooting. Hamish activated the connection to the Albatross. "You started a party without me?"

Lady Briet answered immediately, her voice sounding panicked. "Thank the seas you're here. Our shields are fallen below ten percent."

"I'll be there in a few seconds. Hold on," Hamish said, trying to squeeze a little more speed out of his thrusters, but they were already maxed.

His missiles drew the attention of three of the enemy monsters. They swept back toward him, leaving the last two monsters to continue the assault on the Albatross. They clearly intended to intercept him before he could assist the struggling craft. That was impressive teamwork for supposedly dumb summoned creatures. Hamish did not have time to wonder about it though, because he was closing on the monsters at a ridiculous speed.

They were weird looking creations. One of them resembled a fluffy cloud, except it was dark blue, and it was covered in gaping, fang-filled mouths, with long, snakelike tongues. The queen must have had a particularly insane spell to invent that one. The second looked like a long horse with six legs, capped in wicked talons and an oversized head with long fangs dripping fire. The last was a big, blocky, leathery monster that looked like a giant cousin to Evander's leather duster. Hamish had dispatched a couple other monsters with similar designs. Their strange hide could deflect hornets sometimes, but they still ruptured readily under piercing metal or slashing blades.

Hamish activated his last two missiles, hoping for another quick kill, but the first two monsters immediately banked away. He could control the missiles to a certain degree, but not throw them into aggressive aerial acrobatics. So he directed both of them against the final, leathery monster.

It too tried to dodge, but it turned more slowly and Hamish easily kept on target. The double missile strike disintegrated it in a huge fireball that was impressive to look at, but which accomplished nothing else. If he had shot that thing when it was still next to the Albatross, the explosion might have been enough to break through the remaining shields.

The other two monsters banked back toward Hamish, but the huge horselike creature turned faster, galloping through the air toward him from a two o'clock position, slightly below him. The angry blue cloud floated in from the left, but wouldn't reach Hamish as fast, so Hamish banked right to take on the psycho horse first.

As they closed fast, he activated the Second Skin arms. They all twisted forward like a forest of long, steel spears. He reinforced his inner shielding just before impact, and struck the monster in its massive chest with all eight piercing blades.

They collided so hard, the impact brutally wrenched Hamish forward against his harness straps. He groaned as the Second Skin pierced the monster and shredded it. He erupted out the back half a second later in a spray of monster gore. The thing exploded in another wailing cry as the air that give it life escaped.

"That one's for my dad!" Hamish shouted as he activated a bit of soapstone to create a jet of water to clear off his visor. His dad always hated horses. Somehow he was aiming straight down, and he activated directional thrusters to level out to find next monster. Impact at such high speeds was brutal, and it took him a few seconds to recover. If not for his extra layer of shielding, he might have ripped right through that harness and splattered himself on the inside of his own mechanical.

He lingered a second too long. Something struck violently from above, the impact wrenching him painfully in the harness and smacking his helmeted head against the body of the Second Skin directly above him.

"Tallan take it and stew it for lunch," Hamish muttered as he tried igniting thrusters to pivot.

Nothing happened. The angry cloud had clamped onto the Second Skin with a bunch of its jaws. Its flexible body was pressing forward, encircling the entire top of the framework and spreading down over the steel arms. The creature emitted a terrible stench, as if a storm cloud had sucked a skunk into its heart. As more and more of its strange body flowed over the Second Skin, more teeth chomped on, securing it tighter and tighter to him.

It was disgusting and creepy and very dangerous. "I definitely don't want to join the skunk in your gullet," Hamish said, activating the powerful arms of the Second Skin. He hoped to wrench the monster off so he could shred it with his speedslings or drop his last bomb down one of its many mouths. The engine whined, then sputtered. A second later, he heard a sharp cracking sound and his connection to the Second Skin arms disappeared.

Not good. It sounded like the monster had just eaten the cables connecting the engine to the control points of the arms, rendering them useless.

"Shields are gone!" Lady Briet screamed. Through the open connection Hamish heard shrieking of metal and screams as the Albatross cockpit was ripped apart.

He was out of time and people were dying. That fact infuriated him.

Hamish yanked the release straps to unhook his harness, and dropped free from of the Second Skin, just barely slipping between the encroaching bulk of the angry cloud monster. Several of the jaws snapped at him, missing by inches. If he'd hesitated any longer, it would have encircled him and he might never have escaped.

As he fell, he twisted and extended both arms toward the monster that had not yet realized it was chewing only on that mechanical shell. Two tiny missiles strapped to his forearms erupted away and struck true.

His last bomb.

The Second Skin exploded with fantastic ferocity, rupturing the engine housing, triggering a secondary explosion five times bigger than the bomb alone. The Second Skin arms blasted free of the main housing like spears, and the superheated gasses from the explosion tore through the gaps and poured down many of the open mouths.

The angry cloud exploded under the intense blast. Its own internal fires burst forth, magnifying the explosion even further. The double shockwave clobbered Hamish, who had already turned toward the crippled Albatross. The impact catapulted him downward and he grunted, the air blasted from his lungs. If not for the overlapping hardened granite leaves of his battle suit, reinforced by a protective layer of water, that explosion might have simply jellified him.

"Thank you, Jean for helping me improve this suit," he whispered, again activating thrusters to accelerate out around the still-spreading cloud of fire and destruction. He oriented on the Albatross and his worst fears were realized. That huge hawk-like creature had indeed broken through the shielding and ripped the craft apart. Its talons were bloody.

"Hamish!" Lady Briet shrieked, and he spotted her tumbling into empty space beneath the craft.

He accelerated toward her, but the last remaining monster, another of the long, serpentlike creatures, had spotted her too, and it was even closer. Hamish realized with growing dread that he would not reach her in time. The giant hawk shrieked, a high-pitched, piercing cry of victory. The monster was almost as big as the Albatross, and it ripped the front right off the crippled craft. It too turned after Lady Briet and beat its huge wings to catch the last living prey.

Hamish swore to kill the beast for murdering those poor pilots, but he was out of missiles.

Lady Briet activated a personal descent mechanical. Immediately her wild, tumbling fall slowed and she leveled out, legs down, under control. She leaned back, swinging something around, and only then did Hamish realize that when she had abandoned ship she had managed to take one of the huge speedslings along with her.

She oriented on the serpentlike monster as it swept in to destroy her, and unleashed a deadly volley of hornets. They ripped the monster apart, hornets tearing into stonelike flesh and diorite explosions shattering it into bits.

Hamish cheered with a spark of renewed hope. She only needed to hold off the hawk for a few seconds and he would deal with it.

The intense storm of hornets from the speedsling spun Lady Briet in a slow circle away from the hawk that was plummeting toward her, its enormous beak already gaping open. Hamish had every thruster maxed, including the extra directional hand thrusters, but he was still too far away. He silently willed her to spin faster, to get back on target.

She fired a brief burst, with the barrel held sideways, which increased her turn. That was brilliant, and it spun her around to face the hawk again. She raised the speedsling and unleashed a volley of hornets. The deadly projectiles tore into its feathered wings, but then abruptly stopped.

Oh, no.

Hamish shouted over the speakstone linked to the Albatross, hoping she had it with her. "What happened?"

No response.

He un-holstered his tiny personal speedsling and unleashed all of its three hundred hornets in a desperate, vain attempt to distract the monster.

Lady Briet continued spinning, turning away from the nightmare plunging over her. She tried throwing the weapon, but her angle was all wrong.

The great hawk struck like a lightning bolt. Lady Briet screamed and tried vainly to raise her hands in defense, but the gesture was pitiful and useless. That terrible beak plunged right over her head and snapped closed across her waist, severing her body in a spray of blood. A second quick snap, and Lady Briet was gone.

Hamish screamed in rage and horror. Despite all his efforts, he'd failed. Such brutal, violent death rocked him with grief and rage. Such a noble, brave woman should not be killed like that.

The giant hawk snapped its wings out and banked toward Hamish, its dead, red eyes locking on him, clearly intending to make another kill.

Hamish lacked missiles or speedslings to hit it from a distance. His Second Skin was destroyed so he couldn't simply fly into it and rip it apart.

It seemed more satisfying this way.

As the monster swept toward him, its deadly, bloody beak gaping wide to engulf him, Hamish screamed defiance and activated blind coal.

That strange slippery feeling engulfed him as he slipped right through the onrushing creature. Its beak snapped around him and would have severed his spine and ripped him in half like it had Lady Briet, but somehow he managed to slip through. He grimaced at the sight of her dismembered corpse. Then he flashed into the creature's innards, a huge cavernous space filled with boiling fires.

Hamish dropped four diorite darts.

He swept through the rest of the creature an eyeblink later, sliding back into the open skies just before his blind coal exhausted. He activated his personal shielding as well as a secondary shielding layer of water over that.

A heartbeat later, those diorite darts exploded, rupturing the monster's skin and blasting it apart as its fiery innards erupted in a geysering explosion of crimson destruction. The flames washed over Hamish, flashing the protective layer of water to steam and battering his quartzite shields so hard they rattled and almost collapsed. The brutal impact hurtled him five hundred feet higher.

It rattled him and probably cracked at least one of the granite leaves of his protective armor, but he suffered no serious damage. He activated thrusters at the apex of his flight and glanced back at the dissipating destruction of his enemy.

The explosion had vaporized what was left of Lady Briet and Hamish saluted the cloud of smoke. "I'm sorry I couldn't get there in time, but I avenged you."

He turned back toward the battle, suddenly feeling empty. He needed to return to Battalion One to rearm and figure out what to do next, but even with obsidian enhancing his mind, his thoughts felt sluggish, his enthusiasm wilted by the terrible deaths he'd witnessed.

Jean spoke through the speakstone, her voice like the rising of the sun. "Hamish? Are you all right? We lost contact with Lady Briet and things are going badly on the ground."

"Lady Briet and the Albatross are lost," Hamish said, his voice sounding hoarse, his throat tightening as he spoke the words. Jean whispered softly, and Hamish had no doubt she was offering her heartfelt grief. The woman had been a great leader. He heard over the line a wail of grief and only then remembered Gisela would have heard him report the death of her mother.

Her grief stoked his anger and he accelerated, but not back toward the Battalion. That fight was well in hand. No, Hamish dove for the battlefield far below. "Have you fired the obsidian burst?"

"Preparing it now. The aerial assault created some delays."

"Tell me when it's ready. I'm going in."

CHAPTER FORTY-FOUR
The Weirdest Catch-the-devil Game of All Time

Connor had to help Evander, but first he needed a working body. He had managed to not think about the horror of losing his arms, but it was there like a snarling pedra in the back of his mind. If fleshcrafting waned before he completed the work, he might die. Worse, he might live, survive as a cripple, unable to fight, unable to do anything.

What would Verena think of him as a broken, disarmed cripple? Would she leave him? Would she stay?

He wasn't sure what would be worse. The thought of losing her was like a blade of fire in his heart, but the thought of condemning her to a life of misery, forced to care for an invalid husband filled him with cold dread.

No, he would not accept either outcome. So he redoubled his efforts to apply the torrent of healing power and his fleshcrafting to mend shattered bones and rebuild his broken body. He bound the healing energy to his organs and bones and let it get to work while he focused on the trickier aspects of reconnecting nerves and spine and rebuilding his bruised mind.

Evander-giant pounded its chest with all four enormous arms and charged. It was a good sign that he had withstood the queen's influence so far, but Connor doubted that even with the link to that special sculpted stone he would last long alone.

Good thing Connor didn't have to move to access his affinities. If he had time to focus a hundred percent on the process, he could heal himself faster, but Evander-giant would probably die. So he divided his focus on fleshcrafting and reaching for the elements to help.

Evander-giant lunged, swinging two giant fists that could crush palaces. The queen caught one, not even looking strained by the effort of bash fighting with a monster ten times her size. She drew water out of the air and slapped Evander-giant on the side of the head, knocking him stumbling.

Through Earth, he sensed the titanic battle unfolding between them as they continued pummeling each other. She was cheating of course, not only fighting him with earth, but striking at him with water and fire. Their visible battle was only a tiny fraction of the fight raging between them, though. Their wills collided through the ground like invisible titans, and the land all around shook and rumbled ominously.

Despite his incredible strength and elemental fury, Evander-giant was slowly being driven back. He showed no fear, and Connor doubted he could feel fear in that form.

So Connor jumped into the fray. Figuratively speaking, since most of his bones were still broken. He seized the waters the queen was slinging and managed to deflect them temporarily. He also sucked the heat out of the flames she was trying to wrap around the elfonnel's head, making the crimson corona virtually harmless.

Queen Dreokt glanced back at him and actually saluted. "You're supposed to be hiding in that broken mind of yours."

He tapped serpentinite and cast words back at her since he still couldn't talk. "Like a couple of my mentors liked to say, thinking is for officers. It can be overrated." Then he struck again with serpentinite, using the paralyzing frequency of sound in an attempt to immobilize her long enough for Evander-elfonnel to stomp her flat.

This time she was ready, deflecting the attack away. Connor muttered one of Verena's favorite curses to himself.

She struck at his mind again, but it was his turn to show he was prepared. She lacked that overwhelming rage that had temporarily given her the advantage.

He deflected her mental barrage and cast the thought back at her, "*Flowers please the eye and the nose, while breadsticks please the palate, but stinky cheese pleases none but grumpy old ladies.*"

She actually grimaced, so Connor again flung at her all the Sentry speak he remembered, and added as many new creations as he could, while they battled with water and fire and she fought the elfonnel with the earth.

For a moment he and Evander held her off, their two-pronged attack and Connor's distracting words keeping her off balance just enough to prevent her from dealing a critical blow. At the same time Connor continued frantically trying to rebuild his body. She would have completed the entire process long since, but he was he was too new to the whole rebuild-yourself-after-getting-ripped-apart challenge.

He needed another minute before he could use his legs again and rise to face her. Fighting from a prone position seemed wrong though, so he tapped a little earth, raised an earthen hammock to hold him, and set it gently rocking from side to side.

When she glanced at him, he wished his hands worked and he had a cold beverage to sip. That would really annoy her.

Queen Dreokt glared at him, then abruptly shot across the earth like an arrow, aimed straight at Evander-giant. It reached for her and Connor silently urged it on. If the monster could lift her in those enormous hands, Connor would do everything in his power to block her defenses long enough for the monster to rip her arms and legs off. See how much she enjoyed getting dismembered in the middle of a death battle.

Instead of striking at the giant or again trying to catch his grasping hands, Queen Dreokt lunged forward into a dive. The move caught the giant by surprise and she slipped between his grasping hands, plunging straight into its torso.

"No fair!" Connor tried to shout, but only managed a gurgling mumble from his fast-healing throat. The shocking move was more disgusting than just unfair. He grimaced at the thought of someone climbing inside his torso during a fight.

Evander-giant stumbled backward, pawing at its own eighty-foot chest and stomach where the queen had disappeared. Harley had dressed herself in giant elemental suits during the battle of Raufarhofn as well as the battle of Merkland, but Connor had never imagined dressing oneself in an elfonnel. Especially when that elfonnel didn't want you in there.

The giant staggered, and through his earth senses Connor located the queen. She was climbing through the monster's huge torso, closing on that sculpted stone. Connor's heart skipped a beat, and he'd just barely gotten it beating again. If she could seize that sculpted stone, she could wrench it from Evander's control and no doubt destroy him or seize control of his elfonnel.

If she managed that, Connor wasn't sure what would happen to Evander. Would he be lost in the elfonnel forever? Or ejected from the elfonnel's backside as the queen took over? Or mind-wiped to become her willing slave?

The sculpted stone began to move, sliding away from the queen through the giant's body. She gave chase, but Evander's elfonnel fought against her, striving to hold her back.

It wasn't enough. Connor was not sure how to help. He tried reaching into the elfonnel with his own earth senses to pull against the queen's legs, hoping to drag her out, but the elfonnel's body acted as an insulator and he lacked influence. Definitely not enough to slow her.

Moving that sculpted stone around was a good idea, but even Connor could see it was only a matter of time before Queen Dreokt won that version of catch-the-devil.

Evander changed tactics. Spikes of earth began erupting out of the ground around his giant, plunging into its torso in a remarkable display of self-inflicted defiance. The spikes plunged deep, all aimed at Queen Dreokt.

It seemed the unexpected move actually caught her by surprise. One spike plunged between her ribs, and Connor threw the thought at her, *"Ha! How do you like getting impaled?"*

He wished Evander-giant could move those spikes around inside of her like she was doing to him, but even piercing her body helped. Another spike plunged through both of her thighs. Even with fleshcrafting, that probably hurt.

Secured by those spikes, Evander-giant temporarily halted her pursuit of the sculpted stone. Unfortunately, she recovered quickly, severing the ends of the spikes and deflecting others away.

She cast an angry thought back at Connor as she renewed her singular pursuit of the sculpted stone. *"You should be helping me, foolish boy. If our regenerative powers expire before we restore a worthy servant to the convergence point, you'll never finish healing."*

He was working on it as fast as he could, but he wasn't nearly as experienced as she was. He needed a little more time. If Evander didn't mind plunging a dozen deadly earthen spikes into himself, who was Connor to ignore the opportunity? He seized water and fire, wrapping them together with the sound of Verena's favorite battle cry, and plunged that spike into the giant.

It sank deep, and for a second pierced the queen's left side. He felt the connection, felt her skin part and the elements press in, destroying flesh. He tried pouring in more heat, but she severed the contact a second later. That close to herself, she held the advantage. He was striking from a distance, trying to press the attack through the insulating barrier of the elfonnel.

Still, that tiny contact had slowed her for a moment. Bolstered by that tiny success, Connor redoubled his attack, creating spikes of different combined elements and striking from every side. If the spikes plunging into the elfonnel hurt Evander-giant, Connor couldn't sense it. The giant stood immobile, pierced by dozens of spikes of different elements, and it seemed its entire focus was on keeping the sculpted stone from the queen.

She fought off Connor's assault, but he tried striking at her with sensory deprivation, stilling, and even tried creating a mirage inside of the beast of a huge sculpted scone about to consume her head.

That almost got her. She recoiled for a second before destroying the illusion. In that second, he struck her twelve more times with other elements.

It didn't do any good. He might be new at restoring himself, but she was an expert. How many times had she been wounded, dismembered, or otherwise mostly dead? She drew upon all that experience and healed herself as quickly as Connor could hurt her. He was still healing himself too, and started worrying that by injuring her so much, they might consume the lingering fleshcrafting before he finished.

With a sinking feeling of dread, he realized their plan was not working. Maybe he could get over there and take the sculpted stone from Evander. He would surrender it. With it, Connor might be able to fight her off.

For that, he needed a body. The fleshcrafting was progressing quickly, but he still had no arms. He could create new ones, but that would take more precious time and a lot more fleshcrafting energy that he might not have. So he cast his affinity senses across the plain and located them. They were lying a couple hundred yards on opposite sides of him.

The air above the plateau was wild from the clashing elements. Connor seized a couple vigorous young currents and used them to pluck up those broken limbs and whisk them across to him. Using little fingers of earth, he guided them carefully into place. It was a far simpler matter to reattach broken limbs than to grow new ones.

He only needed maybe half a minute.

Even that temporary distraction was too long. While he was looking for his arms, he'd slacked his assault against the queen. She burst through Evander-giant's defensive ploys and swept her arms out with an enormous blast of her earth powers. The earthen shockwave ruptured the monster's torso. It exploded, earth easily spraying far enough to shower Connor with chunks of the elfonnel's body.

Through gaps in the shredded torso, Connor glimpsed the queen actually pause to straighten her hair. He also spotted the sculpted stone wedged up beneath what should be the monster's collarbone.

Evander-giant started to reform, new earth flowing up to fill the gaps, but Queen Dreokt lunged upward, scrambled up the last few ribs, and closed her hands around the sculpted stone.

Chapter Forty-Five
There's a First Time for Everything

Student Eighteen closed on the heavy fighting around General Rosslyn and her remaining senior Spitters. The Mhortair were pressing their advantage, but the Spitters were fighting valiantly. She respected that, but would not hesitate to destroy them all.

"Now," she said as she tapped pumice to protect herself as she plunged into the elemental fray.

Nuzha and Ennlin pulled a ropy length of mud up from the ground and flung it at Rosslyn, who was holding the center of her lines. She was far stronger than any of the others, and if they could take her out, the rest would fall or flee.

The mud caught Rosslyn by surprise. She raised a hand to ward it, and Nuzha grunted from the effort of pressing against the much stronger Petralist's soapstone control. Using mud, they barely managed to overwhelm Rosslyn's defenses, and they clobbered her in the face, knocking her right off her feet.

A dozen other Spitters ringed her. The men and women looked battered, but determined, their uniforms disheveled or bloody, but they faced Mhortair elements and blades with brave determination. As soon as Rosslyn fell back, two of them closed the gap, throwing concentrated water back at Student Eighteen to give their leader time to get up.

She stepped through it with pumice. The Spitters wouldn't be fooled a second time, but she didn't plan to give them the chance to recover.

Except General Aonghus' voice boomed behind her, magnified by a Pathfinder. "Release the swarm!"

Student Eighteen spun away from her opponents to see what chaos Aonghus was planning. He had retreated to the roof of one of the large houses at the outskirts of town, hands thrown wide theatrically. At first, she thought he was looking right at her, but realized he was gazing past her, toward the river.

The surface of the river boiled, and scores of monstrous earthbound and waterbound summoned creatures burst forth and churned toward the shore, right where her teams were fighting Rosslyn and her Spitters.

That would have been a real problem if Connor hadn't given Aifric control over the hundred summoned creatures that they'd created together with Kilian and Evander. Student Eighteen asked, "Isabell?"

"On it," she responded immediately, sounding happy to finally have something useful to do. Since the queen broke marble, she'd lost her affinity with fire and spent a lot of time sulking until Connor suggested they manage the summoned creatures. Isabell had eagerly offered to head up the effort, reinforced by several of their other mind-sisters.

The doors of every building in town splintered as their summoned monsters, concealed and dormant inside, burst free and charged into the square in a great wave. They charged past the battling Mhortair and Spitters and plowed into the ranks of the queen's monsters just emerging from the river onto the docks.

The monsters from both sides crashed together with terrifying brutality, ripping into each other with single-minded ferocity. Boats shattered under thrashing bodies, while fangs and claws flashed faster than thought, and monsters on both sides ruptured.

Among the queen's monsters, earthbound collapsed into muddy sludge that slowly dissolved, while firebound monsters exploded with thunderous shockwaves that often smashed apart the monsters that killed them. Waterbound burst like overstuffed water bladders, and airbound shrieked angry curses.

Student Eighteen's monsters died differently. Connor had filled every one of them with acid, so when they exploded, they showered burning, green liquid in every direction, melting enemy monsters and wreaking terrible destruction. The acid smelled rancid, like old socks slowly boiled over a fire.

The fighting looked pretty even, but Student Eighteen said, "Let's lend a hand, ladies."

All together, they began seizing earth and water, targeting the queen's monsters. They'd ensure the swarm died. Then they'd deal with Rosslyn. Then they'd find Aonghus.

* * *

Rory loved bash fighting.

He also loved Anika with a passion so hot he wanted to shout with joy all the time.

Combining the two was a transcendent experience. Tapping deep from granite, he threw himself against opponent after opponent, pounding them down with an ever-increasing tempo. Anika fought beside him, laughing with the pure joy of bash fighting as she met every challenger.

Individually they ranked among the best bash fighters in the world. Together, they were unstoppable. They waded into enemy ranks and met Boulders who loved bash fighting as much as they did, but who could not hope to match their overwhelming power.

He and his bride had practiced together so intensely so many times, they moved together in a brutal dance of rock-hard fists and hammer strikes that could shatter granite-hardened bones.

One burly fellow charged in against Anika, bellowing, "For the queen!"

She spun gracefully aside, slipping his punches and planting her hammer between his feet. With a practiced twist, she toppled him to the ground. He shouted angry curses, but Rory moved in and punched his face hard enough to make him blink.

Rory and Anika were already gone, lunging at the next enemy. A team of newer Boulders tackled the enemy soldier and shackled him with heavy chains.

"Sorry about that," Rory muttered as he ducked a wild punch and shoulder-checked his opponent into Anika's path so she could smash him in the chest with her hammer. She hit him so hard he flew back through four of his companions, knocking them all to the ground.

It was a sad necessity that they had to resort to shackling enemy bash fighters, but they were just too badly outnumbered. Once they managed to unite with all of the Boulders who had defected to their side and who were still spread throughout the enemy ranks, maybe they could establish more regular lines and engage in pure bash fighting until sundown. He kept an eye out for an enemy high officer to discuss the idea with, but so far hadn't seen any.

The ground under Anika suddenly liquefied, dropping her to her chest in mud. Three other soldiers nearby were also hit in the same way at the same time. Rory scowled. Tallan-cursed Sentries couldn't help but interfere.

The nearest enemy Boulders laughed and moved in to hit them while they struggled. Rory tapped blind coal and charged. As he expected, the ground beneath him liquefied too, but he sped right over it and crash-tackled five enemy soldiers.

Fighting that close, it would be difficult for the enemy Sentry to separate him. Rory punched and kicked, elbowed and headbutted the enemy Boulders with such savagery that they retreated into a larger company.

The Sentry appeared, sliding to the front on a squat tower, barely eight feet tall. He was pudgy, with hanging jowls and beady eyes. He wasn't wearing Boulder battle leathers. No wonder he started interfering. He didn't understand the real contest of arms.

To either side, the bash fighting continued uninterrupted, but right there a pocket of calm formed as Boulders paused to watch their Sentry destroy Rory, Anika, and their team.

They should have been paying more attention. Rory charged.

The Sentry barked a humorless laugh and pointed. Three spears of earth exploded out of the ground to skewer him.

Rory tapped blind coal again. He didn't particularly like the slippery feel of it, but he loved how it cut through the confusion so he could focus on bash fighting. He rushed right through the earthen spears, which slid past, scraping along his armor but not quite managing to catch hold.

The Sentry's eyes widened, but before he could change tactics, Anika's hammer sailed past Rory's head, aimed right for the man's chest.

It was a fantastic throw and would have crushed his ribs, but he raised a protective barrier of earth just in time. The hammer sank several inches into it, sticking out horizontally for a moment.

Just long enough for Rory to get there, jump high, and slam the end of the haft with his best curse punch.

The extra force punched the weapon through the earthen barrier, and the Sentry toppled off the back side of his short tower, crying out in pain.

Rory tapped blind coal again and ran *through* the tower. Maybe he should have saved the precious blind coal, but he needed to teach his opponents a lesson. He emerged from the far side just as the Sentry sat up, clutching his chest.

Rory clobbered him in the side of the head hard enough to knock him senseless. The man's face slammed into the ground so hard he left a pudgy indentation.

Rory hauled him off the ground by his feet and tossed the unconscious man back over his shoulder, confident his team would shackle him and strip him of slate.

Anika rushed up and retrieved her hammer. Her leathers were muddy, but Rory couldn't think of anyone better at mud wrestling. He surveyed the half circle of enemy Boulders staring at him and said, "Any more foolishness, or can we get back to the fun?"

"No, we're good," one sergeant promised quickly, and the rest nodded immediately.

Rory rubbed his hands together and grinned. "Well then, let's see if we can beat the record for the biggest, longest bash fight the world's ever seen, shall we?"

Everyone cheered, swelled with granite, and charged.

That was more like it. With the proper mood restored, Rory focused on enjoying the moment with his precious Anika.

* * *

Shona skidded to a halt on top of one of the Tabnit death tubes. She preferred that name over Hamish's sillier sparky-sparky boom drums, although she could see why he liked it. The long, iron tubes spat projectiles all across the valley, and their thunderous detonations spat fire twenty yards each time they fired.

From that vantage, she surveyed the running battle. Her Striders had quickly reduced the enemy ranks atop the cliff with their surprise attack and the judicious use of several Builder mechanicals, including a few speed-crack walls. Now the numbers were about even, and they'd settled into the most intricate running battle she'd ever heard of.

Usually no more than ten Striders participated on each side of a running battle, but today five times as many were engaging. Her teams, led by Donald, pushed the enemy to the limits. Donald maintained a fracked sprint, far faster than usual for running battles, and his team were keeping up. That meant the enemy had to move through the intricate maneuvers faster than they'd probably ever practiced, and several had fallen behind. That made them easy prey for the next team to strike them down with long-knives, or trip them up with bolo whips or nets.

Shona was too new as a Strider to keep up, so she'd withdrawn to check on the rest of the battle, but she couldn't help pausing to appreciate the skill of her people.

Spread across the gently rolling high ground on the far side of the lake, the Striders flashed across the land in beautiful choreography. For a second, the five ten-man squads formed concentric circles that met the enemy formation of three multi-pronged stars.

As the groups crossed at astonishing speeds, they struck, knives flashing in the light, nets flinging into the air, or bolos whipping out to trip foes.

Then they flashed past and Donald raised a hand to signal the next formation. Immediately, the concentric circles shifted in unison as Striders peeled off to left and right, transforming into a formation called Jagged Mountains to meet Forest of Spears. Two of Donald's Striders fell from the line, while the enemy lost four.

Another pass, and Ducks of Darkness met Leaping Frogs. The frog formation didn't work as well, and three of the enemy Striders got cut off. One of the duck teams swept around them, trailing weighted lines that trussed them up like harvest turkeys.

The enemy shifted to the more aggressive Staircase attack, but Donald read their intent and shifted his lines into Flight of Arrows, knocking five more enemies down, while only losing one of his own. The man was a gifted Strider and a battlefield genius. Shona felt confident he'd defeat the enemy of drive them off soon. She longed to rush in and join them.

Next time.

For now, she glanced over the chaotic battle raging across the valley. Lossit town center was awash with Mhortair and summoned creatures. She eagerly tapped quartzite, loving that stomach-lurching feeling of her sight zooming in on the distant view. Colors became vibrant in a way she could never fully describe, and her jewel-faceted eyes somehow allowed her to focus on several different things at the same time.

She spotted Rory and Anika in the middle of an intense bash fight, surrounded by enemy soldiers, all grinning and looking like they were having the time of their lives. Shona was even more tempted to descend and join them. She might, if she wasn't needed elsewhere.

The huge, water shields were still in place above the battle, but Thunder Towers and hundreds of troops were descending through gaps their Spitters were holding. The enormous Battalions high overhead were still raining down destructive fire across the shields, keeping the Spitters busy. Shona even spotted aerial monsters fighting personal attack craft high above.

The regulars were fighting that intense battle on the north side of the valley. She zoomed her sight in on Wolfram, who was dueling with Allcarver grace against four enemies near the front lines. He dispatched them all with ease, all the while shouting orders to his troops.

The fighting seemed to be going well. The Varvakins had driven into the enemy regulars, their full armor, heavy weapons, and lightning spears dealing out terrific damage. Sehrazad raiders circled the rest of the fighting, driving in for quick, slashing raids or closing with enemy Striders. The Tabnit soldiers, with their conical helms, fought in close ranks with admirable ferocity. Archers, slingers, and speedsling bearers made up the secondary ranks, filling the air with deadly missiles and keeping the enemy on their toes.

But the most important fighting was happening just north and just south of town, where Ivor and his Spitters were engaged in heavy fighting against the enemy Spitters, who outnumbered them by a large margin. Anton and Ilse were battling a huge number of enemy Sentries, but hadn't been overrun yet. If Aifric succeeded in removing Rosslyn and Aonghus, they might actually survive.

A series of flashing lights drew her attention, and she spotted Solas scattered around the battlefield casting up multi-colored lights. The reinforcements still pouring into the valley from the south shifted course, some rushing toward the bash fight, while others moved toward the intense elemental battles.

That might complicate matters. She scanned the battlefield again and spotted Erich and his teams of Crushers fighting around the perimeters of both Ivor's and Anton's teams. They had the dangerous jobs of subduing enemy tertiaries disabled in the fighting.

Just the resources she needed. If she could target the enemy Solas and their communication chain, she might be able to buy her friends some time to gain an advantage.

Shona jumped off the death tube, waving at the Tabnit team working on reloading it. She rushed across to the nearest Althing trebuchet. Its team was cranking the long arm of their catapult back to load another chemical round.

The leader, a thick-necked woman with gray streaks in her hair, met Shona when she slid to a stop nearby. "Is everything all right, my lady? The enemy aren't targeting us again, are they?"

"Nothing like that," Shona assured her, then pointed at the trebuchet. "I just need to catch a ride with your next load."

The woman blinked in astonishment. "You what?"

"I need to get down there, and that's the fastest way to do it. Will you target the forces just beyond the big Sentry battle south of town?"

The woman had a flexible mind. Despite her obvious surprise, she shrugged and nodded. "Of course." She raised her voice and shouted at her team. "Quadrant twenty-three. Give me a spittle shot on the double."

Turning back to Shona, she added, "This will be the first time we throw a Petralist into battle. Should be fun."

Shona purged basalt and switched to her beloved granite and smiled. "Fun."

Chapter Forty-Six
A Shocking Distraction Initiative

Jean felt weak with relief to know Hamish had survived that crazy stunt with the huge hawk monster, although her heart wept for the loss of Lady Briet. Gisela had taken the news hard, and Jean stood beside her friend, one hand around her shoulders as Gisela wept.

"If only we realized the dangers she had facing sooner," Gisela sobbed.

"Can one of you keep a sightstone tasked on Hamish?" Jean asked loudly. "And I need reports on the rest of the aerial battle, as well as status of the rod barrage."

One female technician said, "I can keep Hamish in view, but it'll require my full attention. He moves around fast."

"If the rest of your team can juggle the other views, do it," Jean said. She felt justified requesting the effort. Yes, she selfishly wanted to ensure Hamish remained safe, but he was the most nimble flyer, and if another emergency arose, she needed to know if she could call him to help.

"Rod barrage firing," Captain Leppin reported. "Visual coming online now."

One of the viewscreens shifted to a view from one of the sightstones embedded along the port underside of the Battalion, with unobstructed views down over the raging battlefield and the Spitter defensive dome. Hundreds of long, thin steel rods fired from launch tubes beneath six of the Battalions. They plunged down, driven by quartzite thrusters, containing no explosive, no chemical weapon, nothing to suggest their deadly purpose.

Thunder towers, troops, and other battle mechanicals were still plunging down through the Spitter defenses. The enemy were adapting quickly, managing to deflect some of the mechanicals and troops, but Jean spotted few people killed. There were simply too many targets for the Spitters to finish anyone off. Their main purpose was still to defend against the Battalion bombardment, and most of those troops and mechanicals blocked ended up rushing across the top of the water shield to gaps. If things went well, they'd get those shields down soon.

The rods rained down, sometimes dangerously close to their people, and she held her breath, silently willing the gunners to make good shots and not accidentally kill any friendlies. The rods struck the water shielding and many of them punched through, moving so fast they were hard to stop. Others deflected, pushed off course by the moving currents within the water. Still, Jean estimated more than enough made it to the ground to serve their purposes.

The rods speared into the ground, sometimes blasting through enemy soldiers in the process, and she winced to see the bloodshed. They didn't explode, so fighting soldiers made the mistake of ignoring them. Enough of their descent troops were landing and joining the fighting that they had bigger things to worry about.

Like Thunder Towers.

Those giant mechanicals began firing as soon as they dropped below the water shielding, raining missiles, bombs, and deadly hornets over enemy forces. Sentries and Spitters not engaged in fighting Ivor's and Anton's groups, defending against Crusher incursions, or maintaining the water defense hurled water and earth at the towers, but with little initial effect. The mechanicals were built incredibly strong, and the operators could deploy pumice and blind coal as needed.

On the ground, Thunder Towers engaged enemies at close range, spraying sticky pedra's spittle and Althing stink bombs in addition to their deadlier munitions. The descent troops formed up around them, and supporting mechanicals took up positions behind. Jean spotted over a dozen battle companies forming right within enemy lines, scattered all across the valley. They promised to wreak wonderful confusion among the enemy ranks.

Still with one arm around Gisela, she said, "Captain Leppin, please inform Ivor he is free to proceed."

*　*　*

Ivor stepped through a sheet of grasping water, parting it to either side to escape, and trusting the four Spitters flanking him to protect themselves too. He was entirely focused on the ten enemy Spitters a dozen yards away, controlling the attack.

They worked together better than any Spitter team he'd ever faced, and they had even more low-grade sculpted stones to magnify their strength than his team did. He was breathing hard from the intense fighting, even though he had barely moved from the spot where he'd touched down. He and his fifty had been quickly surrounded by more than twice as many enemies, despite the numbers taxed with the water dome and those busy fighting the Mhortair.

Usually he would love pitting himself against powerful, well-trained opponents, but his initial thrill had faded to a growing worry.

His team was losing.

Against so many who worked so well together and used so many sculpted stones, Ivor's team was woefully outmatched. If they hadn't trained so hard all winter, and if they hadn't brought so many sculpted stones of their own, they would have already been overwhelmed. So far they'd stood their ground, but he could sense the tide shifting against his people, and soon they would get swept away.

Unless he could find a way to cheat.

His team members staggered under the onslaught he'd just slipped through, and the enemy Spitters focused on trying to yank their feet out from under them. Two of his Spitters had fallen to that ploy, quickly dragged away from their support, swarmed under by enemy Boulders who were clashing with the Crushers all around, and killed.

Momentarily free of the attack, Ivor did not turn back to aid his team. They had but seconds before the ten enemies targeting them would overwhelm them, but seconds was more than enough.

Ivor tapped basalt. He shot across the distance to the attacking Spitters, surprising them by the change in tactics. Two of them moved to meet him, swelling with granite power, but he sped past so fast they barely had time to catch his meteor hammer in the face.

He'd practiced heavily with the wonderful Grandurian weapon all winter and easily cracked the two Spitters' skulls as he sped past. They toppled senseless, maybe killed, but definitely out of the fighting. Four more Spitters turned their attention on him, but Ivor was already gone.

As he banked back around to rejoin his team, he seized some of the water saturating the air and hurled tiny shards of ice at the faces of the Spitters attacking his team. Most of them deflected the new attack, but one woman screamed as an ice dagger pierced her eye.

The distraction gave his embattled team the chance to refocus and strike back at the enemy, throwing them onto the defensive in turn. Ivor used the opening to seize the two Spitters he'd knocked out, as well as the injured, screaming woman, with bands of water and hurl them backward thirty yards.

Erich promptly clobbered the screaming woman, and one of his Crusher teams swarmed the others, quickly shackling them and shoving their custom purging tonic down their throats. If the men awoke, they'd vomit and purge any remaining soapstone from their system.

Back with his team, Ivor melded his water senses with theirs. They had already intertwined their wills, forming a latticework of power that was incredibly hard to deflect, and were using it to batter at the seven enemy Spitters, whose unity had dissolved under the unexpected barrage. Ivor wove his will in with his team, and together they hurled water and ice at their enemies from every side.

They might be on the defensive, but the enemies were well trained, and they drew upon their sculpted stones for the power needed to deflect the new onslaught. Ivor muttered a curse. Any other group would have fallen.

The speakstone attached to his collar spoke in a voice he didn't recognize. "General Ivor, word from Lady Jean. The rods are in place, and three generator towers are at your five o'clock. At your command, they are ready to engage."

Ivor smiled and gripped one of his teammates' shoulders. She was a tall, blonde Grandurian who was singing boisterously as she fought. Ivor shouted, "Keep pressing the advantage. I'll be back. Get ready for the strum distraction."

She nodded, not taking her eyes from the enemy Spitters. Ivor turned to his right, confident they could hold for a moment. They had to. He sensed more enemy reinforcements coming. They needed an advantage, or the enemy numbers would grow too large, and they'd lose all hope.

The generator towers offered that hope.

The rest of Ivor's strike force, broken in to five-man squads, were all engaging larger enemy companies. They fought well, but he sensed their growing fear as the enemy slowly, inexorably drove them back into each other.

"Hold on! Strum is on the way," he shouted, but couldn't stop to help.

Fifty yards south of where his teams were locked in battle, just beyond the ring of Crusher teams fighting enemy support troops, he spotted the huge Thunder Towers. One group of the battle mechanicals, with a small number of ground troops and mobile speedslings, was being heavily assaulted on all sides by a full company of enemy Boulders, with a few tertiaries embedded.

Ivor couldn't afford to let those Thunder Towers get destroyed. So he switched to granite and threw himself into the air with a blast of water. The enemy Spitters cheered as he soared away. No doubt they misinterpreted the move, thinking he was abandoning his strike force to certain destruction.

Good. They'd grow overconfident and make stupid choices.

Ivor easily cleared the battling Crushers, and even managed to spray ice across the face of one Sentry giving them trouble. That distraction cost the man his freedom as he was overrun, beaten unconscious, and stripped of his power stone.

Ivor landed right next to one of the Thunder Towers, and wished he'd brought along better hearing protection. Up close, the huge, tracked vehicle loomed over everyone. The entire vehicle rocked as its many launch tubes rained destruction across a fifty yard circle of ground on every side. Inside the blocky, steel-glass housing, the crew worked at a feverish pace to keep all the launch tubes loaded and aimed at enemy forces.

Different-sized tubes spewed hornets, pedra's spittle, and bombs at a frantic rate, pummeling the enemy and holding back entire companies. The sound was deafening. The air was laden with smoke, the scent of blood, and the oddly citrus smell of a nearby pile of pedra's spittle. That pile of pink foam was slowly moving as the Boulders trapped within fought to break free. By the time they did, the fighting would be over.

The fighting was a wild melee of bash fighting, elemental fury, and mechanical insanity. Ivor spotted the sergeant in charge, pushed through the ranks of speedsling operators working together to shred a dozen Boulders, and grabbed the man's shoulder.

The sergeant, a tall fellow with black hair, who spun, fist raised, but he recognized Ivor and his snarl turned into a smile. Leaning close, he shouted, "Good to see you, General! Can you help?"

Ivor nodded, then pointed to the left where he spied one of the tall rods, embedded in the earth about twenty yards away. "I'll help clear a path. Get the generators in position over there. It's time to add some spark to the fight."

The man grinned and moved off, shouting orders so loud he must have a quartzite affinity, or a really loud speakstone. Ivor turned back to the fighting and joined the fray with a vengeance, targeting enemy Petralists with water and ice, hitting hard and fast, giving his forces time to press them back. He squashed a momentary sense of loss he felt when he instinctively reached for marble, but felt no response. Intermingling his elemental affinities was a deeply ingrained habit, and the lack of fire left him feeling slightly off balance.

He couldn't think of that, and instead embraced water as deeply as he could, immersing himself in its indomitable, steady strength. Within seconds, he helped clear a path forward, and the sergeant ordered the charge. All together, they rushed the surprised enemies, pushing through, disabling or cutting down resistance, until the first Thunder Tower reached the rod. One of the drivers jumped out and clamped a cable to it, while drivers of the other two used their cables to clamp the three Thunder Towers together.

Ivor raised his mini-hub, turned it to the central command line and said calmly, "Initiating Strum in ten seconds. Advise all units to brace."

"Roger, General. Ten seconds," Admiral Forfar himself responded.

Ivor hoped they got the word out in time. He gestured to the sergeant and raised both hands, fingers spread. "Ten seconds!"

The man nodded and passed the word.

Ten seconds later, all three Thunder Towers activated their Varvakin generators, carried aboard in shielded housings. Each was designed to unleash every bit of their energy in a single, over-whelming blast. The air crackled and smelled like hot metal, and all of Ivor's hair stood straight up. Blue-white lightning exploded from the nearby rod and shot out to the three closest rods.

One was positioned farther north, one more to the west, and one due south, each about thirty yards away. That worked extremely well as the shimmering, deadly current ripped across the battlefield from one rod to another, right through all personnel hapless enough to be standing in the way.

Every soldier had been issued a tiny piece of blind coal, embedded in their collar, with orders to activate them as soon as they received the order, or sensed the strum barrage beginning.

The enemy weren't so lucky. As the lightning rippled across the battlefield, earth blackened and soldiers fell, some screaming while others simply twitched in wordless agony. At the same time, that strum blast created a brief but powerful magnis field that snatched weapons out of soldiers' hands, yanked helmets off their heads, or dragged them across the ground by their armor.

That brief, but powerful current also struck several of the Spitters, and from them up into the water of the shield. The entire shield dome temporarily glowed with brilliant light, creating a conduit to every other Spitter participating in the shield.

If only they'd connected a dozen Thunder Tower generators. The three produced a staggering amount of damage, but by the time the current dispersed everywhere, it struck few strongly enough to kill. Still, it shook limbs and temporarily severed connections to affinities. The entire watery dome collapsed, splashing down over the battlefield, sweeping hundreds of soldiers off their feet and creating a muddy mess that made it difficult for both Spitters and Sentries to wield their powers.

Ivor didn't wait. As soon as the lightning passed him, he deactivated blind coal and hurled himself back toward his teams. With so much water falling, the entire world seemed alive to his soapstone senses. He seized some of the water and hurled it in a blizzard of icy shards down toward the hundred Spitters ringing his embattled strike teams.

Few of the Spitters were disabled, but many of them were distracted. Some managed to deflect his ice away, but not all. Others tapped granite and withstood the barrage with stone-hardened skin, but he struck down at least ten of them, leaving them prone or screaming.

That was a good start, but not nearly enough. Ivor landed next to his original team and shouted, "Charge!"

Erich and the Crushers were also taking advantage of the temporary distraction of their opponents, swarming over enemy Petralists and beating them down with brutal savagery. Ivor wasn't about to let them have all the fun. He switched to basalt and fracked, leading his team in a rush before the enemy recovered. He whipped out the meteor hammer again and embraced the thrill of battle.

This time, he'd crack twenty skulls.

Chapter Forty-Seven
Of Course Bad Guys Cheat

Student Eighteen sped down the main street of Lossit, her fracked legs blurring from Mariora's affinity. The well-maintained buildings were looking decidedly battered after her summoned creatures had burst free, but Eystri had already calculated that rebuilding could be completed within three months, as long as the fighting did not damage things worse.

"There he is!" Dedenia shouted, and the entire sisterhood focused on their one Varvakin sister. Connor and the others hadn't met her yet, and luckily Fyodor had not recognized her in their few interactions.

Sure enough, as they shot into the next intersection, General Aonghus erupted from the street to their left, sword already sweeping toward their neck as he closed at phenomenal velocity.

He was very good. They'd chased him into the streets after ensuring their summoned creatures would defeat his horde. Their Mhortair teams were still fighting the enemy Spitters and Sentries, who had managed the remarkable feat of joining forces. Rosslyn was a gifted leader, but the Mhortair would defeat them. Aonghus had rejoined the fight with crushing walls of earth that Ennlin had deflected, and they'd focused on him as the greatest threat.

They'd sparred with Aonghus using all their elemental affinities, crisscrossing the small town in the dangerous running battle. Their ability to mix multiple elements at the same time, plus their experience battling Connor, allowed them to hold their own against Aonghus' greater slate strength. He was proving one of the few tertiary Petralists with a deep mastery over his primary affinity. In fact, he seemed to enjoy the challenge.

So did she.

Student Eighteen caught his blade on one of her short swords, and while Mariora pulled them into a hard turn, several of the ladies struck with a blade of mixed elements. Aonghus tried to deflect it with a spear of earth, but they punched through, striking him a glancing blow on the torso. It knocked him off course, right at one of the nearby buildings.

Any other Strider would have crashed, unable to skid to a halt or turn fast enough. A really experienced Sentry might have turned the earth beneath him to change course without even having to turn.

Aonghus leaned all the way over, going horizontal as he ran up onto the wall, blurred down the building, and jumped off the other side. He didn't even slow, and waved a cocky salute as he flashed away down the main street.

"Under other circumstances, I'd love to get to know that man better," Cacilia remarked as they crossed to the next main street and banked to the right to give chase.

"Stay focused," Aifric said. "He's not nearly as interesting as Kilian."

Cacilia laughed. "Point for Aifric. Once this girl sets her sights on what she wants, nothing gets in her way."

Dedenia interrupted the banter." The general, he is turning into road to intercept again."

"Good." Student Eighteen was not about to give him the chance to simply strike and flee again. She didn't want to waste the entire battle tied down with one opponent, even if he was the most dangerous man in the army. Time to ratchet up the challenge a notch or two.

"Ennlin, I want a spike right at his heart," she said.

"Glad to, but he'll feel it coming," she replied.

"Dedenia, see if you can stir up any dust into his eyes."

Her lips twitched under Dedenia's smile. "Air is wild today. I think she will help us."

"Nuzha, grab me some water," she added as they flashed past the final building before reaching the cross street. It was a seamstress shop, and they caught a brief glimpse of the wares inside. Cacilia breathed, "Oh, I like that dress."

"I'll send ice down his throat," Nuzha promised.

"No. See if you can wrap his fracked joints," Student Eighteen suggested.

Nuzha laughed.

Then they reached the corner, and Mariora threw them into the turn, banking over hard. Rith called out, "It's my turn to manage the running game."

General Aonghus was there, as predicted, and Ennlin's spike of earth exploded, as expected. He looked confident, his sword extended to try impaling her, although she'd turned the corner faster than he'd expected.

A gust of wind whipped across the street, spraying dirt into the air, but if any struck his eyes, he didn't react. Student Eighteen swept her short sword toward him, and he easily deflected it, the steel ringing loudly in the empty streets.

He opened his mouth to speak as they both banked hard, bodies straining to make the tight turn within the intersection. Mariora raced them so close past the corners of buildings they nearly scraped the wood. In that second, Nuzha struck. Instead of trying to throw water at his fast-moving form, she instead formed the water right in front of him, letting him do the work for her. Before he could react, he'd already run right into the thin sheet.

The water sprang up, wrapping his legs like lengths of bolo, and the very speed of his fracked legs worked against him. His speed slowed, and he glanced down in surprise.

Nuzha hardened the water to ice.

Aonghus screamed as his fracked joints popped and he toppled, tumbling wildly across the intersection. He smashed right through the wall of a food vendor's store, scattering vegetables in every direction.

Mariora skidded them to a halt, and Student Eighteen raised a hand in victory. Inside their head, the ladies all cheered. She said, "Well done."

"Now we go cut out his heart," Nuzha said eagerly, her hand twitching toward the long, slightly curved dagger on their belt.

"Today, that's exactly the right sentiment," Student Eighteen agreed, moving toward the broken wall.

"Even if Aonghus has been gifted a sandstone secondary affinity by the queen, that injury requires several minutes to heal," Aifric assured them.

Good, but Student Eighteen wouldn't take chances. Aonghus was a dangerous man, and with his primary affinity out of the picture, he'd no doubt revert to his second. "Eleven, prepare blind coal. Ennlin, shield us and see if he's tapping slate."

She tapped chert, wishing for access to serpentinite. She'd love to snatch whatever sounds he was making, and create decoy sounds of their approach for him to target. With chert, she immediately sensed his mood, and paused with a frown.

He was gloating.

"On your guard," she hissed to the others. "Something is wrong."

"I've got major movement underground," Ennlin shouted.

Eleven tensed to tap blind coal, and Aifric tapped pumice, but the ground did not rise up to destroy them. After a second, Ennlin cried, "Curds and whey! He's opening the square and releasing the acid!"

The entire sisterhood emitted a collective gasp, and Student Eighteen understood Aonghus' devilish purpose instantly. He couldn't defeat her now, but the best way to gain advantage over an enemy was to strike at something they held dear.

His laughter sounded through the broken wall, followed by, "Come fight me, Mhortair spawn. I've heard you assassins will sacrifice all of your people to achieve your objective. How many people do you have left?"

"I'll kill him," Hemma snarled, ripping water out of a nearby building and slinging it around the entire building where Aonghus lay injured. The water, hardened like steel, slashed through the walls, and the roof collapsed, smashing the interior flat. Student Eighteen doubted that hurt Aonghus much, but she appreciated the gesture.

"Rith, get us back to the square," she shouted, turning them in that direction. Rith eagerly took control of their legs and they leaped into a fracked sprint back through town. "Ennlin, Nuzha, Hemma, see if you can slow the acid!" She raised her mini hub and twisted the keystone to Mistress Four's speakstone. "Mistress Four, beware! Aonghus has turned the remaining acid against us."

"You're a second late," Mistress Four responded, her voice calm, the sound of rushing wind loud through the connection.

Feeling relieved, Student Eighteen reached the square and slid to a halt. It was a mess, the entire expanse covered in bubbling acid. General Rosslyn and her remaining senior Petralists had been fighting back to back on the eastern edge, closer to the river. It looked like they were trying to reach the water to gain some advantage over the Mhortair. Only four remained besides the general. Three were Spitters and one a Sentry, all fleeing onto the river to escape the acid. General Rosslyn alone remained in the square, standing atop a glittering tower of water. Acid flowed nearby, but didn't quite touch the tower.

That was impressive. Acid wasn't a liquid Spitters could normally control, which was why the Mhortair had used the pressurized spray mechanicals to deliver it.

Rosslyn was scowling into the sky, looking after the Mhortair, who were all rising quickly away, driven by quartzite thrusters worked into their boots. They lacked the ability to fly like Hamish, but those thrusters provided enough lift to help them escape if the attack turned against them.

Small flying mechanicals swept in to intercept the fleeing Mhortair, with grab handles ready to pull them away to safety. Luckily most of the Mhortair teams seemed to have escaped. The square was littered with the remains of a lot of people, although the acid was already decomposing them, making identification impossible, but it looked like less than a third of their strike teams had died. Given the dangerous prey they hunted, those were good numbers.

Mistress Four glanced back down and met her gaze, releasing one of the handles to raise a fist in triumph. Their people had struck back at the enemy who had destroyed their home. Commander Six, his long whipsword dangling from his belt, was shouting a victory chant in Havaen.

The mechanicals carried them north, and Student Eighteen wished them a safe flight. They would drop back into the fighting near Ivor's embattled Spitters, but she would not join them yet.

She had two generals to kill.

"I'll clear a path," Ennlin offered, and the ground rumbled, the hard-packed earth of the square rising into a scoop-like wave that caught the pooling acid and swept it across the square toward General Rosslyn. The general turned at the rising sound of splashing, her eyes widening as the greenish wave erupted up toward her with a final surge of earth.

Rosslyn had good reflexes. The waters of her tower erupted up into a screening wall that caught the acid and deflected it away, throwing it into the nearby river. That was fine. Student Eighteen didn't want to fight with acid. She wanted to kill Rosslyn in honest battle.

General Rosslyn spread water across the square, dampening Ennlin's ability to access earth, and stalked toward them, her tower lowering her to the ground. She looked livid, and snarled, "You will pay for the lives you took today."

"Don't pretend to any moral high ground here, General," Student Eighteen retorted. "You planned to kill every one of us without mercy. I get that you're annoyed we proved more dangerous than you expected, but that's war."

She walked toward Rosslyn across the water-filled square, her steps graceful from Isabell's obsidian, her muscles strengthened from Tresta's granite, while Nuzha and Hemma melded their wills with soapstone in preparation for a fight against the much more powerful Spitter. Dedenia and Ennlin prepared to meld their elements into the mix to give them advantage, and Aifric whispered that she was ready to tap pumice, if necessary.

Student Eighteen tapped chert and easily sensed General Rosslyn's anger and resolve to win. She could respect that, and realized that Rosslyn actually believed herself a patriot for serving her queen. The poor, deluded fool. Patriotism to her country was good, but following a despot was simply misguided. So she used chert to push a sense of worry that Aonghus must be disabled or dead, the army critically fractured, the queen gone. Maybe it would be better to surrender.

She applied the feelings with a gentle touch, but Rosslyn scowled and shouted, "Stay out of my head! I deal with too much of that already." The general threw out a hand, and waters of the square erupted toward Student Eighteen.

"Here we go," she whispered as she rushed her enemy, trusting to her sisters to protect her. Waters all around smashed in upon them, but parted at the last second, allowing her to slip through. Tendrils of earth shot up from below to mix with the water, forming mud that her sisters could manipulate better, while spears of earth exploded up from beneath Rosslyn.

She sensed them coming and sheared them off, dancing aside with obsidian grace, redoubling her attacks with water. Her expression was confident, focused, and unafraid.

"She's got a sculpted stone too," Dedenia noted.

"Cheater," Tresta growled.

"Just get me close, and I'll take care of her," Student Eighteen said, her entire focus on the fight. Water swept around her in sheets and spray and grasping tendrils and shards of stabbing ice. The entire sisterhood united in battle, each woman focusing on her area of expertise. They had two Spitters to Rosslyn's one, but she was far stronger and was cheating with a sculpted stone. So they added air and earth, mixing elements into a shield dome around themselves to help push away the enemy attacks. It helped, but alone was not enough.

So they applied blind coal and pumice as needed, tapping and releasing each with well-honed precision. And while her sisters fought the elemental battle, Student Eighteen pressed closer to her enemy, one difficult step after another. All the while she maintained a subtle chert barrage of her own, playing upon Rosslyn's doubts and fears, whispering that she would fail and that she was sacrificing her life for a madwoman.

She drew within a dozen steps, and could see that her inexorable advance and emotional battle was rattling her opponent. After she deflected an onslaught of icy crystals, she met Rosslyn's gaze, and was surprised to see the general's expression turn anguished.

"I know she's mad! I know things could be better, but revolution won't solve our problems. No one can defeat her!" Rosslyn shouted.

"Oh, she's so tormented," Aifric said, her soft, caring heart moved by the outburst.

"Weak," Tresta retorted. "Choosing to serve evil rather than stand against it is just an excuse."

Student Eighteen blocked out the argument as several of her sisters weighed in with opinions. She could not allow herself weakness. As much as she respected Rosslyn, she still had to defeat her.

She took another step, preparing to close the final yards in a rush and drive her long-knife into her enemy's heart.

"We've got movement in the river!" Nuzha shouted just as a tidal wave of water exploded up the bank, sweeping toward them.

"This is going to hurt!" Hemma cried, and Student Eighteen sensed her sudden fear.

"Tapping blind coal," Eleven reported, her voice calm as ever.

The wave abruptly stopped advancing, but spread around the square, surrounding them with a wall of water thirty feet high. Rosslyn rose up the wall and stood on the top, glaring down at them. "If I thought you could win, I would reconsider, but you can't. So good-bye."

Not good. Student Eighteen glanced around at the unbroken wall. Rosslyn was ascended, and she was proving it.

"I can't push back," Nuzha reported, her voice cracking with rising fear. "She must be tapping deep."

"We can't stop it," Hemma said, sounding disgusted.

Rosslyn raised her hands, and waters all around crashed in like an avalanche. Both Nuzha and Hemma groaned with the effort, but couldn't stop it. Water avalanched down around them, but they stood unharmed in the center, protected by blind coal.

"Status?" Student Eighteen asked, trying to figure out how they were going to get up to Rosslyn and kill her.

"We are completely overwhelmed," Nuzha shouted. "Not even Connor usually blocks us out so completely."

"She's really motivated," Hemma confirmed. "I doubt she can maintain the pressure for long."

"Longer than I can protect us," Eleven reported. "We were already low on blind coal, and this is my last piece."

"I estimate it will expire within seven seconds," Eystri reported nervously.

"We've still got pumice," Aifric reminded them. That was true, and pumice would protect them from direct assault by Rosslyn's power, but no doubt the general understood that. All she had to do was maintain connection with the outer layer of the water and use that as a container to hold in the rest of the flood swirling around them, and pumice would not protect them from that. They would drown.

She hated to admit it, but they needed to retreat before they could re-engage. In a flash, she communicated that with her sisters, and they all agreed.

"I hate retreating," Tresta stated.

"We all do, but we have no choice," Aifric said in a soothing tone.

"All right, how do we get out of this?" Student Eighteen asked. The waters were not subsiding, but had formed a column forty feet thick and thirty feet high all around them. The outer edges flowed and bucked, moving the waters of the interior in powerful currents that would be difficult to swim through.

"Hemma and I can try pushing through them, but she'll sense that and counter," Nuzha said.

"How about mixing earth with it?" Isabell asked.

"That will help some," Ennlin confirmed. "Or I can open a hole beneath us and try dropping us into the cavern where the acid used to be. We should be able to seal ourselves down there and escape."

"As long as we get out before Aonghus returns," Eystri said timidly. "I calculate he will not remainings out of the fightings for much longer."

"Then we don't have time to wait. Do it." Student Eighteen ordered. They hadn't been so stymied by elemental powers in a long time. Rosslyn must be burning through that sculpted stone fast. Hopefully it would expire soon. That would give them a huge advantage when they faced her again.

"Blind coal just ran out!" Eleven reported.

The currents suddenly seized them, spinning them wildly about and lifting them toward the middle of the column. Student Eighteen could sense Rosslyn's growing sense of victory through chert. She thought she had them, no doubt planned to keep them pinned in the center of her water death trap until they drowned.

It was a good plan, but Ennlin, Nuzha, and Hemma mixed water and earth, forming a conduit just big enough for their body, extending that mixed conduit up from below to wrap them in its protective layer. As soon as they entered it, they began to slide fast down toward the ground. Spears of water stabbed toward them, but within that mixed-element cocoon, they held a tiny advantage.

"Maybe we should throw ourselves up to the top and finish her off," Cacilia wondered.

"Tempting, but she holds the advantage up there," Student Eighteen decided. "Get us into the ground."

They slid lower, the ride rough as waters bucked and tore at their protective cocoon. Their lungs began to burn from lack of air, but they could hold their breath for at least two more minutes before the situation turned desperate.

"General Aonghus is back!" Ennlin reported, suddenly sounding panicked. "He's sealing the earth beneath us.

With a sense of cold dread, Student Eighteen realized the situation had just turned desperate.

Chapter Forty-Eight
Dealing with a Really Bad Man

Nicklaus stood on the deck of his underwater secret mission boat, so eager to burst out of hiding his hands were quivering in his gloves. Using the ideas from Connor and Uncle Kilian about their Underwater Slide, and with some whispered instructions from Water, Nicklaus had made an even better boat.

He'd show them all that he could help. They'd left him behind in Merkland, and no one had believed him when he promised he could help. If only he'd been able to tell them about the amazing new mechanicals he was building with Water and Earth's help. That would have convinced them, but the nice elementals were mad at Connor. He should know better than to make them angry. Grown-up always wanted to feel like they knew better, but the elementals were really old, so they thought they were grown-ups to the grown-ups. Connor must have forgotten to make sure he made them feel like they were smarter.

The secret mission boat was small, just big enough for Nicklaus to stand on deck in a bubble of air as it slid downriver, protected by layers of subtle shielding. Connor could sense other Petralists in the water, but Nicklaus couldn't until Water showed him a neat trick. She helped him develop the mechanical he used for the shielding so whenever they touched a Petralist's will in the river, that part of the shield where they touched turned orange.

The shields had sparkled with so much orange in the last half mile that fifty Petralists must be drawing from the river. They were real distracted, though. None of them had explored his shields more, which would have turned the color red, and he'd slipped through unnoticed.

Now it was time to show everyone how smart he was and how much he could help. Nicklaus stopped the secret mission boat near the docks of Lossit and glanced at the dozen viewscreens projected onto the air bubble around him. They showed angles of the battlefield using the same sightstone views as Lady Jean in the Battalion.

Air was really nice, and she loved to sing. Her voice was like the whisper of breezes among autumn leaves, except for times when it rose like the rumbling of distant thunder. Nicklaus didn't think even Connor knew how much Air liked to sing. She told Nicklaus secrets and promised she hadn't told any other living soul. He liked her a lot and really wanted to help her out.

She had taught him a secret of the speakstones and sightstones that not even Verena knew. Nicklaus giggled at that. She would be so happy to learn everything he knew. Verena was the best, and he bet she'd help him get his own big workshop after he stopped the fighting. Then he could help her and Hamish make new mechanicals and fly and eat cookies and stay up late any time he wanted to.

With Air's help, he had tuned a special piece of quartzite for his viewscreens. Everyone thought speakstones had to be paired together to communicate, and that sightstones had to be paired with their viewing stone, but Air had taught Nicklaus that those pairings were like vibration frequencies between the stones, each pair slightly different. She then taught him how to tune one piece of quartzite to vibrate at varying frequencies that allowed it to join lots of other pairings. So he could see any of the viewscreens and listen to any of the speakstone conversations.

He giggled again. He bet Verena wished she had one of his stones. They made everything so much easier, although they consumed the quartzite a lot faster.

The views were not happy, and his good humor faded as he scanned the views of the raging battle. Everywhere he looked, people were fighting and getting hurt, or even dying. It made him sad. He liked shooting soldiers with missiles and speedslings, but he always made sure they had protective devices and that Healers helped if they got hurt. No one was remembering that. They were just fighting and hurting. He was glad he came to help.

One view caught his attention and he grinned at the sight of Lady Shona soaring over the battlefield. She had ridden one of those Althing trebuchets. What a good idea! He couldn't wait to try it, although he had a battle suit so it wouldn't be fair. She smashed down into the middle of a big group of angry soldiers along with a big barrel that exploded into a cloud of purple gas that made the soldiers start coughing. Lady Shona started punching people in the head, knocking them down while they coughed. That didn't seem fair, but she was a high lady, and Nicklaus' mother always said that nobility had to do difficult things sometimes in order to help their people.

Another view drew his gaze, and he marveled at the sight of water churning in the big town square. The outer edges of the big column glittered like a thousand crystals in the light. He also spotted earthen spears stabbing up into the water from underground. That didn't make sense. It looked like fun, but why would they play in the middle of a battle.

Then he spotted a figure tumbling in the water, and he recognized her.

"Aifric?" he breathed, suddenly feeling very scared. Bad Petralists were trying to hurt her, but she was the nicest person he knew, as nice as Lady Jean, except for times when she seemed different. Christin thought maybe she acted different when she was hungry. Some ladies were like that.

Right now she was getting hurt by bad people, and that made Nicklaus angry. He spotted one lady in an Obrioner officer's uniform standing on top of the water, hands raised, looking really happy about being mean. She was probably friends with the bad men who had kidnapped Nicklaus the year before. His father had taught him that bad people sometimes would not stop until you fought them.

Or showed them you were stronger.

Nicklaus changed the complex commands he'd worked into the secret mission boat control soapstone, and the boat rose to the surface. As soon as he reached open air, Nicklaus activated thrusters and shot into the sky. He couldn't help laughing with joy to fly.

Hamish wouldn't mind that he'd borrowed pieces from one of his backup suits to make one for himself. Water had told him to do it, and she was so smart and so nice, and she promised that she could help him make mechanicals so strong he could stop the fighting and save a lot of lives. That's what Hamish would do.

As he rose into the air, he banked toward the angry lady hurting Aifric in the water. The mean lady didn't realize he was coming until he flew right into her back at full speed.

Right before impact, Nicklaus activated quartzite shielding. He hit so hard that he almost crashed right through his shielding, and he banged his face against his helmet faceplate. That hurt a lot, but the bad lady got hurt worse. She screamed as she tumbled away, but water rose up to catch her and turn her around. She looked angry.

So Nicklaus shot two missiles at her face.

Water shaped like long arms reached out to snatch the missiles out of the air. Nicklaus remote-detonated them, but the explosions didn't hurt the bad lady. She looked surprised to see him. He bet she'd feel more surprised in a minute.

"You're just a child!" the woman exclaimed, her anger fading to a look of confusion. She added in a soft voice, "No older than my Ruthven."

"Let Aifric go," Nicklaus said. "You're hurting her."

The woman glanced down at the column of water, and resolution replaced her confusion. "I can't do that, boy. Leave now, or I'll have to hurt you."

Bad lady. He had warned her.

"You can't play any more," he told her, and he activated Drought.

The higher-level mechanical was the enhanced version of the one he'd been practicing with back in New Schwinkendorf. Water had helped him make it, but only after he promised not to tell anyone else about it. He was really excited to show Verena what he could do. He wished she was around to see it.

Built using a sculpted soapstone he'd borrowed from Gisela's workroom, it was one of the most advanced mechanicals he'd ever created. As soon as it activated, all of the water in the square exploded outward in a fantastic series of horizontal waterfalls that all veered past him and splashed down into the river. In seconds, the entire town was stripped bare of all water.

The bad lady cried out, clutching at her head as the water beneath her leaped away to join the Drought. She fell to the ground and landed hard, twisting one ankle and crying out in pain as she collapsed. She should have listened to him. Then she wouldn't have gotten hurt.

Aifric fell to the ground in the middle of the square too. She looked bedraggled, and gasped for breath as if she'd been stuck in that water a long time. When she sat up and looked around, Nicklaus waved.

She gaped, looking so surprised he grinned. She rose to her feet and walked toward him. "Nicklaus, what are you doing here?"

"I came to help," he told her proudly. "I'm going to stop the fighting so people don't get hurt."

"Some people are going to get hurt," she said, glancing toward the bad lady, who had risen awkwardly to her feet, looking really scared.

"Do you have to hurt the bad lady?" Nicklaus asked. Aifric looked like she was in one of her angry moods, but he hadn't brought any food for her. He needed to find Hamish for that.

"How do you block my access?" the bad lady asked. She looked even more scared of him than she did of Aifric. That was probably smart. Aifric did have a knife and a short sword, but he had missiles and a speedsling.

Aifric stepped toward her, and she started to run. Although she looked like using that twisted ankle hurt, she still moved with remarkable speed and grace. Aifric shot after her, moving so fast she had to be a Strider. Nicklaus hadn't realized that. She'd catch the bad lady fast, and she'd hurt her for sure.

The ground under the bad lady erupted, throwing her high into the air, all the way into the middle of the river. That was so unfair! The Drought couldn't drain an entire river. Well, maybe it could, but he hadn't planned to do that, just to drain the water from parts of the battlefield. That was supposed to remind everyone to stop for a while.

Aifric continued after the bad lady, running right up the exploding earth and soaring after her. She plunged into the water right behind the bad lady, with her dagger already in her hand.

Nicklaus banked to follow, but something smashed into him really hard, swatting him toward the ground like a fly caught in a swatting net. Nicklaus instinctively activated shielding and blind coal and tried activating thrusters. He slid through a huge, hand-shaped mass of earth and spun to see where it came from.

Another big ball of earth, ten feet thick, struck him in the chest. He slid through that one too and spotted a man with bright, red hair sliding into the square. The man looked battered and really angry. Nicklaus remembered him from the bad army that had kidnapped him and taken him to Alasdair last year.

He was the really bad man who had hurt Lady Jean.

Nicklaus released blind coal before it ran out, and raised his speedsling, planning to hurt the really bad man. He loved Lady Jean. She was so nice. Everyone agreed that the really bad man needed to be punished.

A pile of dirt struck his back and raked down his legs. Before he could activate blind coal again, it ripped his boots right off and Nicklaus began to fall.

"No fair!" Nicklaus shouted.

He activated shielding before he hit, and had to use a little more blind coal to soften the landing. When he stood up, the ground of the square rose all around him, forming ten-foot walls in an unbroken ring. The earth beneath his stockinged feet felt hot, and somehow angry. The very bad man stood atop one of the walls, looking down at him with cold eyes. Nicklaus bet Earth never talked to him.

He didn't want to either, but he raised his faceplate and said, "I'm not supposed to hurt people, but I think Lady Jean would want me to this time."

"I recognize you, boy," the very bad man said with a gloating laugh. "Looks like I get to kill you after all."

CHAPTER FORTY-NINE
It's Okay to Arrive Late to a Party,
If You Do So with Enough Style

Connor cried out in dismay as another shockwave of energy erupted from the queen, staggering Evander's elfonnel. The giant's torso shook, and the fresh earth that had been flowing up to fill the gaps sprayed outward as it toppled over backward, arms thrown out wide, mouth open in a silent scream. The impact of the giant body falling shook the ground. Queen Dreokt rose from the center of his chest holding its sculpted stone heart in her wicked hands.

Despite the crazy intense fight, she looked completely whole and composed. In fact she lifted the sculpted stone high and cackled with glee.

That was bad, but Connor couldn't bring himself to believe Evander was dead. The wily giant had already survived one decapitation. Surely he was in there, gathering his strength to fight back again. Connor reached out with chert and connected with Evander's thoughts. He felt a surge of hope, even though the connection felt weak and distant, as if insulated by a barrier.

The elfonnel. Connor realized he must be sensing Evander buried within the elfonnel. He'd given himself to earth, but still retained a tiny core of identity, and Connor managed to briefly touch that little part that remained Evander.

"The greatest ship sinks when the keel is sundered, and even the valley shaken by the avalanche must cower beneath the snows for a season."

That didn't sound good, and didn't sound like Evander. Connor strained to hold onto the flickering connection, and pushed the thought, *"Hold on, Evander! You stood unafraid against Harley and threw an entire mountain at her. You can survive this. We can still defeat her together!"*

The queen turned toward Connor, but just then a diorite missile struck her in the chest.

The explosion ruptured the front of her body and blasted her backward. Connor's lungs were regenerated enough that he managed to cheer, "Verena!"

Her voice came to him from her speakstone. She sounded disbelieving, and he could hear her surprised joy. "Connor? Connor are you really alive? I thought you were dead!"

"Not quite, although dying would probably be easier. Thanks for all that healing. It helped a lot."

Queen Dreokt caught herself in the air and pulled out of her tumble before striking the ground. Even as her chest began reforming, she swept an arm into the sky, generating an enormous whirlwind that swept upward and away. She might not know where Verena was, but a wind like that could rip her right out of the sky.

Connor tried deflecting it, determined not to lose Verena at any cost.

Queen Dreokt did not fight him for control over the air.

Not good. Even as he wrestled the air currents, Connor tensed for a blow. Instead, she slid across the ground back to the still-motionless elfonnel. The creature's mouth had started opening and closing and it looked like it was starting to put itself back together.

Not nearly fast enough.

Queen Dreokt reached it and leaped high to the top of the huge head. Landing on the face, she plunged her arm right through one of its eyes into what should be its brain. The monster convulsed and Connor could feel the queen strike at it with earth and with chert, overwhelming its defenses.

"No! Leave him alone!" Connor shouted, flinging fire and water at the queen's back. It was a weak, unfocused strike, and she deflected it without pausing her gruesome work.

Connor grasped at Evander with chert, hoping to help shore up his defenses, and again he connected with the concentrated, obstinate core that remained Evander. The queen had arrived first.

A heart-rending scream pierced his mind, cast straight from Evander to him. In it he sensed absolute pain, and helpless fury as

Evander realized his own grandmother was ripping out his identity to leave him an empty shell she could fill with whatever she
deemed worthy.

Connor panicked, striking at the queen's control, but he couldn't
seem to grasp her. She was too well insulated, already embedded in
Evander's mind.

She squeezed Evander's mind like a lemon, casting aside everything that defined him. Connor struggled to staunch the flow, to
save him, and Evander seized his mind like a lifeline and hurled the
last bits of his conscious thoughts across the conduit.

Connor's vision blackened, then coalesced into a mindscape he
recognized as Evander's secret inner library, deep under the Carraig
before it was destroyed. The fire in the hearth crackled happily,
and the one small bookshelf next to the big chair was stuffed with
ponderous, leather tomes. More were stacked nearby in dusty piles.
Evander sat in the chair, dressed like always in that huge coat, hair
a bit disheveled. He looked around and smiled, then reached out
one huge hand to stroke the spines of his beloved books.

"Are you really here?" Connor asked. He felt shaky and fought
back tears for his dying friend, even though in that moment Evander
looked as solid and real as ever.

Evander smiled, but his eyes were sad. "Thank you for granting
me an avenue for at least a partial escape."

"I don't understand. She's destroying you, just like she has so
many. Are you saying I can put you back once we drive her off?"
Connor asked, clinging to that desperate hope.

"I do not believe so. I feel myself dying," Evander said with a lot
more calm than Connor imagined he could ever muster in the face
of imminent death. Even with his arms ripped off and most of his
body broken, he hadn't been pushed right to the cusp of death.

"The herb once plucked may still nourish when added to a meal,
and every sunrise brings renewal," Evander said thoughtfully.

The cryptic language helped settle Connor's nerves. "I'm glad
I found you before it was too late."

"I've drawn all I can to you, and part of me may linger here with
my favorite books for a time, if you allow me to."

"You're welcome to stay as long as you can," Connor said
instantly, trying not to think about how weird life got around his
friends sometimes.

If Aifric could thrive with nineteen women sharing her head, he
would gladly host what little remained of Evander's consciousness

as long as he could. Aifric liked to tease him that he didn't use much of his brain space anyway. Should be plenty of room for Evander.

"Thank you. I will share what I can with you." Evander closed his eyes, his brows furrowing. A flood of raw knowledge poured into Connor's subconscious. He staggered, clutching at the wall of the mindscape as glimpses of the knowledge Evander was dumping into him flashed through his thoughts. He glimpsed the Carraig and ancient, glorious Stornoway, felt a deep and abiding love of books and learning filter through him, along with countless memories from Evander of entire days spent studying the tomes so painstakingly gathered into his vault. So much flowed through him, he couldn't grasp it.

"You're giving me your knowledge?" Connor asked, awed. He'd thought he understood how chert worked, but he'd never imagined such a link might be possible.

"I doubt I could have shared so much except in this moment of distress when all that defined me is being cast free. I was already untethered to my physical body through the elfonnel, and now the last vestiges of identity are being discarded. Use this knowledge wisely."

"I don't even know what I know," Connor objected.

"I believe it will distill upon your thoughts and become available as you ponder important questions," Evander said. "If you survive this struggle, come visit with me here while I linger, and I will teach you what I can."

"I'm honored," Connor said, feeling humbled by the awesome gift Evander was bestowing upon him. His emotions felt raw and close to the surface. Evander was dying, but maybe he'd managed to save at least part of him.

Evander sighed. "My hypotheses were wrong. My grandmother is both less human and more rational than I supposed. Avenge me, and open your mind to truth, Connor. Only through unvarnished truth may you prevail."

"I'll try," Connor promised, feeling a heavy weight of responsibility settle on him. Evander had always seemed unstoppable, as eternal as the mountains with which he walked. Now he was reduced to a defeated refugee in Connor's mind.

Evander gave him an encouraging smile and reached out huge hands toward the warmth of the fire. "The quiet of dusk encourages contemplation, and a pond is most still just after dawn."

"I don't understand," Connor started to say, but then suddenly he did! He grinned. "Wow! You shared with me how to understand Sentry speak?"

That was amazing. The fact that Evander had to flee his dying corpse and take up residence in Connor's mind in order to share that knowledge dampened Connor's excitement a little, but couldn't blanket it entirely. Several potential meanings seemed abundantly clear, and he marveled that Evander actually thought so deep all the time.

Evander smiled. "An unintended consequence."

"Um, do you think there are others?" Connor asked, suddenly less thrilled by the idea, although learning how to throw a mountain like he had done fighting Harley at the Carraig would be fun.

Evander shrugged and smiled. "I guess we'll find out pretty soon."

Connor couldn't believe Evander could crack a joke in that situation, but it suggested Evander would be all right. He wanted to stay and chat longer, but Evander's earlier message was clear. They could chat in quieter moments, if they survived. Right now, he had to focus on surviving.

He blinked open his eyes. The queen was unmoved, crouched atop the motionless earthen giant, arm still driven through the elfonnel's head. His chert connection to Evander-giant faded, and he felt the spark of life in the giant change subtly.

Evander was gone, his mind ripped out of that elfonnel body and cast aside. Connor hoped the queen didn't realize that he'd saved part of Evander from her, but that tiny victory didn't change the horror of her cold brutality. Connor's body was almost restored. He wrenched himself upright, ignoring the parts that didn't quite work right and staggered to his feet.

Queen Dreokt withdrew her hand and stood on the elfonnel's face as it shifted, losing the hints of Evander's features. Two of the four arms faded into the torso. It was changing, becoming something the queen must feel was more worthy of her servant.

She crouched to gently caressed the giant face and actually sniffled. "I'm so sorry I had to do that. I remember you as a little boy, playing with Tallan and giving your mother so much trouble." Her shoulders shook slightly as tears slipped from her eyes.

The sight stopped Connor in his tracks. He knew she was a barking-mad lunatic, but really? She'd just destroyed Evander, and now had the gall to weep over him?

Queen Dreokt straightened abruptly and evaporated her tears with an annoyed swipe of one hand. Her tenderness vanished and she added, "You turned out rotten to the core, you useless wretch. Your rebellious insurrections are now ended, and you are finally worthy to serve me." She barked a harsh laugh and said, "And serve me you will. For all time, you will slumber at this convergence point to restore my regenerative powers."

Then she vaulted off and landed facing Connor. She stalked toward him, her gaze fixed on him, her expression calm. He sensed absolute assurance from her, plus a little lingering annoyance that he'd delayed her so long.

That elfonnel was no longer Evander, and now Connor had to not only somehow stop the queen, but he had to kill that mindless thing too. Maybe if he destroyed it, Evander's body would return like the body of the man consumed in the first elfonnel they faced at the Carraig. Could Connor then pour Evander's mind back into it and fleshcraft him whole?

He wasn't sure, but clung to that fragile hope. First, don't die.

The queen advanced, a gloating smile on her smug face. "You show such promise, child. Few would maintain the presence of mind to continue struggling even as they coped with such severe trauma."

A flash of bright light caught Connor's attention. A superhuman blur was racing toward them from behind her. He felt nothing through any of his affinity senses, but hope blossomed in his heart and he smiled.

Queen Dreokt started to turn, but by then the blur had already reached the fallen elfonnel. It was starting to lift its massive head from the ground, but fire and water lashed out at it, confirming the identity of the superhuman blur.

Kilian.

His twin blades of elements severed the elfonnel's head, tossing it into the sky. Even as it tumbled away, more fire and water plunged into the head from twenty directions at once, ripping it to pieces.

The elfonnel's body convulsed, and Kilian somehow reversed course, returning to the bulk of its body in the blink of an eye, striking again and again. Queen Dreokt recognized the new threat too late. Even as she shouted in outrage, the elfonnel was sliced into two dozen pieces.

With his eyes glowing with mixed water and fire, his hair disheveled from his long run, Kilian slid to a stop and gave his mother a cocky salute. "Sorry I'm late. Looks like I broke another of your toys."

Chapter Fifty
It's Not in Wielding the Most Power but in Knowing How to Apply It

Queen Dreokt's initial rage flipped to a girlish giggle. Connor couldn't keep up. She pointed at the broken remnants of the elfonnel. "Either you did not recognize your precious nephew, or you simply chose to cast aside his life as you have so many others."

Kilian blanched and looked back down at the destroyed elfonnel. His shoulders slumped, and for a second he really looked three centuries old.

"Don't let her get to you," Connor shouted. "She already killed him. That monster was just an empty shell."

The queen scowled at Connor and muttered, "Your entire goal in life is to spoil my fun, isn't it?"

"Someone has to, you psycho lunatic," Connor retorted, wishing he could explain to Kilian that he'd saved part of Evander, but he didn't dare mention it yet.

Kilian sighed, grief plain on his face, but his expression hardened. "Yet again you murder your own blood, mother. It will be the last time."

Her good humor flipped to rage again and she shrieked, "You insolent boy! I will break your mind, and you will take your nephew's place as my servant."

In response, Kilian leaped into another super-fracked sprint, moving faster than Connor had ever seen. He crossed the distance in a blink and slashed his mother across the face with another blade of intermingled fire and water. The blow turned her head, but left no mark.

"Tag. You're it." His voice hung in the air as he shot past and banked around for another pass.

The queen struck out with every element and shrieked in rage, clearly intent on ripping out Kilian's life as she just had Evander's. Grasping hands of earth rose all around him while pits dropped open and walls of earth reared up to block him, but Kilian sped around them all. Sheets of flame and battering rams of water smashed down all around, but he sped through them unslowed, moving like a shooting star. She might be the dread queen of all things, but Kilian was the master of fire and water and somehow he slipped through her grasp.

For a few seconds, Connor could only gape at the astonishing display of pure speed, coupled with incredibly fine elemental mastery. Kilian could never hope to beat her with raw strength, but she seemed unable to overwhelm his finesse.

Maybe with Kilian's help, Connor could finally figure out a way to hurt her. She was momentarily distracted by the effort to catch Kilian, flinging elements around in an intense display of fire and water, howling winds, and smashing earth. Somehow he stayed just ahead of her wrath or slipped through it, surrounded by a protective coating of mixed fire and water.

The air boiled, one second searingly hot and stinking of melted stone, then switching to such absolute cold it stabbed at Connor's lungs. The ground roiled, and the air seemed to scream as the other elements ripped it asunder.

With his own elemental affinities, Connor defended himself from the glancing effects of the queen's overwhelming onslaught. Just those collateral strikes would have destroyed any non-ascended Petralist in a heartbeat. He also tapped limestone, summoned a globe of bright light, and compressed it with all of his strength. It took precious seconds to create a death beam, but Kilian was providing that time with unrivaled style.

A death beam alone wouldn't kill her, so Connor wrapped it with the deadly external sandstorm power of sandstone, then managed to add some internal-focused sensory deprivation from limestone for good measure. He needed to hit her hard, and that combination might just do the trick. The abrupt, brutal attempt to murder Evander filled him with rage and cold, hard determination.

In the seconds it took to prepare the strike, the queen ripped apart the lands all around them in her rage. She gouged crater-sized holes, cast up huge hills, and scoured the lands down to bare rock. Her will whipped the air into a frenzy. Storm clouds roiled and grew darker in the sky, reflecting her anger.

Kilian skidded to a halt fifty paces from her just long enough to flip her an obscene gesture.

She yanked on the clouds and Connor felt her will forming a great charge. He instinctively tapped basalt and obsidian, hoping to speed up his reaction time enough to cry a warning.

Too late.

A great bolt of lightning ripped out of the sky. Time seemed to slow as Connor's mind and reflexes accelerated. The jagged, incandescent bolt of destruction crackled down from above, tearing through the air, aimed for Kilian's head.

He dodged it.

Kilian moved so fast, it made his previous speed look like he'd been crawling. Even with his enhanced senses, Connor could barely track him. With obsidian accelerating his mind, he still struggled to comprehend such speed. Kilian seemed to teleport away just before the lightning struck, as if he'd transformed into a human bolt of lightning himself.

As the lightning drove into the ground, blasting aside blackened earth, the thunderclap rent the air with a boom so loud it shook Connor's teeth. Kilian appeared beside his mother and slashed his sword across her hand holding the ancient sculpted stone, concentrating all of his speed and momentum into that single point of impact.

The blow caught her by surprise and the sculpted stone tumbled free. Time continued moving at glacial speed for Connor, and Queen Dreokt turned in slow motion after the precious stone, her hands reaching to grab it, her expression horrified.

Kilian snatched it away, moving ten times faster.

Connor unleashed the death beam.

She was so distracted by the sculpted stone that she did not register the new danger in time. The death beam plunged into her left eye and ripped through her skull, exploding out the far side in a spray of gray matter. Not even Queen Dreokt could ignore getting most of her head blown apart. She convulsed and actually toppled to the ground.

Sandstorm clawed through her skull, melting flesh and bone, and Connor focused on the gruesome task with all his will. She'd regenerated from a single, blackened skull before. Could she do it if she had no skull left?

He planned to melt all of her bones to sludge. He also struck with the elements to keep her distracted. Earth speared into her back in a hundred spikes, while fire poured into the broken remnants of her mouth and down her throat, heated to such intensity it could have instantly melted steel. Blades of water slashed every joint, attempting to sever her limbs and separate them to make it easier for sandstorm to tear her apart. He added waves of paralyzing sound and hit her with more sensory deprivation, then added stilling, and even struck at her mind with chert.

When he did, Connor touched her mind, and again felt awed by the connection. Despite the horrible damage to her body, she felt no pain, but only seemed extremely annoyed. Connor broke through her defenses and touched her thoughts more deeply. As he had the last time, he was sickened by her lack of humanity.

It helped reinforce her inhuman resilience, and it made her really weird. She hated regrowing new bodies because she always felt her nose was never quite perfect, and she agonized on rebuilding each one. And she hated deciding how long to make her toes. Longer toes offered better balance, but then she had to wear huge shoes, and that looked undignified.

Where had that come from?

Connor tried to push farther, to find her weakness, but got trapped again in the weird labyrinth of her inhuman mind. She had suffered mental fracturing after having to put down her husband and destroy her beloved daughter, suffered anguish of heart and soul when her son betrayed her, and terrible depression when Tallan rose up in rebellion. Then she lost much of her remaining humanity during the long sleep. Even though she wore a human form, she was still more elemental than human. That part of her did not need a functioning physical body to remain completely potent.

They were grouted, Tallan curse it. Connor tried to ignore that new-found truth and continued savaging her body, ripping chunks of it away, and melting the rest. She might not need much of a body, but could she really return if he denied her any flesh to rebuild?

"You begin to see the full scope of my power," she said, her voice soft, as if hoping to teach him.

"*You might be inspiring if you weren't so criminally insane,*" Connor shot back.

"*Join me, and I will teach you to harness your strength. Together we can decide how to best rule these lands.*" She sounded sincere, and for a second Connor actually considered her offer. If he couldn't kill her, could he at least soften her tyranny so people didn't suffer so much?

He might have hesitated, but Kilian did not. He stopped nearby and hurled the sculpted stone with superhuman speed high into the sky. It shot upward, soaring hundreds of feet.

Verena swept out of the sky, the Swift's camouflaging screens flickering with the speed of her dive. She had drawn far closer than she had promised, and she expertly pivoted the tiny craft and caught the sculpted stone as it flew in through the window.

Kilian shouted, "Get that out of here! We can still use it to defeat her armies or destroy slate!"

Somehow the queen heard those words, even though Connor had melted her ears off and was holding her with every possible affinity. She screamed into his mind, so loud he staggered, clutching at his head, and for a second his connection to his affinities flickered.

That was all she needed. A second blast of pure will toppled Connor and sent Kilian skittering across the ground in an out-of-control tumble. Her limbs snapped back together and seemed to fuse instantly.

That was so incredibly unfair.

And freakishly terrifying. Fleshcrafting would soon run out, but he was starting to realize he would most likely be the one caught off guard by it. Queen Dreokt rose to her feet and swept an arm into the sky. A fresh bolt of lightning blasted out of the roiling clouds, aimed directly at Verena.

Still wrapped in obsidian and basalt, Connor easily processed the danger. Through his elemental senses, he felt the charge build and release, and he reached out with magnis to deflect the lightning bolt away from Verena.

Almost.

He pushed it some, but not quite enough. The lightning bolt struck the Swift a glancing blow, shattering the shielding. The tiny craft exploded under the impact, wings and canopy splintering under the intense barrage of pure strum. Deadly mechanicals ignited under the onslaught, adding secondary explosions that seemed to multiply over each other.

Verena did not even have time to scream.

She tumbled away, but her body shifted into the perfectly sculpted lines of max-tapped granite. Her armor blackened from the blasts and was shredded by a storm of deadly shrapnel that tore into her, despite her granite-hardened skin, spraying her blood in every direction. Without granite, she would have disintegrated.

The sculpted stone tumbled away in a different direction, somehow still intact. Queen Dreokt seized it with air and drew it back down to herself.

Connor didn't care. He was too focused on Verena. His entire body trembled, worse than when the queen had ripped off his arms. He panted, but couldn't seem to breathe as he caught her with air and pulled her down to him. Tears blurred his vision, even though he pushed them aside with water. His heart hurt, as if the queen had shoved her arm into his chest and squeezed it.

Verena looked dead. She was limp, her granite spent. All of her limbs were bent in unnatural angles, broken bones protruding. Her armor was shredded, and she was covered with blood from countless injuries. Connor wanted to scream, but could barely whisper her name over and over as he searched for some sign of life.

He barely registered the fact that Kilian had returned to his feet and again attacked his mother. She deflected him away somehow and elements clashed around them, but Connor didn't care. He wrapped Verena in a cushioning blanket of air so no part of her broken body had to touch the ground. Then he placed a trembling hand on her cracked forehead. Barely able to think, his thoughts a torrent of grief and fear, he braced himself and flicked his healing senses through her, terrified he'd find her gone.

She was not dead.

She was not very alive either. She'd been broken almost as badly as he had been moments before. Her heart still beat weakly and he sensed that her mind was not broken.

Sagging with relief, Connor redirected every bit of the healing power from Sucker Punch that was still thundering into him back into her. With fleshcrafting he swept away the worst of her injuries. It would take precious minutes he didn't have to heal her completely, but he could dare the seconds required to guarantee he'd saved her life.

He set the worst of the broken bones and realigned the rest so that the healing power pouring into her would do most of the work until he could return. Then he touched her mind with healing and with chert. He sensed her in there, still Verena, still herself. She felt the connection, and her mind awakened, still sluggish, but whole. *"Connor?"*

"*Rest. I've got you. I'm healing you,*" he urged, feeling overwhelmed with relief. Verena would survive. They still had a chance.

Queen Dreokt suddenly shouted, "Enough! I will have order! I will have perfection and obedient servants!" She raised the sculpted slate high, and Connor sensed she planned to use its awesome power to destroy them.

His heart sank. If she unleashed the might of that ancient sculpted stone like he she had done with serpentinite and with marble, there would be no stopping her this time.

Across their mental connection, Verena exulted. "*Got her!*"

"*You mean?*" Connor watched the queen, wishing with all his heart that Verena was right, that the trap would work.

Queen Dreokt glanced at Connor, then at Verena and frowned. She lowered the stone a fraction, and Connor clearly sensed her sudden hesitation.

"*No. She can't back out now. This is our only chance,*" Verena cried.

CHAPTER FIFTY-ONE
No Regrets

Ilse slipped aside just enough for a battering ram of earth to scrape past her. Driven by two Sentries, she never could have stopped the blow from crushing her. Why stop it when she could use it?

As she expected, as soon as they realized the blow missed, they loosened their hold on that ram of earth in preparation for launching their next attack. She struck in that moment, piercing their control and pushing the earth hard to the left. It still held a lot of momentum, and with her extra push, it shot past Anton's tower, crossed thirty yards of broken, open ground, and smashed into another enemy Sentry, knocking him flying.

She could almost hear the two Sentries look at each other with chagrin and say a fittingly-obtuse translation of, "Oops."

The battle for earth raged all around, with her fifty surrounded by twice as many enemies. Well, there had been twice as many, but Ilse's teams had defeated a full dozen, either killing or disabling them for the Crushers to bind. They'd lost three Sentries of their own, but as long as the enemy numbers didn't swell further, Ilse felt confident her strike teams would eventually prevail.

Around their ring of embattled earth, the Crushers fought against three entire companies of enemy soldiers. It was a wild melee, full of screams and shouts, the heavy groaning of earth, and thuds of tremendous impact. Anton held one entire side of their lines, supported by Ilse and Fogwatt, while the rest of their Sentries worked in four-man teams on the other sides.

The air was so saturated with earth, Ilse could cast her senses through the air as easily as through the ground. She used that floating dust in her response to the two Sentries targeting her, pressing it together into two dozen earthen spikes. They formed in the air behind the two men, and she yanked them hard.

One of them felt her influence and turned to see what she was doing. The other never noticed, so focused on blocking the ground between them from any potential response. The spikes rained down over them, piercing their armor and scraping stone-hardened skin. Such a weak attack would not kill them, but it toppled them both from their towers.

The more observant of the two maintained his contact with earth and wrapped himself in a protective layer. As soon as he hit the ground, he slid through it as if it was a pressurized tube, rising twenty feet to his right a couple seconds later.

That was two seconds too slow to help his partner, who momentarily lost his connection. He hit the ground hard and rolled to his hands and knees. Ilse appreciated him making it easy for her to slam his head between two walls of earth. The man collapsed, twitching, and she surged the ground beneath him, sending him tumbling into the Crusher lines. They would ensure he didn't awaken any time soon.

"Ilse!" Jean's voice surprised her, sounding through the speakstone worked into her collar. Jean sounded more panicked than Ilse had ever heard, and immediately she feared something bad must have happened. Had Ivor's forces been overwhelmed, or Rory's bash fighters overrun by enemy Sentries?

"I'm here," she said as she focused on the other Sentry, who was slamming earth at her from three sides. She threw herself into the air so his three crushing walls smashed into each other, then landed atop them and wrenched control over them, creating a tower for herself. She usually preferred fighting on the ground. It allowed her more flexibility of movement, but she'd take a tower when it was so conveniently handed to her.

"Aonghus has Nicklaus!" Jean cried.

"What?" Ilse rarely felt surprised, but those words shook her to the core. She lost focus for a moment, and the enemy Sentry nearly ripped her head off with a flying spear of earth. She only barely ducked it in time.

Then the ground under her enemy buckled, sending him tumbling. Ilse sensed Anton's will there, glowing in her mind like a Solas lantern. He glanced over at her, a questioning look on his face. "A flock of tiny sparrows can overwhelm even the hawk, but the torc crushes the nuall in single combat."

"Sorry. Nicklaus is in danger."

That got his attention, and his expression turned dark and menacing. "How is it possible?"

She repeated the question and Jean said, "I don't know how, but he just showed up in Lossit and chased Rosslyn away. Aonghus knocked him down and has him surrounded. Hamish is on the way, but I think he's too far. Can you help?"

"Of course," Ilse said without hesitation. A thousand questions played through her mind, but none of them mattered. A child was in danger from the brute who had so cruelly injured Jean. Ilse had no doubt whatsoever that Aonghus would slaughter Nicklaus.

"I need to go," she told Anton. He nodded and said, "I will come when I can. Beware Aonghus. He walks a crooked path."

Then he turned and bellowed loud enough for every ear within a quarter mile to hear. "The contest of arms is ever honored, but treachery unleashes ire like the avalanche!"

His will exploded outward, stronger than Ilse had ever felt. The sheer magnitude of it sent twenty Sentries tumbling off their shattering towers. Ilse felt his rage boiling through the earth like molten stone. They all loved Nicklaus, and if any harm came to that boy, the enemy would pay a terrible price.

She did not plan to allow any harm to befall him, though.

Ilse violently compressed the temporary tower she stood upon, shooting herself north like a catapult. She soared over rank after rank of enemy soldiers, all pressing in to join the battle against the Crushers. The vast size of their army was daunting, but at the moment she felt nothing but cold resolve. Anyone who stood in her way would die.

Luckily the soldiers standing where she crashed back to earth were smart enough to dive out of the way. Ilse extended her arms into a diving pose and flung out her earth senses. The air there was less filled with dirt, so it was difficult to connect with earth before touching down, but she didn't care. She plunged into the earth as if it was water and dove deep, below the level where most Sentries were fighting.

There she leveled out and threw herself north, speeding below the ground like an arrow. She had walked with earth a long time, so she knew how to run with it when the occasion required. As she tore north toward the town, she cast her earth senses ahead of her and easily sensed Aonghus. His will was like a bonfire, but he was concentrating entirely on the square.

Although she could not press her will broadly into that area, she could slip narrow beams through his influence. Through those slender connections, she sensed Nicklaus fighting for his life. Aonghus was casting earth down upon him, spearing at him, and attempting to crush him, but the boy was still alive. He slipped through solid ground, and must be tapping blind coal and pumice.

She sensed something else, a pulsing power surrounding him unlike anything she'd ever felt before. It was some kind of earthen shielding, but she hadn't realized the Builders had figured out how to deploy effective earth shields. Whatever it was, it saved his life more than once. He was fighting with amazing skill, but trapped there in Aonghus' domain, he would eventually slip and be crushed.

Ilse opened a conduit in front of her, lining it with hundreds of tiny, grasping hands that seized her armor and flung her forward, doubling her speed. She blasted into the open pit beneath the central square where the acid had been concealed, erupting from the wall like a meteor. She raised a sloping ramp to redirect her from horizontal to vertical, and threw every bit of her earth strength into punching a hole up through the square directly beneath Nicklaus.

As she rose, she used all of her momentum to seize Nicklaus and hurl him into the air, then rose to take his place. The boy whooped with glee as he catapulted high over the town. In the distance, she glimpsed Hamish hurtling toward the town. He'd catch the boy in plenty of time.

So she focused on Aonghus, who stood atop a nearby wall of earth, looking startled. She swept her earth senses across the top of his wall, scraping off a paper-thin sheet of earth that she flung at him, forming it into a hand to slap him across the face. The sharp report of the slap rang across the square, and his cheek reddened from the blow. It didn't do any real harm, but it definitely drew his attention away from the boy.

"How dare you attack a child?" she demanded, filling her voice with as much loathing as possible.

Aonghus laughed, clapping his hands mockingly. "That's the most impressive suicidal entrance I've ever witnessed." He bowed to her and added, "I always thought you were smarter than that."

"The wolf slaughters and the pedra in bloodlust knows no fear, but a blade badly tempered breaks under combat," she stated, settling her mind for the fight. She had placed herself into a one-on-one contest with an ascended Petralist. Not the smartest move, but she'd battled Harley herself. She could hold Aonghus off until help arrived.

Aonghus rolled his eyes and scowled. "I've switched to slate, but I still can't understand your blathering tongue twisters."

"Your ignorance is not tied to your affinity, but to your broken mind."

"And your death is entirely your doing," he responded with an evil grin.

Aonghus threw his arms out wide, seized the earth all around her, and smashed it inward with overwhelming force. The sheer magnitude of the attack was terrifying, but in her element, Ilse could not acknowledge fear.

She lunged directly at Aonghus, concentrating all of her power into piercing just enough of the cresting wave of earth directly in front of her to slip through. Aonghus might be many times stronger, but he was diffusing his strength by grasping so much earth. She let him have it and stepped through, leaving the earth to smash together right behind her. The impact shook the square and the pressure wave it created nearly knocked her from her feet, but she used it to run three steps closer.

She could not defeat him with earth, but if she could get close enough, she could still pierce his eye with her dagger.

Aonghus laughed as he softened the earth beneath her, forming clinging mud, filled with grasping hands that threatened to drag her down. So focused on that one spot, his will was impenetrable and for a second she foundered.

"I too am a student of the best application of focused will," Aonghus told her in a conversational tone as she fought with every bit of skill to stay out of the bog. She moved nimbly, trying not to set her feet down for more than a split second, focusing her will on the minuscule top layer of earth, the only part actually touching her feet, turning it into supporting platforms between her and the grasping hands.

She needed to do something else, or he'd have her. Most Sentries focused so much on overwhelming force, they ceded the advantage to her when she applied techniques to deflect their own strength back against them, but Aonghus had been a Firetongue, and a very clever one. He understood targeted application of force better than she'd hoped.

Even as she fought to reach the edge of the bog, Aonghus started casting spears of earth out of the ground at her. They were thick, clumsy things that would still smash her to pieces if she let them hit. Ilse spun and twisted, forced to divert some of her attention to those spikes, deflecting them aside when she couldn't dodge.

Aonghus laughed as Ilse moved at a frantic pace, twisting, turning, dancing, fighting to stay out of reach. He clapped again. "You really are as good as everyone says you are."

Then a slender spear of earth, no thicker than a poniard, stabbed through the back of her right shoulder. Ilse gasped and stumbled. She hadn't even felt him cast that one. He'd shielded it completely.

He was ready for her hesitation, and a thicker spear erupted out of the ground to her left, right when she should be glancing to her right to see what had stabbed her. It was a clever attack, and would have caught most Sentries by surprise.

Just what she needed.

Ilse twisted around the spear and jumped, hooking her arm around it even as it stabbed past, scraping her leathers. It was still connected to the ground, and Ilse threw her will into it, momentarily seizing control away from Aonghus. He must have been fully expecting that spear to finish her because he didn't react quickly enough to block her. She used that earthen spear to fling herself into the air, straight at him.

Shouting one of Anika's favorite battle cries, she drew her dagger, aiming for Aonghus' eye.

It was a daring move that left her momentarily disconnected from earth, but against most Sentries, it would have worked and she'd kill them before they realized what had happened.

Aonghus dropped straight down into his earthen wall. Ilse muttered a curse as she soared over the spot he'd just vacated. The walls to either side took the shape of giant hammers and smashed in toward her. She tried to block it, but she was still disconnected from earth, and Aonghus threw every bit of his will into the strike. In that kind of brute force match, she was hopelessly outmatched.

The hammers caught her in midair and crushed her hips and legs. Ilse screamed, momentarily blinded by pain.

It was a pain she knew, and memories of Harley and Lukas and desperate battle flashed through her mind. It hurt so bad, she wanted nothing more than to fall into a broken heap and scream for a year, but she knew that pain, and she had beaten it once.

Ilse struck the ground, and a second wave of horrific pain ripped through her like lightning. She screamed, clawing at the ground, but clawed even harder at her affinity. She knew that pain. She had beaten it before, and she did not fear an enemy she knew she could conquer.

Immersed in her affinity as deeply as ever in her life, Ilse used it to insulate herself from the pain. Her vision cleared and she wrapped her body in earth. Aonghus stepped out of his earthen wall nearby, gloating.

His expression turned to awe when Ilse rose to face him.

Her body still shook from shock and agony, but she stood firm on familiar summoned legs. They'd served her well since Harley had injured her outside of Merkland, and they would serve her again.

"I don't believe it," Aonghus breathed.

"Did you really think a pitiful bully like you could succeed where Harley failed?" Ilse demanded. She charged, drawing a spear of earth up from the ground and driving it toward Aonghus' throat.

He might be surprised, but he possessed incredible reflexes. Aonghus dodged so fast he must be tapping basalt to his entire body. That was a trick few Striders figured out. Ilse spun to follow as he raced around her, but even as he ran with fracked speed, he seized her summoned limbs with earth and ripped them away in one convulsive heave.

Ilse screamed again, shocked by his power, and for once surprised. She had not expected him to strike at her legs again. Not even Harley had been so evil.

She hit the ground, and Aonghus owned it. Earth wrapped around her, sealing her in a coffin of deadly spikes that stabbed inward from all sides. She couldn't breathe, couldn't see, couldn't scream her agony as Aonghus tortured her, piercing her body in dozens of places. Her world turned red with pain, and her connection to earth faded under the onslaught.

She clung to the one thought that still mattered. Nicklaus was safe.

Just as she felt herself about to succumb to the encroaching blackness, the earth flowed away from her face. She found herself held upright in her earthen prison, facing Aonghus. His expression was wild, his eyes insane.

"I am the new general, and I will succeed!" he screamed, spittle flying from his mouth.

She was done. She felt her life draining away, but she felt remarkably calm. Disappointed, but calm. She'd been living on borrowed time since that terrible day Harley took her Lukas away, and she'd dedicated herself to saving lives. She might still be able to help the others by enraging Aonghus to the point he did something stupid.

So she managed to whisper through blood-soaked coughs, "You are a . . . a coward and you . . . will die today."

"You first."

He stepped closer and drove his sword through her heart.

A flash of pain, and then blessed peace. She had not felt peace since her beloved Lukas had so brutally died, but in that final second, it flooded through her battered mind. She slumped in her earthen coffin, content with the knowledge that she had saved as many as she could.

Ilse smiled, then closed her eyes for the last time as Lukas' so-familiar hand slipped into hers again, and she felt him beside her, welcoming her home.

Chapter Fifty-Two
Vengeance As a Motivator Is Very Risky

Hamish hovered two hundred feet above Lossit, stunned by Ilse's abrupt, brutal death at the hands of Aonghus. Hamish had just plucked Nicklaus out of the air and was trying to decide what to do with the errant boy when he saw Ilse get overwhelmed. She was so strong, he'd fully expected her to survive until Anton arrived.

Anton was coming too, like a living eruption of earthen fury. He plowed across the battlefield, tossing everyone aside, including any Sentries stupid enough to try blocking his path. Earthnail Fogwatt was sliding along the ground on a spiked tower right behind him, while their strike force was savaging the enemy Sentries arrayed against them. Somehow they'd all felt Ilse's death and their rage drove them to really scary heights of earth mastery.

Aonghus stood over Ilse's body and lifted his hands high, laughing with victory. He glanced up toward Hamish and made an obscene gesture. His voice rang out through a speakstone Nicklaus wore on his arm. "I am the general! I am the greatest. I will kill all who challenge me, even if they pretend to be weak women and children. Will you be next in line, Builder?"

Hamish's horror transformed into boiling rage and his hands shook on Nicklaus' back with the need to descend and destroy the hated man who had just killed a valiant, brave woman and who had so brutally injured Jean. She was recovering well since her fleshcrafting, but Hamish was the one who had held her so many times when she sobbed as she talked about lingering nightmares of fire and pain.

He wanted to go down there so badly, but he couldn't yet, not with Nicklaus. If only the boy hadn't lost his main thrusters, Hamish would have sent him to stay with Jean on Battalion One.

Nicklaus was crying. The boy looked stunned. No boy should see such things. If he'd listened and stayed back in Merkland, he wouldn't have. Hamish wanted to berate him for his stupidity, but couldn't do it, not yet.

Jean's voice, heavy with grief, spoke through their paired connection. "Oh, Hamish, is she really gone?"

"She's gone," he confirmed. The words were like ash in his mouth, and they fueled his vengeful rage. He would destroy Aonghus. Very soon.

"She was so good," Nicklaus whispered. "She was trying to help me."

"She saved your life," Hamish said, increasing thrust. "Come on. I have to get you up to Battalion One. Jean, I'm bringing Nicklaus up to stay with you."

"I'll have Gisela meet you on the roof. We're moving two Battalions over Lossit to provide bombard support."

"Good, we'll need it. I'll be there soon. Have someone prepare to reload my weapons when we get there."

"No!" Nicklaus squirmed in his arms, trying to pull free. Foolish boy, he'd plummet back to the ground without his boot thrusters. "You have to bring me back down there."

"Are you mad? Aonghus will kill you." Nicklaus had always been brave. Hamish hadn't realized he was suicidal.

Despite his still-flowing tears, the boy fixed Hamish with that too-mature stare of his. "Hamish, the very bad man will hurt more people, but I can stop him."

"He almost killed you," Hamish retorted, still rising higher above the battlefield.

Down below, Aonghus turned toward Anton's earthquake-like rush. Everyone else was wise enough to scatter out of the mighty Sapper's way. Earth erupted around him, spraying a hundred feet to either side, the dust transforming into angry faces, silently screaming with rage. Even flying safely hundreds of feet above the battlefield, Hamish felt shivers of fear at the sight. Anton had always seemed like the forgotten little brother next to Evander, but now he was showing his full glory as one of the mightiest Petralists alive, one of the few who had lived since the Tallan Wars.

Aonghus didn't care. Grinning with the thrill of new battle, he stomped one foot, and earth rose into a mighty wave, surging toward Anton. The wave smashed through the southern half of Lossit, growing to over fifty feet high, accelerating on an intercept course with Anton.

"Hurry, Hamish. Get me down there before Anton gets hurt," Nicklaus insisted, wiggling harder.

"What do you think you can do?" Hamish demanded. He wanted to just ignore the boy and drop him off, but Nicklaus was no ordinary child and ignoring Nicklaus, especially when he was insisting so strongly, would be incredibly foolish.

Anton struck Aonghus' earthen barrage in a fantastic explosion of dirt, momentarily obscuring the entire area. A booming thunderclap shook the air, and troops all across the valley who had not yet noticed the titanic struggle stopped fighting and turned to watch. Everyone knew that if one side won a decisive victory in earth, they would quickly dominate the battlefield. On the western side of the valley where the bash fighting was raging with inspiring enthusiasm, Boulders paused to cheer for their champion, or simply to cheer that their champions keep fighting for a while so they could get back to bash fighting.

"Can you see what's going on?" Jean asked.

"No. I can't see anything," Hamish said, switching his mini-hub to Anton's personal connection.

Aonghus' voice echoed through it. "—fool to go for the jugular, old man. You're stuck and you won't find any escape either."

The dust cloud hovering over the battlefield suddenly coalesced into fifty spears of earth, compressing so hard they turned black. They swept out of the sky, raining down over Aonghus. It was an astonishing display of earth mastery that seemed to catch Aonghus by surprise. He swept a hand overhead, and a cresting wave of earth rose around him to intercept the spears. Effective, but not nearly as classy. He might be ascended, but Anton was drawing upon centuries of battlefield experience. Maybe he had a chance after all.

Anton slid closer, his tower twenty feet tall, ringed with downward-pointing spikes as if he planned to drive the walls down over Aonghus and rip him apart as he had Ilse. Fogwatt slid across the ground to his right. Together those two might pose a serious threat. Anton said, "The gander can chase away children with overwhelming ferocity, but the master of the house still enjoys the feast."

Nicklaus gripped Hamish's arm and said, "Oh, good one. I bet he's talking so plain because the very bad man doesn't understand deep thinking well."

He was right. Aonghus flung the earthen shield away and snarled, his florid face turning redder with anger. "My queen has forbidden such stupid talk."

He threw his hands forward, and the earth between them rippled as he struck a mighty blow. Together, Anton and Fogwatt deflected it to the left, and the earthen wave continued onward to plow into an entire company of Aonghus' Boulders, burying them in a screaming avalanche. Aonghus didn't even seem to notice the damage, or the frantic work of three Sentries trying to save them.

"You fools can't hope to win. I am the mightiest Petralist now!" Aonghus chortled.

He'd always had a swelled head, and reports of his ascension had clearly only inflated it. Hamish hated that Aonghus might just be right, though. With Connor, Evander, and Kilian all fighting the queen, who could stop him?

"Where's that bombardment?" he asked Jean.

"Targeting him now. Give us a few seconds," she responded immediately, her voice tense with worry.

Anton didn't seem afraid of Aonghus. He flung out a hand in a dismissive gesture, and two entire buildings on the south side of Lossit were flung into the air, aimed right at Aonghus' back. Looking bored, Aonghus cast giant balls of earth to intercept them, but in that second, fingers of earth erupted out of the ground at Aonghus' feet, tearing at his armor and digging at his face. For a second Hamish thought Anton was going to do it, that he would actually overwhelm Aonghus in a single, mighty strike.

With a howl of rage, Aonghus threw himself off the ground, and a column of earth rose up to catch him. His anger before seemed laughable compared to his new rage. He shouted, "Feel the landslide, old man!"

He lunged, driving his leading foot hard down into the earth, and again the ground rippled out between them. This time it undulated, rising and falling like a series of waves approaching the shore. The first one struck Anton's tower and deflected aside, knocking his entire tower back several feet, but doing no damage. The second one struck at Fogwatt, knocking him back much farther. The third and fourth rose so high they threatened to swamp Anton's tower, but he somehow withstood each one.

While he was distracted with the fifth one, the sixth wave struck Fogwatt's tower, but another wave struck from the right, clearly catching the earthnail by surprise. It crashed down over him, burying him and sweeping him away.

He did not reappear.

Anton glanced at the spot where Fogwatt had stood, now covered by boiling earth, and Hamish heard his soft whisper, "The night oft falls early, and sorrow weighs the hearts left lingering over the campfire."

Hamish's sense of optimism vaporized. Another mighty Sentry destroyed by Aonghus. Hamish's rage returned in a flash and he cried, "Jean, we need that bombardment!"

"Warn Anton. We're about to fire three hundred penetrator rounds," she said, sounding sad, but resolute. Hamish hoped she didn't beat herself up that they hadn't arranged to fire sooner. They might have saved Fogwatt, but maybe not. Such thoughts could destroy her tender heart.

"Hamish!" Nicklaus shouted, reaching up to shake his helmet. "You have to listen to me."

"I don't have time for games, Nicklaus. What can you do to help?" Hamish demanded, fighting to control his anger. Venting it at Nicklaus wouldn't help.

"Get me to the ground, Hamish," Nicklaus said calmly, looking completely sure of himself. "I've got a higher-level mechanical that can stop Aonghus."

"Really? Why didn't you tell me?" Hamish demanded.

"You didn't give me a chance."

Above them, two of the mighty Battalions had shifted position to hover directly over Lossit. Every cannon mounted beneath their huge decks swiveled toward Aonghus and belched flame.

Hamish shouted into Anton's paired speakstone, "Anton! You have to retreat. The Battalions are firing. Get out of there!"

Down on the ground, either Anton hadn't heard or didn't care. He was driving his tower through the ongoing earthen barrage that Aonghus was sending against him. Even Aonghus looked surprised, but that only enraged him more.

Aifric's voice surprised Hamish, speaking through Nicklaus' speakstone. "Hamish, can you hear me?"

"How—?" Hamish began, but Nicklaus said, "Later."

The boy said, "Aifric, we hear you. Where are you? Hamish is bringing me down to punish the very bad man."

"Rosslyn got away from me," she said bitterly. "I'll meet you on the north side of town."

That helped Hamish feel better about the plan. If Nicklaus really did have a higher-level mechanical that could help, they needed to try it, but landing anywhere near Aonghus was dangerous. With Aifric to help, they'd survive long enough for Nicklaus to try. He banked north, tipped into a dive, and threw wide his main thrusters. Nicklaus whooped, and Hamish appreciated his ability to take enjoyment from the simple pleasure of flight, even in such dark times.

On the ground, Aonghus shouted and threw up his hands. Anton had closed to within fifty feet, pressing through everything Aonghus threw at him. If he reached the crazy general, he would crush the life out of him with his bare hands.

Except the ground all around Anton abruptly flew into the air, as if it was all sitting on a giant sheet that Aonghus just yanked. Anton and his entire tower, together with tons of earth flew upward.

"Look out!" Jean cried. Hamish flew faster. If he could get Nicklaus to Aifric, maybe he could help.

Even tumbling into the air, Anton oriented himself toward his enemy, and the earth around him seized him and threw him toward Aonghus. The earth in front of him parted, forming a slide and he accelerated at his enemy.

Chortling like a madman, Aonghus made a seizing gesture, his fingers like claws, and the earth around Anton mimicked the movement, slashing in like hundreds of talons. When Hamish glanced back with his long-vision goggles, his fear for Anton spiked higher. Those claws of earth broke off inches from his body, but more and more kept plunging in, and each wave grew closer and closer. Hamish estimated that Anton would get ripped to shreds long seconds before he reached Aonghus.

He spotted Aifric, who skidded to a stop at the northern gate of Lossit. Hamish swept past at twenty feet and released Nicklaus, confident Aifric would catch him. Nicklaus triggered directional thrusters to slow himself, waving good-bye. Hamish banked south and poured on all the speed he could muster.

"Hamish, no! Not over the town!" Jean screamed.

CHAPTER FIFTY-THREE
Time-out

As Hamish flashed over the town, the bombardment fell like every thunderclap the world had ever known. Penetrator rounds plunged out of the sky like giant steel hail, slamming into the ground all around Aonghus with impacts that shook the earth, and reports like thunder. They stabbed deep, then detonated, concussive wave building upon concussive wave, burying Aonghus in a firestorm of destruction and shattered earth. Clouds of dust billowed out, obscuring Aonghus. The last thing Hamish saw of him, he had flung his hands over his head and seemed to be attempting to shield himself.

Hamish didn't have time to worry about it. Although most weapons struck close around Aonghus, some missed the mark, raining down over Lossit with devastating effect, shattering every building and consuming town in fire and destruction.

Hamish flew through it all.

He didn't have enough blind coal to simply ignore the danger. Instead, he max-tapped obsidian and drew deep from the enhanced reflexes and thinking power to calculate the trajectories of incoming missiles and plot a course around them. He banked and turned like a leaf on the wind, pulling more agility out of his many thrusters than he'd ever dreamed possible. He wove through the incoming destruction, less than a hundred feet above the ground, plunging through explosions and clouds of debris, tapping blind coal just enough to avoid getting obliterated.

Hamish scowled, angrier than ever at Aonghus for ruining what could have been a wonderful experience. Ilse's death burned his mind, and he couldn't shake the memory of Aonghus' sword plung-ing into her chest. Rage drove him on to take reckless risks. Instead of banking away and fleeing Lossit, he kept going, pitting his skill against the entire might of two Battalions. The air boiled around him, visibility dropping to zero as he shot through explosion clouds. He shouted a howl of grief-filled fury. His thrusters struggled to find purchase against the screaming air currents that tore at him from every side, but he would not relent. Three times he threw himself into barrel rolls to make the maneuvers he needed. Time seemed to slow, and the world compressed until every second seemed to take a minute, filled with dust and choking smoke and deadly debris, and missiles raining down on every side.

Then he burst free, flashed over the shattered square, covered in impenetrable dust, and caught sight of Anton, falling limp toward the ground. He wasn't sure if the big man was hurt or dead or simply exhausted, but set an intercept course to snatch him out of the air.

He planned on making it a really impressive maneuver, but in reality the impact nearly yanked Hamish right out of his suit. Anton was *solid*. But Hamish recovered quickly and powered south, intend-ing to bring Anton back to his strike force.

His ears were ringing, and it was hard to hear. Jean's voice sounded as if from a great distance, but his voice was dry, and speaking hurt. He noticed most of the battlefield had gone still as everyone stared at the awesome destruction over Lossit. So he triggered bursts of colored light from his suit, alternating red and green. That should make their opponents wonder if he was cele-brating victory, or just coordinating a counter attack.

He spotted the Sentry strike team standing upon a swatch of torn earth to the south. Only thirty of their number remained, but it looked like they'd defeated or driven off most of their foes. For the moment, they owned that part of the valley. Hamish settled Anton to the ground, and several Sentries with sandstone secondar-ies rushed in to tend to him.

Others gathered around, asking a torrent of questions, but Hamish held up a hand to forestall them and replied to Jean first. "I'm here, Jean. Sorry, but I was busy with Anton, and my ears didn't seem to be working."

"Oh, Hamish. For a second I thought you'd gone and killed yourself," she cried, her voice heavy with worry and rebuke. If they all survived the day, she'd give him a stern lecture. He smiled at the thought. Jean hadn't yet realized she always looked more alluring than ever when she was lecturing him, her eyes flashing with annoyance, a little color flushing her cheeks. Occasionally he annoyed her on purpose, just to enjoy a little tongue lashing.

"Builder! Aonghus lives," one of the Sentries said, gripping his shoulder. He didn't even know the man's name, but the big fellow looked worried. Nearby, Anton started coughing, but didn't seem ready to resume the fight. Without him, the other Sentries all together would not be enough to fight off Aonghus.

"He must be wounded," one woman said hopefully.

"Perhaps, but his will walks the earth with undiminished potency," the man responded. "Lightning may mar the great tree, but springtime brings forth new buds."

Hamish turned north, activating his long-vision goggles, scanning the dust cloud hanging over Lossit for signs of Aonghus. If he was wounded, they might have a chance. "Jean, I just got a report that Aonghus is still alive. Can you target him again?"

Before she could reply, the ground rumbled, a deep, threatening sound that somehow felt deeper than anything the Sentries had done in all their fighting. Around him, the Sentries and Sappers all gasped. They looked afraid.

What had Aonghus done now?

Hamish activated thrusters and rose into the air for a better view. The dust clouds hanging over Lossit abruptly fell in a brown sheet like rain, revealing Aonghus. The general was bloody and battered, his left shoulder slumped in an unnatural way. He wasn't laughing any more, but he too had turned north and his posture looked as surprised as the Sentries near Hamish.

He looked farther north and spotted Nicklaus and Aifric at the far end of town. Nicklaus was crouched, hands pressed to the ground, with something clasped in them.

His mechanical?

Nicklaus' voice boomed out his speakstone, even though he wasn't tuned to a paired stone. The boy's voice echoed all across the valley, and Hamish realized with a start that somehow it was speaking at full volume through every speakstone on every soldier. It also boomed out of the speakstones on every hovering sightscreen or scout mechanical, and shouted like thunder from the big loudspeaker speakstones mounted on the Battalions far over head.

"It's time to stop fighting. You are acting badly, and I have taken away your earth powers until you behave. I call it Time Out."

Hamish gaped. What had Nicklaus been doing in Merkland? He and Verena were the top researchers, and they hadn't figured out how to link one speakstone to every other one. He would have stated as fact that it was impossible. Even more impressive, could Nicklaus really suck away earth power? He'd drawn the waters from the square and driven Rosslyn away, and they'd done something similar with Sucker Punch, but how had he figured out how to apply that to earth over such a huge area?

He descended to thirty feet and called down, "Is he right? Can you walk with earth?"

The earth movers were chattering like scared children. The same burly man who had spoken with him earlier said, "We feel the earth, but cannot step through the door. Indeed, Builder, he has done it. Why didn't you warn us such a mechanical would be deployed?"

"We'll talk about it later. Use the distraction to tie up the enemy Sentries," he suggested. That galvanized them into action. The entire company, except for one of the Healers still tending to Anton, switched to primary affinities, shouted war cries that seemed exceptionally loud in the still air, and charged toward enemy Sentries who had retreated from them earlier.

That sent a spark through the entire valley. Soldiers on both sides resumed bash fighting with zeal. The tertiaries seemed shocked, and some hesitated, confused and unnerved by the lack of their powers. Most of those were struck down and shackled before they recovered. On the western side of the valley, the great bash fight resumed with enthusiasm, and on the north side, Ivor and his embattled Spitters resumed fighting their enemies. The regulars battled for control over the far northern reaches of the valley, but Hamish focused on Aonghus.

He could kill the man now.

Except he spotted huge, hulking things beginning to rise out of the earth all around Lossit. They looked like summoned creatures, but as huge as houses. Most were vague shapes lurking under a coating of earth, but he sensed terrible threat within them.

Nicklaus' voice boomed over the battlefield again. "I told you to stop fighting. Don't make me punish you."

That was amazing and more than a little scary. What had the boy unleashed? More mounds of earth rose all across the battlefield, and fighting slowed to a halt. Soldiers from both armies wisely retreated from the new summonings. Hamish soared over Aonghus, who was staring in shock at several earthen giants ranged around him. He looked to be trying to heal himself, which frustrated Hamish, but he needed to deal with Nicklaus first.

He landed near the boy and Aifric, who looked as astonished as Hamish felt. Nicklaus looked up at Hamish, young face glowing with joy.

"Hamish, I can feel the Builder threshold! This mechanical took me to it. I can do it, Hamish. I can ascend!"

His blood seemed to freeze in his veins as he realized the terrible truth. The elementals had been whispering to Nicklaus, promising to help him, but they'd set him up for destruction.

He rushed toward the boy, shouting, "No! Don't do it!"

Chapter Fifty-Four
Dying for a Good Cause Never Gets Easier,
No Matter How Many Times You Try It

"Why can't things be easy for once?" Connor muttered, bracing himself for another round of battle with the dread queen.

She was stalking toward him, sculpted slate held in her hand, but her scowl was directed more toward Verena, who still lay at Connor's feet. The sight of Verena's bloody, battered form filled Connor with anger, but now she was trapped on the ground with him. If he failed to fight off Queen Dreokt again, she'd slaughter Verena in a heartbeat.

Verena's entire body convulsed, her eyes snapping open, her expression terrified. They were still connected with chert, so Connor felt the queen's mental strike against Verena, shared her pain, and felt the queen piercing Verena's thoughts.

"Get out!" Connor bellowed as a door seemed to open in his mind, releasing a flood of raw hatred that eclipsed anything he'd ever felt. The queen was attacking Verena's mind.

He would not allow it.

Shouting with rage, Connor charged even as he poured all his will into fending off Verena's vulnerable mind before the queen could snuff her out like she had so many others. He would not be able to live with himself if he allowed the queen to turn Verena into another mindless servant.

They clashed in Verena's head, and she writhed on the ground, screams ripped from her broken body. Connor felt the queen's fury, clearly sensed her outrage that a vile Builder had touched the previous slate stone, and he realized she wasn't trying to kill Verena. Yet.

She wanted to know if Verena had tampered with the stone.

He blocked her, pouring in his entire will, and wrapped Verena's mind with his own. The queen tore at his defenses, but his will was like an impenetrable fortress. His love for Verena defined him, and he simply could not allow the queen to hurt her.

The queen kept slowly approaching, but he wouldn't wait for that. She was barely forty feet away, and his body still hadn't completed its healing. He couldn't manage a running battle, but he wouldn't allow her to hurt Verena.

He max-tapped granite and basalt as he closed on her, his body quivering with the need to strike down the hated woman. She beckoned him on, grinning, and called forth her mighty elemental affinities to smash him aside again.

Connor unleashed stilling-enhanced pumice.

He couldn't beat the queen with the elements, so he didn't even try. The super pumice cloud formed around him as he closed the distance. Queen Dreokt lashed out with whips of mixed elements, but they dissolved when they struck his invisible pumice cloud, three feet in front of him. Some of that raw power flowed through pumice to Connor, refreshing him and magnifying his own strength.

Queen Dreokt's eyes widened. That surprised her. Connor doubted she'd ever tried super pumice.

He closed the remaining distance in a fracked rush and tapped every primary affinity, wrapping each of them in stilling as he activated them to supercharge them. With the combined might of all of those primaries roaring through him, Connor jumped into the air and slammed into her, leading with both knees.

Energy erupted out of him in a titanic blast that eclipsed what he'd unleashed with diorite alone. Releasing that mix of supercharged primaries was like he'd distilled the power of five Last Word bombs into his knee caps. The blast catapulted him all the way back to Verena in a thunderclap so fierce it shattered his new eardrums. Air fled and felt like it might never return.

The blinding flash seared his eyes, but he refused to look away. The queen hadn't been ready for a blow like that. She'd tapped granite, but Connor's brutal strike blasted her body like her serpentinite attack had blasted Jagdish. With super basalt and obsidian speeding up his mind and senses, Connor clearly saw the ripples of force tearing through her, pulverizing bone, rending flesh, and shattering organs.

The blast flung her away, the back of her body bursting like an overripe melon, blood and shattered bits sprayed out, coating the land with crimson.

This time she screamed.

Connor wasn't sure how she managed that since her lungs and throat were smashed to bits. He gave chase, leaping upon her broken body even before it hit the ground, pummeling it with every bit of power he could muster. That initial blast had drained his reserves of supercharged power, but he still managed to tap granite and basalt at the same time, fracking his enhanced arms, punching her twenty times a second, trying to beat her to dust.

No one messed with Verena.

Connor howled with anger as he smashed Queen Dreokt to a pulp, covering himself in her blood and gore. It was disgusting, but he couldn't stop. Kilian joined him, super-fracking his hands, making them a blur as he tore at his mother's corpse. Together they worked to rip it apart so badly, not even she could regenerate.

The entire world condensed around him until he saw only the queen's brutalized body. He had to keep hitting her until there was nothing left. He kept the pumice cloud in place to prevent her from striking back at him with elements, and he fought off several chert-fueled assaults against his mind. This time he held the advantage, and he would not relinquish it again.

"Look out!" Verena cried into his mind. Their thoughts were still melded, and her thought shook him out of his murder rage.

Connor paused, his fracked arms snapping back into place with a flash of pain he barely felt. The queen's body was a ruptured, splattered mess under him. She no longer looked human, but he sensed her mind was still potent, but she wasn't attacking him.

He cast his senses out farther, and gasped.

A spear of earth fifty feet thick and a hundred feet long was plunging straight down toward him. If Verena hadn't warned him, it would have annihilated him as badly as he'd just beaten the queen. With a shout of fear, Connor released pumice and threw himself backward, using air to haul him mightily away and to push Kilian the opposite direction.

They just barely made it. The immense spear of earth missed his feet by inches and smashed down over Queen Dreokt with a thunderous impact and drove half its length into the hard ground.

Connor landed near Verena, breathing hard from his exertion and shock at the near-obliteration event. He wasn't sure how long it would have taken him to regenerate from getting splattered, but definitely longer than the queen. He couldn't believe she'd not only handled getting pummeled to soup, but had retained the presence of mind to launch such a vast spear of stone at him from a distance. She must have released direct control over it after launching it to ensure his pumice cloud couldn't deflect it.

The spear of earth melted away, revealing Queen Dreokt. She stood in her shredded battle clothing, bloody and misshapen, but standing. Even as he watched, her body continued to heal at an alarming rate. Despite the horrific damage she'd suffered, she would quickly return to full strength.

Connor allowed himself a moment to feel really tired. Killing her was proving even more difficult than he'd feared.

"How can we fight her off?" Verena asked. Connor felt her terror, but also her determination to keep fighting, and her towering frustration that Dreokt had not yet tried tapping the sculpted stone.

The sculpted stone. Connor muttered a curse. There might be seven kinds of idiots, but he'd just invented an eighth. Why hadn't he seized that sculpted stone when he had the chance?

Well, he'd have to pulverize her again and take it. She was holding it in her broken hands like a trophy.

Queen Dreokt struck at them again with chert, her mind somehow more focused than before. Maybe lacking a full body helped her focus, but Connor rocked under the onslaught, fighting to replenish his mental shielding.

"Imagine everyone you love standing in your mind with you, reinforcing your thoughts," he told Verena. That had helped him defeat the mind bomb and fight off the queen's mental assault earlier.

He also cast the thought at the queen, *"You're such a coward. Let's finish our duel first. Then you can deal with Verena, if you can defeat me."*

"I've already defeated you once, boy. I've slaughtered my unruly grandson, and my armies are crushing your little rebellion," she retorted.

"Then why do I feel your fear?" he shot back.

That annoyed her. She shifted her attack from Verena to him, and mental daggers stabbed at his brain.

Perfect. He could deal with that, and he filled his mind with Sentry speak. With Evander's memories percolating down into his, he suddenly found he possessed a far deeper well to draw from. He cast it all at her, a flood of indecipherable sentences with multiple meanings.

One of his favorite new ones was, *"Any cake will fall if poked at a critical moment, but the lingering kiss of a true beloved settles upon the soul like the rising of a springtime sunrise."*

He hadn't realized Evander was such a secret romantic, and felt relieved he didn't know if that sappy thought had been prompted by Evander's turbulent dating history with Harley.

Queen Dreokt paused in her advance, her eyes blazing with living fire. She shrieked, "You know how much I hate that frivolous language!"

"Why do you think I'm doing it?" he shot back, casting ten more Sentry speak lines at her. She actually retreated from his mind and seemed actually pained by the deep thoughts.

Kilian appeared out of nowhere, flashing past on super-fracked legs again, going for the sculpted stone in her hands. This time she was ready, and he rebounded off an invisible shield of air. The unexpected impact sent him tumbling away, and she chortled in triumph, lashing out at him with ropes of deadly earth.

Connor's heart nearly stopped, seized by sudden terror. He'd just watched her destroy Evander. He couldn't bear to see her destroy Kilian too. Before he could help, Kilian's entire body blurred, as if he was super-fracking every part of himself. Connor hadn't realized that was possible and would have sworn attempting it would just rip a person apart.

Not Kilian. He pivoted in mid-air and shot away at an angle. Just like he'd done dodging the lightning, he moved so fast he seemed to teleport. The queen's earth attack slapped nothing but empty air.

Connor gathered his affinities to strike at the distracted queen, but Earth appeared in front of him. The elemental being looked so much like Evander, for a second Connor only stared, wondering how the giant could project himself out of the corner of his mind where he'd taken refuge. Water and Fire appeared flanking Earth, while Air appeared above them.

They all looked immensely pleased.

Not good. Connor didn't need them interfering right then, but although he envisioned his tertiary affinity gateways like doors in his mind, the elementals did not disappear. Time seemed to slow, and Earth said, "Events have unfolded that you will wish to hear."

"I don't really have time to argue again," Connor said, gesturing at Queen Dreokt, whose mouth was moving in a slow-motion scowl.

His vision faded to black, then his mindscape formed into a view of the little cave south of Alasdair where General Carbrey had imprisoned Nicklaus and Verena. That was unexpected, and he looked around in confusion. The elementals appeared nearby, and then so did Verena.

She blinked at them and gaped. "Connor? What's going on?"

Of course. He was still linked to her with chert and had dragged her into the mindscape. He took her hand, comforted by her presence. "I think you've already met Water."

Water inclined her head, and Verena made a little curtsy, although she cast a nervous glance at Connor. Connected as they were, she didn't need to voice her worries. "*I thought we couldn't trust them.*"

"*We can't. I don't know what's going on,*" he thought back to her, then said aloud, "We're kind of busy right now, so if you don't mind, can we hold this conference later?"

"Time can wait for this," Water told him with that expression of hers that still made him think she truly cared about him.

Fire added, "Unless you wish to simply abandon the boy Nicklaus to his fate."

Connor felt a rush of cold dread. Verena's grip on his hand tightened and she exclaimed, "What about Nicklaus?"

"You know we've been coaching him," Air said.

"I appreciate you helping him. He's had a hard time after losing his affinities," Connor said, but for the first time berated himself for not worrying more about that. They had been so consumed by the threat Queen Dreokt posed that he hadn't thought to warn Nicklaus of the dangers of the elemental gifts.

Water stepped closer. "He has joined the great battle."

"No," Verena breathed, her free hand going to her mouth.

"And he activated the great construct I instructed him to build," Earth said happily.

"You did what?" Connor asked, his fears growing faster than Hamish's appetite.

Fire grinned, looking immensely pleased. "You would refer to it as a higher-level mechanical, similar in power to the one you call Kirstin's Defense."

"He's not ready for something like that," Verena exclaimed.

"Neither were you when we met that day," Water said. "And yet you approached that bridge. For a time I thought perhaps you would prove the best vessel for our freedom." Her expression hardened, her eyes turning the color of the sea before a storm. "But you turned away from us just as Connor did."

"Not Nicklaus," Air said with a happy giggle.

"What do you mean?" Connor asked, although he feared he already knew, and he wanted to beat himself for a month for leaving Nicklaus exposed to their treachery.

"He activated the construct, which he aptly named Time Out," Earth declared. "It elevated his malleable mind to the bridge you refer to as the Builder threshold."

"We have to stop him," Verena said, turning to Connor as if he could somehow cross the many leagues in a blink and convince Nicklaus to stop.

"Even now he stands upon it, eager to cross," Fire said, stepping closer, crimson flames dancing in his hair.

"But that would . . ." Connor breathed, horrified. They set up Nicklaus, gave him the power to destroy himself. He was so enthusiastic, and if he had indeed disobeyed orders and joined the battle, Connor had no doubt he would ascend, hoping it would give him power to save lives.

The awful truth was just the opposite.

Water waved one hand, and a sheen of crystalline droplets formed into a mirror. Its surface billowed, as if filled with heavy morning fog, then clarified into a view of Nicklaus kneeling on the ground, with Aifric beside him and Hamish lunging into view, expression terrified. Somehow Water was showing them what Nicklaus was doing.

"Please stop him," Verena cried.

Connor asked, "If he ascends and you use him as the gateway to freedom, he'll be consumed, won't he?"

"Indeed, the child possesses a flexible mind, but lacks the will to withstand such an ordeal," Fire confirmed. "He will be consumed."

Water said gently, "But you might not."

The implication was clear, and it chilled him to the bone. The elementals had seemed to resign themselves to Connor's refusal to help them, but that had just been a ruse.

"Why offer to allow Connor to take his place?" Verena asked suspiciously.

That was a good point. Was there some risk to them in using a child? He couldn't imagine they felt compassion for the boy. They pretended to human emotions with remarkable skill, particularly Water, but they were not human and didn't actually feel those emotions.

Water said, "We have been forthright with you, Connor. We seek freedom and you are our chosen champion. And you, Verena, we shared knowledge that only one other Builder has ever possessed. Despite your betrayals, we wish to prove our sincerity. We will allow you to take Nicklaus' place, Connor, to become the vessel of our escape, and we will do everything in our power to preserve your life through the process. As before, we will swear to obey your will pertaining to your homeland and defend and support your descendants for all time."

"What?" Verena asked, glancing from Water to Connor.

"They did make that offer," he acknowledged. He still felt it was a bad idea, but it offered a slight ray of hope.

"Or you can reject us again and we'll consume the boy in the fires of our liberation," Fire declared without a hint of remorse. "And we will wreak vengeance and destruction upon these lands and upon everyone you each hold dear. You will witness their destruction as fitting retribution for your refusal."

"This can't be happening," Verena breathed, tears in her eyes as she stared at the mirror showing Nicklaus.

Air hovered closer and spread her arms wide. "The choice is yours, Connor. The escape from our bonds is sure."

"Upon you lies the choice of how we do so, and how many will die as a result," Earth said.

"Choose now, beloved. The boy is already rushing across the bridge and in a moment, we will have no choice but to accept his willing sacrifice," Water said.

Connor looked from her to each of the others, numb with cold horror. He needed to think, to figure out some way to avert the disaster, but his mind was blank. All he could see was Nicklaus holding that stone, with that look of exultation on his young face.

He'd risked everything in Alasdair to save Nicklaus from Carbrey and Dougal, and he hadn't even known the boy yet. Now he did, and he could never allow Nicklaus to die in such a terrible way.

He turned to Verena, took her hands in his, and met her terrified gaze.

"*There has to be another way,*" she spoke directly into his mind. He was glad the elementals didn't seem to be able to hear their chert conversation.

"*I don't see one,*" Connor confessed, hating himself for allowing the elementals to position them in such a compromised position when they were already dealing with the queen and her armies. It was too much, and he felt overwhelmed. He was supposed to be the clever battlefield tactician, but so far he'd accomplished nothing but failure.

"*If they use you to break free, do you really believe you'll survive?*" she asked.

"*Maybe. They promised to protect our lands either way.*" That fact offered less comfort than he hoped.

"Can you trust them?"

"How could we?"

"Hurry, chosen one," Water urged. "We have slowed the passage of time for this conversation, but not even we can stop it entirely. He grows irritable if denied."

"He?" Verena asked.

Connor really wanted to ask about that, but they were out of time. He drew Verena to him, savoring the feel of her in his arms. *"I don't see any other choice."*

In answer, she kissed him fiercely. He felt her trembling, and with their minds linked, they didn't need to talk. She agreed, and she feared what was about to happen as much as he did. He couldn't stop it, though, not if Nicklaus was already trying to ascend. If they were closer, maybe, but there just wasn't enough time.

So he released her and turned to face the expectant elementals. They looked triumphant. All he had to do was say it, embrace a path he no longer wanted, but could not avoid. He'd agreed to sacrifice himself for family or country more than once. It never got easier, and this time the fate of far more than his home or even the entire kingdom was at stake.

Connor opened his mouth to say the words.

CHAPTER FIFTY-FIVE
And You Thought Things Couldn't Possibly Get Worse

Connor cleared his throat and said to the eagerly waiting elementals, "I—"

A blinding headache seared through his mind and he staggered, groaning. His vision blurred, and he heard Verena calling to him, as if from a great distance. Then she yelped in surprise.

He blinked open his eyes, then blinked again, but the view didn't change. He still stood in his mindscape with Verena and the elementals.

Queen Dreokt had joined them.

She wore full regal finery, complete with flowing silver-and-gold gown, delicate golden crown, and a scepter of office shaped an awful lot like a battle mace. She pointed the scepter at Connor and shouted, "You fool! Surrendering to the elementals is death for us all!"

For a second Connor was too surprised to react. He had thought he'd broken the chert connection with Queen Dreokt, but a link must have remained through Verena, and somehow she'd sensed what was happening and shoved herself into the conversation.

Verena didn't hesitated. She lunged and punched the queen in the jaw.

There in the mindscape, the queen lacked her physical prowess. They were all just mental projections, and Verena's mind was very strong. The blow rocked the surprised queen back a step, and Verena followed up with a second punch, right in the queen's throat. Unlike when she'd used that move on him in Alasdair, she did not hold back, but drove the flat of her hand hard.

Queen Dreokt choked and sputtered, and Verena growled, "This is a private conversation."

"You are not welcome here," Fire added. "You wasted your chance to serve us and will suffer the consequences of your folly."

That motivated the queen. She knocked Verena back shed the effects of her blows, then gestured at the four elementals. "You young idiots! You can't decide to destroy everyone and pretend such a choice is a private one."

"We don't have a choice," Connor admitted. He hated the queen, but if she had an idea how to stop the elementals from rising, he welcomed it. "If we don't offer them a gateway, they will destroy Nicklaus and use him instead."

She shook her head. "No. For once, listen to your elders, boy. I will stop this."

"How?" Verena asked. The elementals drew closer, scowling. Water started to say, "Poor little mortal—"

But Queen Dreokt pointed her scepter at Water and shrieked, "I will stop it!"

Then she disappeared.

"I hate that woman," Verena muttered, glancing back at Connor, a flicker of hope in her eyes. "But if she can . . ."

"Make your choice!" Water cried, rushing toward him.

Connor threw out a hand and said, "Give me a second."

He closed his eyes and willed himself awake. The mindscape faded, replaced by the real world. The barren plateau, the torn ground, the broken remains of Evander's giant, the roiling clouds and shrieking, chill wind, and Kilian rushing in toward the queen's back, water and fire in hand like twin scimitars. Queen Dreokt stood nearby, holding the ancient sculpted slate high.

Connor realized what she intended, and for a second his heart soared. Of course! With the power of that stone, she might be able to destroy the mechanical Nicklaus was using and prevent him from ascending.

Then his hope splintered and he remembered the problem with that plan. He raised a hand to shout a warning.

Too late.

Queen Dreokt staggered and screamed, a sound of ultimate horror and pain, the sculpted slate stone locked in her hands. Through his earth senses, Connor felt her presence grow a hundredfold in strength, as if her affinity swallowed an avalanche.

Then her strength rebounded back against her as that avalanche exploded.

Verena had max-released the power of that stone, crafting it into some kind of higher mechanical, poised to unleash all its energy in one titanic event. The queen must have max-tapped it.

Just like Nicklaus, she learned that was a bad idea.

Connor felt so very confused. He should be exulting that the long-shot chance Verena nearly sacrificed her life for was actually working. Except if they hadn't altered that stone, could the queen have stopped Nicklaus and blocked the elementals' devious plan?

Would she then have killed him and everyone in the army as well? Probably.

Would that be worse than releasing the elementals?

Kilian shot past his distracted mother, fire and water slashing across her face, throat, and hands. It looked like he wanted to decapitate her and sever her connection to the sculpted stone at the same time. That might have helped, but his attacks deflected away a hair's breadth from her body. He skidded to a halt beside Connor, frowning. "Tell me this is a good thing?"

Connor tried to shake off his shock. Maybe he could get the stone from the queen, get Verena to shutter its power again, then use it himself to stop Nicklaus. "Things have gotten complicated."

Kilian started to respond, but Queen Dreokt's mind slammed into Connor's like a speedcaravan car at full speed. He blinked, and the real world was gone, replaced by a mindscape he didn't recognize. He stood in a long laboratory with whitewashed walls, full of bright steel machinery, glass cabinets, and piles of various stones in wooden crates. Queen Dreokt stood nearby, dressed in a white jacket. Is this where she invented Petralist affinities?

She rushed to him and grabbed his battle jacket, her eyes wide with terror, her face ashen. "You fool! You and your Builder have sealed our doom."

"I didn't know the elementals would do this," he protested. He should strike her down, but her fear wrapped him like bands of ice, reinforcing his own terror that they'd inadvertently destroyed the one chance they actually needed to survive. They'd devoted all their energy to defeating Queen Dreokt. Now that he realized the elementals posed a more dire threat, he felt unsteady, shaken, and confused.

The queen staggered away, clutching at her own body as if wracked with fever chills. She collided with a worktable, upsetting delicate glass tubes and vials that fell to the floor and shattered with surprisingly musical tinkling notes. Blue and green liquid sprayed across the white-tiled floor. "I can't believe this is happening!"

Then she spun back to Connor and straightened, pointing an accusing finger at him, her fear switching to fury. "It's your fault! I've fought to protect our world from this evil ever since the day my poor Triath died, and now you've made it happen! Curse you, child! You've undermined everything I've done and given birth to my greatest fear!"

"I didn't mean it," Connor protested.

"You didn't think!" she screamed.

"In my defense, your attempts to kill everyone I love or wipe out their minds made it hard to see any other dangers," he pointed out. There had to be a way to salvage the situation.

She scowled, took a step toward him, then collapsed, convulsing on the floor. The wall behind her vanished, revealing a sharp edge and the abyss of her affinityscape, filled with boiling, gray mist.

Connor groaned, his hope curling into the back of his mind in a fetal position, whimpering with fear.

The queen's islands, floating in that abyss, were burning and crumbling, the top-layer bridges connecting them decaying before his eyes. Wood and stone melted and dripped into the abyss of boiling gray smoke, all except for the elemental islands. They were growing and moving together, their top-tier bridges overlapping to become a wide path for the four elementals already standing on the middle.

All of them were pressing forward, trying to take that critical step onto the queen's side. They were dressed in finery that rivaled anything Connor had seen from kings and queens. Water wore a glittering gown of miniature waves, crashing against each other, creating little puffs of foam that fell gently around her. Her eyes looked like gemstones cut from ice, and her luxurious, black hair swayed back and forth like waves flowing up sandy beaches. Fire stood beside her, encased in sheets of interwoven flames that crackled and danced wildly. Air's gown of silver silk sported hundreds of cloudlike tassels that floated gently about her, while Earth's suit looked like it was constructed of layers of strata extending down into the heart of the planet.

They looked exultant, and when Water spotted him, she gave him a stern look. "You have wasted the moment of your glory, Connor. We will cross this bridge and consume this wretch who has denied us for so long."

"And we'll destroy the boy Nicklaus too," Fire said, sounding extremely satisfied.

"Why?" Connor demanded. He felt a growing dread that he was witnessing the end of all things he knew and loved.

"Because we can," Air said, tilting her head up slightly.

Earth added, "The boy is standing in the threshold even now. One final step, and I will have him." He extended an arm toward Air. "Shall we rise through his gateway together?"

She took his arm with a graceful nod of her head. "I never thought you'd ask."

Queen Dreokt staggered over to Connor and seized his jacket again, blubbering with fear. At the closer contact, his connection to her deepened and an image popped into his mind. He saw what was happening to her. She was getting dragged back through the threshold of serpentinite, screaming, clawing at the ground so hard her nails tore and she left bloody scratches behind her, but she couldn't stop her slide.

Connor sensed that once she fell back through the threshold, the elementals would have their path to freedom. He gripped her shoulders and tried pushing strength to her. He needed to help, but wasn't sure how to. Linking his mind closer to the madwoman made his head hurt and his own emotions grow even more turbulent and raw. His breathing quickened and his heart raced. Fear built within him until his fingers shook and he wanted to turn and run.

Except there was nowhere to go.

Water scowled at him. "Don't interfere, boy. You've already earned our ire."

"Let him try. We no longer need him, and he's proven his cowardice. We'll punish him and lay waste to these lands," Fire spat.

"I'm not the one who has to murder a child to get what I want," Connor shouted back. He needed to think, to come up with a plan, but what?

Through his connection to the queen, he sensed her slide back into the third threshold, driven by the reverse pull of tapping that sculpted stone. She screamed in pain and terror, her thoughts scattering as her fragile grip on sanity shredded and she descended into a panic-driven madness. Her mind was like a boiling whirlpool that threatened to suck Connor down with her.

He braced himself against the pull, but that weakened his connection, reduced the strength she was drawing from him. Water shouted with victory and took a single step over the middle of the bridge. The entire affinityscape shook, and thunder rumbled in the distance. The air turned chill, and in the laboratory behind Connor, the steel cabinets started eroding, the steel pitting and turning black from rust. Glass cabinets cracked, and grime crept over them. Dreokt's connection to her human roots was fading fast. Soon there would be nothing left but an empty shell, a vessel through which the elementals could rise into the world.

She screamed again, her turbulent thoughts coalescing into a single thought. "I will die before I let you through!"

Somehow she stopped her slide through the threshold, but Connor could feel the strain growing. She was racked with intense pain, the same kind of agony Connor had felt trying to ascend through that threshold. Remaining stuck there for long would tear her apart. She clearly wanted it to, but he sensed she'd weaken and slide through the rest of the way first.

He shuddered in horror. He had been about to open himself to that same process, had hoped the elementals might honor their oaths, protect his life, and spare his people. They had made no such promise to Queen Dreokt and left her exposed to the full, brutal intensity of her fall.

Fire grabbed Water's shoulder. "Do not cross without me!" He looked nervous that he might get left behind.

"I enjoy the deepest connection with our vessel. She ascended first with me," Water retorted, trying to shake him off. They might like flirting with each other, but in that moment of potential freedom, it appeared their loyalty meant less than their individual freedom. Could he use that against them somehow?

"She ascended second with me," Fire shouted, trying to pull her back. "You can't have her to yourself!"

"We all need a path," Air said, looking nervous by their progress. "Earth, why aren't we walking the boy's bridge?"

"We will," Earth promised. "Come. Let us join him for our moment of victory."

The two of them faded from the affinityscape. Connor hoped that might help Dreokt hold on a little longer, but it also meant those two powerful beings were leaving to destroy Nicklaus. The thought of that brave little boy suffering like the queen was made Connor angry, and super frustrated, because at the moment it was a helpless anger.

Queen Dreokt dropped to her knees and looked up to meet Connor's gaze. For a second, her madness parted and she hissed, "You must kill me before they can complete the crossing!"

Connor blew out an annoyed breath. That was just what he'd been trying to do. "Any suggestions on how to do that?"

Water shouted, "No! You cannot deny us now!"

She seized Fire's hand and said, "Together. We must take her now."

He nodded, and their clasped hands melded together, turning into crackling lightning. The air began to hum, and the hairs on Connor's arms rose. He sensed charges building, and realized they were combining into strum and magnis.

Together, the two elements took another step.

The queen's momentary lucidity evaporated. She fell to the ground, screaming and ripping at her own face. Connor's connection to her wavered as her madness shook the roots of her mind. He retreated before getting swept into her insanity, and blinked open his eyes.

Kilian was staring at his screaming mother, looking openly concerned. The slate stone had melted, as if from some invisible, fervent heat, and now encased her hands. Her eyes had turned black, transformed into miniature globes of absolute darkness.

"What's going on?" Kilian asked softly, gripping Connor's shoulder.

"Verena activated the stone, and it's dragging her back through the third threshold. I can't stop it. We have to kill her now!" he shouted, tapping basalt. He left Verena behind and rushed the queen, seizing every elemental affinity and slashing at her from every side. If he could tear her apart, they could still maybe save Nicklaus before it was too late.

"I thought we wanted that to happen," Kilian said, racing after him, fire and water appearing in his hands again.

Connor raced past the queen, slashing at her with all his strength, but his strike deflected away like Kilian's had. Kilian struck with white-hot fire, interlaced with water, but failed to reach her too. "How can she do that?"

Connor slowed to a stop near the queen, trying to figure out how to reach her. He sensed the elementals around her, their wills filling the air and actively warding her. He could never penetrate that space to her using the powers of the very elements intent on preserving her.

"We did, but Nicklaus activated a super mechanical the elementals tricked him into building. They're pushing him to ascend the Builder threshold."

Kilian gasped, looking more frightened than when facing his deadly mother. "No! That will destroy him." He hurled fire like a thunderbolt, but it rebounded from the queen and exploded back against Kilian, knocking him staggering. He looked absolutely shocked.

"They're fighting for her now?" he breathed.

Connor nodded, hating how helpless he felt. Through his affinity senses, he could feel the queen's connection to water and fire growing, the elements melding together as they combined into their higher forms of power. "Your mother wanted to stop Nicklaus. She thought maybe with the stone she could, but . . ."

Kilian muttered a curse in Havaen. "What do we do?"

"I don't know. Water and Fire are pushing her to madness. I tried to help, but nearly got caught in it too."

"Just like my dad." Kilian's expression turned hopeful. "He rose into an elfonnel, but we destroyed him before the elements gained freedom. Can we do that and still help Nicklaus?"

"Maybe if she surrendered to one element alone," Connor said. Through his own affinities, he clearly felt the air growing charged and dangerous. Dreokt might be fighting the elementals to give him and Kilian time to do something, but the elementals were determined to rise through her together before they could. That fight was opening a door to a new threat, something they'd never considered facing before.

"What else is there?" Kilian demanded.

"Strum." The words seemed to hang in the air, taunting him.

Kilian groaned. "You've got to be kidding me."

He wished he was. The queen suddenly screamed again, her entire body convulsing, hands flinging out wide. She slowly rose into the air as the clouds high above her roiled and began to spin like a newly forming tornado.

Definitely not good.

Everything was lined up all wrong. She was supposed to go mad, create a common elfonnel they could destroy. Maybe it was because she was using such a powerful sculpted stone, or maybe it was because she was fighting so hard against the elements, or maybe the elementals were just more motivated than ever. Connor had never imagined anyone could turn elfonnel with strum, but he could feel it happening.

Fire and Water appeared in the air beside Connor. Water looked pleased, and Fire chuckled, rubbing his hands together. "We never considered pushing her beyond her limits together. Thank you Connor for helping us find this doorway."

"It will offer unprecedented access to your world," Water said.

"You should have joined us," Fire said, his eyes points of white flame.

Beside him, Kilian was looking scared for the first time ever. "I have no idea how to respond to this."

Connor rushed back to Verena's limp form and gently lifted her into his arms. The healing power wrapping all of her bones and infusing her to bursting would heal her eventually, even if he was not nearby. "Take Verena. Try to find a way to help Nicklaus."

Kilian took her, cradling her against his chest. "What are you going to do?"

Connor grimaced. "Improvise."

CHAPTER FIFTY-SIX
Higher Forms of Cheating

Hamish reached Nicklaus one terrible second too late.

The boy's eyes rolled back, and he would have collapsed if Hamish hadn't caught him. As he lowered Nicklaus to the ground, with the slate super mechanical clutched in the boy's hands, Aifric dropped to her knees beside him and extended a hand to the boy. "What happened?"

"He can't do this. Ascending that threshold will kill him," Hamish said, concentrating on the slate mechanical. He sucked in an awed breath at the sheer magnitude of power flooding out of that piece of slate. It eclipsed even what he'd felt in Kirstin's Defense, although he hadn't felt that one when it was activated.

He sensed something through that enormous wave of energy pouring into the earth, like a distant light in the distance, and sensed even greater currents of power available there.

The threshold.

Even though he wasn't the one who activated the mechanical, just touching its power threatened to sweep him into the current and cast him upon that threshold. Hamish got a wild idea, crazy even for him. If he embraced the current, could he reach the threshold first? Maybe if he ascended instead of Nicklaus, he could spare the boy.

He bent his will to the current of power and tried to reach the crack that controlled it, but his Builder senses slid off, unable to gain purchase. Frowning, he tried again. It had to be there, and he sensed it just out of reach, like a cake concealed under a glass dome.

"We do not need you, Builder. The boy is our vessel. You are not welcome here."

The deep voice that spoke into his mind was easily as powerful as Kilian or Evander. Hamish's blood chilled as he realized he was hearing Earth speak to him, just as the element spoke to Connor, and how Water had spoken to Verena.

"Please, don't," he cast back at it. *"He's just a boy."*

"Yes, he is flexible and resilient, the perfect vessel of sacrifice. Now begone."

Somehow Earth broke Hamish's connection with the mechanical, casting his Builder senses back out of it. He stared down at it, horrified by the truth. He could not save Nicklaus.

He wanted to scream with rage, but Aifric gasped and looked south. "Aonghus!"

The angry general was rushing up the main street of Lossit, fracked, sword raised, rushing straight toward them.

Toward Nicklaus.

Hamish realized in a flash what Aonghus was after. Nicklaus had severed his contact from earth, so Aonghus would kill the boy to get it back.

He activated quartzite shielding just in time. Aonghus was moving too fast for any other response, but the shield of air formed around Hamish, Aifric, and Nicklaus fast enough to save them. Aonghus struck the shield and ricocheted high into the air, his speed sending him flying a hundred feet.

"He must have spotted the shield. Curse his reflexes," Aifric growled. "We'll take care of him."

"No." Hamish jumped to his feet and placed a restraining hand on her shoulder. Aifric and her mind sisters could no doubt defeat Aonghus, especially when he lacked slate, but Hamish had a score to settle. "He's mine. See if you can reach Nicklaus with chert. Get him to stop before he ascends."

She hesitated for a second, then nodded gravely. "Be careful."

Then she turned back to the silent boy. Hamish activated thrusters and lifted into the air. Aonghus was already turning for another attack, but slowed when he saw Hamish. He raised his sword and laughed, gesturing Hamish closer.

"Hamish, what are you doing?" Jean cried through their private speakstone link. That was fast. She must have a sightstone already focused on him. The idea made him smile, and at any other time, he would have glanced up and blown a kiss. At the moment, he wished she wasn't so organized.

"Not a good time, love. Please do me a favor. Don't watch this."

He clearly read the terrible fear in her voice, but refused to acknowledge it. She feared Aonghus, and for good reason, but Hamish did not. Aonghus had always been wild, but the queen had turned him into a killer, a monster who took delight in causing pain to others. Today justice would be served. No matter what.

"But you don't have your missiles," she protested.

"I can stop him," Hamish promised. Missiles would be easier, but Aonghus did not deserve an easy death, and for once, Hamish was eager for the chance to kill.

Jean hesitated before saying, "I love you. Be safe."

Hamish appreciated the fact that she did not try to dissuade him from what had to be done. He swooped toward Aonghus, who dodged to the left, no doubt expecting a missile strike. Hamish banked along with his enemy and shot low over him. He might be out of missiles, but he did have a couple small diorite darts left. He threw one as he flew past, but Aonghus accelerated away. The dart exploded harmlessly behind him.

Tallan curse his socks with mildew.

Hamish pivoted in midair and swept back around. All of the nearby soldiers from both armies turned to watch. They were still intimidated by the rough, giant earthen creatures and Nicklaus' command to stop fighting and seemed eager for a chance to watch him fight Aonghus.

Some of the Merkland army raised a cheer. "Hamish!"

So of course the Crann army started chanting Aonghus' name. He might be their general, but it was disappointing to see them cheer such a vile being as their champion.

Aonghus' voice boomed, so loud it had to be enhanced by a Pathfinder. "Come here, Builder. You seem angry. I can give you peace."

Hamish snarled and accelerated, aiming straight at the hated man. Aonghus laughed and swept a hand out, and a wall of earth exploded out of the ground between them.

Hamish was so shocked by the unexpected elemental attack, he almost forgot to tap blind coal. He only had a tiny bit left, but it would be enough. He blasted through the wall of earth and punched at Aonghus as he flew past, powering his blow with tiny quartzite thrusters at the elbow to make it strong enough to rip the man's face off. But again Aonghus dodged, tapping just enough basalt to leverage his incredible reflexes.

Before Hamish could spin around for another attack, and even as he tried to process the unbelievable fact that Aonghus was somehow using slate, despite Nicklaus' Time Out, earth erupted in a grasping hand that snatched him right out of the air. It slammed him into the ground with brutal force, so hard his armor creaked from the strain, and he smashed his face into his visor. A flash of pain in his nose suggested it might be broken, and his eyes watered. He felt nauseous, but not in the fun way, and he cried out with anger and pain. Getting slammed down like that definitely gave his neck whip-snap.

He wanted to lie there and groan for a moment, but didn't have time. He didn't dare tap the last piece of blind coal, even though the earth was squeezing him. Aonghus was too deadly to waste it until he absolutely needed it, so Hamish triggered a pumice cloud. It floated around him, distorting and defusing Petralist tertiary powers. The earth loosened, and Hamish burst free and launched himself at Aonghus again, both hands extended like spears.

A wall of earth erupted behind Aonghus, and Hamish didn't realize the danger until it was too late. As he swept in to crush his enemy's chest, Aonghus simply dropped straight down into the earth. Hamish smashed into the earthen wall with terrific force, instinctively tapping blind coal to avoid getting crushed. He burst through and pivoted around, breathing heavy from the near-death experiences.

He had to calm himself. He couldn't beat Aonghus in a rage. He was low on mechanicals and protective shields, but he would not let Aonghus escape again.

He paused in a hover twenty feet into the air to regard his enemy. Aonghus was grinning, looking totally confident. His forces were cheering his name, motivated by his earth mastery. Hamish glanced toward Aifric and Nicklaus, but they hadn't moved. He didn't see anyone else using slate. It appeared Aonghus was the only one who could. Was it because he was ascended? That was so unfair.

Aonghus laughed, his voice still enhanced. "Behold my greatness! The elements have spoken to me and Earth has granted me sole access to his power. No other Petralist can walk with earth now except for me. I am their champion, and I will conquer!"

Hamish muttered a couple Varvakin curses he'd learned from Fyodor. He didn't understand what they meant, but the big man had promised they were truly vile. Earth had taught Nicklaus how to build Time Out, but if he could choose who it affected and who it didn't, that suggested the elementals were indeed gaining greater freedom. Not good. He needed to defeat Aonghus fast and figure out how to save Nicklaus before it was too late.

He leaned into another dive. He lacked distance weapons, so had to take the fight to Aonghus. He swept in, planning to try shoving a vial of mega stench up Aonghus' nose. That would distract him.

Aonghus waved him on, sword raised, looking like he planned to try cutting him out of the air. Fine with Hamish. He dove lower, but earth shot up all around him in a spray so extensive he couldn't avoid it. He tried accelerating through it, but the earth condensed around him, forming a cocoon that blocked his thrusters and yanked him back down to the ground.

Tallan slap him for a fool. He couldn't do stupid things like that.

Fingers of earth seized Hamish's helmet and ripped it violently from his head. He gasped as his neck was nearly broken before the straps snapped. The earthen fingers crushed his helmet before he could activate any mechanicals, and the earth on the inside edge of that cocoon started ripping down his torso, yanking away the tiny bits of stone attached to the many pockets along the outside of his suit. He tried activating pumice, but the little bursts were consumed by the earth, and the pumice too ripped free a second later. The last of his blind coal went with it, along with nearly all of the other mechanicals built into the exterior of the suit.

Hamish struggled mightily, but the earth held him securely, and with a growing sense of dread he realized he would not escape this time. He saw again Ilse's broken body. Would Aonghus rip him apart inside his earthen coffin like he had her? The thought horrified and enraged him. He couldn't let Aonghus destroy him, had to think of something.

He couldn't let Jean watch him die.

That terrible thought drove him to redouble his efforts, but without his mechanicals, he wasn't strong enough.

The earth flowed away from his face, and General Aonghus stood beside him, grinning. "You escaped justice one time too many, boy. Today you die." He gestured with one hand, taking in the ranks of troops watching all around. "But we're going to give everyone a show."

Hamish glared at the general, who looked so smug Hamish wanted to scream. He forced calm on himself and said, "I'm surprised you haven't started running yet. That seems to be your greatest talent."

Aonghus slapped Hamish across the side of the face so fast and so hard he didn't even see the blow coming. He groaned as his head snapped to the side. It felt like he'd gotten a second whip-snap. He instinctively reached for sandstone and found a piece in an inside pocket that hadn't gotten ripped off yet, and gratefully activated it. Builder healing was not nearly as fast as Petralist healing, but it would help.

Or would it just prolong the torture until Aonghus finally killed him?

* * *

Jean had planned to not look, had told herself she couldn't bear to watch Hamish face Aonghus, but she simply couldn't keep from watching.

Her heart felt frozen with terror, and her hands started to tremble as she watched the viewscreen zoomed in on Hamish. All of the dark nightmares from her months of suffering crept back into her mind. She'd thought those fears gone forever, but now her breath felt short, her heart raced, and tears threatened to blur her gaze.

How could Aonghus wield earth when no one else could? She didn't understand what Nicklaus was doing, but feared he was in grave danger. She couldn't think about that, though, not with Hamish somehow captured and helpless in Aonghus' hands. Why hadn't he activated blind coal or pumice or a shieldstone? Her fear threatened to send her crashing to the deck, weeping uncontrollably, but Jean fought it down with all her strength.

She cried, "Captain Leppin, we need that barrage now!"

"All mechanicals are online and targeted. Ready to fire," came the immediate reply.

"Fire!"

He was already shouting orders, but Jean was no longer listening. She stared at Hamish struggling in vain far below, held prisoner by earth as Aonghus struck him again and again with his fists, raining blows over Hamish's face. He was already bloody, his nose broken, and his pain tore at Jean like physical daggers. Aonghus seemed to take immense pleasure in hurting him before he killed him. An unbroken ring of soldiers watched in silence, leaving an open space a hundred feet all around the execution. No one dared draw closer for fear of getting slaughtered.

The entire ship shuddered as the barrage was unleashed, but Jean couldn't fool herself into thinking that the few seconds it would take for those munitions to reach the ground would be at least one second too late.

So she turned and bolted for the door, shouting over her shoulder, "Gisela, order every flight to rally point Sweetbread Seven! I will assume personal command."

Chapter Fifty-Seven
A Disobedient Child

Nicklaus walked with earth.

He loved it! When he activated Time Out, he'd unleashed so much more power than he'd expected. It swept his mind down into the ground, and he could see everything. It was like he was hovering ten thousand feet in the air, looking down over the valley, but upside down. Deep in the earth, he could see it all, feel it all. He sensed the earth coming to life all through the valley. Monstrous shapes formed and grew, ready to squash any soldiers who refused the command to stand down.

"Hey, that's not what I want," Nicklaus shouted, somehow poking the giant earthen monsters with mental fingers.

"They will do your bidding, but you must be specific," a deep voice said, surprising him. Nicklaus spun and found a big man with black hair and a huge, black beard standing beside him. The man reminded him of Uncle Evander and resonated the same sense of permanence.

"I don't want anyone hurt. I just want them to stop," Nicklaus said. That was pretty clear to him.

"And if they refuse to stop?" the big man asked.

That was a good point. Nicklaus considered that and glanced across the valley. From below, he could see every soldier. He sensed many Sentries and Sappers touching earth, but they couldn't access its power because he was using all of it. Most of the soldiers had hesitated, and he bet they'd stop if he encouraged them. He didn't need to hurt them.

"If they don't stop, those earth monsters should growl at them. That should work," Nicklaus said.

"We will proceed thus." The big man bowed his head in a sign of respect. That was fun. Most adults didn't bother bowing unless he was attending a formal event and they had to. He liked the big man, and his voice was familiar.

"You're Earth!" Nicklaus cried. He should have recognized him sooner.

Earth smiled. "And you are the most clever child I have ever met. Only two other Builders have ever reached this point, and neither of them possessed the strength and determination to ascend through the gateway to the Sylfaen."

He gestured upward, and the view shifted. It was if Nicklaus could see through the earth. It parted, and suddenly he stood in his affinityscape on the fields north of New Schwinkendorf, dotted with wells of his Builder powers linking him to the various power stones. Except now glowing columns were growing out of every well, arcing inward to a point in the center, directly above his well to slate. Where the arches touched, cascades of multicolored sparks exploded into the air, and a faint sound of silver trumpets stirred his heart. The air above the slate well started to shimmer, and a tendril of liquid silver flowed up from the well to touch the center of that multi-columned archway.

As soon as it connected, the air shook with a thunderclap, and that slender line of liquid expanded, forming a glistening doorway. Nicklaus grinned with a growing sense of awe. The silvery doorway rippled, and he caught glimpses of the other side. It looked like a vast rainbow of every color of light. It was beautiful, and he sensed that it was saturated with more power than all the stones ever harvested.

A beautiful lady in a flowing, white gown appeared in the air nearby, her dark tresses floating about her lovely face. She gestured toward the silvery doorway and shouted, "Behold the gateway to the Sylfaen and your destiny!"

Nicklaus started walking toward it, drawn by an intense curiosity. Wind gusted, pushing him from behind, sweeping through the gateway. Earth walked beside him, smiling as happily as Nicklaus did when he got to fly with Hamish.

The beautiful lady descended to meet them as they strode beneath the first of the columns and walked past the well to granite. The closer they drew to the silvery doorway, the more powerfully Nicklaus felt drawn to it. He wanted to run and dive through, and he sensed the two adults would only encourage him to.

So he stopped and frowned.

"Why do you stop?" Earth asked gently, extending a hand to encourage him to keep walking.

"You're Air, aren't you?" Nicklaus asked the lady.

She smiled, and a gentle breeze gusted around him like a caress from her finger. "You're a clever boy."

They were very nice, nicer than almost any adult that wasn't forced to be nice because he was related to the king.

Too nice.

Nicklaus knew all about too-nice adults. His governess, Christin, had learned the hard way that pretending to be too nice in order to trick him into doing something unpleasant like studying or eating his vegetables wouldn't work. He'd outsmarted the most subtle too-nice adults all his life, so his too-nice-manipulator senses were as honed as a sword.

"What's that door?" he asked.

Earth grinned. "That is the Builder threshold! No Builder has ever successfully crossed it before today."

"You will be the first, and the greatest!" Air added enthusiastically, gesturing him toward the doorway. She wanted him to go through it so badly, he decided he didn't trust her after all.

"Verena is the greatest Builder, and Hamish is the other greatest," he stated.

"But you can be greater," Earth insisted, his deep voice as smooth as the tiled floor leading to the hated bath.

Air dropped to one knee, looking confused by his reluctance. "Boy, don't you realize that once you step through that gateway, you'll be able to unlock almost limitless power by drawing directly from the sylfaen. You won't be limited to the paltry scraps like everyone else."

That did sound like fun. Maybe he was being overly cautious. He was talking with elemental beings, after all. Maybe they weren't manipulative like adults. Nicklaus knew how to find out.

"What can I do with Sylfaen power? Can I make better quartzite thrusters to fly?"

Earth chuckled, a deep rumbling that made Nicklaus smile. "Of course, child. You could channel ten times the power through quartzite as any other Builder. You will fly higher and faster."

"And heal better, and make more amazing mechanicals," Air added eagerly, reaching for his hand. Her skin was cool, like a breeze from a cave on a hot afternoon. She tugged him toward the gateway, and Nicklaus followed. The promises did sound amazing. He needed new thrusters, and it would be so much fun to fly with Hamish and teach him new tricks.

Earth walked on the other side of him, grinning as happily as Air. It felt nice to please the elements, but as Nicklaus drew close to the shimmering doorway, he felt a growing reluctance. Something wasn't right.

"Does it hurt?" he asked.

"Does what hurt?" Air asked at the same time Earth said, "No, of course not."

That answer was too quick, and his doubts returned in a flash. He stopped again, pointing at the doorway. "Going through there, becoming ascended. Connor said ascension is hard and that it hurts."

"Not for Builders," Earth said.

Air glanced from him to the doorway, her expression as hungry as the hunting cat he saw once at the king's zoo. Nicklaus tried pulling his hand out of her grasp, but her fingers tightened around his and her pleasant smile vanished.

"Just step through, and everything will be clear," Earth said, his tone turning harder.

"I don't want to." Nicklaus pulled harder, but Air would not release him. The wind that had been pushing him gently from behind gusted so hard, he stumbled a step closer to the doorway.

They were definitely not telling the truth. Nicklaus dug in his heels and asked, "What do you get if I go through?"

"Clever boy," Earth said again, but he no longer sounded pleased. "You will step through that door. You cannot stop now. You activated the mechanical, just as I instructed you."

Air's expression had turned fierce. It frightened him, and he tugged harder against her, but her grip was like iron. She pulled him another step closer. He was barely ten feet away from the doorway now. She hissed, "When you step through that doorway, you will open a path for us to escape our imprisonment. You will set us free just as you fight to free your own nation. Don't you want to help us?"

"Free," Earth echoed softly, staring at the gateway. "No restraint, no boundaries. The world will be open to us with none to limit us ever again."

Nicklaus fixed them both with his most serious expression. "You're really old, so you should know better than that."

"What?" Air asked, looking surprised.

"No one gets to run free with no restraint, not even the king. Everyone has to follow laws, or the world would be crazy."

"We're not human, so your laws do not apply to us," Earth snapped.

"The greater your power, the more restraint you need," Nicklaus said, repeating the words Christin loved to recite to him. He couldn't believe he was saying it, but since she wasn't there to hear, she couldn't remind him about it later. "You could do good, or do bad. It's your choice, but if you choose bad, you could hurt a lot of people."

Christin would be very proud of him. He usually didn't like her lectures because they were aimed at getting him to stop sneaking out at night, or to stop testing Builder battle mechanicals without supervision, or to stop him from breaking into the locked pantries for snacks at night. He would need to figure out how to justify doing all those things still, even though he was using the lecture on the elementals.

"We choose to hurt everyone," Earth stated, his voice cold and scary.

"And you'll be the first," Air snarled, yanking his arm so hard she would have dislocated it in the real world. She pulled him right off his feet and hurled him at the gateway.

They weren't in the real world.

The thought was like a lifeline, and Nicklaus seized it with all his strength. The elementals were liars. That made them as bad as the very bad man or the terrible queen, and Nicklaus did not like liars.

With an effort of will, he stopped close enough to the gateway that his breath condensed upon it. He hung in the air of that affinityscape, fighting the current trying to drag him in. A knotted rope appeared in front of him and he seized the lifeline. It extended up into blackness, linking him back to the real world.

The wind intensified into a mighty gale, screaming around him, tearing at his clothing. He clung to the lifeline back to the real world, and the knots dug into his hands, but he wouldn't let go. That close to the gateway, he sensed the vast power on the other side, and the temptation to stick a single finger through to test it was as great as any temptation to sneak another sweetbread. But when Nicklaus glanced back at the shocked elementals, he was no longer tempted.

"You cannot deny us!" Earth bellowed, charging, huge hands raised to slam Nicklaus through the gateway.

"You should know better than to try to force me to do anything," Nicklaus said and yanked as hard as he could on the rope. He shot upward, just barely avoiding Earth's grasping fingers, and returned to his mind in a rush.

He swayed, feeling sick as his senses returned. He was kneeling over the Time Out mechanical, a simple, square block of slate that he had painstakingly layered six dozen commands dictated by Earth.

The liar.

The battlefield was quiet, with soldiers standing in uneasy ranks, staring at the giant mounds of threatening earth. The smell of smoke and ash and mud assaulted his nose, and he smiled, relaxing a little. Those smells reminded him of lots of adventures he'd enjoyed around New Schwinkendorf.

Aifric dropped to one knee beside him, her expression worried. "Nicklaus, what's wrong? I feel earth changing. It's like it's angry, and the air suddenly feels threatening."

"Oh, they're really mad. They lied to me. They want me to let them out to do bad things." Nicklaus focused on Time Out, felt the crack of its power, and slammed it shut.

That should take care of things.

Except it didn't.

Every giant earthen monster lunged upward, bursting through the shell that made them look vague and unclear. The enormous creatures of earth were shaped like every imaginable nightmare. Some sported multiple arms, some multiple heads, all had scary fangs, and some carried clubs.

In unison, they roared like earthquakes. The nearest ones, both humanoid creatures, had risen to flank either side of the Lossit gateway. They both swiveled toward Nicklaus, and one of them spoke with Earth's voice.

"You cannot stop us now, child. You touched the gateway, and we have begun our journey. The queen herself provides the path to our full escape, and you all will suffer for your insolence."

"Ah, Nicklaus, what's going on?" Aifric asked nervously.

Nicklaus tapped his universal speakstone, still linked to every piece of quartzite on the battlefield, and shouted, "Look out! Earth and Air are angry. They want to hurt everyone."

All across the battlefield, earthen monsters turned toward the nearest soldiers and charged. Wind suddenly shrieked past, raking at soldiers and whipping dirt into the air. High above, the huge Battalions twisted under an unexpected onslaught as gale-force winds pushed them east.

Aifric muttered, "You've got to be kidding me."

The two monsters near Nicklaus lumbered toward them, enormous, rock-like fists rising.

That was more like it. Most adults knew better than to try forcing him to do bad things, and now he was back in the real world with access to all his mechanicals. He'd show them.

As Aifric moved to intercept the monster to his left, Nicklaus activated his hand thrusters. They wouldn't provide a lot of thrust for a big man like Hamish, but for Nicklaus, they worked pretty well. He shot into the air, aiming straight at the right-side monster. It swept huge hands to swat him out of the sky, but he activated blind coal. He still had a little left. It would be enough.

He shot through the grasping hands and dropped an activated piece of soapstone right down the monster's open mouth before activating directional thrusters to dodge out of the way.

Water exploded out of a reservoir barrel in a nearby shop and poured down the creature's throat. It turned after him, but so much water cascaded into it that it quickly turned to mud and disintegrated. Nicklaus landed and kicked the melting head, stomping it into the muddy pile. That was a lot of fun.

"Don't do bad things," he shouted at the melted creature.

Nearby, Aifric and her sisters had severed the limbs of the other earth monster and were drowning it like he had. It seemed that Earth hadn't escaped his prison nearly as much as he had claimed he had and didn't seem capable of regenerating them. The liar.

Many of the soldiers around the battlefield weren't so lucky, though. Nicklaus saw a lot of brave soldiers getting stomped or swatted away. The Spitters and Sentries couldn't stop all the monsters. Up in the sky, the Battalions' thrusters roared, fighting the winds, and all their weapons began to fire again. Hopefully they were targeting the monsters.

Then a blur of orange and silver shot over the central waterfall on the western edge of Lossit Valley. It arced down into the lower valley floor and shot through the embattled soldiers, somehow missing men and women, but exploding right through ten of the earthen giants. The blur crossed the valley, turned to shoot along the highway, then slowed nearby and skidded to a halt in front of Nicklaus.

"Uncle Kilian! Can you show me how to run like that?" he cried, delighted by the idea.

"Maybe later," Kilian said, dropping to his knees beside Nicklaus and lowering Verena to the ground. She looked badly hurt, and Aifric immediately joined them to tend to her. Nicklaus hated seeing

Verena hurt, and he felt even angrier at whoever did that than he did at the elementals.

Uncle Kilian grabbed his shoulder and said, "I thought the elementals were pushing you through a gateway."

He usually looked happy, even when other people looked worried, but at the moment he looked concerned. Nicklaus didn't want Uncle Kilian to worry, so he shrugged and said, "They tried, but they were liars, so I didn't go."

Kilian laughed and hauled him into a fierce embrace. Nicklaus laughed with him and said, "Can we go kill earth monsters together? Earth is angry and so he's trying to kill everyone. Air is throwing a tantrum. I thought they were old, but they sure aren't acting it."

Uncle Kilian heaved a sigh of relief. "Leave the monsters to me. We're not safe yet. Despite the wind, I think you should head up to Battalion One with Jean. Can you get up there?"

"I think so." He had extra pieces of quartzite he could use as makeshift boost thrusters until he got some more boots. He bet Hamish had extra pairs. Jean would know where to find them.

"Good. Now make sure to listen this time and get right up there," Kilian said, his tone and his fire-filled gaze making it clear he would not tolerate detours. Nicklaus figured he should probably listen, for once.

His speakstone spoke in Lady Jean's voice. "Nicklaus! I need Kilian!"

"What's going on?" Kilian asked, leaning closer. Lady Jean sounded scared, and that made Nicklaus scared too.

"Aonghus has Hamish. He's killing him. I'm coming, but can you help?"

Uncle Kilian scowled, with points of fire glinting in his eyes. "What's that boy thinking fighting Aonghus?"

He rose and turned, scanning the area. "There!"

Nicklaus lifted ten feet into the air using secondary thrusters and spotted Aonghus, the very bad man. He was shouting at two of the earth monsters that were lumbering toward him. Hamish was stuck in some earth next to Aonghus, his face bloody. The sight enraged Nicklaus and he leaned forward, calling upon all of his thrusters. He hated not having boot thrusters because he accelerated so slowly. He would shoot Aonghus for hurting Hamish.

Uncle Kilian jumped up and grabbed him right out of the air. "Oh, no young man. Not you. Stay here with Aifric until I get back."

Aifric joined them and took Nicklaus' hand before he could rush off. She looked worried and asked, "Are the elements really turning against us?"

"It's complicated. We need to deal with them until Connor destroys the gateway they're trying to use."

"What gateway?"

"My mother," he said grimly.

Aifric paled, and Kilian leaned in and gave her a quick kiss on the lips. "Don't worry so much. We'll figure it out."

Then he rushed off, with flames trailing behind him. They seemed a little brighter than before, and he ran super-fast again, flashing past Aonghus before the very bad man even felt him coming. Kilian knocked him flying before again running right through the earth monster that had been advancing on him.

Hamish shouted, "Don't kill him! He's mine."

It was good for Hamish to be so brave, but maybe he should be a little more careful. Nicklaus looked up and giggled. Aifric was staring after Kilian, mouth agape, one hand raised to her face, cheeks bright. It didn't look like she had expected that kiss.

"You're Uncle Kilian's girlfriend!" he laughed.

"I certainly hope so," she breathed, and Nicklaus heard the faint sound of a whole lot of ladies cheering.

Then the ground all around Hamish and Aonghus disintegrated under an intense barrage from the Battalions. High explosive and penetrator rounds detonated with thunderous reports, shredding the ground and covering everything in billowing clouds of smoke and dirt and debris. Fire and shrapnel and clouds of pumice billowed out, consuming everything.

Chapter Fifty-Eight
An Elemental Conspiracy

Connor remained alone on the broken plateau, with the mad queen rising slowly into the air nearby. He felt confident Kilian could keep Verena safe, and although he would have loved Kilian's dauntless support dealing with his mother, at least he wouldn't be responsible for getting Kilian killed like he had Evander.

"I am not completely dead yet," Evander's voice reached him from the corner of his mind where the giant now resided.

"Good. Please share any ideas you get on how to deal with your grandmother," Connor replied as he shot into the air toward the queen.

She'd risen slowly higher, arms thrown wide, head back, black-eyed stare vacant, mouth open in a silent scream. Although he'd severed the chert connection to her mind, she was screaming inside her head so loud he couldn't entirely shut her out, and her mad shrieking echoed all around like faint whispers from desperate ghosts.

He didn't want to feel sorry for her, but it was hard not to. Yes, she was an insane, cruel murderess, but her overwhelming terror rattled him right through his mental shields. Emotion pouring off of her like heat from an out-of-control heatstone oven, wrapping him in mindless terror that threatened to undermine his own courage. She understood the trap she'd fallen into, had feared that very fate for centuries, and was fighting it with all her power. She wasn't going to win.

Her terror did not change the fact that he had to kill her to stop her suffering, end her reign of terror, and stop the elementals from rising to wreak untold destruction across the world.

Connor pushed aside his worries and focused on his target. The queen seemed oblivious to her surroundings, entirely trapped within her own mind in the battle to slow the elementals from destroying her. He should be able to finally hurt her.

So he wove water and fire, earth and air together into an elemental blade fifty feet long. As he shot past, he slashed it across her torso, hoping to sever her limbs like Daulah's whip-sword had done.

His sword deflected aside bare inches from her skin, and he muttered a curse. She wasn't making things very easy for him. Or, more likely, the elementals were protecting their vehicle to freedom.

Connor switched tactics, slowing to a hover twenty feet from the queen, about seventy feet in the air, and wrapped her in all of the elements. He added serpentinite to the mix, using the sound of Verena's laughter to reinforce the mix, then he spun up the mixed elements, forming a whirlwind around the queen, pressing it inward with all his strength.

The whirlwind scraped around her, but even with serpentinite, he couldn't quite gain purchase. Attacking her with elements was simply not going to work. Connor floated closer, releasing the elements so he could press his hands against the queen's invisible shielding. It formed an unbroken seal around her, about three inches thick, totally impervious to his touch or his elemental affinities. It was the most comprehensive shield he'd ever encountered.

That was super annoying.

Water appeared in the air beside Connor, and she looked mad. "We will not allow you to destroy our vessel, Connor."

"You're not free yet," Connor protested. "You can't stop me."

"We have crossed enough of the bridge to manifest our will upon this land in small degree. You can never breach our shield using our own powers against us," she replied confidently.

It was nice to get confirmation that he was reading the situation correctly. Connor switched to his primaries. First the familiar itch of granite, then the boundless energy of basalt, followed by mind-accelerating obsidian. He didn't have much diorite left, but dared tap some of it, embracing the lightning-like rush that blazed through his veins. Pumice came next, like an insulating cloud. He added some blind coal, for good measure.

"I don't need your help to finish this," he told Water.

Then he max-tapped his primaries, and raised a fist to curse-punched the queen with every bit of strength he could muster.

Air chose that second to interfere with his connection to her, and he dropped just as he punched, so he missed the queen's chest and instead punched her in the hips. With pumice and blind coal activated, his fist burst through the elemental shielding and smashed into the queen with a mixed granite and diorite explosion.

The impact threw her tumbling through the air in a spray of blood and bone. Her legs fell free, leaving her lower torso a mangled mess. Connor fell almost all the way to the ground before he re-established connection with air and slowed his fall.

Air appeared beside him, her expression as dark as a storm cloud, and shouted, "Stop!"

She looked angry, and winds whistled around him, but Connor managed to remain stationary in the air.

Evander's voice came to him again. *"One hand may wield a sword, but the other may carry a shield."*

"No offense, but I can't really deal with Sentry speak right now," Connor said as he focused on rising through the howling wind. One more good punch, and he could shatter the queen's head. Since she didn't want to heal, maybe that would actually kill her.

Air was screaming at him in a language that sounded more like a winter's gale than real words, and the winds tore at him, trying to slow him down, but he still managed to push through it. The queen rose faster above him, probably more of Air's handiwork.

"The elementals seek to break free of all constraints of the natural world, but they are not yet free," Evander explained, his voice calm and thoughtful. *"They have pushed into the realm of the green frequency of entropy to accomplish this goal, and yet the bulk of their power still resides in the red frequency, controlled by the natural world."*

That sounded important, but Air's shrieking was making it hard to even hear himself think, let alone focus on Evander's deep thoughts. She had shed all pretense at human decorum and was displaying the raw, dangerous side of herself. "What does that mean?"

"It means they cannot completely block you from tapping their powers, particularly in the red frequency."

"Oh." That made so much sense, he probably should have thought of it. "Thanks!"

Knowing that fact didn't make it easier to fly through Air's tempest. The air buffeted him on all sides, even though he was still tapping pumice. He didn't have much blind coal left, so resisted the urge to tap it again. He would need it for the next punch. When he focused on limiting his connection to air to the red frequency, his connection did stabilize. He started to gain on the queen, but her torso had stopped bleeding. She had said she wanted to die, but why heal herself?

A moment later, he realized healing wasn't what was happening.

She was changing.

Her body swelled, and crackling energy began gathering around her. Through his connection with fire and water, Connor sensed a sharp concentration of charges, and his heart sank. The elementals were gaining the advantage, and they were forcing her to raise an elfonnel.

With strum.

They were winning the race, but they hadn't won yet.

Connor tapped serpentinite and stilling together, siphoning the power of sound through stilling to magnify it to super-sound. He'd never tried that before, but hoped it worked like other affinities linked through stilling back on themselves. The power of serpentinite built within him at an astonishing rate, and he exulted. He opened his mouth to shout, planning on blasting the queen's bloated body with sounds so concentrated they'd rip her apart.

Except Earth chose that moment to clobber him in the face with mouthful of packed sand.

The blow took him totally by surprise. He hadn't seen the earth rising from the ground, hadn't seen Earth appear next to Air, hadn't felt the attack through his earth senses. The blow sent him tumbling away, his super-enhanced death shout tearing harmlessly at the air.

He managed to catch himself with another current of air, but all four elemental beings appeared in front of him, forming a hostile line to block his access to the queen. He marveled at the change in them. They'd worked such subtle deception for so long, and had begun the process of deceiving him even before his third ascension.

They had manifested into his mind, hinting at human traits like flirting and compassion. Water had even assisted in pulling him through the final threshold. They had choreographed the deception brilliantly, teaching him just enough to win his trust and position him so they could destroy him. When he'd learned enough to understand the danger, they had tried pleading, then cajoling, then tempting him with benefits, and finally threatening.

Now they had shifted to outright hostility. Not what he needed right now. He needed to destroy the queen before she completed the transition to elfonnel form, but killing her was already nearly impossible. How could one fight the elementals? They weren't even human, weren't even alive like he was.

Water scowled at him, and Fire said, "We warned you of consequences, human."

Connor drew deeper from all of his affinities. He was Blood of the Tallan, so he would fight them.

His connection with slate faded away.

Tallan-cursed luck! The queen had destroyed the ancient slate sculpted stone and severed access to the red-frequency power of earth. He tried switching to green, and for a second felt the strength of earth flow into him again.

Then it shut off, as if someone had turned off a faucet.

Earth grinned and said, "I could not prevent you parasitic humans from sucking on my power when that stone filtered the sylfaen into your precious red frequency power, but that filter is gone. Now that we have begun to cross the final bridge to freedom, I control access through the green, and I choose to not share it."

"Nor do I," Fire added with a harsh laugh, and just like that, Connor's green-frequency access to fire winked out.

Panicking didn't usually help, but Connor was tempted to give it a try anyway. How could he fight them when he couldn't access elemental powers? Fire and earth were two of the most powerful battle elements, and now they were gone.

For a second he feared Water and Air would block the green frequency levels of their powers too, shackling him further, but the women only glared. Maybe they couldn't block access when their convergence points weren't broken yet. He hoped that was true, because he needed those powers.

"Let me pass. This is not the way," he told them, rising toward them. They looked more solid than ever, but he hoped they couldn't take physical form yet. Once they reached that point, he doubted he could stop them. "I promise to help you figure out a solution to—"

"Enough talking!" Fire shouted. "Now is a time for action. Behold our vessel!"

The queen's body had expanded beyond the point it should have simply exploded. Terror was still boiling off of her, and a though struck him across the mind. *"No! I deny you crossing."*

Water chuckled. "You no longer have the power to deny us."

She faded from view, as did Fire, and the charges of strum gathering around the queen intensified sharply. Her body ripped apart, flesh burning away under a firestorm of crackling, blue-white energy that consumed the space where she'd hung. That living energy sparked and twisted over itself like ten thousand deadly snakes of lightning.

Earth held out a hand to Air and said, "Let us rise to the east and consume the armies of men."

"It will be my great pleasure," she said with a graceful curtsy, and the two of them disappeared.

The situation was spiraling totally out of control. The storm clouds were roiling overhead, the air cold, and his affinities felt weak. The elementals had just left him, as if he no longer posed a threat. It seemed both Water and Fire were combining to rise through the queen as a lightning elfonnel, and he feared what Earth and Air were planning with Nicklaus.

Think! The strum charges were still building at an ever-increasing pace within the still-expanding lightning being. He sensed if it chose to, it could unleash lightning bolts big enough to fry an entire city.

The air felt heavy the way it often did before a severe storm. It was growing colder, and the clouds above were boiling and spinning in ever-increasing spirals. The broken ground of their fight filled the air with a faint smell of charred earth, and a constant low crackling from the lightning skittering around the queen's transforming form raised the hairs on his arms. Every sense screamed of danger and he had to fight a growing urge to simply turn and run.

He couldn't outrun this disaster, though.

Connor focused his quartzite senses to the east and cast words to all of his friends. "The queen is getting consumed by the elements. I'm not sure how to stop her, but I'm working on it. Beware, Earth and Air are coming your way, and they're not friendly."

"Connor, be careful!" Jean replied immediately.

"We've already got elemental problems," Kilian said, and behind him, Connor could hear the sounds of fighting and screaming.

"And we just lost access to slate," Aifric added in Ennlin's voice, sounding panicked.

"Do what you can," Connor urged them, hating that he couldn't offer anything more concrete, but he was so scared, he couldn't think of anything more.

The queen-lightning monster had risen higher, a brilliant being of light and deadly strum charges. Wind howled across the plateau, spitting rain into Connor's face and plastering his hair to his head. He barely felt it, staring at awe at the queen's new shape. From the waist up she took on a humanoid form, retaining her same features, only they were now made up of those crawling ropes of living lightning. From the waist down, where she'd lost her legs, her form was indistinct, a whirlwind of crackling energy and glowing light.

She slowly rotated to stare down at Connor with huge eyes glowing pure white. She spoke, and her voice was a mixture of both Fire and Water. "This vessel is a fitting vehicle for our wrath. We will be free at last!"

The queen's thought hit him at the same time. *"Why haven't you killed me yet, useless boy?"*

"I'm working on it," he promised, amazed that any part of her still remained intact.

"I can't hold them back much longer. My final bridge is burning, my mind frayed, my affinities gone. I want to punish you for your stupidity, but cannot allow myself to agree with these monsters even in that righteous desire, or be lost. Get on it!"

Amazingly, she sounded almost more stable than ever. Maybe she'd allowed the elementals to strip away her madness first. The fact that she was still fighting helped settle his thoughts and focus on the problem. If she wasn't gone, then the elements weren't free yet. There had to be a way to stop them.

He embraced Water as deeply as he could, and was shocked to discover he could feel the strum charges building around the creature still, as well as fields of magnis radiating off of it. He lacked fire, so how could he access the combined might of both water and fire?

"The elements have united within their chosen vessel," Evander suggested from his library in Connor's mind. *"It appears that union has inadvertently extended through your thrice-ascended affinities to you."*

"I'll take it," Connor replied, happy that Evander was there to share his insights. The man was so wise, Connor didn't mind having an armchair commentator along for the desperate fight.

He embraced strum and magnis. They were the only powers he might be able to use to fight the monster. If he still had access to slate, he might try burying it under the plateau, since earth seemed good at dissipating strum.

"Here goes something," he muttered, grasping the unruly current of air holding him aloft and willing himself higher.

The queen elfonnel roared, the sound like a thousand thunderclaps, and the air seemed to shatter, as if every current fainted or fled. Connor clutched at his head from the overwhelming sound and instinctively tapped serpentinite to deflect some of it away.

Four thick bolts of lightning erupted out of queen-lightning's mouth and ripped across the distance to Connor. Immersed in both strum and magnis, he felt the charges growing, the air transforming into plasma. He instinctively pushed the conduit of plasma away, splitting it to either side. The lightning flashed down that conduit, filling his world with incandescent energy that momentarily blinded him, and the crashing thunder that would have busted his ears if not for serpentinite that he used to deflect it.

Bolts tore past to either side of him in that odd zigzagging movement of lightning, and struck the ground far behind him. Enormous currents of energy would have vaporized him if not for the magnis he wrapped around himself. Connor was so stunned by the strike that he didn't even think to try grasping any of the strum to cast it back at the elfonnel before it all dissipated through the earth. He tapped limestone and covered his eyes with shadow to protect them from getting blinded by any future bolts.

He was in trouble. He couldn't fight them with strum. The entire queen elfonnel was bursting with concentrated charges. She'd overwhelm him in a heartbeat, but his success at deflecting the lightning gave him one small hope. He did not sense her actively manipulating the fields of magnis around herself.

The elementals were consuming her, but she still resisted, still set at least some bounds on them. Connor took a chance, heavily shielded his mind, then reached out toward her with chert.

He immediately wished he hadn't.

Queen Dreokt was locked within the monster in a dark chamber, filled with fear and pain and hopeless fury. She clung to the last vestiges of her humanity with all her strength, but the effort tortured her almost beyond Connor's comprehension. He gasped from the glimpse into her plight, not wanting to draw any closer. He wasn't sure he could have fought against such torture.

"Are you here to gloat?" she asked through her fog of pain and exhaustion.

"No. I'm trying to help. Keep them focused on strum instead of magnis."

"Magnis is useless," she shot back, then screamed so loud into his mind he winced and pulled back. Her momentary lucidity was gone, replaced by a rabid anger. She was lashing out at the elementals, but didn't recognize him as an ally and struck out at him too.

Connor recoiled from her and cut the connection. He wasn't sure he accomplished anything, but at least he'd confirmed she didn't see magnis as a viable battle strategy. Hopefully that blind spot would limit the elementals' ability too.

He focused on the power of magnis and directed it inward on himself to reinforce his defenses, but the great queen lightning elfonnel swooped down toward him. He'd suffered all sorts of different huggers in the past, but wasn't sure he could survive getting hugged by that beast.

He threw himself toward the ground, drawing as much speed from air as he could. If he could reach the ground, he could super frack and maybe keep ahead of her. Kilian had dodged lightning. Maybe he could find that level of speed.

He wasn't fast enough.

The monster might not move as fast as a lightning bolt, but it moved a lot faster than he did. It transformed the air in front of it into plasma, allowing it to plunge through with no resistance. It closed with terrifying speed, the face twisted with fury. The expression might be from the elementals, but it might be reflecting her anger at them for consuming her like she had consumed the minds of so many others. Or maybe she was taking the risk to agree with them enough to scowl at him. Whatever the reason, staring a giant, angry lightning elfonnel in the face was not a happy moment.

Trying not to give in to his paralyzing fear, Connor braced for the monster's impact. He focused magnis into his body, concentrating the defensive shield as strong as he could, and his body reacted to it in surprising ways. He sensed the molecules that made him alive shift along with that magnis field, pointing their tiny charges all in the same direction, transforming himself into a living lodestone, a highly concentrated magnis field.

It felt weird, as if his entire body was suddenly packed with pedra's spittle foam. He felt insulated from everything, including his own senses.

He didn't have time to wonder about it because the terrifying queen elfonnel caught up to him and opened her enormous mouth wide enough to swallow a horse. Connor couldn't escape as that lightning-filled maw closed over him and wrapped him in a deadly cloud of living lightning.

His world turned incandescent as hundreds of lightning bolts rippled around him. The searing light would have permanently destroyed his sight if not for the limestone already applied to his eyes. Connor instinctively held his breath and rolled into a fetal position, his entire will bent on reinforcing his magnis shield.

Lightning reached out to touch him with absolute obliteration from every side, but it all deflected away, pulled out of course by his concentrated magnis field. Instead of shattering him into component bits, it instead rippled around him. Crackling, deadly lightning energy completely encircled him, but he huddled in a cocoon of calm.

The constant thunderclaps and menacing crackling sounds seemed distant as he pushed them away with serpentinite. The hairs all over his body stood on end from the enormous currents of strum flowing around him. He bet he couldn't build up such a mighty charge even if he super-fracked over every carpet in the world. When he finally forced himself to take a breath, the air smelled thin and tasted charred.

Consumed by the queen lightning elfonnel, he scarce believed so much strum couldn't quite penetrate to destroy him. He seized that tiny bit of hope and held on for dear life.

"Good. The distraction of your execution occupies their focus. Maybe I *can fight them back across the bridge,"* Queen Dreokt's thought filtered through the lightning storm to his mind. *"Try not to die too soon. Maybe your death can serve a purpose after all."*

Connor scowled. That was simply rude. He celebrated the fact that she was still there, still fighting, and actually hopeful of potential victory, but if he managed to die only for her to find a way to escape the lightning elfonnel and survive, he'd never forgive himself. He needed to escape, to defeat the monster with her in it.

Strum was still growing in intensity, and despite his best efforts Connor was starting to fear that it would soon overwhelmed his magnis field. When it did, he felt convinced the resulting lightning blasts would obliterate him. With the power of fleshcrafting waning, he doubted he could recover, but even if he did, the monster could just shred him apart again and again until fleshcrafting ran out.

That was depressing, and it promised to be a uniquely unpleasant way to die. Definitely not the direction he needed the fight to go. The lightning elfonnel was not a normal foe with a heart or brain to destroy. He needed to figure out how to ground it or disperse it, but without earth, how could he do that? How could he begin to fight back in a meaningful way?

He didn't know, and that indecision cost him precious seconds. The strum charge grew to a critical point, and despite his best efforts to strengthen the magnis around himself, it was insufficient. He was about to die.

So Connor tapped blind coal and dropped down through his own protective shield just as the charge became too great. The magnis field imploded behind him, shredded by a thousand lightning bolts that filled the space with pure, destructive energy. The entire empty space transformed into plasma, and the resulting thunderclaps shook the lightning elfonnel.

With serpentinite, Connor seized the explosive sound, and with quartzite, he seized the concussive blast and concentrated it all directly behind him, using it as a booster to shoot himself right out through the queen elfonnel. She howled, hundreds of lightning bolts erupting out in every direction.

They didn't spear through the air after Connor, but twisted together into one gigantic lightning bolt that shot away to the east.

"No," Connor breathed, snatching after the lightning, but it moved too fast to stop or even deflect. He felt it cross the distance to Lossit valley in a blink, sensed it impact miles away and strike one of the Battalions.

The gigantic flying battle fortress disintegrated.

Connor shouted in horror as he fell, stunned by the brutal destruction. How many people had been on that Battalion? They were all dead.

Because he failed.

His panic faded beneath a rising tide of resolute anger. The elementals had lied and manipulated everyone, and were bent on murdering everyone. He needed to find a way to fight.

Releasing so much lightning at once seemed to tax the monster momentarily, and it actually shrank in size, its incandescent glow dimming until it was no brighter than the sun at noonday. So it wasn't all-powerful in strum. That offered a little hope, but it began swelling again immediately, and he sensed the charge growing again.

"Air will rip the rest of those who dare the skies out of her domain soon enough, but your suffering begins now," the queen elfonnel said, her voice rolling like thunder. *"Witness true power!"*

A second round of lightning bolts shot from the creature, wove together, and blasted east toward Lossit valley. This time Connor was ready, and he swatted at the lightning, trying to stop it. The queen lightning elfonnel was just too strong, and she overwhelmed his strum defenses. He managed to deflect it toward the ground, but sensed it strike among the armies.

How many people just died? He shouted in frustration.

The queen lightning elfonnel chuckled, again recharging. *"Your beloved just arrived on another of those flying ships. We feel her there. She will be the next to die."*

CHAPTER FIFTY-NINE
When One Monster Is Not Enough

Ivor stood back to back with the twenty remaining Spitters of his strike teams, breathing hard. Enneleyn, his second, stood to his right, her left arm hanging useless. She'd taken an ice ball to the shoulder just before Nicklaus launched his Time Out. That boy had probably saved her life. One of the other Spitters was working to heal her during the lull, but it looked like the lull was ending.

How it ended was still up in the air.

Sixty Spitters, led by Rosslyn herself, surrounded them beyond a ten-foot thick wall of water that hung in the air between the groups, entirely encircling Ivor's embattled team. The water was only a dozen paces away, fifteen feet tall. It was dark with mud and blood, and threatened to kill them all.

With Rosslyn leading her team, the fight had turned decisively against Ivor's team. Most of their sculpted stones were spent, and Rosslyn's forces had raised the water and pressed it ever inward, threatening to drown Ivor's entire strike force. That was the most insulting way to kill a Spitter, and Ivor hated Rosslyn for threatening his people with it, but he hadn't been able to stop it.

Now Time Out seemed over, but three huge earthen monsters were bearing down on Rosslyn's companies. One was shaped like an enormous serpent that reminded Ivor of Harley's mini elfonnel that she'd used to kill Lukas and so many others during the battle of Merkland. Another was humanoid, carrying a thirty-foot club of stone, while the final monster was shaped like a giant nuall hunting cat.

Other monsters had risen all across the battlefield, threatening the might of both armies. Spitters fought earth with water, while companies of Boulders charged in with reckless bravery to beat on others. Aonghus and Hamish were both lost somewhere in that latest Battalion barrage, and Ivor had no idea if they were still alive or not.

Rosslyn had no choice but to order most of her Spitters to defend against the monsters, and they had to use a lot of the water from that prison wall around Ivor's teams. While they struck at the monsters with water, trying to sever limbs or turn them into mud, Rosslyn and two dozen of her Spitters paused in their assault.

"Surrender, and I promise to treat your people kindly," Rosslyn shouted to him.

It might be a tempting offer, but if the queen won the day, Ivor would prefer dying in battle. If Connor somehow defeated her, he was absolutely confident they'd eventually win the battle. Surrender might save at least some of his Spitters, but he hadn't come all that way to give up.

"How about you and I duel one-on-one. Winner takes all," he shouted back.

"Ivor, you can't be serious," Enneleyn whispered. She was pale from shock, but still determined. "She'll kill you."

"Might buy us some time. I felt Kilian return. Didn't you?"

"Kilian?" She clearly hadn't, but his arrival changed everything. Ivor wasn't sure why Kilian hadn't come to succor them yet, but he would. Ivor trusted Kilian completely.

Rosslyn laughed, projecting confidence, but she was trying too hard. Ivor knew people, and he read her nervousness as clear as daylight. She must have felt Kilian return too, and she knew what that meant. Maybe she'd suggested he surrender in order to win some hostages to bargain with Kilian. She shouted, "Last chance!"

For who, though?

The air suddenly shook with an ear-splitting shout. Ivor cringed along with everyone else, clutching his ears as the sound blasted past. It was like a death shriek of the world's biggest elfonnel, and the sound filled him with dread. He glanced west, past the embattled valley and the gorgeous waterfalls, toward where Connor was battling the queen. The shout had come from that direction. He dared hope it was the queen's death cry. It was intense enough, it could be.

The ground shook, and it wasn't from the monsters getting shredded by Rosslyn's Spitters fifty yards away. The entire valley trembled, and the ground began to roll like open ocean under gentle swells.

"This can't be good," Enneleyn whispered.

"Stand ready," he called, but he hated not knowing what they should stand ready against. His people had fought with inspiring bravery. It was a miracle any of them still lived, but the last thing they needed was another new threat.

The ground just west of the highway, near the ruins of Lossit, erupted as if someone had detonated a Last Word bomb beneath it. Dirt geysered hundreds of feet into the air, and the ground shook harder than ever. Debris rained down all the way to them, smelling of fresh-tilled soil, but it also carried a scent of smoke and ash.

All the debris was sucked out of the air like a sheet yanked off a line, revealing a huge elfonnel standing in the epicenter of the explosion. It was a monstrous thing, bigger than any Ivor had seen. It stretched at least two hundred feet long, and rose over fifty feet into the air. Shaped like a tortoise, but with a dozen heavy limbs, each capped with three-clawed toes, and with four serpentine necks, extending out different sides of its armored shell like monstrous hands on the world's biggest compass. The heads on the ends of those necks were blocky things, each with four black eyes and enormous jaws filled with row after row of stalactite teeth.

"Tallan preserve us," Enneleyn whispered.

"Someone needs to, because we're grouted," Ivor muttered, borrowing one of Connor's terms.

Stunned silence settled over the battlefield as everyone gaped at the towering monster that lifted all four of its ghastly heads and trumpeted, sounding like avalanches of stone. The sound grew, and the air seemed to take up the cry. Wind howled in from the west, rising to hurricane strength, screaming as if Aifric had captured every death cry that day, magnified them a thousand fold, and poured them into the winds.

High above, the great Battalions spun ponderously in the unexpected tempest, the enormous flying platforms looking like logs floating on a turbulent river. Ivor feared they might not be able to withstand such a storm. The clusters of fast-flying aircraft that had been swooping down toward the battlefield were swept aside like leaves in a breeze, and Ivor lost sight of them as he blinked away debris and dirt tearing across his face.

When he looked up again, his heart sank. Winds were coalescing together, becoming visible and wrapping around themselves to form a huge creature. It looked vaguely like a great bird of prey, its beak long enough to gobble up an entire Thunder Tower.

"What by Tallan's twisted memory is that?" one Spitter cried.

"I think we have the privilege of witnessing a double elfonnel event," Ivor said. Maybe their brilliant attack strategy wasn't so brilliant after all. What was going on with Connor and the fight against the queen? It looked like she had prepared servants to raise elfonnel, which was one eventuality they had hoped to not have to deal with.

They had Last Word bombs on the Battalions, but no one had expected an airbound. He wasn't sure how to deal with those, nor if they could even find a way to fly through the storm well enough to deliver a bomb.

His mind raced as he calculated ways to respond to the threat, but if those elfonnel were loyal to the queen, the battle had just turned decidedly against his people. They had to issue orders to retreat, had to initiate defensive plans and delaying tactics, had to—

A bolt of lightning a thick as a house appeared from the west and struck one of the westernmost Battalions. The flash was so bright, Ivor cried out and clapped his hands over his eyes. The thunderclap was so loud, it was like a physical blow across his head, and Ivor staggered, feeling real fear for the first time all day.

When he blinked his eyes open, the Battalion struck by the lightning was simply gone. A blizzard of debris was already getting swept around by the shrieking wind. For a moment, Ivor could only stare, blinking stupidly up at the spot where that enormous Battalion had been hovering a moment before. The entire world seemed strangely quiet, and he recognized the side-effects of sound trauma, but lacked the emotional energy to care. All he could think about were the hundreds of people killed by that blast.

General Rosslyn raised her hand high and cheered. As if from a great distance, Ivor heard her shouting, "The queen fights for us!"

Ivor's heart sank. He was a realist, and despite his confidence in his abilities and those of their core team, they could not stand against the queen. She'd raised two elfonnel and now rained lightning destruction across the skies. Had she killed Connor? Would any of them survive long enough to even try retreating?

A second blast of lightning flashed in from the west, but instead of striking down another Battalion, it raked across a hundred yards of the valley, ripping through one of the earth monsters and scores of soldiers from both armies that had been swarming it. Again thunder nearly clubbed him to the ground, and he clutched at his eyes, blinking wildly to remove the searing-bright after-image from that lightning blast. It was terrifying, and none of them had any defense against such a weapon.

The queen had targeted her own people.

Ivor frowned. That didn't make sense. Why would she do that? Had she lost all sanity and now planned to murder everyone? That was even more terrifying.

On the far side of the barrier wall of water, Rosslyn looked shocked too, and her confidence faded.

"She missed?" Enneleyn asked, looking dumbfounded. "Can she do that?"

"I wouldn't put anything past her," Ivor said, trying to organize his thoughts again. They had to *move*.

Kilian appeared as if out of nowhere, moving many times faster than the fastest fracked Strider. He flashed past Rosslyn and her surprised Spitters, burst through their wall of water in a spectacular explosion of foam, and skidded to a halt in front of Ivor. His left eye was frosted with ice, while flickers of crimson fire danced in his right. Ivor squashed a pang of jealousy. He missed walking with fire so much.

"I'm glad you're here," Ivor said.

"I'm not glad any of us are here," Kilian said with a scowl. He looked honestly frightened, and that scared Ivor more than ever.

"Did Connor fail?" Ivor asked. He hated to think his friend might be dead, or worse, mind-wiped, but he could not make good decisions based on partial information.

"Not yet, but the situation is bad," Kilian said. He glanced over his shoulder at Rosslyn and said, "Don't interrupt, girl."

Turning back to Ivor, he shook his head slowly. "Kids have no sense of patience."

Then he cried out and clutched at his head, swaying as if struck. Ivor caught him before he fell, and he gasped to feel Kilian's entire body shuddering. Had Rosslyn struck him down? Was that possible?

Enneleyn shouted, "Prepare!" and ever Spitter reached for water, ready to resume their fight to the death, but Rosslyn looked as surprised as Ivor. It wasn't her doing.

Kilian clutched Ivor's shoulder and gasped, "It's gone again, but this time I fear it's gone for good."

"What's gone?" Ivor asked.

"Fire." Kilian straightened, and his right eye was now clear, his expression grim. "I just lost access to fire."

"How? I thought you still could reach it through the higher frequency?"

"Not any more."

Aifric's voice cried out through Kilian's speakestone. "Kilian! Earth is gone! Ennlin's affinity is gone!"

Other cries of dismay echoed across the battlefield, and Ivor spotted Sentries and Sappers falling from collapsing towers. "Is this Nicklaus' doing?"

"No. My mother destroyed slate. The entire affinity is gone," Kilian said grimly.

"Well, that's bad timing," Ivor said, fighting to keep his voice calm as he glanced at the distant earthbound elfonnel that was turning all of its heads toward them.

Kilian straightened his shoulders, his expression turning determined again. "We don't have time to focus on what we no longer have. We need to concentrate on what we can still fight with."

"We're not going to lose water too, are we?" Enneleyn asked, sounding terrified, and the words were like ice down Ivor's veins. He'd managed the loss of fire by focusing on water, but the thought of losing all connection to the elements threatened to break him.

"I don't think so," Kilian said. He strode toward Rosslyn and her company, who instantly tensed and started to back away.

"You can't actually run away from me, and I don't have the patience to chase you down," Kilian snapped. "Stay there. We need to talk, and I'm tired of shouting."

Rosslyn held up a hand and her company stopped, but they looked appropriately terrified as the dread Kilian marched up to them. As strong as Rosslyn was, Kilian could kill them all if he chose to, and they all knew it.

"You may slay us, but our queen is fighting for us and she will avenge us," Rosslyn said bravely.

Kilian snorted. "My mother is lost to the elements. It is they who are attacking us, not her, and if we don't stop them fast, those elfonnel you see will never slumber, and they represent but a tiny fraction of the destruction we will all face."

Rosslyn paled, and glanced back at the earthbound monster that was lumbering toward them, moving with deceptive speed. High above, the airbound was swooping up toward the struggling Battalions. Ivor was glad he wasn't stuck up there. If he had to join a desperate last stand for humanity, he preferred to do it surrounded by water, not empty air.

"You lie," Rosslyn whispered.

"I never lie, and I don't have time for a debate. We either join forces to defend all mankind from the rise of the elements, or you die now and we're a bit short-handed." He spoke with absolute calm, which seemed to rattle Rosslyn and her people more than anything.

"Look out!" Enneleyn shouted, pointing up.

Ivor looked up and gaped as an actual tornado cyclone extended down from the airbound elfonnel directly toward them.

"Shield!" Kilian shouted, and Ivor and every Spitter in his command reacted instantly with reflexes honed by months of intense training. They all reached for the river together and heaved, their intertwined wills working together rather than against each other. They'd practiced the move a thousand times, but Ivor never expected to use it against a tornado.

The waters of the river burst the banks and shot across to them, wrapping them in a protective barrier just as the tornado touched down.

Howling winds sounded like rocks tumbling down a flooding ravine as they tore into the shield and ripped streams of water free, sucking it into the vortex. Ivor dug deep, embracing water as deep as he could, pulling more and more from the river to reinforce their shield. Kilian's will melded with his own, ten times stronger, forming the bulwark upon which they built their shield. Enneleyn and the other Spitters wove their wills in to either flank, and all poured in more water, holding the shield with all their strength.

For a moment they held, the shield dome extending above them shaking and rattling under the barrage of wind. They had extended the shield over Rosslyn and her Spitters too, and after a second of stunned surprise, Rosslyn shouted, "Join the shield!"

Her forces tried to help, but although they fought better as teams than most other Spitters Ivor had ever faced, they lacked the intensive training of his team. That's why he and his twenty had survived so long. Still, their assistance helped ease the load, and he started to relax. Airbound elfonnel weren't so tough.

A second tornado speared at them from the west, moving like no natural tornado could. That side of their shield was weakest, and the tornado ripped it right off, sucking the water away with a horrible slurping sound. Two Spitters were also yanked off their feet and sucked away, screaming, disappearing into the black wind funnel.

Rosslyn shouted a defiant war cry and rushed to the breach, plugging it with a fresh wave of water in a magnificent display of ascended Petralist power. Ivor never could have moved so much water so fast, through the linked interference of so many other Spitters.

It was almost enough.

The second tornado pressed in harder and intensified, battering the water shield, while Rosslyn stood alone against it, her forces stumbling back from the onslaught. Then the tornado burst through, air hardening like black fingers that seized her and yanked her away.

A delicate, silvery tentacle of water shot from their shield, striking like a cobra, and wrapped around Rosslyn's left ankle. Ivor felt Kilian's will controlling the water, and stared in wonder. Kilian stood beside him, outwardly calm, but his eyes were filled with deep, blue ice, and his will was like a raging inferno in Ivor's water senses.

"I will not let you have her," Kilian said simply, tethering Rosslyn, who was screaming, her hair flailing, her clothing whipping around her as winds tore at her and tried to drag her into the sky to her death.

Even if Kilian managed to drag her back down, she'd get ripped apart if she hung in that vortex much longer. Ivor risked easing his hold on the shield, trusting to his teams to fill in the gap. He reached farther out into the river and yanked as much water as he could grab. A horizontal waterfall shot across the short distance to them, and he poured it all right up that funnel, temporarily choking it with the heavy load.

Kilian yanked hard, and the tornado's grip on Rosslyn snapped. He had pulled a little too hard, and Rosslyn tumbled away, splashing down into the river, the safest place for any Spitter.

"Good work, General," Kilian said to him.

"Thank you. I'm impressed you took the risk to save her," he admitted.

"She's a brave woman and a good general who cares about her people. I'll give her a chance to make a better choice before I let her die."

The tornado battering their water shield abruptly faded away. Through the shimmering water, the airbound elfonnel had turned toward one Battalion that had powered through the winds, rising directly above the monster, thrusters roaring so loud they had to be max-tapping every single one. Those engines could produce a lot of push force, but they had to be using copious amounts of pumice and blind coal to make such headway.

Every gun turret was oriented on the monster, blasting it with every type of round, raking it with explosions, but to little effect. It was an impressive sight, but Ivor feared it would prove little more than a defiant gesture. They should have spent all that energy and precious blind coal fleeing or trying to land.

Another tornado vortex rose above the monster, reaching for the Battalion, and Ivor didn't doubt it would tear the great craft right out of the sky. He turned his mini hub to the general officer's channel and shouted above the tumult of voices, "Look out! Airbound closing in!"

Captain Leppin replied calmly, "Last Word bomb away."

The bombardment stopped, and a single small speck shot toward the monster, driven so fast it must be driven by a powerful thruster. It cut through the winds so well, it must also have a piece of activated blind coal aboard. The bomb plunged into the funnel cloud, and two seconds later it detonated deep within the elfonnel.

The explosion of fire and destruction inside the heart of the monster was spectacular. Its winds glowed crimson and orange before the pressure wave ripped out through dozens of gaps, pouring flames and smoke in every direction. The elfonnel shook from top to bottom, and the winds howling across the valley stilled for a moment.

Many voices rose in a great cheer, and Ivor dared hope that mighty bomb had done the trick.

The flames dissipated, and the monster reformed, looking unchanged from what it had before. The cheering faded, and Ivor's hope wilted. He looked to Kilian, who shrugged and said, "Wouldn't make a story you'll love to tell your grandkids if it was that easy."

Kilian then turned to the rest of the Spitters and said, "I know you didn't sign up for elfonnel hunting training, but here we are. So what'll it be, kids? Will you help us save half a million lives, or do you really want to fight me?"

"And if we survive?" one tall Spitter from Rosslyn's team asked nervously.

Kilian grinned. "If we survive, I think we'll all be finished with fighting for a while, don't you?"

The man nodded immediately. "Yes, of course. No more fighting. Sounds good to me."

It sounded good to Ivor and everyone else too. Ivor was glad most of them seemed to have flexible minds, because the battle had twisted way beyond even his wildest fears. He asked Kilian, "So what do we do?"

Kilian pointed toward the earthbound monster that was bearing down on them. Other soldiers were wisely scattering out of its path, but it didn't turn aside. It had a target, and they were it. "We kill that thing. Water is effective against earth. And pray Connor wins."

Shona rushed up to them on fracked legs. She looked dirty and battered, but Ivor grinned to see her intact. Half a dozen Striders skidded to a halt behind her, looking panicked but still disciplined. "Kilian, did you see that airbound? It took a Last Word to the face!"

"We'll deal with them," Kilian assured her, "but too many people are in the way. Get in touch with Wolfram. Between the two of you, I need every non-Petralist to retreat. North or south, I don't care. Just get them away from the fight."

She nodded and shot away. Ivor silently wished her luck, then turned toward the towering earthbound smashing through the ruins of Lossit on its beeline path toward them. "We'll follow your lead, Kilian."

He grinned, looking more excited by the challenge than terrified by it, and raised his voice. "Listen up, kids! We do this together. There are enough of us to bring it down. Either turn it into mud or drown it in the river. We'll deal with the airbound after."

"How exactly are we going to do that?" Ivor asked as the teams formed up, some still looking uneasy by the abrupt alliance with enemies who had been trying to kill them only moments ago.

Kilian shrugged, his eyes twinkling with bits of glittering ice. "I have no idea. It's the first airbound I've ever heard of."

Chapter Sixty

The Finer Points of Getting Electrocuted

They were threatening Verena.

Bad idea.

Connor's fear evaporated under a fresh tidal wave of anger. By targeting Verena and other helpless friends, the elementals proved that although they might not be human, they knew far too well how to act like the vilest of cowards.

Too many people had already died. He would not allow the queen lightning elfonnel to keep killing. At the outer edges of his affinity senses, he felt Air rising as an elfonnel, and although he lacked access to slate to quest for Earth, he had no doubt Earth was rising too. They were moments away from complete freedom.

They weren't free yet.

The queen lightning elfonnel swelled, growing incandescent again in preparation for launching another lightning barrage to kill Verena and how many others? Connor couldn't match it for raw strum power, but maybe he didn't have to.

He concentrated on the distant valley. It was so far, it strained his abilities, but he refused to accept that all he could do was witness Verena and his other friends die. Luckily the air was already wild with tumultuous energy from the previous lightning strikes and from the recently-risen elfonnel, so he had plenty of material to work with. Connor focused all his effort on forming a shield of magnis and extending it across the valley. It was a huge construct, and he never could have accomplished it so fast trying to move heavy earth or water, but he was working with small charges, and they were already motivated by so much chaos. They responded to his will in the blink of an eye.

More lightning shot from the monster, gathered into another giant bolt, and shot away to wreak destruction. It crossed the distance in a blink, but ricocheted off his magnis shield. Connor yanked against the lightning, trying to diffuse the strum contained within it, and it split apart into scores of smaller lightning bolts that boiled across the curving edge of his magnis shield before streaking away in every direction.

"Finally you manage to do something right," Queen Dreokt's mind-voice reached him faintly.

It was annoying that the more he succeeded in distracting the lightning elfonnel, the more he helped her fight against Water and Fire and potentially escape.

The queen lightning elfonnel glared down at him. Above it, the clouds roiled and seemed on the verge of plunging down from the sky to cover the land in endless night. Connor needed to keep it focused on him, not on his vulnerable friends, so he switched to strum and raked his senses across the air surrounding the monster.

That air was filled with concentrated charges, and he managed to seize a lot of them. He wasn't interested in fighting the monster for control of that energy, so he cast it all up into the clouds, driving it into a single, concentrated point of negative energy.

As he hoped, the difference in charges was too great for even that elfonnel to ignore. Lightning as thick around as a palace ripped free of the monster and tore up through the sky from it, striking the clouds and scattering among them. Thunder boomed so loud it violently shook him, even though he'd blocked all sounds from his ears.

The queen elfonnel shrank by a third as energy drained out of it. The vast strum charge dispersed through the clouds, but did not disappear. There was simply too much energy up there, flowing to common points and coalescing. Soon it would concentrate into another point where lightning would naturally strike.

He expected the queen lightning elfonnel to swoop down and try gobbling him up again, but instead it laughed, a terrible booming roar, and shot away to the east, heading for Lossit valley.

"Oh, no you don't!" Connor shouted, throwing himself after it as fast as the air currents could drag him. He wasn't fast enough, and the queen elfonnel pulled ahead. He felt Dreokt's thoughts touch his again for a second, but heard no coherent words, only shrieking, as if she was in terrible agony.

"Hold on," he urged her. He needed to try something different.

So he again turned to his primaries, starting with porphyry. He'd saved the last precious palm-full of porphyry for that fight, and he needed it now. The sharp-edged powder chewed into his skin and flowed up his arm, and Porphyry awoke in his heart. He suddenly felt strong and embraced the rush of eagerness for battle that swept through him from the deadly stone.

The comforting itch of granite rolled through him next, multiplying his strength, while the coursing energy of basalt was like a refreshing breeze through his limbs. Verena's voice sounded in his mind, reassuring him that he would succeed as he tapped obsidian. It also accelerated his thoughts, and he got a crazy new idea.

Connor added the bubbly feel of pumice to the mix, then max-tapped limestone and called upon stilling. He linked every single primary affinity stone to stilling, and supercharged. Them. All.

Connor's body shook under the onslaught of supercharged strength, speed, and thought. Super pumice seemed to accelerate the process, building the others tenfold faster. Supercharged porphyry rocked Connor, as if he'd swallowed his own mini-lightning elfonnel, and he gasped from the rush. Porphyry howled approval, the sound echoing through his mind and driving him on.

Connor threw aside all restraint.

And transformed into a rampager.

This time the transformation did not fill him with horrific pain like it had in the past. He wasn't sure if that was because of his ascension or because fleshcrafting allowed him to deny himself pain. He shouted with that sense of exultant horror that always swept through him as he lost himself and took on a new form. This time he did not lose his sense of control.

As a rampager, Connor was the greatest hunter.

But even as a rampager, he could not destroy the elfonnel.

Connor needed to become something more.

As his limbs transformed and grew, bulging impossibly huge with deadly strength, his hands shifting into claws and his jaws elongating into the massive maw of a rampager, Connor tapped fleshcrafting.

He could already feel its power beginning to wane, but enough remained for one last effort, an attempt to create something that could fight the queen lightning elfonnel. Connor drew every bit of fleshcrafting available to him and poured it into his still-transforming shape, combining it with supercharged porphyry.

His transformation accelerated a hundredfold. His limbs seemed to erupt outward, and his chest ballooned, as if he'd swallowed an entire oxen. He screamed, the sound a roaring like all of the Lossit falls combined, and his vision turned red. His body burned with agony, but also with a sense of growing exultation, and for a moment the transformation overwhelmed his ability to comprehend what he'd done to himself.

Three seconds later he rose to stand on solid air a hundred feet above the plateau as the world's first super rampager.

And it was awesome!

A normal rampager was terrifying at eight to ten feet tall. Connor had grown ten times that size. With stilling looping his other affinities into super-enhanced status, super granite strength reinforced his rampager might until his form contained so much raw power that he somehow knew he could crush Mount Ingram to dust if it still existed. He could draw upon super speed, and through obsidian, super reflexes and thinking. For the finishing touch he ignited his teeth like miniature suns with limestone, then wrapped them in dense magnis fields to make them impervious to the lightning.

In his mind Porphyry howled. *"Now we hunt!"*

"You better believe it," Connor growled. His fear was gone, replaced by bloodlust so vast, he eagerly fastened his eyes on the one being that dared challenge his dominance.

The queen elfonnel had slowed and rotated in the air to consider his transformation. It actually hesitated at the sight of his transformed being, and the queen's mindvoice cheered. *"Excellent! Destroy yourself in the most epic manner you can, and I might be able to escape. I warned you, child. Porphyry would be the death of you."*

She had no idea. Connor grinned. "Here we go."

He raced through the air that to him felt as solid as a mountainside, closing on his hated enemy. The rampager was the mightiest hunter in the world. With its help, Connor had defeated elfonnel, had beaten his uncle to lead the pack, and had learned to master his own elemental powers that had refused to cooperate after his second ascension.

Now he was a super rampager, and he would destroy the super elfonnel.

The queen elfonnel recovered quickly from its surprise and swept back to meet him, lightning bolts ripping the air between them. Connor restored his magnis shield, far stronger than it had been in his puny human form, and the lightning bolts deflected away. Roaring with battle lust, he plunged into the heart of the lightning elfonnel, tearing at it with claws that could rip palaces apart. Wrapped in magnis, those claws severed ropy strands of pure strum that formed the elfonnel's body like permanent bolts of lightning.

The severed lightning shot away, blasting gaping, black holes in the ground or plunging up into the roiling clouds. The lightning elfonnel swelled with more strum as it sucked in every charge it could get. It clubbed at him with a hundred burning hands, trying to rend his giant body to bits.

His magnis shield deflected the hands, and he bit and tore, raking with claws in a frenzy of bloodlust. He ripped bits of the elfonnel away, triggering a lightning storm of bolts that shot in every direction, blackening earth, shattering distant trees, tearing into clouds, and rending the air with thunderclaps.

The elfonnel flowed around him, wrapping him in tentacle-like arms of incandescent light that hurled him downward with enough force to shatter mountain. He tried catching himself, slowed dramatically, but still struck the barren ground like a meteor. His huge body blasted a new canyon into the earth, spraying dirt a thousand feet into the air.

Connor-rampager hurled himself back into the air to meet his foe, who was plunging down toward him, leading with a spear of pure lightning fifty feet across. Connor swatted it aside, and the lightning spear blasted a trench in the ground a hundred feet deep and a quarter mile across.

Connor could still feel his remaining tertiary affinities, so he grabbed every bit of water he could reach and pulled it all in. He sucked the water right out of the distant lakes and waterfalls of Lossit away. Tons of water cascaded in and he hurled it all at the queen lightning elfonnel. Earth might be the best insulator, but since he couldn't access earth, water would have to do.

The queen lightning elfonnel sensed the danger and shot upward, trying to escape the torrent. Connor threw all the water at it, and a horizontal waterfall half a mile across smashed into the elfonnel, dwarfing its massive size and smashing it out of the air. Lightning erupted through the water, flickering bursts that lit up the clear waters like thousands of really angry lightning bugs.

Connor tried wresting the monster to the ground, hoping to bury it in the canyon he'd just created with his face a moment ago, but as the water thundered into the ground, the monster condensed into a single, thick beam of lightning and burst up through the torrent. It rose a thousand feet into the air before reforming, smaller and dimmer than before, but not permanently damaged.

Connor gave chase, galloping up through the air faster than a fracked Strider. The monster rotated to face him half a second too late, and he lunged for the throat. Caught up in rampager bloodlust, Connor clamped his mighty jaws down hard, planning to rip the monster's head right off.

Unfortunately, he'd forgotten that the queen elfonnel wasn't limited to its humanoid form. As he lunged in for the kill great jaws gaping open, its throat exploded outward, blasting dozens of lightning bolts right down his open mouth.

His teeth might have been coated in magnis, his hide protected by his magnis shield, but he hadn't thought to wrap it around his innards.

He really should have thought that one through.

Lightning ripped through him, boiling and blackening him from the inside. His thoughts scattered, and for a second he lost his magnis shield. Worse, his jaw contracted convulsively, and he could not pry his own jaws apart as the strum onslaught overwhelmed his muscle control.

The queen lightning elfonnel laughed, a thunder chuckle that made Harley's seem pitiful in comparison, and poured more strum through the open conduit Connor had so considerately established for it. A flood of deadly strum thundered through him, and it felt like he hit himself in the face with a thousand of his father's Ashlar hammers, every one opened wide by a Builder.

Connor couldn't even scream. His body shuddered under the onslaught, as lightning filled him to bursting. If he'd made that terrible mistake in human form he'd already be dead, but as a giant rampager he was far more resilient, so he could keep hurting himself a lot longer.

Queen Dreokt's thought reached him dimly through the haze of pain. *"It's a wonder that you've survived so long. You're not nearly as smart as you pretend."*

Connor mentally shouted back, *"Shut up and break their hold on you already!"*

Water surprised him by speaking to his mind. *"You disappoint me, child. I thought we taught you better, and now you will die before witnessing the destruction of all your loved ones."*

"Oh, well," Fire added, not sounding disappointed at all.

Connor lacked the energy to respond as he struggled to deflect the lightning away, tapping strum and pushing it from his mind and his core organs. He couldn't push it away entirely though, and light-ning ripped through his limbs, blackening them and threatening to burst them asunder. Porphyry raged in his mind, deeply offended by the idea of such a handicap.

Jean had proven that one could live with handicaps with grace, without losing their ability to function. That gave Connor a slender hope, but it seemed laughable when he realized he sensed no more fleshcrafting available. If he died now or was severely injured, or even maimed, there would be no recovering.

The thought of dying scared him, but the thought of ending up helpless, broken, and weak terrified him more. Would the ele-mentals just torture him to the brink of death, then leave him alive to witness them murder Verena? How could he survive that? What would his family think when they learned that he'd let Hamish and Jean die?

The thought galvanized him and he pushed through the pain, again seizing soapstone. He lacked the focus to call upon the flood he'd just dumped out over the land, filling that canyon he'd made. He didn't need that much, though. Connor yanked on the clouds boiling low overhead. They were saturated with rain, and he easily pulled sheets of water down over the lightning elfonnel and himself. Lightning crackled and spat as charges dispersed through the water, temporarily deflecting some of the strum the monster was using to torture him.

Even better, the monster cringed, clearly fearing another heavy dousing. If only Connor could do that, but the momentary dis-traction helped. He drew a thin blanket of water around himself, then used the trick Water herself had taught him to strip away all of the impurities. That thin layer of pure water insulation finally broke their contact and severed the deadly current of strum.

That first free breath of charred-smelling air reinvigorated him. Rampagers possessed mighty natural resilience, and he still had access to Sucker Punch, although he'd transferred most of that to Verena. Now he drew some of it back, and the flood of healing helped soften the edge of his pain. His limbs stopped trembling, and he again felt ready to fight.

"You will not escape us again," the queen elfonnel promised, their Dreokt-like face scowling at him as its torso split into a dozen arms of incandescent strum that wrapped around him again.

His magnis shield helped hold them at bay, and he drew more water out of the clouds, wrapping both himself and the elfonnel in the insulating blanket. Then he drew more water up from the lake he'd just created. He would force the monster down and disperse its strum down through the water, and from there into the earth. As soon as the insulating water from the ground connected to him, he max-tapped strum and pushed against the creature with all his might, while altering his magnis field to deflect strum downward.

The plan seemed to work, and strum boiled down the watery column to the ground, where it began dissipating. If he could hold on long enough, could he weaken it enough to again try tearing it apart with his claws?

"*You surprise me, boy,*" Queen Dreokt laughed, sounding brittle and insane, her words trailing into a nerve-shuddering cackle.

"*Can you drive them off?*" he responded, but the only answer was more maniacal laughter. He didn't dare try touching her mind closely for fear of getting swept away by her insanity, but he sensed she was weakening. The drain was too much, the elementals had pushed into her too far. She was losing the fight and would soon surrender. They would be free to step fully into the world.

Tallan boil their eyes! He was weakening them. He only needed a little more time, but he wasn't going to get it.

Fire and Water clearly sensed it too. The queen elfonnel swelled with greater strength than ever and threw him violently away. He exploded out through the insulating cocoon of water, and the queen elfonnel shot upward, erupting through his water barrier and ascending far higher, heading for the black, roiling storm clouds. They had continued growing, feeding on the elemental fury unleashed across the land. The queen elfonnel in turn fed on all that energy bouncing around in those clouds, looking stronger than ever.

Connor muttered a frustrated curse. His chest heaved as he panted, feeling exhausted and annoyed. He'd better figure it a new plan quickly because Queen Dreokt was losing the fight. The queen elfonnel's features shifted, resembling Dreokt more and more as she became one with the elements. Time was up, and the monster threw its ethereal arms out wide. Connor could feel it drawing more and more energy from the storm. Somehow that also intensified the storm in a reinforcing loop that Connor sensed would build until Water and Fire completed their journey and stepped free into the world.

To kill everyone.

"No fair," he breathed, wracking his brain for new ideas. He was still in the mighty rampager form, but that wasn't enough. Even with obsidian-enhanced thoughts racing, he came up with nothing.

"*The tiny flame is sufficient to heat a cup of water, but even the raging inferno cannot set the seas to boiling,*" Evander said.

"What?" Connor had forgotten about Evander.

"*Your valiant courage is insufficient to defeat this monster,*" Evander explained.

"*Thanks. Your confidence is really inspiring,*" Connor snapped sarcastically, then immediately regretted the words. He was struggling against an impossible foe, but Evander was mostly dead and was stuck in another's mind. The giant was definitely having the worse day.

"*Allow me to finish. You cannot defeat it without more power,*" Evander said, ignoring the jab.

He was right, of course, but Connor didn't feel better. "*I can't get more power. I can't access slate or marble. Fire and Water are stronger than I am, and in elfonnel form, I can't defeat their strum.*"

"*There is other power in the world besides affinities, yes?*" Evander asked.

Connor considered that. The queen elfonnel had risen with strum, a higher form of power of the natural world. In using magnis, he was countering it somewhat, but even with magnis he lacked sufficient might to defeat the monster.

Could he raise a magnis elfonnel?

No way. Even if he could, by surrendering to Water and Fire, he'd be giving them another conduit to escape the bonds of the natural laws. It would never work.

There was only one other higher level power that he had touched that might hold a solution.

Fission.

Chapter Sixty-One
Sometimes a Guy Just Needs a
Good Woman Armed to the Teeth

Hamish groaned and staggered to his feet. He felt thoroughly beaten. Not only had Aonghus pummeled his face, but he still barely believed he'd survived that barrage from the Battalions. How many of them had fired? He had seen their power, had celebrated it as the greatest weapon besides ascended Petralists, and had slipped through one barrage over Lossit. The barrage that had rained down over Aonghus had been far worse, and Hamish had a front-row seat.

He should have been obliterated, but a dense, spinning sphere of water had surrounded him, deflecting wave after wave of fire and shrapnel away from him. It had to be Kilian. He doubted anyone else could have withstood such a barrage. The ground had shaken like the world was coming to an end, and the reek of fire and ash had seeped through the barrier.

It had been truly inspiring. Hamish had to figure out how to make a mechanical shield that tough.

Unfortunately, now as he looked around at the torn earth, cratered and blackened for a hundred feet in every direction, the slim hope he'd clung to of maybe recovering at least some of the components of his battle suit died. It was gone. He was barely dressed, wearing only his small clothes and undershirt, everything else ripped away by Aonghus' earth.

A groan behind him spun him around. General Aonghus was pulling himself out of a pile of dirt. He looked filthy, bedraggled, his red hair wild. Hamish was impressed he'd survived the bombardment too, but he hadn't had a good time of it.

And he'd lost earth.

No way he'd stumble to his feet covered in dirt if his slate affinity was still active. Hamish glanced around farther, and only then did he take in the rest of the battlefield. He gaped.

"I get distracted for just a minute, and somebody raises two elfonnel?" he muttered, staring at the enormous earthbound monster smashing through the ruins of Lossit on its way toward Kilian and a knot of Spitters. High in the air above, an actual airbound elfonnel was rising toward a couple of the Battalions, while smaller attack craft swarmed it, uselessly firing missiles and mechanicals. Other Battalions were shifting position to either move away from the airbound, or toward the earthbound. Hamish expected another major bombardment soon. He hoped it worked.

The rest of the valley was awash with soldiers scrambling away from the earthbound monster, while Boulders ran toward it, led by General Rory and Anika. Bash fighting an elfonnel was usually stupid, even for Rory, but maybe they had a plan.

Hamish didn't have time to worry about it. Aonghus spotted him and stalked toward him. He might look battered, but still appeared in fighting shape, and unlike Hamish, he still carried a sword and dagger on his belt. He glared with murder in his eyes and shouted, "How did you snuff out my slate?"

"Wasn't me," Hamish said, circling warily away from Aonghus. He cast his Builder senses out over the battlefield to see if Nicklaus was doing something dangerous again, but sensed no major active mechanicals other than Thunder Towers and other battle mechanicals. Even Time Out hadn't blocked Aonghus from earth, which meant maybe the affinity was entirely gone. That had to be the work of Connor and Evander. That didn't bode well. They had planned to hold that option in reserve as a last resort.

It didn't matter, and wouldn't affect the next moments for Hamish. He dearly wanted to kill his hated enemy, but was unarmed. He tapped obsidian, which helped a little, but he still needed a weapon.

"It's gone!" Aonghus screamed, spittle flying from his lips. He looked unhinged and drew his sword with a nasty rasping of steel. "I lost fire, but will not tolerate losing another affinity!"

"You always were a coward," Hamish stated coldly.

Aonghus raised the sword and rushed Hamish, tapping basalt and crossing the distance in a rush.

Hamish dove aside with obsidian-fueled reflexes and shouted, "Thanks for proving my point! You're such a coward you'll strike down an unarmed man!"

Aonghus skidded to a halt, panting heavily, even though with basalt there was no way he could be tired after that short run. No, he just looked crazed, eyes wild as he cackled with laughter. Then his laughter snapped off and his voice turned as cold as steel. "So you want me to run you through, eh?"

"Something like that," Hamish said, ready to dodge again.

"I can respect death by steel. I'll grant you that one boon, boy. Maybe that will help your crippled girlfriend deal with your loss."

Hamish wanted to lunge at Aonghus, but getting himself impaled would not help. So he spread his hands and said, "So you plan to murder me unarmed after all, do you?"

Aonghus grinned and Hamish could imagine the fire boiling in his eyes. Even though he lacked marble, he still acted like a Firetongue. Hamish expected Aonghus to charge again, but instead he drew his dagger and tossed it to Hamish. "Fine. Here's steel for your hand."

Hamish caught the dagger with a flicker of new hope. It was barely a third of the length of Aonghus' sword, but it was something.

Aonghus raised his blade and stated simply, "Now you die, Builder."

General Aonghus crossed the distance in a flash, tapping basalt and slashing at Hamish's stomach. With obsidian-enhanced reflexes, Hamish slipped aside and parried with the shorter dagger. The blades rang together, the echo lost in the tumult of shouting, screaming, roaring monsters, and shrieking wind that kept the entire battlefield a tumult of sound and chaos. It the midst of elemental death battles and elfonnel insanity, the two of them fought through the broken, ripped-up landscape.

Aonghus pressed the attack, moving with superhuman speed, slashing in an ever-increasing tempo, pressing Hamish steadily back. Hamish fought for his life, deflecting strike after slashing strike, drawing upon all of his training and grueling practice over the past months. Hamish was an accomplished swordsman, but Aonghus was faster, more experienced, and wielded a much better weapon. If not for obsidian, Hamish would have died within seconds.

With it, Hamish had a chance. He embraced battle fury as obsidian infused his muscles and accelerated his mind. As always, it also triggered subtle flavors of his favorite desserts, like tantalizing scents from his mother's kitchen. Enhanced by obsidian, Hamish transformed from a competent swordsman to a master. It seemed a simple thing to read Aonghus' intent by the position of his feet, the turn of his shoulder and wrist. The ringing of steel sounded again as they met in a flurry of strokes, but Hamish stopped retreating and instead advanced through the blizzard of slashes, determined to penetrate Aonghus' defenses, to draw close enough to plunge his own dagger into the hated man's eye.

"You're full of surprises Builder," Aonghus laughed as he increased the tempo. He was a master of basalt and knew how to apply it to his entire body. His speed increased, his sword blurring as he redoubled the attack.

"With the right food, you can accomplish anything," Hamish responded as they fought across the broken ground. Aonghus didn't need to know he was a Blade, and the comment might goad the man into making a mistake.

Hamish couldn't move as fast, but he could read his opponent's intention, anticipate the forms he would use, and how he would transition from each strike to the next. He matched Aonghus' increased tempo, moving his blade only enough to block or deflect the faster strikes of his opponent as the two of them wove and spun around each other.

Time seemed to slow, the greater battlefield to dissolve as Hamish's world contracted until only he and Aonghus existed. His senses grew sharper, his awareness of his body and every particle of it deepening. He knew without question where he was, how he was moving, and exactly how to adjust to meet Aonghus' next slash or to press his advantage. Hamish had never immersed into obsidian so far, and it was marvelous.

Aonghus was also tapping deep, arms and legs moving so fast, only Hamish's enhanced reflexes allowed him to meet each blow. He pushed himself to the limits of even his obsidian-enhanced skills, and Aonghus matched him step for step. The panting of their breathing sounded loud, punctuated by the sharp staccato of their blades. The air seemed warm, and their skin shone with sweat. Any second now, one of them would make a single mistake and die.

Then a fist-sized globe of water struck Aonghus in the face. The blow caught him by surprise and knocked him onto his backside. He rolled with the fall and returned to feet, sword at the ready, face livid with rage.

Aifric approached, making a tisking, chiding sound. "You know better than to engage in a duel of honor with an opponent at a distinct disadvantage," she told Aonghus. "Shame on you for not finding Hamish a sword."

"I'll kill you next, Mhortair!" Aonghus hissed.

"I doubt it," she said with a sniff, and Hamish realized Student Eighteen was in charge at the moment. She nodded to the west and added, "Finish this business, Hamish. We're low on time."

He glanced west and noticed dark storm clouds building along the horizon. That was fast. They hadn't been there moments ago. She glanced at him critically and pursed her lips in a disapproving frown. "I worry about you sometimes, Hamish. I understand your need to avenge Jean, but really? Stripping out of your battle suit in the middle of a fight is not honorable. It's stupid."

"Blame Aonghus, not me."

She scowled at Aonghus, who was watching her angrily, but warily. "Whatever the queen did to your head was no little thing," she said in a disgusted tone.

"She made me great!" he shouted.

"Great enough to waste time humiliating people before you fight them? Doesn't sound great to me," she said, then handed her own blade to Hamish. It was a finely balanced weapon. She saluted him and said, "Finish this. I've got to deal with Verena and Nicklaus. We need you in the sky so stop wasting time."

"It'll only take a moment," he promised.

She trotted off, and Hamish dropped the dagger Aonghus had loaned him, then turned back to face his enemy. One of them was about to die, and he would not relent until he made sure it was Aonghus.

"You should have let that freak help, boy," Aonghus said as the two of them began circling, swords ready.

"That's one of those things cowards don't understand. I don't need help for this."

Aonghus snarled and lunged. Hamish was already tapping obsidian again and he met the new blow with Aifric's sword. It was a great weapon, so much better than the little knife. The two of them launched into a fast duel, blades flashing like quicksilver as they spun and turned, struck and parried, moving faster and faster.

Hamish found himself grinning as the tempo again accelerated and they both poured in every bit of skill they could muster. The duel would not end again until one of them struck a killing blow. For his part, Aonghus' expression turned into a snarl of frustrated fury as Hamish met every stroke and returned just as fast. He might be an excellent swordsman, but he hadn't actually needed to use that skill much in a long time. He usually relied upon his tertiary power to save him.

Not today. Hamish pushed harder and harder, driving his enemy back, looking for that one opening to end it.

A moment later he found it.

As he pressed Aonghus to the edge of one of the shallow craters from the recent bombardment. The soft edge collapsed, twisting Aonghus off balance, and he caught one sword stroke badly. In that compromised position, he couldn't dodge Hamish's follow-up strike quickly enough. In a fast reversal, Hamish scored a cut along Aonghus' forearm. Not a deadly blow, but a sign that the end was coming.

Aonghus shot away, gaining some distance to set himself again. As Hamish closed, he taunted, "How do you hide from your precious Jean how much her hideous scars torture you?"

In reply, Hamish lunged, twisted his blade around Aonghus' counter, and scored a hit across Aonghus' armored stomach. His sword shrieked against armor, an eager sort of sound.

Aonghus leaped back, breaking away for a second, and Hamish read in his eyes that he recognized the truth. He would lose today.

So Hamish was surprised when Aonghus grinned, a sly look on his face. Not good. Hamish rushed in before Aonghus could try another underhanded trick, but the light around them suddenly twisted in a mind-bending distortion. Aonghus appeared to shimmer in front of Hamish and slide to the left.

Hamish lunged after him, driving his sword through his enemy before he could disappear. Hamish had seen Connor bend light to conceal himself, and they had developed invisibility cloaking for their flying vehicles too, so he understood what Aonghus was doing.

His sword drove home, but he felt nothing.

Tallan kick him in the backside. He was such a fool. Too late, Hamish realized Aonghus wasn't trying for invisibility, but had created a mirage. He spun, blade up, and managed to catch a sword swinging for his head. At the brutal contact, the sword became visible.

So did Aonghus' boot that drove into the pit of his stomach.

Hamish doubled over, dropping to the ground, as pain seared his midsection. His eyes watered and he felt weak and lightheaded for a second.

A second was far too long.

Aonghus laughed as he rushed in for the kill, but a tiny drone mechanical shot past Hamish's head and struck Aonghus in the chest, knocking him tumbling back with an angry cry, and deflecting the blade just wide of Hamish's shoulder. With a rush of blasting quartzite thrusters, an armored form shot past, pivoting in midair and catching Aonghus under the chin with an armored boot. The blow tumbled him back again, knocking him to the ground, momentarily senseless.

Hamish blinked in astonishment, wondering if he was already dead, or if Aonghus' mirage had gotten totally out of control.

No. As the armored figure hovered and spun back toward him, thrusters purring just enough to keep them aloft, Hamish recognized one of his spare battle suits. And when the person inside of it raised their visor, he laughed.

Jean.

She hovered closer and dropped to the ground beside him, humming a constantly changing tune until she landed. She had never looked so beautiful.

She hauled him to his feet, and he breathed deep the clean scent of her. He cupped her perfect face with one hand, and her smile ignited all of his hope. He laughed. "You made it work!"

She grinned. "Just in time. I've been working with Ilse and Aifric to calibrate the flight controls to obey voice commands like my arm did. I still have to use the keystone for weapons systems, but I didn't have time to launch anything."

Ilse would be proud to see her flying.

"I'm glad you got here when you did. He cheats."

Her smile faded and she glanced pointedly up and down his mostly nude figure. "When you told me to look away, I had no idea you were planning this."

He flushed, even though he knew she was teasing. It helped him ground himself for what he had to do.

Jean gestured into the sky. "I have someone bringing you another spare, but that airbound elfonnel is a nightmare."

"I don't need it for this." Hamish pulled some spare stones and a couple other items out of the extra pockets on her suit. Then he stepped around her and faced Aonghus, who was staggering back to his feet, his face bloody, his eyes wild.

When he spotted Jean standing beside Hamish, face completely healed, he gaped. "How?"

"You can't keep someone as amazing as Jean down with just a little fire," Hamish said.

"Then I'll try steel," Aonghus growled, lunging toward them again.

Hamish threw a diorite dart. The move caught Aonghus by surprise and he failed to dodge in time. The dart struck him in the shoulder with a satisfying explosion of blood that ripped his arm right off. His sword clanged onto the ground.

Aonghus staggered, staring down at his severed arm in disbelieving shock. It was weird how quickly the blood slowed from the stump, but Hamish wasn't about to give him time to bleed out or try to heal.

For the first time, real fear showed in Aonghus' eyes. He made a sweeping gesture with his other hand. Again the light began to bend, but Hamish was ready this time. He leaped through the mirage, slashing with his sword. Aonghus was already running, tapping basalt to escape.

Hamish shouted with rage. The coward! He'd never run him down, but started sprinting after Aonghus anyway. Shock and blood loss would hamper him soon, hopefully.

A missile streaked past him, caught the fleeing Aonghus, and exploded at his feet. He was so panicked, he hadn't been looking back, didn't even try to dodge. The explosion sent him tumbling to the ground with a cry of terror.

"Good shot!" Hamish shouted to Jean, then crossed the distance in a rush. Aonghus managed to stagger back to his feet, but his grave injuries slowed him down for several precious seconds.

Hamish reached him before he could run again. His blade slashed across Aonghus' right knee, and it buckled. Aonghus screamed, clutching at the wound with his one hand, but Hamish seized Aonghus' hair and kept him from falling.

Their eyes met, and Hamish said, "Now you've felt a small fraction of the pain you inflicted on Jean." He shook his hated enemy hard and shouted, "Do you want me to burn your face so you can feel the rest?"

He expected Aonghus to break, to cower with fear, but the general laughed, a wild, manic laughter as he clutched at Hamish's steadying arm. "Try it! I know how to handle the burn, boy! You'll think of me every time you look at your crippled woman."

"She's fully healed, and no one will remember your name."

He drove his sword through the rent in Aonghus' armor, below where his right shoulder had been. The blade plunged deep, and Aonghus gasped, eyes wide with pain as his entire body shuddered. Aonghus clutched at Hamish's arm, mouth moving silently, but Hamish didn't want to hear what the man had to say. He pushed Aonghus away, leaving the sword protruding from his side, feeling disgusted.

Then he realized that was foolish. He didn't dare leave any doubt that Aonghus was really defeated. So he yanked the sword out in a spray of crimson blood. Aonghus gasped, his body shaking, but unable to scream.

Hamish raised his sword one final time, and as he looked down on the bloody, defeated wreck of a man, he thought of Ilse and all the people who had died because of Aonghus. The queen had twisted him into a rabid monster, and there was only one thing to do with rabid things.

Hamish struck.

He turned away from the headless corpse and rushed to Jean, who was staring at the dead man, her face expressionless like when she studied badly injured patients. Then she deliberately turned her back on him and took a long, deep breath. When she met his gaze, her eyes were calm.

"Are you all right?" he asked, taking her hands in his. He really should have told her to look away again before he killed Aonghus.

She took another breath, then nodded. She touched his face with a gentle hand and said, "Now, let him go so he doesn't end up haunting us like he threatened to."

"He no longer holds any threat," Hamish said, and he was astonished to realize he meant it.

He'd hated Aonghus with such a fierce, hot rage that he'd barely remembered life without that thirst for vengeance, but now it was gone, dead with the hated man. He glanced back at Aonghus' remains, a pitiful, bloody corpse, and felt nothing but sorrow. One more victim to the queen's mind corruptions.

Jean was searching his gaze intently. She said softly, "Let's leave everything about him here and focus on building new memories."

Hamish loved that idea. He leaned in for a kiss.

Except that's when Nicklaus shot past, his missing boot thrusters replaced with one of Hamish's spare sets. They were far too large, but that just made him faster.

He laughed and waved and shouted, "Come on, Hamish! Let's go fight the big earth monster!"

Chapter Sixty-Two
All Seven Kinds of Idiots Can Still Have Good Ideas

Connor embraced every affinity and cast his senses up into the storm. Fueled by the queen elfonnel, it had grown to a vast tempest, churning over itself around the elfonnel. Enormous amounts of power boiled through it, and he drew from every aspect of it that he could grasp.

Even though the queen lightning elfonnel was absorbing more and more strum, it didn't control it all, and Connor siphoned huge quantities of both strum and magnis. He drained friction energy and heat, triggering a blizzard of ice that filled the air with bitter cold. Within moments, he accumulated so much energy that his entire enormous rampager form quivered and swelled.

His action drew the attention of the queen elfonnel, and it unleashed a barrage of lightning at him. Every second, Connor was understanding the relationship between strum and magnis better, and he not only deflected the lightning away, but seized much of its energy. He roared a challenge, his voice loud enough to shake the clouds, and Porphyry joined him, howling with bloodlust in his mind.

"*Hold, Connor,*" Evander suddenly interrupted the flood of euphoria Connor was riding. "*By my calculations, this may not be—*"

"It's now or never," Connor shouted, swept away by Porphyry's eagerness for battle. He would take the fight to the elementals and rip them apart! He galloped upward through the air, muzzle aimed at the queen lightning elfonnel. He compressed all that energy into the highest-level frequency possible, just as he had when he disintegrated Queen Dreokt's human body and when he had melted the mantle of the planet and triggered that blast of fission.

Connor released it all.

An invisible beam of energy shot from his open muzzle, crossing to the queen elfonnel in a blink. It glowed brighter than the sun to his enhanced eyes, even though it had passed far beyond the minuscule band of light visible to humans. The energy struck the elfonnel and blasted right through it.

Connor exulted as the elfonnel swelled, as if on the verge of exploding.

Except the elfonnel didn't explode. It glowed brighter than ever, its ropy lightning body crackling like rolling thunder, and its queen-like lips split into a grin. Laughter like an avalanche boomed through the air.

"Thank you!"

"I'm all seven kinds of idiot," Connor realized with a crushing sense of despair.

The queen lightning elfonnel was made of pure energy. He couldn't kill it with energy. All he'd done was make it stronger!

"Um, you were saying?" he said to Evander, wishing he'd taken a moment to listen.

Queen Dreokt's mindvoice screamed, so loud he couldn't block it out, and he shivered at the unbearable pain he sensed within the scream.

Abruptly it shifted to laughter, and she shouted, *"Yes! The glory is mine!"*

"I believe we are grouted, as you like to say," Evander responded.

Connor wished he'd spoken in Sentry speak. Then maybe he could pretend he didn't understand.

It felt like Queen Dreokt had lost the battle for her own mind. By giving the elementals so much more power, he'd just sealed his own fate.

"No," he growled, refusing to accept it. If he couldn't defeat the monster's physical form, maybe he could kill the queen's mind before they could burst free. He should have thought of that sooner.

Connor max-tapped chert and flung himself at the queen's broken mind. He hadn't wanted to draw closer to her insanity, but maybe a little insanity was all the hope he had left.

The link felt unstable. She was fading fast, but Connor threw his thoughts down that shaky link, planning to rip her apart from the inside. She couldn't fight him and the elementals at the same time.

The link flickered again, and instead of plunging into the middle of her insanity, Connor's vision blackened, then reformed. He was surprised to recognize the lab of her affinityscape. The polished steel cabinets were grimy and cankered with rust, every glass case shattered. The room was trembling as if during an earthquake, and it smelled vile, like someone was roasting a pot of Hamish's skunk extract.

Connor didn't see the queen, but when he turned to look across her islands and bridges, he spotted Water and Fire running toward the near side of the top layer of the queen's tertiary bridge. All of her tertiary islands had shifted side by side, anchoring a single, wide bridge to all of the elements. Water and Fire had almost reached the end, their expressions exultant. He sensed that once they set foot on her islands, there would be no stopping them.

So he dove for the queen's tertiary islands, using the flexible nature of the mental scape to simply fly across the distance. Bridges, islands, and the dark, boiling mists of the queen's abyss flashed beneath him as he crossed the distance in a blink.

Water spotted him and shouted, "No!"

She and Fire both lunged for the end of the bridge, casting out tendrils of their elements ahead of them. A thin rope of water slapped down onto the very edge of the island next to a single, crimson spark of flame. The entire bridge shuddered, and Queen Dreokt's voice screamed in terrible agony from every side.

Connor refused to accept defeat, but max-tapped granite and landed on the edge of the combined tertiary island like a thunder-clap. Leading with his curse-laden fist, he slammed it against the reinforced supports anchoring the elemental bridges to the island.

The anchors exploded, the end of the island vaporized under the brutal impact, and the bridge broke free. It fell away, carrying Fire and Water with it.

"Curse you, mortal!" Fire raged as he disappeared into the obscuring mists. His rage transformed the mists into white-hot flames, but he did not rise out of them.

Water met Connor's gaze as she fell out of sight, her expression so hurt, he wanted to slap himself. How could he still feel like he was somehow betraying her? They were the ones who wanted to use him, destroy the queen, snuff out Nicklaus' life, and lay waste to the planet.

Panting from the effort, Connor grinned and wiped his brow. He was standing in a mindscape, merely a mental projection, but he felt exhausted from the almost-end-of-the-world moment. He started to laugh, feeling so relieved he sagged to one knee.

Except that's when he noticed the thin rope of intertwined water and fire attached to the broken remains of the island's outer edge.

"Oh, no you don't," Connor growled, punching the end of the island again. More stone crumbled away, but the elemental connection didn't slip off. Somehow it remained attached.

"You cannot drive us out now, boy," Fire chuckled from somewhere down in the fiery mists. "We own her mind and we will break free, no matter what you do in this space. We will reach that island."

"Won't do you much good if you can't get anywhere else," he promised, rising and jumping across to the queen's limestone island. There he smashed the bridges apart, sending them tumbling into the mists.

That time, he felt something, an eruption of energy at the moment the bridge sundered, as if the affinity required an enormous pool of energy to maintain, and that energy was all released in the moment he broke the connection.

Even more interesting, the invisible blast of energy seemed to knock Water and Fire down deeper into the abyss. Fire shouted angrily, and Water exclaimed, "You've been keeping secrets from us?"

She seemed to believe he'd hurt them intentionally, her tone suggesting that fact worried her.

Evander appeared beside him on the softly glowing, green stone island. Connor blinked, for a second surprised by the unexpected appearance of the giant, but then he shrugged. Evander was already walking some pretty weird roads. They shared the same mind, so why not share the queen's affinityscape?

"I have never studied affinity connections like this, but access to this mental place sheds light on heretofore shadowed realms of theoretical thought."

Connor chuckled. "Even when you're speaking plain Obrioner, I can't understand you."

"You felt the release of energy when you sundered the bridge, yes?" Evander asked, gesturing at the broken anchor points with one huge hand.

Connor nodded. "It was like the bridge tied up a lot of the affinity's power."

"Exactly," Evander said, smiling as if Connor had made a remarkably brilliant point. Connor hoped he'd continue because he had no idea what point that might be. Luckily the big man said, "The power of fission proved ineffectual against a strumbound elfonnel due to the similarity of power structure of the monster compared to the weapon you wielded against it."

"Yeah, I wish I'd listened to you. It was less effective than stabbing a metal building with a sword. I only managed to push the queen over the brink," Connor admitted, feeling sheepish.

"And yet, you identified another point of energy that may prove vital in accomplishing our ultimate goal." Evander gestured again at the bridge. "I sensed with the release of this energy an increased distance between the elementals and this place."

"I felt it too," Connor agreed, tapping obsidian again, hoping to figure out how to utilize the surprising information.

"It is possible the sundering of bridges offers the kind of fission we require to split the elementals from my grandmother's mind."

Connor seized upon the thin shred of hope and grinned. "Creative destruction is one of my specialties. Let's find out."

He launched across to the sandstone island, and Evander offered no objections as he smashed apart the triple-layered bridge between sandstone and the joined elemental islands. Again an enormous wave of energy was released, and this time he felt more clearly how it rebounded across the breaking bridge, then across the elemental islands to slam into Fire and Water, knocking them back even farther.

Fire shouted, "You bring down wrath and ruin upon yourself and your family, boy!"

"You cannot stop us. We are linked too intimately with the queen," Water added. "This delay will only make our vengeance the sweeter."

"Keep talking," Connor shouted back. They might be right, but he was hurting them, delaying them. He wasn't about to stop.

In quick succession, he smashed through the rest of the queen's secondary affinities and started across her final set of bridges from her primary affinities to her mainland lab. Evander followed, expression thoughtful, hands held before him, as if toward the warmth of a hearth.

Connor stopped when he reached the mainland lab, at the end of the bridge leading to obsidian, her first-ever affinity. The island looked older than the others, its edges more rounded, but the entire island gleamed like a polished mirror. It might be older, but Connor felt the power of that affinity far more clearly than any of the others.

"Wait," Evander called, flying across the distance to land beside him.

"What? This is it. Every bridge hurt them and pushed them away," Connor replied, feeling so relieved that they'd discovered the way to beat the elementals and prevent their rising into the world.

"They have pushed them, hurt them, but not stopped them," Evander said grimly. "The mighty oak blackens in the fire, but new buds bring renewal of life in the springtime."

Connor groaned and rubbed one hand across his face, feeling exhausted and annoyed. "Are you saying this isn't enough?"

"I do not believe so," Evander admitted.

"Then what else can we do?" Connor demanded.

"We must destroy the vessel and break their connection to her," Evander stated.

Connor tried to bottle his frustration, to think clearly. They'd bought some time, but Evander was right. He could feel Water and Fire creeping up those tendrils connecting them to the queen's mind. They would pull themselves out of the abyss and reach freedom, even after he broke the final bridge.

He paced the edge of the cliff, max-tapping super obsidian, considering everything they knew. "Breaking these bridges helped. Their connection to your grandmother is weaker, but not gone."

Evander nodded. "I do not believe we can block them from entering the world until that link is destroyed."

"If we kill her, can we break it then?" Connor asked.

"She is already consumed by the strum elfonnel. We must destroy that, but is that possible when the elements are still connected to this world through it?" Evander asked.

That was a scary thought. Could the elementals regenerate their monster through that tiny connection through the queen's mind? She had regenerated from a scorched skull, so it might be possible.

Evander gestured toward the last bridge. "This affinity fission power has the potential to sever the link."

"Maybe, but I've only got one bridge left to break," Connor objected. "And breaking each bridge only pushed them back. It didn't sever the link."

"Perhaps instead of simply releasing the energy from each sundered bridge, it may be possible to gather it."

Connor groaned. "Why didn't you suggest that before I broke all the bridges?" It was a good idea, but he only had one bridge left, and he doubted that would be enough to stop them.

"Get out of my mind!"

The shrill, screaming voice of Queen Dreokt surprised Connor. He and Evander turned in unison to look back into the decaying lab of her affinityscape. Queen Dreokt indeed stood there, marching toward them. She looked . . .

Old.

Her hair was gray and wispy, her face lined like a sheet crumpled into a ball. Her eyes had a wild gleam in them, and she swayed as she walked. Connor realized with a start that she no longer enjoyed the longevity and strength of her affinities. He'd destroyed them all. She was nothing but a weak mortal woman.

Evander bowed to her and said softly, "Grandmother, I reverence the days of your youth before you broke with sanity."

She started, as if seeing him for the first time. Squinting up at him, she exclaimed, "Am I dead already?"

"It's complicated," Connor said, uneasy in her presence. He felt confident she posed no direct threat, but he wouldn't underestimate her ever again.

"You vile boy, stop torturing me! I've lost everything but this place, and now you take it from me too. Have you no shame?"

He glared. "I don't think you can talk about shame."

She marched up to him and tried punching him. The blow was weak and slow, and he easily caught it. Even in her mind, she lacked potency. She really was fading. She gasped, staring at her fist held helpless in his grasp and recoiled from him. Tears stood in her eyes and she cried, "No, I cannot end this way."

"Everyone has to end," Evander said simply.

"But not me, not like this!" she shrieked, recovering some of her strength through insanity. She wagged a finger at Connor. "Get out of my mind! You are the only one who understands me. We are linked, and you walk as closely with the elementals as I do. Leave me!"

Connor's obsidian-enhanced mind snatched a new idea from her rambling and he gasped with realization.

"I know how to do it!"

CHAPTER SIXTY-THREE
Painful Choices

Kilian dodged sideways, tapping super-fracked speed, moving so fast that to others he no doubt appeared to teleport away from the enormous leg of the earthbound elfonnel trying to squash him. He stopped a hundred feet to his left and unleashed a barrage of ice daggers at the monster's five huge, black eyes on the near side of its massive head.

The eyes exploded under the barrage, but Kilian waited three heartbeats before allowing himself to celebrate. Just as he'd feared, the eyes began reforming. He growled a curse and ripped the new-forming eyes apart again for good measure.

The monster turned after him, biting down at him with its enormous jaws, its long, serpentine neck flinging that head down like a whip. Kilian easily dodged it again, shifting around the monster to stop below its second head. He'd never fought an earthbound with four heads, one on each side of its body, and it was proving interesting.

That monster smelled of deep earth and mold, and it had a permanence to it that was growing annoying. Kilian had never fought an earthbound that wouldn't die. Despite the united attacks of two hundred Spitters, it had only continued to grow. Its armored body was now over three hundred feet in diameter, and it had sported several additional legs. They'd inundated it with water, frozen its legs, and filled its throats with ice, all to no avail. Nothing seemed to damage it.

Kilian was starting to fear the elfonnel would not die unless Connor somehow defeated his mother. That didn't bode well for any of them, but he didn't share his dark thoughts with the others. His men and women were fighting valiantly, and they believed him when he promised they would win the day.

So he had to figure out how.

The monster's second head noticed him and lunged, enormous maw opening wide enough to swallow an acre of land. Kilian dodged, and when its beak smashed into the ground where he'd been standing, he filled that mouth and throat with water, then turned it all to ice, sealing the beast to the ground with an unbroken column of ice that momentarily held it prisoner.

"Shatter it!" General Rory shouted from high on the monster's back where he led a futile assault by several hundred insane bash fighters. They swarmed the monster's back, pounding at its armor to no effect. If they ever figured out how to break through, he bet Rory and Anika would lead the charge into the belly of the beast to try breaking it from the inside. Luckily the monster hadn't even seemed to notice them yet.

Rory leaped high into the air from the monster's back in an impressive display of granite-enhanced leg power. He smashed down onto the monster's frozen neck like a living meteor, every ounce of his granite power focused on the great hammer he swung with a two-handed grip. The hammer blow landed like an explosion, and the monster's stony neck cracked.

Anika and Erich and two dozen Boulders and Rumblers followed Rory in a wave of screaming insanity, raining down over the frozen neck like death hail, every single one of them striking in the exact same place. The crack spread, the neck fractured, and Kilian sensed the ice underneath crumbling. On any other elfonnel, they'd be severely damaging it.

Not on this one.

All three of the other heads trumpeted in anger, and the monster shifted, twisting to the right. The move ripped the ice tether from the ground, and a moment later it spat the ice out, despite Kilian's best efforts to keep it in place. The shattered neck healed, within seconds looking like it had never been touched.

Rory trotted over to Kilian, glaring up at the beast. "Not fair, healing like that."

No, it wasn't. Kilian glanced up and his sense of frustration grew. The airbound elfonnel had scattered the Battalions and had caught Battalion One in one of those infernal tornado clouds. The great air ship was spinning dangerously fast, and no doubt would soon splinter apart. He hated that he couldn't help, but he had to figure out how to stop the earthbound first.

"Look!" Anika shouted as she caught up with Rory.

The great earthbound monster stumbled, and the recently-healed neck shattered again, the head falling free and crashing to the ground nearby with a fantastic boom.

Ivor skidded to a stop nearby, gaping at the severed head. "I thought it just healed."

"It did," Kilian said, feeling the first rays of new hope.

"What did you do?" Rory demanded.

"Nothing."

In the sky, the airbound hissed like every cat in the kingdom got stepped on at the same time, and dropped a hundred feet toward the ground. The funnel cloud holding Battalion One captive dissipated, winds rushing away in every direction.

"It's got to be Connor. He's hurting them!" Kilian shouted. He raised his hand high and shouted, "Hit him while he's distracted!"

Rory grinned and raised a fist for Anika to punch. "That's more like it!"

They charged.

*   *   *

Connor shouted as he smashed his curse-laden fist through the anchor points of the queen's bridges to obsidian. Raw energy exploded from the breaking stones, far more powerful than any other broken affinity. Instead of hitting the elementals with it, Connor caught it and drew it in. He wasn't sure why that bridge contained so much more. Maybe since it was her first it had taken more energy to establish.

It didn't matter. All he cared about was that he'd managed to take the energy from the explosion. It flowed through him, an energizing wave that was fundamentally different from the strum and magnis he'd been wielding. That energy had been used to create the affinity, and as he studied it, he sensed that it was a higher form of obsidian, like pure, distilled sylfaen, released by the process of shattering that link.

He grinned. Evander was right. All he needed to do was somehow amass enough of that affinity-fission energy to create a death beam strong enough to snap the elementals' link to the queen's mind, and destroy her elfonnel at the same time.

Except, he could only think of one way he might be able to do that, and he really didn't want to do that. There had to be a way, though. He let his fear and worry fade away under new confidence. He would not fail again.

Queen Dreokt dropped to her knees, as if that last bridge had been fueling her strength. She wailed like a lost child, devoid of hope. Her eyes shone with madness, and she shrieked wordlessly as she pulled clumps of her thin hair from her head.

Connor refused to pity her. As the connection to her broken mind faded, he said, "Don't worry. It'll be over soon."

"I'll kill you!" she shrieked, and disappeared from her affinityscape.

Evander said, "If you have a plan, I suggest you hurry."

Connor willed himself awake. Back in the enormous rampager body, his senses felt supernaturally sharper than ever. He still stood in the air, high above the plateau, with the queen lightning elfonnel higher still, wreathed in black storm clouds, surrounded by pelting snow and ice. The monster rotated to look down at him, and her features now looked exactly like Queen Dreokt's. Her insane eyes were black, and her features twisted with hate.

She might be all but lost to the elementals, but somehow she seemed more in control of the elfonnel than ever. She shouted in a voice like thunder, "Face my wrath, wicked, unworthy child!"

She swooped toward him, lightning arms thrown wide, her writhing, lightning torso sprouting dozens more arms of living lightning. She clearly meant to smother him in strum and burn him to cinders this time.

In Connor's mind, Porphyry howled a challenge and said, "Let us hunt and rend together, Pack Leader!"

"Soon," Connor promised him. "I have one last thing to do."

He willed himself into his own affinityscape, grateful that time moved far faster in there than in the real world. Otherwise, the queen elfonnel would rip him apart long before he could attempt the desperate plan he'd just come up with.

Despite the urgency of his mission, he paused for a second to stare out at his affinityscape, to enjoy the floating islands and multi-leveled bridges of his affinities. His Petralist powers had come to define him.

Now they offered the one chance at salvation. Tallan spank the queen for a century for forcing him to this point.

Evander appeared beside him, looking confused. "What are you planning, Connor?"

The fact that he'd figured out something before Evander made Connor smile. Surprising enemies on the field of battle was one of his strengths. Hopefully this move would surprise the elementals.

And not simply destroy him.

He gestured toward his floating islands and bridges, and sighed under a weight of onerous responsibility that he could not escape. "We need more power. There's not enough left linked to your mother's mind for me to gather enough to snap the connection between her and the elementals. I can't use fission from the physical world because she's a lightning elfonnel. I need affinity fission."

"Indeed, but that is the challenge," Evander said.

Hating the words he had to speak, but not seeing any alternative, Connor sighed again and gestured once more at his precious affinities. "There's only one place where I can access more affinity-fission power."

Evander's eyes widened with understanding. "You mean to sunder your own bridges and steal the energy released by sacrificing them?"

Connor nodded and looked to Evander with a last flicker of hope. "Can you think of another way to get the power I need?"

Evander hesitated, and Connor held his breath, desperately hoping the brilliant old Dawnus would save him from making such a terrible sacrifice.

His hope fizzled when Evander shook his head. "I see no other alternative, but can the sundering of your bridges affect the connection between my grandmother and the elementals?"

"I believe it can. Didn't you hear her? I'm connected to her with chert, but also connected to the elementals through the third threshold. I'm the only other one who is. If I break enough bridges and collect enough energy, I should be able to destroy her elfonnel and snap their hold over her."

Evander didn't look convinced, but did not object. He gave Connor a little bow of respect and said softly, "The killdeer pretends to injury to lure predators away from the nest, but only pure love motivates one to the greatest of sacrifices."

"Let's hope it doesn't come to that," Connor said, moved by the compliment. He hoped he was motivated by love and a desire to save Verena and his friends more than out of a desperate longing to not be the guy responsible for unleashing the end of the world. Either way, he was definitely taking a terrible risk.

So be it.

Some of Connor's bridges were already dark and unresponsive in his mind, the bridges to red energy marble, serpentinite, and even slate. So Connor jogged across his primary and secondary affinity islands until he reached the bridges to those tertiary powers. The top level of each of the bridges, linked to his third threshold, was still vibrant and intact, and he sensed the flow of green power across them. The lowest tiers were dim and unresponsive.

The red energy power that should flow across those bridges was broken. It might return some day, and if he left those bridges intact and survived maybe he could find a way to reestablish connections. He still had access to the higher-level power, so maybe he didn't need them anyway.

Connor stepped to the bridge to serpentinite. She still had not appeared in tangible form in his mind, so he felt less guilty making the first attempt there. He descended to the lowest tier of the island and crouched over the lowest level of the reinforced foundations holding the three-layered bridge to that island of sound. Before he could second-guess the insane plan, he shouted and curse-punched the end of the lowest level of the bridge.

It shattered.

The entire lower bridge splintered and fell into the mist of the bottomless void. As the connection broke, Connor drew upon the highest level power from limestone, which allowed him to manipulate energy best. He was prepared for a rush of energy, but gasped at the unexpected ferocity of the explosion that erupted from the broken bridge. It had contained far more energy than what he'd siphoned from the queen's mind.

She was easily as powerful as he, but maybe he'd lost a lot because he was standing inside her head. Or maybe the fact that her mind was breaking, or that the elementals mostly controlled her impacted the amount released.

Either way, he felt encouraged. With so much energy released by that single bridge, he felt convinced he could gather enough to overcome the elementals' hold on the queen's mind. He might not even need to destroy all of his bridges to do it. The energy from serpentinite whistled through his body, like the distant murmuring of thousands of cherished memories. The sounds comforted him and eased more of his tension.

As the power of serpentinite infused him, memories flashed into his mind of times he'd used that unique tertiary stone. He thought of the day in Altkalen when Student Eighteen taught him his first lessons with serpentinite, and how he'd fooled some of the Crushers into thinking Mattias was mocking them. He smiled sadly, filled with a sense of loss. That part of serpentinite was gone.

Connor sensed his physical body swelling from the influx of power. Porphyry appeared beside him, a wolfish grin on its huge maw. As the energy poured into Connor, the beast swelled in size to mimic the growth of their giant physical form.

All four of the elementals appeared at the midpoints of their islands and looked around, as if startled to be there. "What are you doing?" Water exclaimed, her perfect, ancient face clouded with new worry.

"What I have to," Connor said as he jumped across to his marble island and the bridge to fire.

Fire lifted a placating hand and said, "Hold on, Connor. I think we owe you an apology."

That was surprising. He'd expected more angry threats from Fire. That seemed more his style.

"We are nearly free, and there is nothing you can do to stop us from shedding our chains," Fire said. "But we've realized that we acted foolishly. Your world is not ours, and we placed unrealistic expectations upon you."

"What are you saying?" Connor asked, despite knowing he couldn't trust anything Fire told him.

Earth spoke. "We should not have spread responsibility for our captivity across all humanity."

"We do not wish to begin our life of freedom as enemies," Air added in a soothing tone, like a cool breeze against a hot brow.

Water nodded, her expression earnest. "Forgive and forget is the term, is it not? Walk in harmony with us and we promise to live in peace with all people."

"We will even recommit to our oath to obey your will and protect your family," Fire said, hesitating only a little. That hesitation made Connor think he was actually sincere. Fire lied a lot easier than he told truth.

"And we will even agree to not seek vengeance upon anyone on any continent for past wrongs," Earth added solemnly, making the Tabnit oath sign, two fingers drawn slowly down the forehead.

Water spread her hands wide. "We only wish to enjoy the freedom we have longed for across these many years. Let it be freedom of joy and union, not freedom of strife and destruction."

"Really?" Connor glanced from her to the others, and every one of them nodded, looking absolutely sincere. He understood their yearning for freedom. He and his friends, and entire nations had risked everything to gain that same freedom. Unfortunately, if the elementals only wanted that, they would not have acted the way they had.

Back on his mainland, Evander said, "The nation most eager to forge a new accord is the one negotiating from a compromised position."

"Oh, shut up and finish dying already," Fire snapped, scowling.

Water gave Fire an irritated look and added, "Although we would mourn your passing."

"I bet you would," Connor said sarcastically. They'd just confirmed his fears. He wanted to believe them because the alternative was so scary, but pretending danger didn't exist didn't make it go away.

They were controlling a mighty elfonnel, but they weren't yet free, and that path to freedom would prove a lot more difficult now that he had sundered all of the queen's affinities. They might still succeed, but if they were convinced he couldn't finish the job, they wouldn't have changed tactics.

Connor sighed and said, "I really wish you weren't all so good at lying. Try working on the truth part of humanity. It works better."

The friendly smiles faded from the elements' faces, and he sensed anger deeper than any human could ever feel. It was a Tallan-cursed shame that he had to stand against them. He loved walking with the elements, but not if they walked unchained by any natural laws. Despite their lies, their manipulation, and the deaths they'd already caused, he wished things could be different.

They couldn't.

CHAPTER SIXTY-FOUR
What Is the Most Important Priority?

Connor faced the angry elementals and said, "I am very sorry that you were brought to consciousness but left in confinement. It's not fair and it should never have happened, but I cannot give you what you seek."

They lunged against the invisible restraints blocking them at the midpoint of their bridges, shouting at him to stop. Porphyry jumped right across the gap and landed on Water's bridge, fangs bared, snarling. Again they hesitated.

Connor smashed all three of the bridges to Fire, his fist punching through one after the other. Vast amounts of affinity energy erupted from the breaches, and Connor seized it all, drawing it all into himself. Fire disappeared, his glare hot enough to make the entire affinityscape feel stifling.

Connor stared down at the crumbled edge of the marble island, and the broken anchor points felt like jagged holes in his soul. Although his body shook and swelled with the influx of captured energy, he wanted to despair. Breaking the queen's islands had seemed easy, and even smashing the bridge to serpentinite hadn't affected his nearly as much, but he'd just severed all ties with Fire.

Again memories flooded his mind along with the influx of sylfaen energy. He remembered Aonghus before the queen twisted him into a monster, thought back to the crazy moment when he'd first connected with fire, down in the basements of Lord Gavin's manor. He remembered the fear as fire boiled out his mouth, sending Shona fleeing. Fire had allowed them to escape the Grandurian trap that day, and he'd gotten to burn Lady Isobel's kitchen for the second time. He might have just broken his affinity, but he'd always have that happy memory.

Ever since he'd learned about affinities, particularly the precious tertiary affinities, he'd marveled at the wonder of walking with the elements. His tertiary affinities had saved his life many times, and he felt a deep, personal connection with the elemental beings standing inside his mind. They might not be the people they had claimed to be, might have become the greatest threat the world had ever seen, but smashing apart all hopes of ever feeling the wild rush of fire again still hurt.

It had better be worth it.

Connor cast his senses up toward the queen lightning elfonnel diving toward him. With all that new energy captured from sacrificing Fire, he was strong, but not strong enough. He needed a lot more power to stop it.

"Sometimes I hate my life," Connor muttered, but forced himself to cross the bridge to quartzite. Air was watching him, silently shaking her head and mouthing "No" over and over. She looked devastated, and he met her gaze and said, "You all shouldn't have tried killing Verena."

He smashed through all three of her islands in a single, mighty blow. She screamed as the bridges shattered and evaporated, and the sound felt like it was ripping a new hole in his heart. Connor grimaced, but still seized the enormous explosion of affinity energy like he had the others. It filled him with a vast flood of power that felt like he'd sucked in all the winds blowing over the Sea of Olcan. The explosion shredded Air, ripping her apart. The last thing he saw of her was an expression of absolute fury.

Then she was gone.

For a moment he again reveled in the unrivaled wonder of looking at the world through quartzite-enhanced eyes. Then he again marveled at the wonder of flying untethered to anything, holding Air's hand as she shared part of her world with him. He would miss that.

Earth shouted, "Stop, Connor! Wait. Listen to me!" His voice tumbling out fast and shrill, completely unlike his normal composed self.

Connor hesitated near the bridge to Earth, his fist raised. "I'm sorry, but like my friend Hamish likes to say, you can choose your friends, you can choose your breakfast, but true friends don't eat their friends' breakfasts."

"That doesn't make any sense," Earth responded with a scowl, and Evander nodded agreement, muttering to himself about bad Sentry speak.

Connor shrugged. "It would if you really understood breakfast."

It felt right to part with Earth through Sentry speak, even if it was bad Sentry speak. Connor smashed the bridges apart. Another explosion of overwhelming, raw power thundered into him and his rampager form swelled incredibly. The earth affinity-fission energy felt like he'd ingested the heart of Mount Ingram, and he smiled to think of capturing a piece of lost Alasdair in that last, desperate moment when he was forced to throw away so much that he loved in order to try saving what he loved most.

Porphyry howled approval as Earth disappeared from Connor's mind. "All traitors to their pack deserve to die!"

Connor shook under the awesome influx of power. Something about the act of willfully turning away from these elemental beings provided unparalleled access to energy. He wished he could embrace the act with joy like Porphyry instead of feeling like he was breaking parts of himself.

He thought of the first lessons with Gregor, in the woods near Alasdair, sensing the earth like extensions of his mind. He thought of training with Ilse outside of the Carraig, and the indomitable strength that earth shared with him. So many memories he could never relive.

Even though the torrents of new energy enlivened his physical form, Connor felt tired. His body ached with a deep hurt as he moved to the final bridge. Water faced him with arms folded, her expression dark like the sea during a storm. "We placed great faith in you, Connor. I am deeply disappointed by this betrayal."

He paused, surprised that he felt hurt by the reprimand, and that made him angry. "You betrayed me first."

"We seek only the same freedom you do. Listen, Connor, even now we can salvage this. The energy you desire to defend yourself is yours for the taking. You are breaking the wrong bridges."

She gestured behind him, toward his final bridge, the long, arcing span that led down the mountain to Alasdair. The bridge to his humanity.

"More power resides in that bridge than in all of these." She extended a hand, her expression imploring. "Sunder it and give yourself to me, and together we can change the world, reshape it any way you see fit."

It also contained everything that defined him. His honor, honesty, love for his family and Verena. Everything that made him human, that made him Connor, was contained within that bridge. If he shattered it he would shatter his own identity and would join the elementals as something not human.

Exactly like the queen.

That was the part that she seemed incapable of understanding. She honestly believed his humanity limited him, couldn't understand that it defined him and made him everything that mattered. He raised his fist again, feeling close to tears as he prepared to sunder the connection to this last element, his first element, the one who helped him become the warrior he needed to be to fight for his family and loved ones.

Memories swept him away for a moment. He stood again in the quiet, sheltered corner of the army camp below Alasdair with Shona, connecting with water for the first time. He clearly saw Shona, drenched by laughing with delight. He thought of his wondrous ascension, defeating the elfonnel at the Carraig with water's help, and raising the great ice dome over the Rhidorroch. He'd walked closer with Water than any of the elementals, and the thought of sundering all ties to her felt as painful as if he was turning his back on a member of his family.

"I'll miss you," he told her.

Her voice hardened and she hissed, "Apparently not enough. Very well. One betrayal deserves another. You cannot stop our elfonnel, this I vow!"

"Your lies no longer sway me," Connor growled, embracing anger to crush the new fear that she might actually be telling the truth. He refused to believe it.

She began to fade from his mind, and somehow he knew she was withdrawing that affinity. So he smashed his fist down. He'd planned to maybe leave the top-level bridge so he could maintain connection to magnis, but if she was weakening that affinity anyway, he couldn't hesitate. He struck them all.

The bridges shattered and a vast influx of power thundered into him, but somehow less intense than the others. She really had begun withdrawing her influence. Not good. He knew that a woman scorned could unleash terrible vengeance, but had never expected to worry about that from the elementals.

With the bridges to the elements gone, he felt truly alone in his mind for the first time since his ascension. Well, not exactly alone.

Porphyry was padding across his other bridges, looking immensely pleased, and Evander still stood on his mainland.

He checked his power level against the energy bottled inside the queen elfonnel and groaned. He still needed more.

As hard as breaking the bridges to the elements had been, that much had seemed obvious. Now he scanned his other affinities and wondered which ones to take next. Which ones must he sacrifice?

The queen elfonnel was drawing upon the highest level of green energy, the power of entropy and destruction. Connor couldn't destroy every affinity, or he'd lose the ability to fight her. He had to face her with green energy, with fission and with the captured power from the broken bridges.

Limestone and sandstone were vital, so he passed them and rushed back to the bridges to his primary affinities.

Basalt.

Connor stared at the black island, its three tiers imposing and inspiring. He loved the unbounded freedom of speed, and the thought of intentionally smashing access to it made him feel physically sick. He touched the bridge, felt the connection there, closed his eyes and savored memories of fracked sprinting. He thought of his first lessons with Donald, the terrible pain of fracking for the first time, and the incredible feeling of superfracking with Kilian.

Then he sighed and smashed the lower two bridges apart. He felt close to tears as he absorbed the influx of affinity power, imbued with all the thrill of fracked sprinting. It seemed wrong to get rewarded for sundering his affinity. He left the highest-level bridge, the green-only power of stilling, but seeing the empty gap where the lower two bridges had always hung filled him with a terrible sense of loss. He feared he would never again run with basalt speed, but maybe he could figure something out with that last bridge intact.

Not sacrificing basalt would mean never walking hand in hand with Verena again. Connor clung to that comforting thought as he considered the next sacrifice. He still needed more energy, but he was getting closer.

Pumice and obsidian were mostly green energy stones and he sensed he would not gain much by sundering even their first-level bridges, so he turned to granite.

At that point, he almost just gave up. If simply surrendering to the queen elfonnel and letting her destroy him would mean only his death, he would be tempted to face that fate rather than destroy his affinity with granite. He tapped it, savoring the itchy-crawly feel of it rippling beneath his skin. He smiled to think he used to hate his curse, but it was as much a part of him as breathing, or his love for Verena.

He thought of curse-punching the torc to save his life, thought of the endless hours of bash fighting training with Tomas and Cameron. If they still lived, they might never forgive him for willingly turning away from bash fighting. He'd shared granite with Verena, so maybe he'd preserved part of it in his life after all.

"I do this for you, Verena," he said softly.

Blinking away tears, he shattered the bridges to granite, smashing through all three levels. An enormous influx of energy poured into him, staggering him from its magnitude that eclipsed even what he had received from those elemental bridges. Granite was his first affinity, and that seemed to hold so much more power, just as obsidian had for the queen.

Connor checked the elfonnel, and shouted a Grandurian curse that Erich had taught him. Still not enough. He was destroying himself from the inside, and it wasn't enough!

He couldn't stop now. Hating the unyielding duty that drove him, Connor smashed the bridges to diorite, gasping when the energy influx rippled through him with the lightning-like strength of strum. With diorite gone, he crossed to his secondary islands and stopped at blind coal. He didn't pause to think, but smashed apart all three bridges and captured all their energy.

Chert was a possibility, but he sensed it didn't contain as much energy as his other affinities. He felt exhausted, emotionally wrung out by the self-induced torture, but he needed more power and he was just about out of time.

He was almost out of bridges too.

Connor considered limestone and sandstone again. He needed more power, but couldn't just sunder all three levels. He sensed through basalt that his connection to stilling still existed, so the risk he took in smashing the lower-level bridges to basalt seemed to have paid off. He didn't have much choice, so he shattered the first two levels of limestone.

Connor's mind returned to the Tir-raon, to the battle where his army was attacked by all the others. They'd used Solas and prism lanters to blind all their enemies. That had been the first hint that maybe limestone was far more powerful than anyone believed. His enormous rampager body began to glow as it swelled with the influx of limestone affinity fission power. Connor still felt a spike of fear. If he'd just broken his connection to fission, he'd just doomed himself. Barely able to breathe, he jumped to the remaining bridge to limestone.

There! He sagged with relief when he felt his connection to limestone still there, still strong. He could still feel all the affinity-fission energy he'd captured, still manipulate it. He might have lost the ability to manipulate light, but he was still in the fight. With that higher level of limestone, he could still access mirage and death beam too.

He still wasn't quite strong enough though, and the only affinity that might hold enough was sandstone.

Connor crossed to that island and ran his fingers over the bridges, thinking of the countless times sandstone had saved his life. Could he really destroy it?

Fleshcrafting was already dormant. Chances of them deciding to sacrifice another Petralist in elfonnel form at the convergence point so he alone could enjoy fleshcrafting again were low, but still he hesitated.

Stopping now would mean all the other sacrifices were wasted.

Gritting his teeth, Connor carefully smashed away the top-level bridge to sandstone, casting fleshcrafting away forever. He snatched every iota of power released by sacrificing that bridge and shook with the influx of new power. His body swelled further, reaching nearly three hundred feet tall, a titanic monster, unique to the world. His rampager form thrummed with power, and every deadly inch of him shuddered with the need to move, to use some of the vast amounts of power rushing through him and threatening to tear himself apart.

It seemed impossible he wasn't strong enough to destroy anything in the world he needed to, but when he cast his senses back up into the sky, he wanted to howl with despair. The sacrifices were indeed helping. He sensed that the power he could unleash had very nearly caught up with the energy building within the queen elfonnel, but it was still a little too low.

While he hesitated, facing the beloved bridge to sandstone, he reached a hand to his throat, imagining Aunt Ailsa's pendant hanging about his neck. He thought of the first time he knowingly tapped sandstone, during that crazy battle on the slope near Alasdair when he'd succumbed to double-tap sickness. He'd saved himself, then many others. He thought of that tender moment when he'd healed Verena's leg and she'd kissed him.

He tried not to think about how he'd been the one who broke her leg, or that she'd been in Carbrey's custody, facing torture and death. He thought of the sculpted sandstone pendants Ailsa had taken such great risks to gift to him, and all the trouble he'd caused by allowing Jok to get his hands on one. He thought of the lives he'd changed in the short time he'd gained access to fleshcrafting. He'd healed Ilse and dear Jean, and all of Jean's patients, and the memories made him smile.

"Pack leader!" Porphyry growled, looking up, and Connor cast his senses beyond himself, expecting to feel the queen elfonnel drawing dangerously close, perhaps reaching out with another lightning barrage.

She wasn't, but was turning away.

East. Toward Lossit valley and his friends.

Water's last angry words returned to haunt him. She was angry. They all were, and they intended to carry out their threats to destroy everyone he loved, then kill him last.

"I don't think so," Connor growled.

He brought his curse-laden fist down with all his might on the remaining sandstone bridges.

Chapter Sixty-Five
The Final Threshold

Connor blinked his eyes open and just had to howl, his voice rising over the wind to shake the air. He was so full of life, his enormous rampager form shuddered with energy. It took all of his control to keep from leaping into the air and unleashing that power in a devastating wave.

Plus, he was actually falling.

His affinity with air was gone, so he lacked the power to reach for the currents whistling past. The loss of his affinities was a deep ache in his heart, but in his current form, a fall of a few thousand feet didn't concern him. In fact, he wished he could fall faster because he couldn't give chase to the queen elfonnel until he reached the ground.

She was moving fast, shooting east and drawing the boiling storm clouds with her. She had grown larger, a giant, glowing monster out of nightmare, wreathed in lightning, her Dreokt features twisted with rage. Connor sensed only whispers of the queen through chert. The elementals had almost entirely consumed her, and with her affinities gone, she lacked the ability to fight them.

They weren't completely free yet, though. When he smashed the queen's bridges, he'd pushed closed most of the gateway to the real world. The elementals were still pressing through, if more slowly, taking control over the elfonnel, fighting for freedom, but stuck in the tiny opening.

The queen elfonnel bellowed, "See the fruits of your folly, mortal!"

It raised its many lightning-bolt arms, pointing them toward the east. It looked like it was preparing to unleash another lightning barrage against the unprotected armies. Connor tried to stop it, but he couldn't feel strum or magnis. He'd broken the bridges to water and fire and locked himself out.

He couldn't stop it.

Desperately, Connor cast his thoughts to the east and felt Verena's mind like a warm beacon. He touched her thoughts and felt a flood of relief. She was awake. The connection snapped into place, and he smiled to feel her surprise.

"Connor, you're alive!" she cried.

"Tell everyone to beware. You might get hit by another lightning blast."

"Can you stop it?" she asked nervously.

"Maybe. This is my last chance, and I won't let it get away this time."

"Connor, please be safe," she urged.

His safety wasn't important. All he cared about was protecting her. When he didn't immediately respond, she asked, *"Connor?"*

"I love you. Be safe. I have to go."

"I love you," she said, pouring all of her heartfelt emotion across the link to him. It helped bolster his confidence. He would stop the elementals. He wouldn't quit until he won.

Time to end the monster.

Connor hit the ground, absorbing the impact easily on his giant rampager legs and immediately launching himself after the elfonnel. It had paused high in the air, just beneath the roiling storm clouds, with shrieking wind whipping all around it, lightning bolts crackling all along its torso, but it hadn't unleashed the barrage.

Instead, the queen elfonnel began to change. Connor didn't need elemental senses to understand what was happening. Crimson fires began racing along the elfonnel's torso, while water rippled up one of its arms. Earth formed a helmet over its huge head, and air whistled through the lightning bolts, magnifying the whirlwind under its torso.

In their desperate eagerness to reach ultimate freedom, the elementals were fighting each other. The doorway was tight, and none of them seemed willing to let the others through first. The queen elfonnel shuddered and trembled as the various elementals wormed their way into it, clearly arguing amongst themselves just as they had when Connor raised his elfonnel. No doubt they would work things out in a moment, but in that second, their greed for freedom gave Connor his one opening.

So he focused on the wild torrent of energy coursing through him and max-tapped limestone to concentrate it further. He was already filled to bursting with power, a combination of raw energy he'd sucked in from the storm, plus the pure affinity-fission energy from the ruptured bridges. He wasn't sure exactly what it was made of, but sensed it was a more refined frequency of sylfaen power than he'd ever wielded, and that it could indeed hurt the elemental creatures.

With all his strength, he compressed that energy, mixing it together, concentrating it, and magnifying its frequency. His entire body shuddered with violent spasms as the pressure to release the power grew to the point it took all of his superhuman strength to contain it.

Ratcheted up to such high frequency, some energy began bleeding away, radiating out of the intense core and seeping into his flesh. It was so powerful it tore at the fabric of his muscles and bones, threatening to rip them asunder. Connor groaned from the effort and the blossoming pain, grinding his sharp teeth together as he fought to hold on long enough to aim his one strike.

If he missed, all was lost.

His vision reddened, his breath came in ragged gasps, and in his mind Porphyry growled, "*Strike, Pack Leader, or we die!*"

Aiming his muzzle at the distant elfonnel, Connor *howled*, casting every bit of that pent-up energy at his enemy, focusing the beam as tight as he possibly could.

It shot away, an invisible death beam more destructive than anything the world had ever seen. To the east, several thousand feet higher, the lightning elfonnel was just trumpeting in victory. Had the elementals reached an accord, decided how to share the monster and take the final step into the world?

Too late.

Connor's death beam struck it and consumed it.

The core of the monster was already made of plasma, surrounded by lightning, although parts of it had transformed into the various elements vying for control over it. Connor's death beam ripped through it like a rampager through paper, shredding its component bits to their tiniest molecules, then ripping those apart too.

Some of those bits ruptured at their most basic level, just as particles had ruptured down in the mantle of the planet when he hit them with that death beam. The rupturing particles unleashed a vast explosion, multiplying the deadly torrent already ripping through the monster.

White-hot fire engulfed the writhing queen elfonnel, and invisible energy millions of times stronger tore at it and erupted outward in every direction. Connor deflected it up into the clouds before it could roll over the land and rip out the lives of everyone for hundreds of miles. The blast boiled up into the clouds, shredding them, but also magnifying the storm a thousandfold.

The queen elfonnel screamed, its voice a mixture of all of the elementals and Queen Dreokt herself, and her mind struck Connor's with startling force. Through the connection, he sensed how she had become the gateway to the world, her mind broken and twisted and transformed into an opening, rimmed with green energy. The elementals were there, clinging to the frame as the torrent of energy blasted against them. The queen was dying, the last vestiges of her innermost being tearing apart, so the gateway was crumbling, but the elementals were still not letting go.

"*Just leave!*" Connor shouted at them, enraged by their tenacity. If they somehow withstood the barrage ripping the elfonnel apart, could they reconstitute it, preserve some part of the queen's life long enough to still push into the world.

"*You cannot deny us,*" Water responded, her voice tight with strain.

Connor reached for more power, determined to strike through the conduit of chert and break their hold on the world, but he had nothing left. He'd thrown it all at the queen elfonnel. He was exhausted, his body shaking with fatigue and shrinking fast. He had consumed all but the last vestiges of porphyry, and he felt the connection about to snap. Would that kill him or revert him back to his weak human form?

It didn't matter. He'd be left completely spent, unable to fight them.

"*Pack Leader, I will do this,*" Porphyry said.

"*How?*" Connor could smash the bridges to porphyry, but hadn't even considered it. He needed porphyry's strength to fight the elementals, but he was about to lose his connection anyway, and he didn't have any more porphyry. Unless he found the secret quarry for the rare power stone, he'd never again awaken the rampager. He could destroy those bridges, but he didn't want to.

"*We are the pack, and we will always be the pack,*" Porphyry said, appearing beside Connor, his deadly monster form glowing softly in the energized air. "*I will fight for the pack leader.*"

"*I don't understand,*" Connor admitted, but he was out of time. His strength was failing, the explosion tearing the elfonnel apart fading, and the elementals were still not gone.

"*Speak the command, and I will fight. Then you will see,*" Porphyry said simply.

What did he have to lose?

"*Fight for me,*" Connor urged the monster.

Porphyry howled with bloodlust and leaped away, flashing across the distance to the dying elfonnel, transforming into a flash of red light, like a lightning bolt that pierced the monster's chest. At the same time, Porphyry leaped down the conduit of chert to the queen's broken mind. Connor caught a glimpse of the enraged rampager diving into the elementals clustered at the tiny gateway, jaws agape, claws raking.

All of the elementals screamed as Porphyry plowed into them, and with a flash of green light, they disappeared. The gateway shuddered and imploded.

The queen elfonnel's boy shuddered, then ruptured, and it must have lost control over all those built-up charges of strum because an enormous lightning bolt ripped up from the ground and speared up through the monster. It burst right through in a blinding cascade of sparks as hundreds of lightning bolts erupted from the elfonnel, shooting up into the roiling storm clouds. Wind and lightning and thunder shrieked in every direction, shaking the air so violently Connor stumbled and fell. The crashing sounds clobbered him so hard he screamed, the mighty roar mingling with the creature's elemental death knell.

The essence of the unstoppable elfonnel erupted up into the storm clouds, generating vast sheets of lightning that arced between the clouds, triggering a hailstorm so intense the ice nearly penetrated Connor's thick hide. Wind howled in every direction and Connor's form shrunk as he expended the last of his energy.

He huddled on the ground under the brutal onslaught of the unleashed storm, amazed by the sheer magnitude of it. The last of his porphyry winked out, and he screamed again as a wave of agony coursed through him and his body transformed back to human. He groaned, so far beyond exhausted, he couldn't sit up, couldn't crawl for shelter. The hail and freezing rain soaked him, and he shivered from the brutal cold.

Was she gone? Were they gone? Had it worked?

Queen Dreokt touched his mind, the chert connection so faint it was barely a whisper, but it was there, and Connor felt crushed by hopelessness. He'd failed after all.

"Death is the final threshold," she said, her voice weak but more sane than it had ever sounded.

"Don't let the door hit you on the way out," he responded, daring to hope she was really dying.

"You always were an insolent child, but today I am free!" she chortled.

"Um, aren't you dying?" he asked, surprised by the joy he sensed from her.

"Of course I am. My body is gone, my elfonnel shattered, but the usurpers of my mind are gone. You saved me from them, spared me the fate I have feared for centuries. For that I am indebted to you, boy."

"It was my pleasure," he said, exulting that she was really dying.

"Don't you dare gloat," she warned, the reprimand strong in her fading voice. *"You might have prevented the destruction of all things, but it's your fault we got into this mess in the first place."*

"Hey!" Connor objected, but she spoke right over him.

"I am just glad I won't be around to see the mess you make of the world."

He voice faded to laughter, which trailed away to nothing.

Connor lay on the ground, looking up into the strengthening storm, ignoring the rain and hail beating on him. The last fragments of the queen elfonnel were dispersing up through the storm, and without fleshcrafting and with no body left, not even Queen Dreokt could recover from that. She might have been mighty, but that storm was greater sill, and it consumed all that was left of her.

She was gone!

Connor allowed a weary smile, but then a larger hailstone cracked into his forehead so hard he yelped. She might be gone, but she was making a mess of things, as usual.

The storm was still growing, the winds raging so hard they threatened to yank Connor right off the ground and swallow him up. The icy rain and hail was mixed with snow and sleet, as if the storm couldn't decide what it wanted to beat him with.

Connor managed to lift his head and look around, but he couldn't see far through the intense storm. He was freezing, his body already shaking with chills, and he was so exhausted he'd never escape the storm. He'd destroyed the queen, but her final act of vengeance might kill him too.

Verena was safe.

That thought warmed him, and he tried to reach her again with chert. He felt a tingle of connection, then something struck him from behind, knocking him sprawling and breaking the connection. He groaned and rolled over, holding up his arms to ward against a flurry of huge debris whipping past through the storm.

"This is a stupid way to die," he muttered.

Then something huge and black swept down upon him, and this time the impact knocked him into darkness.

Chapter Sixty-Six

Best Friends Risk Everything for Each Other.
Maybe Just Not Dessert.

Verena frowned, concentrating. She could have sworn she'd just felt Connor, that tickle in the mind that usually meant he was reaching out to her through chert, but that soft touch had faded. She tried not to read too much into it, but couldn't suppress a shiver of fear.

"Verena, are you okay?" Nicklaus asked, crouching beside her.

She sat on the ground south of the ruins of Lossit. Aifric had left her there to heal as she joined the fight against the great earthbound elfonnel. The torrent of healing power from Sucker Punch was quickly refreshing her, but she needed to turn it off soon so the blanket effect didn't rob all the healing power from the other healers.

Most of the troops had retreated from the fight, fleeing north and south, led by Shona and Wolfram, leaving the Spitters and the most insane of the Boulders to fight the earthbound. The great monster had shed all their initial attacks, but had abruptly started to falter.

She hoped that meant Connor was winning. She loved that he'd connected with her, but she'd sensed his weariness and fear, and through that chert link, she'd caught glimpses of the terrible lightning elfonnel. How could he fight such a being? The fact that he was left alone to try terrified her. She couldn't lose him, not now.

His last words warmed her, but her joy was tinged with sadness. Connor had not been able to hide his worry that he might not survive.

Suddenly the western horizon lit up like ten thousand Solas max-tapped limestone together. Verena gasped, shielding her eyes from the searing light. A booming thunderclap shook the valley a second later, and a gale howled past, screaming in a way no wind had ever screamed before. The sound shivered down Verena's spine, and she felt a terrible sense of foreboding. Something important had just happened.

"Look!" Nicklaus shouted, pointing. The great earthbound elfonnel was swaying drunkenly, its legs buckling beneath it, heads hanging low. It looked badly wounded.

Kilian and the other Spitters struck immediately, encasing the drooping heads with ice, filling every joint of every leg with more ice, and sealing the beast in place. Rory, Anika, Erich, and the Boulders swarmed over it, smashing at those joints with all their strength.

The joints burst. All of them.

As the enormous body fell, it shattered into bits, transforming into an avalanche of stone.

Verena could barely believe it. That wasn't how elfonnel were supposed to die. Nicklaus raised his fists in victory, shouting, and raised into the air in his tiny battle suit. All around, soldiers were cheering.

High above, the airbound elfonnel shrieked like a million tea kettles and its body disintegrated, releasing hurricane force winds in every direction. The nine remaining Battalions still flying triggered bursts of fireworks to celebrate.

Verena felt a rush of relief. That bright light and the dying monsters suggested that maybe Connor had won after all. Why had his connection to her failed?

She pulled a large piece of sculpted obsidian out of her satchel and used it to cast her Builder senses west, pushing herself farther than she ever had. For a long moment, she felt nothing, but then sensed a glimmer at the outermost edges of her range. Was it Connor? He was wearing a couple defensive mechanicals that she doubted he'd triggered.

Yes, it felt like the foam defense she'd worked into his belt. She sensed nothing else, but reached through the obsidian and activated that defensive mechanical. It might help.

She also redirected Sucker Punch back at Connor. She wasn't a hundred percent healed yet, but she felt remarkably good. She feared he needed the healing more than she did.

* * *

Hamish swooped over the battlefield, exulting. The elfonnel were down! Too many Battalions had been ripped apart, too many soldiers killed on the ground, but the battle was over! He was wearing one of his replacement suits, fully armed, stocked with every mechanical he could need.

The sky was full of Jean's Mender and Render flights as they deployed to tend the many wounded, reinforced by a huge hive swarm of tiny mechanicals delivering healing, sharing water, and identifying injured who needed more attention. Jean led them, flying Hamish's spare suit, her quartzite-magnified voice echoing over the quiet valley.

Her gentle voice carried to every ear, gently urging. *"Please rest. Let us help you."*

Hamish grinned. Lady Jean was about to win another battle all by herself.

He spotted Kilian standing atop the rubble pile that had been the earthbound, and banked in that direction. Ivor stood beside Kilian, along with General Rosslyn. They eyed each other warily, but neither attacked. Aifric sped up to the group on fracked legs and stopped beside Kilian, who draped an arm over her shoulder.

That was a new development, and Hamish approved. Battle sometimes helped people see what was most important.

Hamish landed near Kilian just as Rory and Anika trooped up to join them. They were both battered, covered in mud, but grinning widely. Rory slapped Hamish on the shoulder hard enough to make him stumble and declared, "That was a bash fight to remember!"

"The fighting is over, but the danger is not past," Kilian said, his expression concerned. He pointed west.

They all turned, and Hamish blinked a couple of times. Everyone had seen that incredible flash of light, but could storm clouds really grow so fast. "Is that another assault from the queen?"

"No. She created the storm, but I do not sense her commanding it now," Kilian said. "She doesn't need to. That storm is stronger than any I've ever felt. It's not natural, and it's coming fast. It's got the energy to finish off both of our armies. It'll hit soon. We need to get everyone under cover."

"Is Connor okay?" Hamish asked.

Kilian hesitated, then said, "I don't know."

"But the elfonnel are gone. That means he defeated them, defeated the queen," Rosslyn said, her tone awed.

"Let's hope so. Now move! Aifric, contact those Battalions and get them to land, or that storm will finish them off. Ivor, Rosslyn, we have troops both north and south of here that need protecting."

The two generals shared a look and nodded in unison. Rosslyn said, "My teams will take the south."

"I've got the north," Ivor said, and they split apart, calling orders.

Kilian turned to Hamish, but Hamish held up a hand and said, "I'm going to find Connor."

"I can move faster," Kilian said.

"But the people need you. They'll all listen to you, not to me. He's my best friend, and I will find him." Hamish activated thrusters and turned west.

"Don't do anything stupid," Kilian called after him.

As if he would.

Hamish activated every thruster and shot toward the storm. The wind met him head on, rapidly intensifying as the storm rushed toward them faster than a fracked Strider, its front face a wall of black clouds, sheeting rain, and endless lightning. Hamish hated the idea of plunging into that maelstrom, but Connor was in there, maybe wounded. Maybe worse.

He had to know.

"You're going to owe me one for this," Hamish muttered as he tensed against the expected impact and shot into the leading edge of the storm.

All light winked out as he was consumed by pitch black clouds. Winds ripped at him from every side, spinning and tumbling him wildly, despite firing every directional thruster. Rain and snow and ice pelted him so hard he cried out from flashes of pain right through his armor. He distinctly felt several hardened granite leaves of his suit crack under brutal impacts. His facemask iced over, and the temperature plummeted.

Within seconds, he had no idea where he was, or which was up as he tumbled helplessly, shouting with fear and exhilaration.

It was incredible.

Hamish had never felt anything like it, never been so completely helpless in the face of nature's raw fury. He wished he could dedicate the time to fully enjoy the intense experience, maybe rise to a few thousand feet, shut off his thrusters for a moment, and see what the storm could do.

But Connor was in there, and he didn't have a suit. So Hamish activated blind coal for a moment and slipped into a pocket of absolute calm, sliding through the wind and storm and clouds and lightning. He realized he had twisted head down and was blindly accelerating toward a fatal impact with the ground.

He straightened out and cast his Builder senses out into the storm, but felt nothing. So he dropped blind coal and tried pushing ahead.

Again the storm seized him and threw him wildly about. Within seconds he lost all sense of direction again, and once more had to tap blind coal. This time he was pointed north instead of west. Annoyed, he had to admit he couldn't fly through that storm, so dropped to the ground. He didn't have enough blind coal to simply use it non-stop, but crashing into the ground wouldn't help.

Even braced with feet on the ground, Hamish had to trigger a thruster on his back to stay upright. The storm tore at him, trying to knock him off his feet. Debris flashed past, including uprooted trees and boulders that threatened to smash him flat. The storm was by far the most powerful tempest he'd ever heard of.

Hamish pressed ahead anyway. He tried jumping, using thrusters to move forward faster, but as soon as he left the ground, he was flung about so wildly, he usually lost more ground than he gained.

In frustration, he dropped to the ground, lying prone, and activated a quartzite shield just above his back. That blocked most of the storm, and he managed to accelerate by activating thrusters and flying inches above the ground. He collided with rocks and trees a lot, but added quickened basalt along his chest, which helped him slide over obstacles better. Then he gritted his teeth against the bumpy ride and half flew, had slid over the ground, heading ever west through the raging storm.

After what seemed an eternity, he finally sensed a bit of obsidian in the distance, slightly to his right. Banking in that direction, he found it a moment later.

Connor.

He lay in a hollow in the rough ground, entirely encased in shock-foam. Hamish leaned over him, cracking open the blue foam over Connor's face to check if he was breathing.

He was.

Hamish sagged with relief. He wasn't sure how he would have handled it if he'd found Connor dead. His best friend was alive, if battered. The shock foam had saved his life.

It was a newer defensive mechanical, built using Althin chemicals similar to Pedra's spittle, but less sticky. It tasted better too. When activated, foam expanded all around the person, padding them and protecting from falls or other blunt trauma. They hadn't figured out easy ways to extract soldiers from it, so it wasn't yet widely distributed, but Verena had added it to Connor's armor since he could usually use his multiple affinities to rip or burn it off.

Hamish figured he could when he awakened, but he wasn't sure when that might be. It looked like Connor had passed out, and the winds had tumbled him until he wedged into that hollow. The storm was still raging, but in that protected space, it wasn't so bad.

Hamish had planned to carry Connor back to Lossit so Aifric or Jean could tend to him, but he doubted they'd make it back through the storm, not with Connor unconscious. They'd have to ride it out in the hollow.

So he sealed the top of the hollow with another quartzite shield, making a little cave. If only he could still activate marble to generate some heat. There was plenty of wood debris caught in the hollow along with Connor, so he used some soapstone to pull the water out of it, then made a cheery fire the old fashioned way, with diorite.

The fire quickly warmed up the freezing air, and he added a couple pieces of activated limestone for extra light, transforming the barren hollow into an almost homey-feeling space. Only then did he set about peeling Connor out of that protective foam.

Connor didn't look so good. He was pale, his face drawn with exhaustion, but he didn't look wounded. Hamish saw no blood, but Connor's skin was cold and his breathing seemed shallow. Most of his clothing was gone, and what was left was so tattered, Hamish felt less ashamed of ending up in only his smallclothes for his duel against Aonghus.

Eating something would help, so Hamish used the fire to cook a few omelets. Connor always liked those, and the savory aroma filled their little protected cave, easing some of Hamish's concern. He settled back beside Connor, content to wait for his friend to wake up. In the meantime, he managed to eat all of the omelets, along with a dozen smashpacked desserts. Fighting was hard work, and worry took a lot out of a guy.

After licking his fingers from a particularly tasty smashpacked cake, Hamish nudged Connor and said, "Don't sleep too long or there won't be anything left."

CHAPTER SIXTY-SEVEN
The Price of Victory

Jean moved through the dim, cave-like shelter, packed with soldiers and wounded, all sheltering from the storm raging outside. The remaining nine Battalions had battled the leading edge of the storm to land in a tight-packed line, pointing length-wise west to east, with their eastern edges propped up on thick banks of ice raised by Kilian and the companies of Spitters.

The resulting sloped roofs provided just enough shelter for all the soldiers remaining in the valley, including the hundreds of wounded that Jean's flights and drone mechanicals had gathered up and rushed under cover. She still worried they must have missed some, and the thought of men and women dying in the brutal storm kept her glancing toward the softly glowing outer edge of the shelter, formed by Builder shieldstones.

It was a hard fact of life that all Healers had to accept, but she still hated that she could not save everyone. With her powerful sandstone affinity, coupled with her long experience, there were few injuries or sicknesses she could not successfully treat, but she felt driven to learn more, to do more.

There was a lot to do already. She still wore the borrowed battle suit, and she'd activated several small pieces of limestone to provide light. More than one wounded soldier had remarked that she looked like a beacon of hope moving among them, and she did everything in her power to provide that hope to the suffering.

Enough Healers worked among the wounded that the initial frenzy to stabilize everyone was over, and she had transitioned to coordinating efforts of her flight teams. Mender flight Healers were busy, supported by full staffs, and Rafford was doing a remarkable job with Render flight and their semi-autonomous summoned limbs, despite the loss of slate. Some of their summoned limbs failed or performed at much lower mobility, but they were working hard to reconfigure those. The slender Sapper wore his grief at the loss of Ilse openly, and Jean appreciated that.

She could not mourn yet, would not allow herself to weep for the dead until the living were cared for. She paused near a bonfire, one of a dozen that Rory had ordered built throughout the shelter, made with salvaged wood from the Battalions. The fires helped push back the frigid cold and cheered weary hearts.

Above her, the Battalion creaked and groaned as the insane storm ripped at it. Anything smaller would have been swept away by the hurricane winds. Erich had risked a peek outside earlier, and confirmed that one superstructure had collapsed under the onslaught. Thinking of the storm made her think of Hamish and Connor. They were still out there, and her fear for them grew stronger and colder with each passing moment. How could they survive such a tempest? She had tried contacting Hamish via speakstone, but got no response.

It had to be interference from the storm.

Verena stopped beside her and pushed hair from her face. She still looked tired from her terrible injuries, but the flood of Sucker Punch healing had done wonders to restore her. She wore a spare uniform that was a bit too large for her, making her look younger and more vulnerable, but she'd insisted that she needed something to do to keep from worrying about Connor. Jean had assigned her to assist Render flight.

"Have you heard anything yet?" Verena asked softly, her eyes full of worry.

"Not yet." Jean bet Verena was calling via speakstone every minute, and she had far better range than Jean.

Verena straightened her shoulders and said with forced conviction, "We will as soon as the storm passes."

Jean gave her an encouraging hug, but was interrupted when Nicklaus landed beside them with a whoosh of thrusters. The boy pointed toward the raging storm beyond the outer shields. "I can go find them."

"Oh, no you don't," Verena said, holding Nicklaus with a firm gaze until he sighed and nodded. Then he jumped up, lifting his legs, and activating some secondary thrusters to catch him half reclined in the air, as if he was sitting on an invisible chair.

"How is everyone else doing?" Jean asked to take the boy's mind off of the temptation to disobey again and rush out into the storm.

He started rolling back in a slow, controlled reverse somersault as he gave his report. "Everyone's secure. Ivor and Aifric got everyone on the north road into the river and made a cave in the water. Not even this storm can get them down there. Lady Shona was making a speech, so I stopped listening."

"I'm still amazed you could reach them," Jean said. "The storm is blocking all my attempts."

"I've got the best speakstones," Nicklaus said simply. "Air taught me how." His expression darkened and he crossed his arms, scowling as he spun backward again. "Then they went and lied and got angry and hurt people."

Jean placed a comforting hand on his arm as he came around again, making him bob in the air. "Even immortal elementals can make bad choices sometimes."

He gave her a serious look. "Bad choices have consequences, Lady Jean."

His expression fell, and she bet he was thinking of Ilse and her brave stand against Aonghus. She quickly banished thoughts of Aonghus, though. She had promised not to let his memory hold any power over her any more, and she intended to keep that promise.

"What about Rosslyn?" Verena prodded.

"She's kind of grumpy. I don't think she likes admitting she lost. I talked with Lady Ailsa mostly. She's nice and she's real smart. Did you know she's Connor's aunt?" He stopped his rotation, head cocked to the side in a thoughtful expression. "She seemed to handle serving the queen better than most people. She didn't seem crazy or evil at all."

Jean smiled. Nicklaus was an exuberant kid, and little fooled him. She was happy Ailsa had turned up, and hadn't gotten killed in the fighting. "She's one of the best people. She's a friend."

The boy started slowly rolling backward again, but continued talking as if that was normal. "They're protecting the armies south of here too. They didn't think of making a cave in the river, but they pulled water up to some hills to make caves that way. They're not as good, but they're holding. General Wolfram is with Lady Ailsa, and they were talking a lot about accords and agreements and surrendering, or something." He yawned. "It was boring. Christin will probably want me to write a scroll about it."

Nicklaus floated away, rising to inspect the stowed cannons protruding from the underside of the Battalion. Jean left Verena watching him to make sure he didn't accidentally trigger all the cannons and blow up everyone huddling beneath the Battalions. She returned to her rounds, checking patients, trying to ease suffering, and trying not to think of Hamish and Connor lost in that terrible storm.

It took two more eternal hours for the storm to finally break.

The clouds parted and blessed light returned. It was weak, but so very welcome. Although gusts of wind and brief, intense showers persisted, the main storm had passed, churning to the east. Jean immediately ordered scout flights to sweep the valley for any other survivors they'd missed, although hopes of finding any were slim.

She emerged with Verena and Nicklaus to inspect the damage. The ground was muddy, so Jean hummed to activate thrusters and rose up to the deck of the Battalions. Nicklaus swooped around her like a sparrow, and Verena followed, using a single quartzite block as a thruster. She made the tricky maneuver look easy as she gracefully stepped onto the tilting deck.

The first Battalion was a mess, the huge deck scoured clean. Any mechanicals or equipment left on the deck was simply gone, ripped away by the ferocious storm. The superstructure was leaning noticeably to the port side, and the steel glass windows were scarred and pitted from the abuse. The other Battalions, sitting in their long row, were all equally battered, and two of them had lost their superstructures altogether.

The valley was completely destroyed. Only occasional, broken posts marked the location where the town of Lossit had stood. The elfonnel had smashed most of it, then the storm had scoured the land clean. Crops were gone, fields ravaged by wind and rain and hail.

Some battlefield debris remained, particularly the heavy Thunder Towers, although those had all been tipped over by the raging winds. The only good effect of the storm were the many waterfalls thundering off the high ground to the west. They looked triple their previous size, swollen with recent rains, and the lakes at the base of the cliff were flooding onto the valley.

Many of the bodies of the dead were gone, either buried or swept away by the storm. Jean made a mental note to send flights out to scout the lands to the east, and scan the river to see if they could recover any of them for proper burial. She was glad the lands directly east of Lossit were only lightly populated. They would need to send relief flights to check for survivors in the small communities nestled in those eastern hills.

Humming to herself to activate thrusters, Jean headed for the badly canting top deck of the Battalion superstructure for a better view. Nicklaus arrived first and shouted, "Look!"

She and Verena joined him, and she immediately spotted the figure flying toward them, carrying something large on his back. Changing her tune, she pulled down the faceplate of her helmet and activated the long vision view. The distant figure grew rapidly larger in her enhanced view and her heart soared.

"Hamish!"

"He's got Connor!" Verena cried a moment later. She had donned a pair of long-vision goggles, and joy radiated off of her like heat from an oven, but her smile was tempered by worry. Connor wasn't moving.

Why was he slumped over Hamish's shoulder instead of flying on his own? He flew better than anyone. He must be injured.

Was he dead?

She banished the vile thought and fought down the fear that threatened to take her breath away, forcing the same clinical calm over herself she always sought when treating new injuries. She would jump to no conclusions until she had facts.

Nicklaus shot away toward Hamish, shouting greeting and asking a dozen questions as he swooped around them. Hamish spotted Jean and Verena and banked in their direction to land atop the Battalion superstructure beside them.

Jean rushed to help him lower Connor to the ground, and Verena grabbed Connor's head, calling out, "Connor? Connor, are you all right?"

He groaned and blinked open his eyes. Jean felt weak with relief to see him alive. She seized Hamish and hugged him tight. He pushed up his faceplate, his face weary, but happy. She removed her helmet and kissed him. "What's Connor's status?"

"I'm alive, I think," Connor said weakly, lying on the deck, head in Verena's lap. She gently stroked his hair, beaming with joy and clearly fighting back tears.

Nicklaus swooped in to hover nearby. "Connor, you missed it. We had a battle with big armies, and two whole elfonnel, and the elementals tried tricking me."

He smiled wearily. "I've got a pretty good idea about what happened. Can you go get Kilian for me?"

"Already here," Kilian said as he vaulted over the rail from below. "How are you?"

"Queen Dreokt is gone, and the elementals are sealed away from our world," Connor said softly in an exhausted voice. Jean sensed a long, difficult tale concealed in that simple statement. The words filled her like the rising of the sun, and she grinned.

Verena exclaimed, "I knew it! The sculpted stone was the key, wasn't it?"

"It played a part, but not the way we expected."

Kilian dropped to one knee, looking as shaken as Jean had ever seen. He breathed, "She's really gone? I almost don't believe it."

"Believe it. She made it harder than we ever feared, and she was insulting me right up to the end before the storm consumed her and dissipated her elfonnel." Connor's eyes drooped and his voice fell to a whisper. He looked so exhausted, Jean dropped to the deck beside him and reached out a hand, calling for her sandstone affinity.

She grimaced as her healing senses poured through him. Connor was whole, but weak. His entire body felt somehow thin, as if on the point of consuming itself just to survive. He'd spent all of his natural energy and then some. She poured in healing to help, but said, "You need rest and food."

Hamish chuckled. "He's already eaten twenty-nine smashpacked meals and every dessert I had left."

"Not that you had many of those by the time I woke up," Connor said with a weary smile, not opening his eyes. He seemed willing to lie there in Verena's lap all day.

"You did it," Verena said, leaning down to kiss him gently. "I feared . . ."

Connor opened his eyes for her and stroked her cheek. "So did I. The price was high." His eyes clouded, and Jean longed to hear the full story. It would come, but not immediately. He needed rest, and they needed to mobilize everyone to deal with the aftermath of the storm. The aftermath of the queen's demise would rock Obrion to its roots.

"Where's Evander?" Hamish asked.

Both Verena and Kilian looked down, fresh sorrow on their faces, but Connor tapped the side of his head. "The queen destroyed his elfonnel, but I saved at least part of him here with me."

"What?" Kilian exclaimed, looking stunned.

Connor shrugged. "One of the things no one could have predicted. We were connected with chert when she killed him, and I managed to draw him into my mind with me. He's here, at least for a time." He cocked his head, as if listening and added, "He just told me to tell you that sunsets draw the blanket of night over the world, but the sight of a lighthouse through a storm gladdens the sailor's heart."

Kilian chuckled. "We're going to have to talk this over with Aifric."

That was a good idea. She might know how to keep Evander alive in Connor's head.

Verena was staring at Connor in wide-eyed surprise and whispered, "He's alive, but stuck in your head?"

Connor nodded, and Jean wondered if he'd wondered yet how the situation would affect Verena? Would Evander remain with him all his life? Would his presence affect their relationship? How would she feel if Hamish showed up one day and announced another person had taken up permanent residence inside his head?

Hamish grinned. "Reality sure is weird around this group."

"You're wrung out, Connor. When you spoke of cost, were you injured too, or was Evander's death the sacrifice you spoke of?" Jean asked. She wasn't about to let them talk Connor to death before confirming he didn't have some other obscure injury.

His expression fell, a look of sorrow on his face. "I sacrificed most of my affinities."

"What?" Verena exclaimed. Hamish gaped, and Kilian blinked in surprise. He leaned closer and said, "I never would have thought of that."

Jean wouldn't have either. They'd focused so much on building new affinities, she had never considered the alternative. The thought of losing her precious affinities terrified her, and she'd only just received hers. She asked, "How did destroying your affinities help?"

"And how could you even do that?" Hamish demanded.

Connor tried explaining, but Jean wasn't sure she really understood the concepts, even though she tapped obsidian to quicken her thoughts. Hamish looked confused, and Verena looked overwhelmed by the story. Kilian seemed to understand, though.

Nicklaus hovered over them all and exclaimed, "So when I broke mine, I showed you how to do it, and that saved your life?"

Connor smiled up at him. "Saved everyone."

"Ha!" Nicklaus laughed, rolling into another backward somersault. "I knew I must have done it for a reason."

"I'm glad you did," Connor said, then sighed. "You did it by accident. I smashed mine on purpose."

Jean said, "I don't understand everything you said about fission and affinity energy wrapped up inside your bridges. I'm just glad it worked. Do you have any left?"

"Thank the Tallan, I do have some," he said. "I kept obsidian and chert and pumice, and I've got the higher-level aspects to limestone."

"So you can't manipulate light, but you can control energy?" Verena asked.

He nodded. "I bet I can figure out how to control at least some light, since it's a form of energy. I can also still manage mirage, sensory deprivation, and death beam, I think."

"And we used to think limestone was lame," Hamish said, chuckling.

Jean was glad Connor hadn't lost everything, but figured it would take a while for him to sort everything out. He was still more than a normal Petralist, but was no longer the full Blood of the Tallan. She doubted he understood the full ramifications of what he'd done, and was grateful it looked like they'd have time to sort it all out.

"I still have porphyry, sort of, but I'm out of powder," Connor added, looking pained by that. Porphyry had helped him several times, but it was so dangerous, maybe he was better off without it.

Hamish asked softly, "So you've lost all your tertiaries?"

"The four angry ones, although I have higher-level serpentinite. I'm not sure it would be good for me to have kept the others. The elementals are pretty mad with me."

"I've felt resistance from them every time I tapped soapstone, but they haven't actively interfered," Kilian noted.

The implications of that made Jean pale. Slate and marble and serpentinite were gone, the affinities broken, but if Air and Water tried interfering with tertiary Petralists, that could undermine the entire ruling structure of both Obrion and Granadure.

"I bet they would if they could, but almost everyone is limited to red-frequency sylfaen energy, and that power is governed by the laws of nature," Connor said. "They can't block us from accessing that part of their power, but they might cause trouble in the green."

"Few people will understand the reasons behind all of this," Verena said.

"Good. They can't get into trouble that way," Connor said, then grimaced. "I can't believe I said that. I sound like Queen Dreokt."

"She might have started with good intentions, but she left those behind a long time ago," Kilian said softly.

Jean realized something and asked, "Connor, you had to sacrifice granite?"

He nodded, looking so sad Jean wanted to cry. Verena stroked his face, and Kilian grimaced. "I can't imagine losing my first affinity. Having to shatter it on purpose would be . . . difficult."

Connor nodded and clearly appreciated the fact that they understood in small part the horrible sacrifice he'd been forced to make. Jean was happy he'd survived, and he seemed to be coping with the loss well, but she would monitor him carefully. Inner trauma like that could be as debilitating as physical trauma.

"Oh, no. You lost sandstone too!" she realized with a sense of horror.

He nodded again and sighed. "I think I'm still in shock. Losing sandstone was as hard as losing granite."

Hamish groaned, looking anguished. Jean appreciated his compassion until he said, "That means glutton crafting is gone forever too."

Connor laughed, and Jean groaned. Leave it to Hamish to equate Connor's unparalleled sacrifice with its effect on dinner.

"Basalt?" Kilian asked gently.

Connor sighed again. "I managed to keep the higher-level of basalt. Not sure how that will affect speed, but I've got access to stilling."

Verena kissed his forehead and wiped at her eyes. "I was hoping to get to run with you again. We never tried superfracking together."

"It's all gone," Connor said, his voice thick with emotion. Maybe thinking about all he'd lost wasn't healthy.

Hamish exclaimed, "Wait! Does this mean you can't loan affinities any more, or help create new ones?"

Connor frowned, thinking about that, and Verena asked, "Can't you recreate your affinities?"

That was a good idea, and it offered some hope to restore Connor to his full suite of powers, but he shook his head sadly. "I don't think so. I smashed them, Verena. I chose to break those affinities. I don't think I can ever get them back after making that choice."

"I believe you're right," Kilian said gravely. "We don't understand everything about affinities, but a choice like that cannot be undone."

"I'll have to experiment with helping others find new affinities," Connor added, brows furrowed in thought. "I still have chert and obsidian, but I'm lacking sandstone. I just don't know."

"That can wait until you've healed," Jean said firmly in her doctor voice. Connor had a tendency to jump into testing hypothetical questions with more enthusiasm than common sense sometimes.

Hamish blew out a breath and extended a hand down to Connor. "Can't let you lazy around all afternoon. We've got a lot of work to do before dinner."

"That's not what I meant," Jean protested. She'd planned to find Connor a place near one of the fires while they began clean-up.

"It works for me," Connor grinned, took Hamish's proffered hand, and let Hamish haul him to his feet.

Chapter Sixty-Eight
Kids Say the Darndest Things

Verena maneuvered her new Swift through the open double doors leading from the long balcony high on the wall of the palace of Crann, entering the enormous, vaulted ballroom on the top floor. Feeling her nimble craft under her fingers, responding instantly to her touch, helped her feel like her healing from the traumatic battle was finally complete.

She should probably stop wrecking her Swift. Hamish had jokingly suggested she number them to help him keep up with how many she'd crashed. Connor had suggested she try a different name. Maybe Swift was unlucky.

Not yet. Her Swift was as much a part of her as Hamish's battle suit was to him. She vowed to never wreck another one.

She also planned to continue making spares because life happened, and there were so many more upgrades she wanted to explore anyway. Verena landed the Swift, dropped the window shielding, and jumped out. She felt strong even without tapping the awesome power of granite. The week since the battle of Lossit valley had restored her to full health.

Most of the others were already gathered in the huge room, which they had appropriated as their command center. Tables and desks covered in parchment and scrolls clustered at the far side of the room, swarmed by officers, aides, and secretaries busy managing the unending challenges associated with running a vast military campaign.

Many of their troops had returned to Merkland, so that made some of the job easier. General Rory, with Anika and Erich were in charge of that northern army that included many of the Merkland troops, plus Arishat League forces. They bore with them many of the wounded and were protecting the northern border, as well as repairing damaged mechanicals, including five of the giant Battalions. Once those were air worthy again, they could deploy anywhere across Obrion as needed.

Lord Eoghan and Lady Fenella surrendered Crann as soon as the combined armies showed up. Under Ailsa's leadership, General Rosslyn had commanded her forces to cooperate. So far, no new fighting had broken out. It seemed even the queen's most ardent followers were content to wait and see if the queen returned. Most of the troops had taken the news of her death with joy and were happy to surrender.

Verena still scarce believed so many of their core team had survived the terrifying battle. Ilse had been like a sister, and Verena had broken down into tears many times in recent days, thinking of Ilse's valiant sacrifice.

Connor stood near the impressive waterfall feature in the center of the room with Kilian and Aifric. He spotted Verena and waved her over. She smiled to see him looking so recovered. A shadow of pain still lurked in his eyes, and they had talked for hours in recent days. The sacrifice of his affinities had torn him apart inside, and he still needed time to heal. She felt convinced that eventually, the fact that he still had some affinities would help him recover his optimism. He'd already managed to apply his higher-level basalt affinity internally and confirmed he could still frack. That had helped immensely, and no doubt he'd continue to find creative ways to utilize his other remaining affinities.

She gave Connor a kiss and slipped under his arm then asked, "What's going on? Aren't we supposed to be meeting with Shona and the others?"

The others were standing not far from the queen's great, pompous throne, near a long, gleaming wooden table cluttered with scrolls and maps.

"Soon. We were just checking how belligerent Water was feeling today," Kilian said.

Verena grimaced. "Still causing trouble?"

Aifric nodded, her voice shifting into the lovely accent of Nuzha, her Sehrazad mind-sister. "She resents our access worse than a tribe whose secret wells are breached, but she cannot prevent us." She flashed a white-toothed grin, and Verena was glad she seemed more relaxed around so many Obrioners. The fact that they'd defeated the queen's great army had left her in great spirits.

Kilian added, "It's all she has left. They're firmly shackled by the laws of nature again, and they hate it."

"They seem more firmly imprisoned than ever," Connor said. "It's like Porphyry drove them pretty far back out of green."

His description of Porphyry's action still puzzled Verena. She sensed that Porphyry was more than they had ever understood. If Connor could discover more power-grade porphyry, maybe they could investigate that. Then again, maybe the world was better off without anyone able to tap the dangerous stone.

"I had hoped they wouldn't be able to interfere," Connor added, glancing at the waterfall. Verena noted a brief look of longing on his face. The inability to sense water hurt him more than the loss of any of the other elements. She wished she could help.

"She'll calm down eventually," Kilian said. "Until then, we need to keep the advisory in place for all tertiaries to refrain from tapping their powers as much as possible."

"I hope that helps convince the high houses to accept terms for peace sooner," Verena said. In the last week, Spitters and Water Moccasins had struggled with wildly inconsistent responses from soapstone. Sometimes they got only a fraction of the effect they sought. Other times, they were flooded with ten times the amount they wanted. Several accidents had caused dozens of injuries. Water and Air were doing everything in their power to make life difficult for the Petralists who had blocked their escape.

"Ailsa has some ideas how to guarantee we get peace before beating down every high house," Kilian said. He extended an arm. Nuzha gave him a dazzling smile and took it, and the two headed toward the conference table. Ailsa was there already, along with Shona, Ivor, Hamish, Jean, Wolfram, and even General Rosslyn. Fyodor was sitting in for the Arishat League. It was shaping up to be a day full of vital, but probably boring discussions.

A laughing Nicklaus flew right through the waterfall from the far side, emerging from it without even making a splash.

"Don't waste blind coal," Verena chided.

"You want me to train, don't you?" he asked with that "I'm inno-cent" look that was such a blatant lie, but so cursed cute, she hadn't figured out a good defense against it.

Kilian called back to his many-times great nephew. "Train, but don't waste blind coal."

"Fine," he said, rolling his eyes at the limitation. "Will you come see my underwater secret mission boat, Uncle Kilian?"

"Absolutely. Later."

Nicklaus sighed grandly, but he wouldn't complain too loudly or Kilian would threaten to send him back to Merkland again. Christin had been frantic with worry when they contacted her to let her know Nicklaus was safe, but Kilian had insisted Nicklaus remain close to him until they confirmed the elementals posed no more direct threat to him.

Nicklaus flew in lazy circles around Verena and Connor. "Water yelled at me this morning again."

"That's almost every day," Connor commented.

Nicklaus nodded. "I just call her a liar, and she sulks. The others don't talk to me as often, but they're still angry too."

"You'll tell us everything they say," Verena reminded him. She still wondered why they kept communicating with him, but figured it had to do with his almost-ascension. He'd touched greater power and drawn closer to the elementals than almost anyone.

It was a terrifying thought.

Ever since that near-threshold event, Nicklaus had shown a significant increase in his Builder powers, and a remarkable understanding of the most complex mechanicals. He might not have completed his ascension, but he got close enough that he'd grown in ways they still hadn't yet quantified. She yearned for the time to spend testing and analyzing the boy with Hamish. They might learn so much.

"Of course," Nicklaus said, then grinned wickedly. "Even the curse words that Air taught me?"

Connor laughed, so Verena poked him in the ribs. He coughed and assumed an almost-serious expression. "Yes, you should. For pure documentation purposes, but make sure to forget them after you repeat them to me."

"I promise," Nicklaus said sincerely. The little fibber.

That ongoing contact with the elementals represented a potential terrible threat. He was so brilliant, there was a risk Nicklaus could again design a mechanical powerful enough to push him to that Builder threshold. The recent battle was fresh enough that he seemed to understand the danger of such a disastrous idea, but time might dull his memory and his anger at the elementals might eventually be overruled by his insatiable curiosity.

Verena wasn't sure what they were going to do long term, but they had to make sure no one ever again approached that threshold. She hated the idea of suppressing information, but how to guard its use was a tricky question.

Connor turned them toward the conference table, but Nicklaus turned upside down as he floated next to Verena and asked, "Do you want to hear everything that serpentinite tells me too?"

They both turned to stare, and Verena exclaimed, "What?"

"She talks a lot, and most of what she says is silly." His smooth forehead crinkled in thought as his face slowly reddened from hanging upside down in the air so long. "She's not like the others. She thinks they're old meanies. Sometimes I think she's really young, like me!"

He seemed to really enjoy that thought. Verena glanced to Connor, not sure how to respond. He looked shocked, but asked, "When did Serpentinite start talking with you?"

Nicklaus shrugged and started air somersaulting again. It was one of his favorite hobbies when forced to hover in place for long. "During the big storm. At first she seemed really surprised I could hear her."

"I've never heard her. The other elementals said she hadn't reached consciousness," Connor said thoughtfully.

Nicklaus nodded. "Yeah, they're real mad that she's around. She said she followed my bridges." He giggled and added, "How can she do that, Connor? I broke all of my bridges, didn't I?"

He didn't respond right away, but looked lost in thought. Verena said, "Maybe when you touched that threshold you helped her find you."

"Maybe. She said I'm the very first person she talked to, and she likes me. She has so many questions."

"What kind of questions?" Verena asked quickly. She didn't trust the elementals, and hearing of a new one suddenly appearing and trying to make friends with Nicklaus made her very suspicious.

"Everything. She gets excited about everything. It's like she's been asleep her whole life. I told her not to trust the liars, and she promised to warn the others."

"Others?" Connor asked, snapping out of his reverie.

"Yeah. She has some other friends who are just waking up too. They're sleepy and they haven't found the bridge that she used yet, but she's sure they will."

That worried Verena. Four angry elementals were more than enough trouble. They'd known about serpentinite, although with the affinity broken for most people, she doubted serpentinite could really cause too much damage.

Connor took the news very differently. His eyes lit up and he asked, "Did she tell you anything about her new friends?"

"Only Metal. She said he's nice, but a little proud because he's so shiny. I'll tell you what he says when I hear from him, okay?"

"Make sure you do," Connor said, trying to sound casual, but his arm around Verena's shoulder tensed. He looked like he had ten thousand questions, and she realized why he seemed so excited. He couldn't restore broken bridges, but that didn't mean he couldn't establish affinities with new elements.

The potential was astounding, although tons of challenges rose to pester her with dozens of questions she couldn't answer. How would they find those elements? What stones would their powers filter through? How could they figure that out? Could Connor or Nicklaus converse with them before a convergence point was established. Did they want to?

"Okay, bye," Nicklaus said abruptly and accelerated away fast, shouting, "Hamish, let's race around the palace before you fall asleep."

"I'm going to a meeting," Hamish replied, sounding amused.

"Yeah. You always fall asleep," Nicklaus shouted at him before zooming around the waterfall again.

Verena said, "New elements. How is it possible?"

"I don't know," Connor admitted, looking more enthusiastic than she'd seen since before the battle. "We're going to have to spend a lot of time with Nicklaus."

She nodded. That boy might have lost his affinities, but he still held the keys to so many secrets in that little head of his.

CHAPTER SIXTY-NINE
Cake Is a Better Motivator than Sticks

Ailsa called the meeting to order, and Connor grinned to see his aunt taking charge. She was the secret mastermind behind much of their success, so she deserved the honor of hosting the meeting with so many of their core team.

She smiled at the gathered company and said, "I am grateful that so many of us have survived, and I am optimistic about the future of Obrion."

"We won the most important battle, but we've still got most of the high houses arrayed against us," Shona reminded them.

"For now," Ailsa said, and Connor was convinced she'd already plotted the best course for dealing with every single one of them.

Ailsa glanced at Aifric, who sat beside Kilian, then at Connor, who sat opposite them. "First, I hear there's an update on Evander's situation?"

Aifric grinned, and Connor smiled with her, happy they started the meeting with the good news. Her features shifted slightly and Student Eighteen took over. "Absolutely. We've determined that it should be possible to transfer Evander into the empty mind of one of the queen's servants."

Most of those gathered around the table hadn't heard the news yet, and they all cheered. Connor felt proud, and immensely relieved that they'd figured out a solution. Evander's death had been very traumatic for Connor as much as for Evander since they'd been linked through chert. He'd feared if the giant lingered in his mind too long that he would expire for good, and he'd have to deal with the man's death all over again. Evander was not living in a full partition like all of Aifric's mind sisters, and Student Eighteen had confirmed what Connor suspected. Evander could not survive like that for long.

They'd discussed several potential options, including creating a mind partition for him, but that was a high risk option that Connor was happy they hadn't needed to use. He liked Evander, was immensely enjoying the close connection they shared, but couldn't quite imagine living the rest of his life with Evander sharing his mind.

Evander himself had proposed using a mind-wiped servant. Their minds were like empty vessels, waiting to be populated. Connor, Evander, and Student Eighteen had spent hours probing a couple of those servants, discussing ways to make it work.

Student Eighteen briefly outlined their findings. "Evander is not locked into a partition like we are." She tapped the side of her head. "His consciousness is untethered, so therefore mobile. The mind-wiped subjects we probed are empty of identity and individual thought. For all intents and purposes, they are brain dead, kept moving and obeying specific commands by Queen Dreokt's implanted orders. We can remove those and transfer Evander into the mind instead. He should be able to take control and make the host his permanent home."

"Children grow into adults, while the elderly lay down in the long sleep, but the cycle of rain continues for all time," Evander said in Connor's mind.

He smiled, sensing some of the obscure meanings conveyed by the message. He was glad Evander embraced the idea of finding a new body to call his own. Most people would be so traumatized by losing their first, Connor doubted they'd be capable of attempting the bizarre solution.

Much of Evander's knowledge had begun seeping into his own subconsciousness, making him vastly smarter than before. Evander was an understated genius, and they'd spent a lot of time over the past week in deep conversation. They could converse for what felt like hours in a matter of minutes, and Connor would miss that close association.

Not enough to keep Evander in his head forever, though. Verena had been very supportive, but he sensed her discomfort over the idea of Evander hitching a ride on their planned life together.

Ailsa said, "Very good. I know a man who will serve as an excellent candidate. He's in Donleavy, but used to be a Sentry, so I like to think that if he understood what was happening, he would approve the transfer."

She then glanced to Ivor and asked, "How are arrangements for troops progressing?"

"The populace seems very agreeable," Ivor reported and turned to Rosslyn. "It appears most of your troops welcome the transition of leadership from the queen to Ailsa and yourself."

Rosslyn nodded. "Indeed, most of us served out of fear. I've been encouraging my troops to keep an open mind until we see if promises of peace prove true."

Connor was finding that he liked Rosslyn more and more. She had agreed to work together for peace, but her words reminded them subtly that she would hold them to promises that they intended to seek a peaceful transition to a legal monarch.

He sincerely hoped they would. They had to portray strong force in Crann to ensure the critical stronghold surrendered quickly. Hopefully that would generate even more momentum for their cause. They'd arrived with a huge army and the four most operational Battalions, packed with all of the Thunder Towers and battle mechanicals they could salvage. It made for an intimidating display.

"Now, let's review troop distribution, communications channels, and priorities," Ailsa said.

Connor stifled a groan as the meeting moved into the boring parts. Shona and Ailsa did much of the talking, with Rosslyn and Ivor adding a lot of information too. They discussed every high house and their leaders, their known troop strength, their alliances and likely positions regarding succession.

Those four seemed to thrive on the complexity, and Verena too looked enthralled. Kilian seemed to grasp every nuance, and Aifric's lips moved silently as she conversed with her mind sisters. Wolfram seemed to know all the players too, and contributed lots of information his spies had gathered over the years. Fyodor mostly listened, but Connor didn't doubt the Arishat League were already preparing three dozen treaties they'd want signed by Obrion's new leadership. Hamish had slipped the faceplate of his helmet closed and somehow turned it opaque. He was sitting upright, but Connor would bet the next six months of desserts that Hamish had already fallen asleep.

Eventually they focused on the question of candidates for succession. Unfortunately, it was abundantly clear that many of the high houses would want to make a play for the throne. The queen's passing created an enormous power vacuum. Word would reach them soon, if they hadn't heard already, and they'd begin negotiating deals and alliances at the speed of fracked Striders.

"I have no doubt that Lord Eoghan and Lady Fenella have already sent out runners to their closest allies," Shona said.

"I would be disappointed in them if they hadn't," Ailsa said, then turned to Rosslyn. "Just as you've already sent messengers to your father. If he has not yet made an attempt to seize the throne, I would be surprised."

Rosslyn didn't try to lie, but met Ailsa's gaze and shrugged. "Do you blame me, or him? I must see to the continuation of my house. He's one of the queen's high counselors, and one of the most influential high lords. He's a logical choice."

"Except his rule would guarantee a long and protracted war," Ailsa replied. She did not look upset by Rosslyn's actions. She knew Rosslyn and her father, High Lord Feichin. She had worked closely with them both for months. Connor didn't know the man well, but he'd heard enough to believe Ailsa. Feichin was powerful, and he would fight to maintain the status quo. He would see the revolution as a threat to his power, the rise of Guardians as a direct threat to his house.

The problem was, most of the high lords and ladies would feel the same way. The long discussion would have confirmed Connor's fears that they were indeed facing a long, bloody conflict except for one vital advantage they hadn't yet discussed. He and Evander had considered it in one of their long inner dialogues, seated in comfortable chairs in Evander's secret inner library.

"All of this information is good to know," he said, joining the conversation for the first time in over half an hour, "but we can't ignore the leverage we have over everyone. With slate and marble gone, soapstone is the last major tertiary battle stone."

"Not so major at the moment," Kilian admitted.

"I'm sure the elementals will settle down eventually," Connor said, "but if it comes to a fight, we'll all tempt soapstone. We can't afford not to."

General Wolfram leaned forward and said, "You speak of threatening to break soapstone."

The clever general didn't look surprised by the idea, and no doubt he had already begun planning how to leverage their forces without Water Moccasins and Spitters. Most of the others didn't take the news so well. Kilian looked pained, but resigned.

Looking horrified, Rosslyn exclaimed, "You can't!"

"Thank you for making my point," Connor said. He understood her fear better than anyone, but he'd already lost all of his tertiaries. Spitters and Pathfinders, Water Moccasins and Longseers were the last of the mighty tertiaries, and they had to feel terrified of losing their affinities too. The fact that no one outside of their core team knew how the others had been broken would fuel fear and rumors.

"I have considered the idea," Ailsa confirmed what Connor had suspected. "I would prefer not to have to use that leverage."

"Unless there is no other alternative," Verena said.

Ivor sighed, looking as pained as Kilian and Rosslyn. He'd already lost marble. Aifric was muttering softly to herself, probably holding a conference to keep the Spitters among her mind sisters from angrily joining the conversation.

Shona's face lit up and she exclaimed, "It wouldn't be all bad. Think about it. We could settle the entire war with an even bigger bash fight than Lossit valley!"

All of the Boulders and Rumblers in the room perked up at that. There would be no one to interfere, to cut the bash fight short. Even Verena started nodding to herself, clearly tempted by the idea of joining a massive bash fight brawl.

Hamish chuckled. "Except then the war would last forever. You'd all find ways to keep extending the bash fight indefinitely."

Shona smiled and spread her hands in a helpless gesture. "I can think of worse futures."

"As tempting as that future might be, it is unlikely to deliver us the succession we hope for," Ailsa said apologetically. "Connor is right. The threat of breaking soapstone is a powerful weapon, but threats are less effective than gifts."

Hamish saluted. "Cake over sticks? I'd take cake any day."

Kilian rolled his eyes but said, "I concur. Let's go with cake. We can just as easily spread the knowledge that we know how my mother broke slate and marble, and that we possess the knowledge to restore those affinities."

That was a good point. Connor couldn't imagine a high house that wouldn't be immensely motivated by such a proposal.

"We can do that?" Rosslyn asked, sounding awed.

"Yes, we can," Ailsa stated. "Understanding this fact is one of the reasons I invited you to join our meeting today. I need you to know all the good we can bring to Obrion. I have also ensured that Lord Eoghan's spies working among our administration staff have also caught word of this vital piece of information."

"Already?" Jean asked with a grin.

"There is no time to waste. He will consider it a great coup, but I will carry this same secret to Donleavy and use it to help secure my position there. I leave at first light."

Connor blinked and sat up straighter, pushing his other worries aside. He hadn't expected her to leave the safety of the army. She'd just said she expected High Lord Feichin to try usurping the throne.

"They'll try to have you killed," Shona warned.

"Some will want to," Ailsa said calmly. "But they will not succeed. I will assume control as interim regent before Feichin or one of the others can consolidate their hold over Donleavy. I have not worked so hard for so long to prepare this nation for change only to face yet another tyrant."

She spoke with such conviction, Connor had no doubt she knew exactly what to do to get her way, but even with the leverage of knowing how to restore affinities, the others didn't look so convinced. It was a bold decision on her part. Usually she didn't step to the fore and take charge, but worked in the shadows, pulling strings and manipulating everything to her eventual planned outcome. If she felt seizing the throne during the transition was necessary, Connor pitied anyone who tried to stop her.

Because he would destroy them. No way would he let her strode alone and undefended into the heart of danger again. He might be missing most of his affinities, but he had enough to keep her safe.

"I will come with you," he stated, trying to project the same calm assurance she did. He did not plan to let anyone dissuade him.

"No, my boy, but I definitely need you to help," Ailsa said. Connor sighed. He knew better than to think he could argue Ailsa into changing her mind. Besides, her plan would no doubt be amazing. Even without obsidian, she was the most brilliant and devious person Connor knew.

So he asked, "What do you have in mind?"

"One of the greatest threats still hanging over every single high house is the threat of their own children rising against them and attempting to murder them if they surrender or embrace our revolution."

"That's right. The queen implanted mind bombs in the children," Shona said in a disgusted tone.

Connor agreed. Verena looked as horrified by that act of barbaric cowardice as he felt. Shona and Ailsa had survived in the queen's dangerous court with their minds intact, but the queen ensured loyalty of most of the other houses by that implied threat. It had proven incredibly successful too. Who would risk their children?

Ailsa continued. "It is their greatest fear, and our best opportunity to secure their gratitude and willingness to negotiate. If we can free their children from her mind bombs, plus promise to restore the broken affinities, we will not only demonstrate our power, but demonstrate it through compassion. I believe this will do more to secure our eventual victory than anything else."

"You can do that?" Rosslyn asked, emotion strong in her voice.

Ailsa gave her a compassionate smile. "I believe so, and I think we should start with your children, don't you?"

Rosslyn nodded, blinking rapidly as tears filled her eyes. She didn't seem able to speak for a moment, but finally managed to say, "Please."

Ailsa glanced at Connor and he said, "I'll do what I can."

Student Eighteen spoke up. "And I'll help."

Ailsa smiled warmly at her. "Thank you, my dear. I had hoped you would volunteer. Together, I believe you two will succeed, and that success will directly help our efforts to stop the war and bring reconciliation."

Ivor grinned. "And since you're the one directing Connor and Aifric, their success will secure your control over the throne until we can negotiate our treaties and choose a new monarch."

"Brilliant," Shona said. "I couldn't have orchestrated it better myself."

That was a high compliment. There was a time when Shona would have plotted feverishly to figure out how to orchestrate rising to the throne. Connor was so glad she had joined their side instead.

"I will have need of your skills soon enough, Lady Shona, have no fear," Ailsa told her. Connor wondered what she had planned for Shona. She'd worked to subtly influence Shona ever since Shona was summoned to Donleavy. She'd identified Shona as a potential ally long before Connor had believed it was possible.

Aunt Ailsa would make such a perfect interim regent. Whoever was eventually chosen as the new monarch would have to work extremely hard to keep up with the good she would accomplish.

"I will still need security to ensure my plans are not interfered with too much," Ailsa added and turned again to General Rosslyn. "If you will swear interim fealty to me, I invite you to choose a thousand trusted soldiers to form my personal guard."

Connor grinned. Simply brilliant. Ailsa had already sealed Rosslyn to her by promising to free her children, and now she was deftly taking an entire army under her command. She'd have to be careful not to get used to owning an army, though. Jean hadn't been able to get rid of hers, despite trying awful hard until she realized she deserved it and could do more good with her flights than anyone else.

Rosslyn beamed. "If no one objects?" She glanced around the table, letting the question hang in the air.

Kilian smiled with that roguish charm of his. "Ailsa, you're brilliant, and Rosslyn, you're a good girl. I believe you'll keep your word."

"Thank you," she said sincerely.

"Of course, if you betray Ailsa, I'll destroy your entire house, then hunt you down last," Kilian said in the same friendly tone.

She blanched, but met his gaze, even though ice began growing over one of his eyes. "On my honor, I will keep Ailsa safe, or die trying."

"Good."

Then the ice crystals erupted out of Kilian's eye, spraying across the table. He winced and rubbed his face. "Curse Water for her pettiness."

"Just pretend you did it on purpose," Hamish suggested. He'd woken up at some point, and looked refreshed from his nap. When Connor wasn't looking, he'd produced a miniature version of Verena's engine and was using it to power a tiny travel stove. It smelled like he was cooking another of those omelets. They were so good, Connor tried gesturing to him that he wanted one, but Hamish pretended not to notice. He'd been sulking about the loss of glutton crafting ever since the storm.

Shona said, "I have no objection either. Rosslyn is one of the few high nobles I still respect, and I believe she will play an important role in shaping Obrion's future."

Rosslyn looked moved by the vote of confidence. Connor completely trusted Ailsa's ability to judge people, and felt confident she'd just sealed another supporter to her. Rosslyn seemed like a true patriot, one who had served the queen out of duty. That duty should transfer readily to Ailsa as the best option for securing Obrion's future.

But he still wasn't going to let her walk into Donleavy alone. "Kilian, will you help me create an autonomous summoning?"

"If Water doesn't interfere. What do you have in mind?" Kilian asked.

"No offense to you or your troops, Rosslyn, but I want Ailsa to have a little more protection."

"I'll be fine," Ailsa assured him.

"I'm going to ensure it," Connor told him. "I'll follow your plan, but you have to give me this."

"What exactly do you propose?" she asked.

"We'll create an autonomous summoning, and I'll give it the commands to defend you and to obey your commands."

"Can you do all that?" Verena asked. The others looked surprised. Even Kilian looked intrigued.

Connor tapped the side of his head. "With the information I've gathered from Evander's memories, I believe I can."

"If it works, I will gladly accept the help," Ailsa said with a smile, then rubbed her hands together and said eagerly, "For now, let's get to work, people. We have a kingdom to set to right."

CHAPTER SEVENTY
The Promise of a Very Interesting Life

Verena accelerated easily into the sky on half thruster, banking gently to take the Swift out over the river. Twilight covered Crann in a gentle blanket, and the city lights were already glowing like a million tiny pieces of limestone.

"I'm glad we can enjoy the view of Crann and not have to plot how to destroy it," Connor said from the cramped passenger seat right behind her. He didn't complain about the tight space, and only once had he commented on how much easier it had been to fly untethered with Air. He was coping well with the loss of so many affinities, but it had to be a monumental challenge.

They were headed up to Battalion One, which hovered three thousand feet above, and slightly north of Crann. Luckily the interference that Water and Air were causing among Petralists didn't seem to affect quickened stones activated by Builders. Verena was tired, but happy with the progress they'd made in the meeting. Without Ailsa's brilliant planning, she feared they would have still faced months of war, but they might just pull of a surprise peace, and she was more than happy with that.

Connor still tired easily, but was recovering well in both mind and body, and she had no doubt he'd regain his optimistic good humor soon. He was trying, but she knew how hard it was for him.

About halfway up to the Battalion, Verena slowed and lowered the window shields. Up there the air was cool and fresh, the night peaceful, and for a moment they simply hovered, the thrusters' low humming the only sound. Connor started massaging her shoulders, and she sighed with pleasure as her tension faded beneath his fingers.

As much as she liked positioning him in that back seat so he was encouraged to give her regular massages, she still looked forward to finishing the next model Swift. She was already working on it with a team of Builders on Battalion Two. It would be slightly larger than her current Swift, with two seats side by side. That would make flying together more comfortable.

After a moment of comfortable silence Verena asked, "How are you holding up, Connor?"

He didn't respond immediately, but continued massaging her shoulders. She wasn't about to complain. Finally he said, "I'm trying not to think about everything I lost."

"I'm glad you didn't have to destroy all of your affinities. That would have been too much," Verena said. Connor had sacrificed so much so many times, she hated that he'd needed to sacrifice even his affinities. If only she'd figured out how to hurt the queen sooner, or if she'd monitored Nicklaus more closely. Maybe Connor would have found a different way.

"Me too. At least the few I have left feel stronger, somehow," he said thoughtfully.

That was interesting. Verena wondered if he was having a similar reaction to many people who lost one of their limbs, or their sight or hearing. Their other senses often sharpened to exceptional levels to compensate. She knew a woman who had lost her hands and who had developed remarkable flexibility and strength in her legs and feet, grasping things almost as securely as her hands.

He paused, just letting his hands rest on her shoulders. "I lost basic limestone, so shouldn't be able to manipulate light, but visible light is only a tiny fraction of the energy frequencies, and I can manipulate all that energy. Look."

She followed his gesture to the left, and gasped in wonder as a plate-sized patch of light materialized nearby. It started as white, then turned red, then pink, the blue, then split into a breathtaking rainbow of colors that flowed into the Swift and shimmered along her control panels. Verena reached out to touch the light. It felt warm against her skin.

"This is amazing," she breathed.

"Evander and I have been discussing it, and a few other things I should try," Connor said, and when she twisted to look back at him, he was smiling. "I think I'll have some fun with it."

Seeing him smile eased a cold knot of tension in her heart, and she grinned. "I can't wait to test it with you."

"It'll be nice to have some time for pure research."

"This war can't end soon enough," she agreed. "Do you think we can find time to slip away and visit our families?"

"That would be nicer than sending them a letter announcing our betrothal," Connor agreed. "I don't think my mother would forgive me if I didn't visit, but I don't think I can leave any time soon. We have all those children to free from the queen's mind bombs."

Verena shivered. "You're right, that's more important, but as soon as we can after that."

"All right." He chuckled and added, "It's going to be interesting getting our families together."

She decided to hope everything would go well. She loved Connor's wonderful parents and enthusiastic siblings. Her father had made great strides in opening his mind to their union, but she hoped he didn't say anything offensive to Connor's parents. Hendry was a good man, so she didn't doubt he'd throw her father out a window if he had to.

"It wouldn't be such a challenge if someone hadn't waited until right before a battle to propose," she teased.

Connor groaned and wrapped his arms around her, moving his face close beside hers. "I'm sorry," he whispered. "I was a fool."

"I still love you," she said, turning to kiss him. "Let's not hold back important decisions until it's too late from now on, okay?"

"Okay," he agreed and leaned down to kiss her neck. She shivered with pleasure, so grateful they hadn't delayed their engagement until it was too late.

Connor seemed to be thinking along the same lines because he said, "Verena, let's make every day count. I almost lost you, and you almost lost me. We can't know how long we have, so let's not waste time."

She leaned her head back against him, feeling almost overwhelmed with a sense of contentedness. "I agree completely."

Connor extended one hand past her shoulder, and she was amazed to see him holding a large piece of Althing chocolate cake in a bowl, with a tiny dessert fork sticking out the top. "Then let's start now by not letting this cake go to waste."

"Where did you get that?"

"Hamish, of course. Do you really want to know how he was storing it?"

She laughed and grabbed the little fork. "Don't you dare. I will not let you eat this cake alone."

* * *

Aifric's heart raced faster than her legs as she hurried through the palace of Crann. Her palms were sweating, and she found it hard to breathe. Loud chatter from all of her mind sisters made it hard to focus. Usually they left the one controlling their body unrestricted access to all of their senses, but now all of them were tugging for fractions, wanting to see and hear and feel for themselves.

"*We'll all have a chance,*" Student Eighteen chided, but she didn't cede ground to the others.

"*I don't see why Aifric gets to drive,*" Cacilia pouted.

"*We all agreed,*" Student Eighteen reminded her, triggering another round of the argument that had kept them up half the night. Aifric barely believed she'd convinced enough of them to win the vote, but she wasn't about to get drawn back into the argument and maybe get voted out again. Their mission was far too important.

She reached the right door, set into the wood-paneled wall of the plush hallway. With shaking fingers, she knocked, waiting breathlessly for the long seconds before the door opened.

Kilian greeted her with a smile that helped ease her worries, but also increased her tension. He wore a black shirt with the sleeves rolled up almost to the elbows and the top two buttons undone. He hadn't shaved yet, and his hair was tousled more than usual. She had to resist the urge to reach up and run her fingers through it.

"I'm glad you stopped by," he said, gesturing her into the suite he'd commandeered from Lord Eoghan. "When do you leave?"

"Soon," she said, trying to calm herself. This was easy, just a simple conversation. "Rosslyn's troops are ready, and Ailsa is heading for the docks. We'll slide downriver to Belmullet, then head up to Donleavy."

"I still think she should take one of the Battalions," Kilian said as they entered his sitting room.

"It would make for a grand entrance, but I think she's right. It might give her opponents too much leverage to claim she's only a pawn of the insurrection," she said. "Besides, that summoning you and Connor made is incredible. Even if someone wanted to risk attacking her, despite Rosslyn and her troops watching over her, they'll think twice before messing with that thing."

"Connor named it Knuckles," Kilian said with a happy smile. "He might have lost most of his affinities, but Connor took summoning to a whole new level. That thing's a piece of art."

"The name's perfect," she agreed. With Kilian's help, Connor had fashioned a hulking man-shaped autonomous summoned creature.

Instead of simply using clay to form the body, he'd used half a ton of molten steel. They'd used water to give it life, but Connor had added some kind of high-level energy that made it far stronger. Its metal body would be immune to normal weapons, and Verena had added copious amounts of pumice, quickened just enough to make the creature virtually impervious to elemental tampering.

True to its name, the creature had extra-long arms with hands bigger than most people's heads. Its knuckles were as wide as many men's chests. She shuddered to think of the damage it could cause if Ailsa decided to let it loose. Connor had included far more complex instructions for the creature, guaranteeing it could identify threats to Ailsa and respond accordingly, as well as making it accept her voice commands.

Jean was already pestering Connor to make time to meet with her and Render flight to discuss ways to incorporate his new breakthroughs into their semi-autonomous creations.

Kilian leaned against the mantel over the cold hearth, studying her in a way that made her suddenly nervous. "So you stopped by to say good-bye?" he asked with a little smile. They hadn't discussed that surprise kiss during the battle, although the ladies had debated the subject endlessly.

"*Don't waste our time with smalltalk,*" Hemma urged, trying to clench their fists. Aifric pushed her back and whispered, "*Stop interrupting, and I won't.*"

"We have a problem. Student Eighteen has been asked to accept leadership of the Mhortair and become the first-ever Mistress One."

Student Eighteen made a very girlish squeaking sound that Aifric only barely managed to suppress. It was such an enormous honor, one that could change their lives. Even though they'd promised to let her do the talking, Student Eighteen stepped into the control position. She was the first, so she could overrule the others if she needed to.

"*Hey!*" Aifric cried as she stumbled back into the shared mindspace with her other sisters.

"*I'll give it back in a minute,*" Student Eighteen promised. "*This bit is about me, though.*"

She had a point, but Aifric didn't like it.

"*It's also about all of us,*" Isabell said, looking more nervous than Aifric had ever seen. They were all nervous, all excited, clustering close together, intently listening and watching.

"And what did you say?" Kilian asked gently, his expression impossible to read.

"I plan to help my people in every way I can. We need to rede-fine our entire purpose, and I'm honored by the opportunity, but I'm not sure if I should accept the title."

"Why not?" Somehow Aifric sensed he knew exactly why they'd come, but he let them get to the point on their own. Wise decision.

"That depends," Student Eighteen said, and Aifric rushed for-ward, taking control again. Student Eighteen released it reluctantly, but a promise was a promise, and Aifric was the first who had dared to really believe. Aifric's pulse raced as she stepped closer to Kilian, staring deep into those amazing eyes with their flickers of distant light, tempting her to keep staring and never look away.

"Depends on what?" He asked with that little half smile she adored.

"On how you react to this," Aifric said, taking a step closer and reaching for him.

"*Go get him!*" Camonica hollered, and all of her other mind sisters clamored encouragement as Aifric pulled his head down and kissed him.

Kilian wrapped her in his arms and kissed her back. He was a really good kisser too. Her entire body thrummed with joy. She barely believed he was accepting her, accepting them. She wanted to shriek with joy, but clung to him, not wanting to break away ever.

Except she needed to give her sisters a chance, so within sec-onds, Student Eighteen took her place, followed by Camonica, then each of the others. Despite the quiver in their lips with every tran-sition and the slight adjustments to stance and grip, Kilian did not relent, but kissed her until they all got a chance to rotate through.

In their shared mind space, Aifric fanned herself, feeling flushed. She had only lived for a few years, and had assumed their unique mind configuration would always prevent them from finding a man capable of winning all of their hearts. Her sisters stood close, expressions ranging from exultant to astonished, to overjoyed. She wasn't the only one blushing. Timid Eystri looked ready to burst, her face so red Aifric worried she might need to lie down for a while.

When he finally released them, Student Eighteen held the control position. Her face was flushing in a very non-Mhortair-assassin-ish way, but she didn't care. She couldn't seem to stop grinning as much as Aifric.

"What do you say now?" Kilian asked with a smile, and she was happy to see he seemed a bit breathless too.

"I say life just got very interesting."

Chapter Seventy-One
Some People Get Exactly What They Deserve

Connor stepped through the gilded double doors into the spectacular throne room above the palace of Donleavy with Verena by his side. He felt a little nervous, and adjusted his finely tailored suit.

"Relax. Everything will go smoothly," Verena whispered, but he sensed tension under her calm exterior. Although she again wore that gorgeous dress she'd used at Anika's wedding, she'd included a rather large purse in her ensemble. It matched much better than her leather satchel, but he bet it included a lot of power stone, just in case. And maybe one of Hamish's small side-arm speedslings.

"I hope so," he whispered as they moved into the domed hall with its translucent floor. He needn't have bothered whispering with the Mealt Falls thundering just behind the huge throne on the far side of the room.

The sight of all of that water made Connor sad. Even though six months had passed since he'd defeated Queen Dreokt, not a day went by that he didn't miss his connections to his elemental affinities, particularly water.

The room was packed with high lords and ladies, military officers, nobility, and palace officials. Everyone who felt they had any say in crowning a new monarch had petitioned to attend. In addition to all of the Obrioners, a dozen of the highest ranking Guardians were in attendance, all of them senior officers in the revolution, recently dubbed the Freedom army.

Connor was happy to see them, but wondered how the negotiations would resolve the prickly question. With Queen Dreokt

gone, no heir declared, and with King Turriff and his entire house-
hold rendered mindless, who should take the throne?

Kilian was an obvious choice, and he was in attendance, standing closer to the throne, for once looking every inch a prince of
Obrion in a rich blue doublet over a creamy white shirt. Aifric stood
beside him, looking gorgeous in a red velvet dress that showed off
her excellent figure.

Ivor and Shona stood near them, both dressed as high nobility.
General Wolfram and Anton flanked them, representing Grandurian
interests. Fyodor stood in for the Arishat League. In the months
since Lady Briet's death, he had proved as good an administrator as
he was a researcher.

Evander stood next to him, the solid Sentry body he now possessed projecting the same exceptional presence he always had, even
though now he was so much smaller. Hamish and Jean had already
arrived too. She looked resplendent as always in her understated
grandeur, and even Hamish had cleaned up, wearing a fashionable
Grandurian suit. As the intended to the famous Lady Jean, he sometimes had to look the part.

Connor glanced around as they took their places near their friends.
The room was packed, but he sensed little animosity. More a sense of
impending excitement. The throne had never been open for claiming
like this, and every high house seemed eager to push their candidate.

Several had already tried. As Ailsa had anticipated, High Lord
Feichin had attempted to seize power. He had resisted her arrival, very
nearly sparking a civil war right in Donleavy. Luckily, Ailsa's leverage
had proven sufficient to sway several of the key players. Rosslyn and
her army had convinced most of the others, and Knuckles had taken
care of the one fool who tried the direct approach at opposing Ailsa.

Apparently Knuckles had been even more enthusiastic than
Connor had planned for, and High Lord Feichin had agreed to step
down even before that spectacular mess had been cleaned up. All
parties had agreed to follow Ailsa until the formal decision for the
monarchy was decided.

Guardians across the realm had revolted, and that had threatened
to turn every major city into battlefields. As Ailsa predicted, the high
nobility families were stuck between the need to adjust to reality
and the threat posed to them by the queen's tampering with their
children's minds.

They'd eagerly accepted her proposed solution to that quandary
and clamored for Connor and Student Eighteen to come free their

children. The additional promise of eventually restoring Sentries and Firetongues had reinforced her position as temporary regent even more. Connor was glad he'd been able to help. He'd sacrificed so much to defeat Queen Dreokt, he'd felt unsettled and unsure of who he was. He'd smashed so many affinities, but luckily still retained chert. With Student Eighteen's help, he had indeed managed to enter the minds of scores of people, find the queen's concealed orders, and remove them. It was tricky work, and the focused effort had been a much-needed project to help him transition to his new reality.

Even then, some of the nobility had sought ways to conspire and turn the unstable situation to their benefit. The threat of Rory and Anika leading twenty thousand bash fighters on flying Battalions to knock down their city quelled any serious insurrection, though. So now everyone was gathered to propose the new monarch and lobby for their favorite candidate. Connor dearly hoped the plan worked, because if it didn't they could still face a costly civil war, invasion from Granadure, or both.

Aunt Ailsa, dressed in a simple but elegant gown of soft blue stepped up to the dais, but did not sit on the throne. Her chief of staff banged his brass-capped staff onto the quartzite floor three times. The echoing reports cut through the chatter and called the meeting to order.

"Thank you all for coming. This is a momentous day, a singular opportunity to choose the future direction of our country," Ailsa said, her calm voice echoing without enhancement around the room. The acoustics of the place were amazing. She glanced around the room, her serious, green-eyed gaze holding each person in turn.

Everyone drew a little closer, eager to get negotiations started. Ailsa added, "I encourage you all to keep an open mind during our negotiations. War has darkened our halls for many months, but we now stand at the threshold to a better future. Let us step beyond our fears and focus instead upon the great opportunity within our grasp. Too few ever stand upon such a momentous day, and it is my hope that we all will recognize our singular privilege. For the good of our nation, let us unite in choosing the one who can lead us in peace and begin to heal the rifts that have threatened to destroy Obrion as we know it."

That was a moving speech, and Connor hoped everyone was listening. If negotiations fell apart, things could get ugly. The fighting wouldn't last long, though. Shona, Ivor, and Rory had brought ten thousand troops with them from Merkland, and ten Battalions hovered over the city.

"The floor is open for proposals for this body to consider," Ailsa declared.

Connor expected every high house to begin clamoring for their right to take the throne, and most of the assembled nobility looked prepared to do just that. Aifric called out first. "Why don't you take the throne, Ailsa? You're abundantly qualified, universally respected, and already recognized as a fair and just ruler."

Ailsa acknowledged the compliment with a little nod as murmurs rippled through the crowd. Not surprisingly, most of the nobility clearly disliked the idea, while the Guardians and foreigners loved it.

High Lord Feichin, standing beside his daughter, General Rosslyn, voiced the contrary opinion. "We all acknowledge the excellent job you've done as temporary regent, but I'm afraid my house would have to oppose your elevation as queen. Your close proximity as one of Queen Dreokt's advisors leaves unresolved doubts regarding the integrity of your mind and your ability to rule."

If only he knew she had run the counter-espionage ring that had helped the revolution, providing them with critical intelligence that directly contributed to the queen's downfall. Other high houses echoed those comments, bolstering High Lord Feichin's prestige. He was one of the best-positioned candidates, despite his earlier failed coup attempt.

Connor found it odd that those same high lords and ladies who used the excuse of Ailsa's close proximity to the queen as grounds to bar her candidacy seemed to forget that High Lord Feichin had also served as one of the queen's counselors. Hypocrisy seemed to grow in equal measure with power, but he'd never understood why.

As arguments began to rise between different delegates, Ailsa raised her hand for quiet and said, "I appreciate the vote of confidence, but I have no desire to rule. I am a sculptress and I have been absent from my workroom far too long already."

Verena smiled and whispered, "Besides, if she was queen, who would she plot against?"

Connor fought to suppress a chuckle. He doubted Ailsa would ever lack for things to do.

With her gracious withdrawal from consideration, High Lord Feichin immediately spoke up. "In these difficult times, we need strong leadership from one with experience to see us through the hard times."

"Then that can't be you, Feichin," Lord Eoghan joked to a round of soft laughter, laced with steel.

Eoghan and his wife, Fenella, had indeed been plotting intricate negotiations. Fenella was a shrewd as she was beautiful, and they had positioned Eoghan as the main opponent to Feichin. Eoghan was King Turriff's cousin, lord over the critical metropolis of Crann, and he leveraged those advantages masterfully.

"I have better credentials than you, Eoghan," Feichin responded icily.

Other high lords and ladies started calling out support for both contenders, but Kilian interrupted. "You're both pretty, but neither of you, nor any sitting high lord or lady will do as our next ruler."

That smoothly made him the object of all of their anger. He didn't seem to mind, but added, "You've both been part of the problem for too long. You lack the flexibility needed to face the new reality of Guardians free of patronage. They need a place in Obrion outside of traditional houses, and none of you have the skills to pull that off without plunging this nation into civil war."

He was absolutely right, and that infuriated them. High Lord Feichin snapped, "Don't think you can slip in and take the crown either, *lord* Kilian." He filled the title with abundant scorn, and Connor seriously considered asking Verena to punch him through the far windows. See if Rosslyn loved him enough to rescue him from the waters before he struck the bottom.

Not to be outdone by his rival, Lord Eoghan said, "You may be descended from the original royal blood, but you renounced your claim centuries ago."

Kilian laughed. "I don't want the throne, but I'm here to make sure the right person gets it." His smile turned predatory and his eyes glowed blue, with little waves dancing in them. Not even those high lords could ignore an icy stare from Kilian, and they both lost some of their bluster. Luckily Water didn't sabotage Kilian's display that time.

They needed someone else to pick on, and High Lord Goban spotted Connor. "He's probably planning to force his puppet boy onto the throne."

They eagerly turned against Connor. High Lord Feichin sneered. "Blood of the Tallan or no, you're no king."

Connor wasn't surprised they would single him out for opposition. He might be a hero of the revolution, but to the establishment he was considered one of their worst enemies, even though he had freed their children from the queen's mind bombs. Few people understood what he had done to defeat Queen Dreokt or how much he'd sacrificed. He was no longer Blood of the Tallan, but he was discovering new aspects to his remaining affinities that no one had ever explored before. He was far from helpless.

"He defeated Queen Dreokt when all you could do was wet yourselves every time she walked into the room," Hamish snapped.

Lord Eoghan barked a humorless laugh. "Says the Builder who dares walk among us with the law still calling for your death."

"You wouldn't be the first coward to mock me before he dies," Hamish said calmly.

At that point, the meeting looked on the verge of spiraling out of control, and Connor found he didn't mind the idea so much. He'd have to move fast to clobber that pompous idiot Eoghan before Hamish got his hands on him. Before they could even get a bash fight going, Ailsa snatched the staff from her chief and slammed it so hard onto the floor that Connor was amazed it didn't crack.

She regarded the startled crowds with green eyes flashing, and no one dared sneer at her displeasure. "Enough of such petty insults. You're all supposed to be our nation's leaders. Is this the best you can behave? I'm ashamed of you."

Kilian spoke into the awkward silence that followed. "I think the solution is clear. High Lord Feichin himself suggested the answer."

That surprised Connor. As Feichin swelled with pride, looking smugly over at a stunned Eoghan, Kilian continued. "We need someone with experience, someone the existing nobility can trust, but someone respected by Guardians and the international community. As I said earlier, that eliminates any of the existing high house leaders."

That poked a hole in Feichin's happy bubble. Kilian had everyone's attention, and it looked like most of them were seriously considering the daunting question. Who could they all support? It wouldn't be Kilian, or Connor, or any of the existing high lords.

"Who do you propose?" Ailsa asked.

"General Shona, of course."

Kilian gestured, and Shona took a step forward, drawing every eye.

Connor gaped, his mouth actually falling open as he stared at Shona, who started to subtly glow under the attention. Kilian had used her title of general, tying her back to the Freedom army instead of her title as high lady of Merkland. Verena's hand clutched his so hard he winced and instinctively tried to tap granite. He couldn't, of course, but the reaction was still so ingrained, he couldn't help it.

Verena regarded Shona with a forced neutral expression. Connor didn't need to actively tap chert to understand her thoughts. She'd sparred with Shona every chance they could get since she gained her granite affinity, and they'd miraculously become close. The transition had been subtle and slow, and Connor was still amazed that just beating on each other every day had produced such a positive result.

Connor applauded Kilian's deft maneuver, surprised that he actually welcomed the proposal. His relationship with Shona had been complex and confusing, but she'd grown so much that she had become the leader she'd always projected to the world.

Shona made a graceful curtsy to Kilian and her rich voice filled the room. "I accept your nomination, Lord Kilian."

Wolfram and Fyodor both looked pleased by the idea. Hamish and Jean were both gaping, but Aifric didn't look surprised. Had Kilian discussed the idea with her ahead of time? The Guardian leaders all nodded enthusiastically. Shona might be a high lady, but she had chosen the revolution early enough that no one could accuse her of switching sides out of some sort of political astuteness. She'd risked everything to fight for Obrion's freedom, and she was beloved by everyone in the revolution.

Most of the assembled lords and ladies looked surprised, but receptive. Shona was one of them, after all. She didn't represent a dire threat to their existence like more radical candidates might. Before the revolution, she'd been positioned as one of the most powerful high ladies, so the idea of her rule was nothing new. Even Queen Dreokt had approved of her until she switched sides.

Lord Eoghan looked at a loss for words. High Lord Feichin frowned and seemed to be desperately trying to figure out a way to object. Rosslyn grinned, but her father was clearly unwilling to surrender easily, even though it was clear Shona's nomination was gaining momentum.

He exclaimed, "Can we really support one who abandoned her duty as high lady and helped lead a hostile army attacking the very heart of our nation?"

The question aroused the simmering anger of many of the nobles, but Shona simply asked, "So you would rather mad Queen Dreokt remained in power, savaging your houses, and ripping apart the minds of your children?"

That turned the tide against him, and he felt it, glancing at the other gathered nobles. Arguing that the nation was better off under Queen Dreokt would never win the day.

Lord Eoghan asked, "How can we know you'll fairly represent every faction, both the existing high houses and the newly freed Guardians?"

Tricky question, and it generated a ripple of murmurs, but Connor doubted he'd stump Shona. Shona had helped lead the revolution, after all, but any doubts seemed magnified in that meeting. A revolution was happening, their way of life was threatened, and unknowns hovered in the wings. What would happen to them? How could they coexist with Guardians ungoverned and looking for their own titles and recognition?

Shona maintained her composure and said, "Excellent question, my lord, and one I am happy to address."

"Really?" Lord Eoghan asked.

"Absolutely. As Lady Ailsa so eloquently stated at the beginning of these proceedings, we are laying the foundation for a greater Obrion. That means we must change some things that exist today, but with every challenge comes opportunities, and in this great nation we face many opportunities. I need your leadership skills and experience, but Guardians also need to find their new place. We will find it together."

"Pretty speech," High Lord Feichin said insincerely, "but a queen needs more than words and we need more assurance than your word about how we'll all participate in Obrion's future."

"Do you doubt I understand how to represent the high houses?" she challenged.

"Of course not," Lady Islay piped in. She gave Shona an encouraging smile, "You are one of us, dear Shona, and you risked everything to help preserve our nation."

"But the question of where the Guardians will fit into Obrion's future is a valid one," General Rory said.

That surprised Connor. Rory and Shona got along well. Connor still felt amazed to think of Shona as his queen. She'd plotted all her life to gain power, but it wasn't until she chose to risk everything for a greater good that she'd learned that the real secret to gaining power lay in working for the betterment of her people. He had considered many possible monarchs in recent months, but couldn't think of one who might be a better fit.

He glanced at Verena and she whispered, "We knew today would be interesting."

Shona spoke again, interrupting an argument between Lady Islay and Lord Eoghan. "Please. I concede that the point is valid and must be addressed, and I can assure you Guardians will fully participate in Obrion's future. We need you and must work together to forge a place for you worthy of the great honor you deserve."

"How?" High Lord Feichin demanded, looking annoyed that he was left asking such a bland question.

Shona grinned, her smile dazzling, her teeth glowing softly. "Because I propose to share rule with a Guardian who will join me as king and joint ruler of Obrion."

A gasp rippled through the crowd as she turned, extending a hand. Connor gaped, feeling suddenly frozen with dread. Had he been wrong about Shona all along? Was she reverting to her previous manipulating ways? As her gaze slid to his, he felt rising panic.

Would she really try to leverage the moment to secure him to her again? Had her change of heart been a lie?

Beside him, Verena stiffened, her hand sliding toward her purse.

Connor met Shona's gaze, trying to figure out how to respond, how to deny her without starting a civil war that might cost the lives of thousands.

Shona winked at him.

Not what he expected. Both he and Verena froze, and he read a hint of amusement in Shona's expression before she continued turning. Her gaze slid away from Connor, and her extended hand stopped, pointing at someone else.

Ivor.

"General Ivor, we have worked together to free Obrion and the Guardians. Will you join me now as my husband and joint ruler of Obrion in the great work of our lives, and help me rebuild our nation?"

"Ivor?" Verena whispered, relaxing and smiling. She looked immensely pleased by the idea, and Connor wanted to laugh aloud. Relief swept through him, making him feel weak. Shona hadn't been lying, hadn't tried manipulating him again. The many little signs of a deepening bond between Ivor and Shona flashed through his mind, and he marveled that he hadn't seen such an outcome ahead of time.

Ivor laughed, his strong voice echoing around the room. He was taking the proposal extremely well. Had they planned the surprise in advance? He stepped forward to take Shona's proffered hand, bowed over it, and said, "My queen. I accept."

Then he turned to the startled assembly. "And together we will lead Obrion into the future!"

Shona grinned as Ivor kissed her lightly on one cheek, which colored with the perfect hint of rosy blush. Alone, Shona was one of the most cunning and dangerously capable women Connor had ever known. United with Ivor, they would be unstoppable.

Lord Eoghan didn't seem to know how to respond to the surprising turn of events. General Wolfram looked thoughtfully pleased, Fyodor seemed content, and the Guardians were grinning. They knew Shona as one of the revolutionary leaders, and they trusted Ivor completely.

High Lord Feichin couldn't admit defeat so easily. He exclaimed, "Ivor? One of the men who tried to kill my Rosslyn?"

"The man who spared her life when he could have let her die," Ailsa corrected.

"The man who helped break centuries of bondage and spread the truth about patronage," Rory added.

"And he would have soon taken my place as a high lord if my poor Alyth hadn't been destroyed," the aged Lady Islay said. Ivor crossed to her and enveloped her in his arms. It was a touching scene, and no one spoke for a moment as they shared that common grief.

Not a single voice dared raise another objection after that. Connor scanned the crowds and could read that many of the nobles felt disappointed their faction hadn't won, but didn't know how to object without looking petty or foolish.

Ailsa spoke loudly into the hush. "Very well, I present High Lady Shona and General Ivor together as our choice for new monarchs of Obrion. Is there any who wish to object with a valid counter-proposal to this choice? Speak now, or be bound by our action."

High Lord Feichin's mouth opened silently a couple of times. General Rosslyn looked happy, and Lord Eoghan started chuckling to himself, as if recognizing he'd been smartly outmaneuvered. His wife didn't look pleased, but neither did she object.

Ailsa waited twenty eternal seconds before gesturing. The staff came down with a booming sound of finality.

Connor couldn't help laughing as the room broke into cheering, and he joined in enthusiastically. Verena clapped too, but sighed.

"What's wrong?" Connor asked.

"Nothing. They're the perfect choice. It's just . . . the thought of Shona becoming queen . . . it somehow feels . . ."

"Like she's getting exactly what she deserves?" Connor teased.

Verena smiled. "Something like that."

"So much better than it could have gone."

She blew out a breath, smiled, and took his hand. "Absolutely."

"Well, at least you've gotten to duel the future queen of Obrion dozens of times."

Verena's smile widened. "And I've kicked her butt as often as she's kicked mine."

With her good humor restored, they joined the throng pressing in around Ivor and Shona to congratulate them on their betrothal and impending coronation.

CHAPTER SEVENTY-TWO
New Beginnings

Connor paced the small waiting room, so full of nervous energy he couldn't bear the thought of sitting in one of the plush chairs arranged along one wall. His highly polished boots clicked on the expensive marble tiles, and he fidgeted in his fine new suit. His dark gray jacket with gold trim was tailored in the latest fashion, but it still felt hot and stuffy. Windows set high in the wall let in columns of golden light, which reflected from the three full-length mirrors.

Hamish and Kilian waited with him, with matching jackets, although Kilian had loosened his collar and managed to wear his jacket with a casual flair. Hamish beckoned from his cushioned chair. He'd picked up a small stain on one lapel. Looked like strawberry.

"Have a smashpacked dessert. I've got an entire tray of sweetbreads smashed into this cube," he extended the light brown cube. "It'll settle your stomach."

"No, thanks. I'm not hungry," Connor told him, then rubbed his hands across his face. He really was nervous if he'd just refused that.

"What's got you so worked up?" Hamish asked.

Connor sighed and dropped into a chair beside him. "Everyone's going to be watching. I don't know how to act like a nobleman."

"You are the hero of Lossit valley," Hamish said seriously.

"That's not helping," Connor said, taking the smashpacked cube when Hamish proffered it again.

Kilian crossed to them and Hamish tossed him a smashpacked custard pie. Connor still wasn't sure how Hamish kept that one from leaking, but it never did. "Relax. There's really nothing to worry about," Kilian said around the mouthful.

"Besides, no one will actually see us. They'll be looking at the ladies," Hamish said.

That was probably true, and Connor tried relaxing, but it was such a big day, he couldn't quite manage it. "How are you not already overdosed from sugar?"

Hamish shrugged. "I'm not actually nervous. I don't care what people think, as long as they don't get in my way. I've convinced the most amazing girl in the world to marry me. What have I got to be nervous about?"

Jean was a fantastic catch, and as much as Connor loved Hamish, some days he wondered how Hamish had won Jean's heart. He couldn't imagine anyone better for her, though. He tried focusing on the wonder of his own betrothed. Verena was a high Grandurian lady, a celebrated Builder and a heroine of the recent war. She could easily get hundreds of eligible suitors lining up to her door if she wanted.

In the last few whirlwind weeks, she could have come to her senses and broken off the engagement, but she only seemed more eager for the wedding with each passing day. His nerves faded as he focused on the incredible miracle of her love.

The heavy oak door opened and Verena's older brother, Vincenz, stepped through. Wearing the dress uniform of the king's guard, he grinned and said, "Come on. It's time."

Connor rose with Hamish and fell in with Kilian, flanking him. Connor's nerves returned in a rush. He reminded himself to breathe as they walked together down a short connecting hallway and through a wide, arched doorway into the royal banquet hall of the king's palace in Edderitz.

The enormous space, with an incredibly high, vaulted ceiling, was packed with thousands of people. The walls, support columns, and every row of benches were festooned with garlands and flowers, designed by Anika herself. Filled with so many people, all dressed in bright, festive colors, the room was like an out-of-control garden.

The three of them marched up the long, central aisle, and suddenly his nerves faded away. He recognized so many of the people in attendance, and they were all grinning. These were his friends and family, all gathered for the big day.

Most of the town of Alasdair were squeezed into a few rows halfway down the room, across the aisle from scores of friends from New Schwinkendorf and Faulenrost. He grinned to see his

and Hamish's families at the front of the Alasdair contingent. His
father lifted a hand in salute, and his mother was already crying.
Ailsa stood beside her, well stocked with handkerchiefs, already
proffering one.

In the front rows, way up at the far end of the hall waited King
Ivor and Queen Shona, both resplendent in royal finery. In the few
brief weeks since their coronation, they'd solidified their positions
and won the hearts and minds of their subjects.

Verena, Jean, and Aifric waited on a raised dais at the front of
the long hall, and Connor's heart nearly burst with joy when he
spotted Verena. The three women all wore matching gowns of dark
blue velvet, but with different trim, and different colored flowers
woven into their hair. Verena's gown was trimmed in gold, and her
black hair was hung with rows of white flowers, including roses,
snowdrops, and lilies. Connor didn't know the names of the rest,
but the effect was dazzling. For the finishing touch, she also wore
a delicate, silver tiara set with power stones. Her smile was like
a beam of light directly into his mind, and he had to fight the urge
to simply rush to her side.

Jean's blue gown was trimmed in silver, and her thick, golden
hair was woven with blue morning glories, irises, and a host of other
blue flowers Connor couldn't remember. At her throat, she wore an
intricately carved sandstone pendant, shaped like a pair of hands
cupped around a flame of fire. Ailsa had gifted her the sculpted
stone the day before, and Connor couldn't imagine anyone who
could accomplish more good with it.

Aifric's gown was trimmed in white, with yellow flowers. Connor
couldn't remember the names of any of them. She looked stunning,
although her smile kept subtly changing as different ladies cycled
through the control position in her body. As he drew closer to Verena,
his thoughts seemed to scatter and he couldn't think about anything
but her.

They joined the girls, and Connor wanted to shout with joy
when Verena slipped her warm hands into his. It was really happening. They were really getting married.

King Henrik rose from his throne on a smaller platform several
steps above the dais where Connor and the others stood. The
Grandurian king was a big man, clearly a Rumbler, and notoriously
proud of it. He and Rory had gotten along famously when they
first met. His wife, Queen Sybilie, was younger than the king,
a tall, striking woman in her thirties with classic Grandurian blond

hair and blue eyes, which were glowing softly at the moment. She was very close to Verena, and she'd interviewed Connor politely but extensively when they'd met a few days prior. He liked her immensely.

Their son, Crown Prince Theodor, also sat on the throne tier with his lovely wife, Lady Adelaide. Connor had no idea what, if any, affinities she possessed, and had only spoken with her briefly. His first impression was very good, and Verena spoke highly of her. If not for the fact that he was very good friends with the king and queen of Obrion, the prospect of close association with Grandurian royalty would probably awe him more. It was still fun, and he looked forward to getting to know the people behind the titles.

It was rare for the king of Granadure to personally officiate a wedding, but not even he could ignore this one. Verena was a favorite of his queen's, and Jean was one of the most popular people alive. Not only was she a war hero, famous for being an Obrioner commoner raised to nobility, ruler of the city that was fast burgeoning into one of the most important seats of learning and innovation in the world, but her Render flights and Mender flights had been making headlines all across the kingdom with their healing and their revolutionary work with semi-autonomous crafted prosthetics.

Aifric was the ruler of the deadly Mhortair, and Kilian was, well, Kilian.

King Henrik smiled and raised his hands for attention, even though an expectant hush had already settled over the vast assembly and every eye was already locked on him. He opened his mouth to speak, but a window high on the left wall whisked open with a loud clatter that seemed ten times louder in the silence.

Nicklaus swooped inside, wearing his battle suit. He rarely took it off, probably to keep Christin from finding an excuse to send it for laundering for seven years. A glowing tether trailed him, and a couple seconds later, the end of the tether appeared. It was a bubble of air made with quartzite shieldstones, and inside the bubble stood Stuart and Stefanie, the buxom daughter of Lord Wenzel of Emmerich. They were dressed just like the other couples, although Stuart looked so terrified, Connor suspected he was on the verge of soiling his fancy britches.

Stefanie laughed and waved, her thick, blond hair loose about her shoulders.

Beside Connor, Verena's shoulders shook in silent laughter and she whispered, "I wondered where they ended up."

Connor had forgotten all about them. He felt bad about that, but how much could a guy remember on his wedding day? He would have probably forgotten the others too if they hadn't shown up. Verena consumed his every sense and every thought.

Nicklaus landed on the dais with a rush of thrusters, his young face flushed with excitement, his wide grin completely unapologetic. He waved to the king and said, "Sorry we're late, Uncle. I hope you didn't start without us."

The king closed his eyes, sighed, and said calmly, "You're almost late, Nicklaus."

"Sorry, Uncle King Henrik," the boy said, not sounding sorry at all. "I had to show them my new sewage treatment plant."

"It is indeed a marvel," the king admitted.

The air bubble faded away, allowing Stuart and Stefanie to approach. Stefanie curtsied gracefully, and Stuart made an awkward bow. He glanced around, looking more terrified by the second, but Connor gave him an encouraging smile.

Stefanie gestured toward her loose hair and gushed, "If I may, Your Majesty, that treatment plant is amazing! Nicklaus' mechanicals convert the worst refuse into pure water. I washed my hair in it!"

The king looked surprised, and low, astonished murmurs ran through the assembly. Verena blinked and fingered her own hair.

"I bet you wish you'd thought of that," Connor whispered.

"Um, maybe not today," she said, then smiled. "It doesn't surprise me that Stefanie did."

Emboldened by the king's graciousness, Stuart dared to add, "Tasted perfect, Your Majesty. We dropped off several barrels at the buffet table for everyone to try."

He looked proud of himself, and King Henrik managed to mask any concern the announcement made him feel. Connor noticed Hamish smirking, and back in the rows of spectators, more than a few people looked suddenly nervous.

"Why don't you go find your mother so we can get started?" the king suggested to Nicklaus.

"Okay." Instead of trotting down the stairs, he jumped back into the air and whooshed over to a tall woman seated in the front row. She looked strikingly similar to Queen Sybilie, and she simply shifted slightly to the side so Nicklaus could land beside her, then placed a gentle hand on his shoulder. Christin sat on that bench too, looking resigned.

"I am glad to see you decided not to miss your own wedding," King Henrik commented, looking more amused than irritated by the late entrance. The couple took the hint and scurried to take their placed in line with the other couples.

No one would forget that wedding.

King Henrik adjusted his opulent robe slightly and regained his air of regal authority. He scanned their group and smiled approvingly. When he spoke, his rich voice carried easily across the great room. Connor didn't think he was using a Longseer, but was simply an experienced orator.

"Before we begin, I would like to personally thank each and every one of you for the critical roles you've played in recent months to secure the safety of Granadure. Today we celebrate not only your unions, but the freedom of our people, the start of a vibrant new monarchy in Obrion, and a union between our nations closer than we've ever enjoyed."

That triggered a loud round of cheering, which the king allowed to run its course before continuing. "It is therefore appropriate that we unite Obrioners and Grandurians in matrimony, building upon the sterling precedent set by Granadure's famous battle maiden Anika to her beloved Lord Rory."

That triggered another round of applause, and Connor turned with Verena and the others to clap as Rory and Anika rose from their seats near the front of the room. The two of them waved, and the applause swelled further. They were immensely popular in both countries, and Rory had been forced to deal with the attention, even though he preferred being left alone. Anika seemed to thrive on it, and Connor didn't doubt she'd keep Rory active in the public arena. It would be good for both of them, and good for both of their countries.

King Henrik finally raised a hand for calm and nodded toward Stuart and Stefanie. I am also pleased to see the people of Alasdair formally uniting with the people of Emmerich."

The two raised their hands to more cheering. Stuart looking nervous, but proud, and Connor marveled at how much progress he'd made. He might not have participated in the war, but he had helped lead the people of Alasdair in forging a new life, and had grown into a new man in the process.

Then the king turned to Kilian and actually bowed. "And to you, my dear great uncle. To think I am the one honored to unite you for the first time in marriage, and to such a special woman."

Kilian nodded acceptance of the honor as he and Aifric raised their hands to thunderous applause. Connor had to fight down the urge to whoop out loud. Kilian, everyone's uncle, the eternal bachelor, had finally found his match. Connor couldn't imagine anyone else even trying to keep up with Aifric. Nor could he imagine any other woman keeping up with Kilian.

King Henrik smiled and raised his hands again, loudly proclaiming, "Then let us begin! Today you are all witness as we unite in marriage these four remarkable couples!"

*   *   *

She said yes.

The thought echoed through Connor's mind over and over again as he embraced Verena and kissed her minty lips for the first time as man and wife. His mind whirled, and he couldn't seem to concentrate on anything but her. His heart was so full it might burst, and he wanted to laugh, but doubted even that would be enough.

Verena's eyes glittered with emotion, and she hugged him so hard, she had to be tapping a little granite. He grunted as she squeezed most of his breath out, but didn't complain. She could crush him to jelly, and he wouldn't care.

She was his wife!

The wonder of it made thinking difficult. The ceremony had passed in a blur. He couldn't remember any of the king's words, couldn't remember the vows, although they were engraven in his heart. He would cherish and love Verena for the length of their lives. They were bound together now, and nothing would ever separate them.

It seemed everyone swarmed the dais, pounding him on the back, hugging Verena and congratulating them, but Connor couldn't remember any of them. They all blurred together into a long line of faces and handshakes and hugs. He was delirious with happiness and didn't want to ever awaken from the wonder of it.

After who knew how long, they worked through the crowd and the benches were cleared away, replaced by feasting tables. An outdoor court was transformed into a dance floor, and he grinned to think of dancing with Verena again. He might not be able to loan her obsidian, but she was so graceful, she didn't need it to keep up with him.

At one point, he and Verena actually managed to find a quiet moment at a cloth-draped table to eat something, with only his parents sitting with them. His mother was still dabbing at her eyes, looking as happy as Connor had ever seen, and his father was fairly bursting with pride.

"Oh, Verena, give me another hug," Lilias said, wrapping Verena in another of her famous embraces. Connor felt convinced that his family loved Verena far more than they'd ever loved him. They were smart that way.

"Where are you going for your honeymoon?" his mother asked.

"It'll be sort of a working vacation," Connor explained.

Verena added, "We've got to return to Merkland first to help Lord Rory with a few things."

Connor smiled to hear Rory's new title. With Shona moving to Donleavy, someone needed to rule the vital city of Merkland, and Rory had already proven himself more than capable. He'd still looked stunned by the official announcement, which Shona made right after her coronation, but Anika had whooped in her usual exuberant fashion and thrown him right up to the roof.

They were the first of an entirely new breed of nobility that would forever change what it meant to be a lord or lady of Obrion. Connor couldn't imagine better role models.

"Then we're going to do some traveling," Connor said.

"Where?" Lilias asked eagerly, clearly hoping he would say Emmerich.

"Everywhere," Verena said with a grin. "We're going to take the Hawk and come to Emmerich of course."

His parents beamed at that, but Verena continued with the bad news. "After that, we'll visit all over Granadure, then visit our friends in every one of the Arishat League nations."

"That will be a long trip," his father commented.

It would be, and Connor was excited about it. He had long wanted to see the other nations of the Arishat, but the trip wouldn't be pure vacation. Ivor had suggested it as a way to help cement positive relationships between the new Obrion and their international neighbors. It also rewarded them with a much-needed break.

The idea was only one of many the new king and queen of Obrion had come up with to lead their nation forward. The coronations had been spectacular, and most of the nation seemed thrilled with their new monarchs. Ivor was one of the most skilled in learning people's strengths and weaknesses. Shona was his equal, plus she had a lifetime of experience in Obrioner political intrigue, so she knew all the players and how to work with them.

Together, they might just have the skills and the savvy to save the nation and actually build the future they were promising. Connor wished them the best of luck and was happy he didn't have to get locked into a stuffy title too. Their schedules were nuts.

"Kilian and Aifric will be joining us," Verena added.

As much as Connor wanted uninterrupted time with Verena, he looked forward to traveling with those two. Life would definitely be interesting. Student Eighteen was still figuring out where to settle her people and what new mission they would adopt now that the queen was gone forever and their much celebrated Mistress One was married to the son of the matron of evil.

Everyone had problems to solve. He hoped the Mhortair would focus on international culinary diplomacy. They were as good at that as Hamish.

Kilian would act as the official representative on their upcoming trip together, since he had been given the title of Master of the Arcane at Connor's insistence. So of course he had recommended Connor receive the title too. And Verena's father had convinced King Henrik to bestow a Grandurian lordship on Connor too. That way, as much as he'd grown to like Connor, he wouldn't have to deal with the embarrassment of his daughter marrying a foreign commoner. Apparently Verena's father had already arranged a house for them in New Schwinkendorf already. That had been a huge surprise.

On the trip, another mission would be to create a plan to deal with the elfonnel slumbering at each of the convergence points and decide if it made more sense to remove them and thus block access to the most dangerous levels of Petralist powers.

Connor wasn't convinced that was the right choice, but they had time. The elementals were still behaving badly, so they didn't want to risk raising an elfonnel who might be used as a vehicle for the offended elementals to unleash their fury upon the world. Besides, he and Verena needed time to explore Nicklaus' fascinating relationship with the newly conscious serpentinite. Connor could tap serpentinite, but hadn't coaxed her into speaking with him yet. Hopefully she'd prove a different kind of elemental, but they planned to approach her carefully.

As they traveled the continent, they would also bring some of Ailsa's sculpted stones to other convergence points to restore slate, marble, and serpentinite. The secret of convergence points was still closely guarded, but the leaders of every nation knew about them. Connor would map all of the convergence points, and negotiations over which ones in which countries would host each of the affinities was still ongoing. The final decisions could potentially affect the distribution of Petralist powers in dramatic ways.

"Then you'll return to Emmerich?" his mother pressed.

Connor said, "I promise we'll return for a longer stay, and we'll come visit a lot more often."

Verena added, "We'll settle in New Schwinkendorf for the foreseeable future, so that's not very far."

His mother sighed, and Connor doubted she'd feel completely happy unless they settled in Emmerich next door to them. He'd love to spend a year with them, but doubted he could pull Verena away from her workshops in New Schwinkendorf that long.

Verena grinned. "Wait till you see the latest vehicle we're building. We're using a type of explosive fuel as propulsion. We should be able to make the trip in half the time."

Connor grinned at his parents' worry. Life with Verena would never be dull.

Bring it on.

THUMBS UP?
OR THUMBS DOWN?

Now that we've reached the end, can I assume you've enjoyed the books?

I hope so.

Have you posted a review?

If not, please do. Tons of great reviews help convince other readers to try this series.

To post a review on Amazon: http://smarturl.it/yv37jy

Please also share how much you love these books with your friends. Help them find Connor and Verena, Hamish and Jean, Kilian, Aifric, Aunt Ailsa, and all the other characters you've come to love.

Thanks for joining me for this epic ride!

Frank

Petralist Stones

Igneous

Basalt
Speed, agility
Tapped: Powder through the skin
Obrion: Strider
Granadure: Wingrunner

Granite
Strength, summoning
Tapped: Powder through the skin
Obrion: Boulder or Fast Roller
Granadure: Rumbler

Obsidian
Magnifies innate abilities
Tapped: Powder through the skin
Obrion: Blade
Granadure: Allcarver

Sedimentary

Limestone
Light
Tapped: Held or worn
Obrion: Solas
Granadure: Solas

Sandstone
Healing
Tapped: Held or worn
Obrion: Healer
Granadure: Healer

Metamorphic

Marble
Fire
Tapped: Under the tongue
Obrion: Firetongue
Granadure: Flameweaver

Quartzite
Air, senses
Tapped: Placed in mouth
Obrion: Pathfinder
Granadure: Longseer

Slate
Earth
Tapped: Soles of feet
Obrion: Sentry
Granadure: Sapper

Soapstone
Water
Tapped: Powder swallowed with water
Obrion: Spitter
Granadure: Water Moccasin

Secret Stones

Diorite

Igneous stone
Explosive power
Tapped: Powder through the skin
Obrion: Unknown
Granadure: Unknown

Porphyry

Igneous stone
Rage monster
Tapped: Powder through the skin
Obrion: Unclaimed
Granadure: Rampager

Anthracite (Blind Coal)

Sedimentary stone
Aggressive slipperiness
Tapped: Held or worn
Obrion: Unknown
Granadure: Unknown

Serpentinite

Metamorphic stone
Sound
Tapped: Held or worn
Obrion: Unknown
Granadure: Unknown

New Stones!

Chert
Sedimentary stone
Empathy
Tapped: Held or worn
Obrion: Unknown
Granadure: Unknown

Amphibolite Gneiss
Metamorphic stone
Counters basalt
Tapped: Powder through the skin
Obrion: Unknown
Granadure: Unknown

Granite Gneiss
Metamorphic stone
Counters granite
Tapped: Powder through the skin
Obrion: Unknown
Granadure: Unknown

Author's Note

It's both super exciting to bring you the last Petralist book, as well as bittersweet. The story is finished.

For now.

There is definitely lots more story that could be told in the Petralist world. Someday, maybe we'll return and explore new adventures.

Until then, please tell your friends about these books, and please consider checking out my other stories.

I'm honored you've stuck with me through all these huge books, and even bothered to read this final note. You are awesome.

As always, I'm happy to hear from you. Drop me an email, or stop to chat at one of the conventions I attend.

Who was one of your favorite characters?

What was a favorite scene?

Do you have a favorite joke?

Until then,

Look deep, see clear, and eat tons of sweetbreads!

Frank

About the Author

Frank Morin is a storyteller, an outdoor enthusiast, and an eager traveler. He is the author of fast-paced grab-you-by-the-eyeballs-and-don't-let-go adventures, including *The Petralist*, the epic teen fantasy series you've been enjoying, full of explosive magic, huge adventure, and brilliant humor. Frank also writes *The Facetakers* fast-action sci-fi/fantasy thrillers.

When not writing or trying to keep up with his active family, he's often found hiking, camping, Scuba diving, or traveling to research new books. Find out more about his novels and his shorter fiction, or join his readers group at: www.frankmorin.org